THE

MANDALORIAN

A Random House SCREEN COMIX™ Book

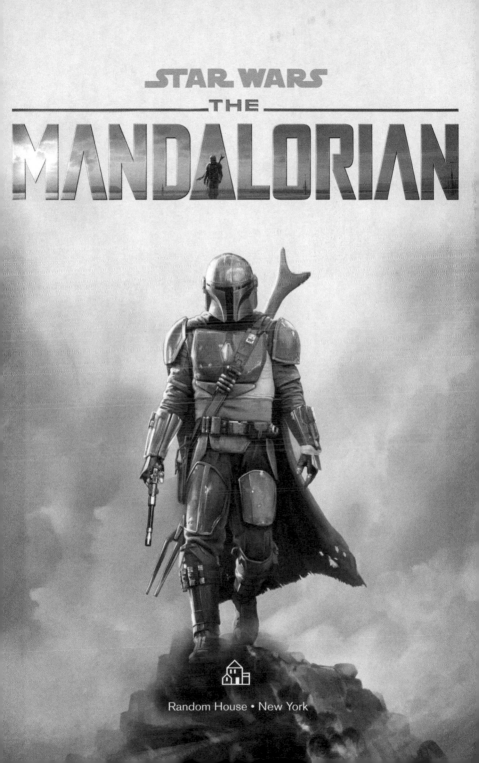

STAR WARS
THE
MANDALORIAN

Random House • New York

For Lucasfilm
Senior Editor: Robert Simpson
Creative Director: Michael Siglain
Art Director: Troy Alders
Project Manager, Digital & Video Assets: LeAndre Thomas
Lucasfilm Art Department: Phil Szostak
Lucasfilm Story Group: Pablo Hidalgo, Matt Martin, and Emily Shkoukani

ISBN 978-0-7364-4141-4
rhcbooks.com

Printed in the United States of America
10 9 8 7 6 5 4 3 2 1

Chapter 1

THE MANDALORIAN

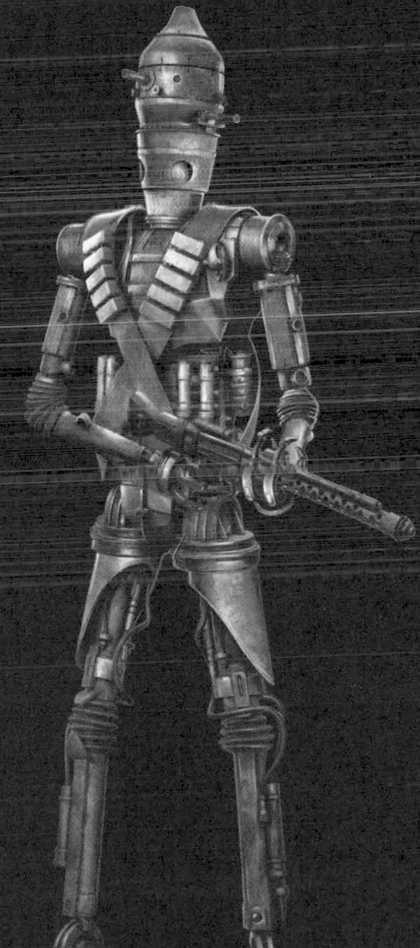

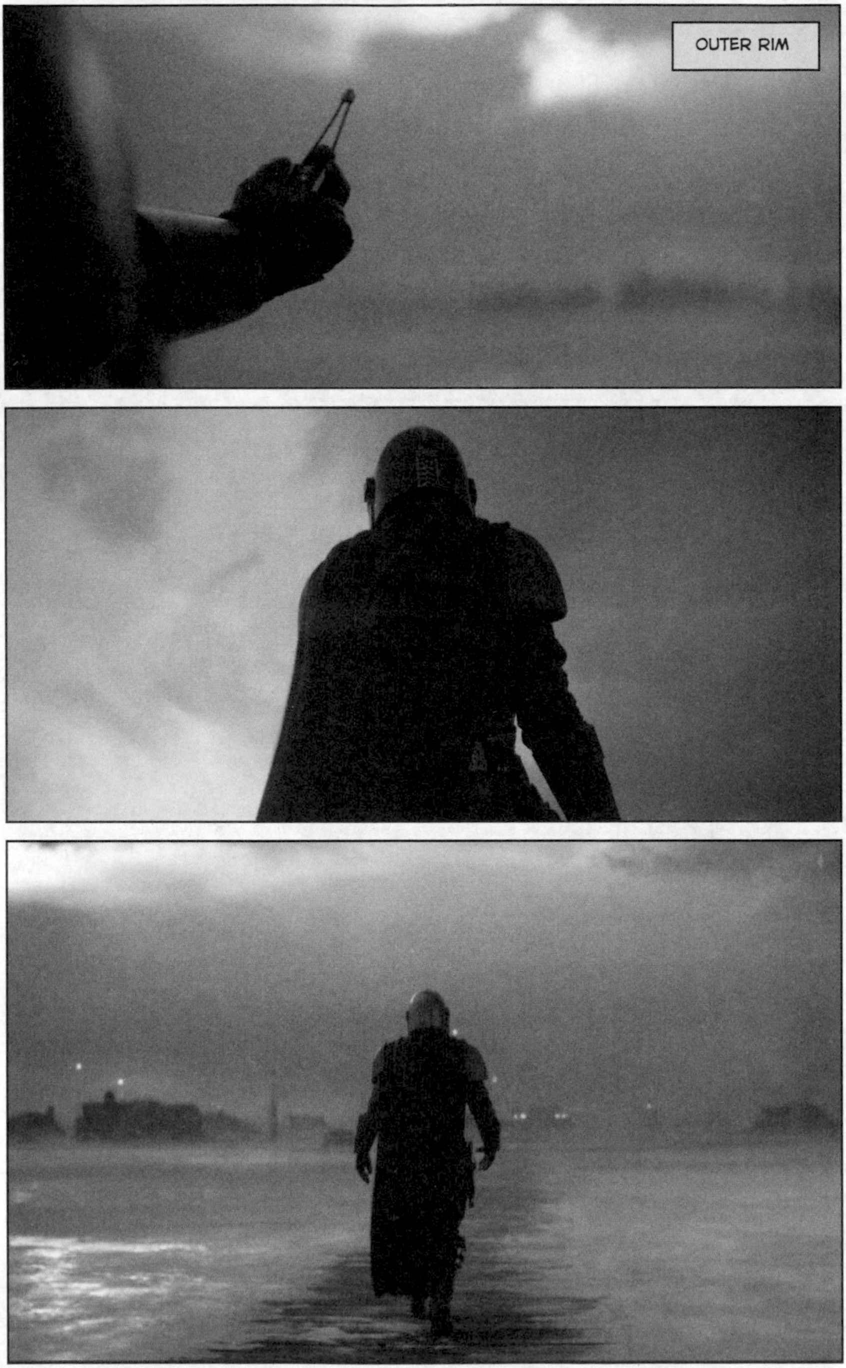
OUTER RIM

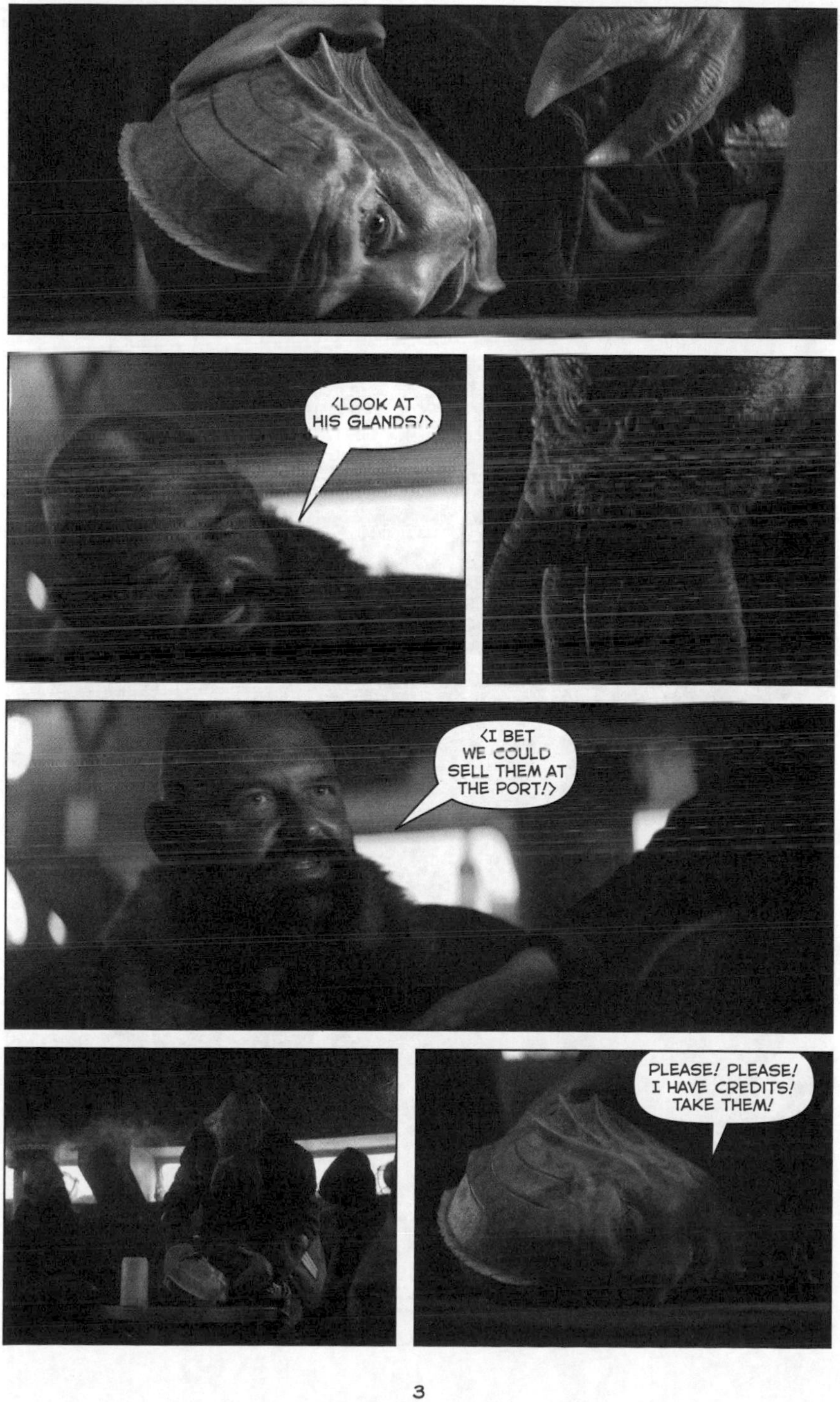
<LOOK AT HIS GLANDS!>
<I BET WE COULD SELL THEM AT THE PORT!>
PLEASE! PLEASE! I HAVE CREDITS! TAKE THEM!

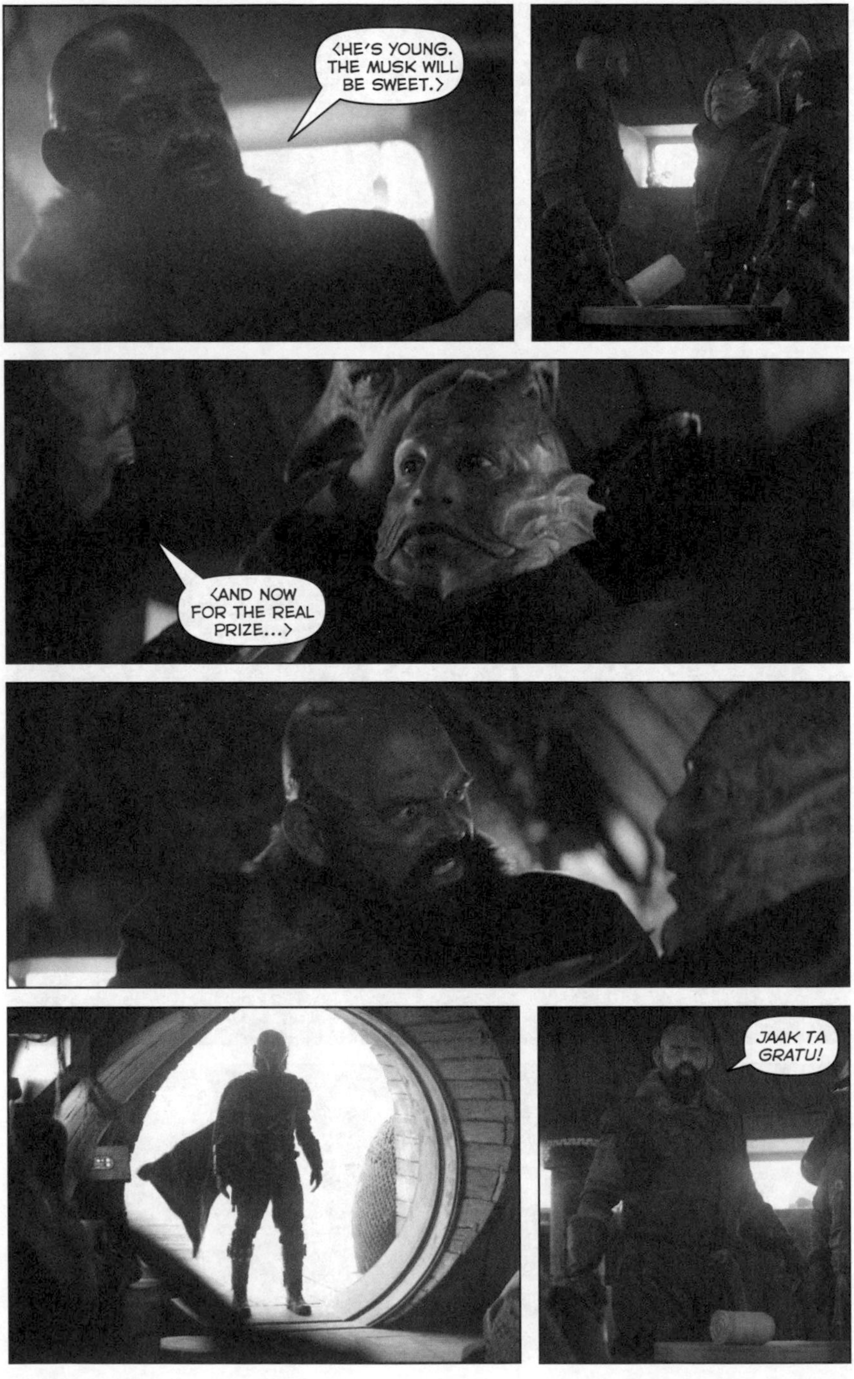
<HE'S YOUNG. THE MUSK WILL BE SWEET.>
<AND NOW FOR THE REAL PRIZE...>
JAAK TA GRATU!

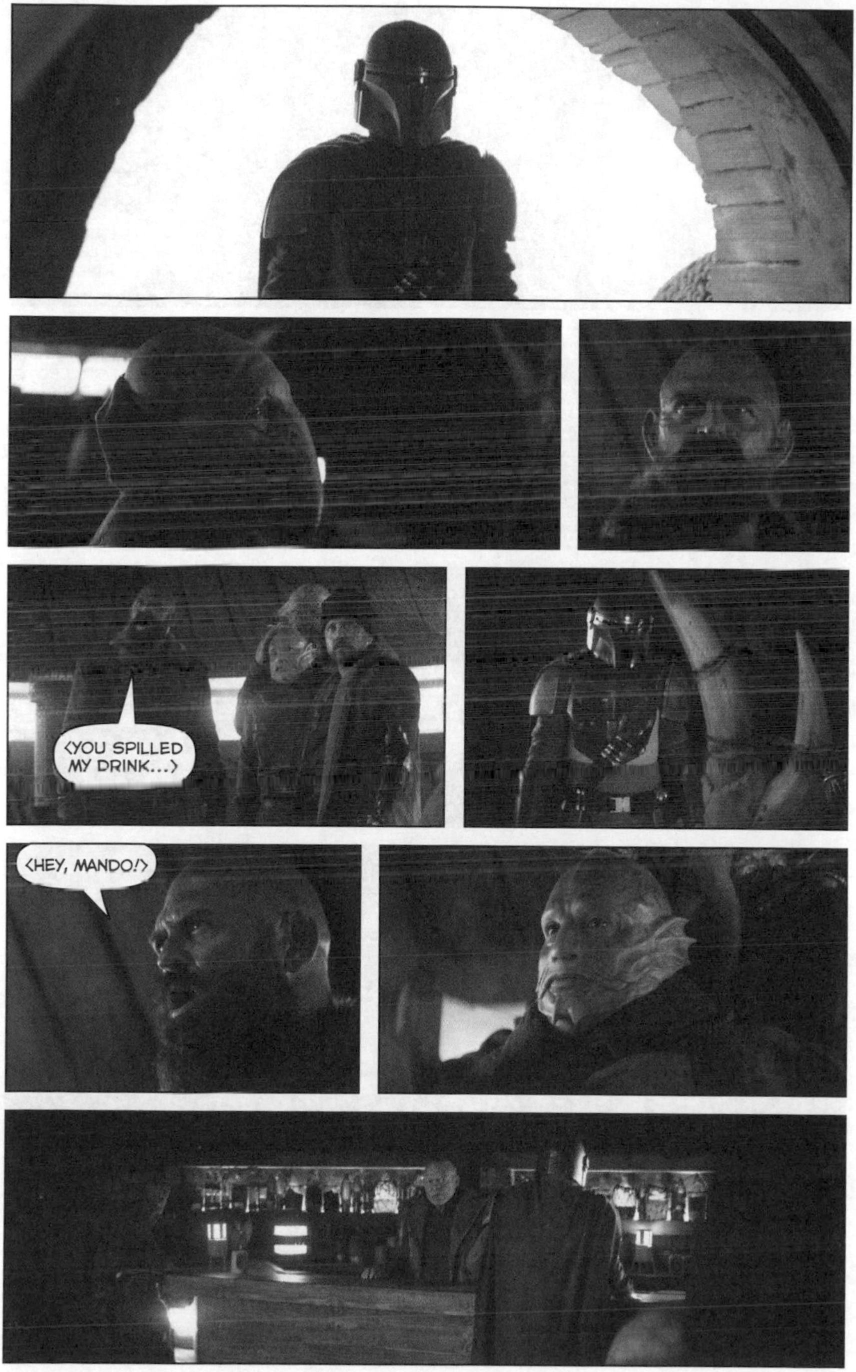
<YOU SPILLED MY DRINK...>
<HEY, MANDO!>

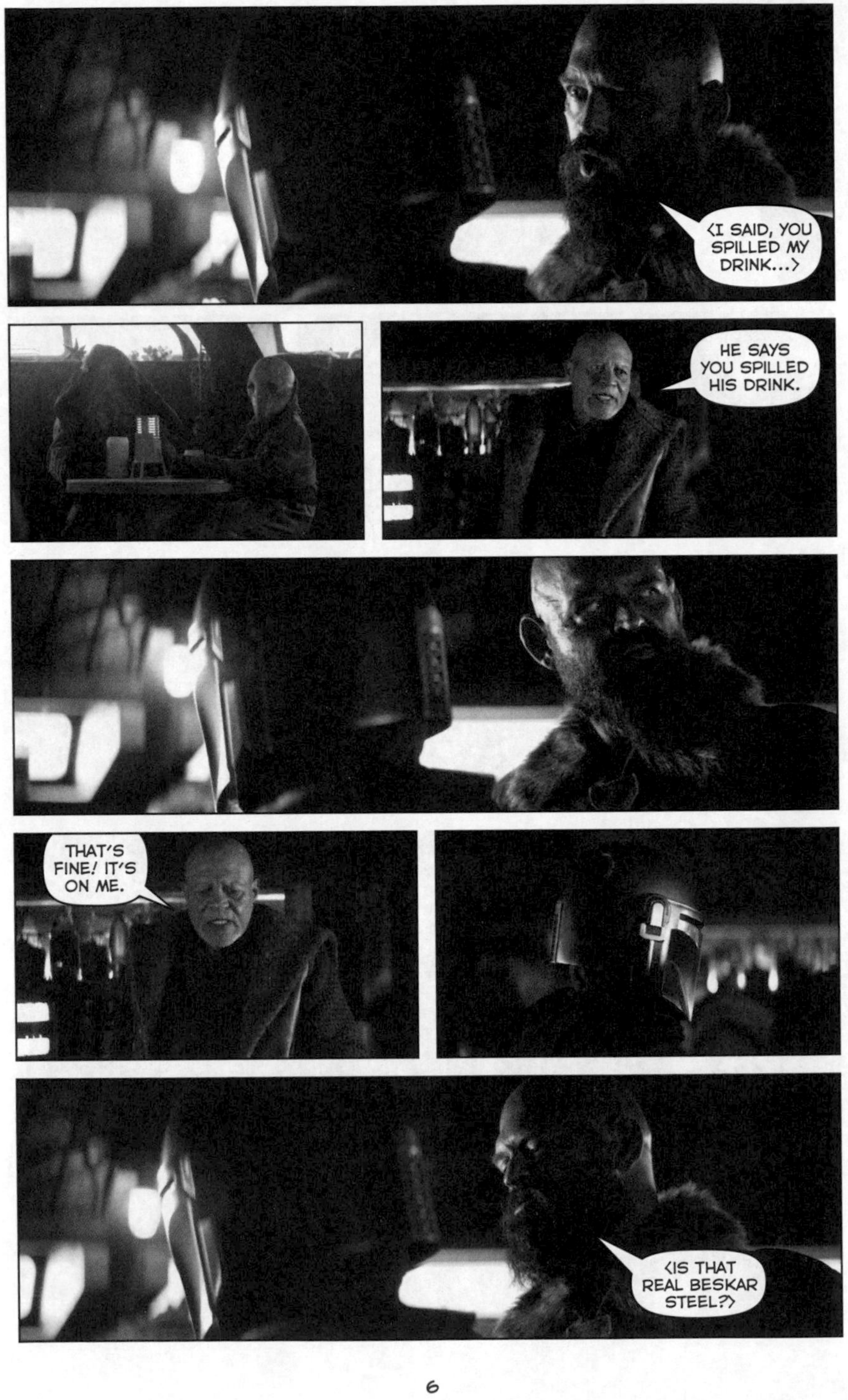
<I SAID, YOU SPILLED MY DRINK...>
HE SAYS YOU SPILLED HIS DRINK.
THAT'S FINE! IT'S ON ME.
<IS THAT REAL BESKAR STEEL?>

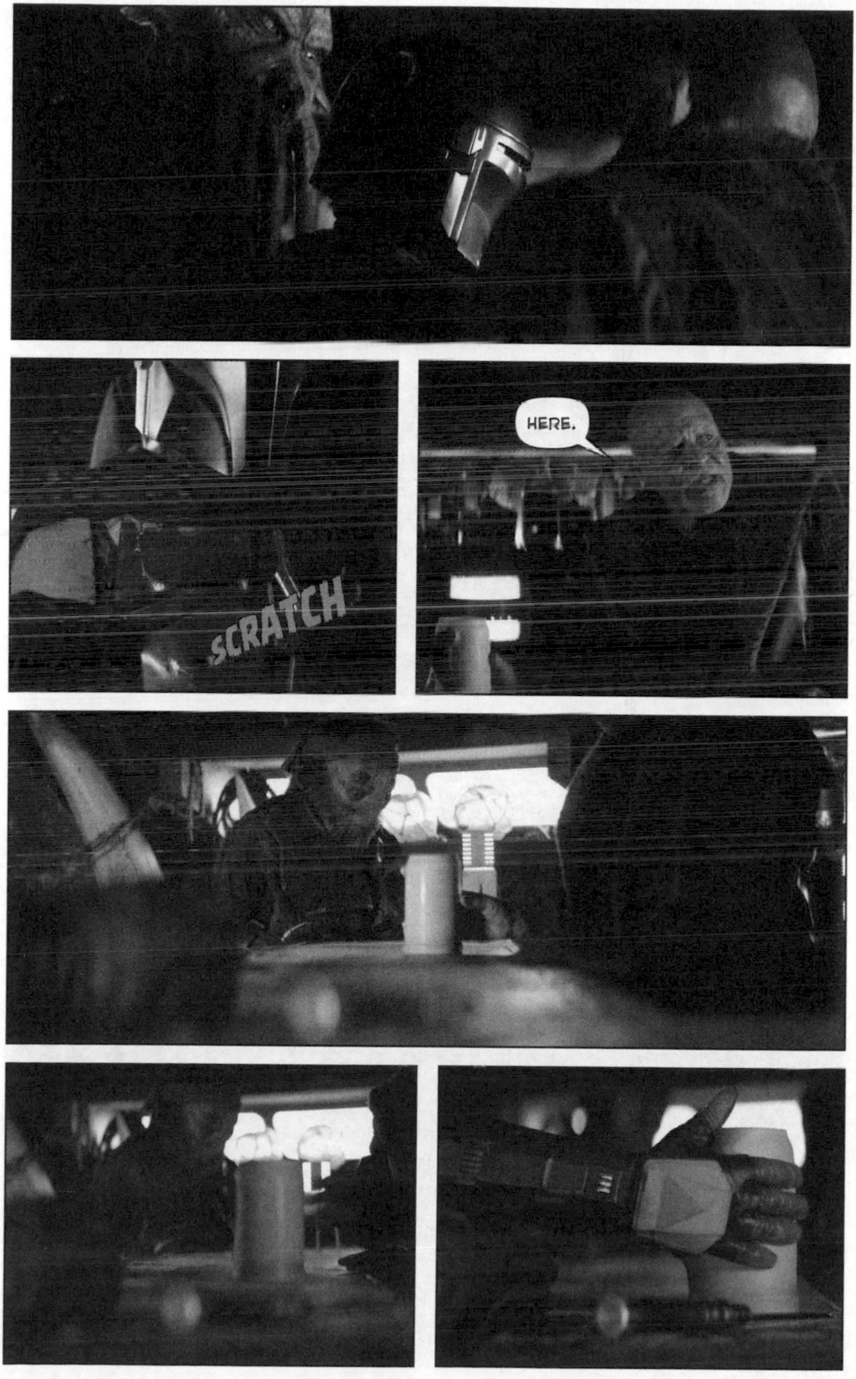
SCRATCH
HERE.

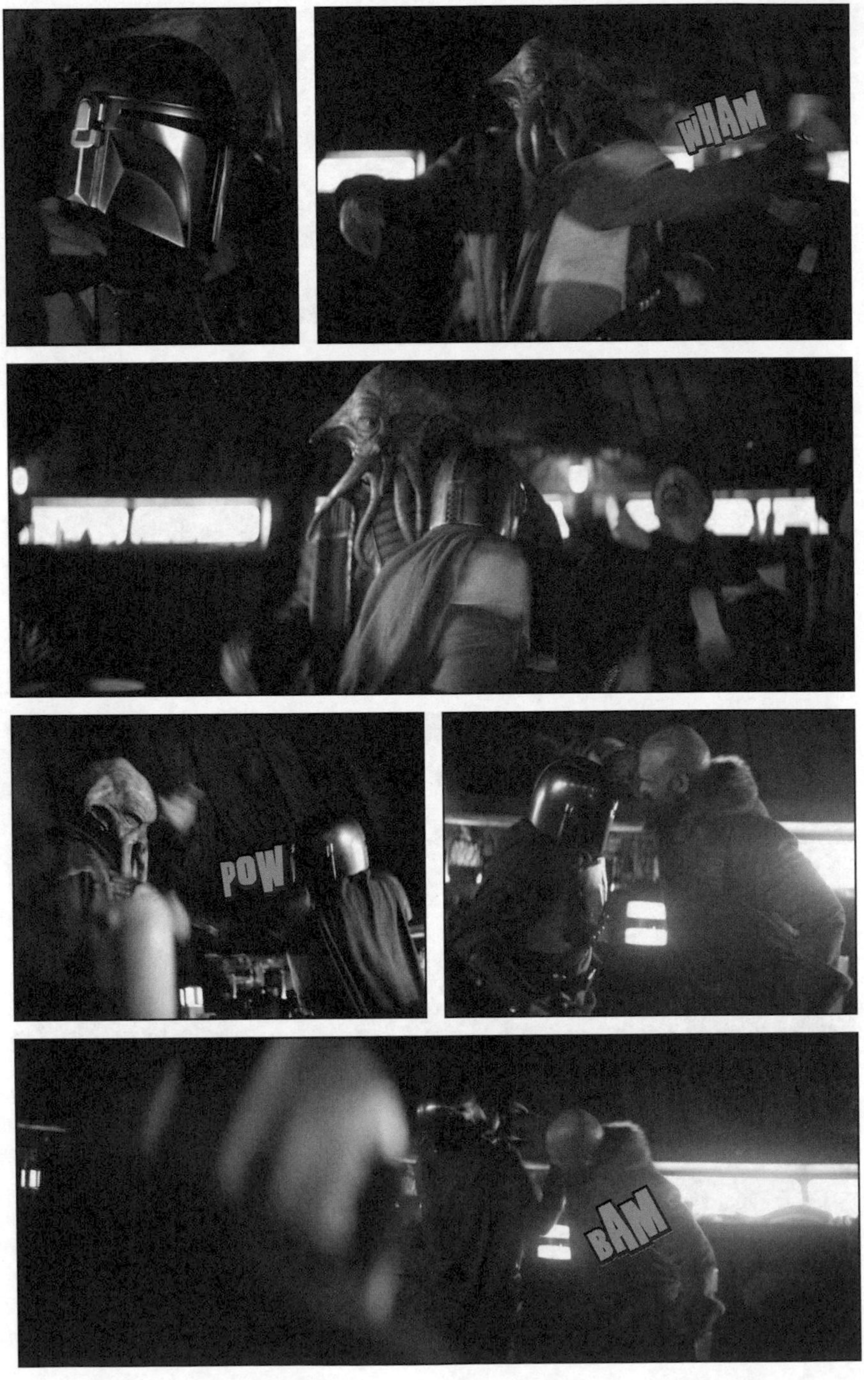
WHAM
POW
BAM

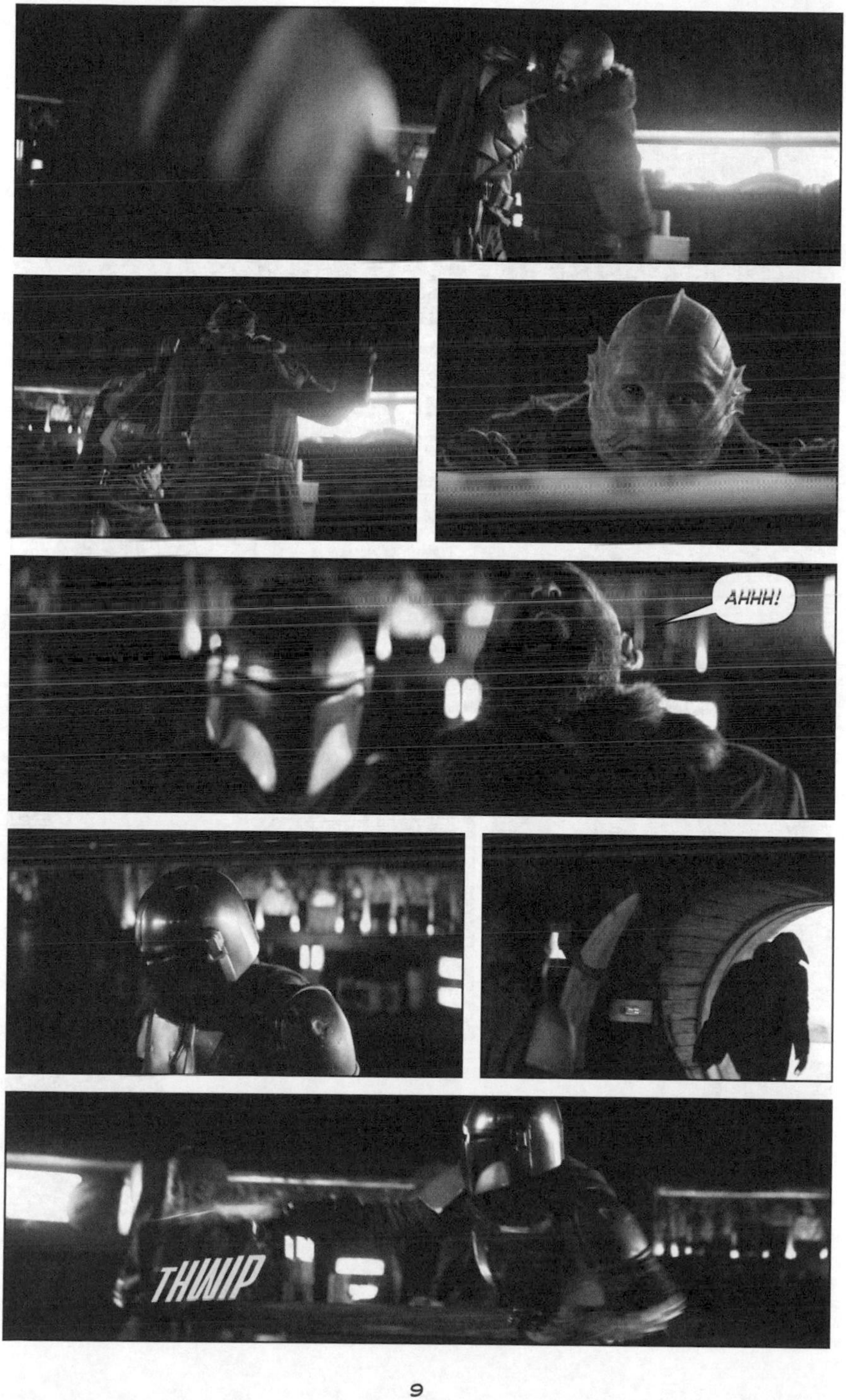
AHHH!
THWIP

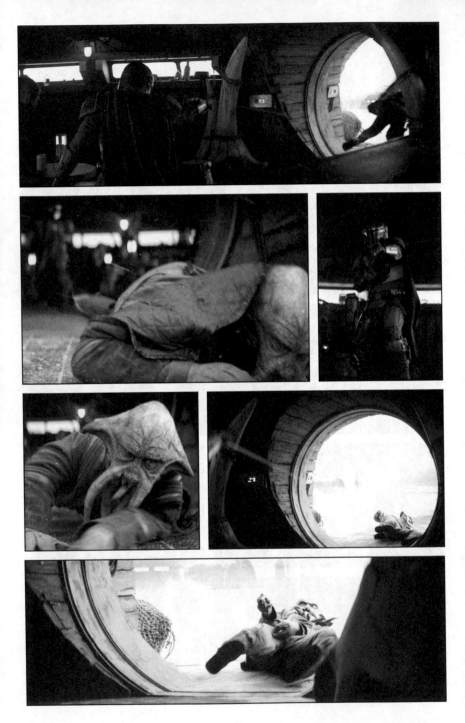

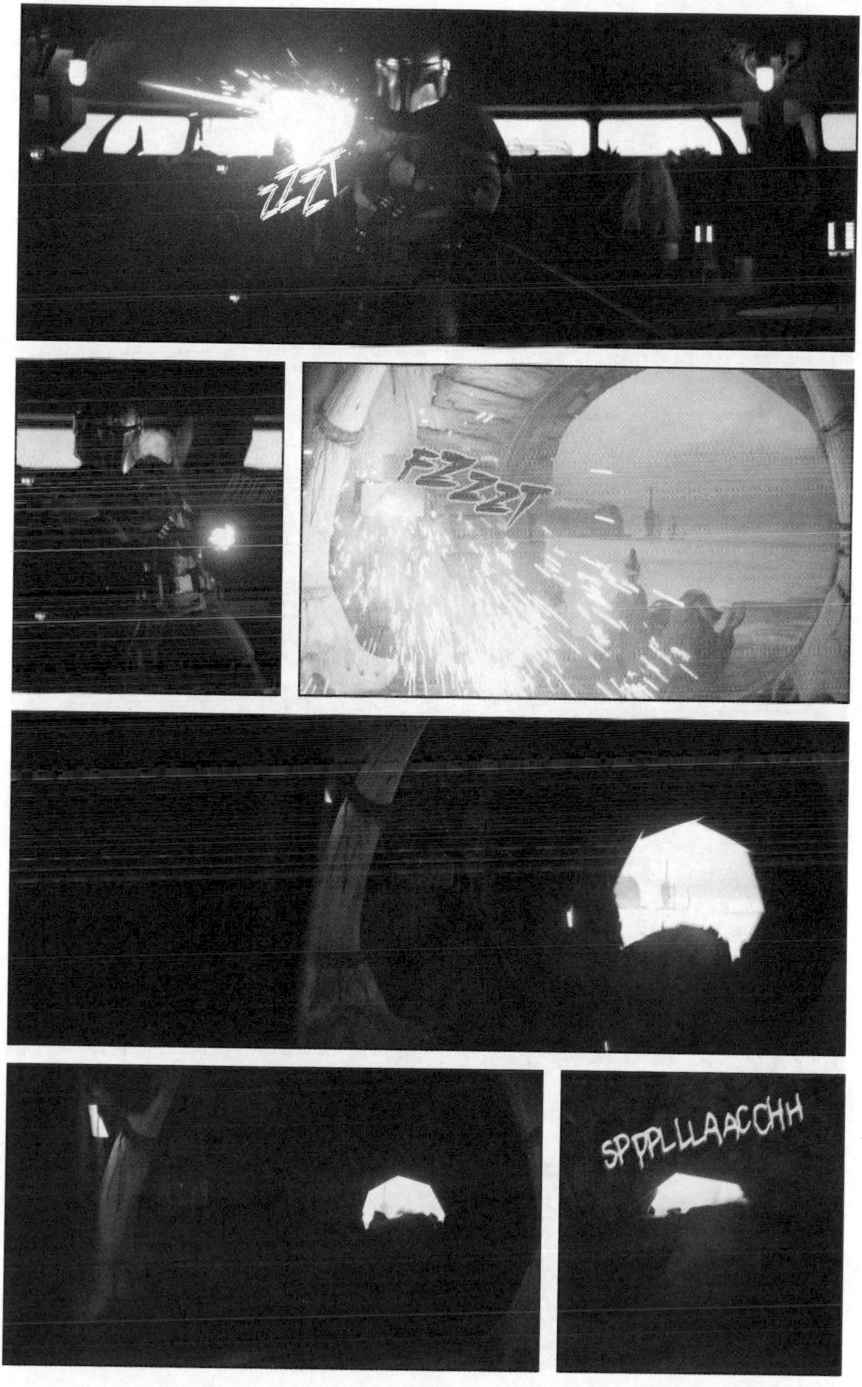
ZZZT
FZZZT
SPPPLLLAACCHH

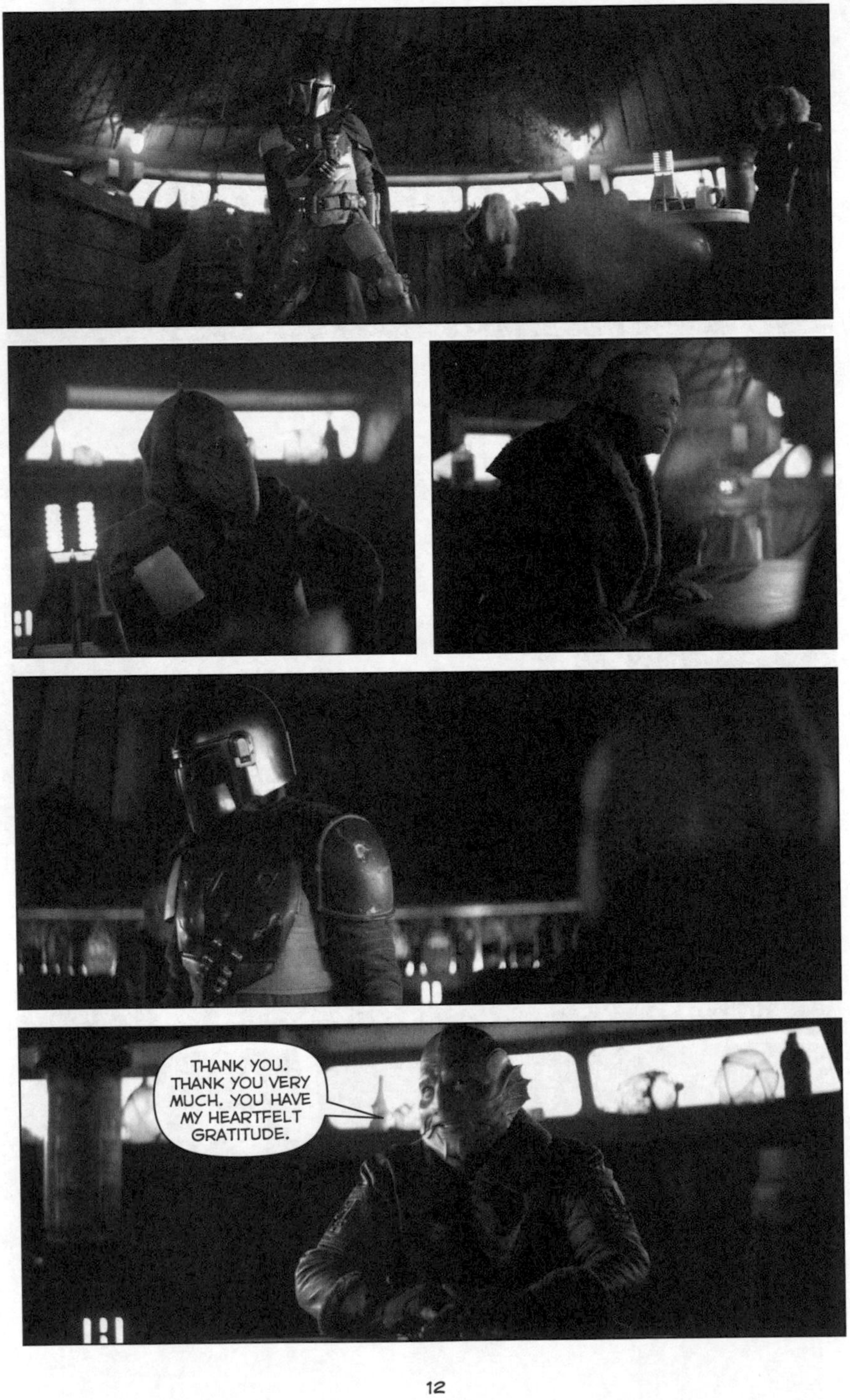
THANK YOU. THANK YOU VERY MUCH. YOU HAVE MY HEARTFELT GRATITUDE.

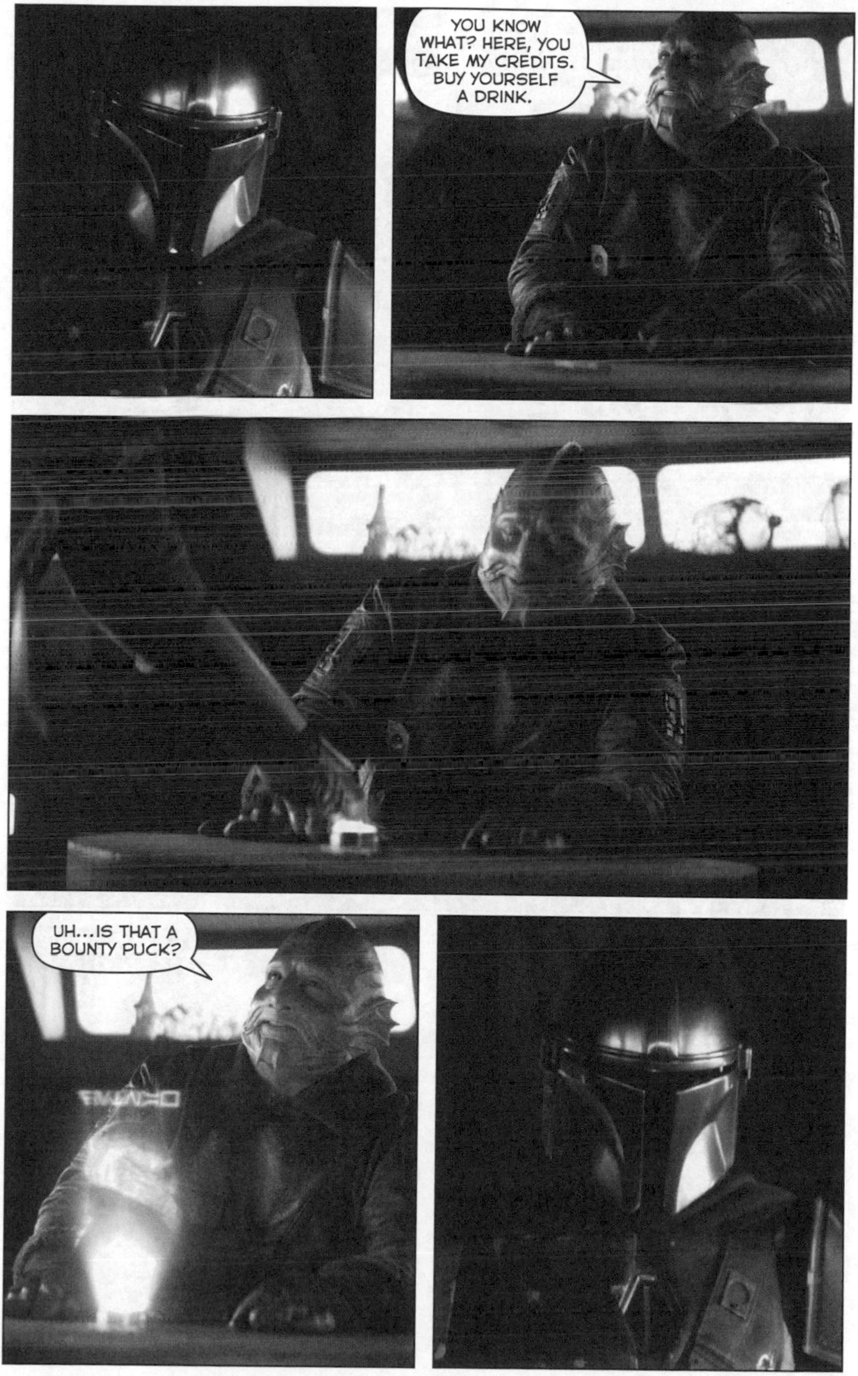
YOU KNOW WHAT? HERE, YOU TAKE MY CREDITS. BUY YOURSELF A DRINK.
UH...IS THAT A BOUNTY PUCK?

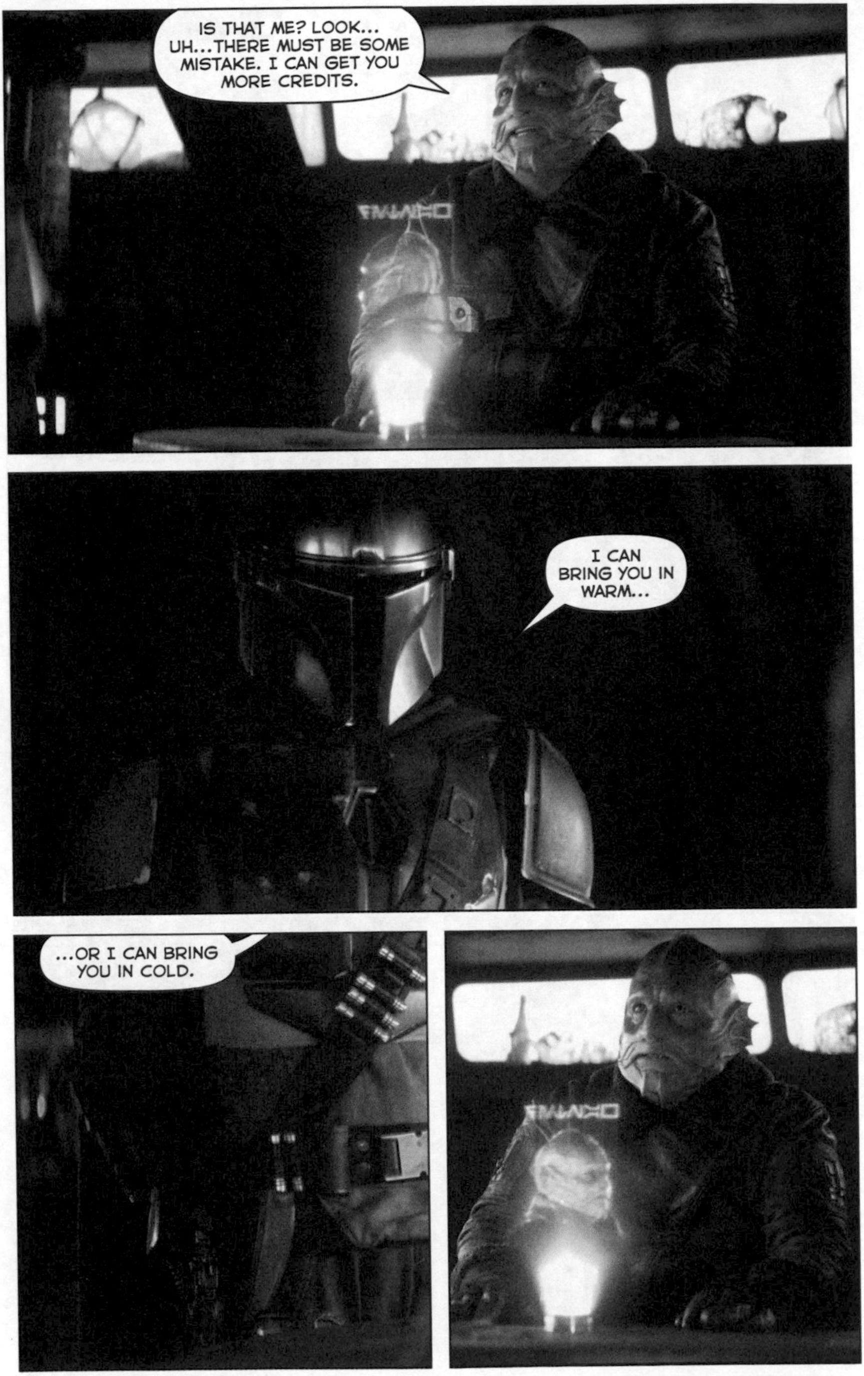
IS THAT ME? LOOK... UH...THERE MUST BE SOME MISTAKE. I CAN GET YOU MORE CREDITS.
I CAN BRING YOU IN WARM...
...OR I CAN BRING YOU IN COLD.

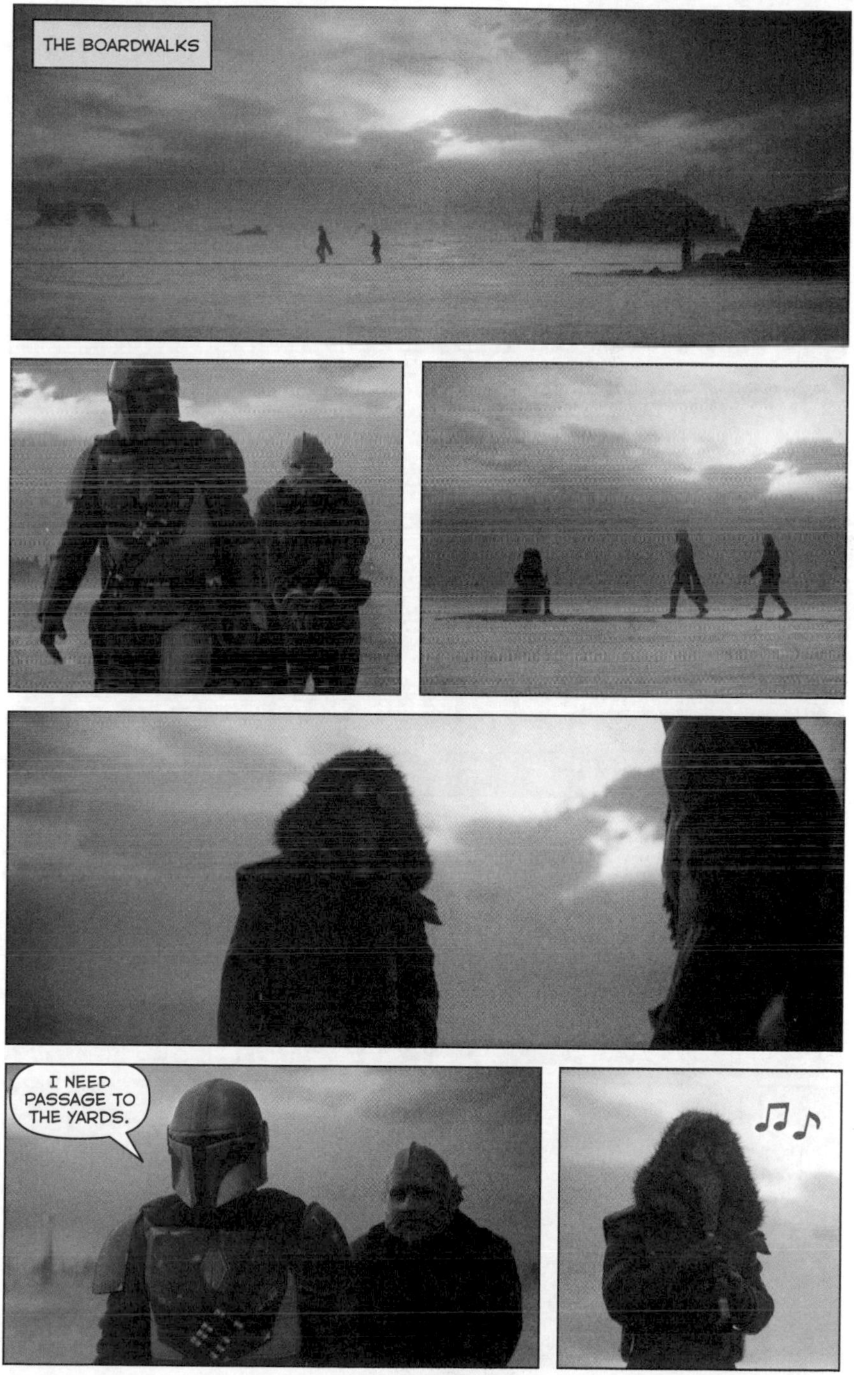
THE BOARDWALKS
I NEED PASSAGE TO THE YARDS.
♫♪

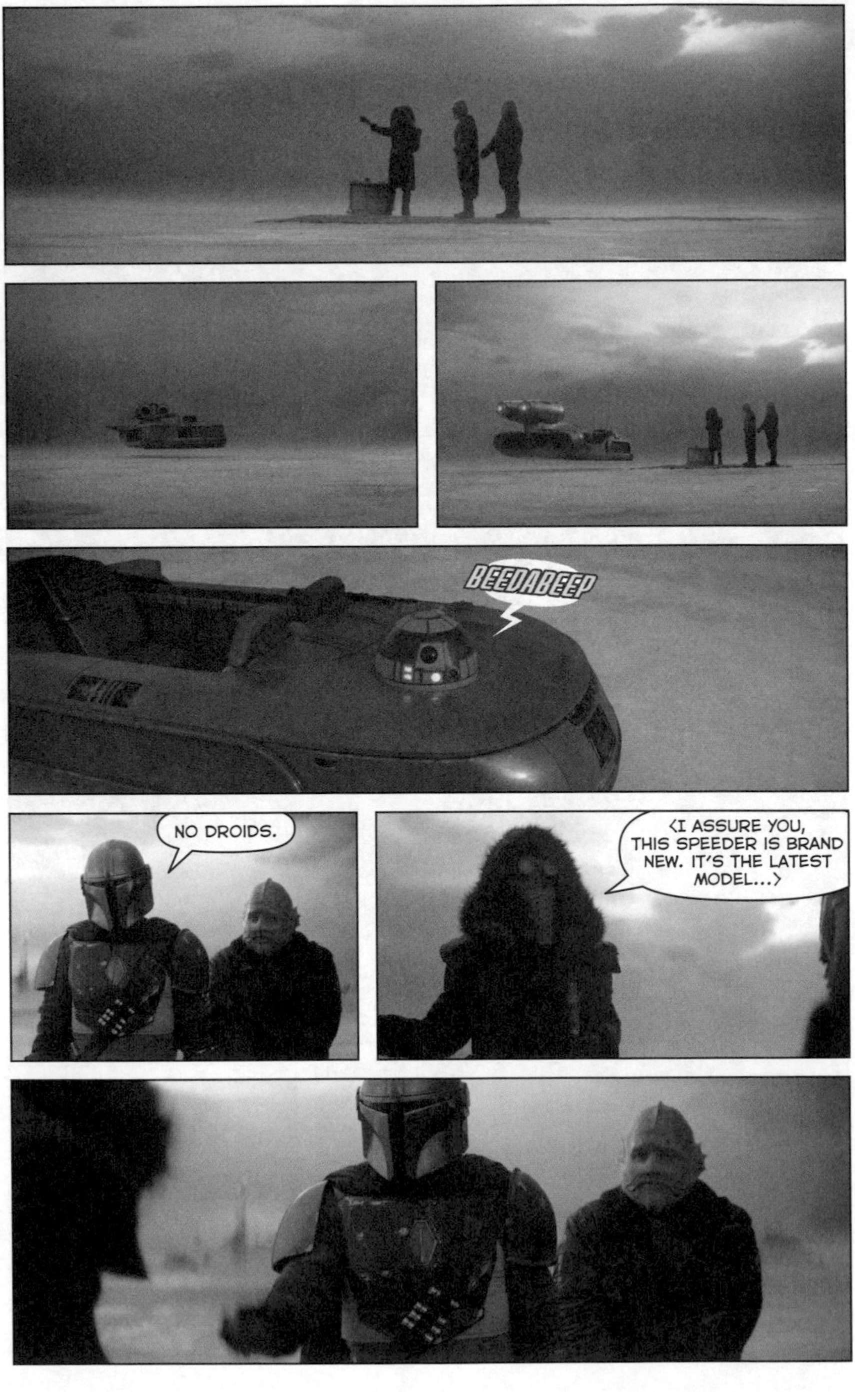
BEEDABEEP
NO DROIDS.
<I ASSURE YOU, THIS SPEEDER IS BRAND NEW. IT'S THE LATEST MODEL...>

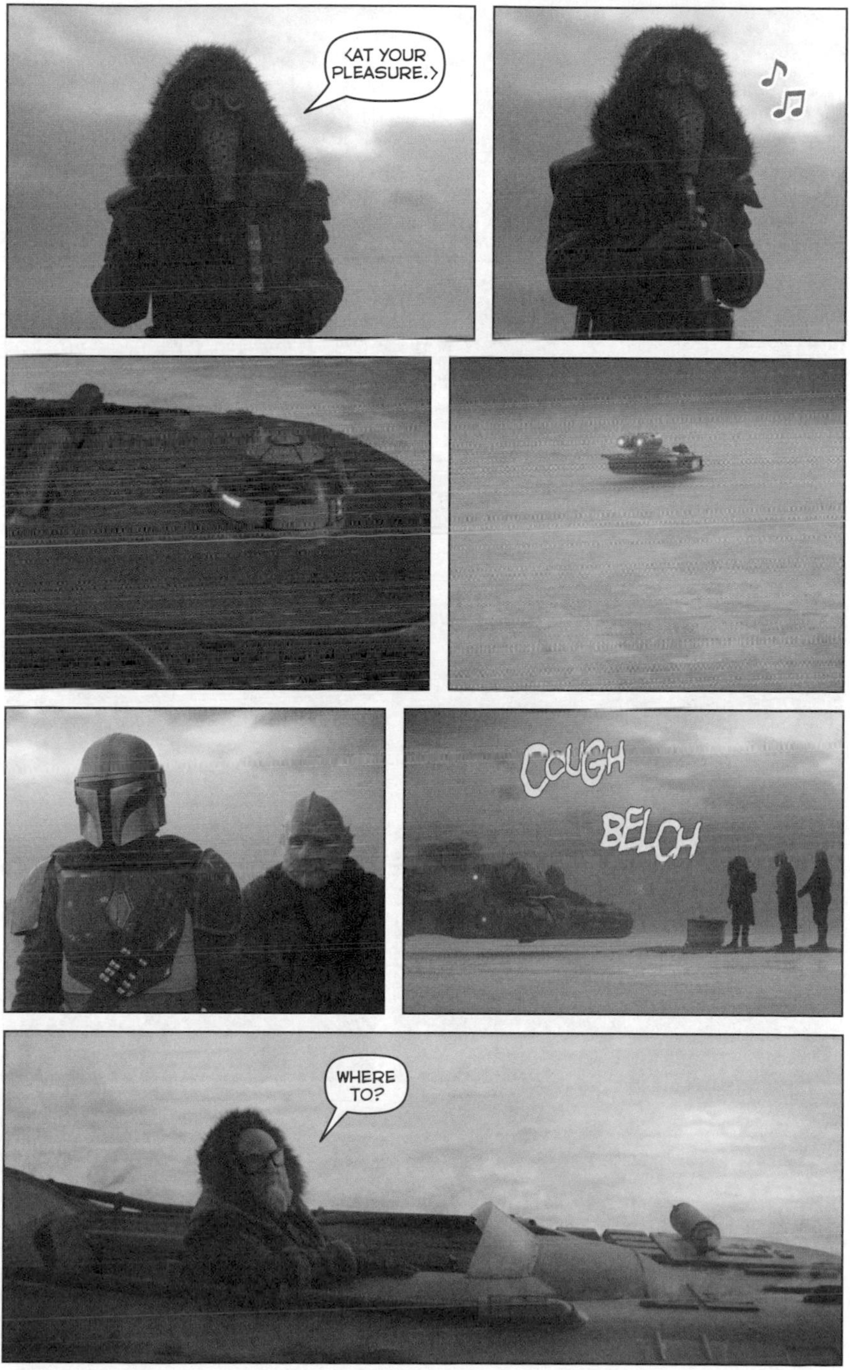
‹AT YOUR PLEASURE.›
COUGH
BELCH
WHERE TO?

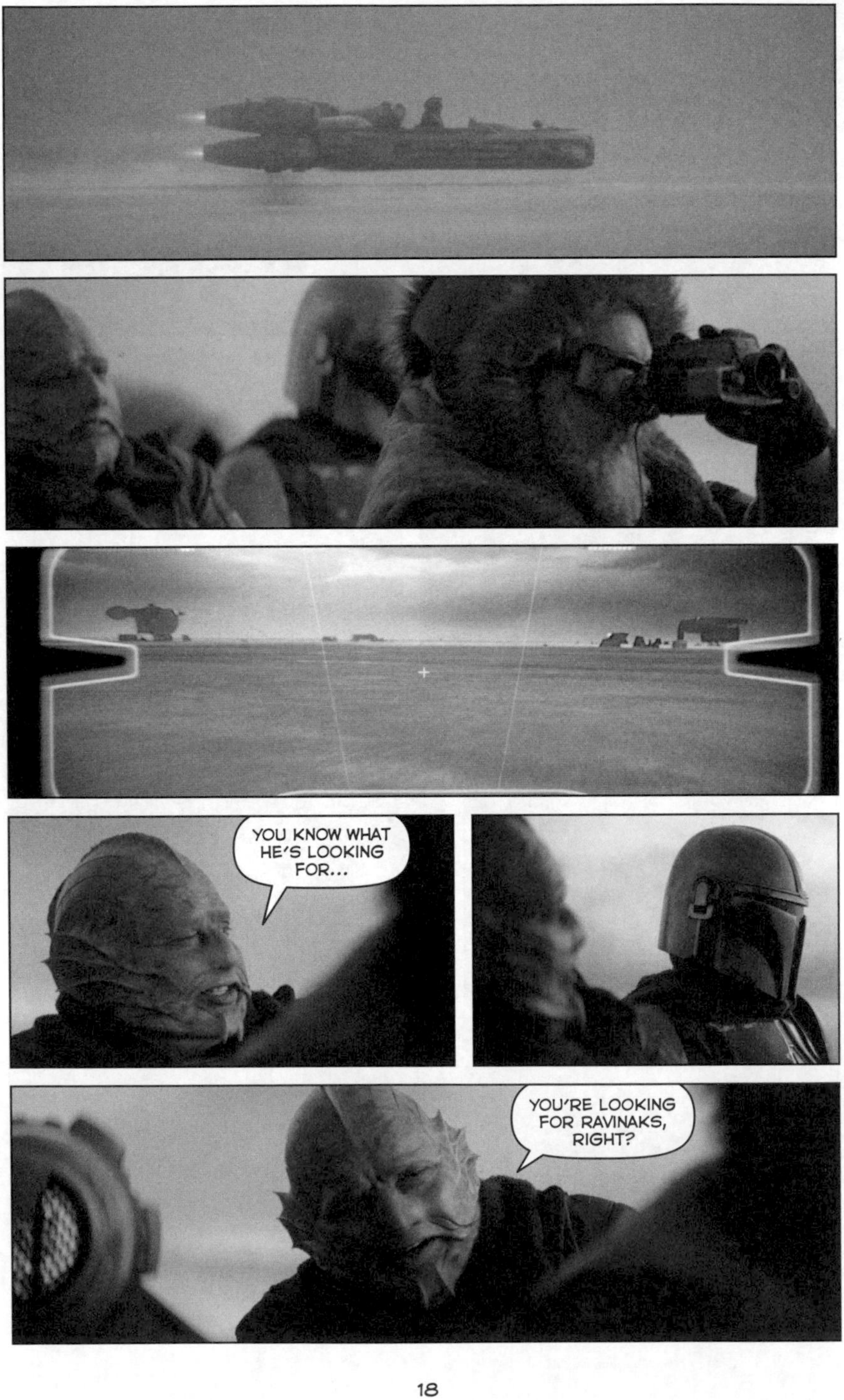
YOU KNOW WHAT HE'S LOOKING FOR...
YOU'RE LOOKING FOR RAVINAKS, RIGHT?

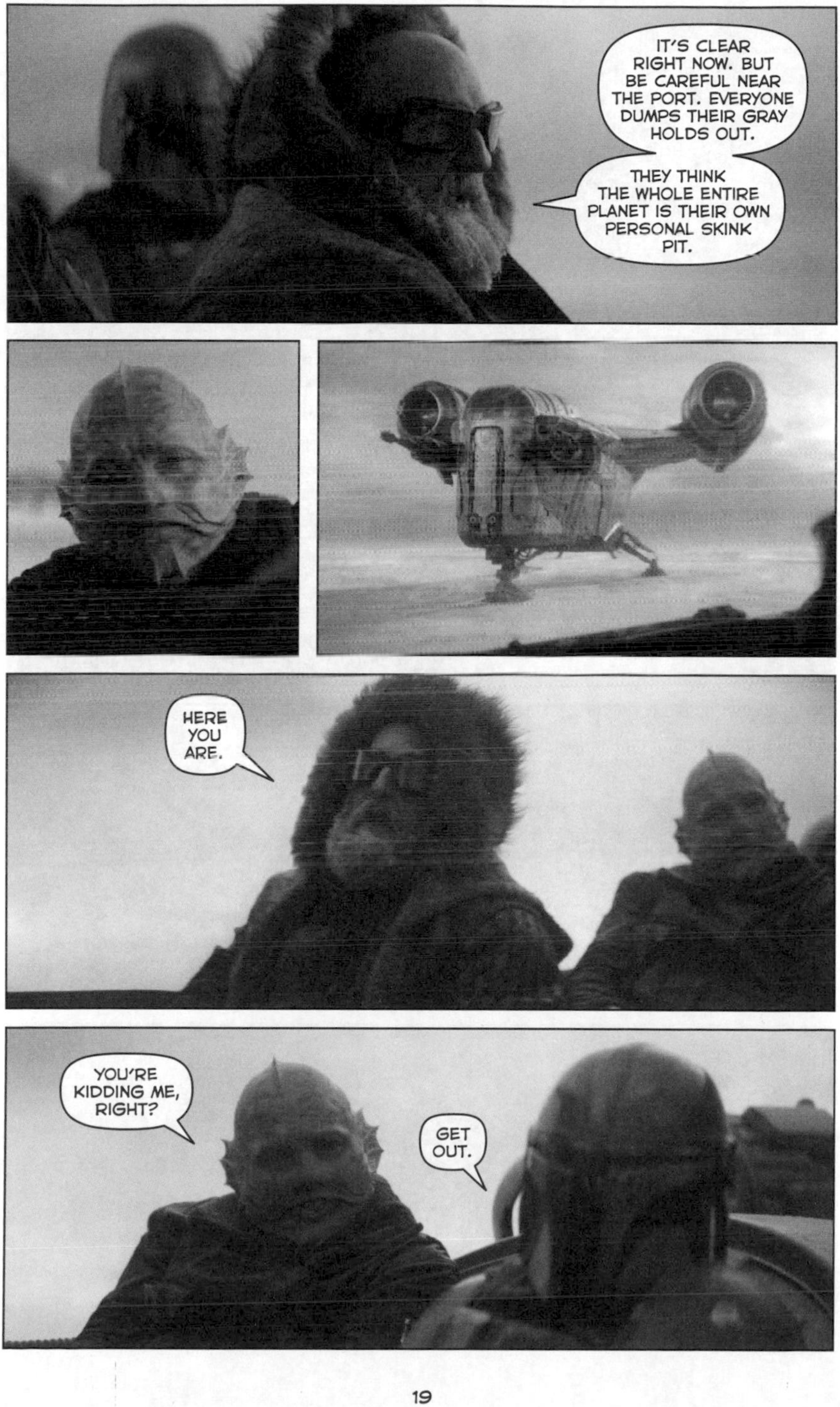
IT'S CLEAR RIGHT NOW. BUT BE CAREFUL NEAR THE PORT. EVERYONE DUMPS THEIR GRAY HOLDS OUT.
THEY THINK THE WHOLE ENTIRE PLANET IS THEIR OWN PERSONAL SKINK PIT.
HERE YOU ARE.
YOU'RE KIDDING ME, RIGHT?
GET OUT.

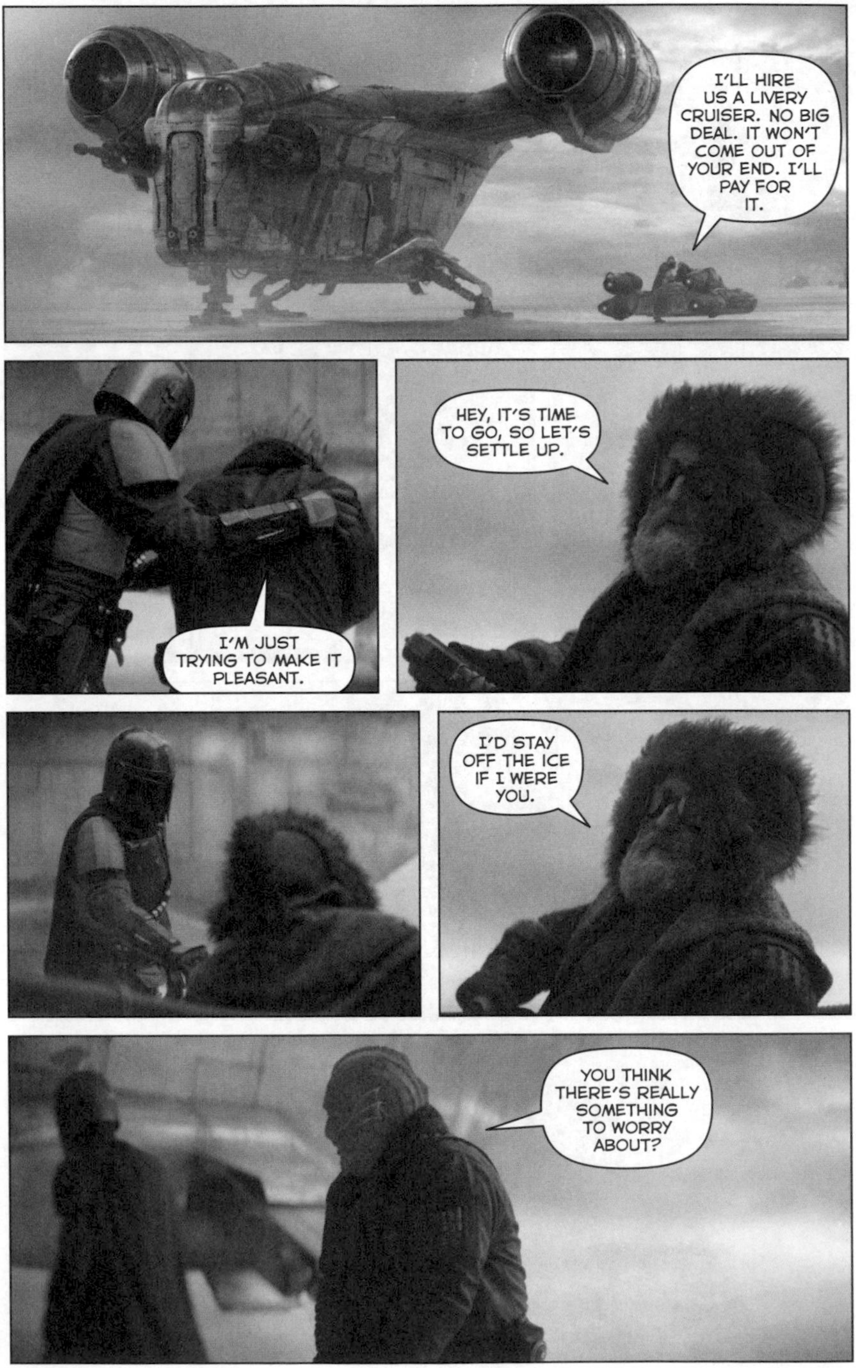
I'LL HIRE US A LIVERY CRUISER. NO BIG DEAL. IT WON'T COME OUT OF YOUR END. I'LL PAY FOR IT.
I'M JUST TRYING TO MAKE IT PLEASANT.
HEY, IT'S TIME TO GO, SO LET'S SETTLE UP.
I'D STAY OFF THE ICE IF I WERE YOU.
YOU THINK THERE'S REALLY SOMETHING TO WORRY ABOUT?

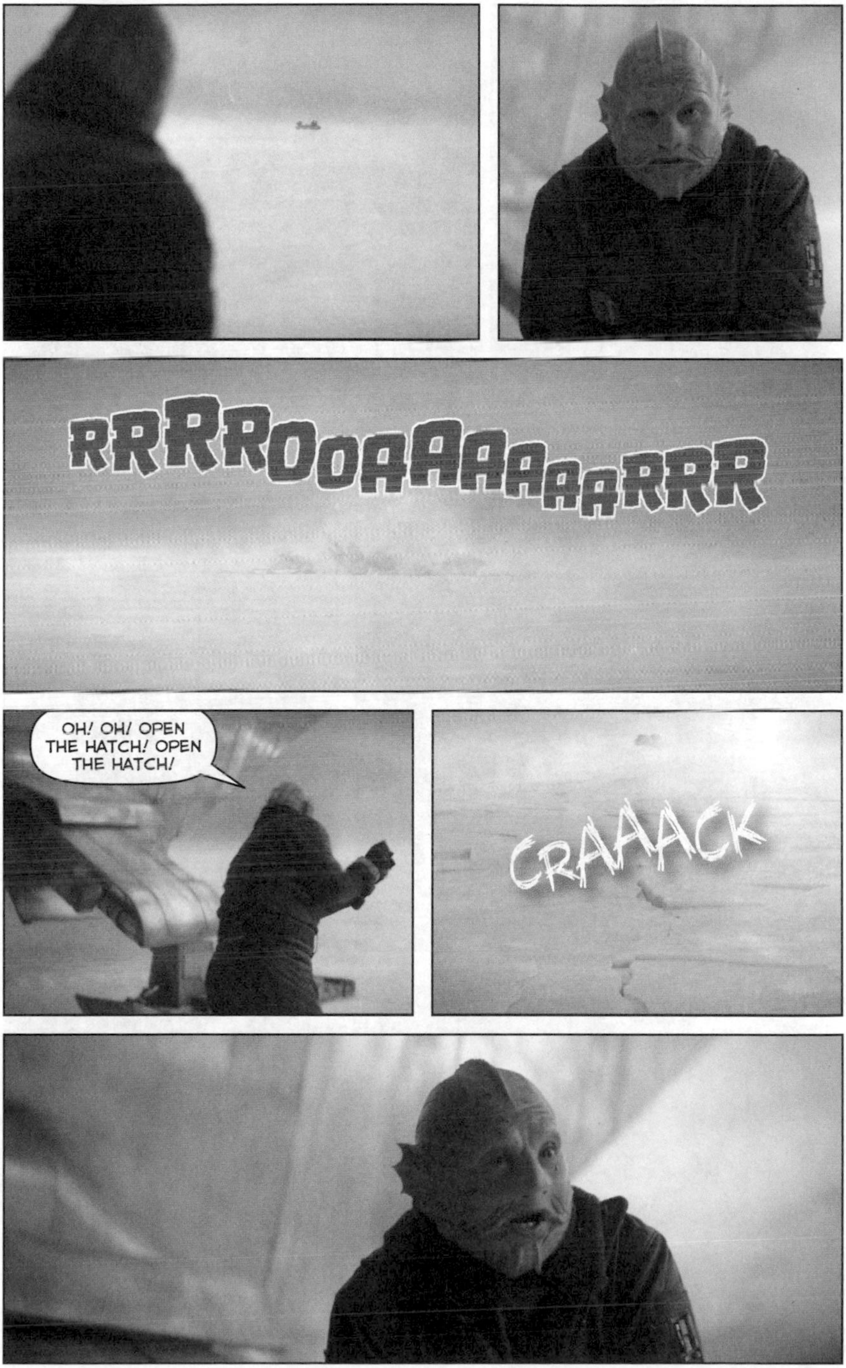
RRRROOAAAAAAARRRR
OH! OH! OPEN THE HATCH! OPEN THE HATCH!
CRAAACK

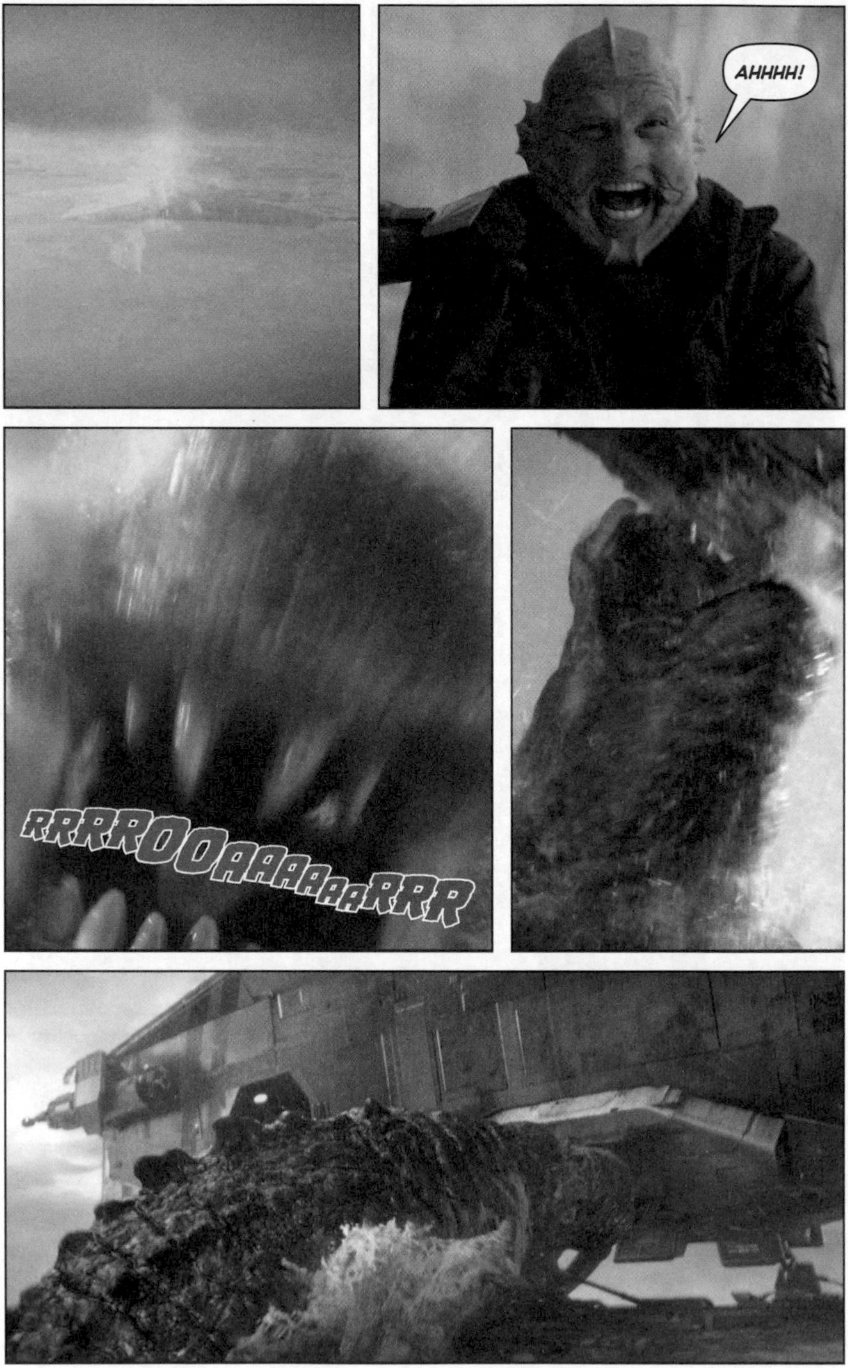
AHHHH!
RRRROOAAAAAAARRR

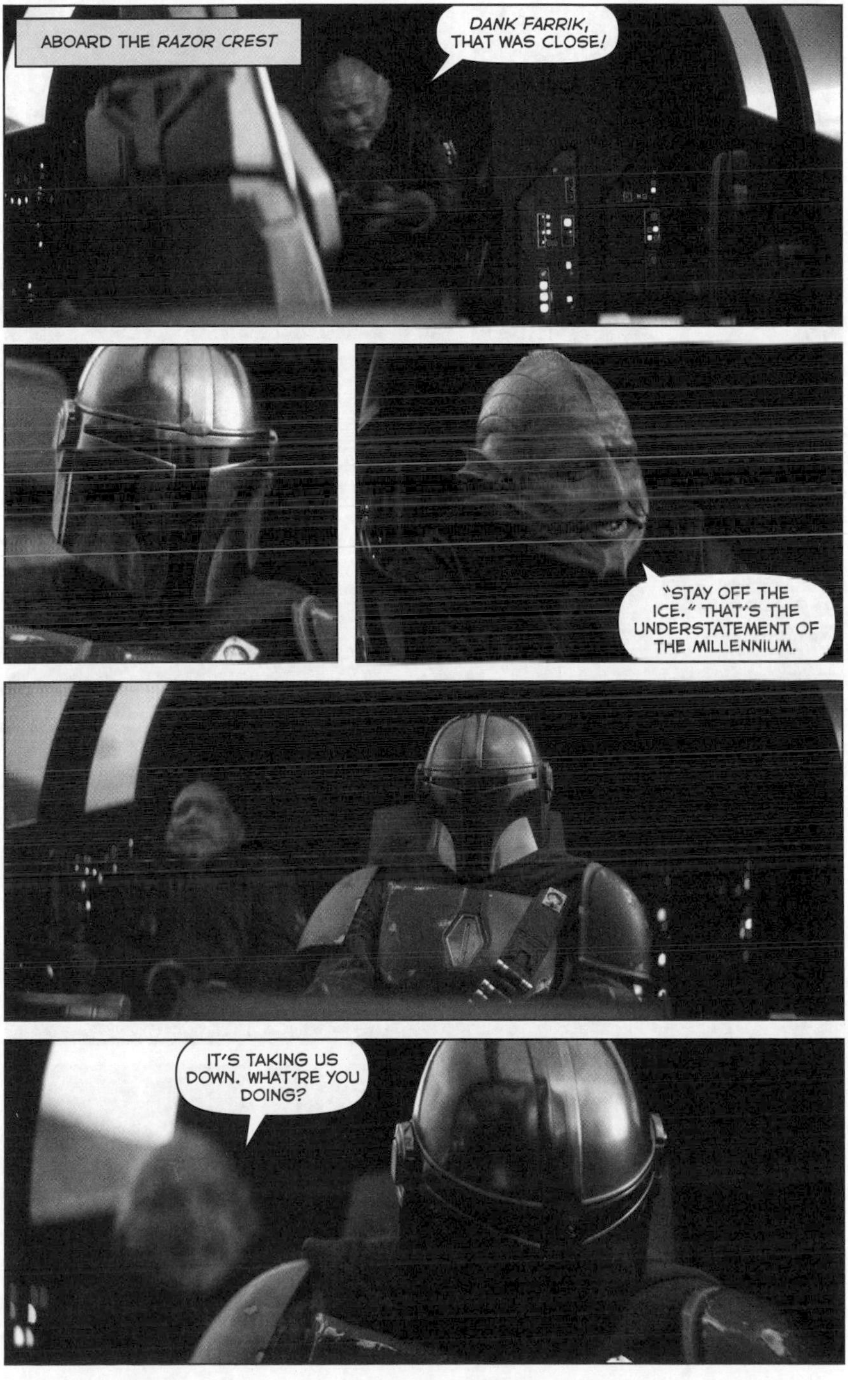
ABOARD THE *RAZOR CREST*
DANK FARRIK, THAT WAS CLOSE!
"STAY OFF THE ICE." THAT'S THE UNDERSTATEMENT OF THE MILLENNIUM.
IT'S TAKING US DOWN. WHAT'RE YOU DOING?

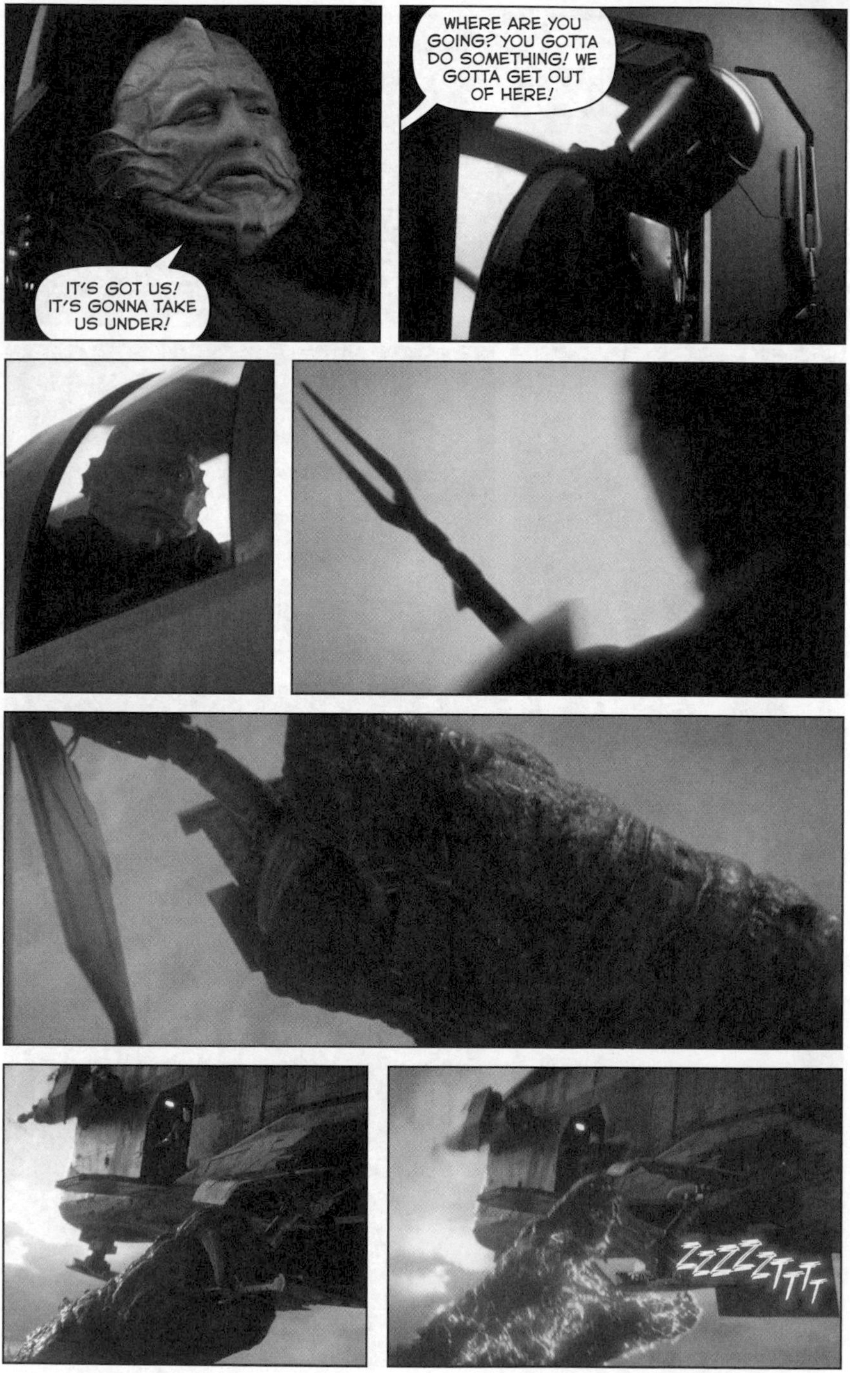
IT'S GOT US! IT'S GONNA TAKE US UNDER!
WHERE ARE YOU GOING? YOU GOTTA DO SOMETHING! WE GOTTA GET OUT OF HERE!
ZZZZZZTTTT

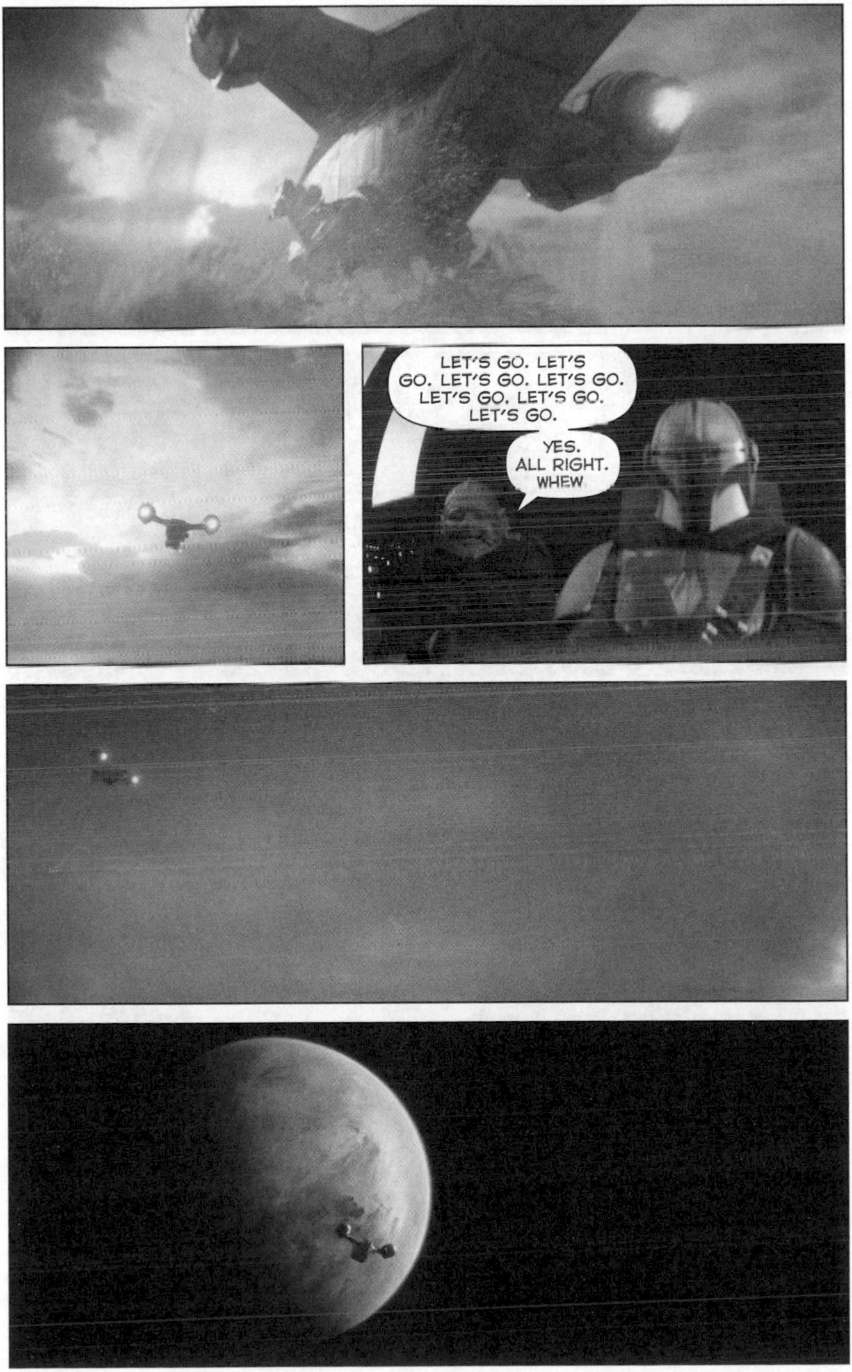
LET'S GO. LET'S GO. LET'S GO. LET'S GO. LET'S GO. LET'S GO. LET'S GO.
YES. ALL RIGHT. WHEW

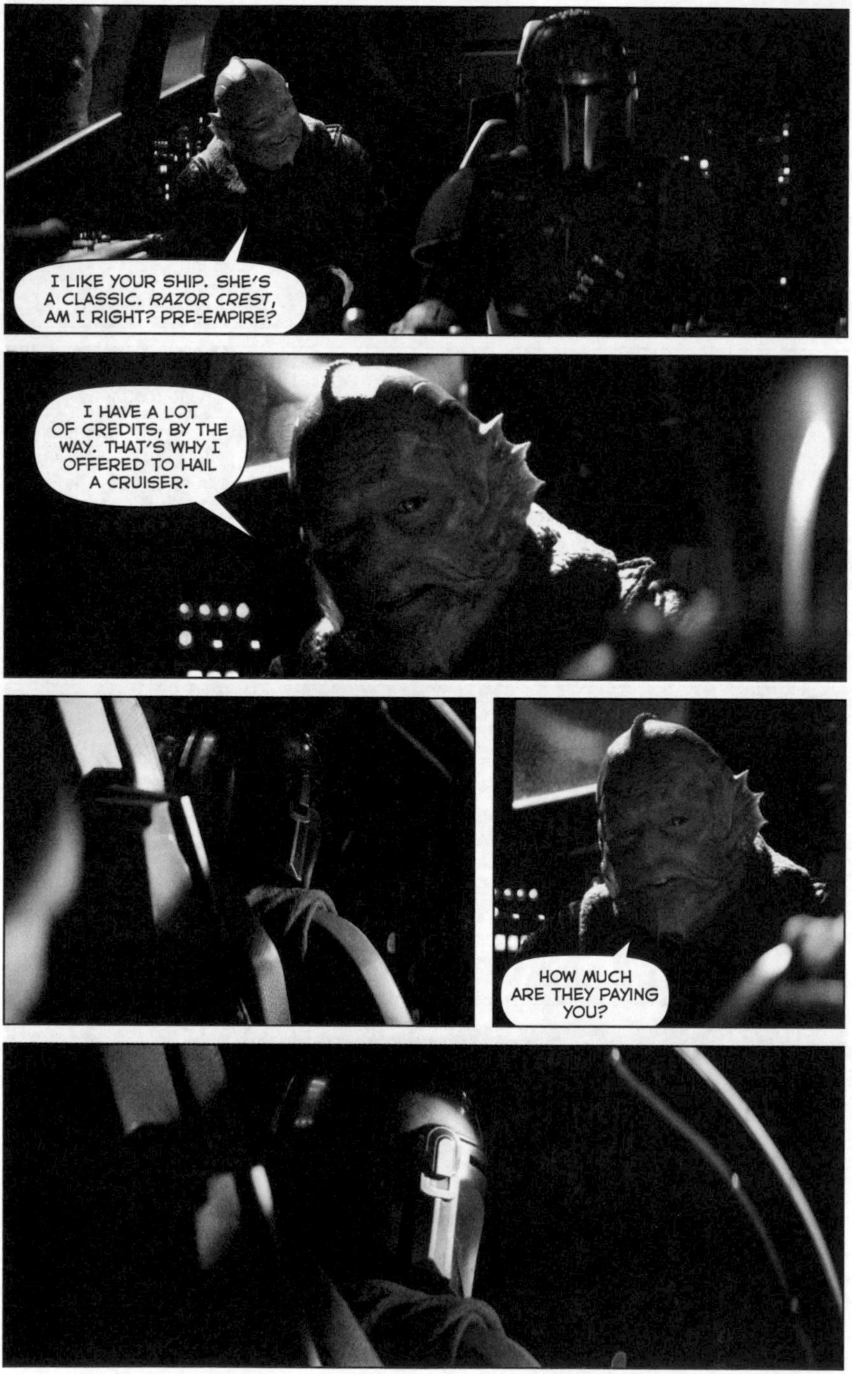
I LIKE YOUR SHIP. SHE'S A CLASSIC. *RAZOR CREST*, AM I RIGHT? PRE-EMPIRE?
I HAVE A LOT OF CREDITS, BY THE WAY. THAT'S WHY I OFFERED TO HAIL A CRUISER.
HOW MUCH ARE THEY PAYING YOU?

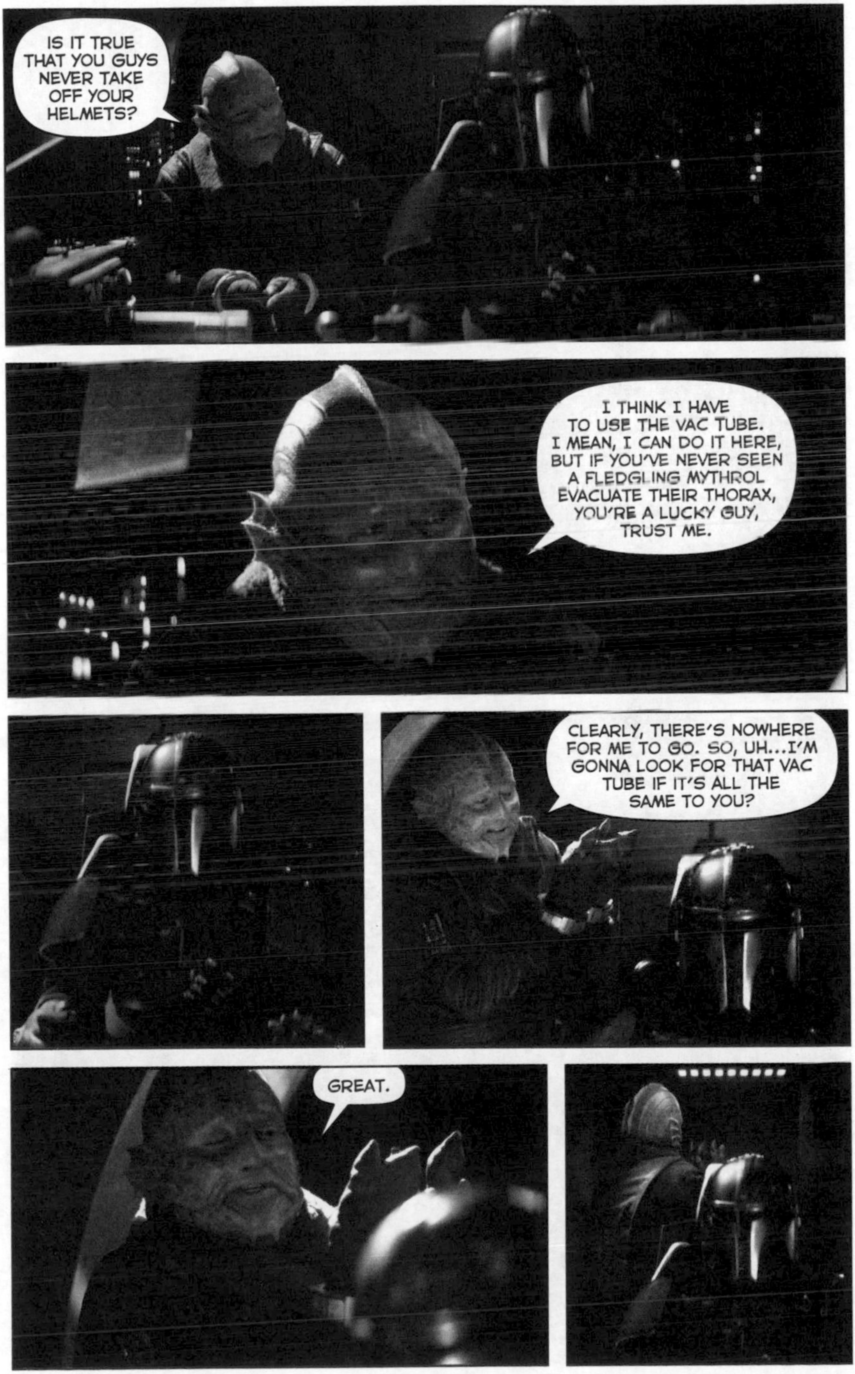
IS IT TRUE THAT YOU GUYS NEVER TAKE OFF YOUR HELMETS?
I THINK I HAVE TO USE THE VAC TUBE. I MEAN, I CAN DO IT HERE, BUT IF YOU'VE NEVER SEEN A FLEDGLING MYTHROL EVACUATE THEIR THORAX, YOU'RE A LUCKY GUY, TRUST ME.
CLEARLY, THERE'S NOWHERE FOR ME TO GO. SO, UH...I'M GONNA LOOK FOR THAT VAC TUBE IF IT'S ALL THE SAME TO YOU?
GREAT.

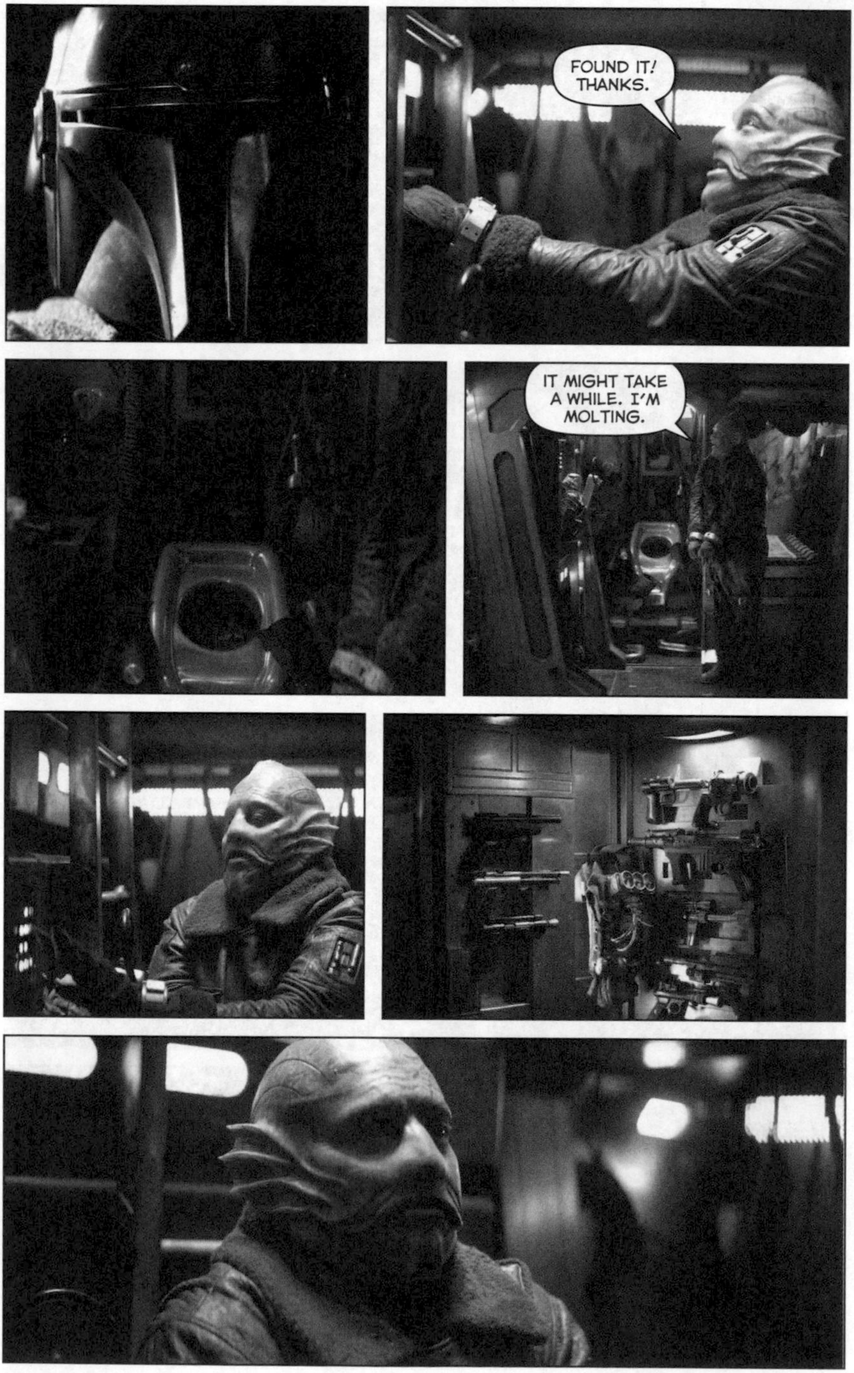
FOUND IT! THANKS.
IT MIGHT TAKE A WHILE. I'M MOLTING.

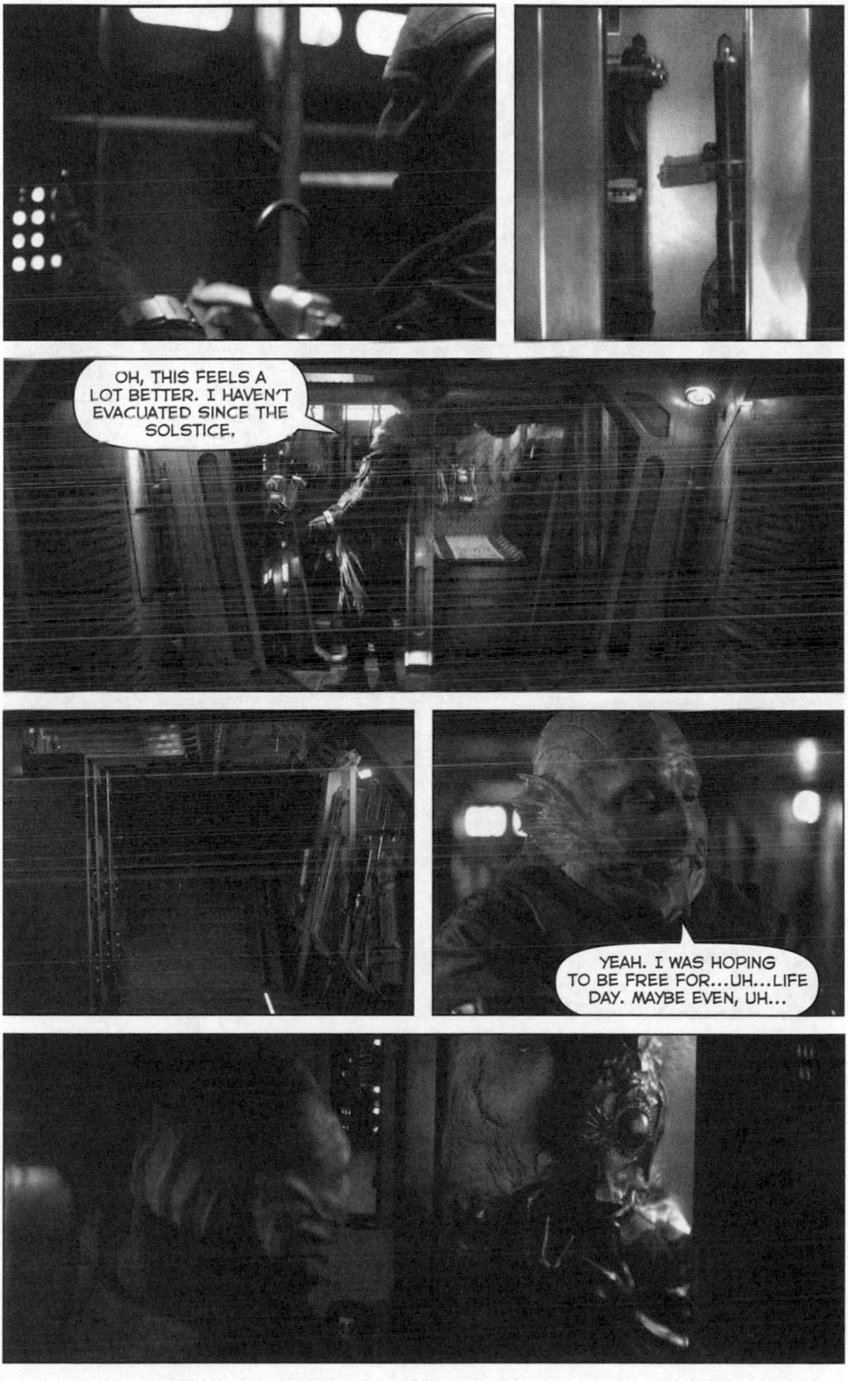
OH, THIS FEELS A LOT BETTER. I HAVEN'T EVACUATED SINCE THE SOLSTICE.
YEAH. I WAS HOPING TO BE FREE FOR...UH...LIFE DAY. MAYBE EVEN, UH...

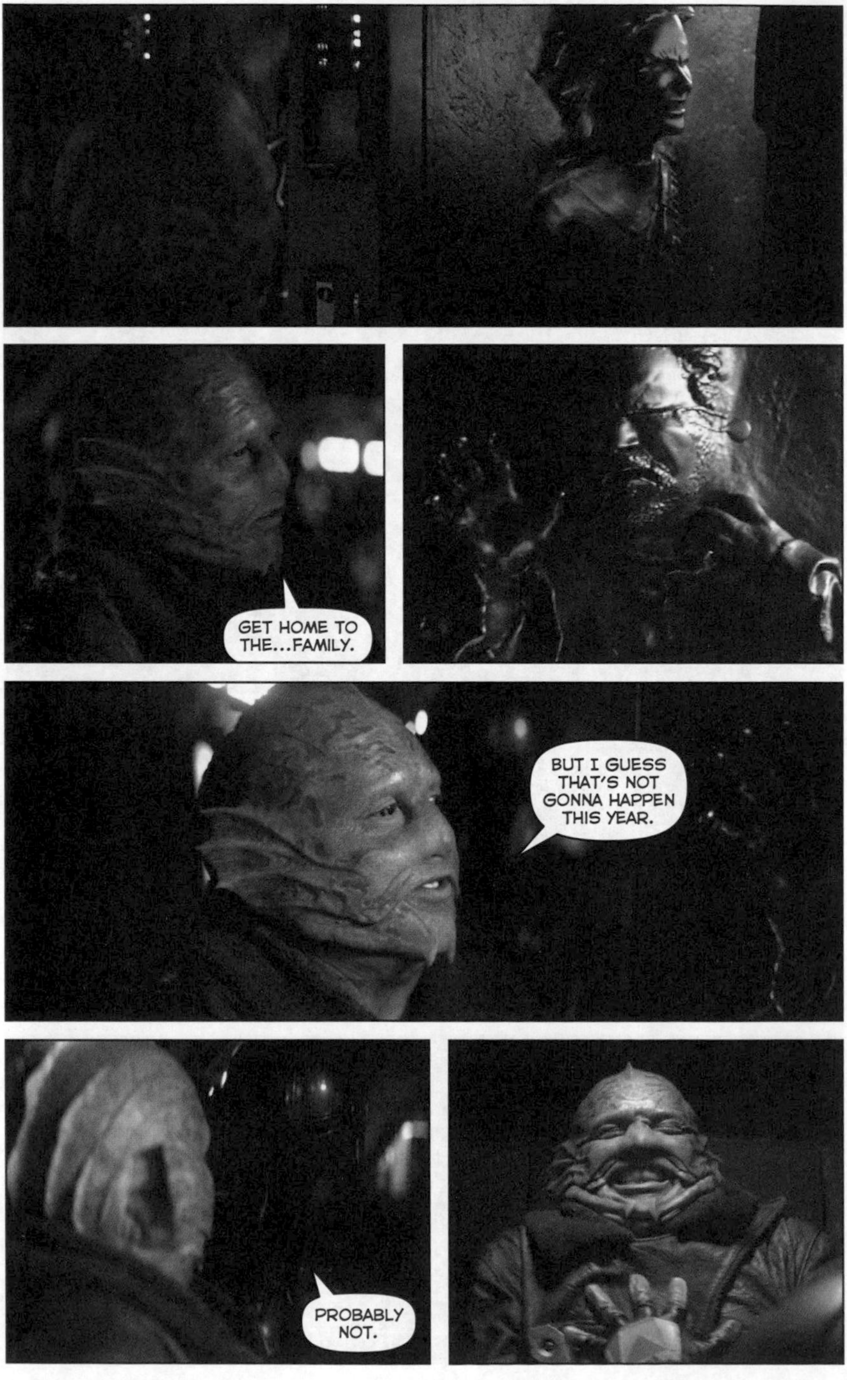
GET HOME TO THE...FAMILY.
BUT I GUESS THAT'S NOT GONNA HAPPEN THIS YEAR.
PROBABLY NOT.

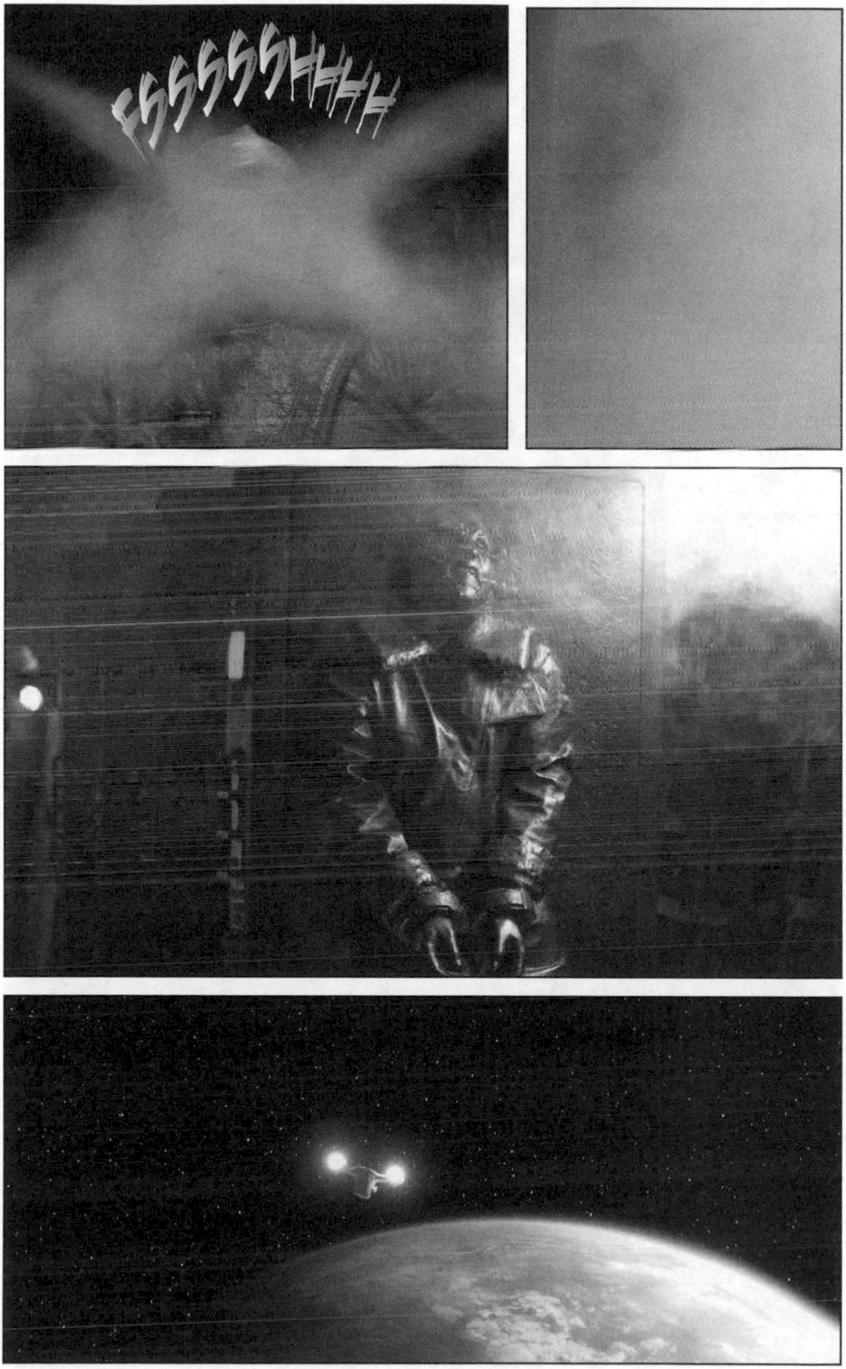
FSSSSSHHHH

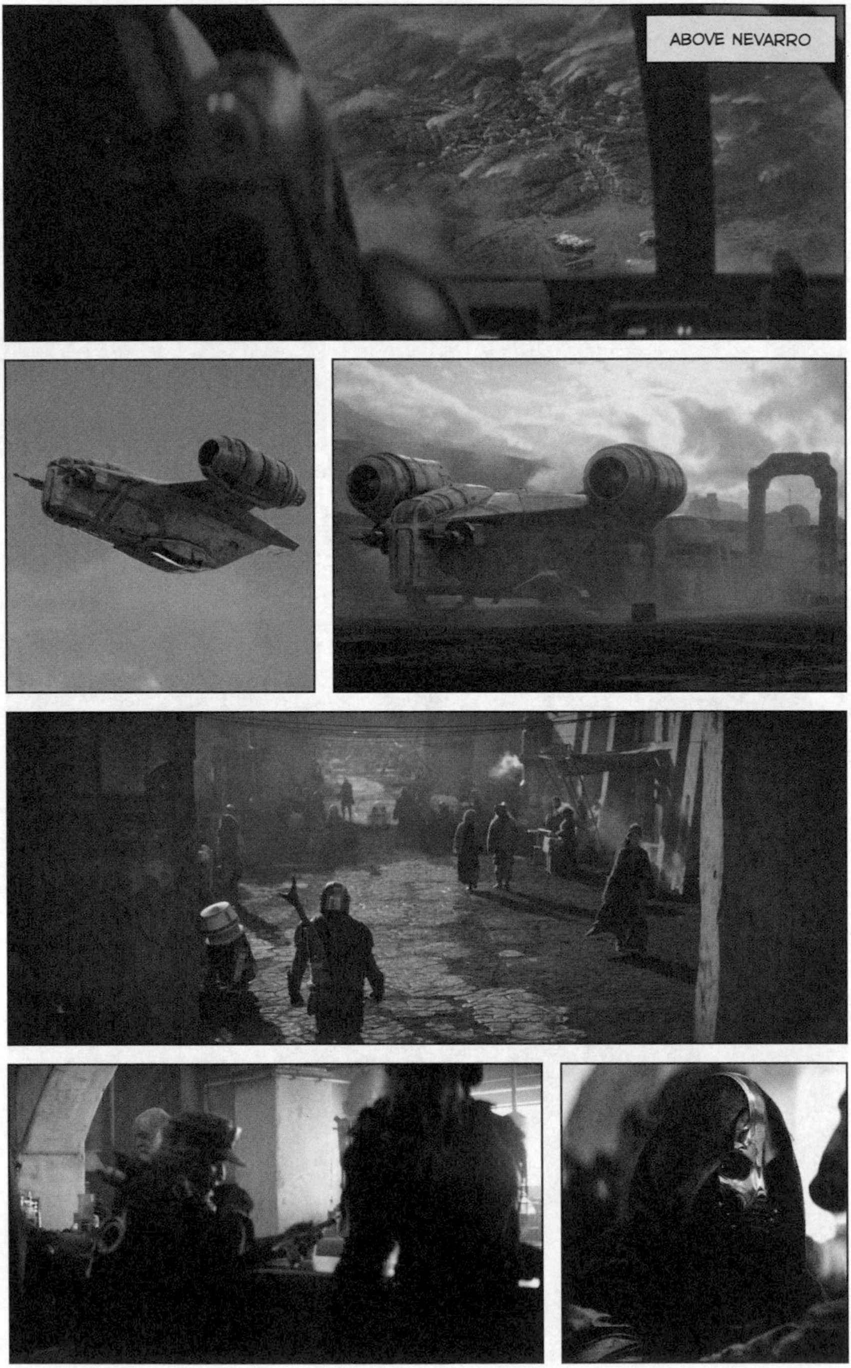
ABOVE NEVARRO

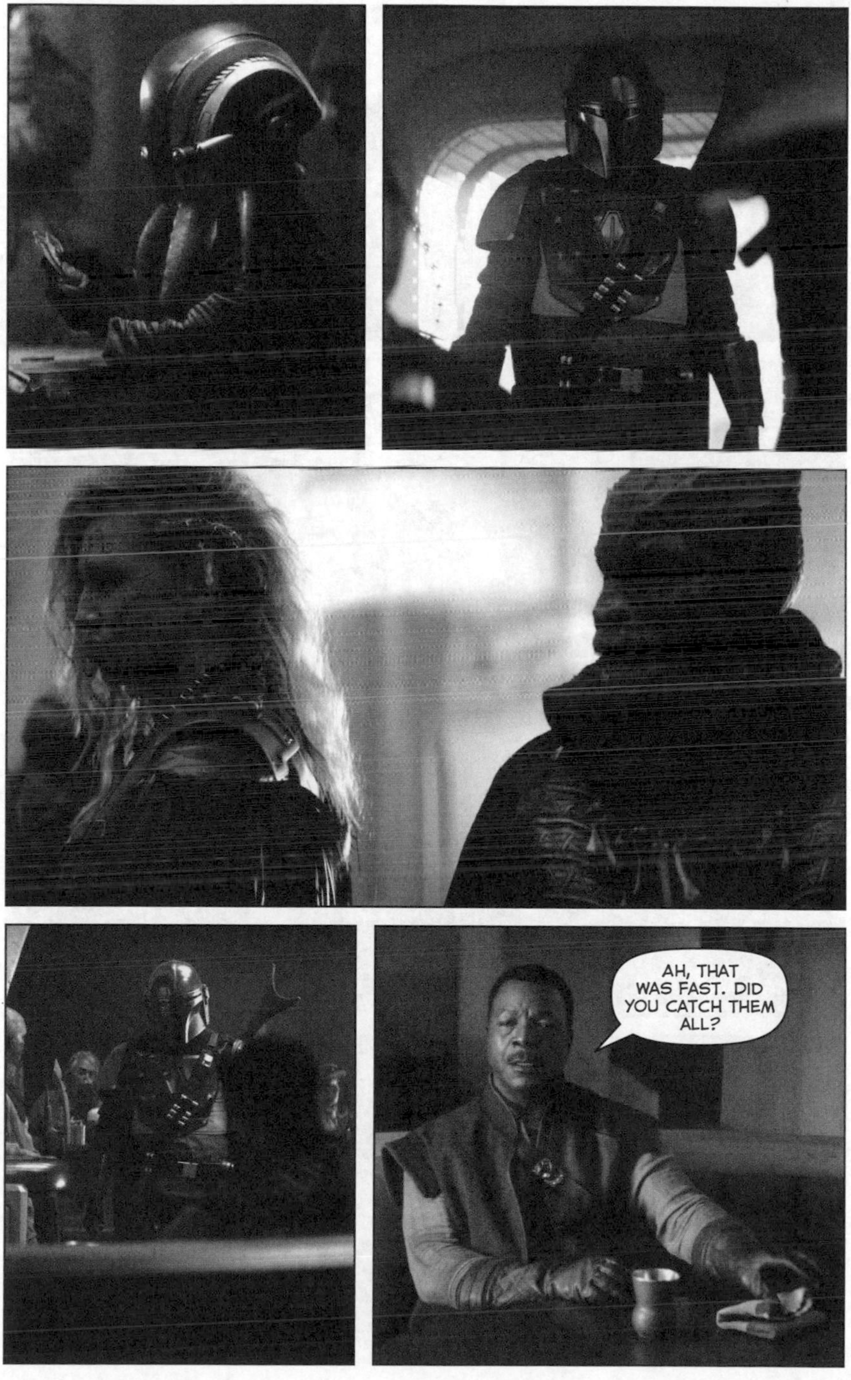
AH, THAT WAS FAST. DID YOU CATCH THEM ALL?

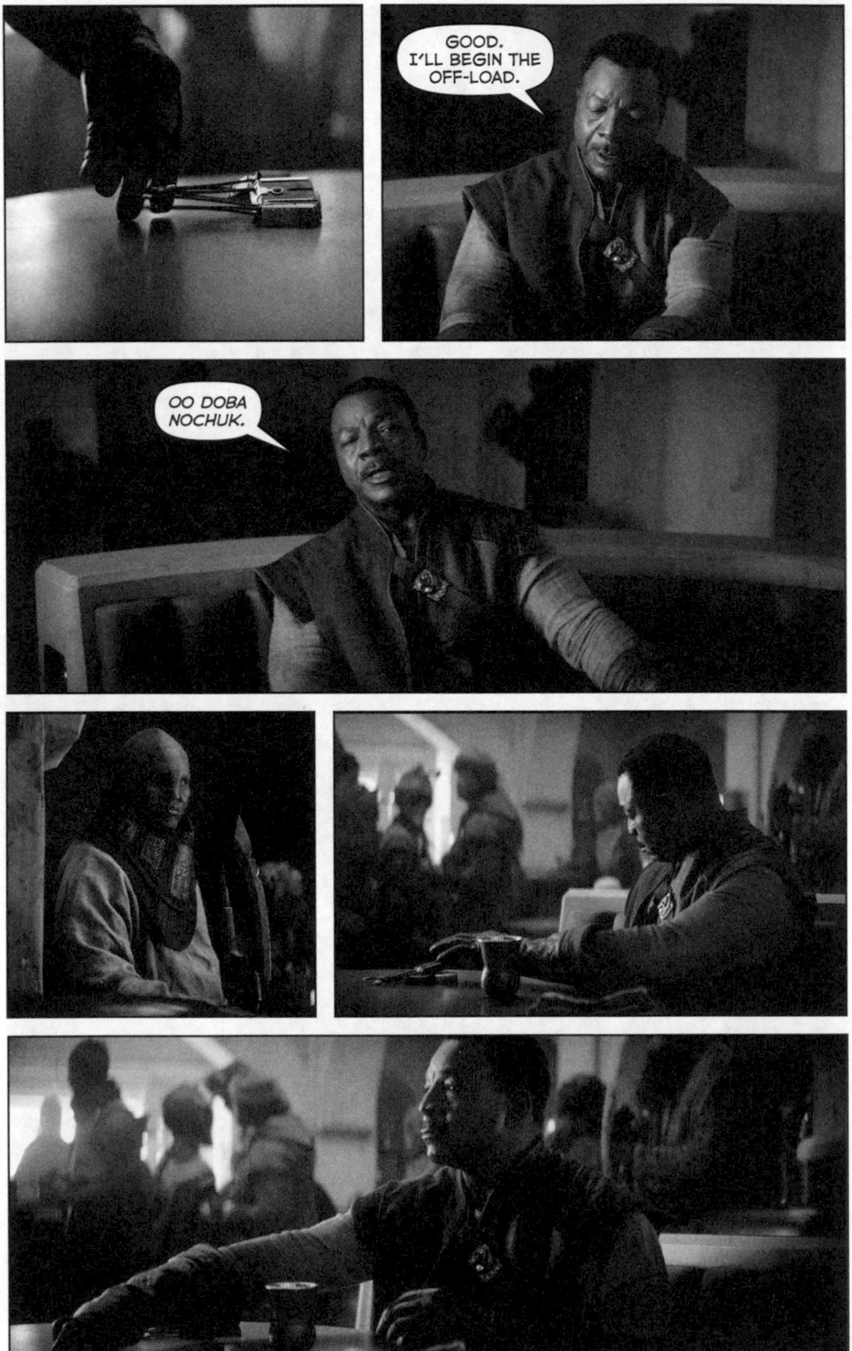
GOOD. I'LL BEGIN THE OFF-LOAD.
OO DOBA NOCHUK.

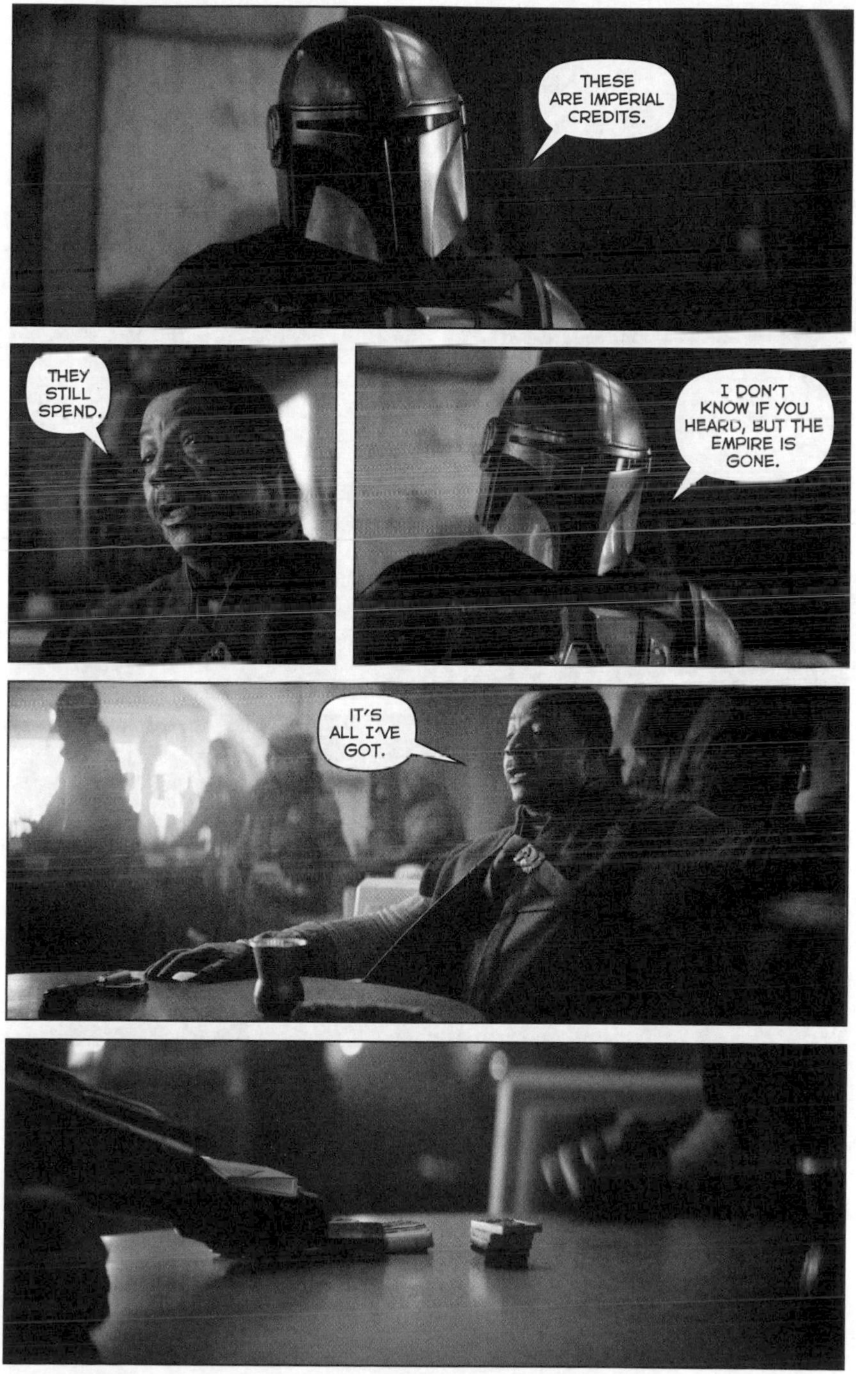
THESE ARE IMPERIAL CREDITS.
THEY STILL SPEND.
I DON'T KNOW IF YOU HEARD, BUT THE EMPIRE IS GONE.
IT'S ALL I'VE GOT.

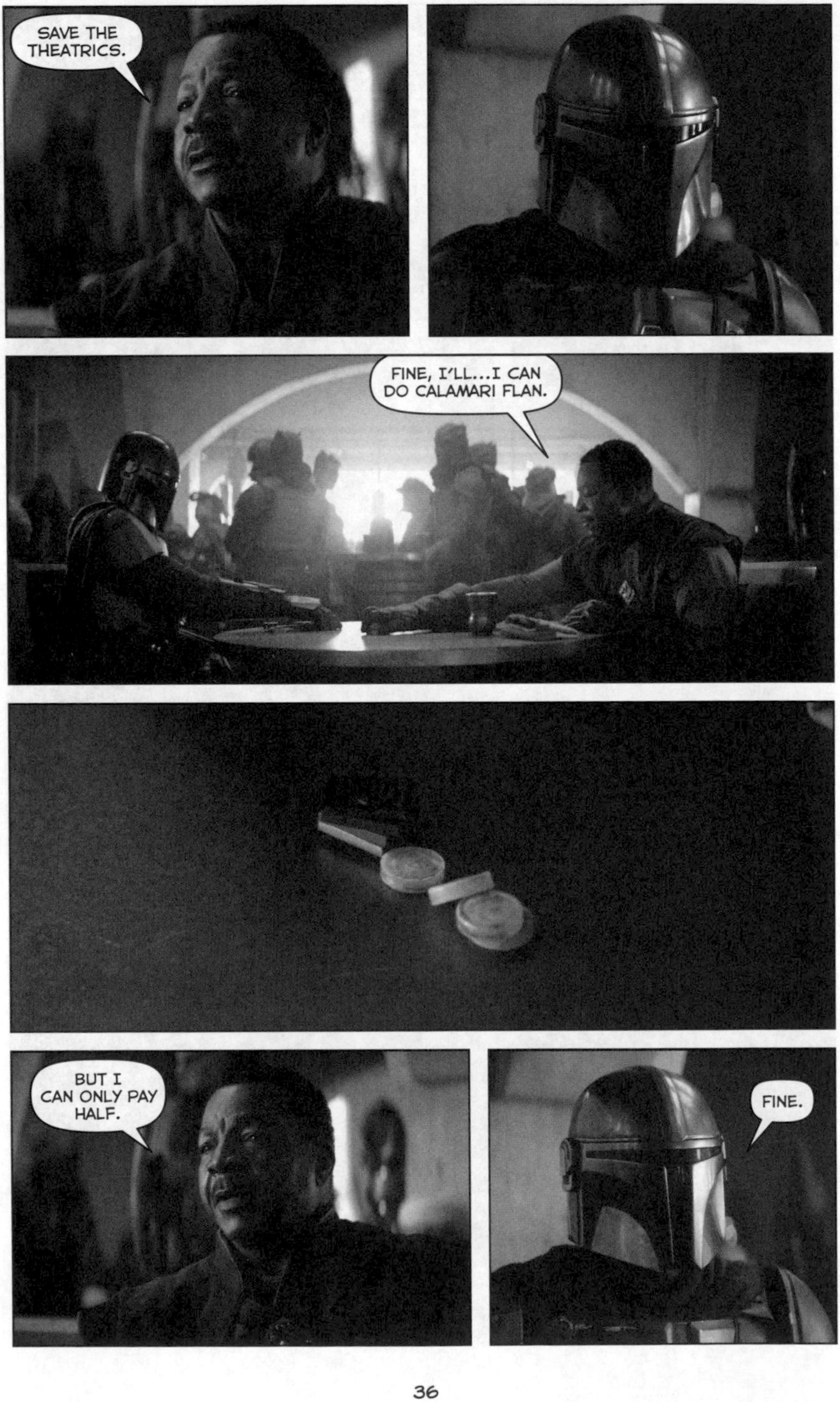
SAVE THE THEATRICS.
FINE, I'LL...I CAN DO CALAMARI FLAN.
BUT I CAN ONLY PAY HALF.
FINE.

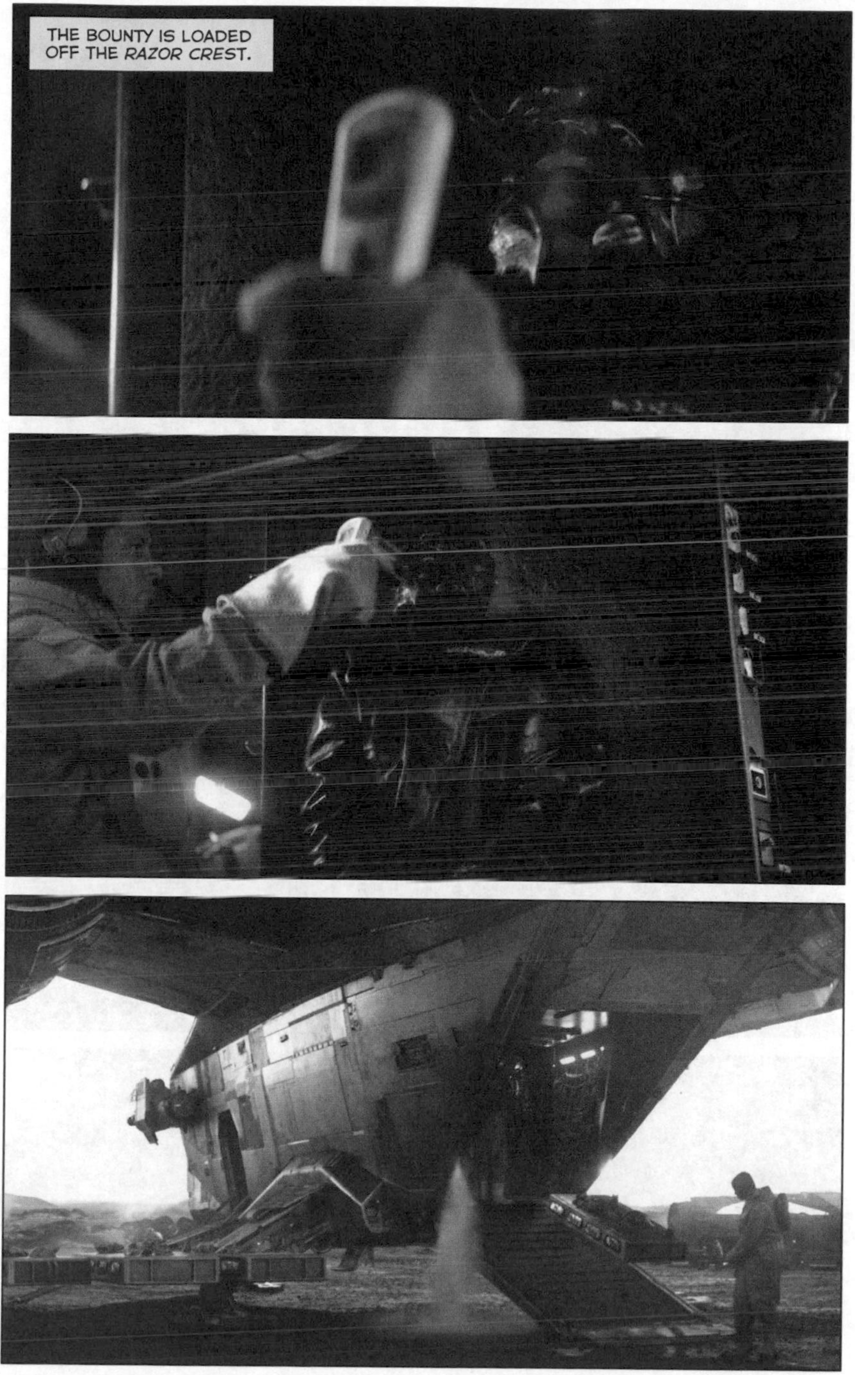
THE BOUNTY IS LOADED OFF THE *RAZOR CREST*.

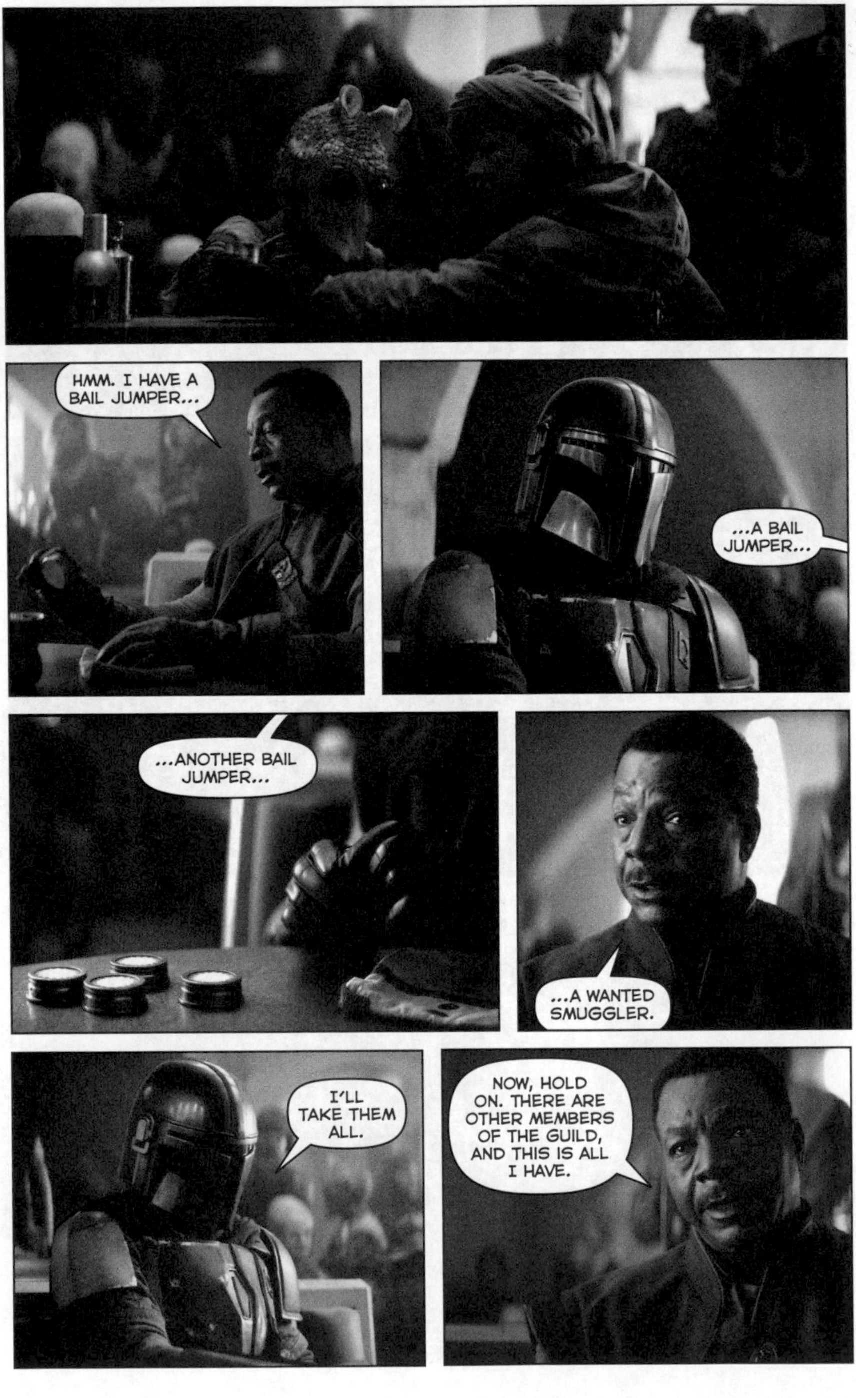
HMM. I HAVE A BAIL JUMPER...
...A BAIL JUMPER...
...ANOTHER BAIL JUMPER...
...A WANTED SMUGGLER.
I'LL TAKE THEM ALL.
NOW, HOLD ON. THERE ARE OTHER MEMBERS OF THE GUILD, AND THIS IS ALL I HAVE.

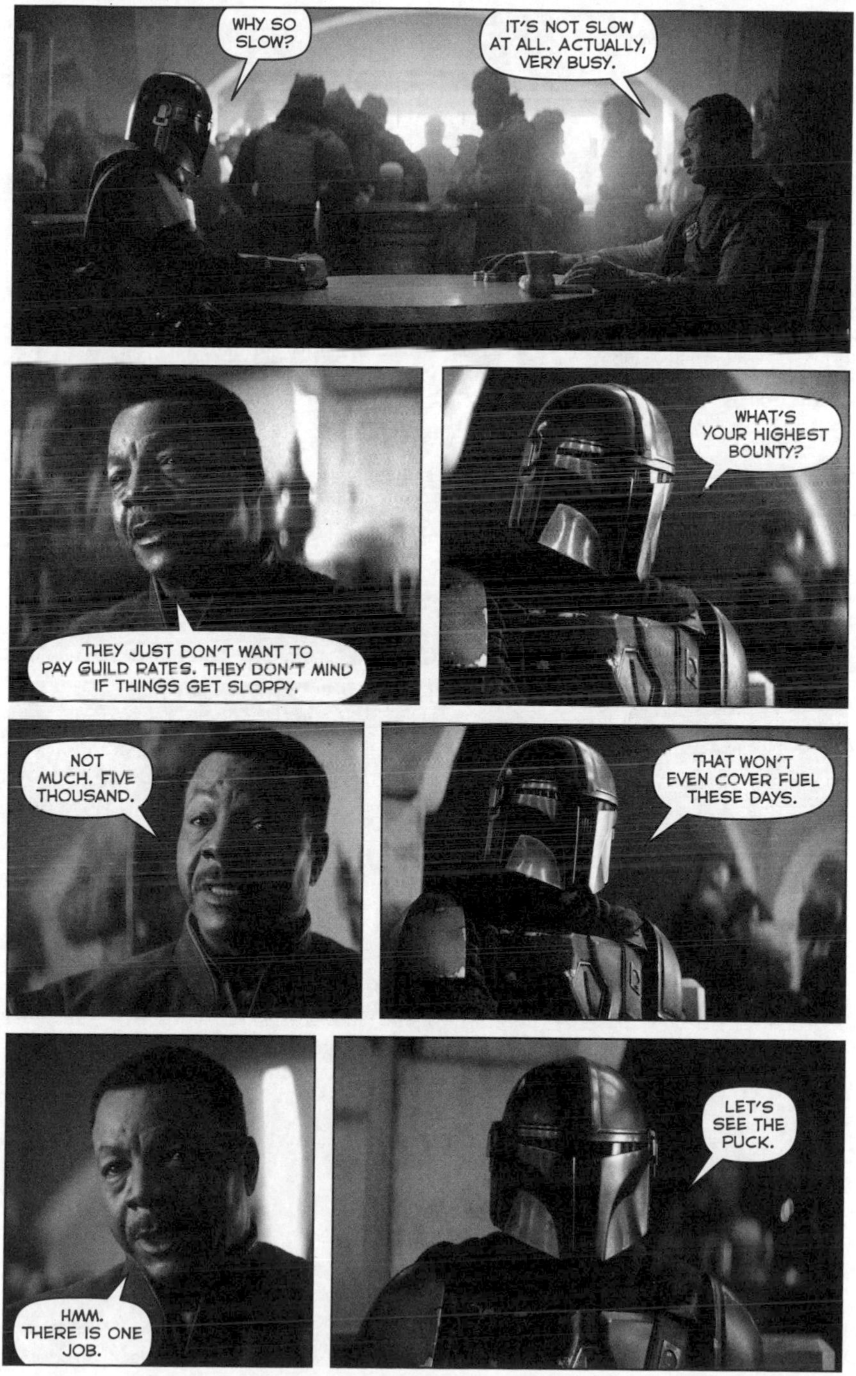
WHY SO SLOW?
IT'S NOT SLOW AT ALL. ACTUALLY, VERY BUSY.
THEY JUST DON'T WANT TO PAY GUILD RATES. THEY DON'T MIND IF THINGS GET SLOPPY.
WHAT'S YOUR HIGHEST BOUNTY?
NOT MUCH. FIVE THOUSAND.
THAT WON'T EVEN COVER FUEL THESE DAYS.
HMM. THERE IS ONE JOB.
LET'S SEE THE PUCK.

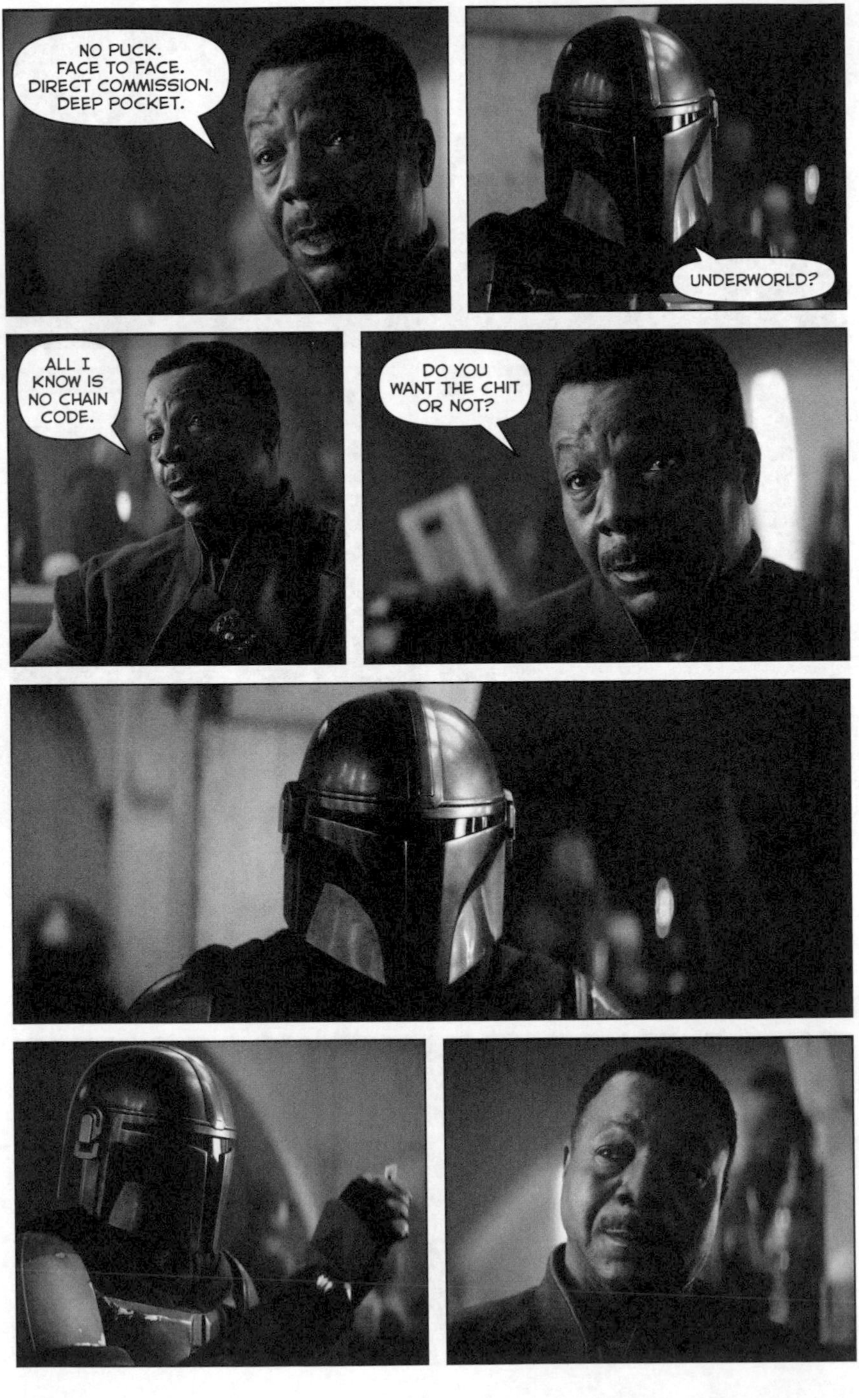
NO PUCK.
FACE TO FACE.
DIRECT COMMISSION.
DEEP POCKET.
UNDERWORLD?
ALL I KNOW IS NO CHAIN CODE.
DO YOU WANT THE CHIT OR NOT?

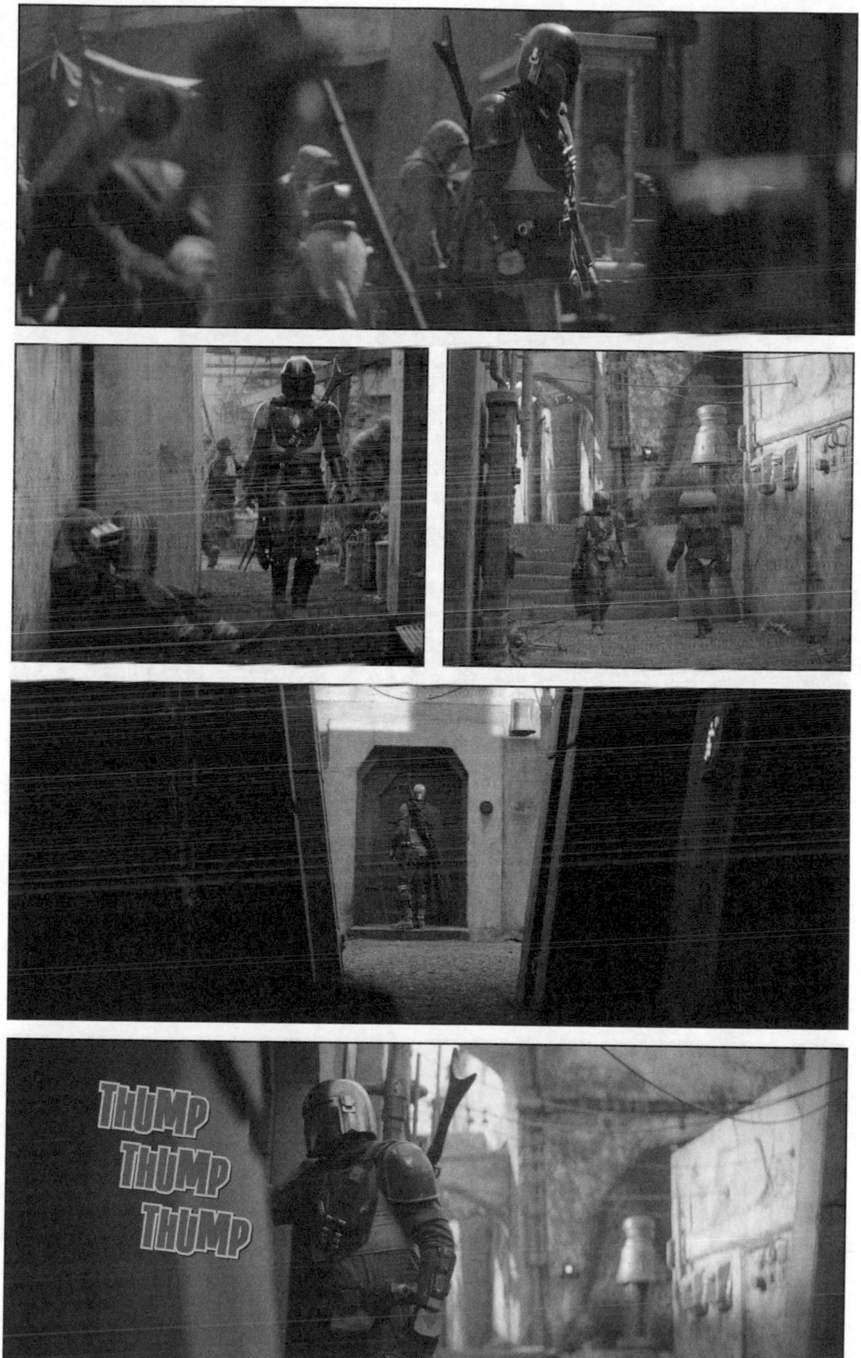
THUMP
THUMP
THUMP

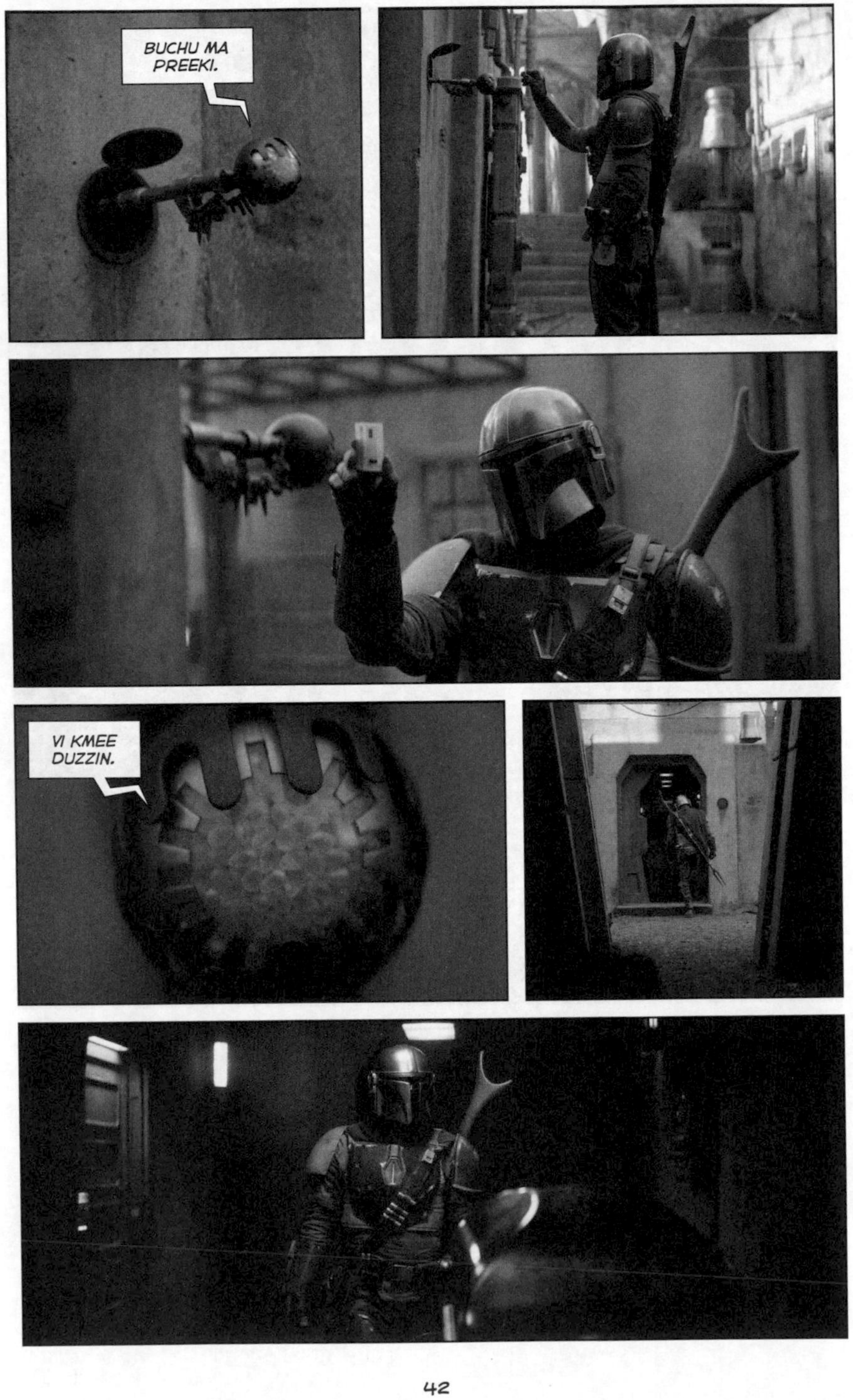
BUCHU MA PREEKI.
VI KMEE DUZZIN.

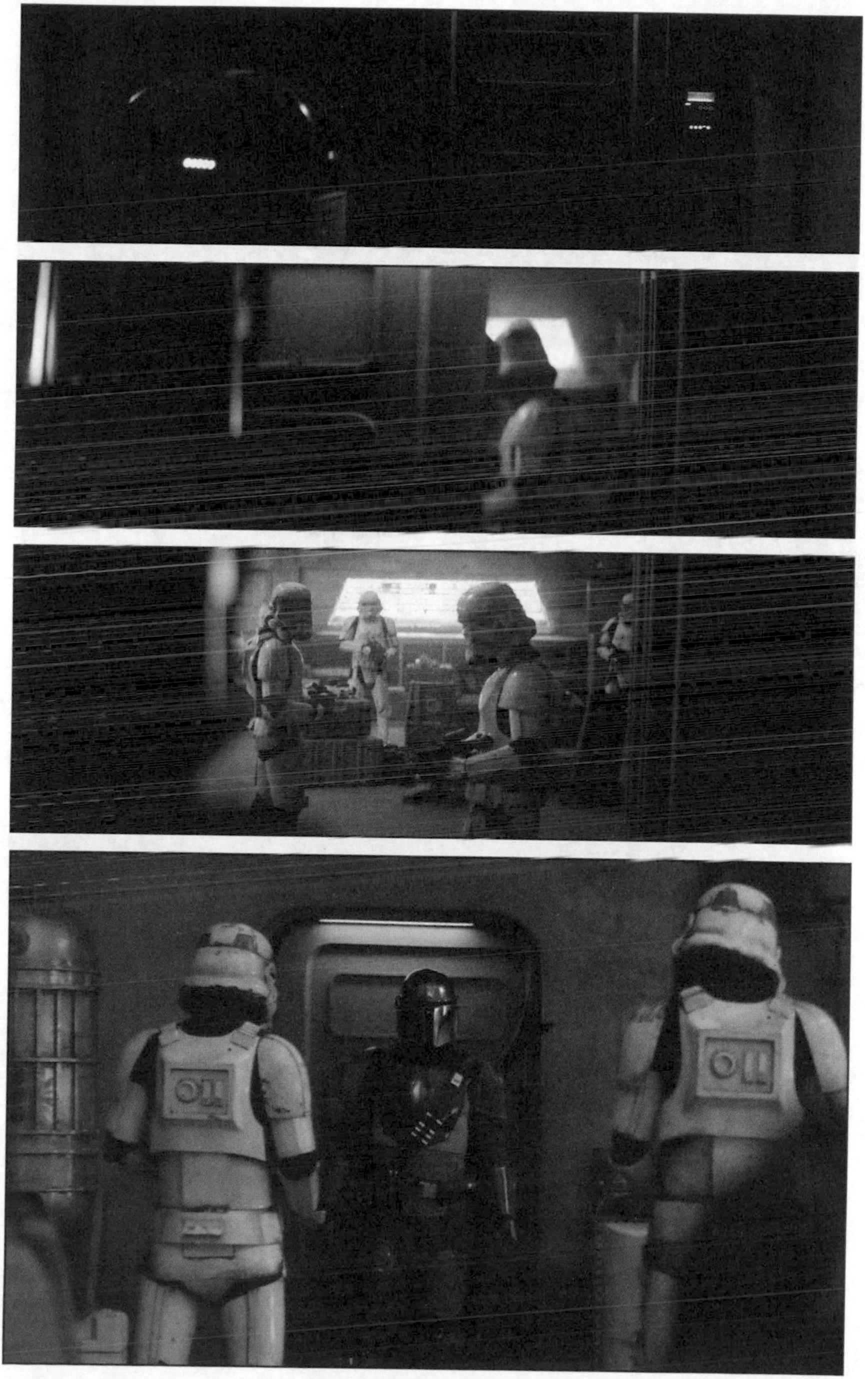

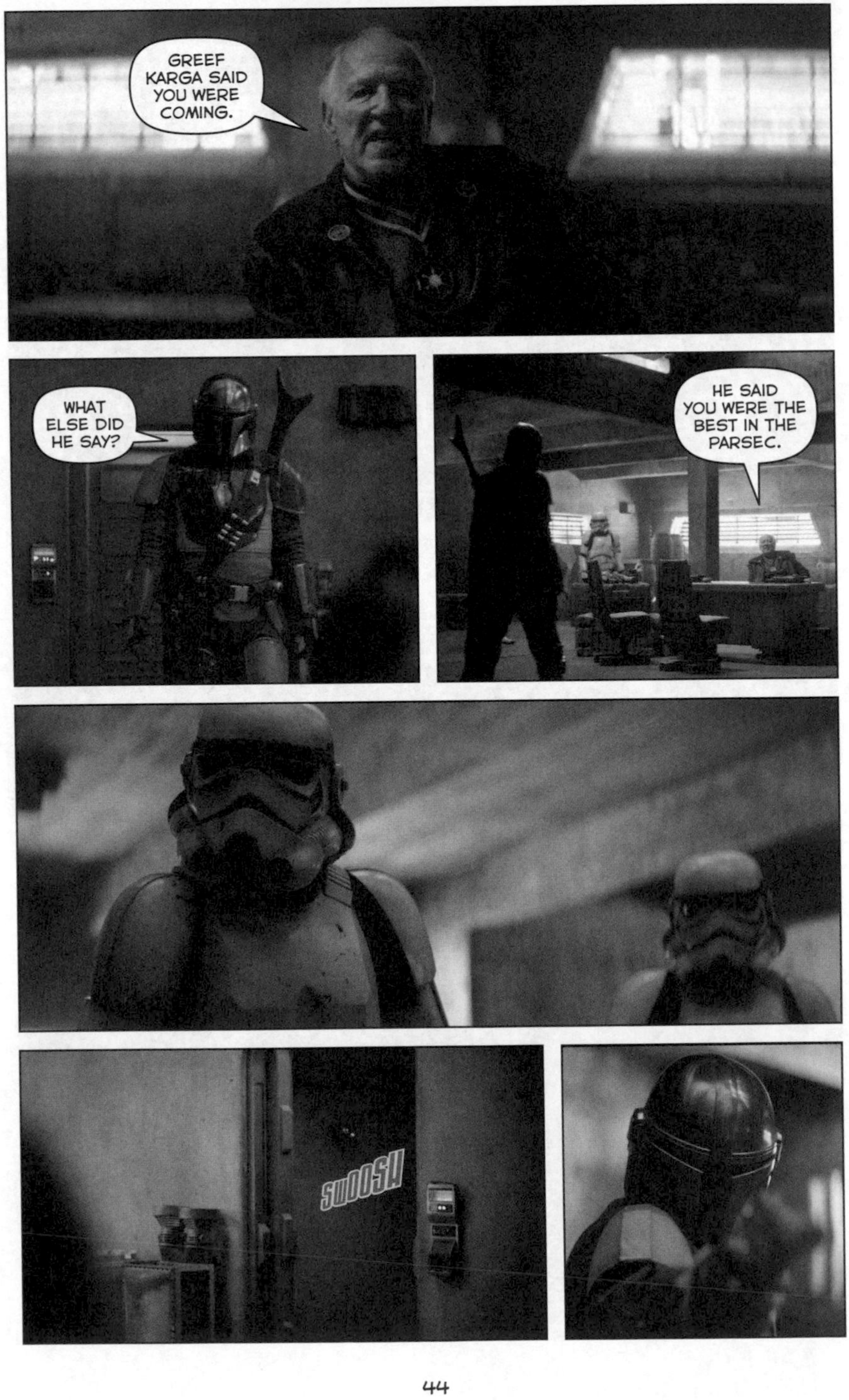
GREEF KARGA SAID YOU WERE COMING.
WHAT ELSE DID HE SAY?
HE SAID YOU WERE THE BEST IN THE PARSEC.
SWOOSH

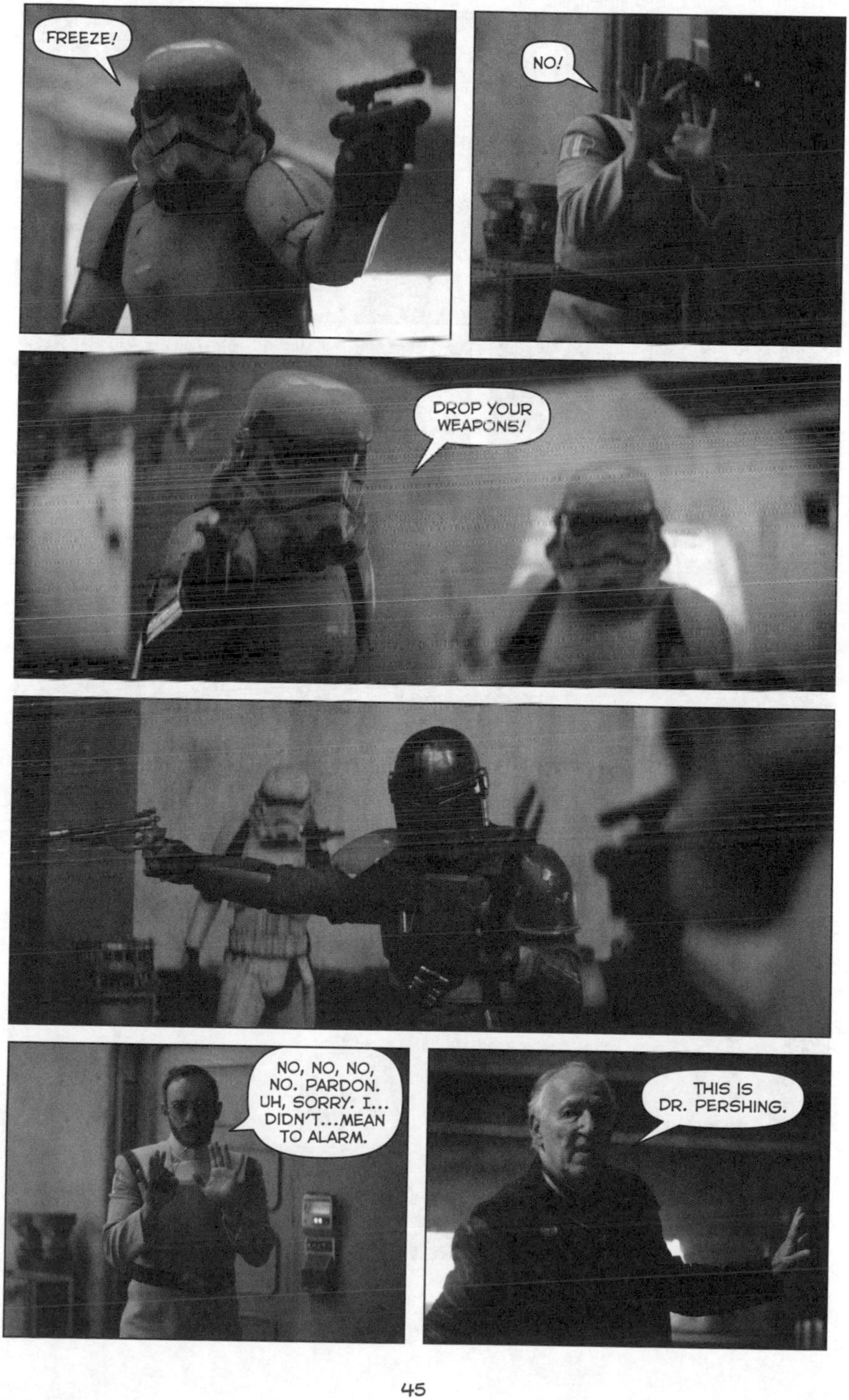
FREEZE!
NO!
DROP YOUR WEAPONS!
NO, NO, NO, NO. PARDON. UH, SORRY. I... DIDN'T...MEAN TO ALARM.
THIS IS DR. PERSHING.

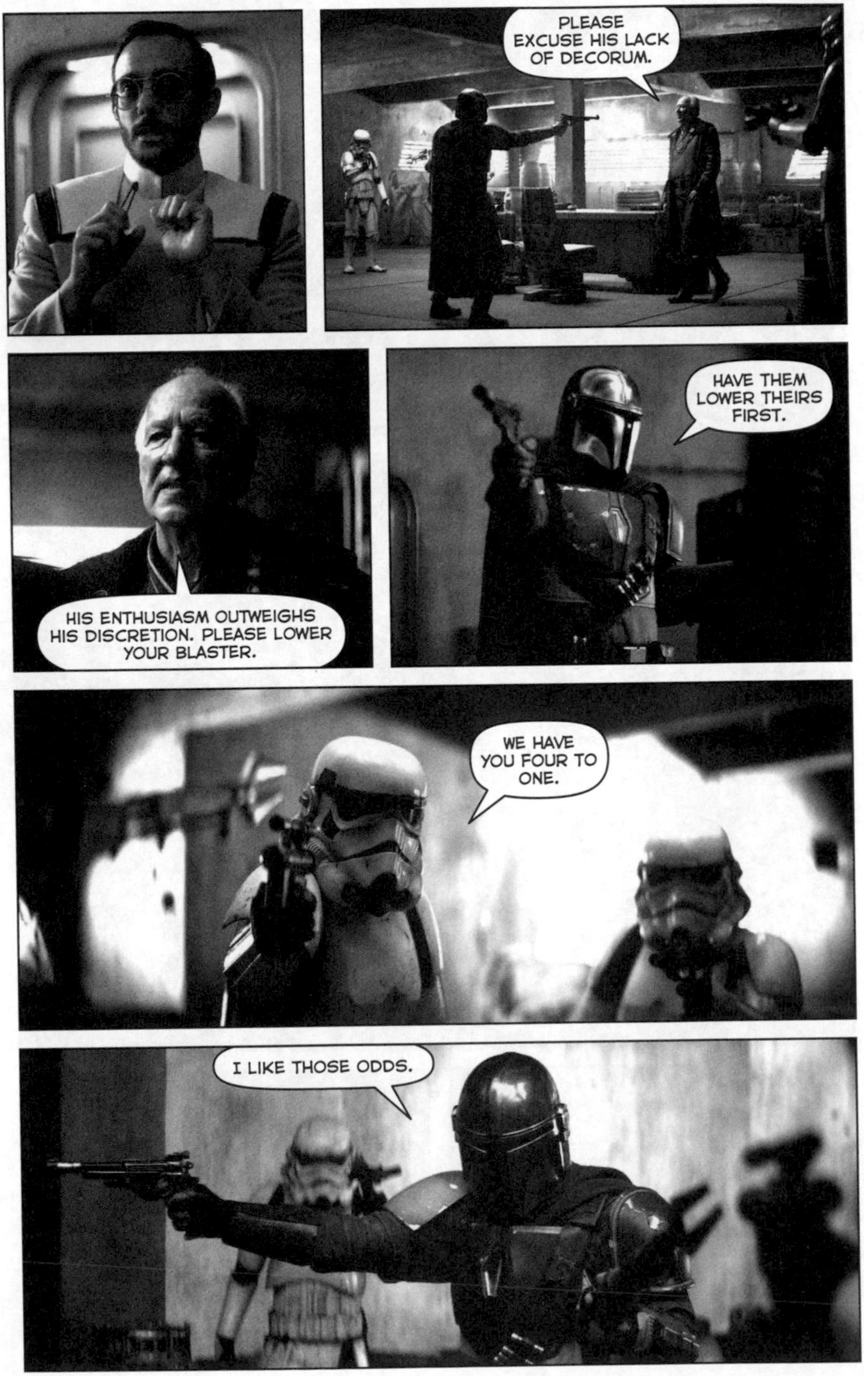
PLEASE EXCUSE HIS LACK OF DECORUM.
HIS ENTHUSIASM OUTWEIGHS HIS DISCRETION. PLEASE LOWER YOUR BLASTER.
HAVE THEM LOWER THEIRS FIRST.
WE HAVE YOU FOUR TO ONE.
I LIKE THOSE ODDS.

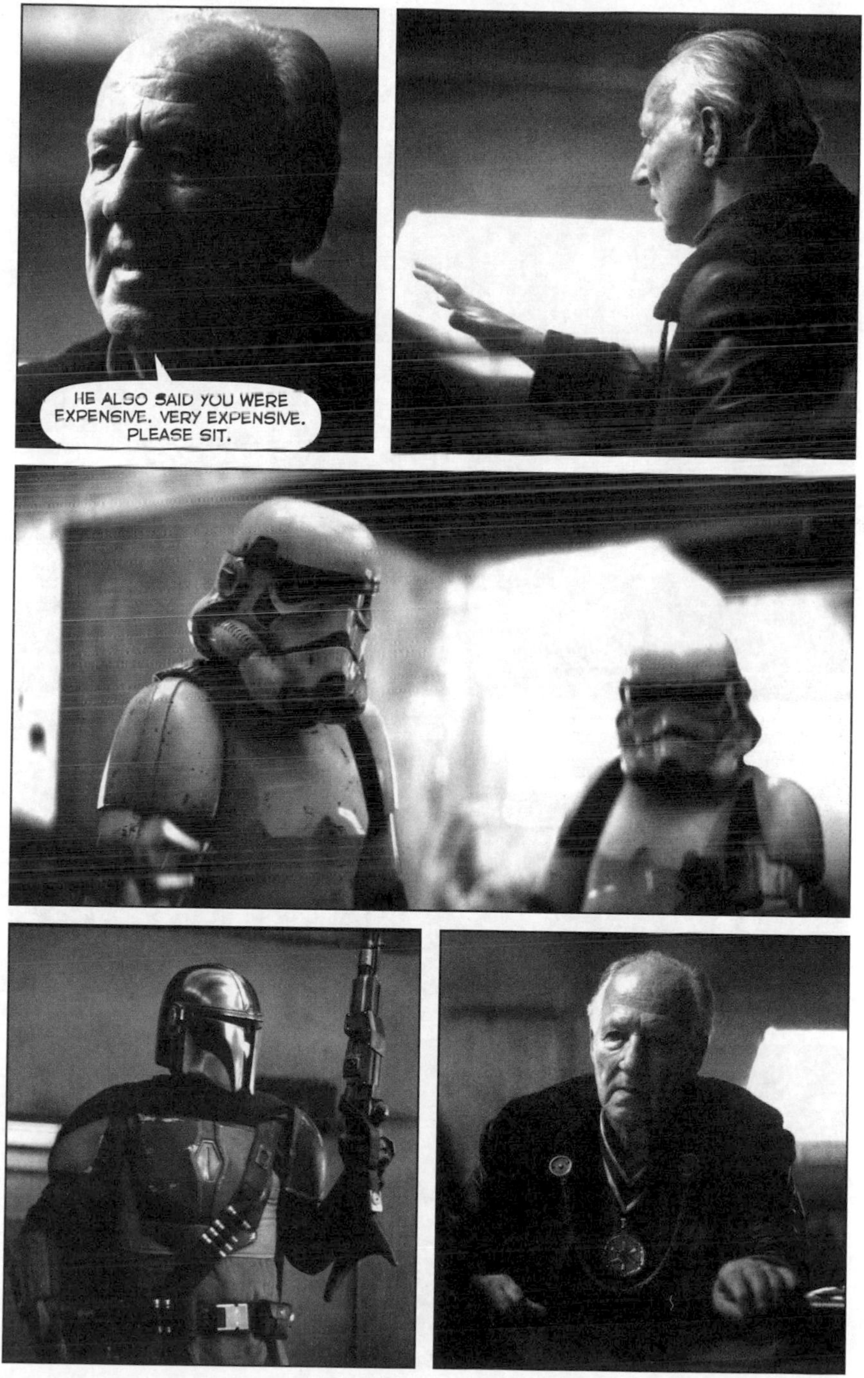
HE ALSO SAID YOU WERE EXPENSIVE. VERY EXPENSIVE. PLEASE SIT.

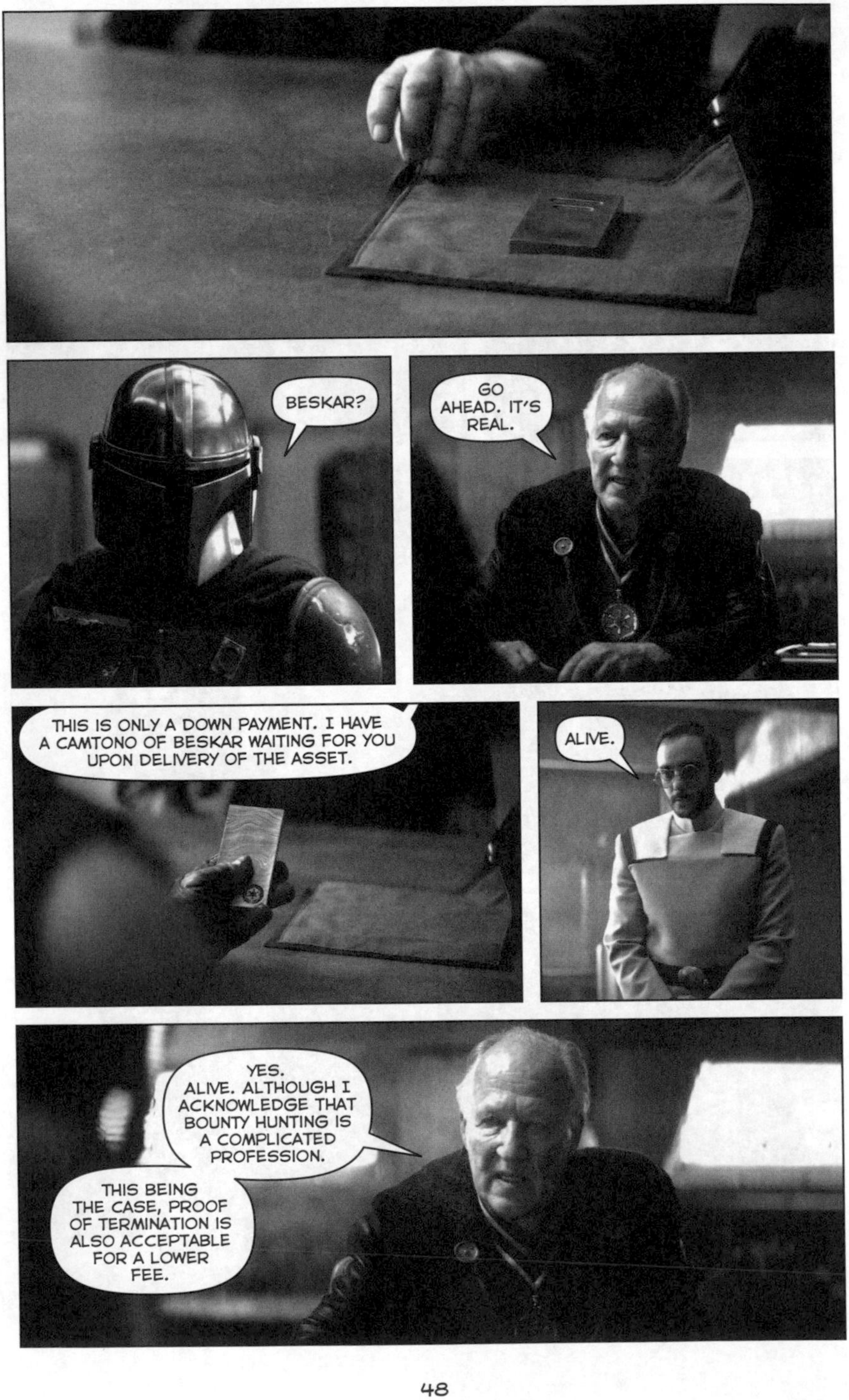
BESKAR?
GO AHEAD. IT'S REAL.
THIS IS ONLY A DOWN PAYMENT. I HAVE A CAMTONO OF BESKAR WAITING FOR YOU UPON DELIVERY OF THE ASSET.
ALIVE.
YES. ALIVE. ALTHOUGH I ACKNOWLEDGE THAT BOUNTY HUNTING IS A COMPLICATED PROFESSION.
THIS BEING THE CASE, PROOF OF TERMINATION IS ALSO ACCEPTABLE FOR A LOWER FEE.

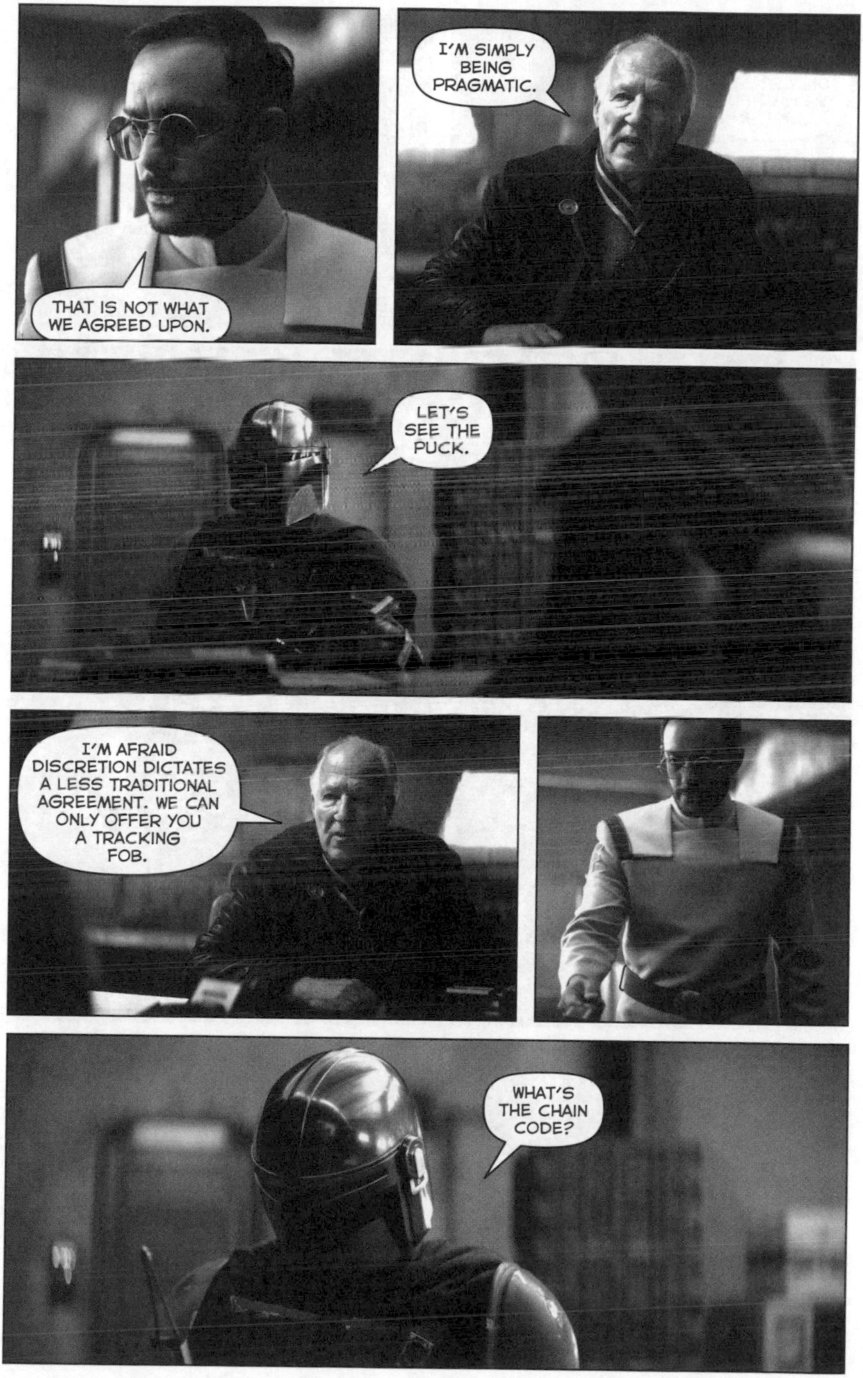
THAT IS NOT WHAT WE AGREED UPON.
I'M SIMPLY BEING PRAGMATIC.
LET'S SEE THE PUCK.
I'M AFRAID DISCRETION DICTATES A LESS TRADITIONAL AGREEMENT. WE CAN ONLY OFFER YOU A TRACKING FOB.
WHAT'S THE CHAIN CODE?

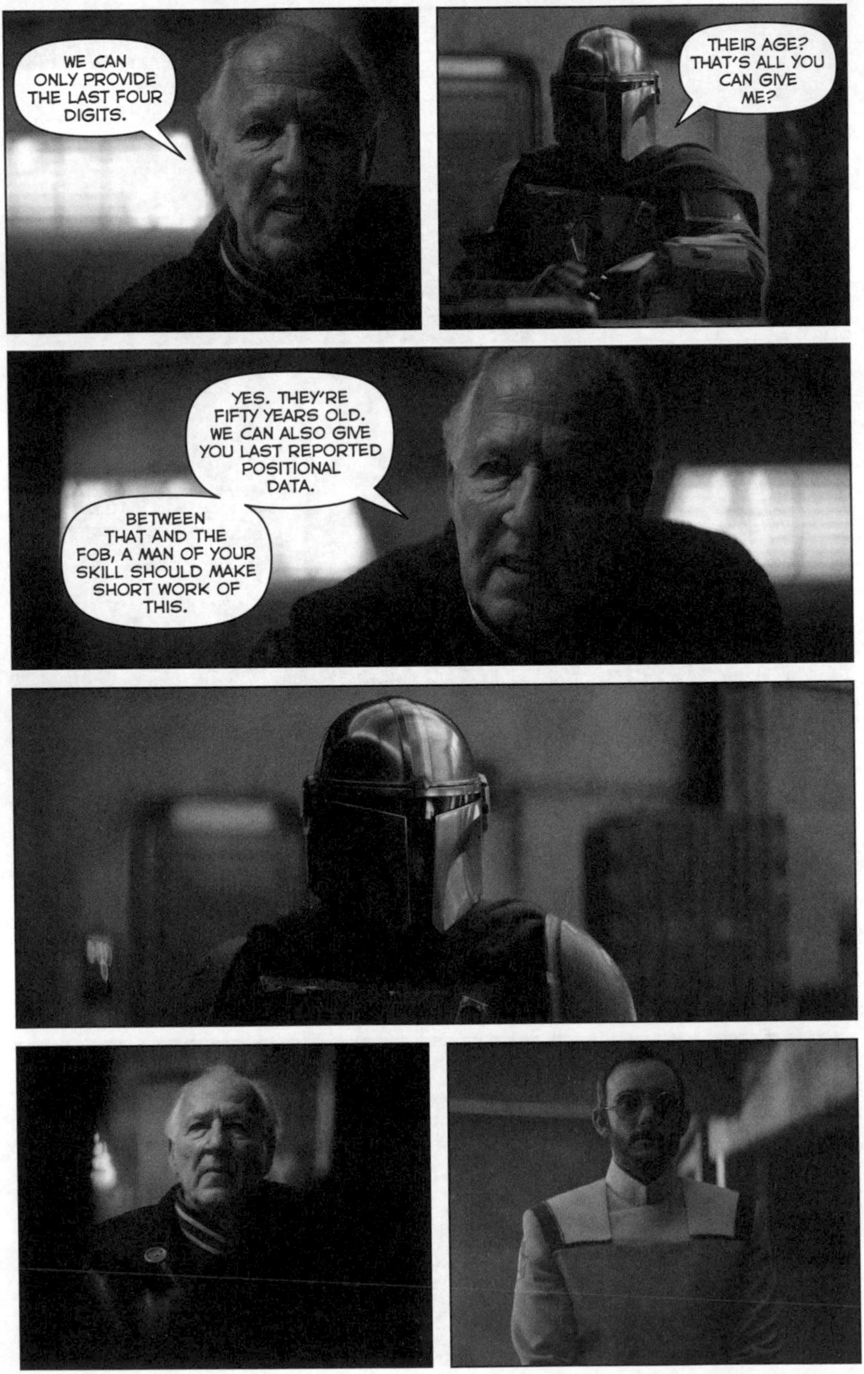
WE CAN ONLY PROVIDE THE LAST FOUR DIGITS.
THEIR AGE? THAT'S ALL YOU CAN GIVE ME?
YES. THEY'RE FIFTY YEARS OLD. WE CAN ALSO GIVE YOU LAST REPORTED POSITIONAL DATA.
BETWEEN THAT AND THE FOB, A MAN OF YOUR SKILL SHOULD MAKE SHORT WORK OF THIS.

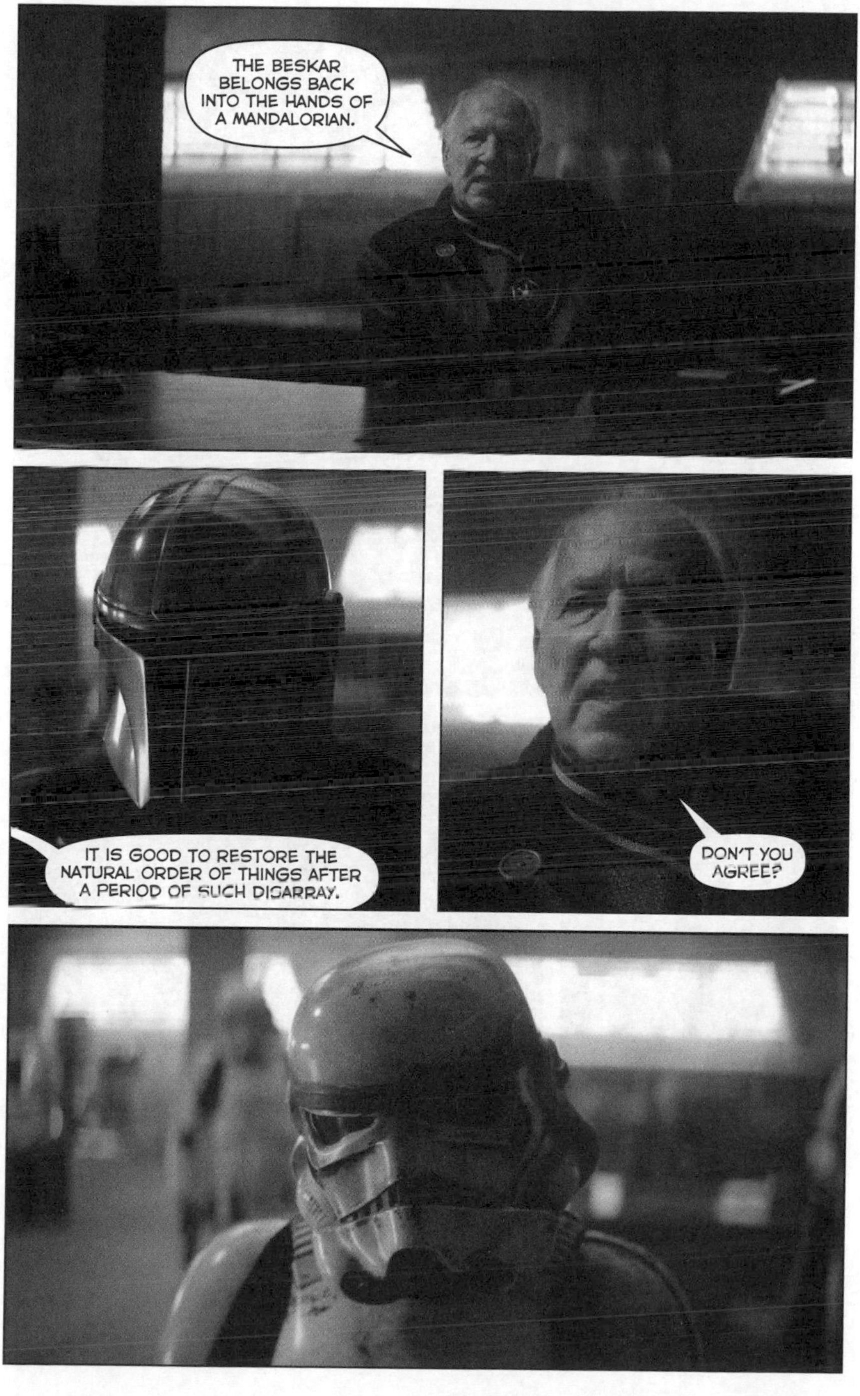
THE BESKAR BELONGS BACK INTO THE HANDS OF A MANDALORIAN.
IT IS GOOD TO RESTORE THE NATURAL ORDER OF THINGS AFTER A PERIOD OF SUCH DISARRAY.
DON'T YOU AGREE?

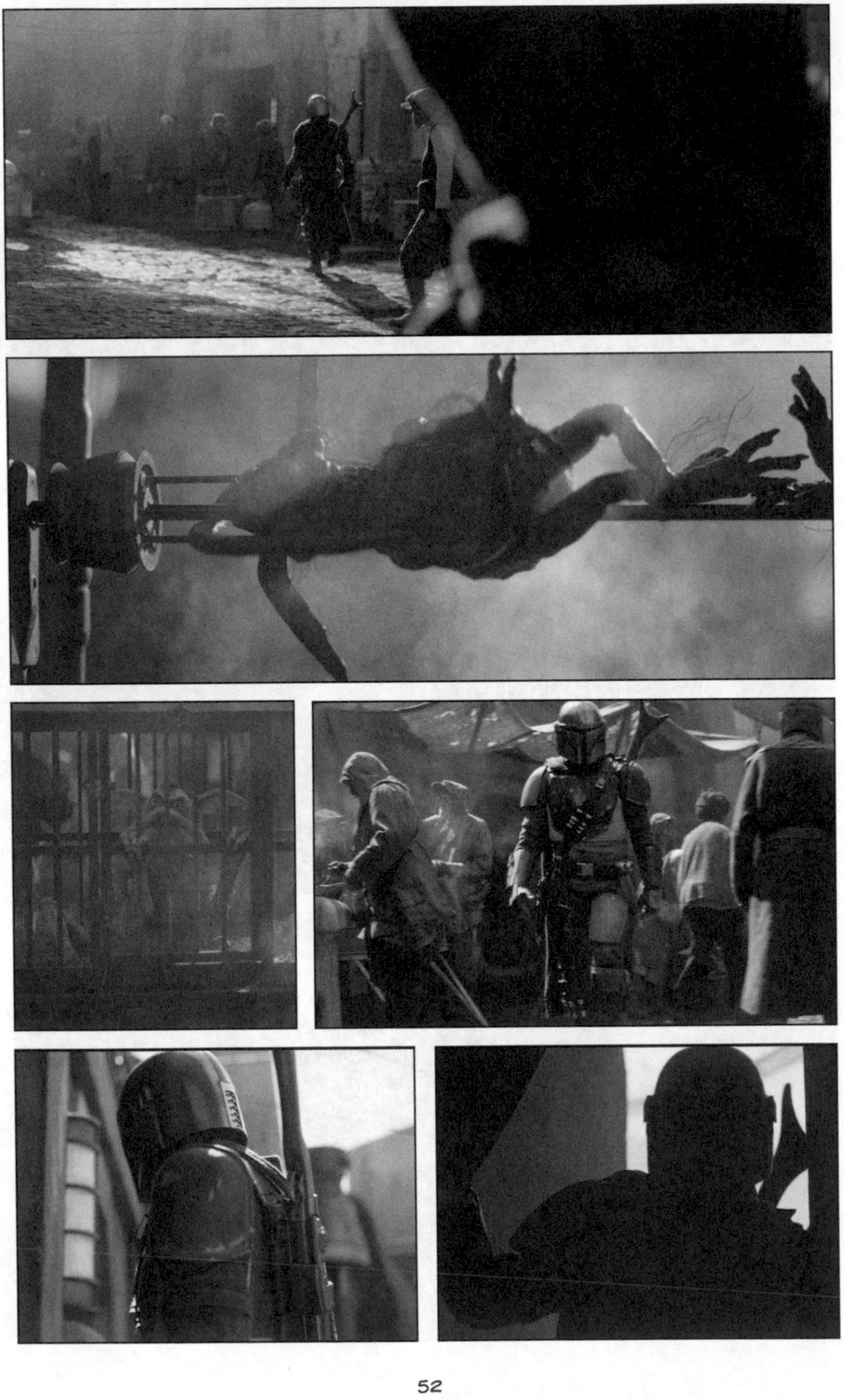

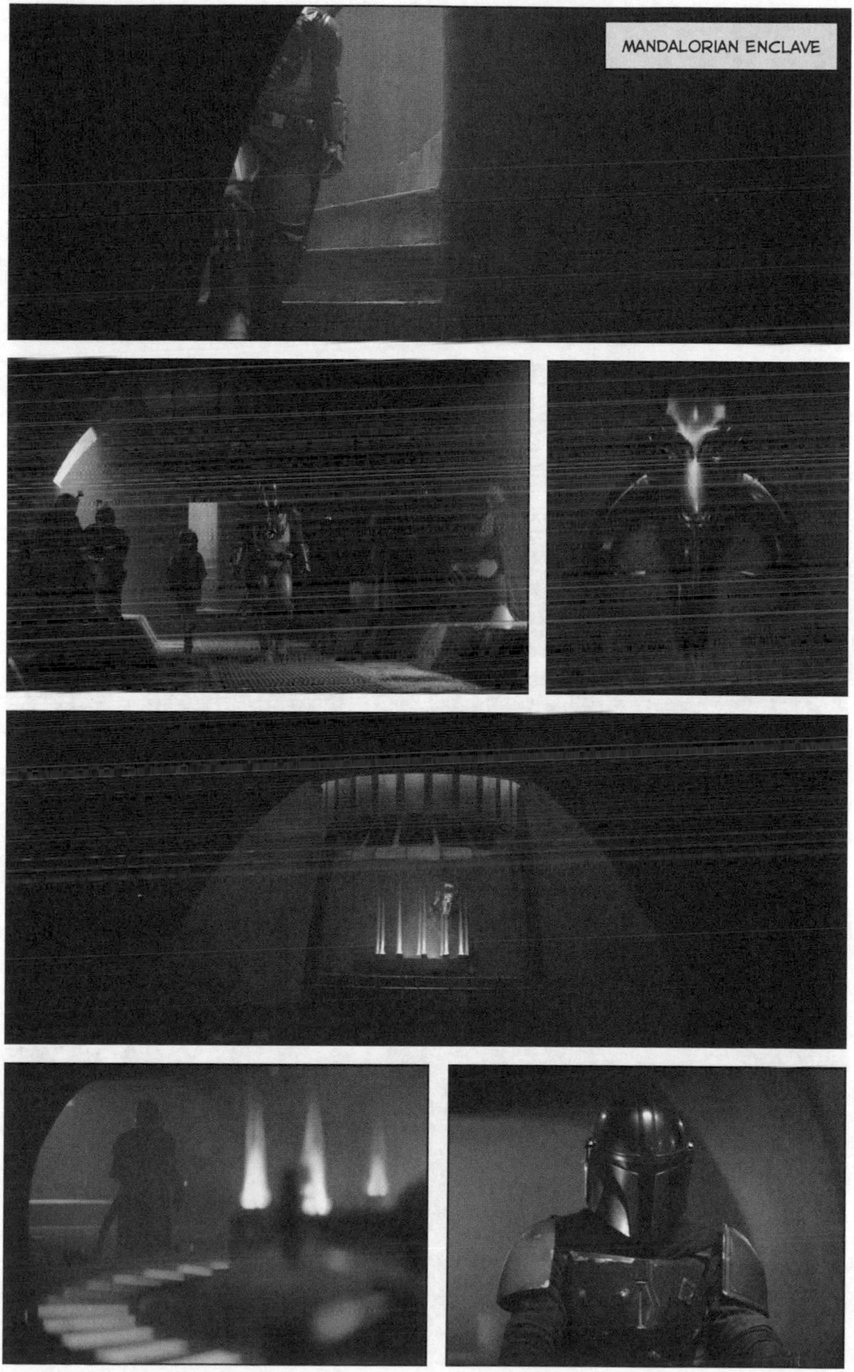
MANDALORIAN ENCLAVE

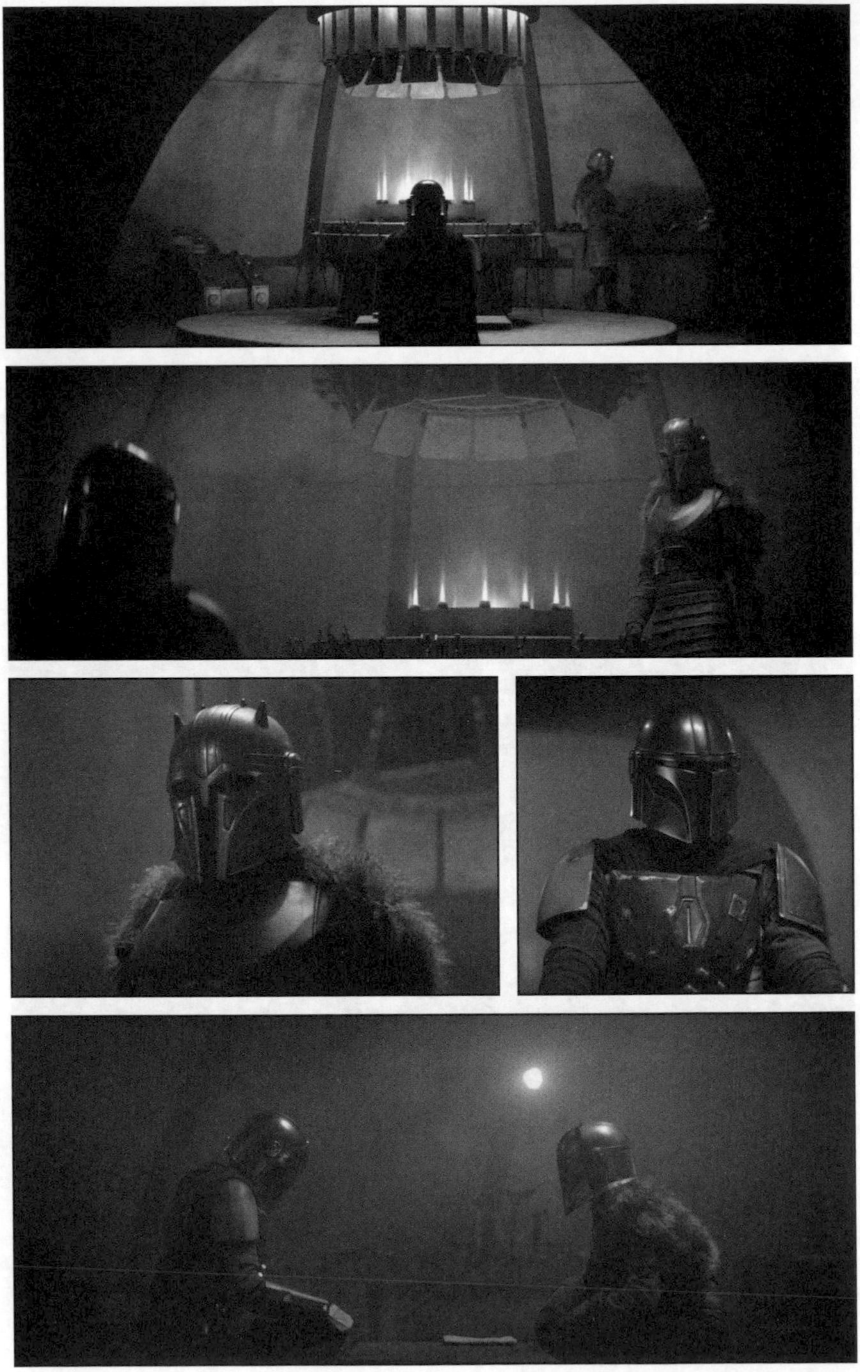

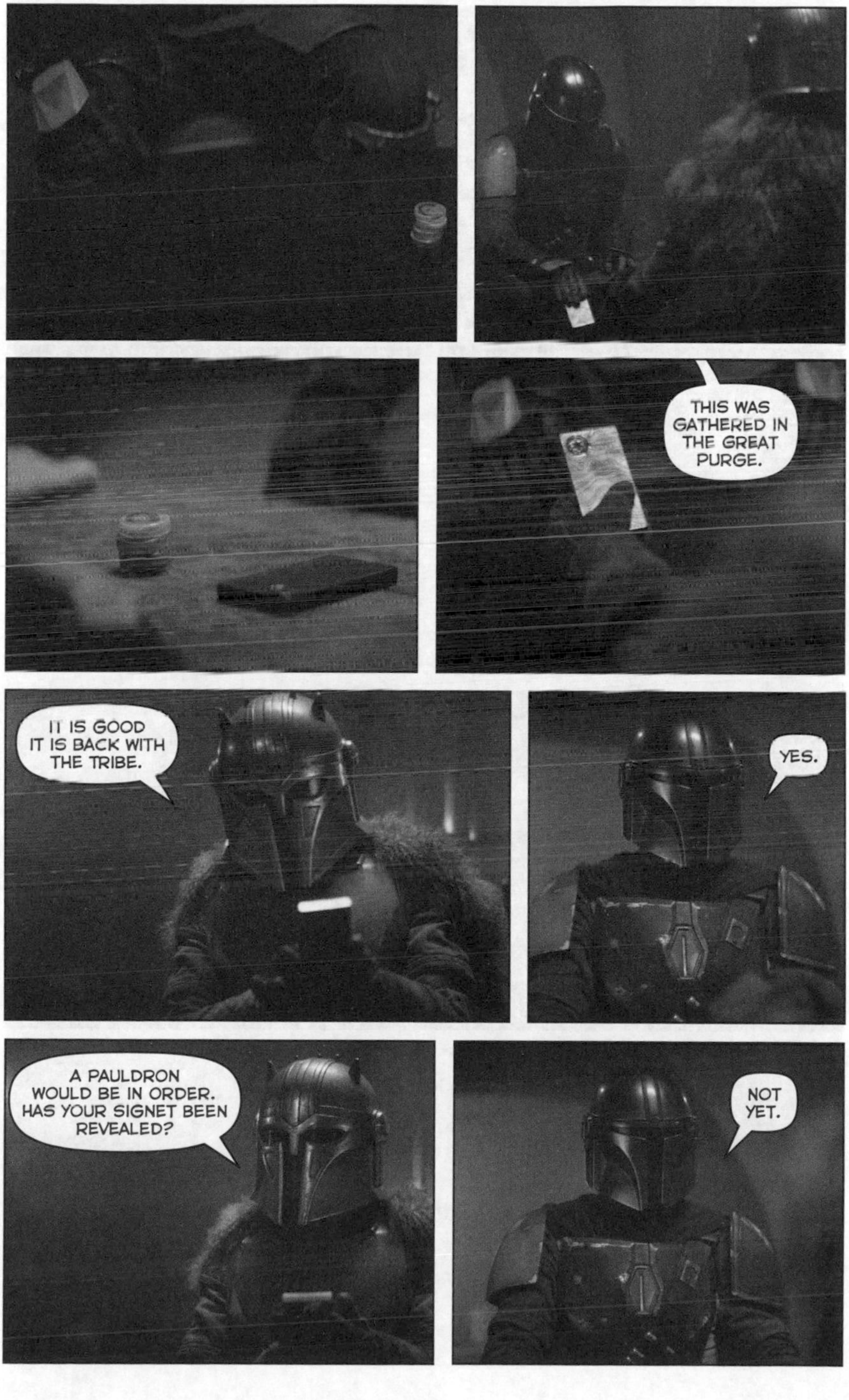
THIS WAS GATHERED IN THE GREAT PURGE.
IT IS GOOD IT IS BACK WITH THE TRIBE.
YES.
A PAULDRON WOULD BE IN ORDER. HAS YOUR SIGNET BEEN REVEALED?
NOT YET.

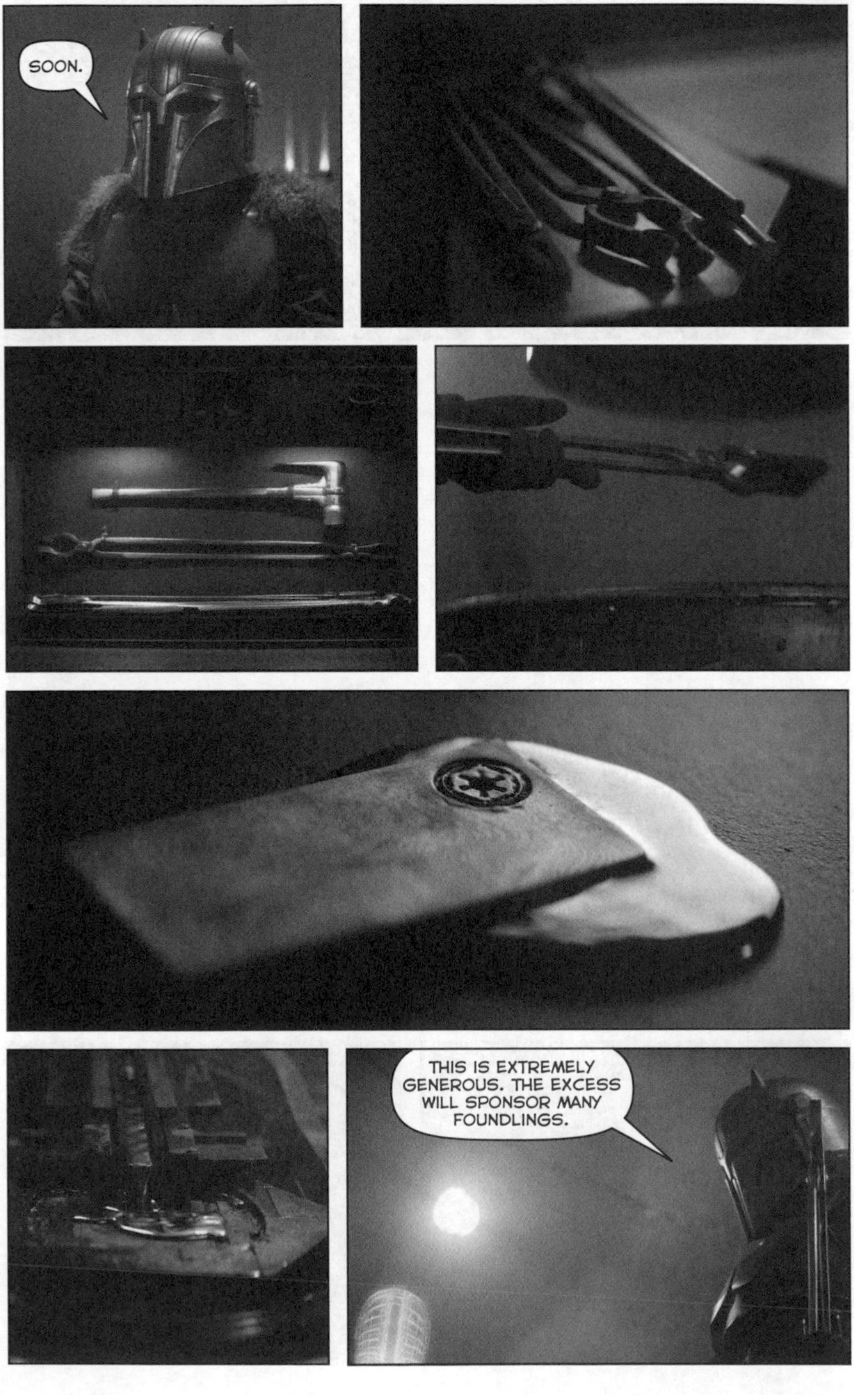
SOON.
THIS IS EXTREMELY GENEROUS. THE EXCESS WILL SPONSOR MANY FOUNDLINGS.

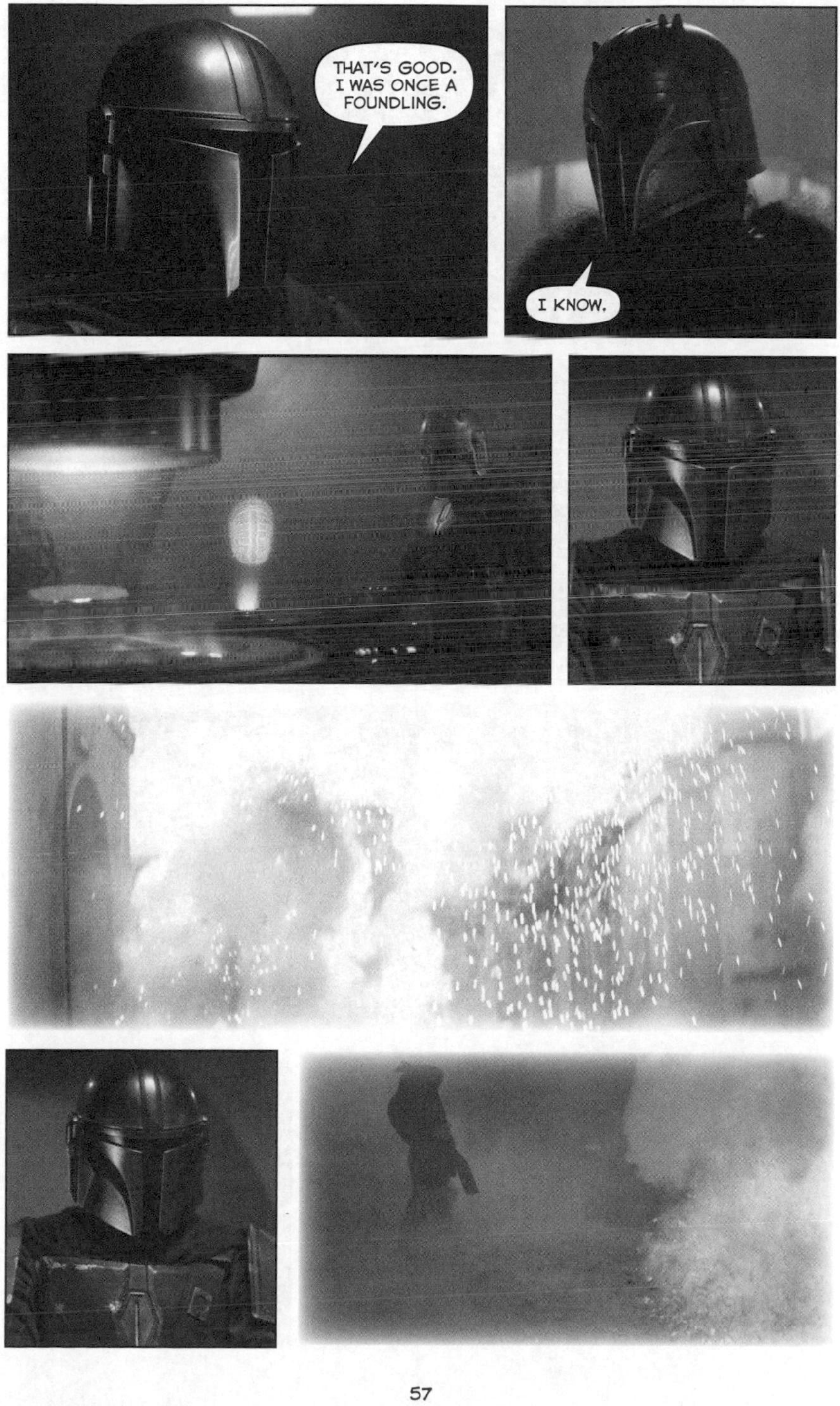
THAT'S GOOD. I WAS ONCE A FOUNDLING.
I KNOW.

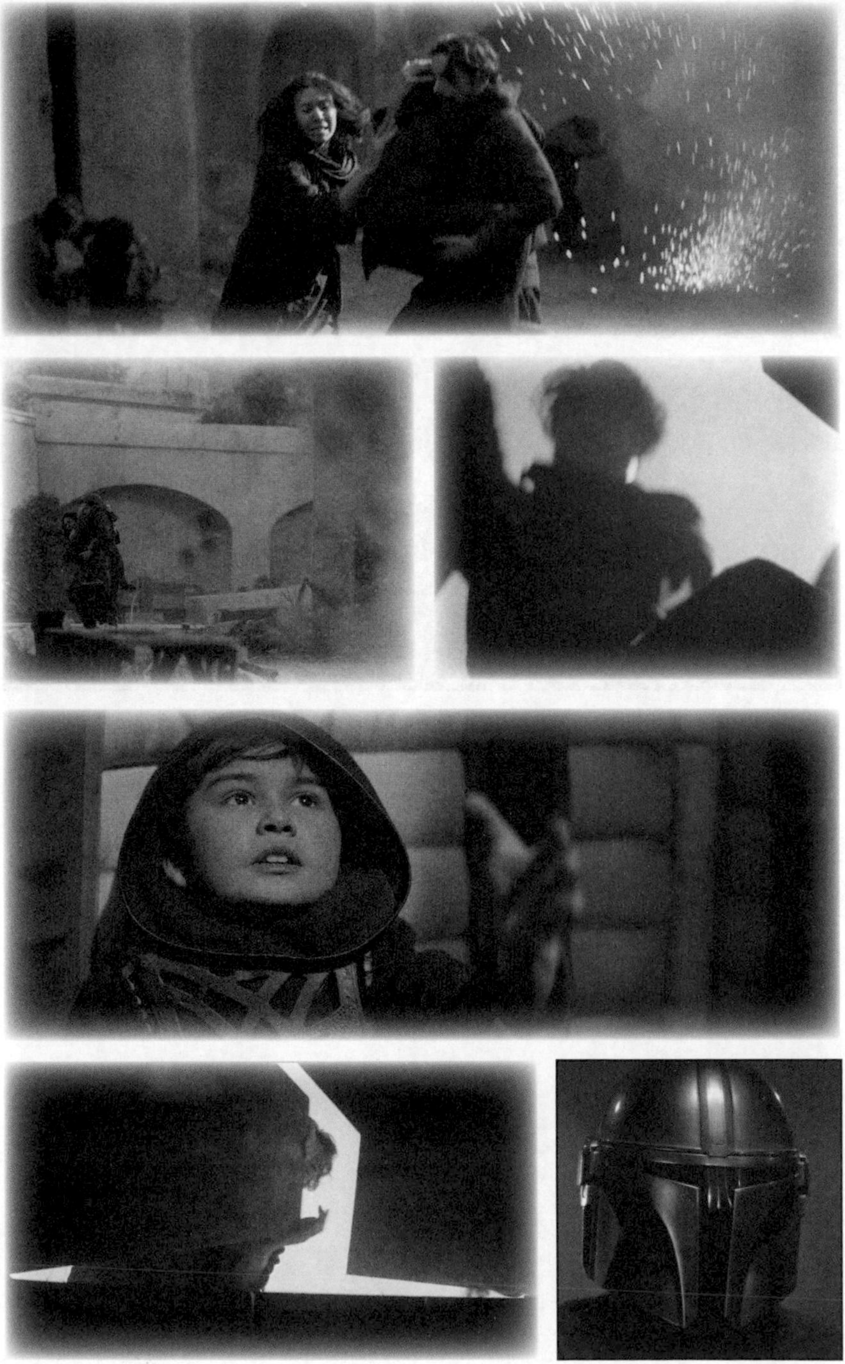

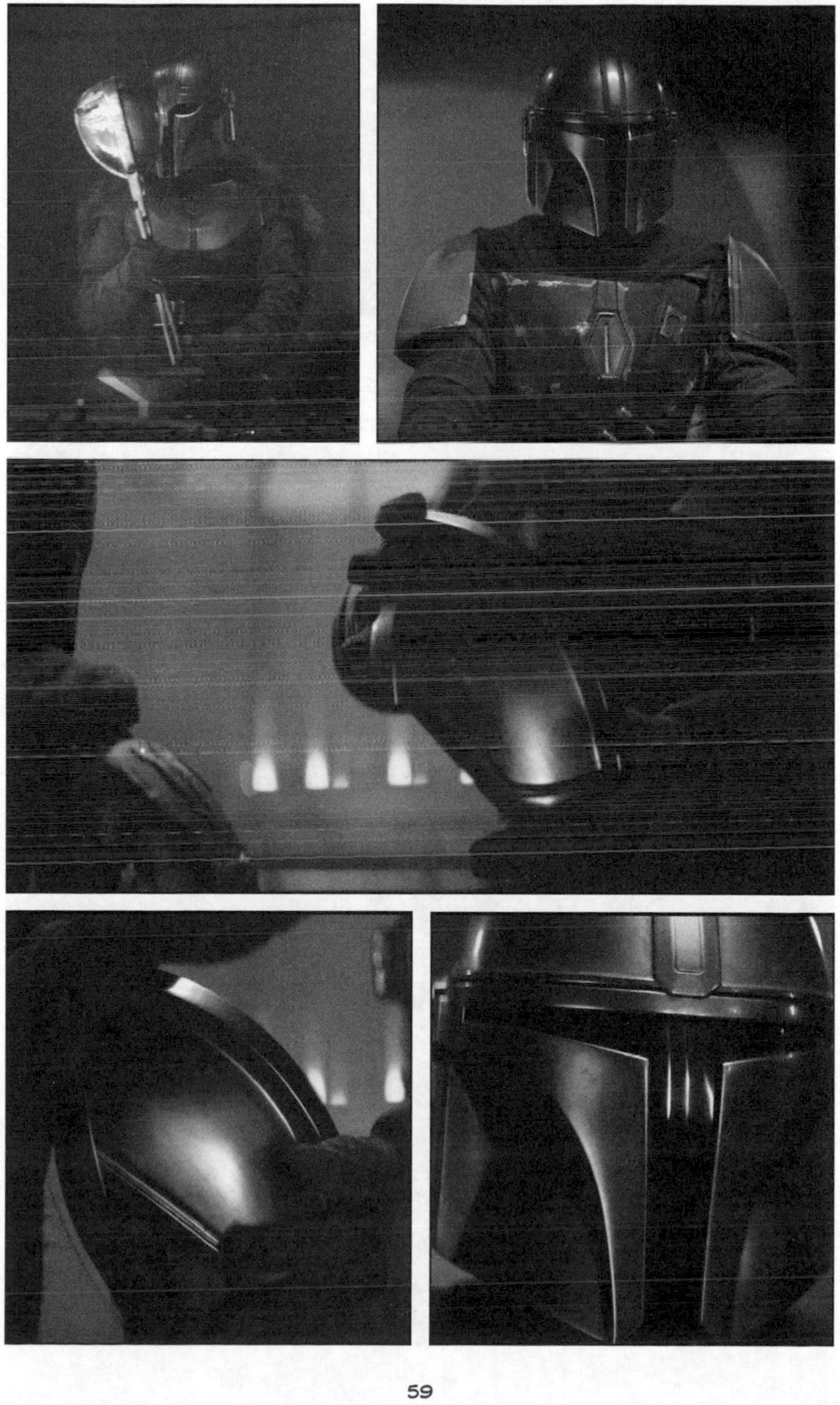

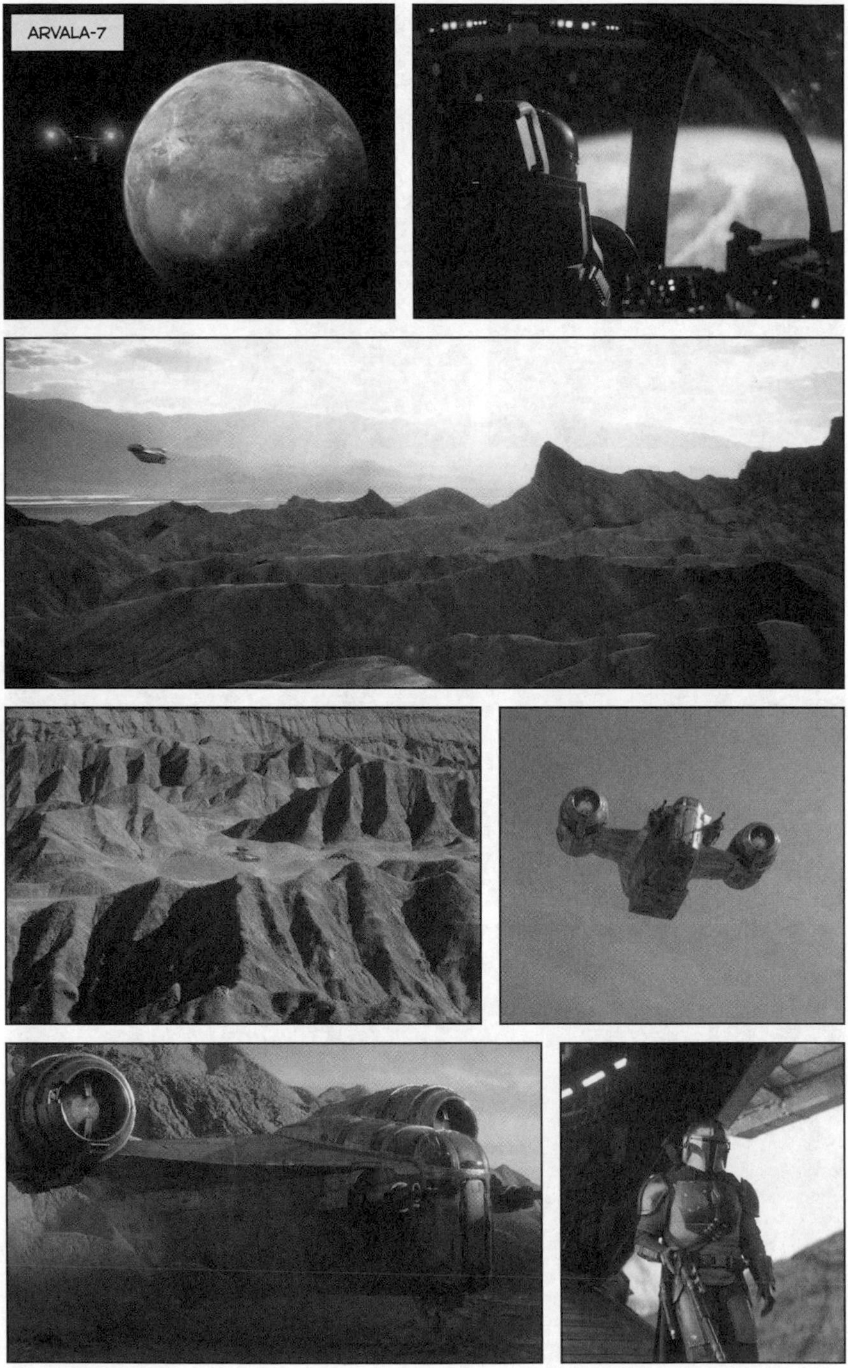
ARVALA-7

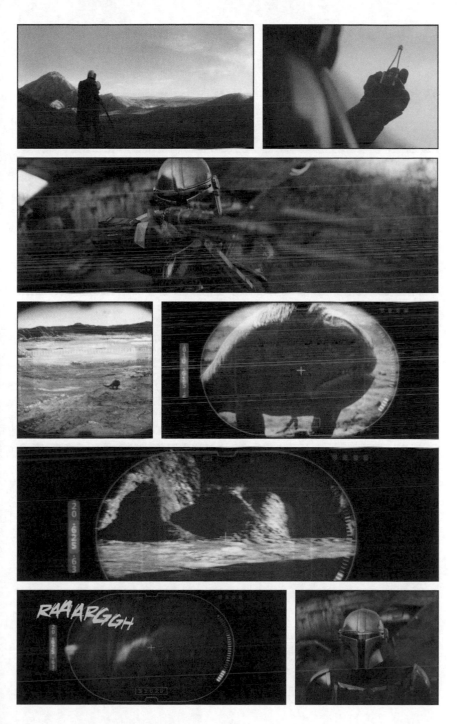

RAAARGGH

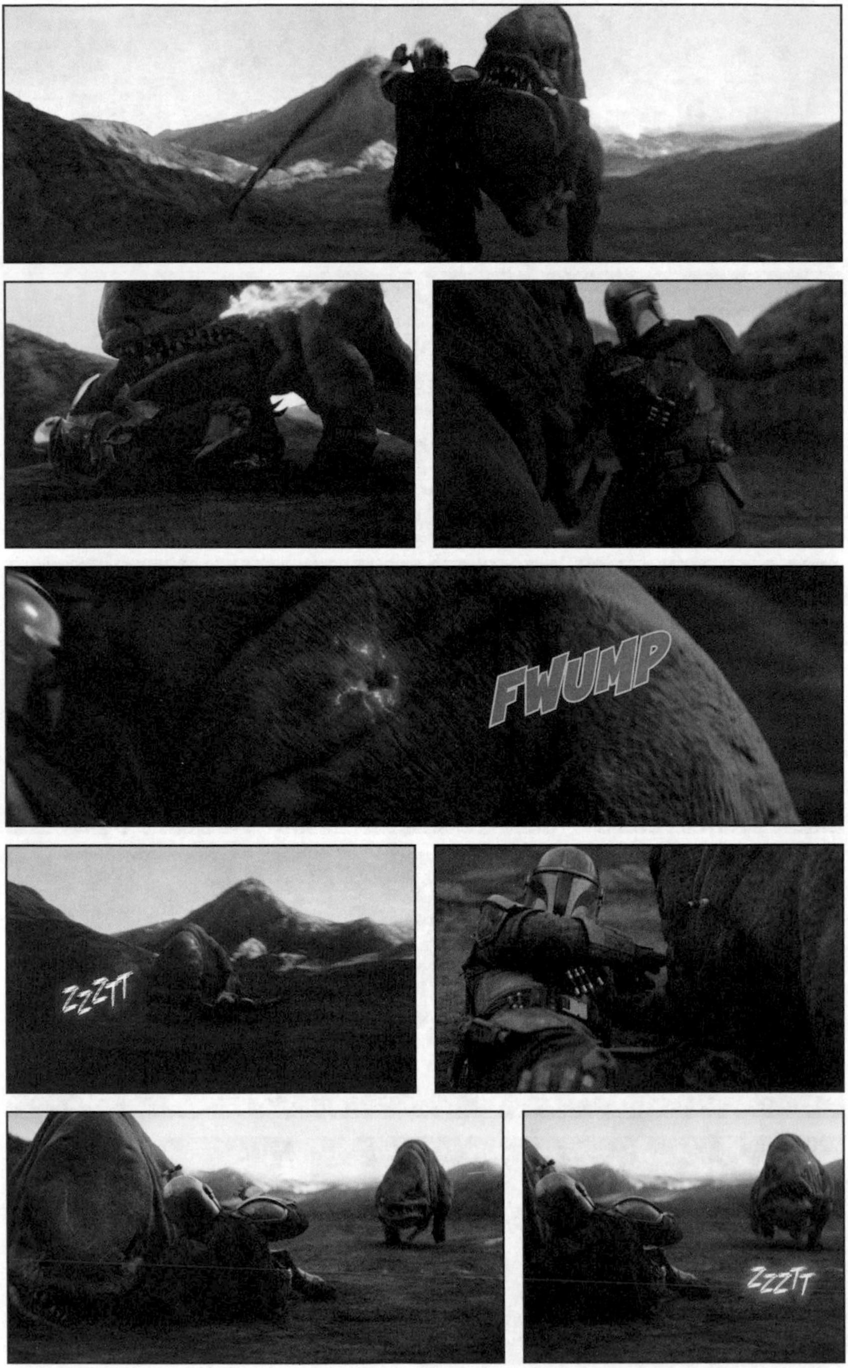
FWUMP
ZZZTT
ZZZTT

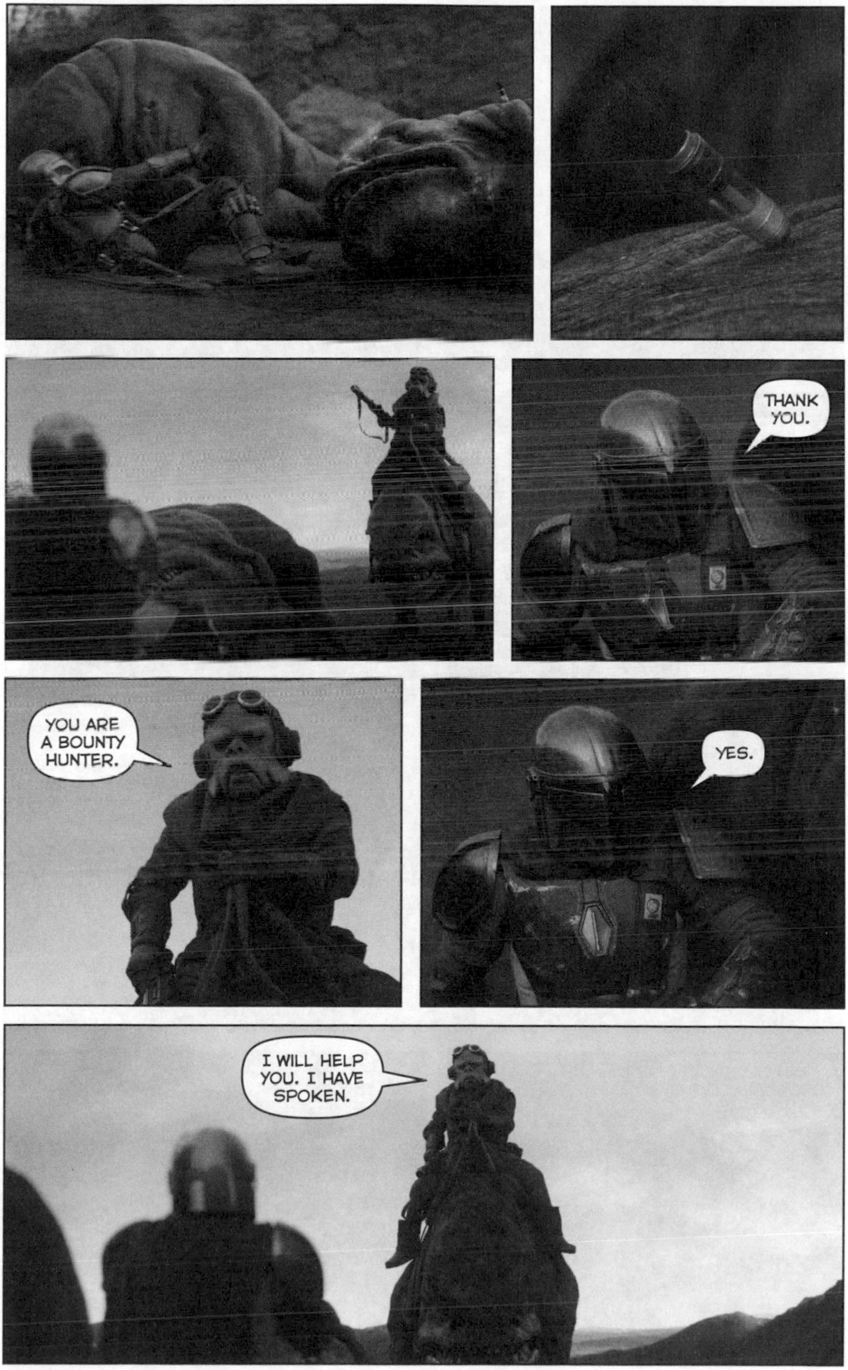
THANK YOU.
YOU ARE A BOUNTY HUNTER.
YES.
I WILL HELP YOU. I HAVE SPOKEN.

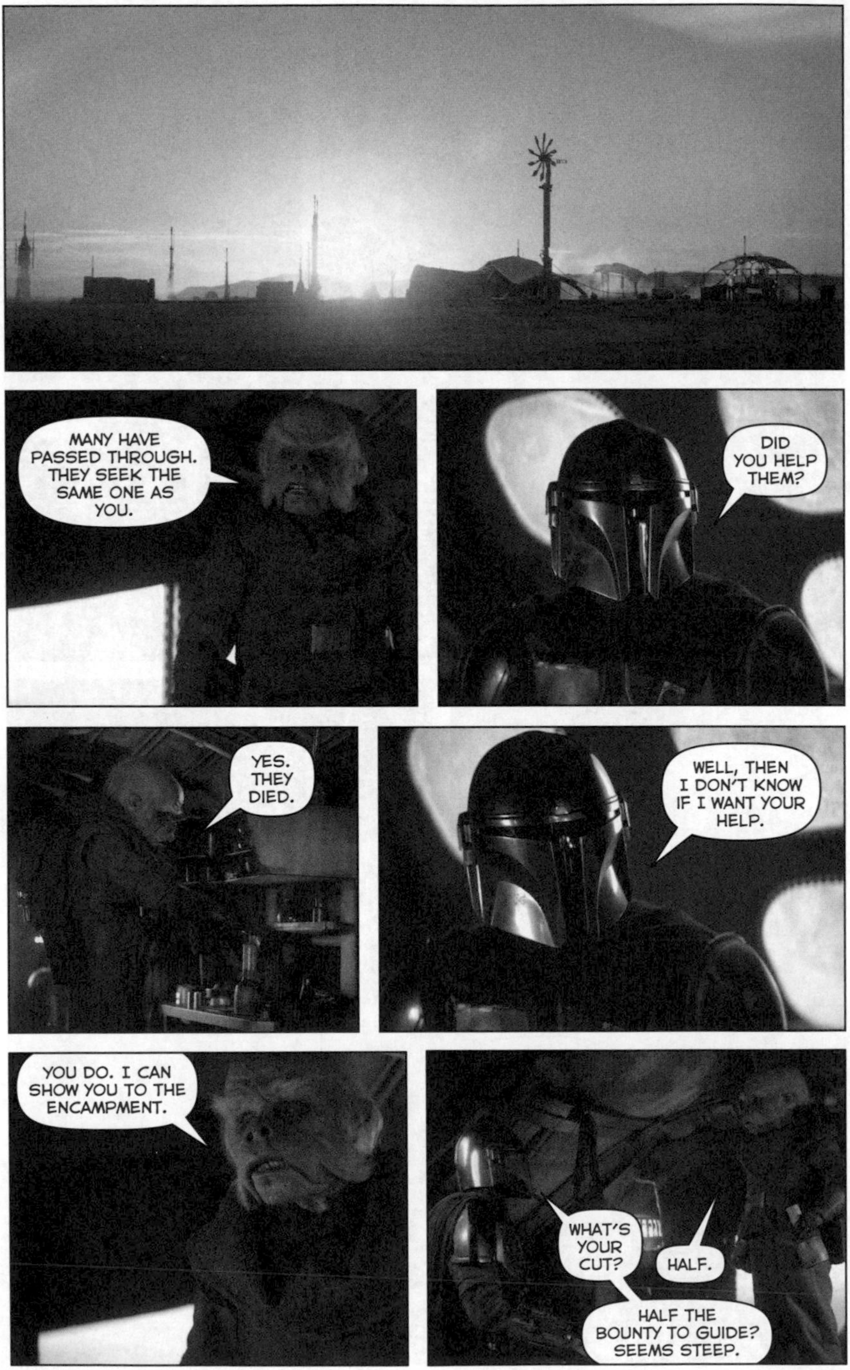
MANY HAVE PASSED THROUGH. THEY SEEK THE SAME ONE AS YOU.
DID YOU HELP THEM?
YES. THEY DIED.
WELL, THEN I DON'T KNOW IF I WANT YOUR HELP.
YOU DO. I CAN SHOW YOU TO THE ENCAMPMENT.
WHAT'S YOUR CUT?
HALF.
HALF THE BOUNTY TO GUIDE? SEEMS STEEP.

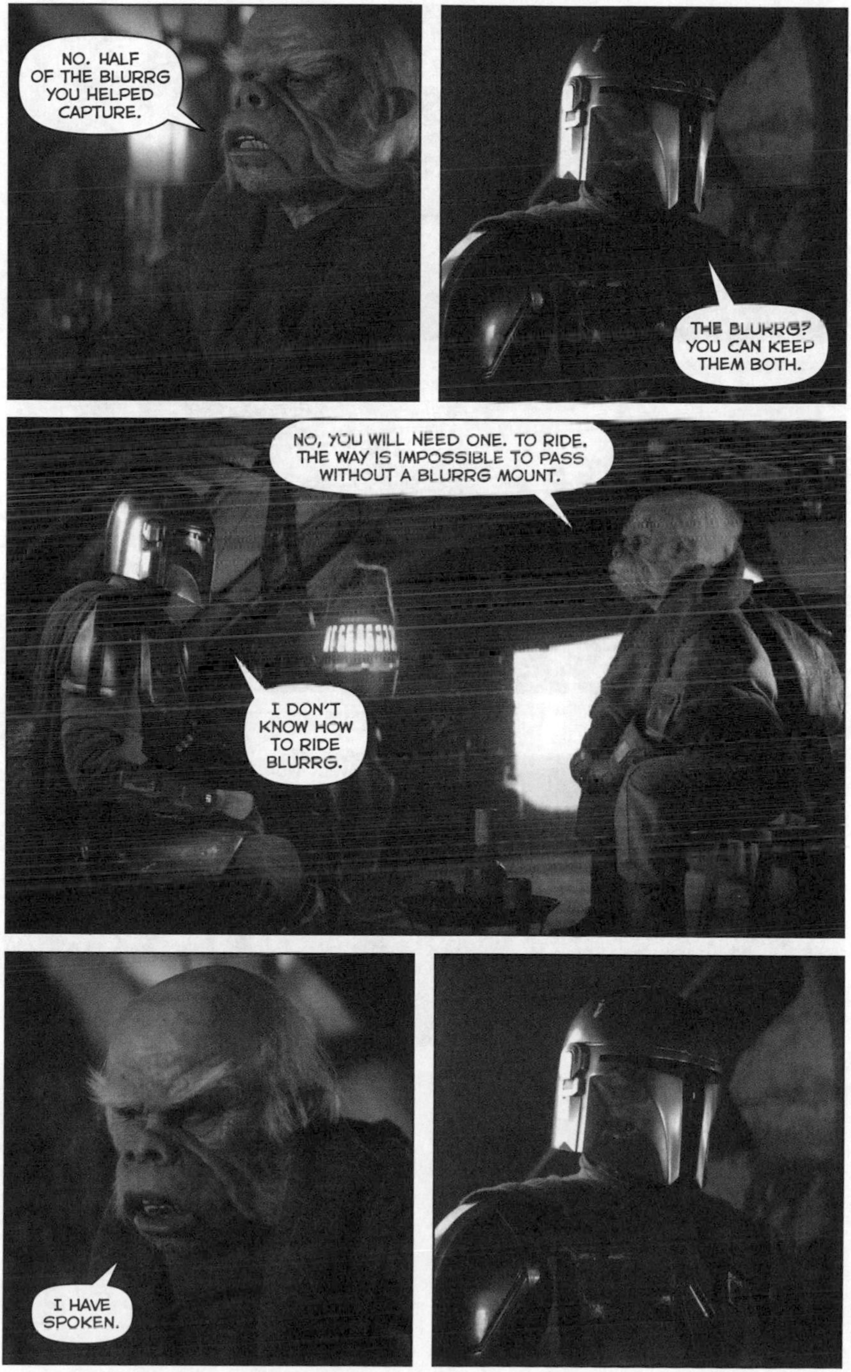
NO. HALF OF THE BLURRG YOU HELPED CAPTURE.
THE BLURRG? YOU CAN KEEP THEM BOTH.
NO, YOU WILL NEED ONE. TO RIDE. THE WAY IS IMPOSSIBLE TO PASS WITHOUT A BLURRG MOUNT.
I DON'T KNOW HOW TO RIDE BLURRG.
I HAVE SPOKEN.

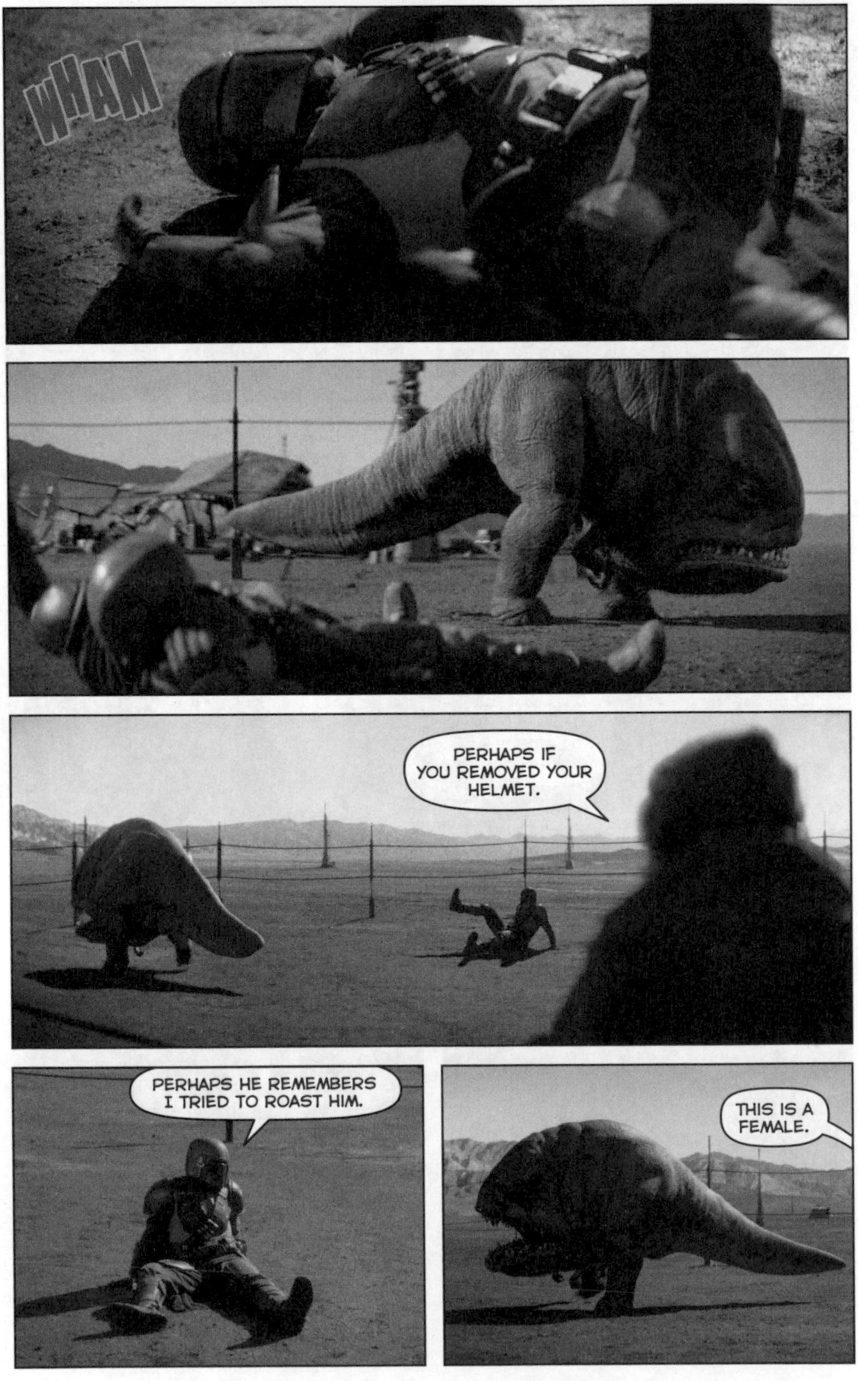
WHAM
PERHAPS IF YOU REMOVED YOUR HELMET.
PERHAPS HE REMEMBERS I TRIED TO ROAST HIM.
THIS IS A FEMALE.

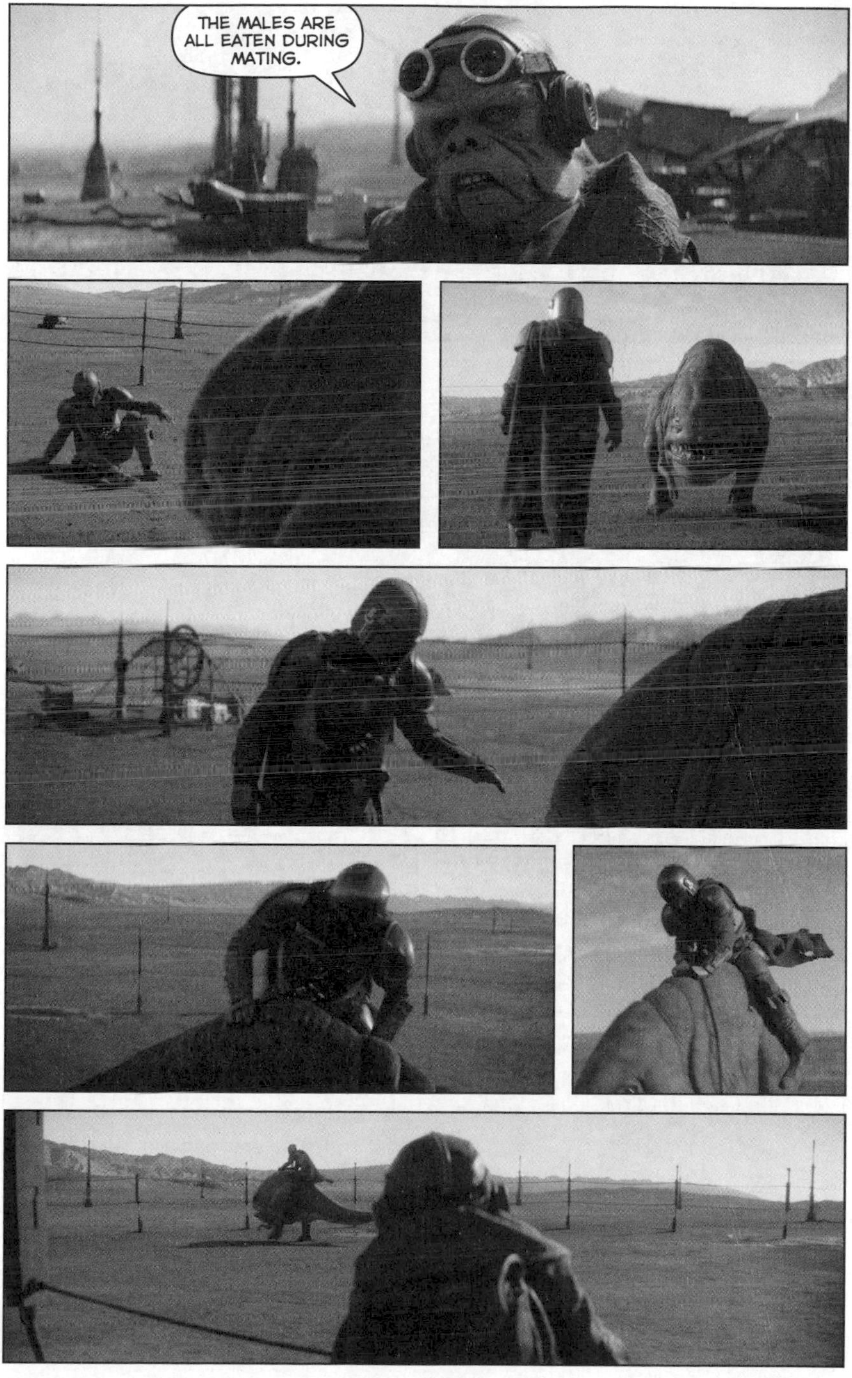
THE MALES ARE ALL EATEN DURING MATING.

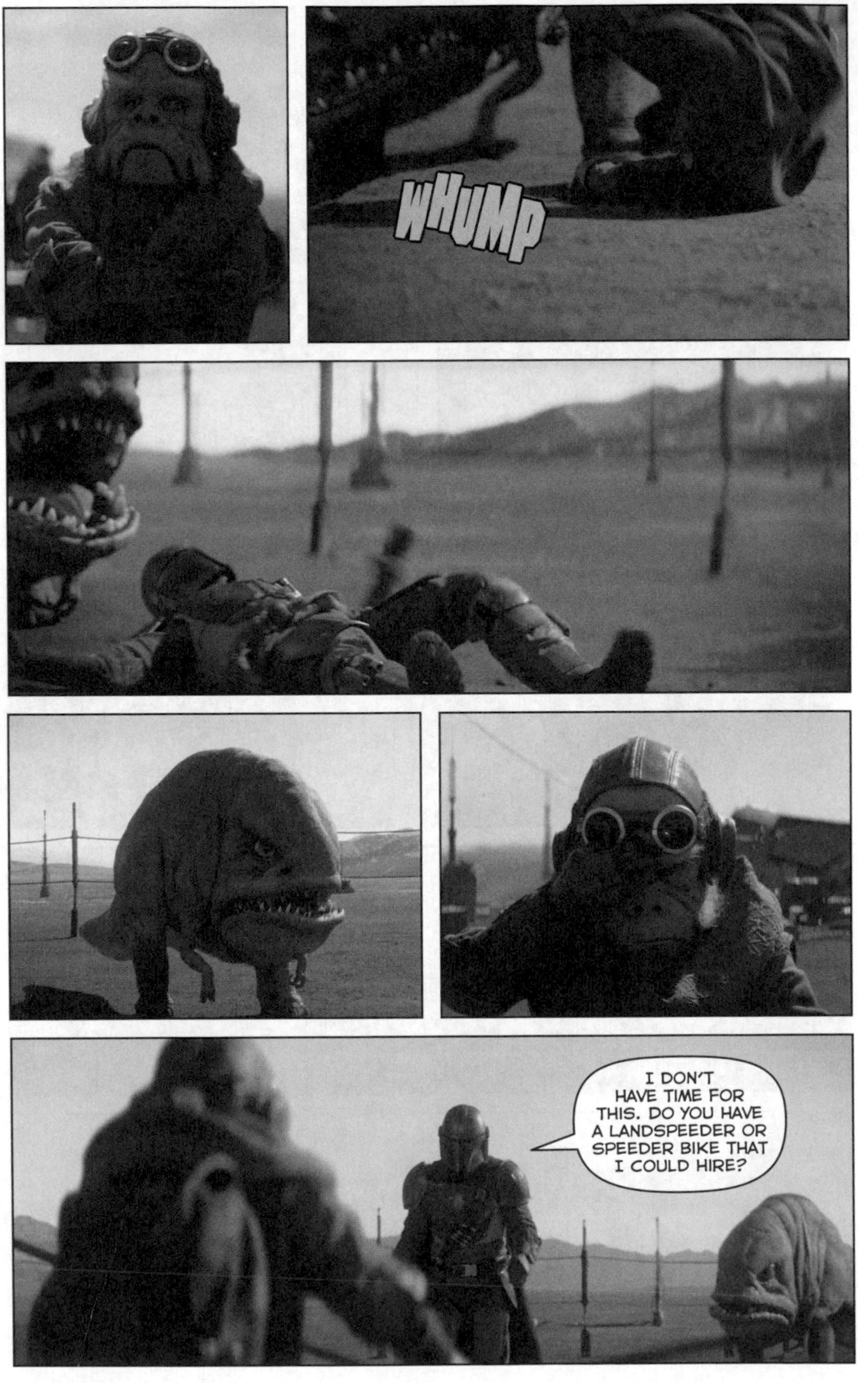
WHUMP
I DON'T HAVE TIME FOR THIS. DO YOU HAVE A LANDSPEEDER OR SPEEDER BIKE THAT I COULD HIRE?

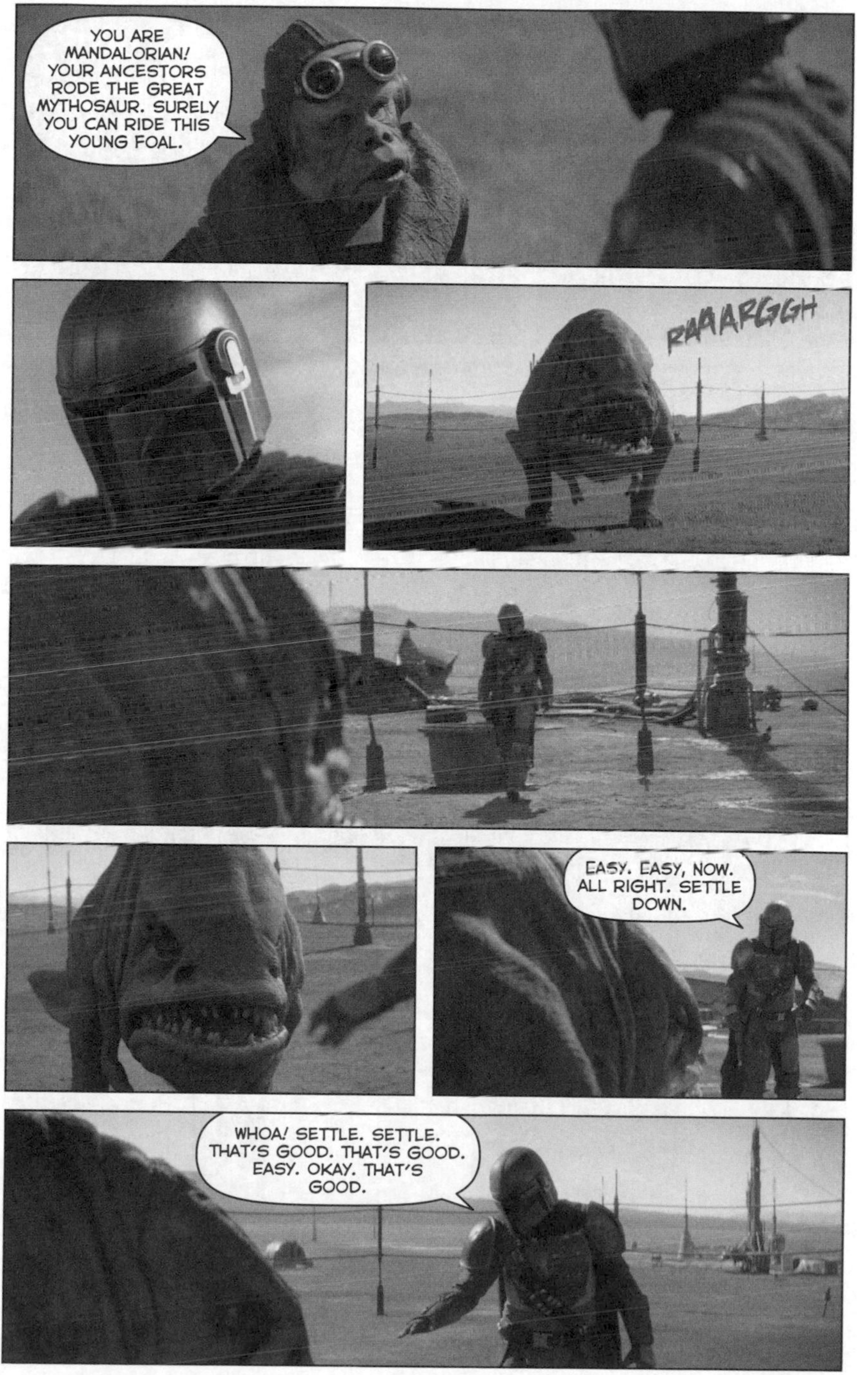
YOU ARE MANDALORIAN! YOUR ANCESTORS RODE THE GREAT MYTHOSAUR. SURELY YOU CAN RIDE THIS YOUNG FOAL.
RAAARGGH
EASY. EASY, NOW. ALL RIGHT. SETTLE DOWN.
WHOA! SETTLE. SETTLE. THAT'S GOOD. THAT'S GOOD. EASY. OKAY. THAT'S GOOD.

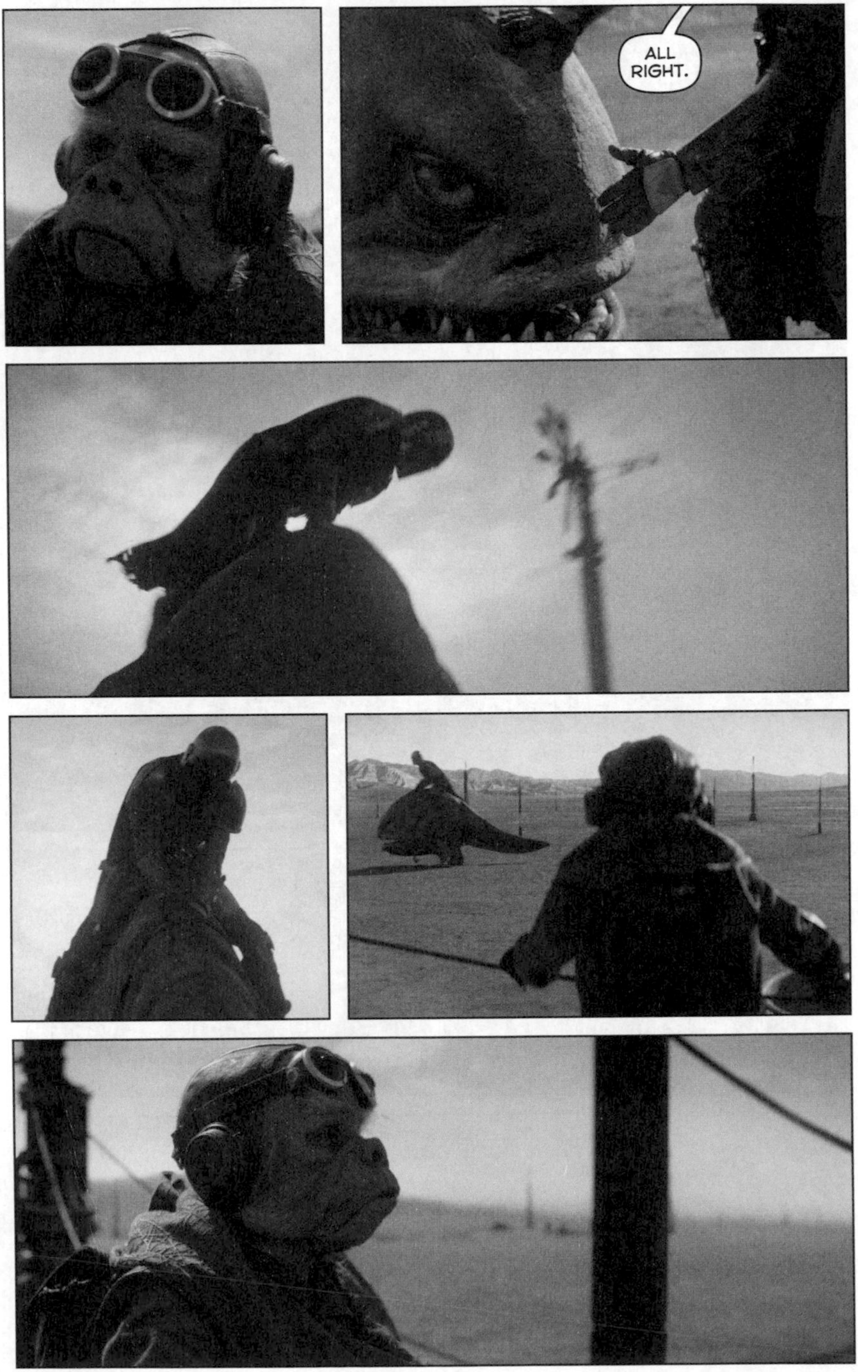
ALL RIGHT.

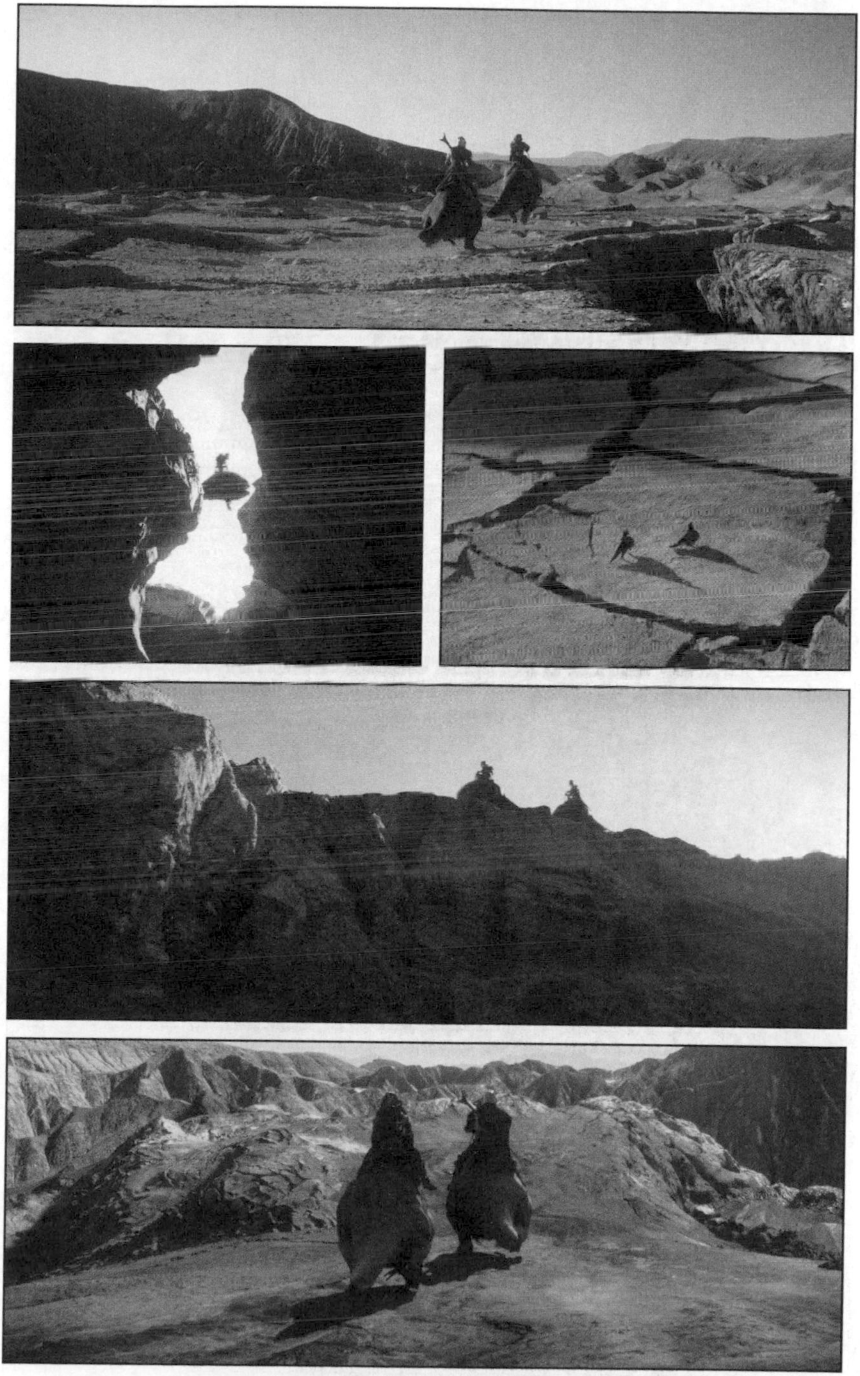

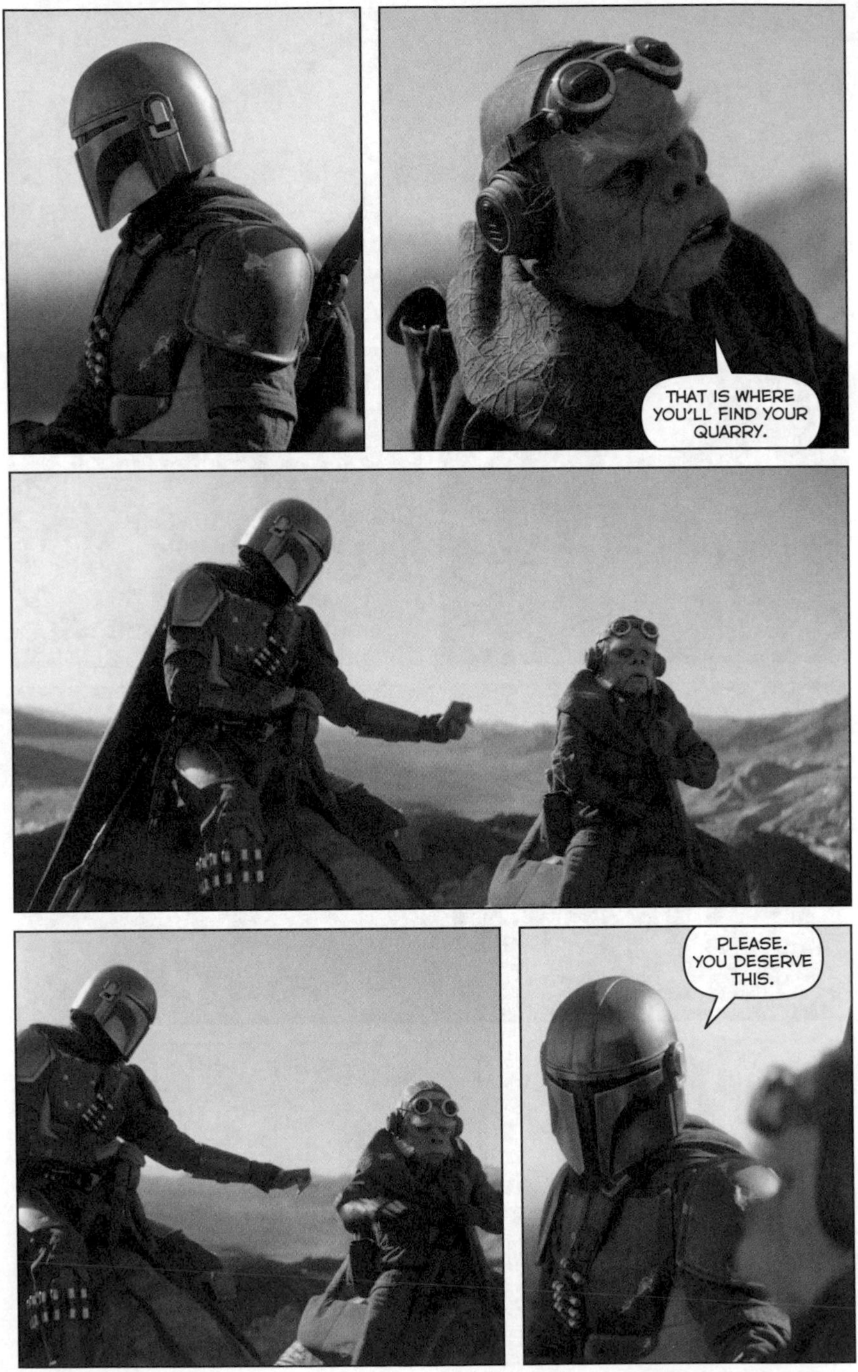
THAT IS WHERE YOU'LL FIND YOUR QUARRY.
PLEASE. YOU DESERVE THIS.

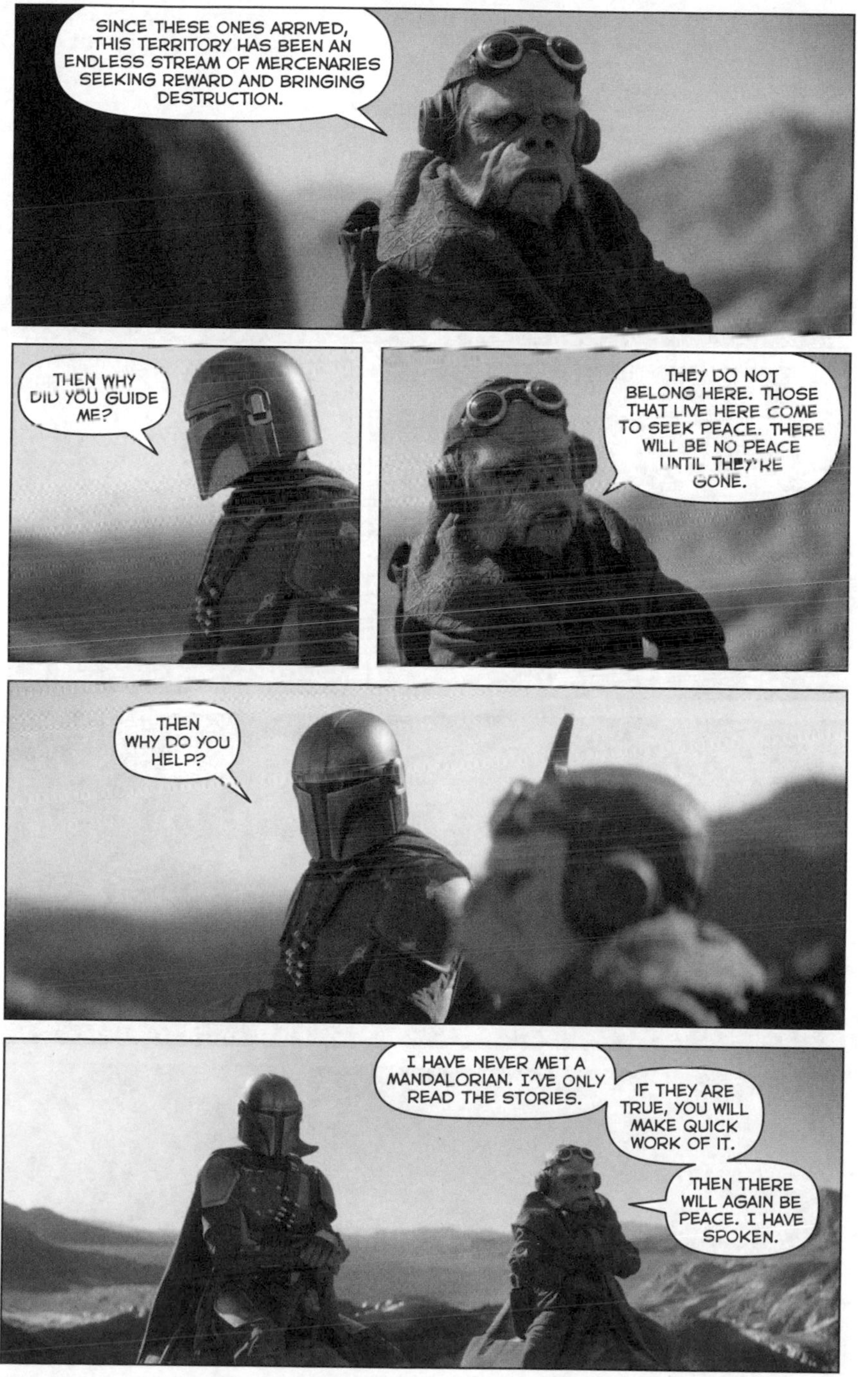
SINCE THESE ONES ARRIVED, THIS TERRITORY HAS BEEN AN ENDLESS STREAM OF MERCENARIES SEEKING REWARD AND BRINGING DESTRUCTION.
THEN WHY DID YOU GUIDE ME?
THEY DO NOT BELONG HERE. THOSE THAT LIVE HERE COME TO SEEK PEACE. THERE WILL BE NO PEACE UNTIL THEY'RE GONE.
THEN WHY DO YOU HELP?
I HAVE NEVER MET A MANDALORIAN. I'VE ONLY READ THE STORIES.
IF THEY ARE TRUE, YOU WILL MAKE QUICK WORK OF IT.
THEN THERE WILL AGAIN BE PEACE. I HAVE SPOKEN.

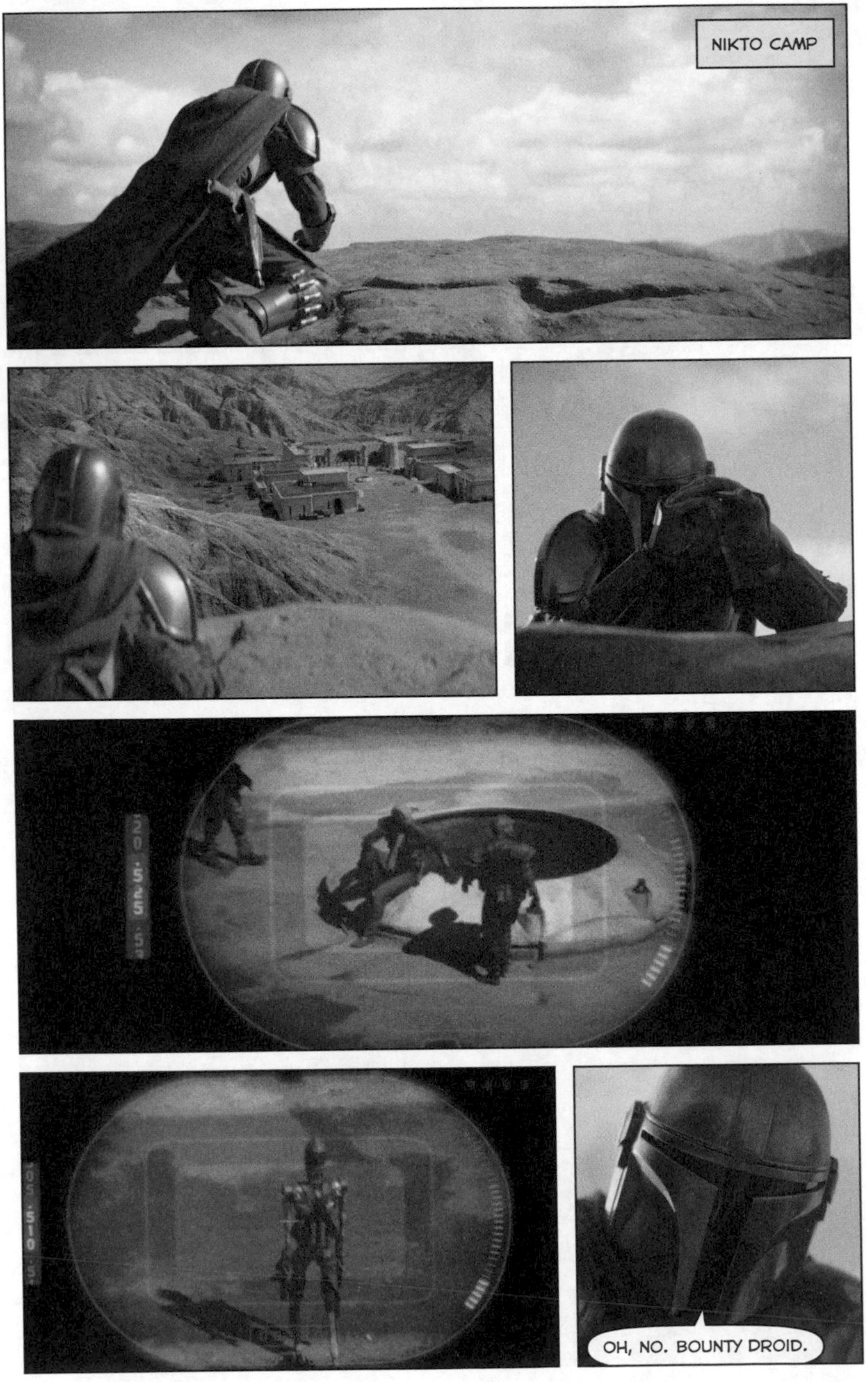
NIKTO CAMP
OH, NO. BOUNTY DROID.

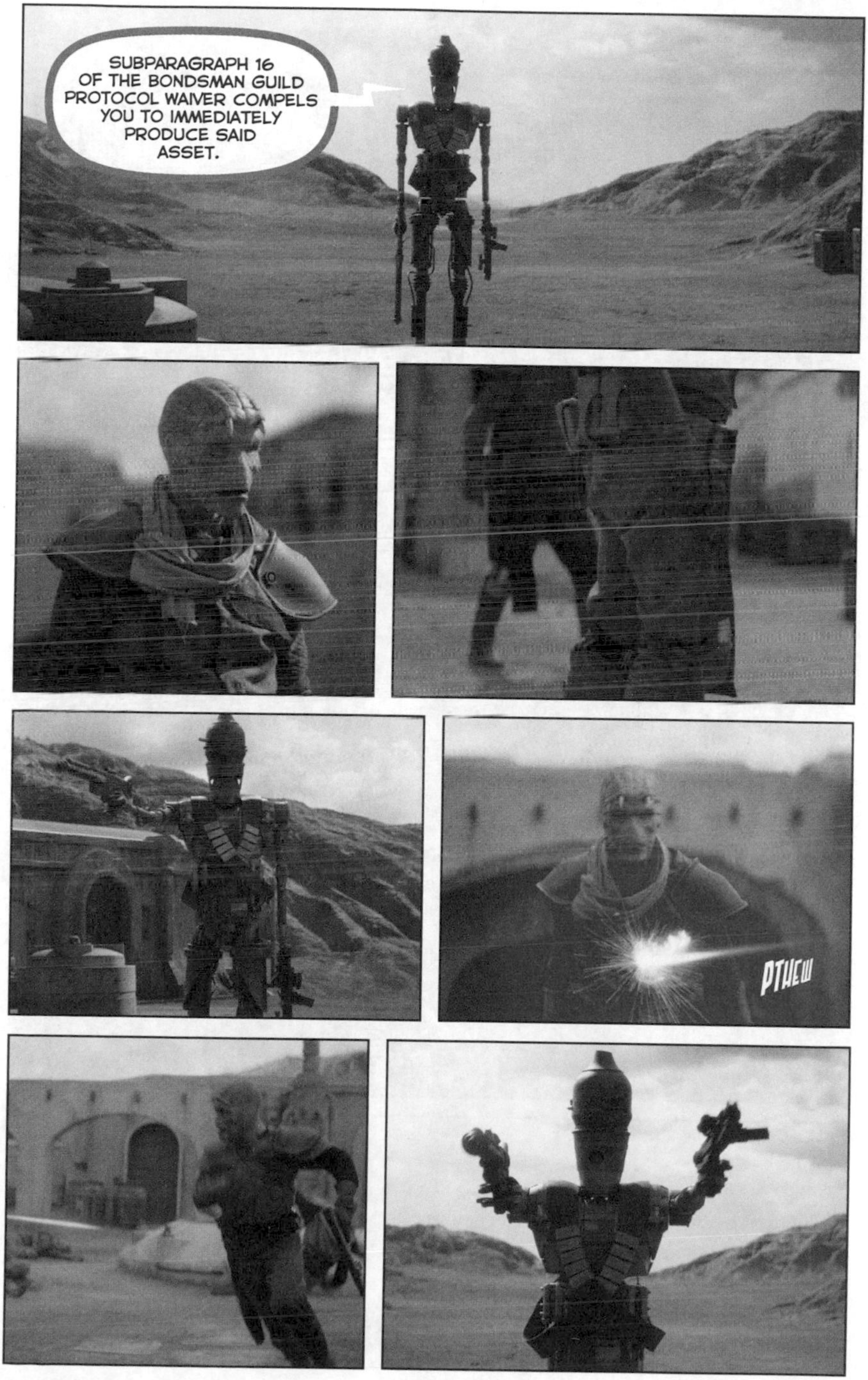
SUBPARAGRAPH 16 OF THE BONDSMAN GUILD PROTOCOL WAIVER COMPELS YOU TO IMMEDIATELY PRODUCE SAID ASSET.
PTHEW

76

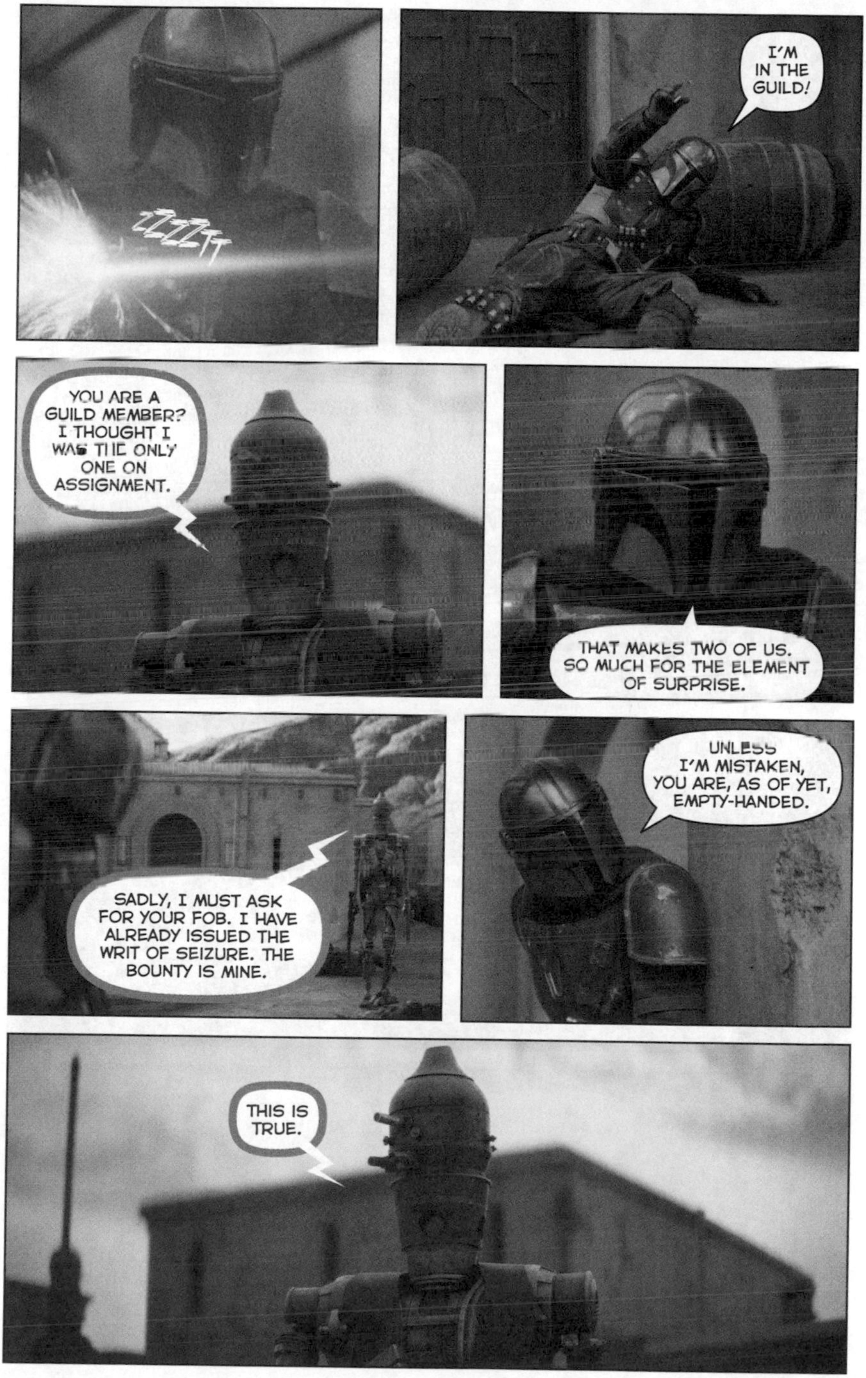

ZZZZTT
I'M IN THE GUILD!
YOU ARE A GUILD MEMBER? I THOUGHT I WAS THE ONLY ONE ON ASSIGNMENT.
THAT MAKES TWO OF US. SO MUCH FOR THE ELEMENT OF SURPRISE.
SADLY, I MUST ASK FOR YOUR FOB. I HAVE ALREADY ISSUED THE WRIT OF SEIZURE. THE BOUNTY IS MINE.
UNLESS I'M MISTAKEN, YOU ARE, AS OF YET, EMPTY-HANDED.
THIS IS TRUE.

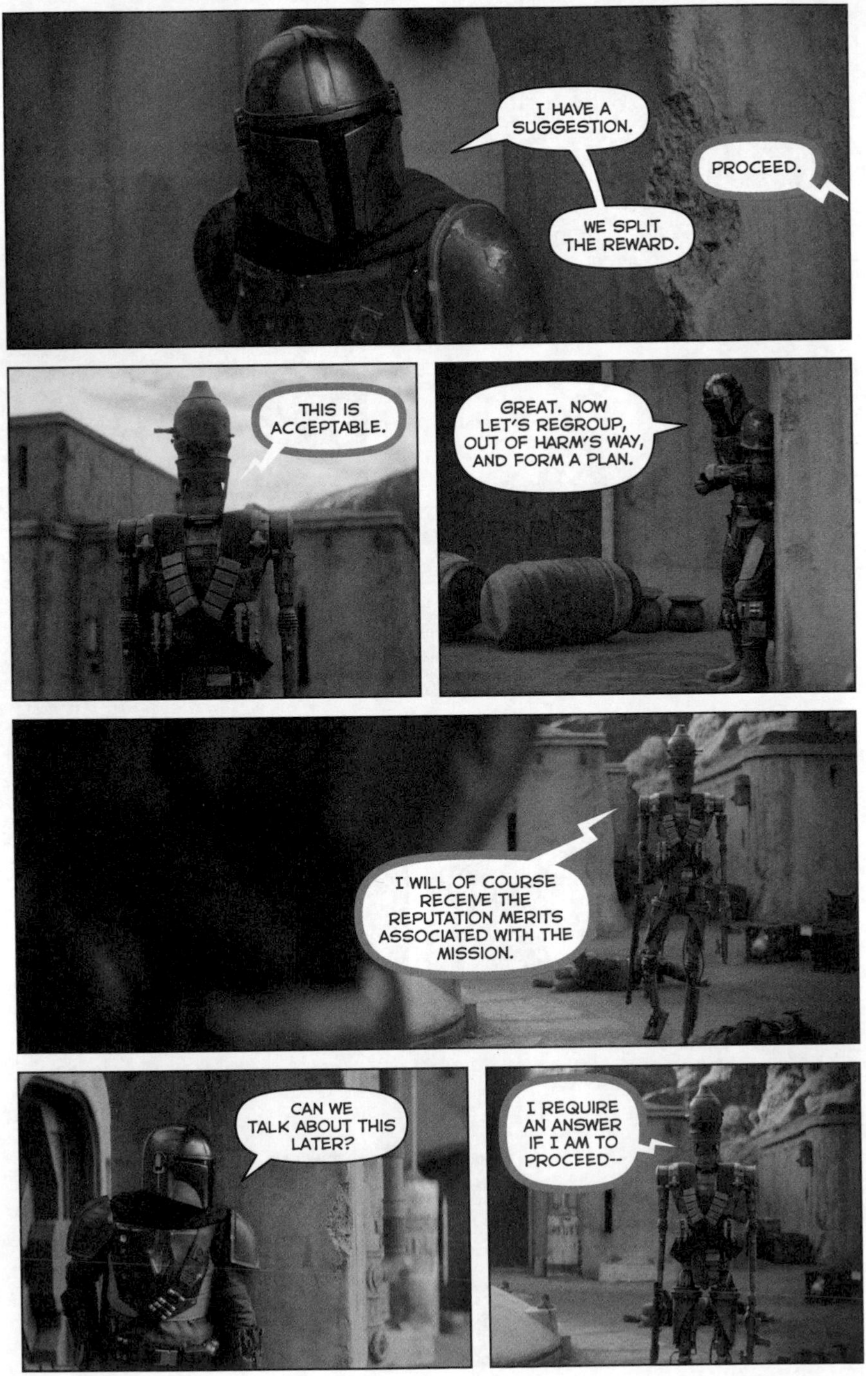
I HAVE A SUGGESTION.
WE SPLIT THE REWARD.
PROCEED.
THIS IS ACCEPTABLE.
GREAT. NOW LET'S REGROUP, OUT OF HARM'S WAY, AND FORM A PLAN.
I WILL OF COURSE RECEIVE THE REPUTATION MERITS ASSOCIATED WITH THE MISSION.
CAN WE TALK ABOUT THIS LATER?
I REQUIRE AN ANSWER IF I AM TO PROCEED--

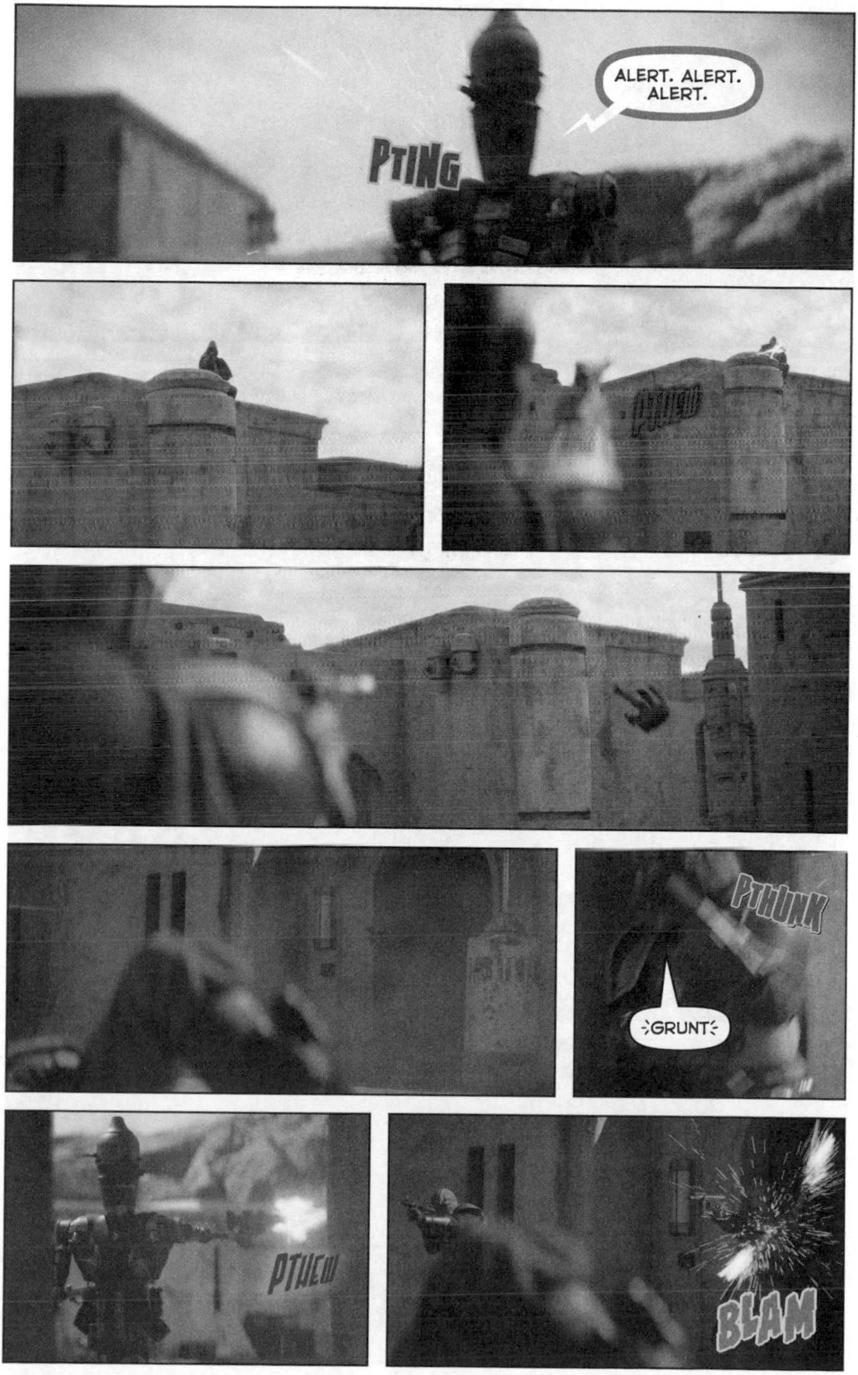
PTING
ALERT. ALERT. ALERT.
PTHUNK
GRUNT
PTHEW
BLAM

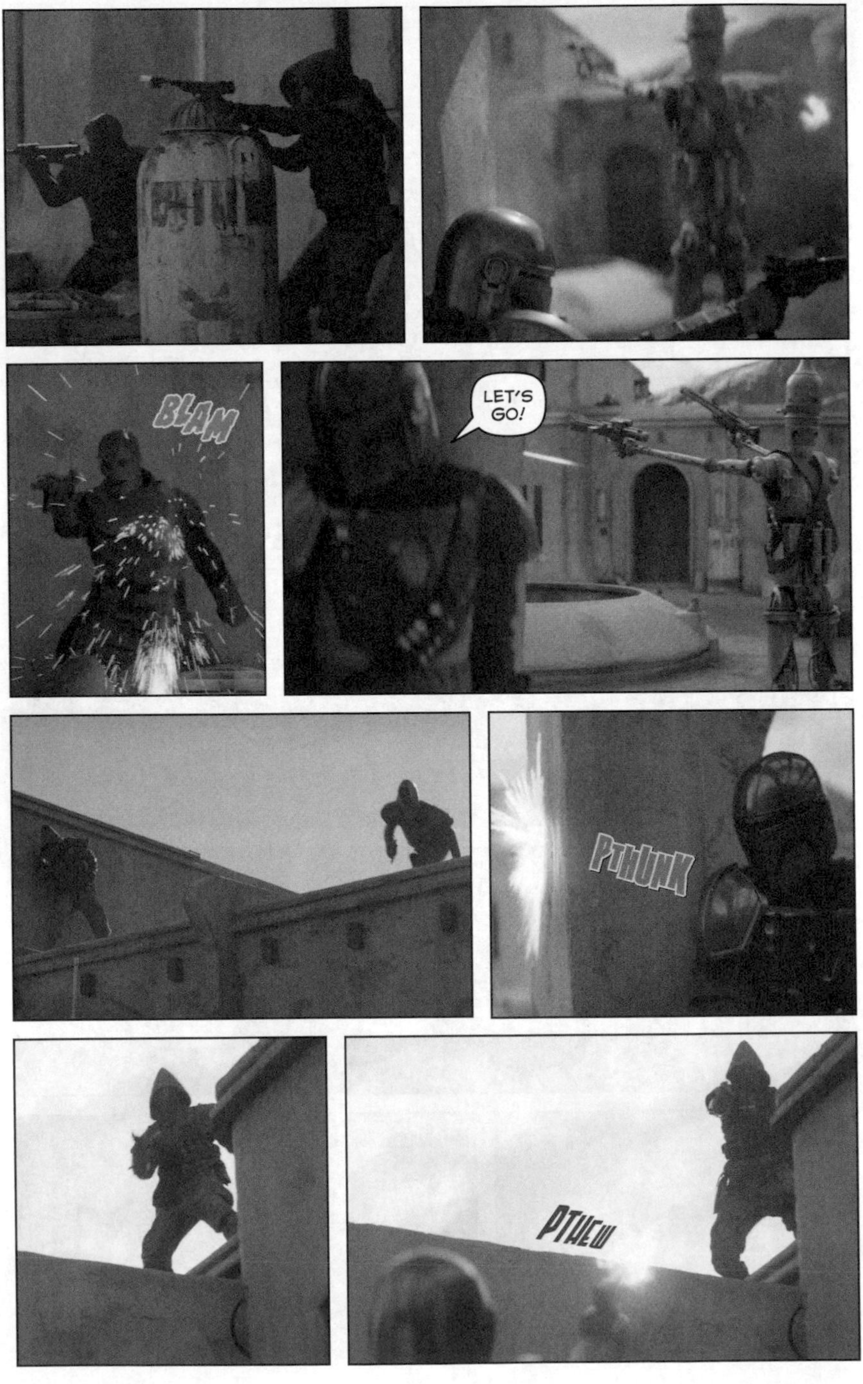
BLAM
LET'S GO!
PTHUNK
PTHEW

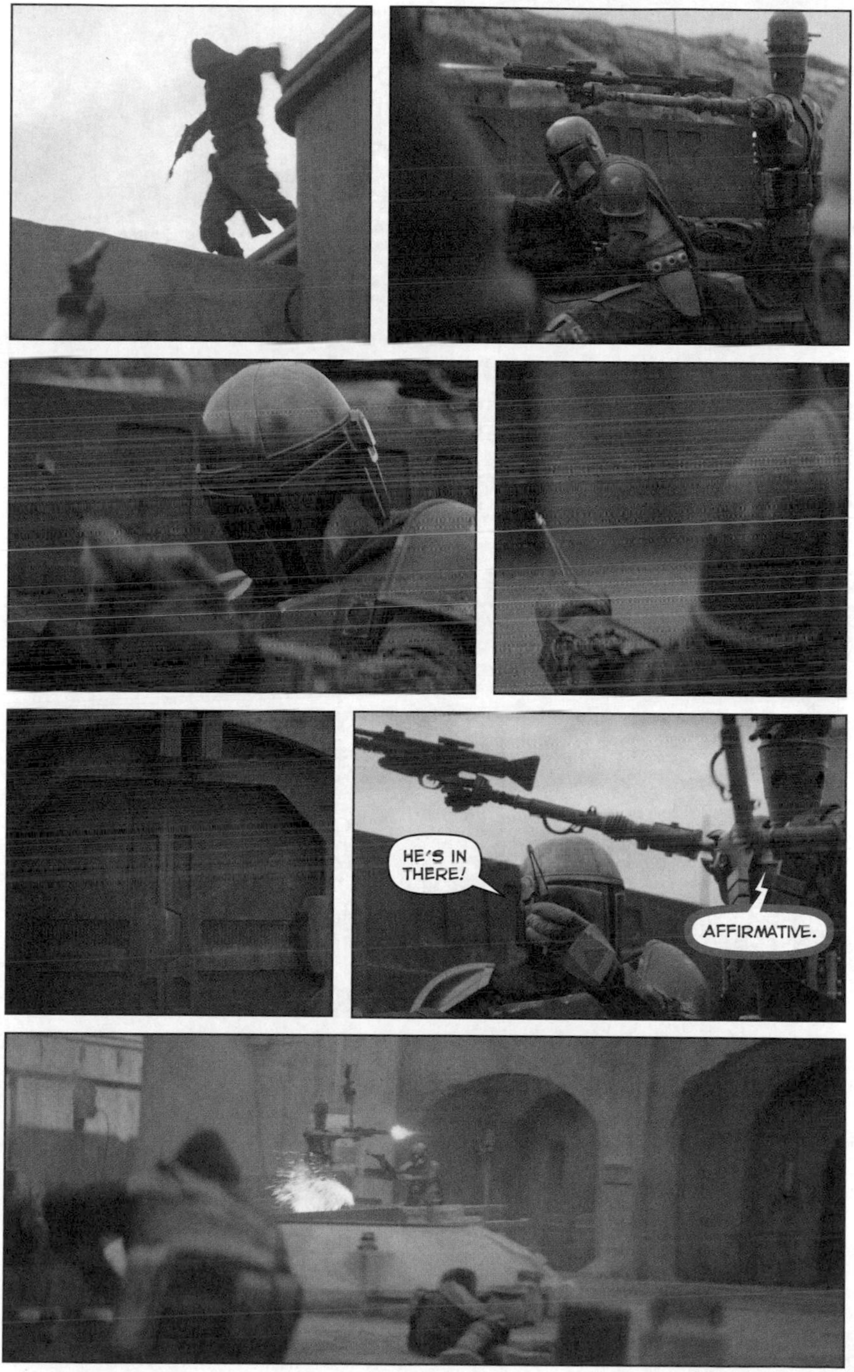
HE'S IN THERE!
AFFIRMATIVE.

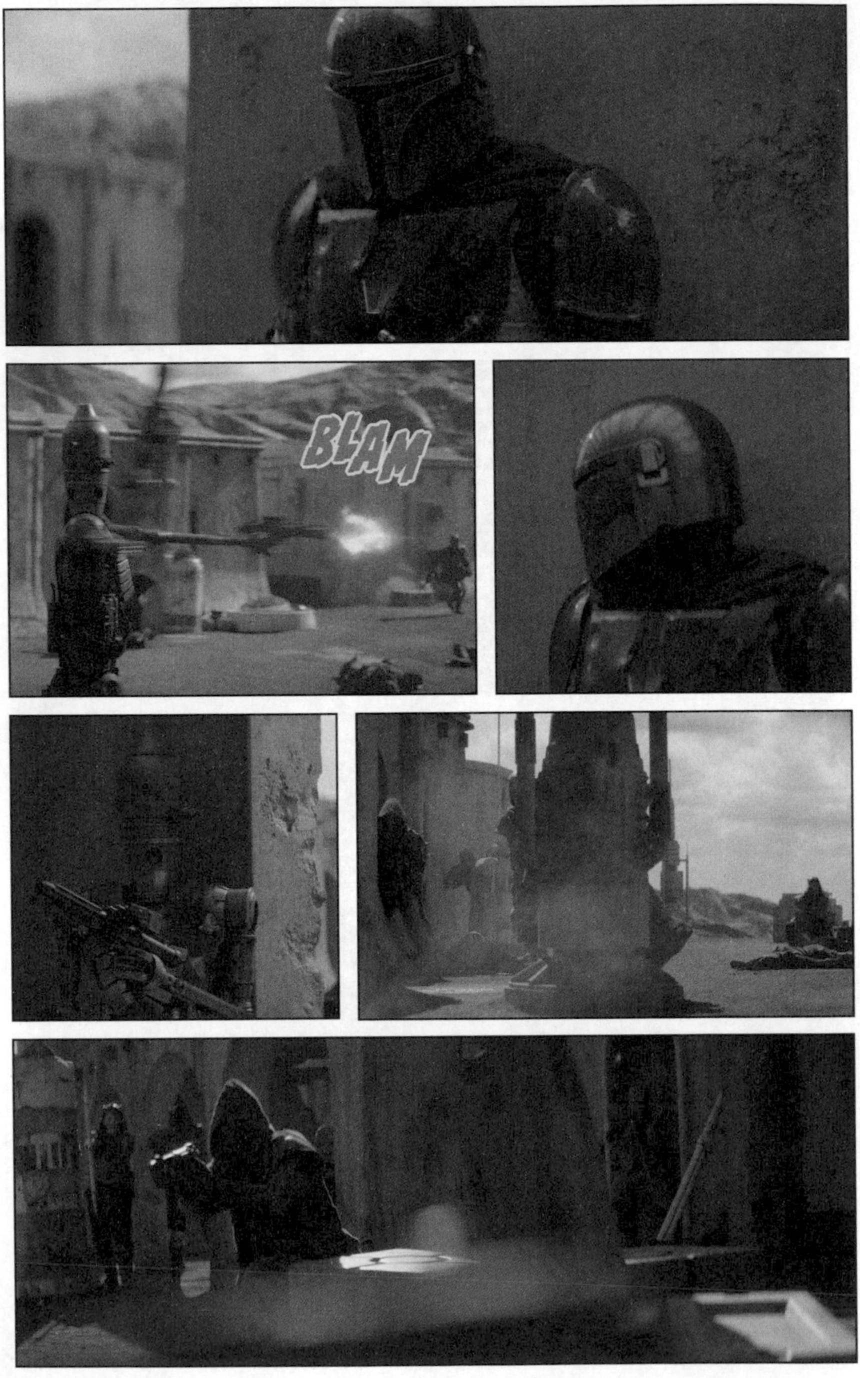
BLAM

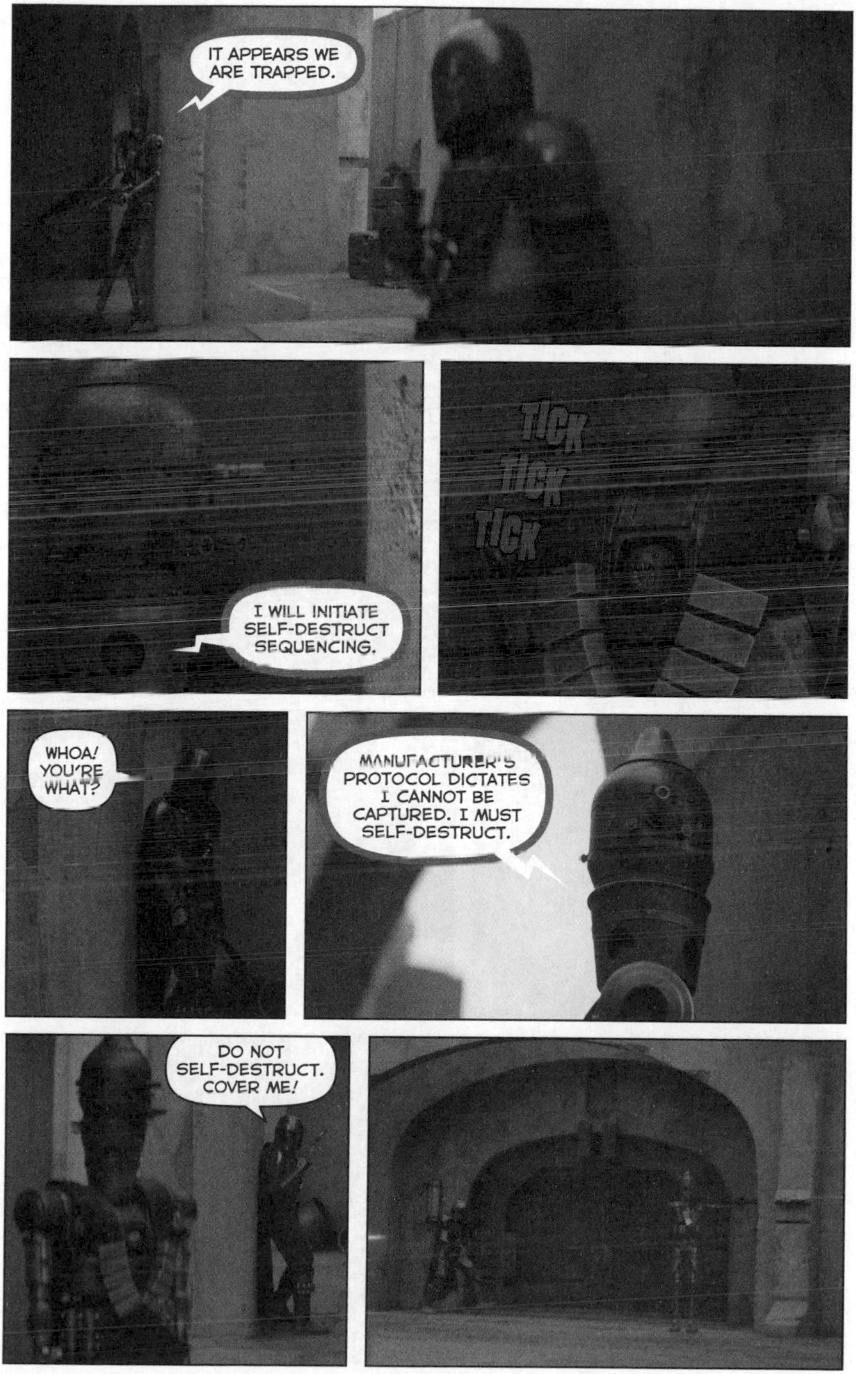
IT APPEARS WE ARE TRAPPED.
I WILL INITIATE SELF-DESTRUCT SEQUENCING.
TICK TICK TICK
WHOA! YOU'RE WHAT?
MANUFACTURER'S PROTOCOL DICTATES I CANNOT BE CAPTURED. I MUST SELF-DESTRUCT.
DO NOT SELF-DESTRUCT. COVER ME!

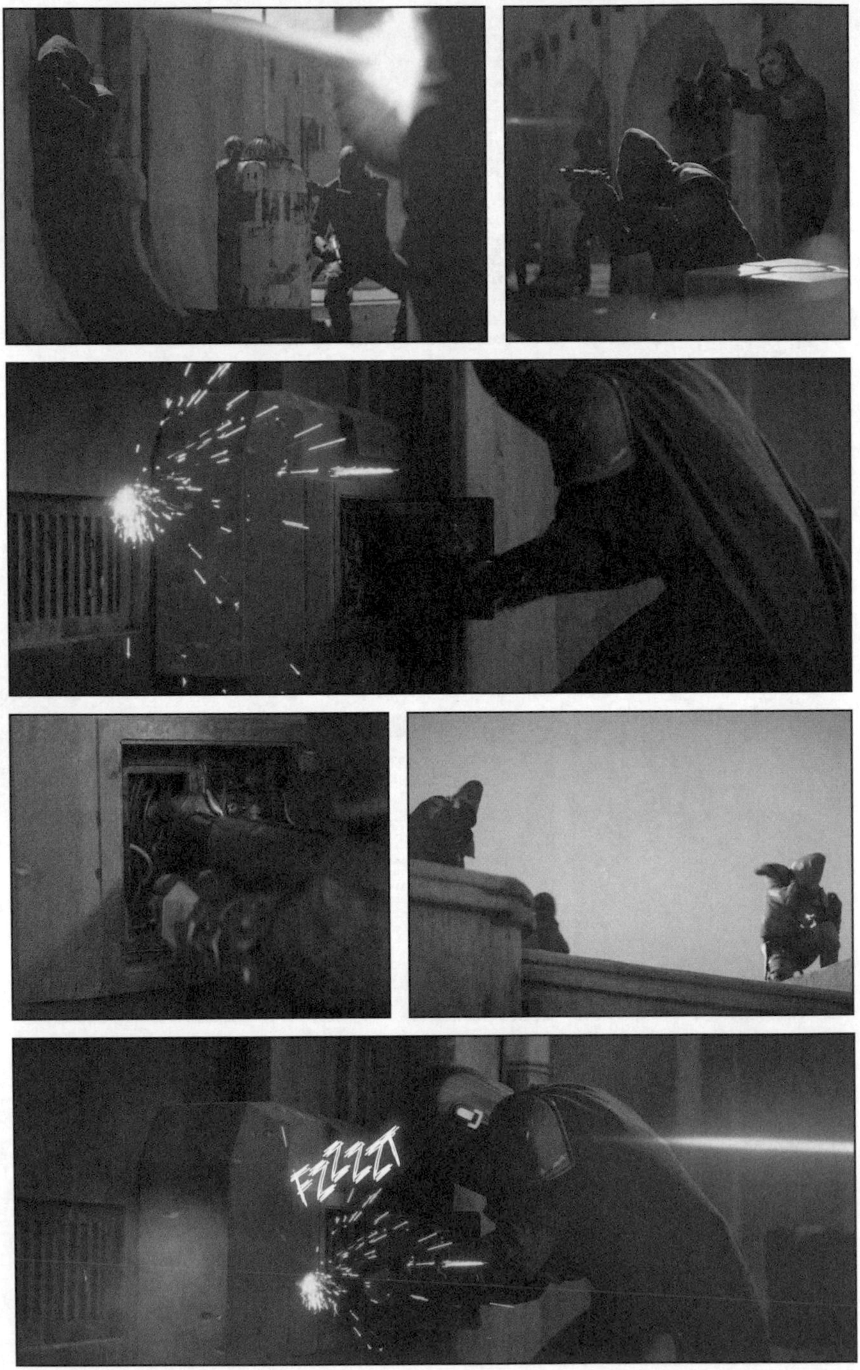
FZZZZT

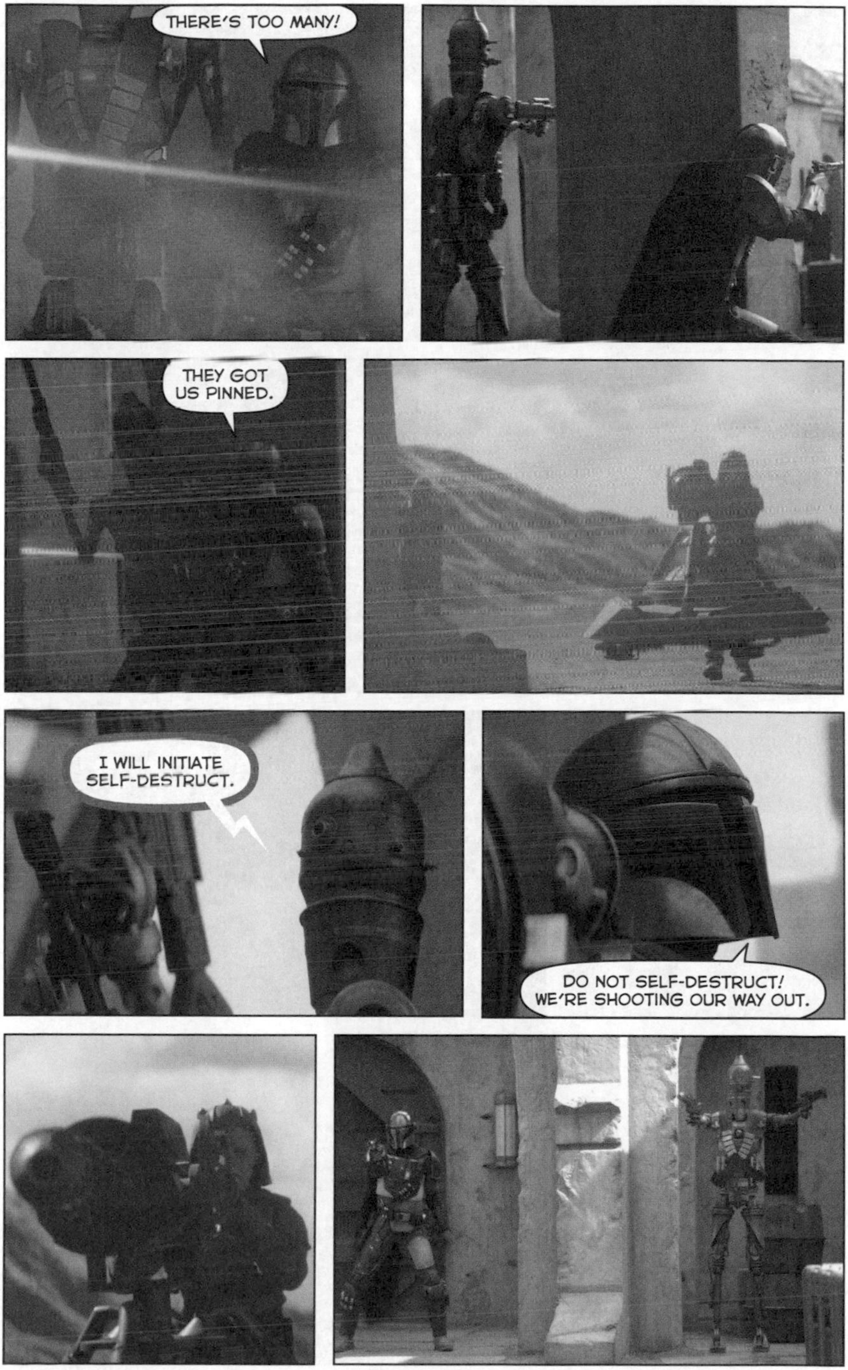
THERE'S TOO MANY!
THEY GOT US PINNED.
I WILL INITIATE SELF-DESTRUCT.
DO NOT SELF-DESTRUCT! WE'RE SHOOTING OUR WAY OUT.

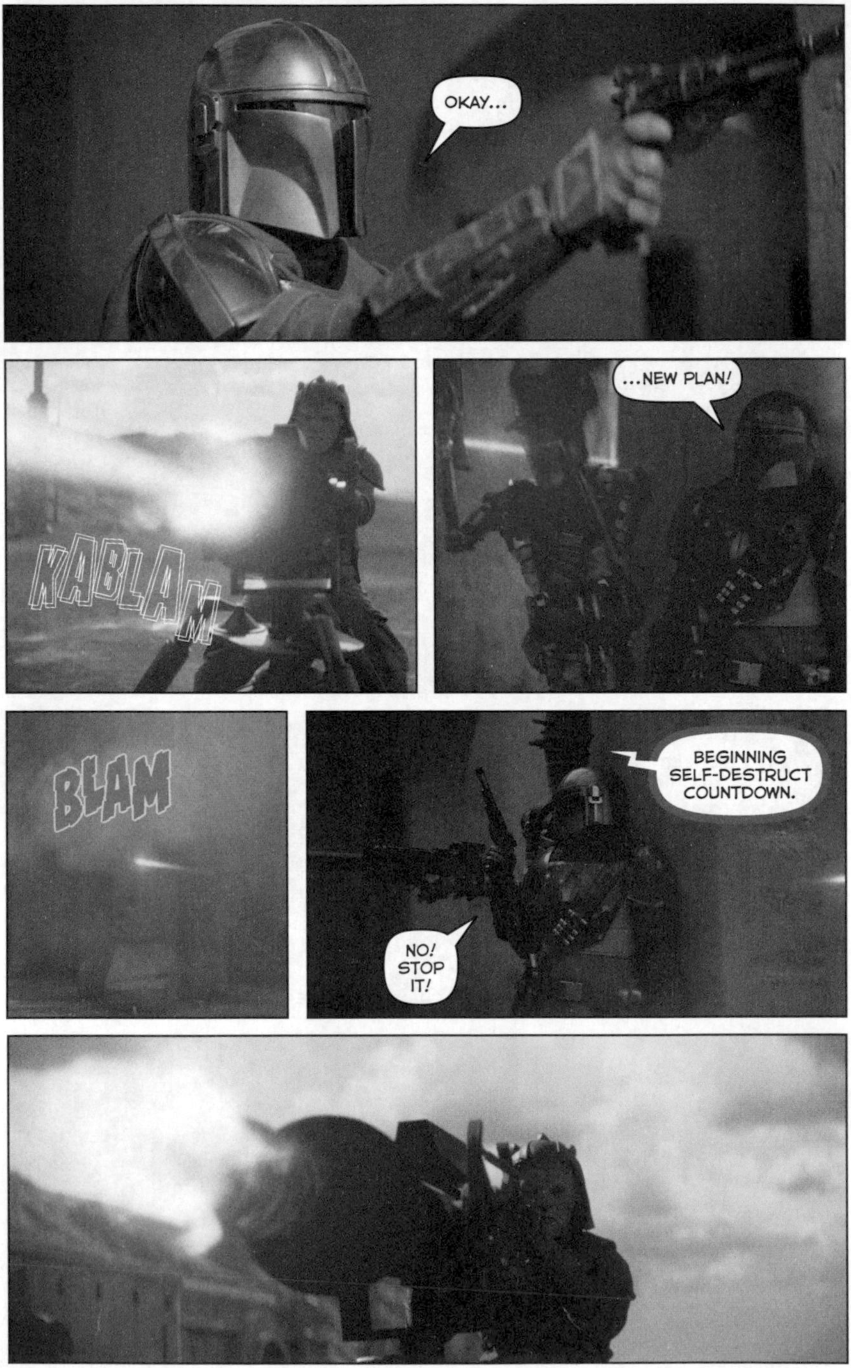
OKAY...
KABLAM
...NEW PLAN!
BLAM
BEGINNING SELF-DESTRUCT COUNTDOWN.
NO! STOP IT!

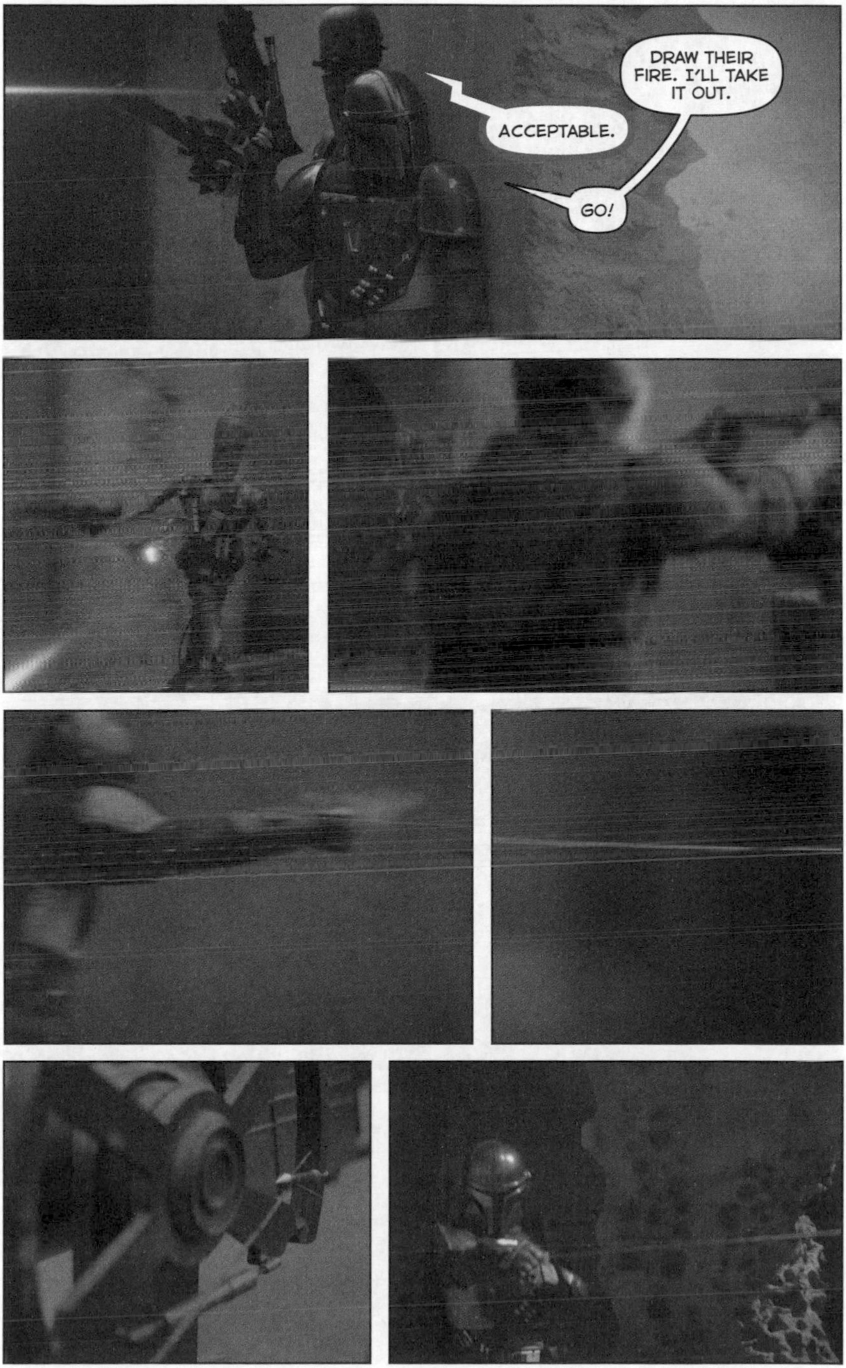
DRAW THEIR FIRE. I'LL TAKE IT OUT.
ACCEPTABLE.
GO!

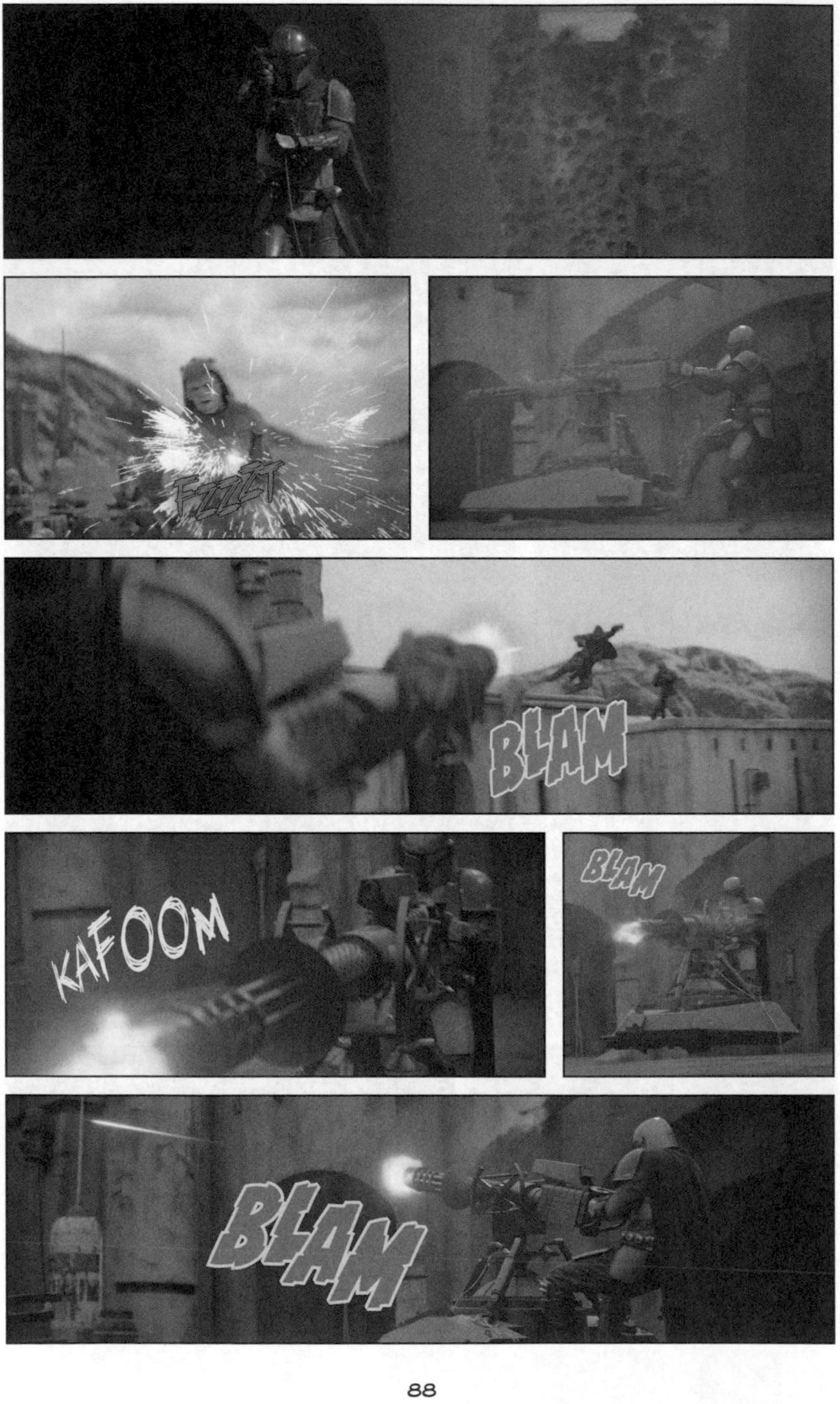
FZZZT
BLAM
KAFOOM
BLAM
BLAM

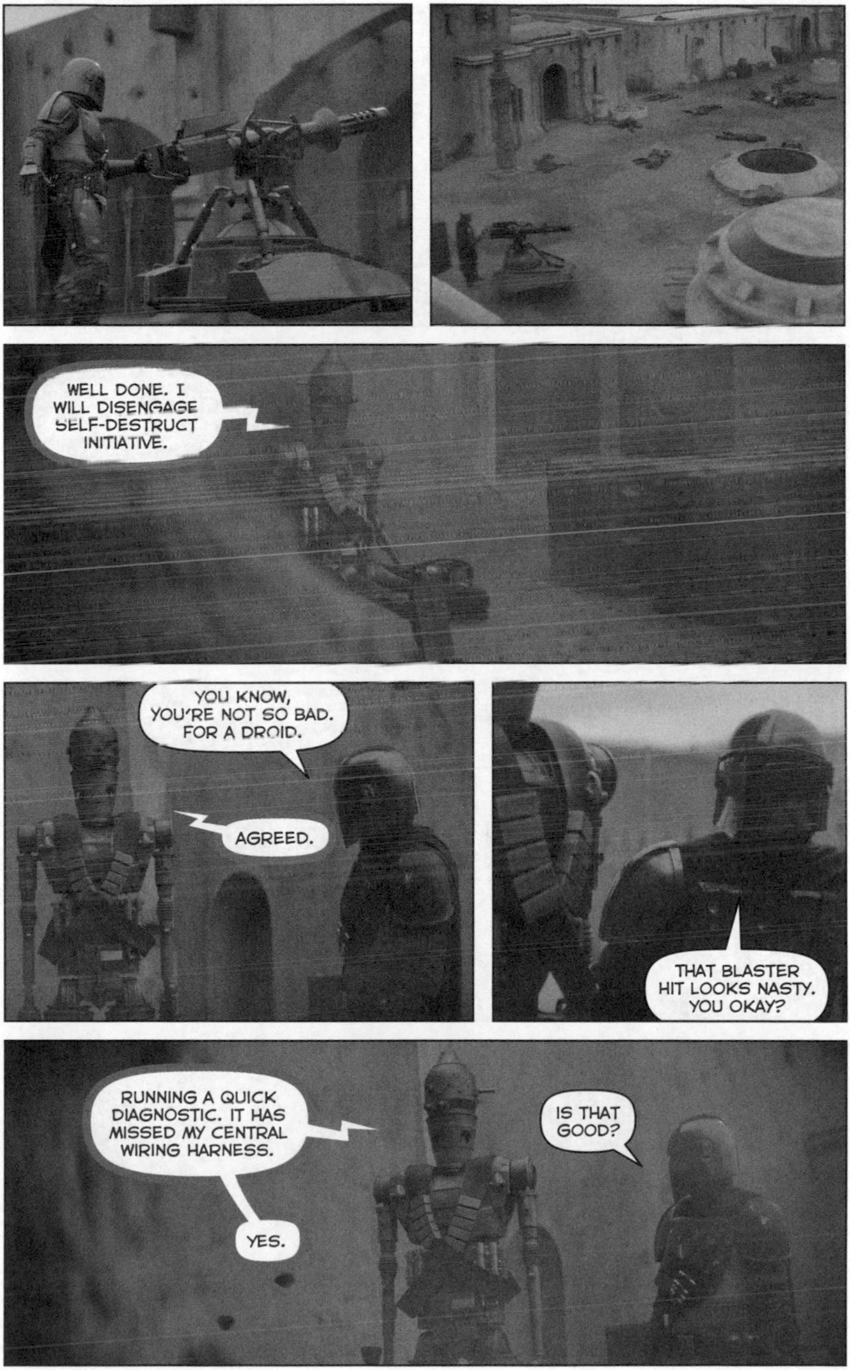
WELL DONE. I WILL DISENGAGE SELF-DESTRUCT INITIATIVE.
YOU KNOW, YOU'RE NOT SO BAD. FOR A DROID.
AGREED.
THAT BLASTER HIT LOOKS NASTY. YOU OKAY?
RUNNING A QUICK DIAGNOSTIC. IT HAS MISSED MY CENTRAL WIRING HARNESS.
IS THAT GOOD?
YES.

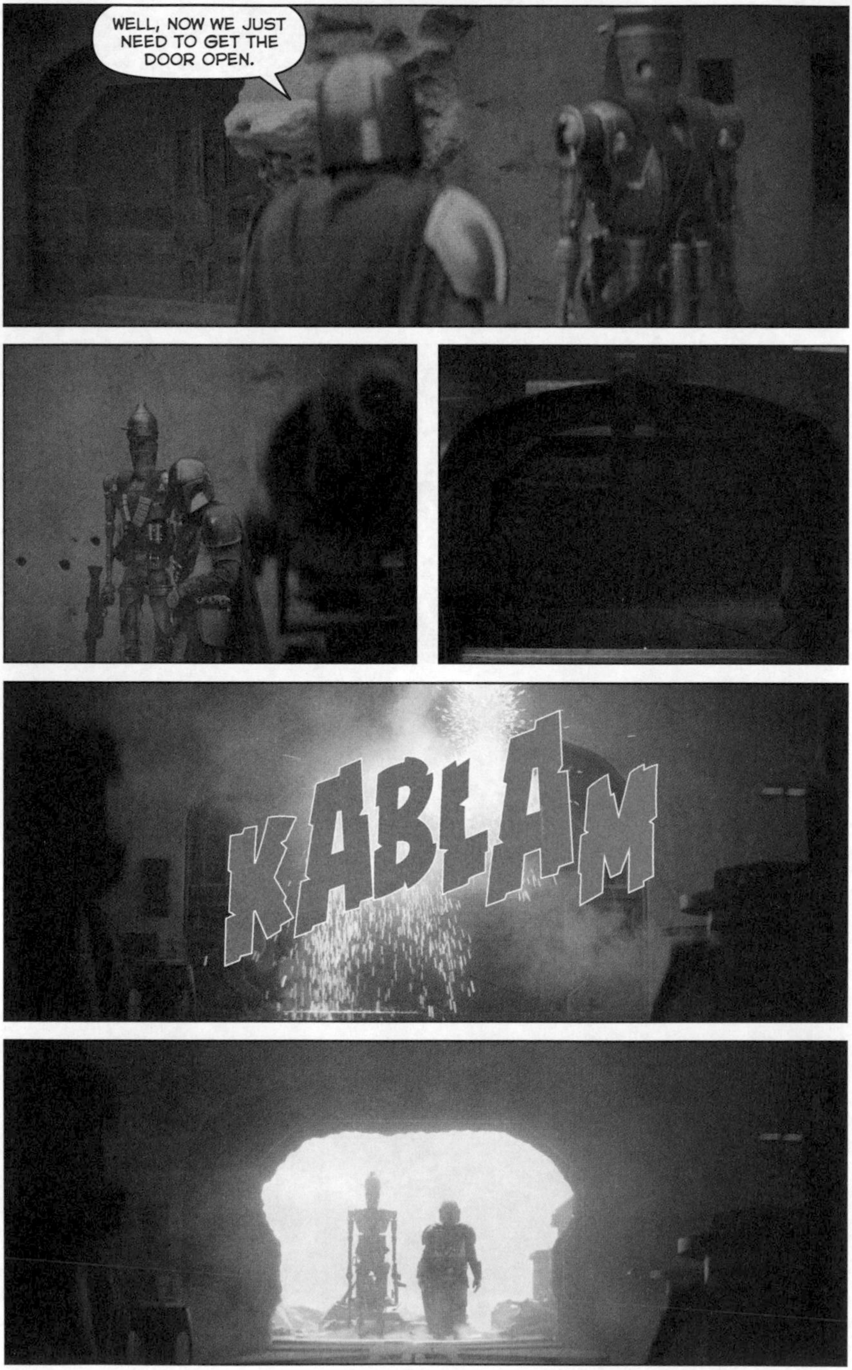
WELL, NOW WE JUST NEED TO GET THE DOOR OPEN.
KABLAM

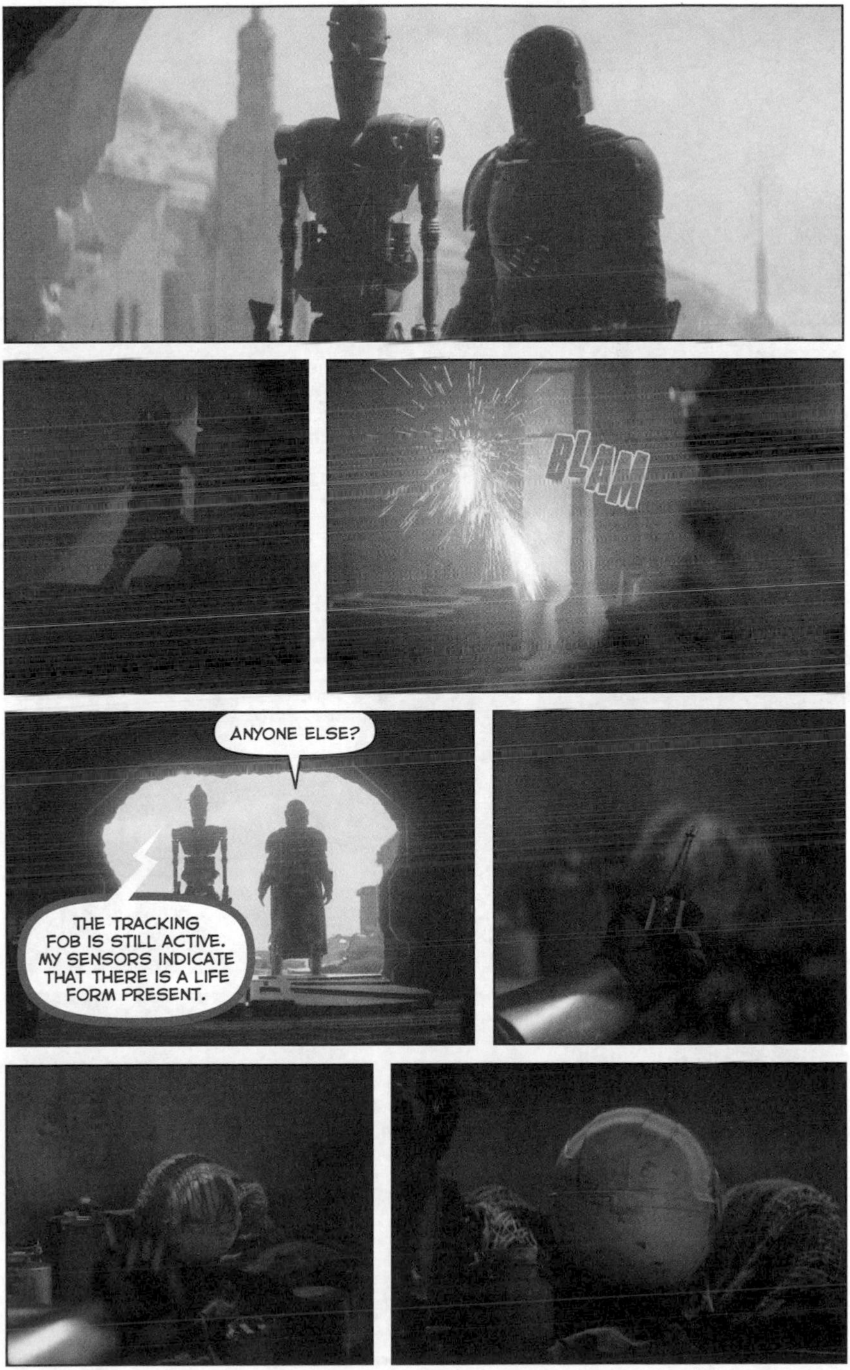
BLAM
ANYONE ELSE?
THE TRACKING FOB IS STILL ACTIVE. MY SENSORS INDICATE THAT THERE IS A LIFE FORM PRESENT.

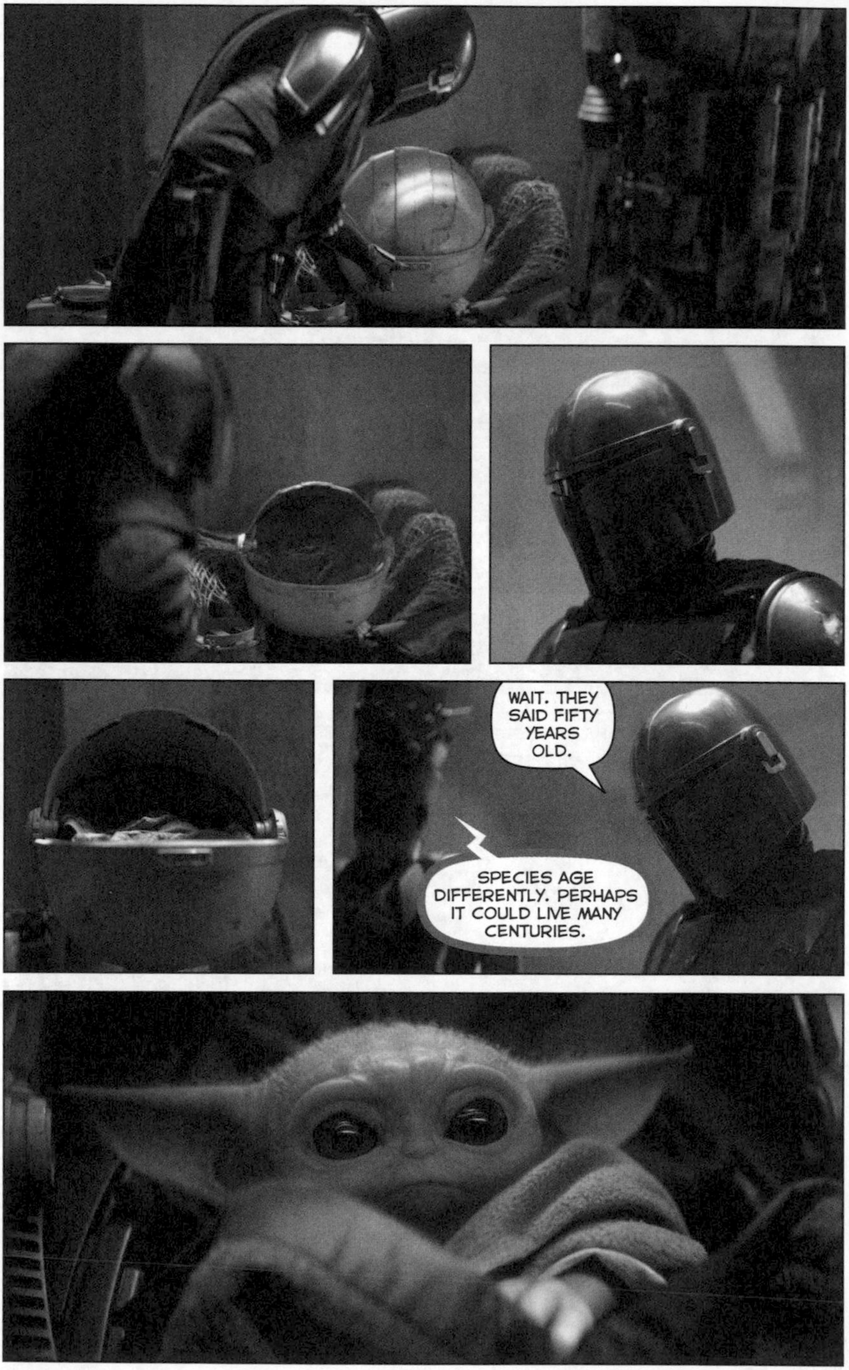
WAIT. THEY SAID FIFTY YEARS OLD.
SPECIES AGE DIFFERENTLY. PERHAPS IT COULD LIVE MANY CENTURIES.

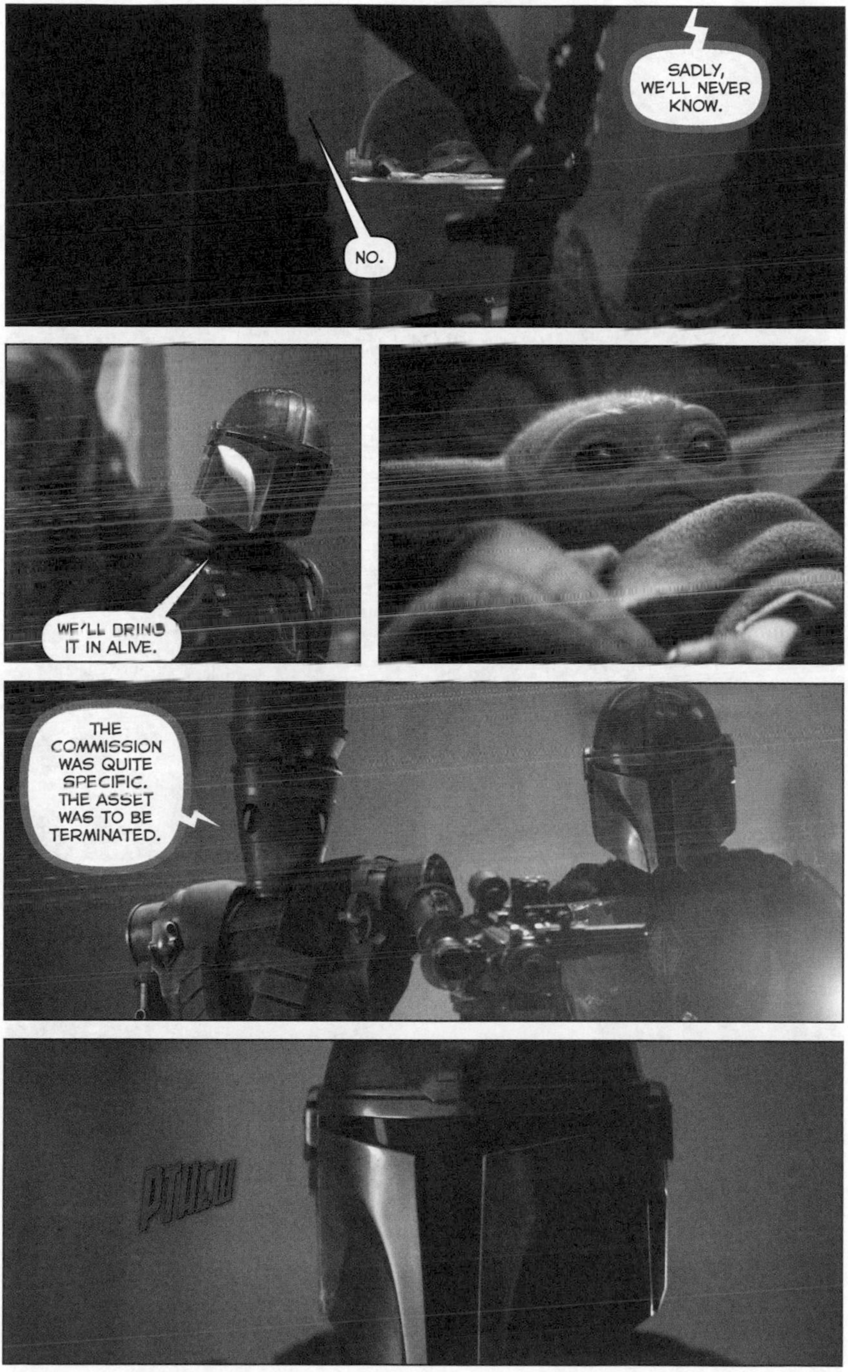
SADLY, WE'LL NEVER KNOW.
NO.
WE'LL BRING IT IN ALIVE.
THE COMMISSION WAS QUITE SPECIFIC. THE ASSET WAS TO BE TERMINATED.

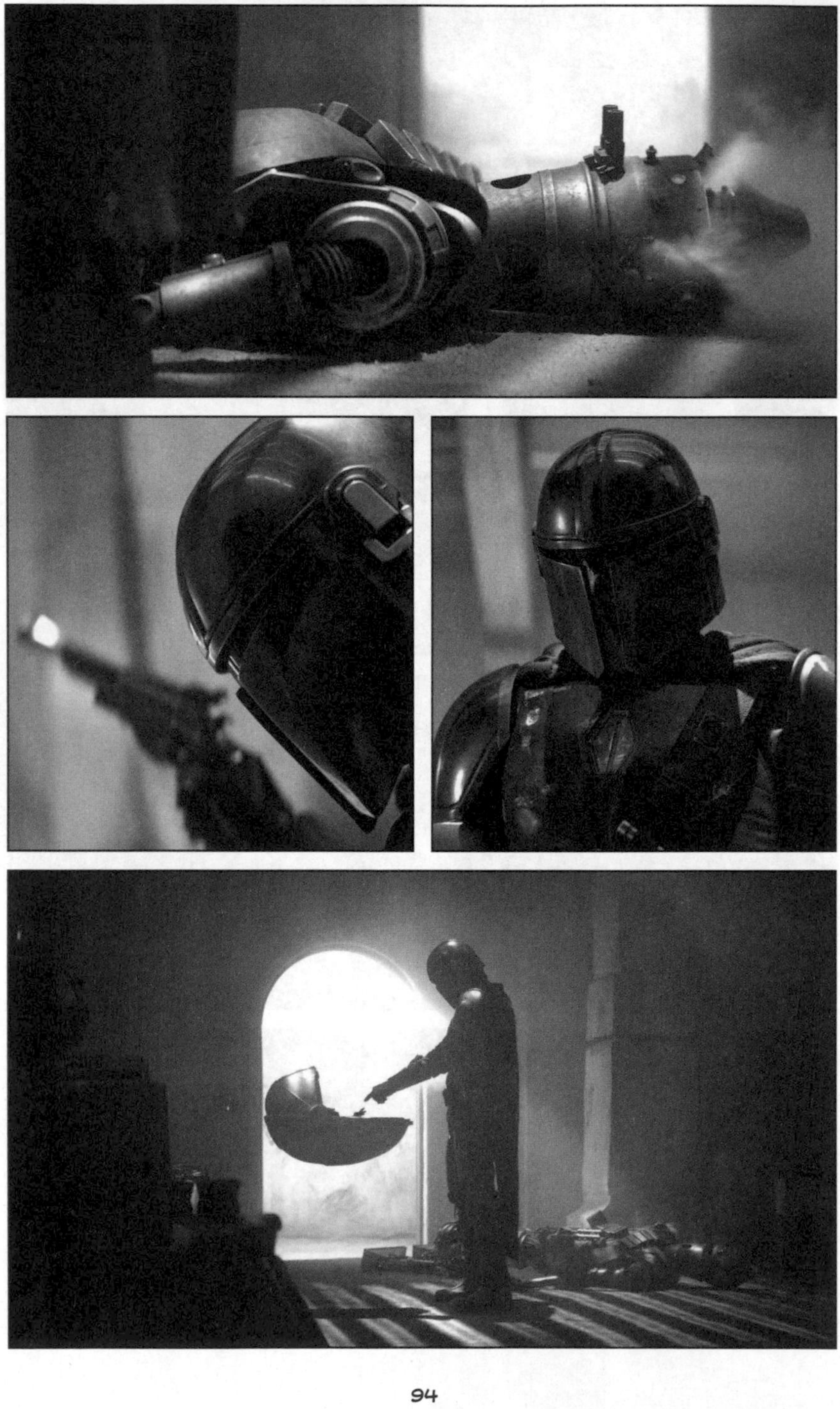

Chapter 2

THE CHILD

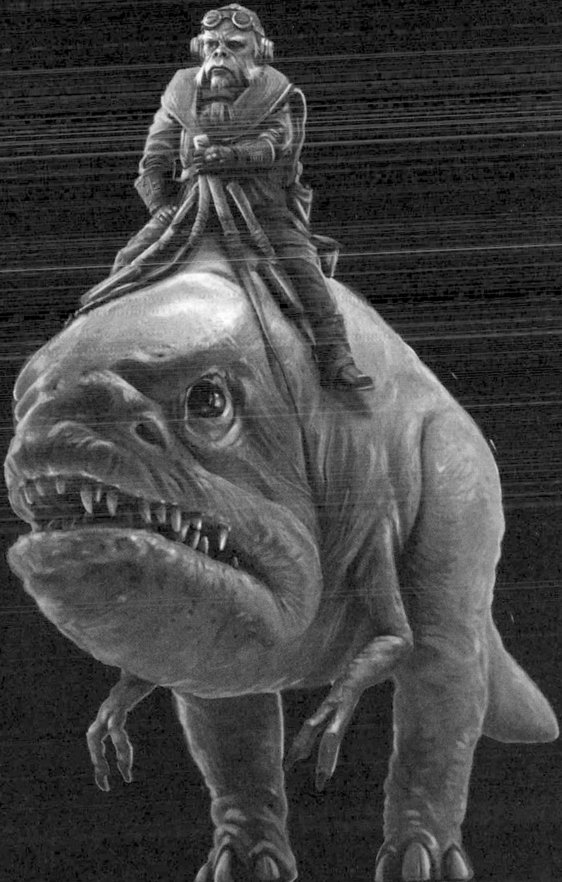

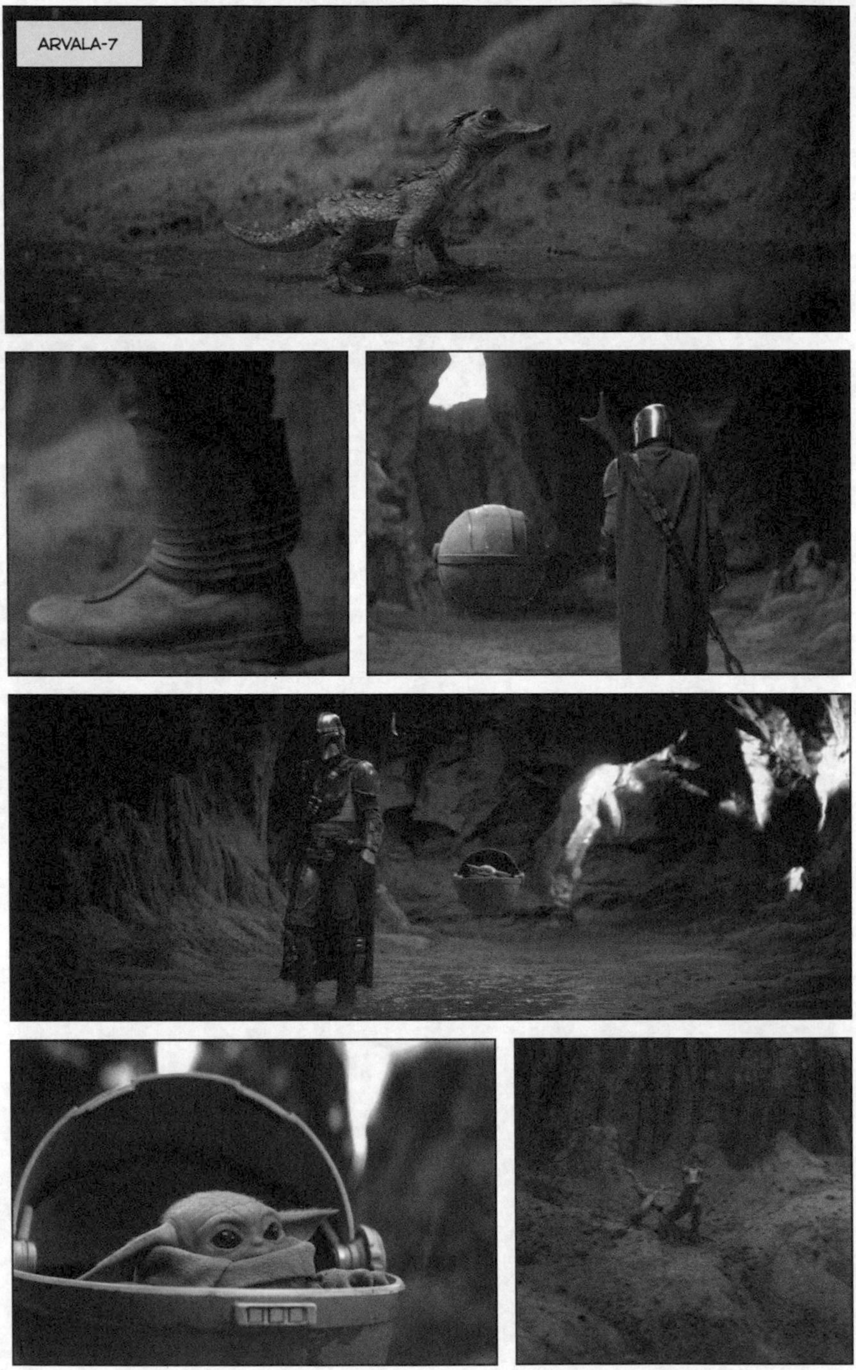
ARVALA-7

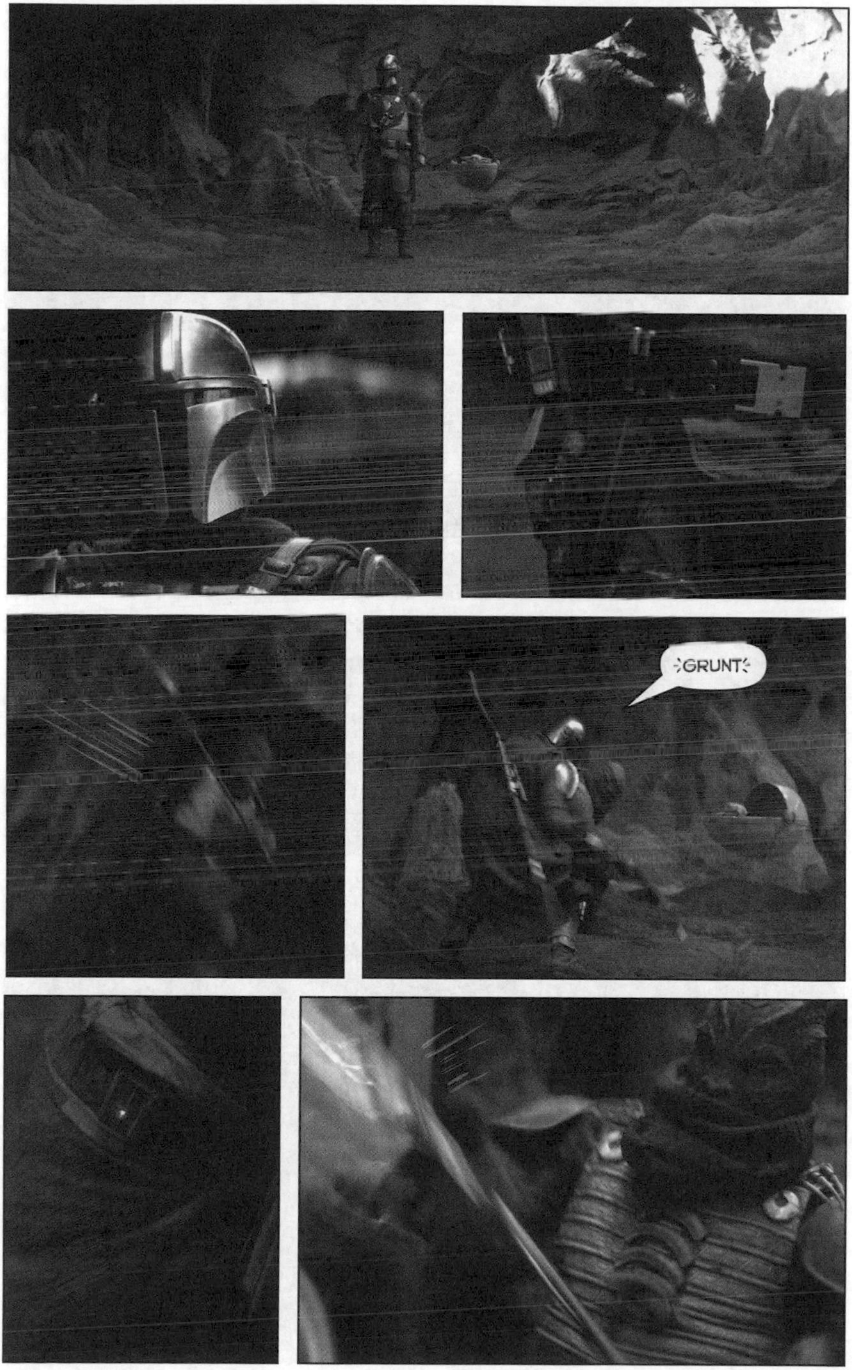
GRUNT

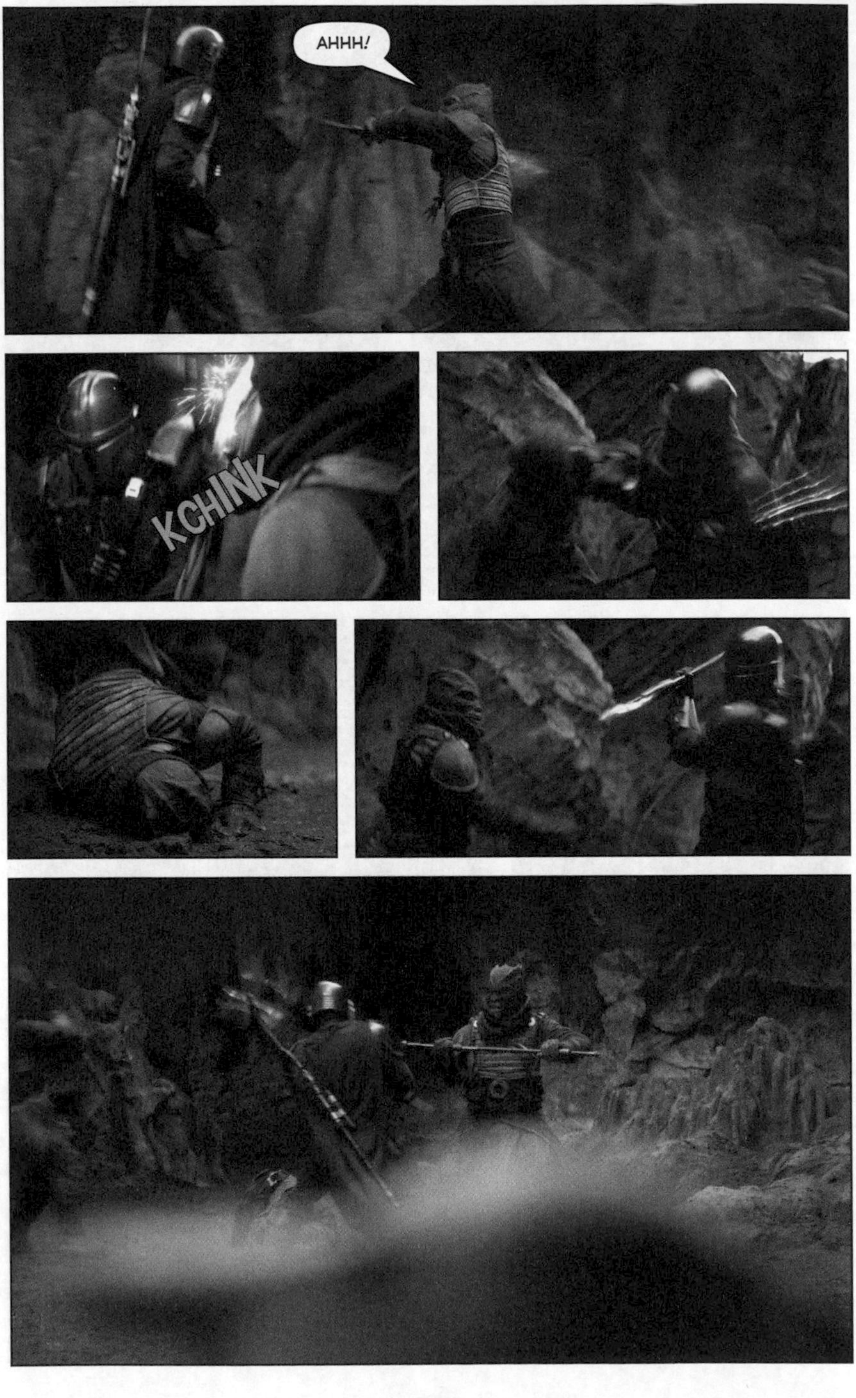
AHHH!
KCHINK

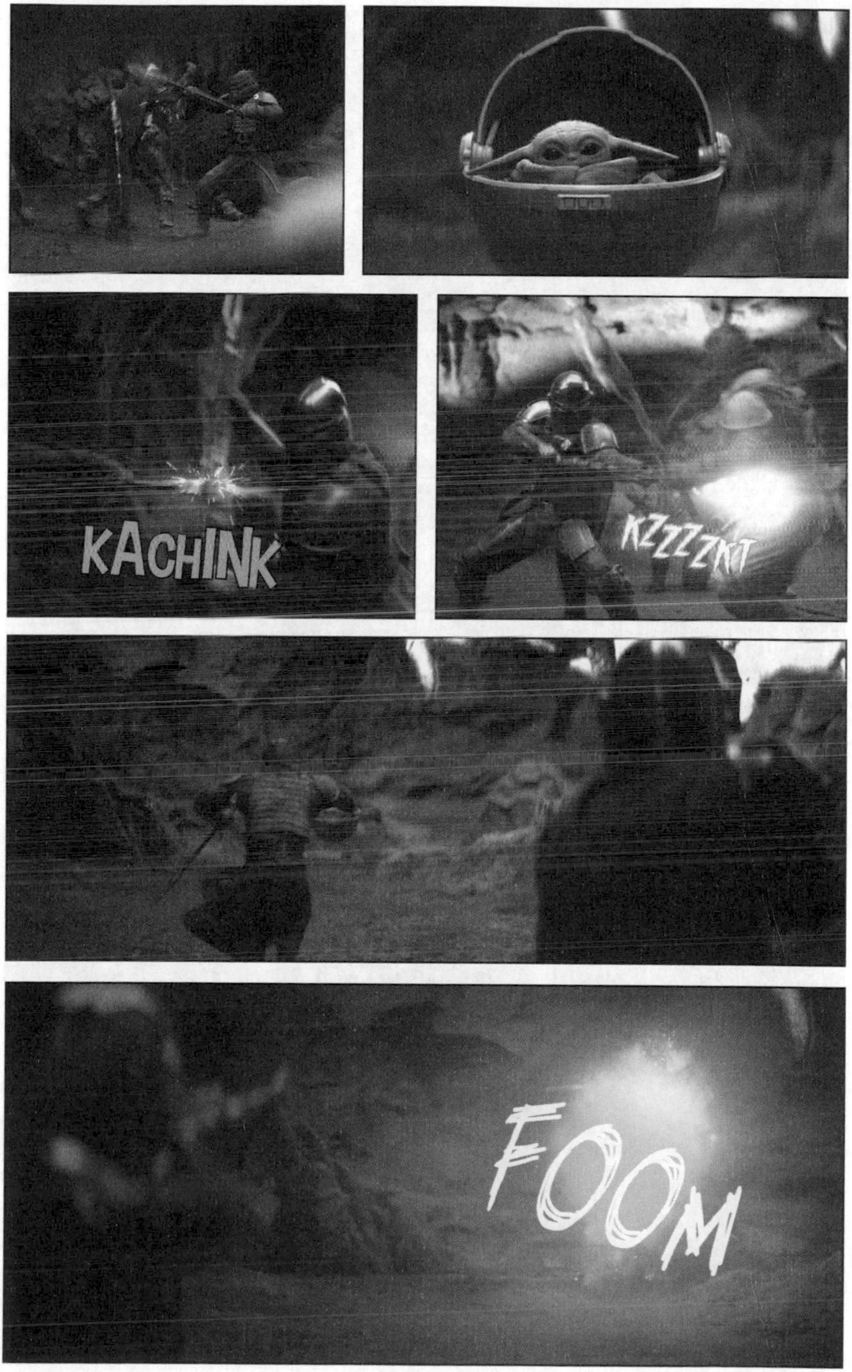
KACHINK
KZZZZKT
FOOM

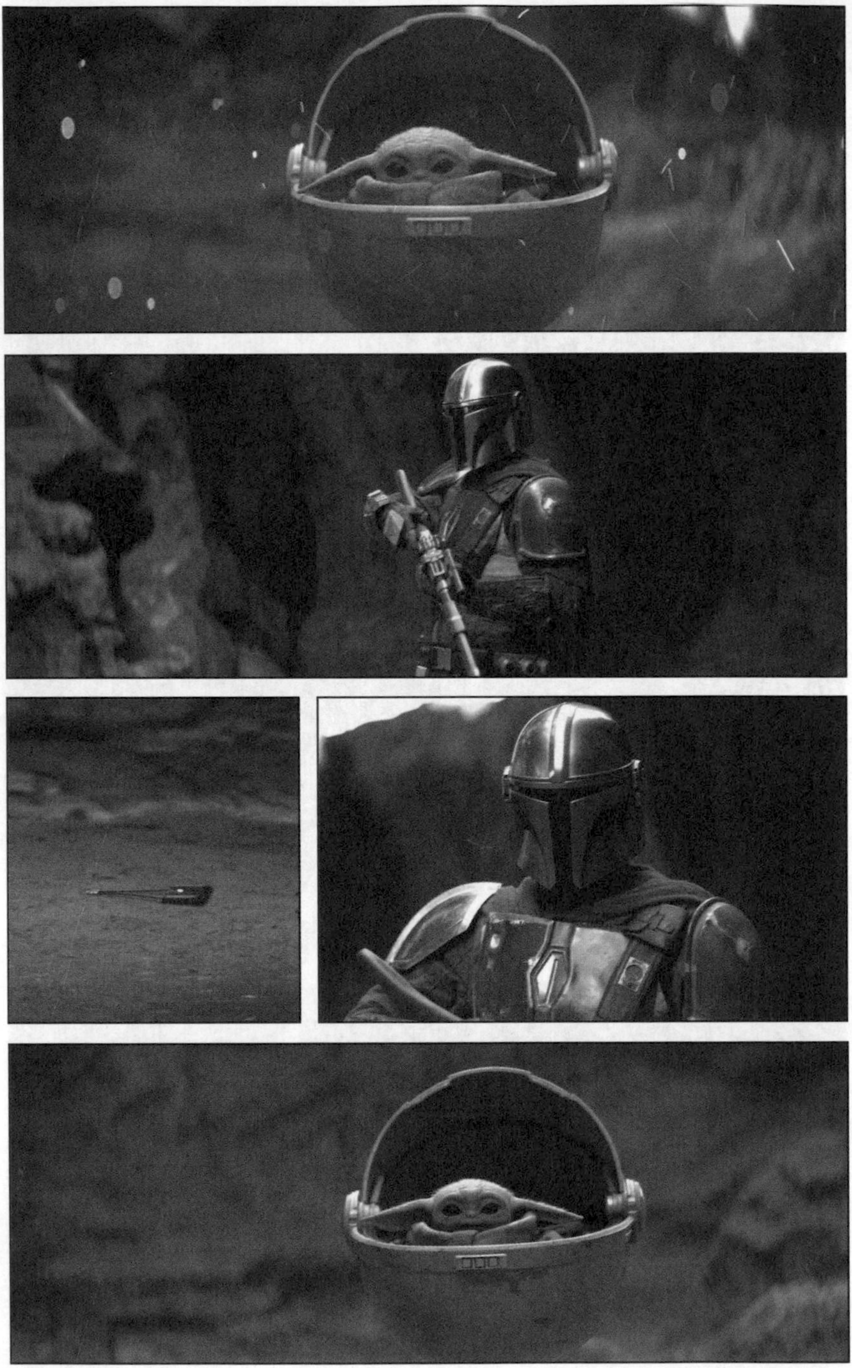

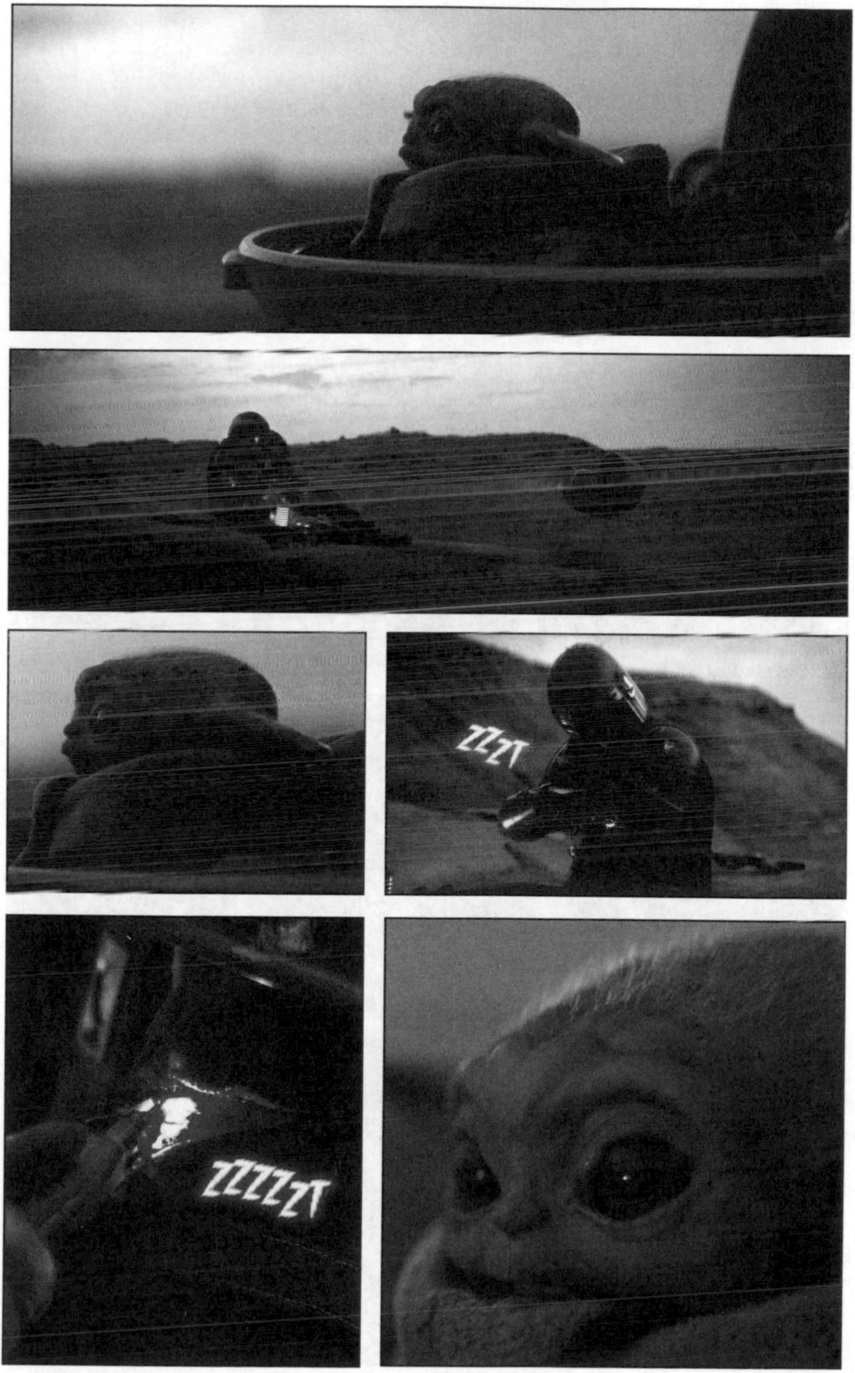
ZZZT
ZZZZZT

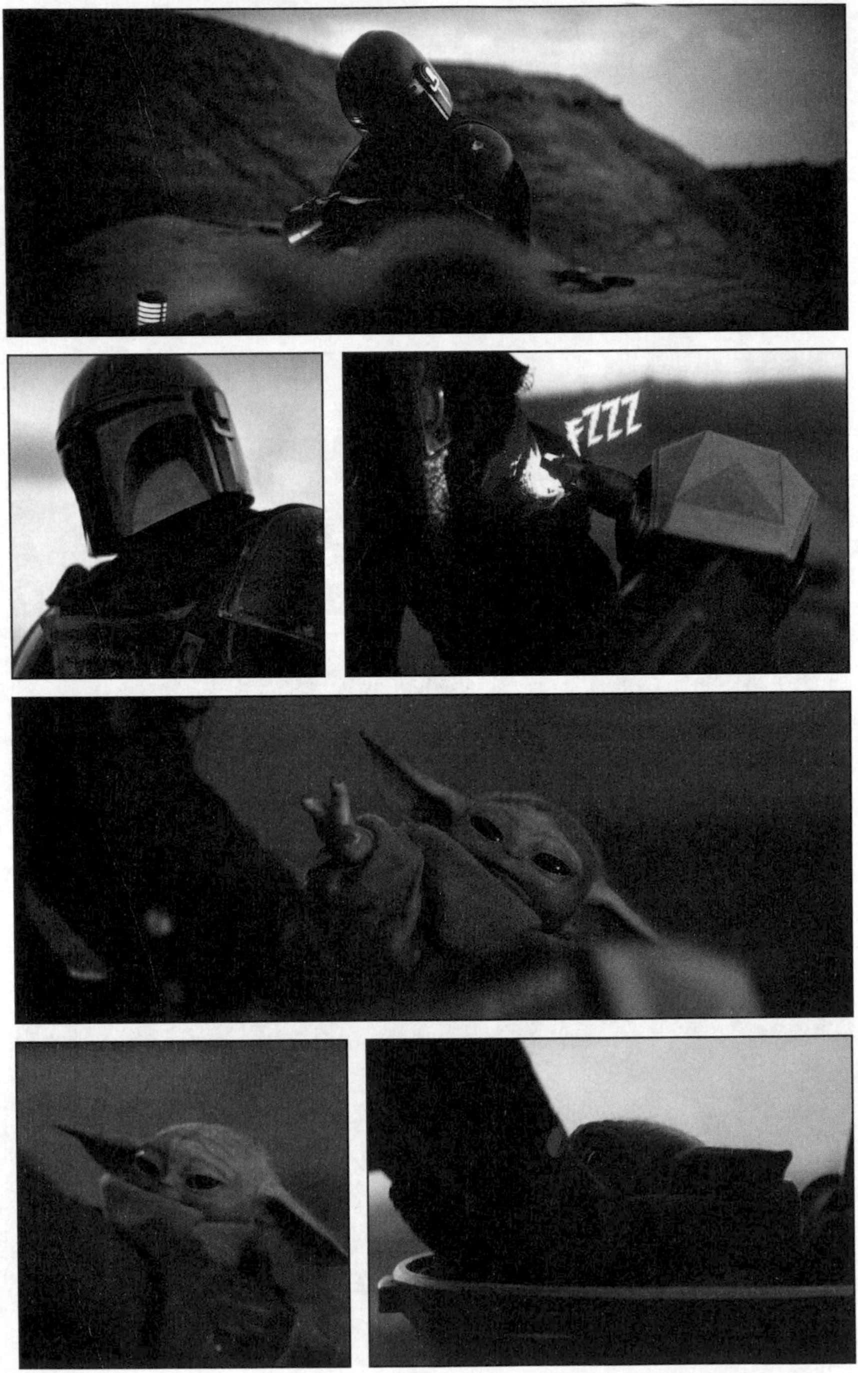
FZZZ

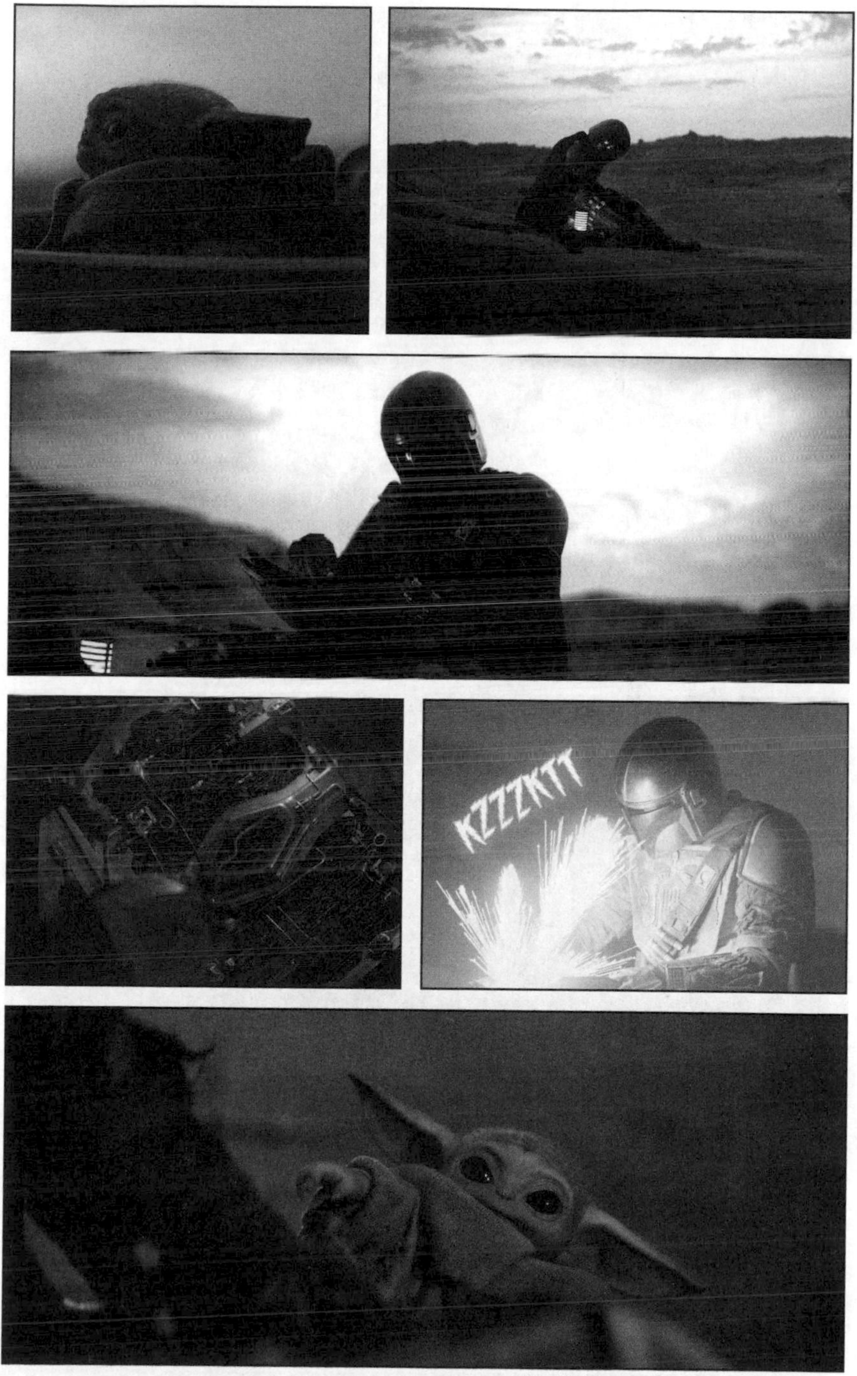
KZZZKTT

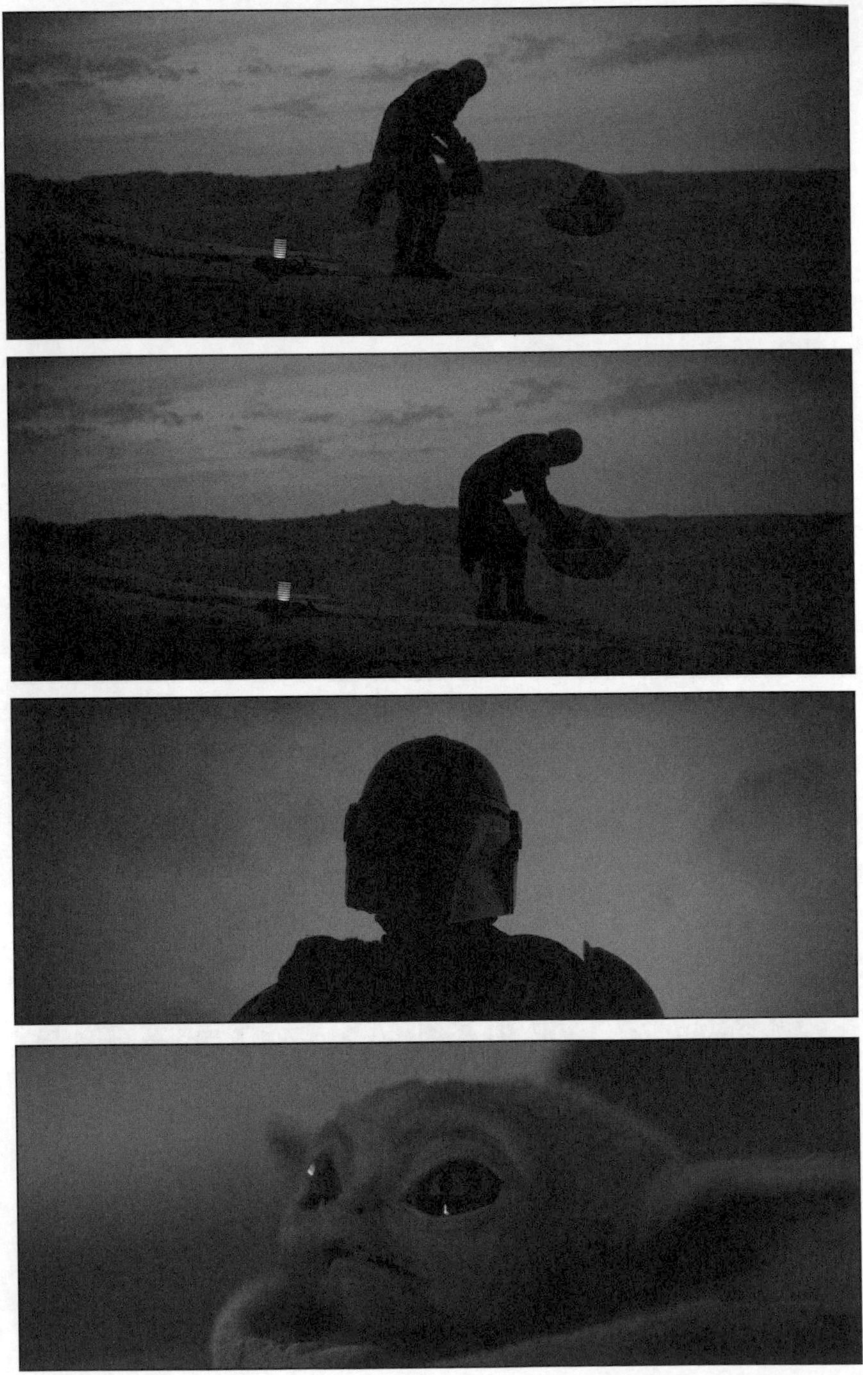

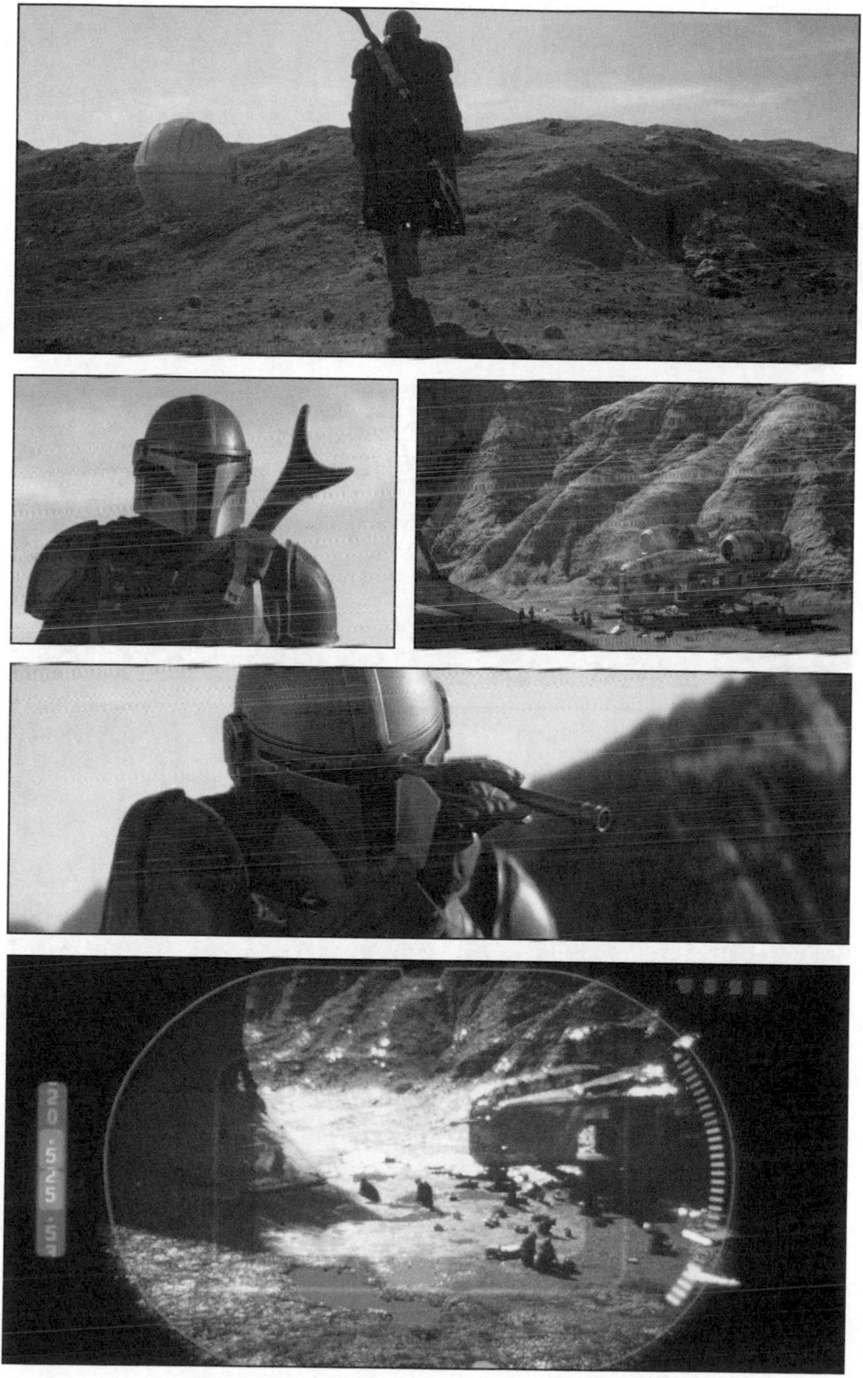

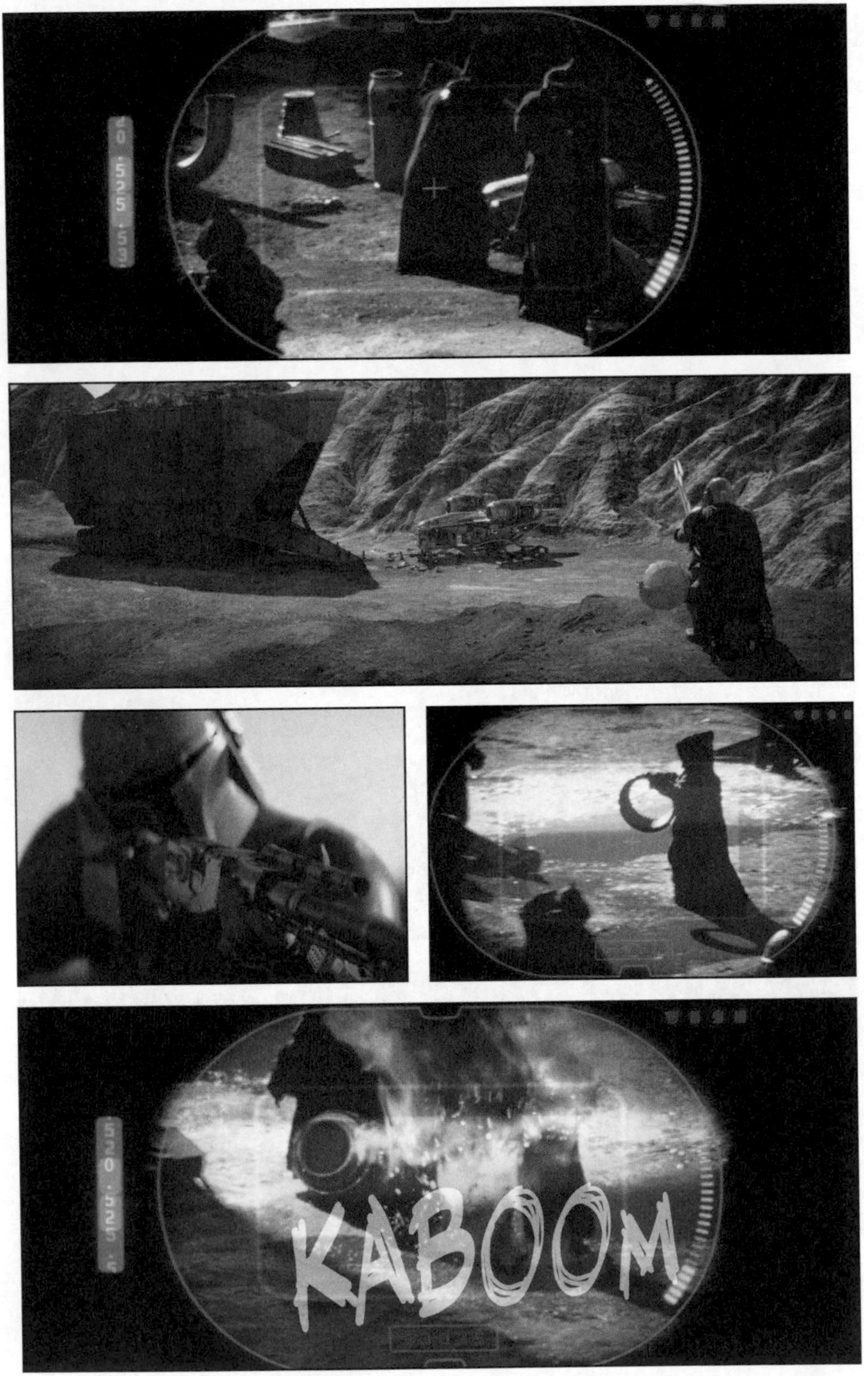
KABOOM

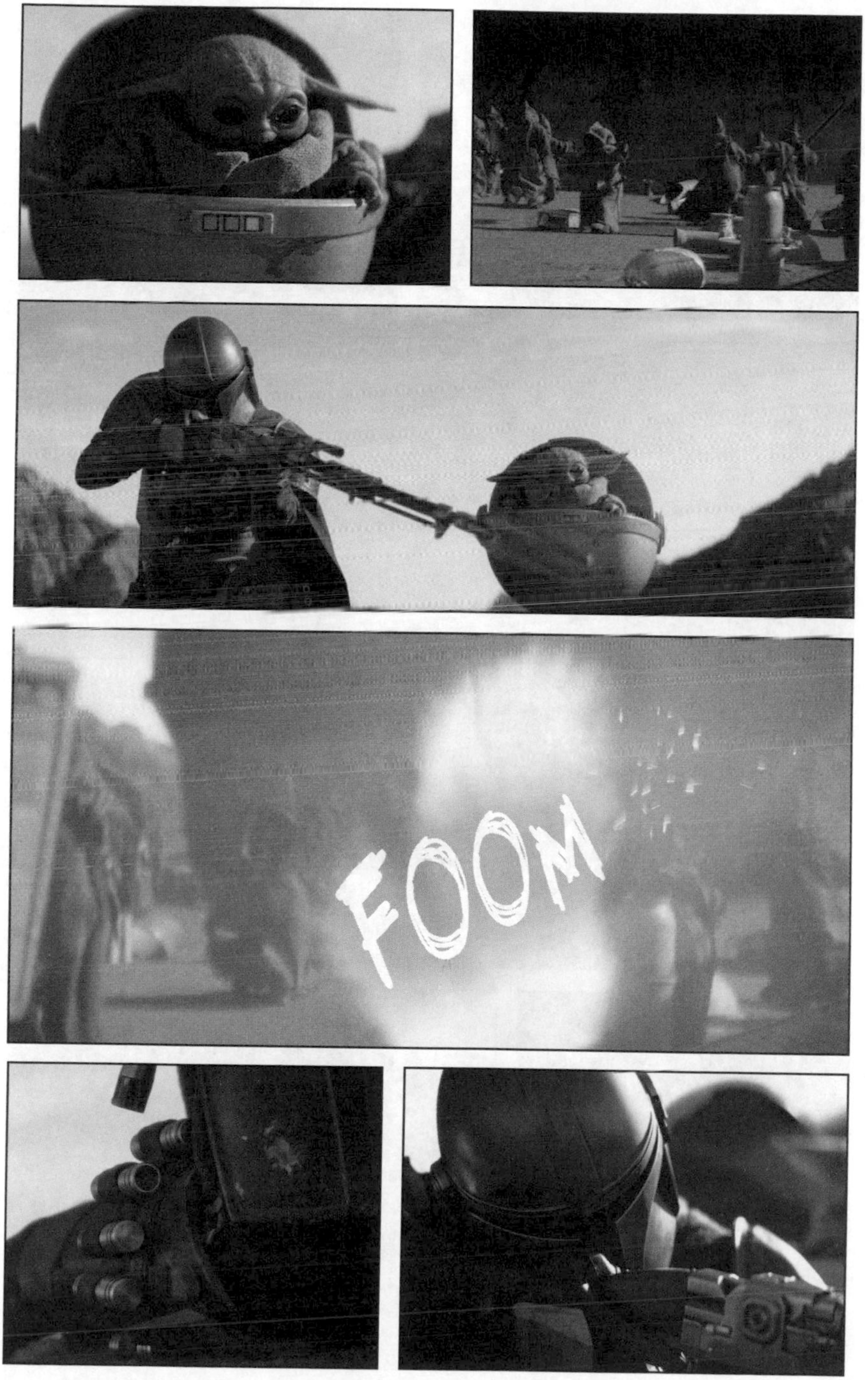
FOOM

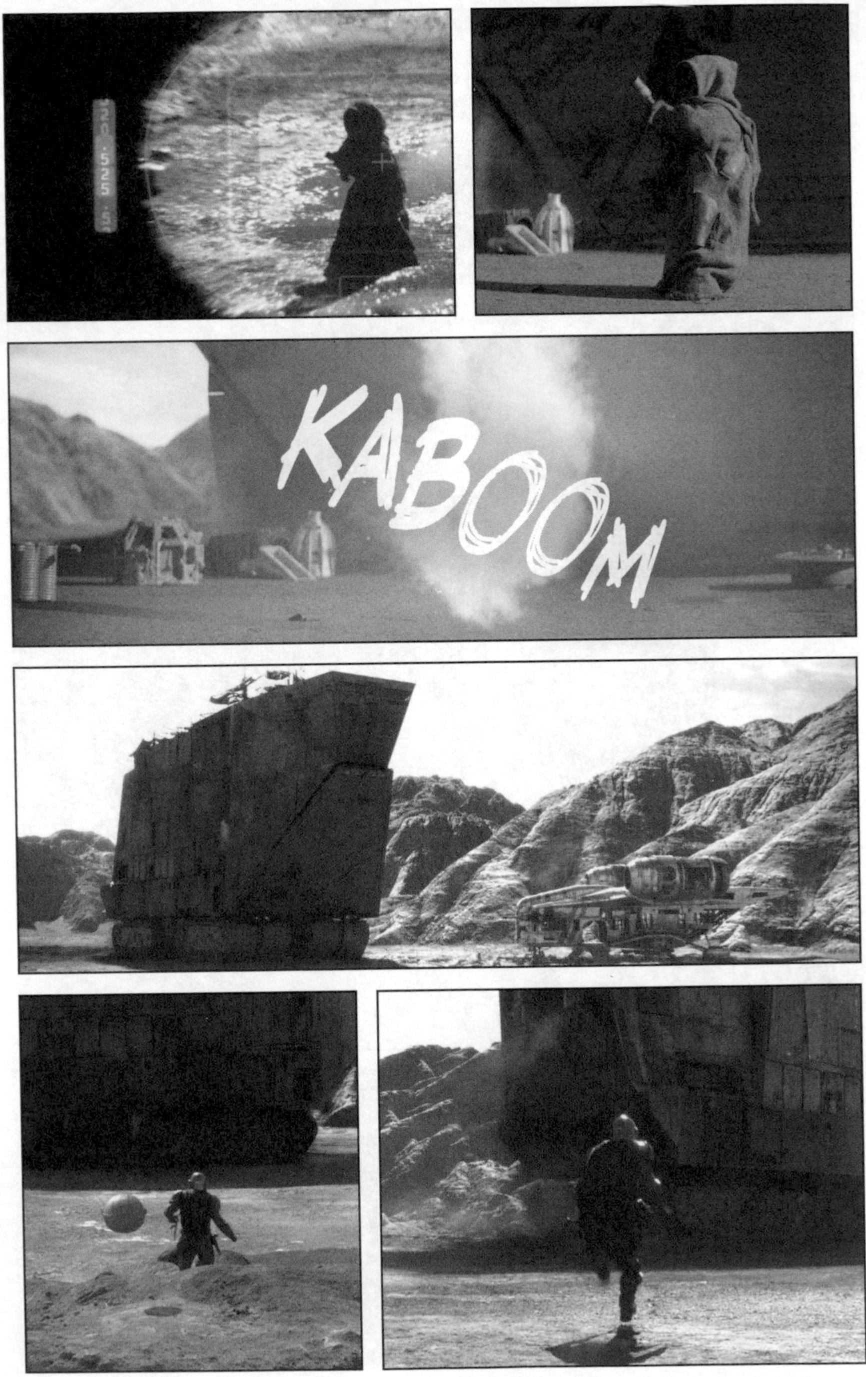
KABOOM

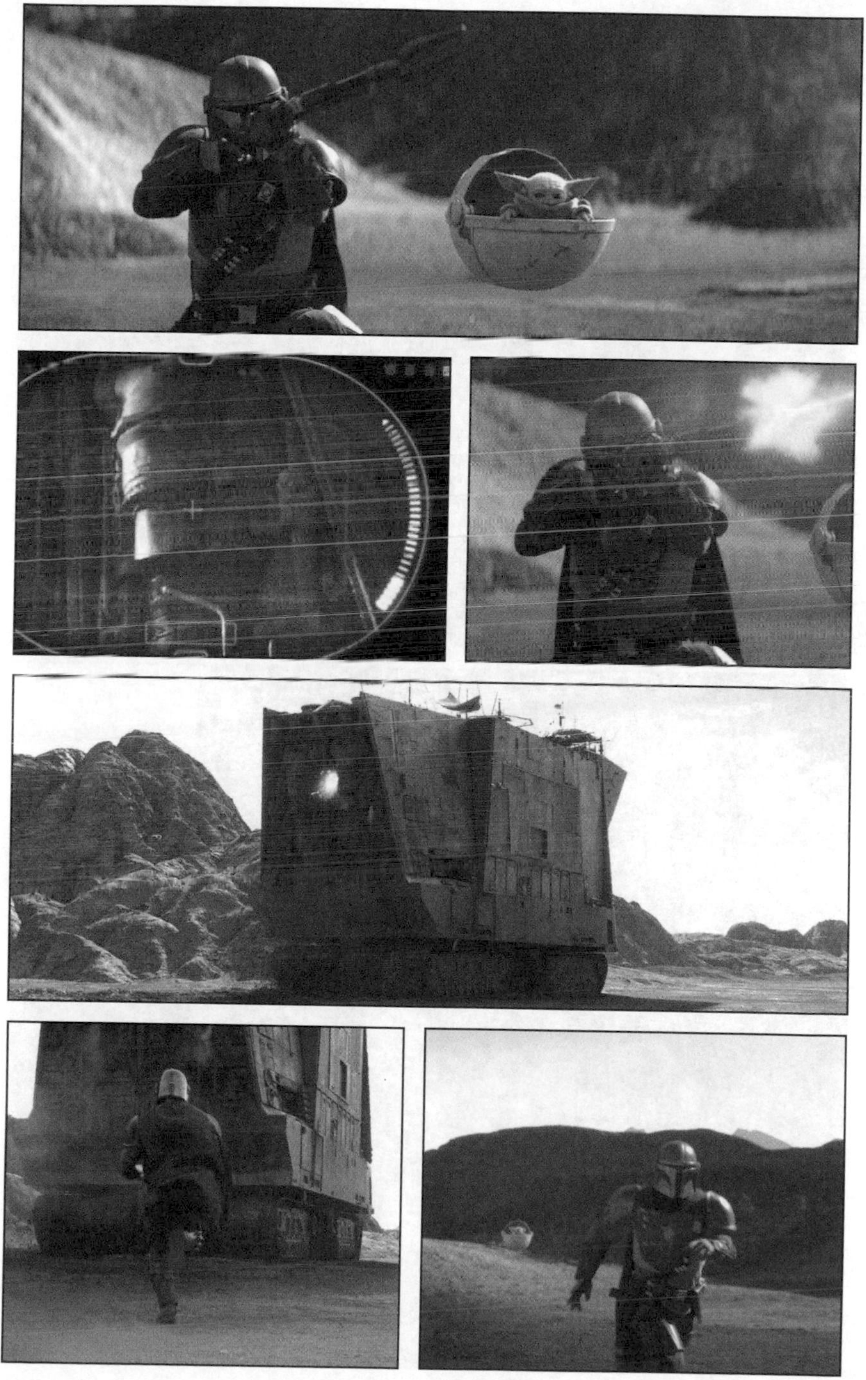

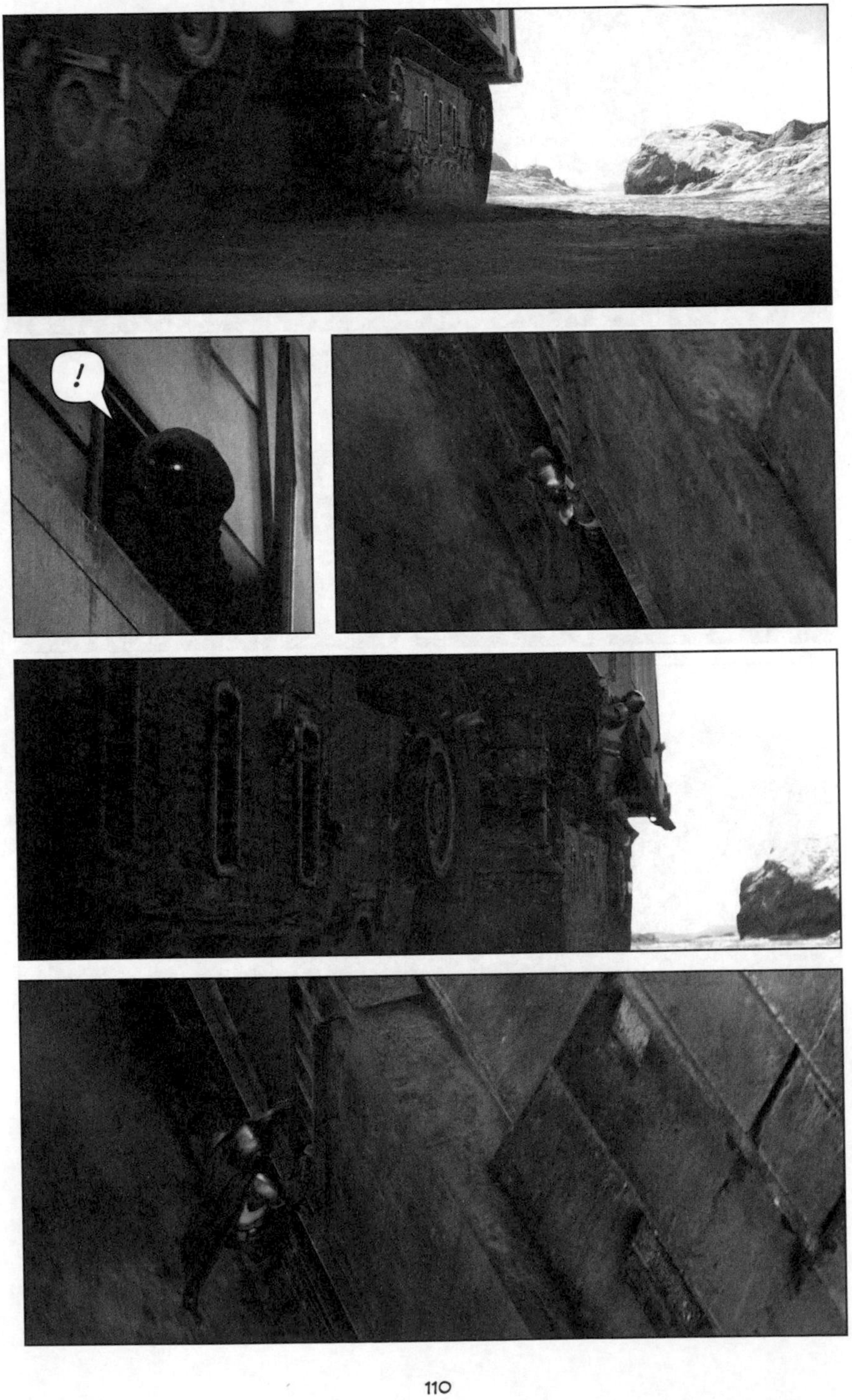
!

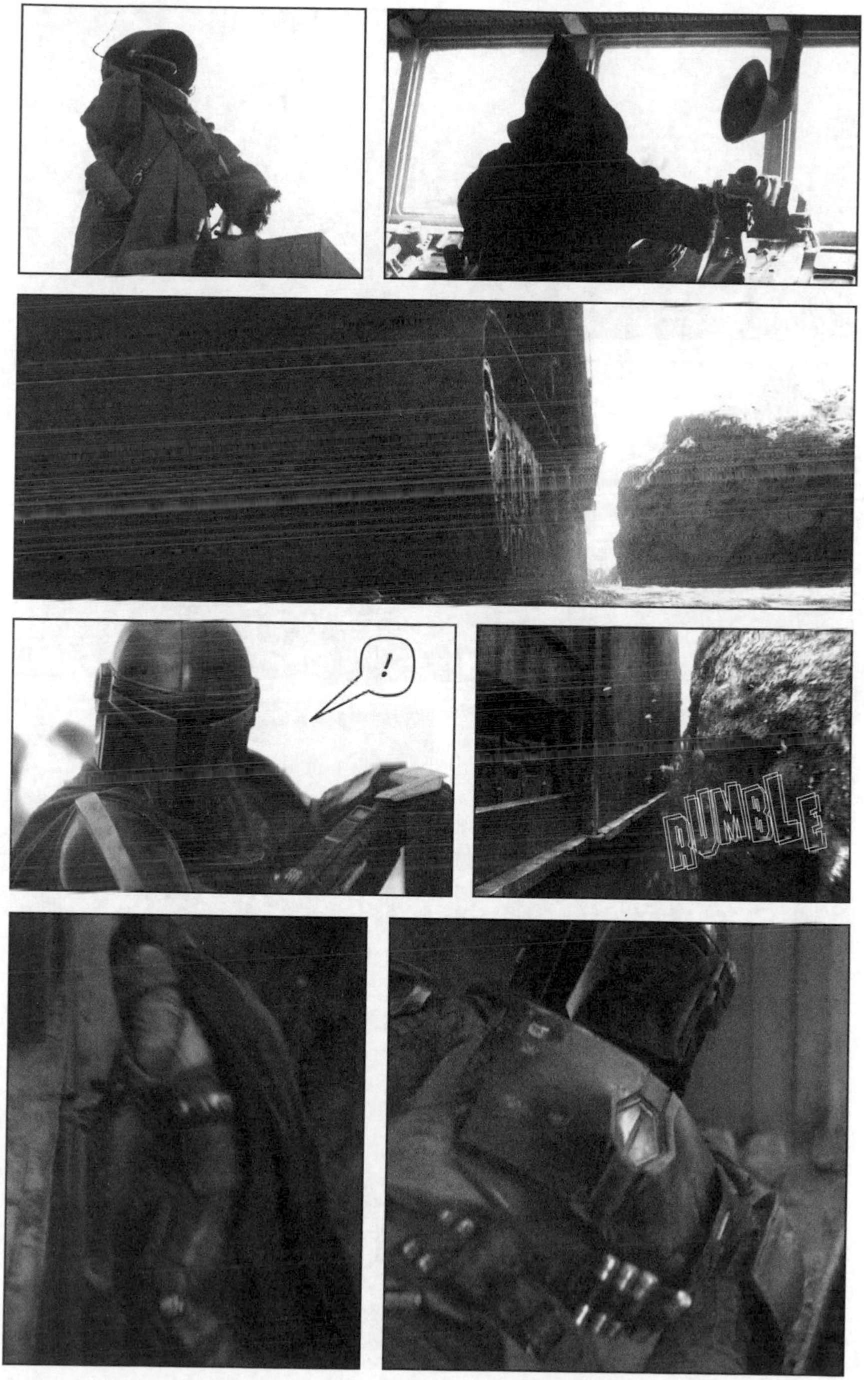
!
RUMBLE

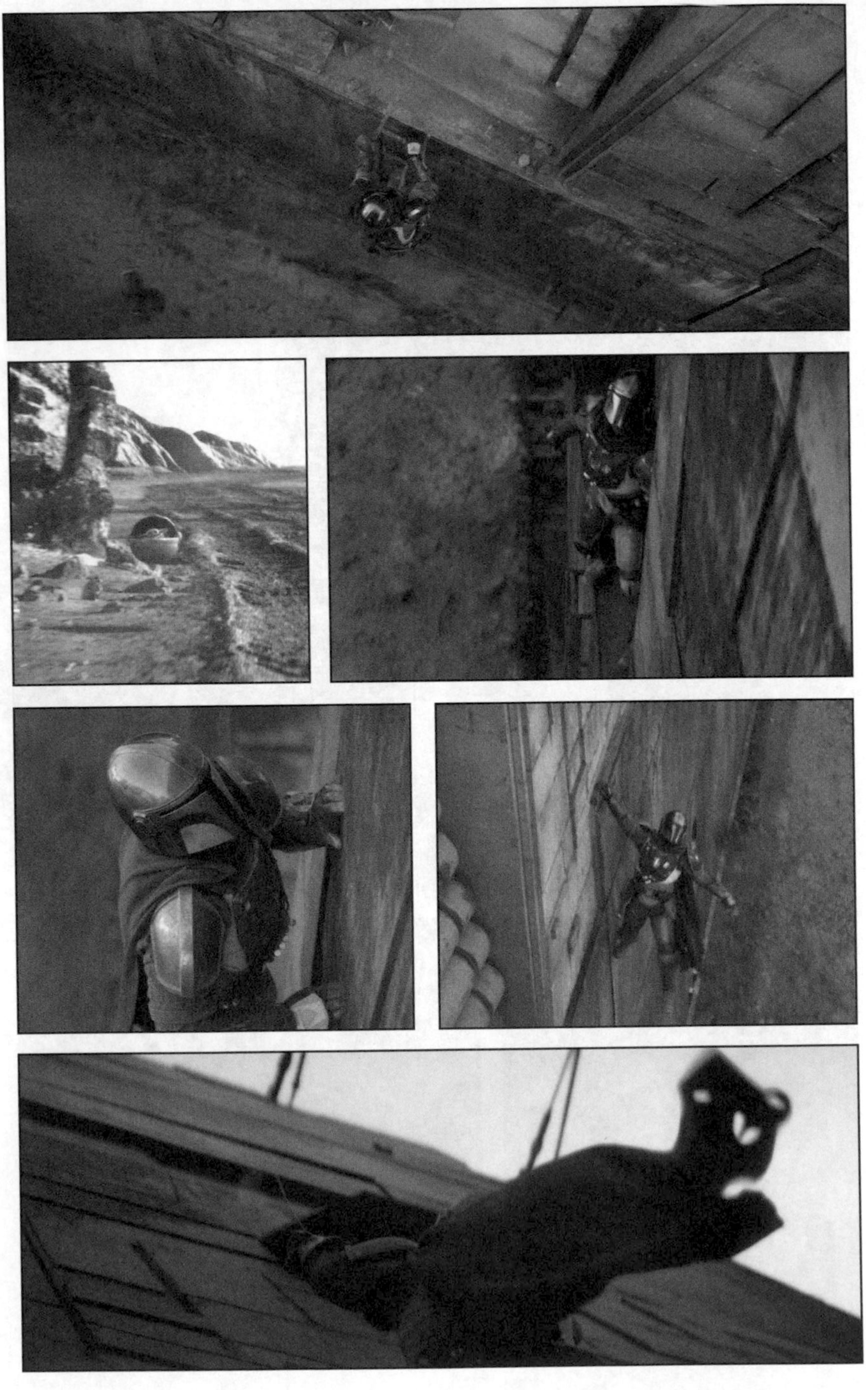

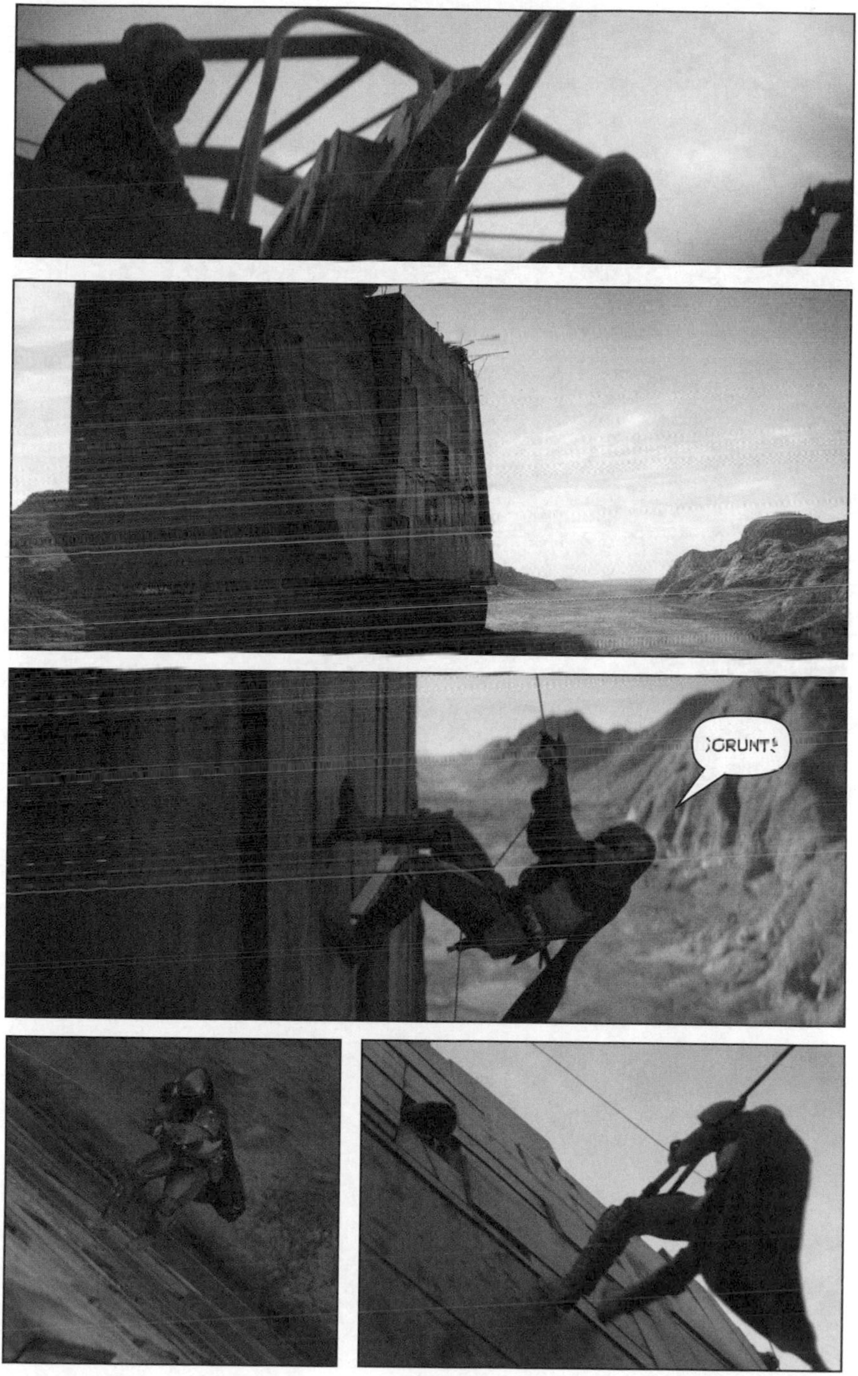
GRUNT

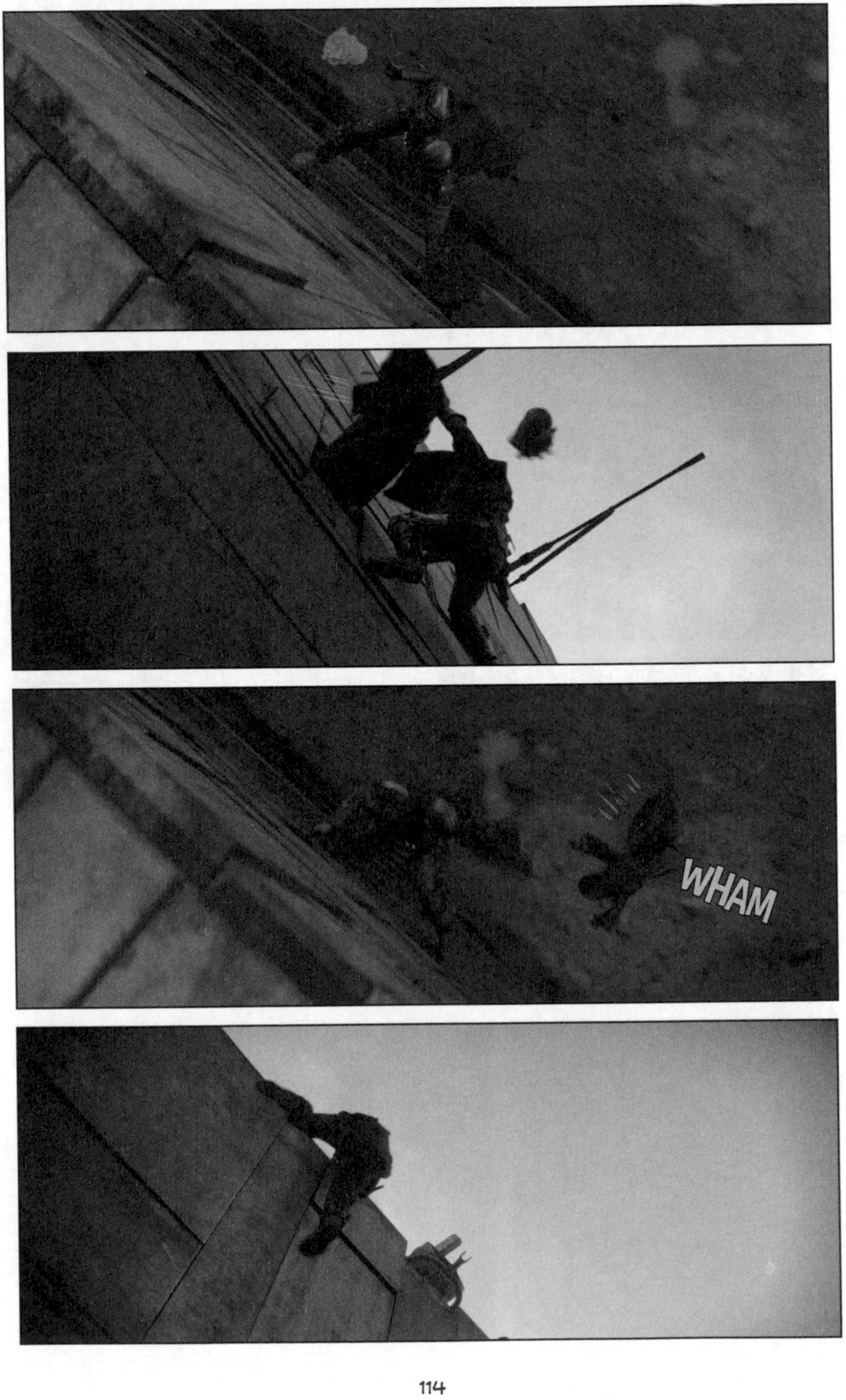
WHAM

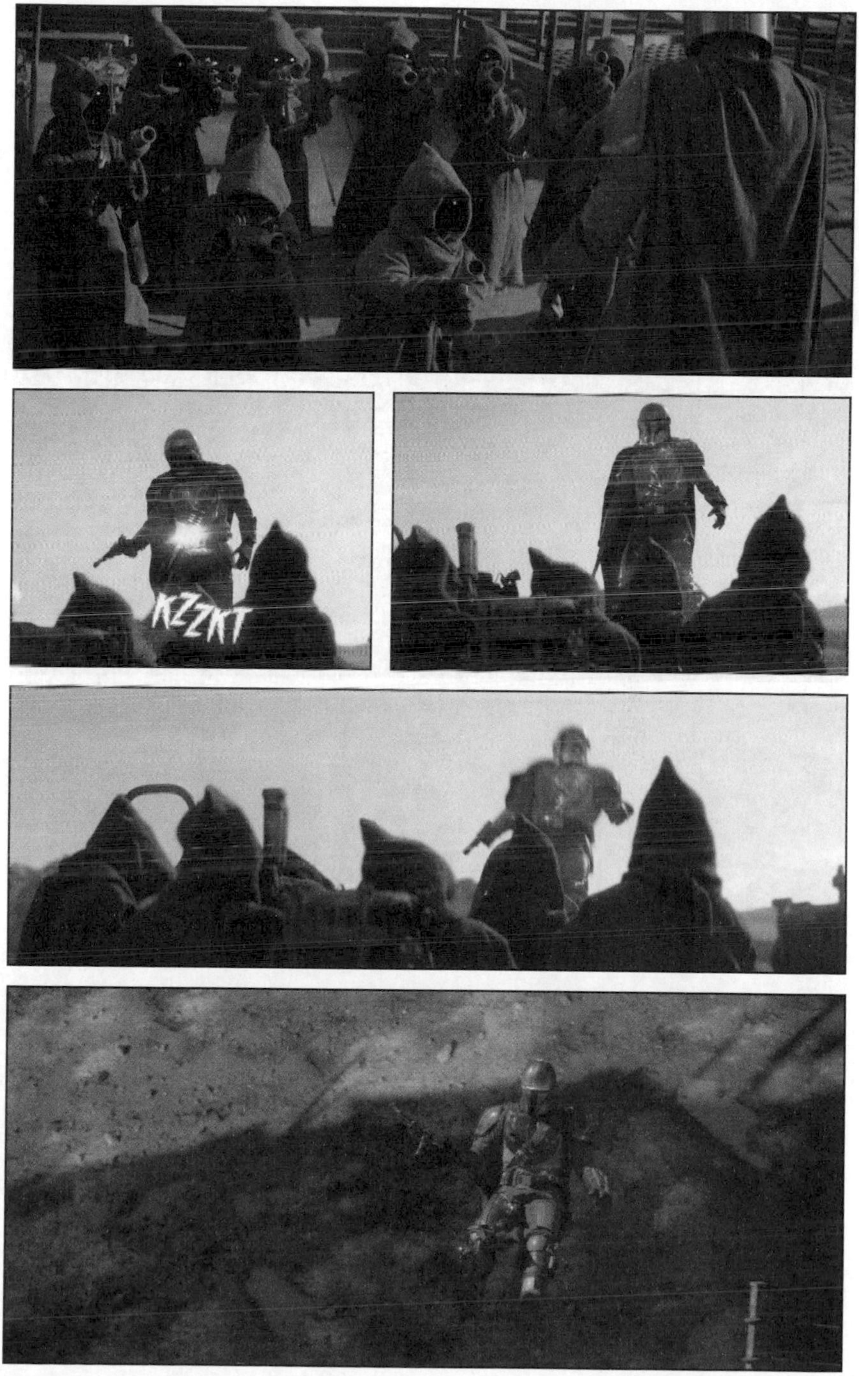
KZZKT

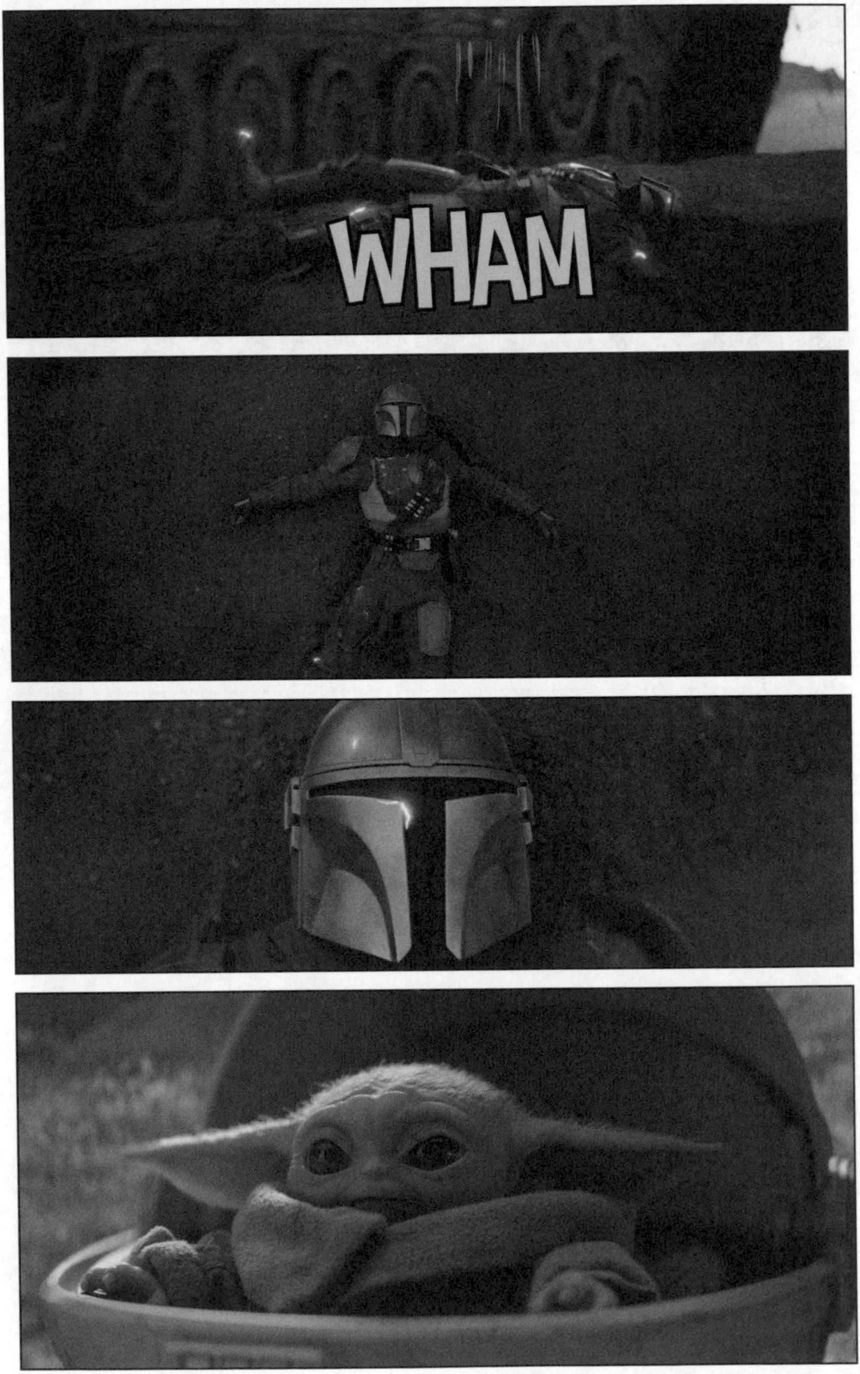
WHAM

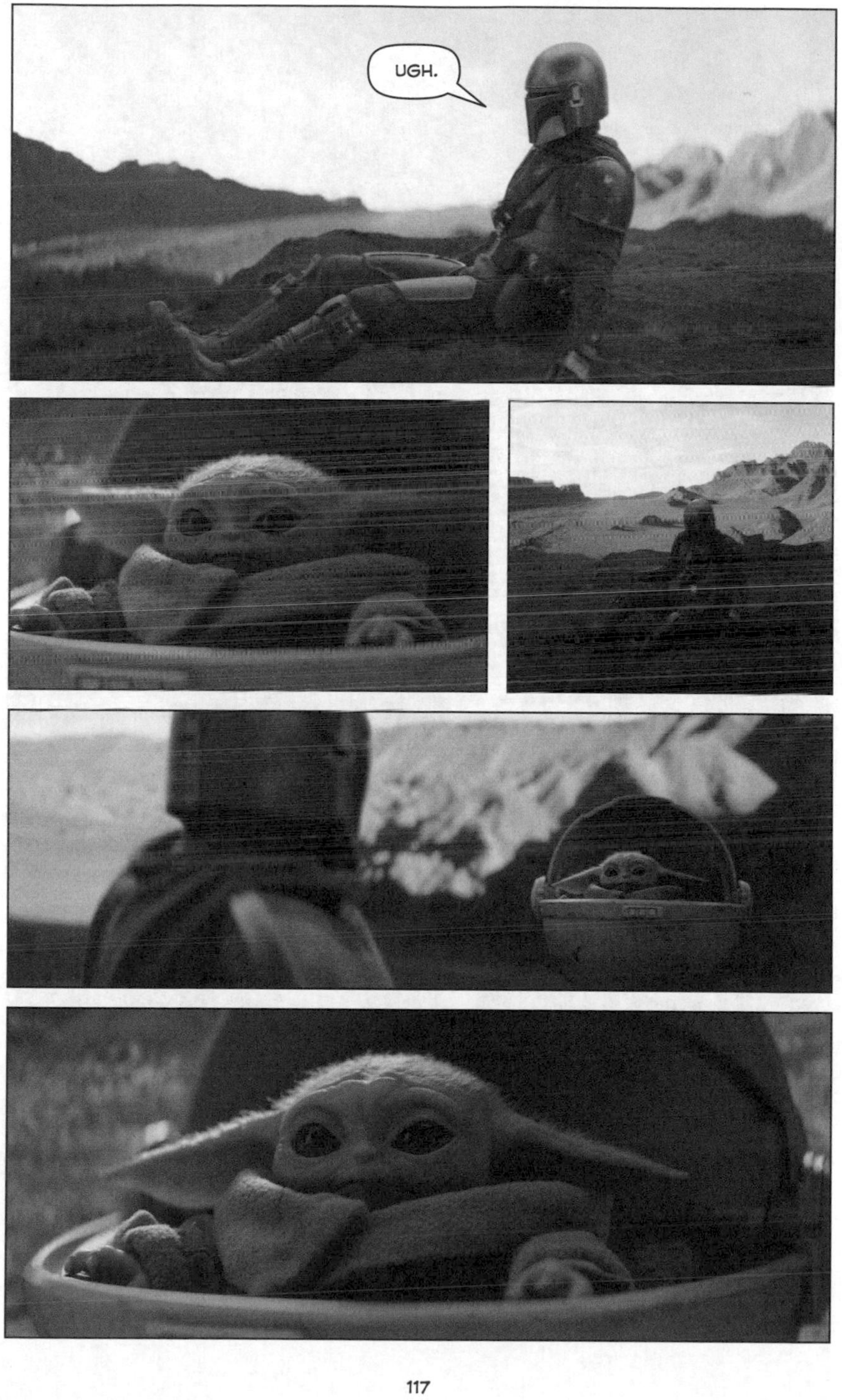
UGH.

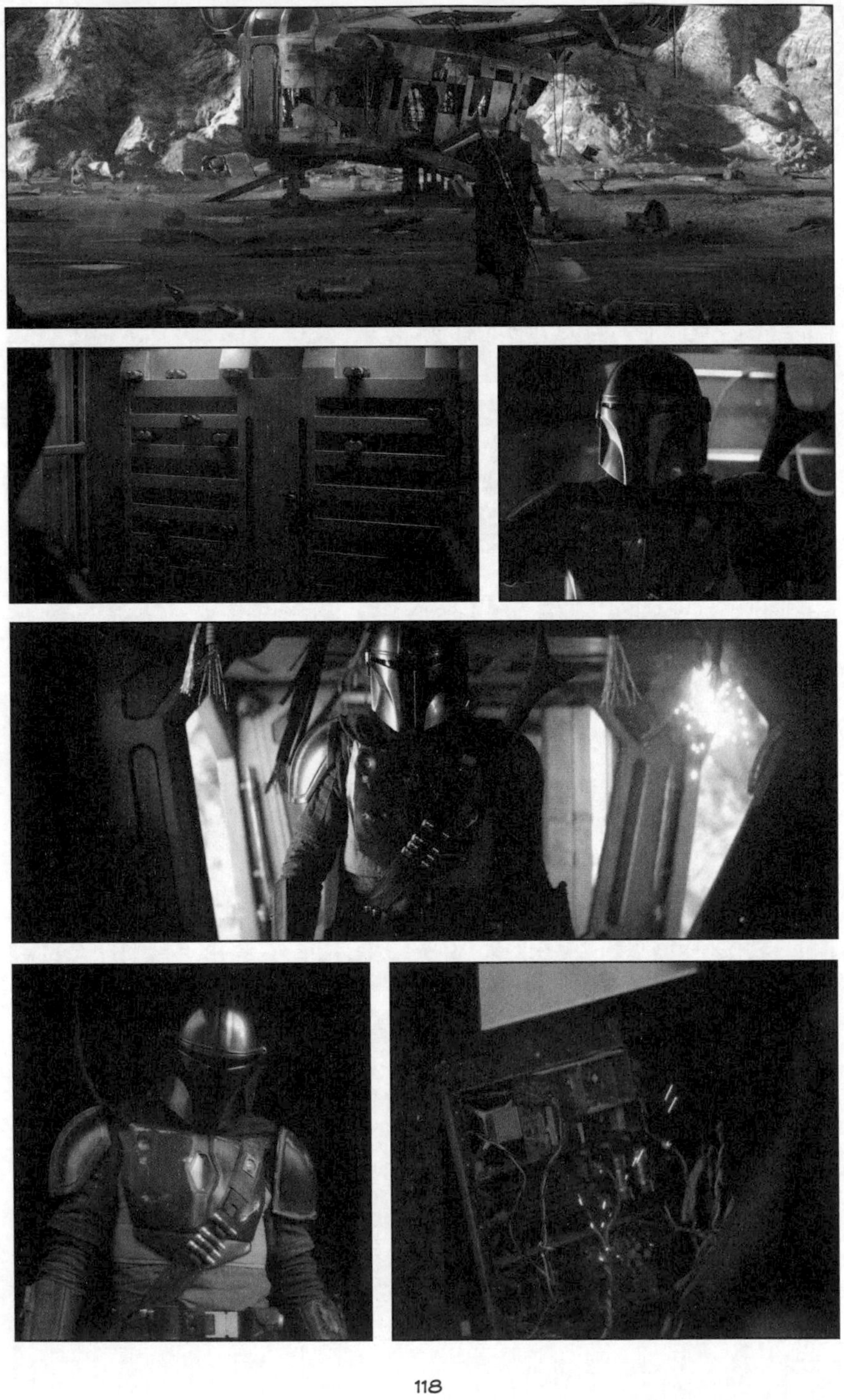

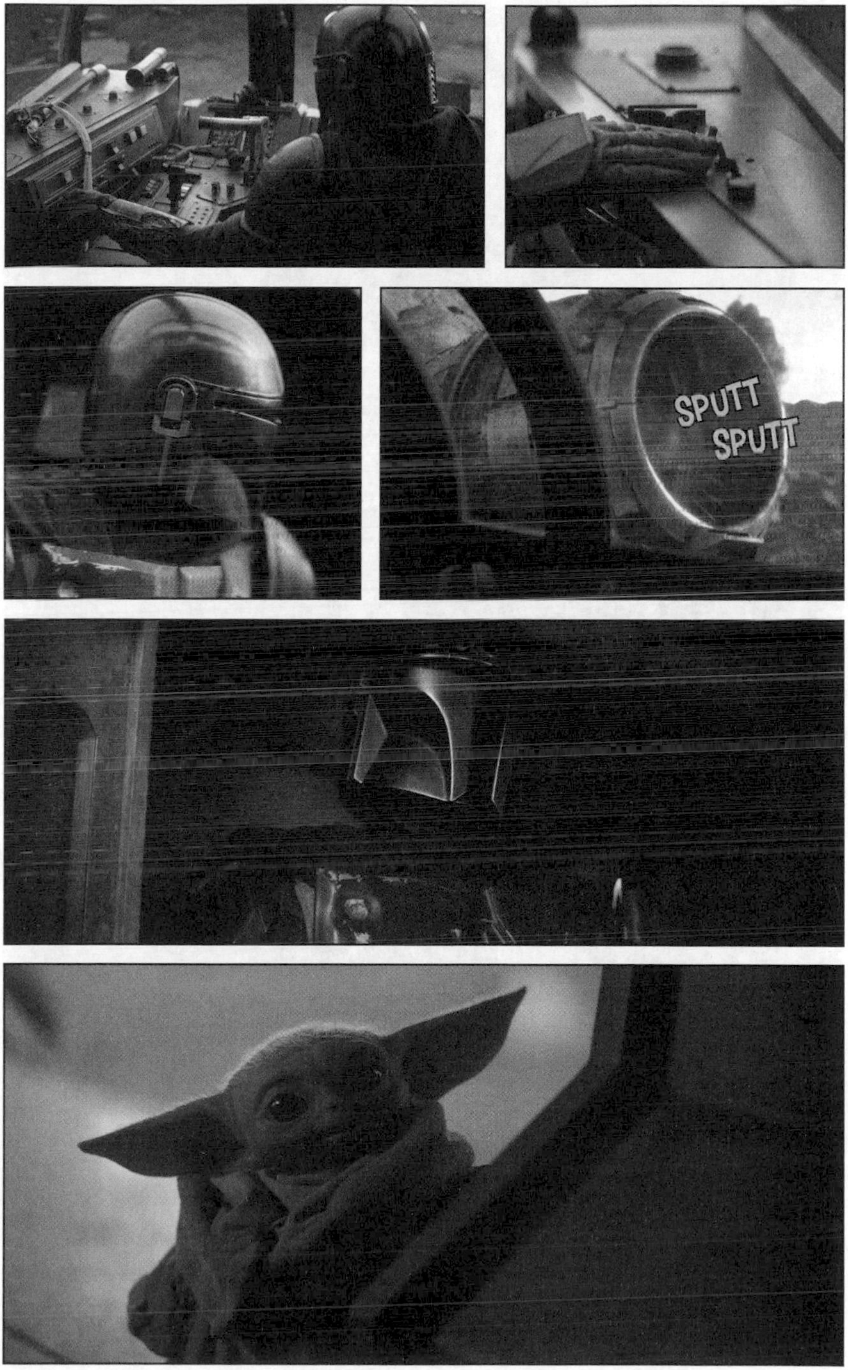
SPUTT
SPUTT

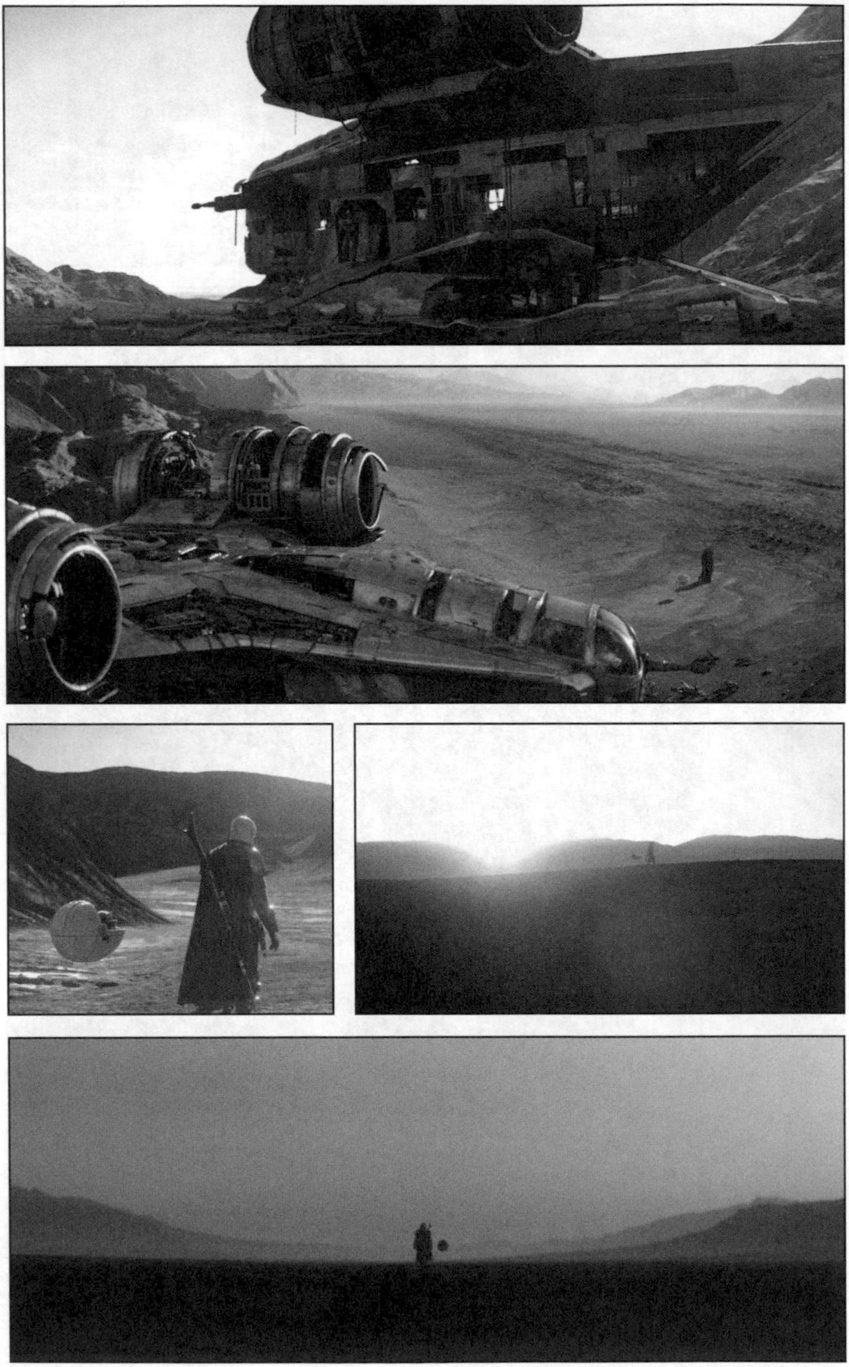

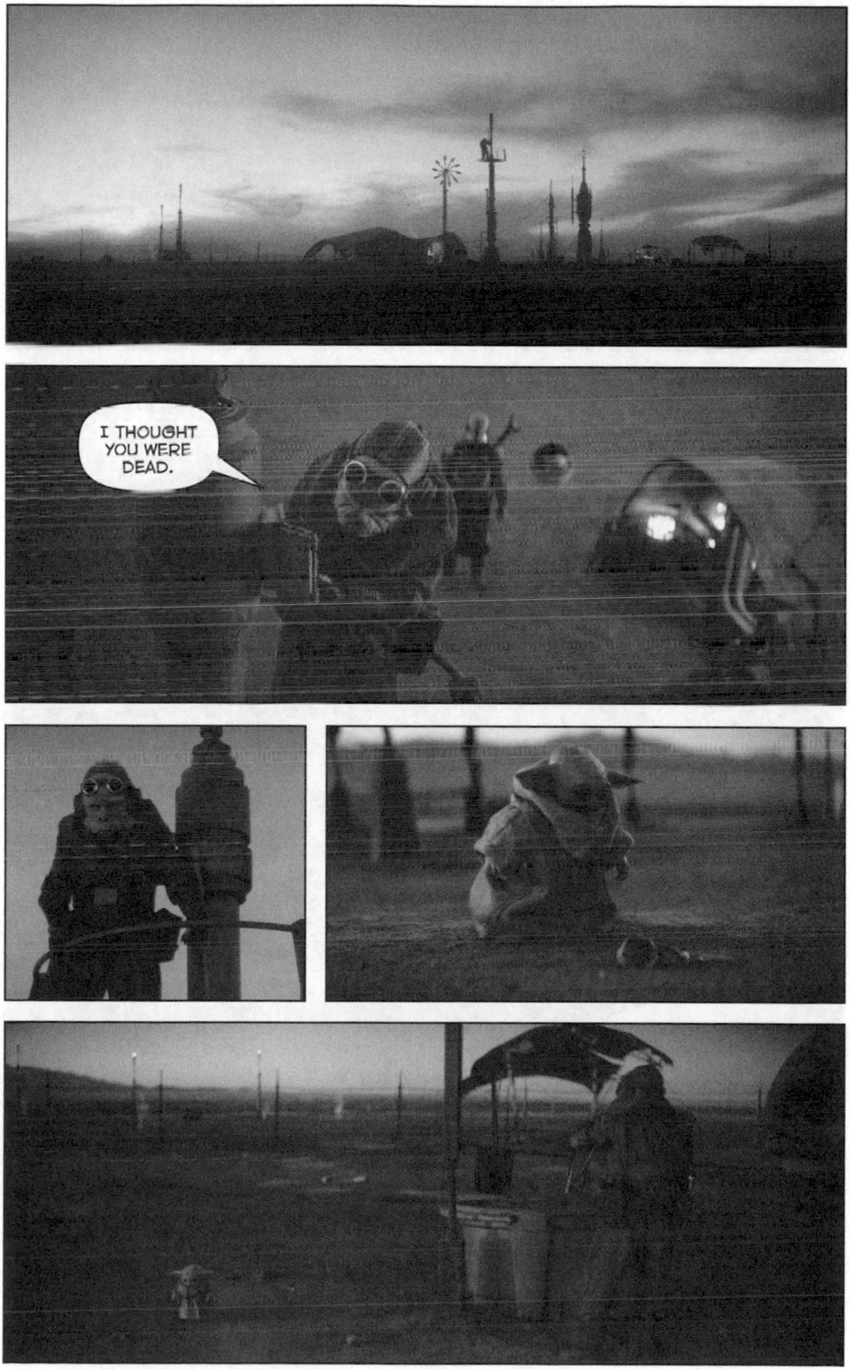
I THOUGHT YOU WERE DEAD.

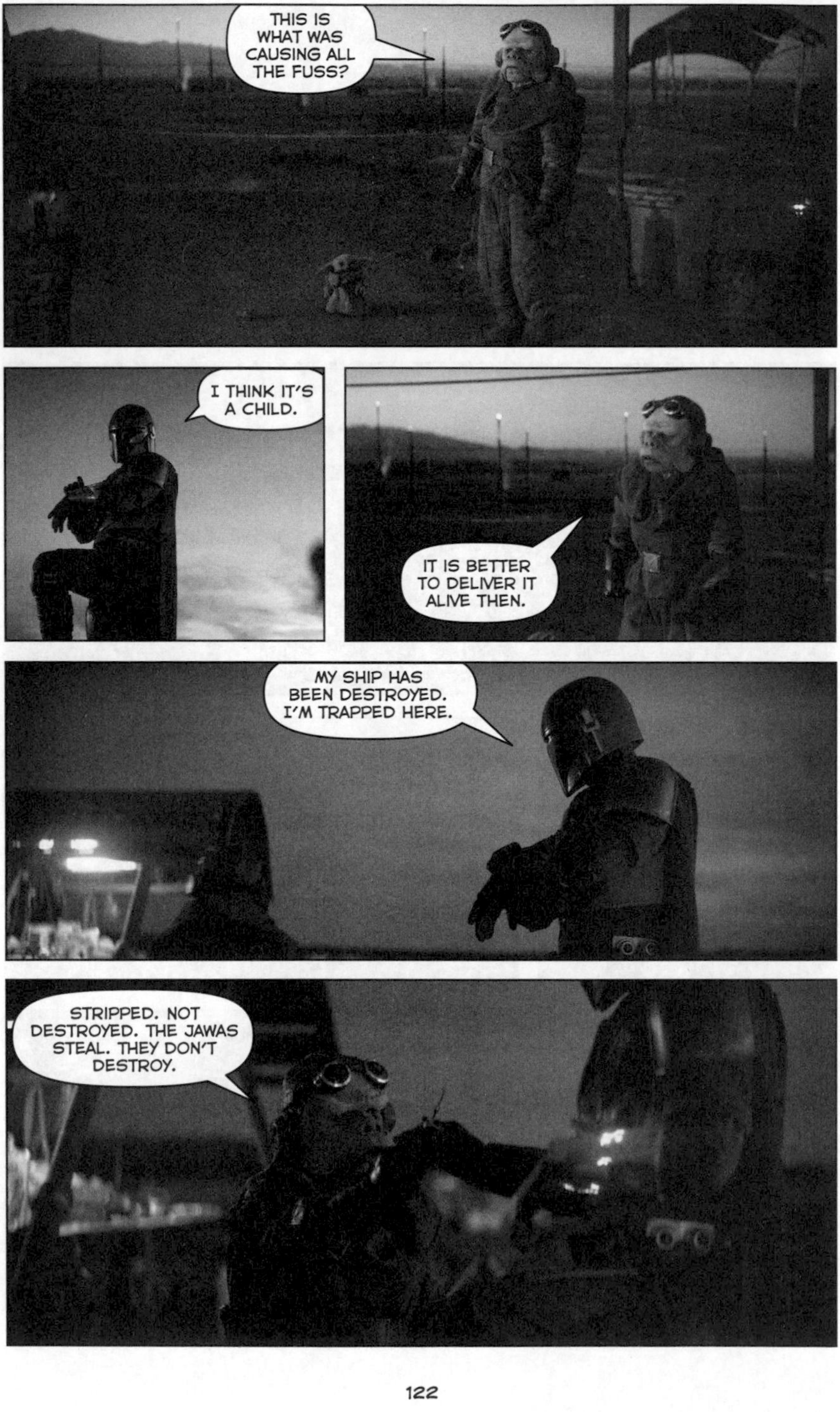
THIS IS WHAT WAS CAUSING ALL THE FUSS?
I THINK IT'S A CHILD.
IT IS BETTER TO DELIVER IT ALIVE THEN.
MY SHIP HAS BEEN DESTROYED. I'M TRAPPED HERE.
STRIPPED. NOT DESTROYED. THE JAWAS STEAL. THEY DON'T DESTROY.

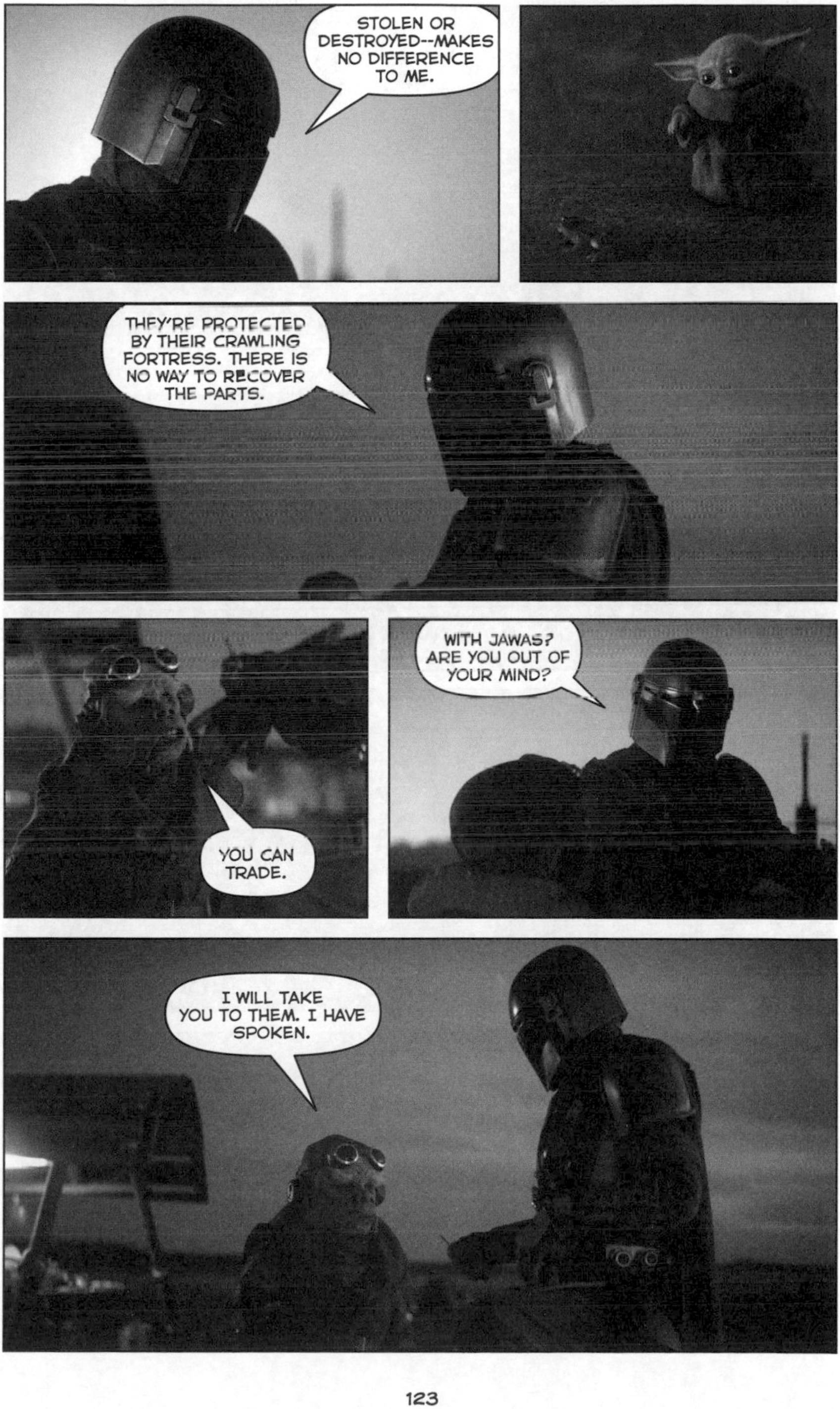
STOLEN OR DESTROYED--MAKES NO DIFFERENCE TO ME.
THEY'RE PROTECTED BY THEIR CRAWLING FORTRESS. THERE IS NO WAY TO RECOVER THE PARTS.
YOU CAN TRADE.
WITH JAWAS? ARE YOU OUT OF YOUR MIND?
I WILL TAKE YOU TO THEM. I HAVE SPOKEN.

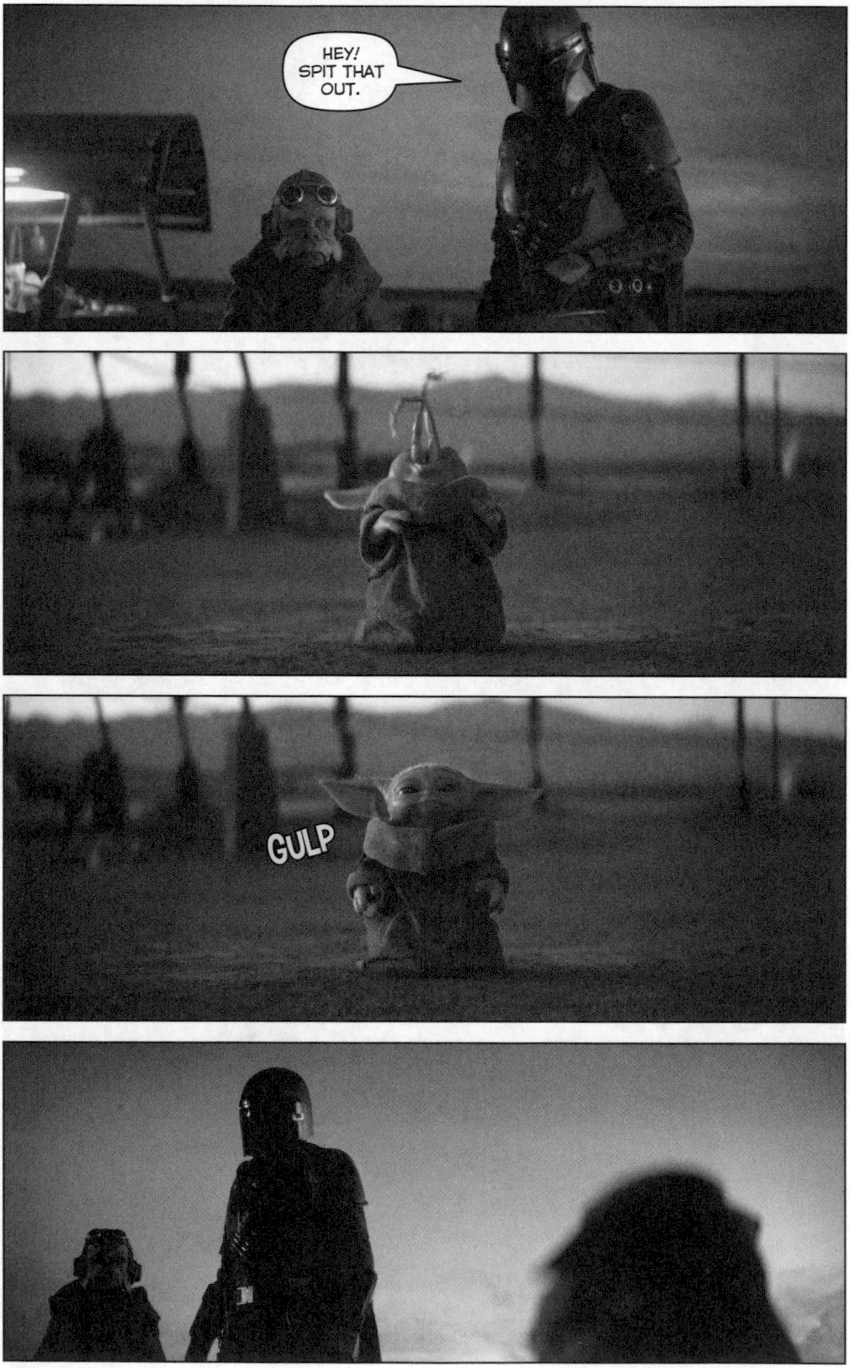
HEY! SPIT THAT OUT.
GULP

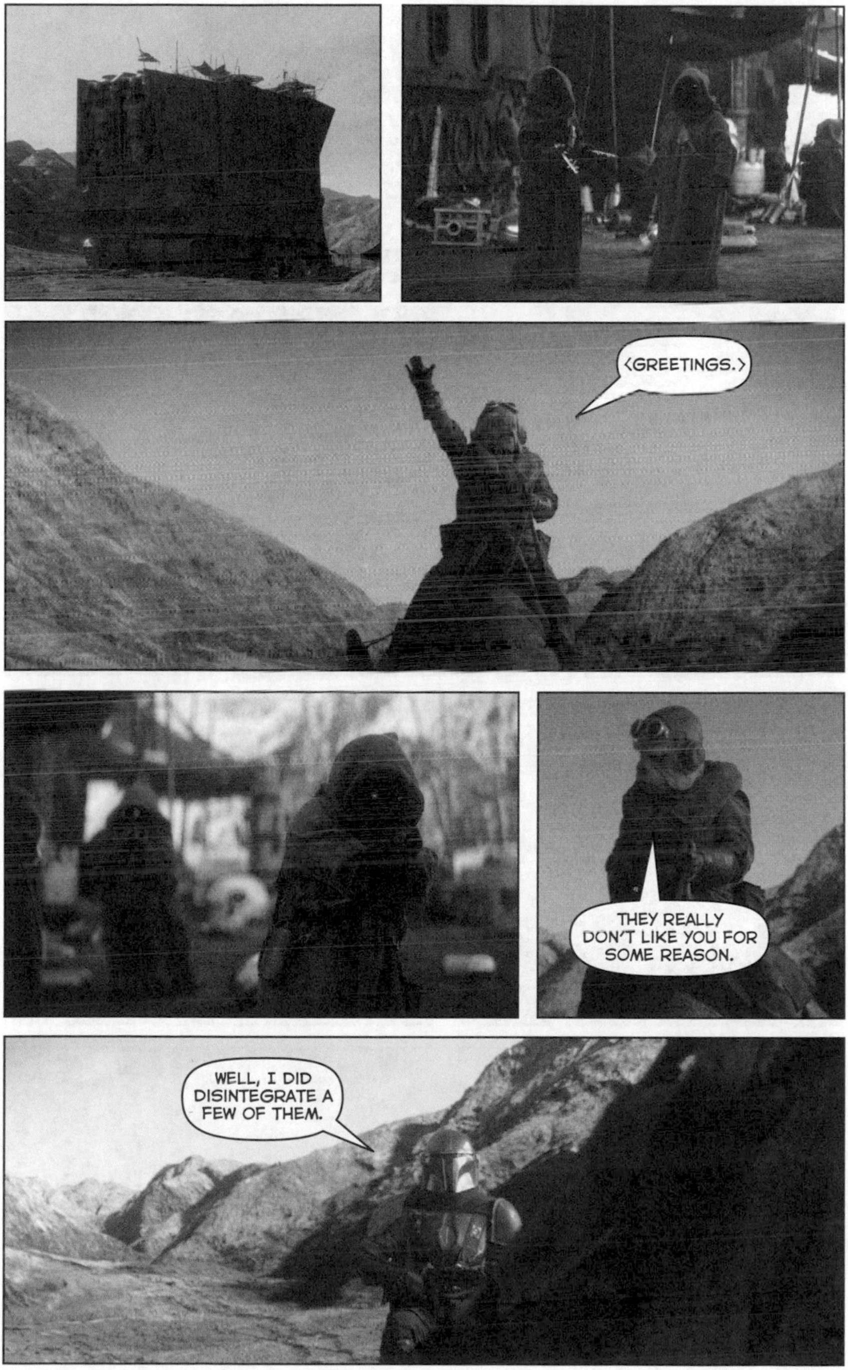
<GREETINGS.>
THEY REALLY DON'T LIKE YOU FOR SOME REASON.
WELL, I DID DISINTEGRATE A FEW OF THEM.

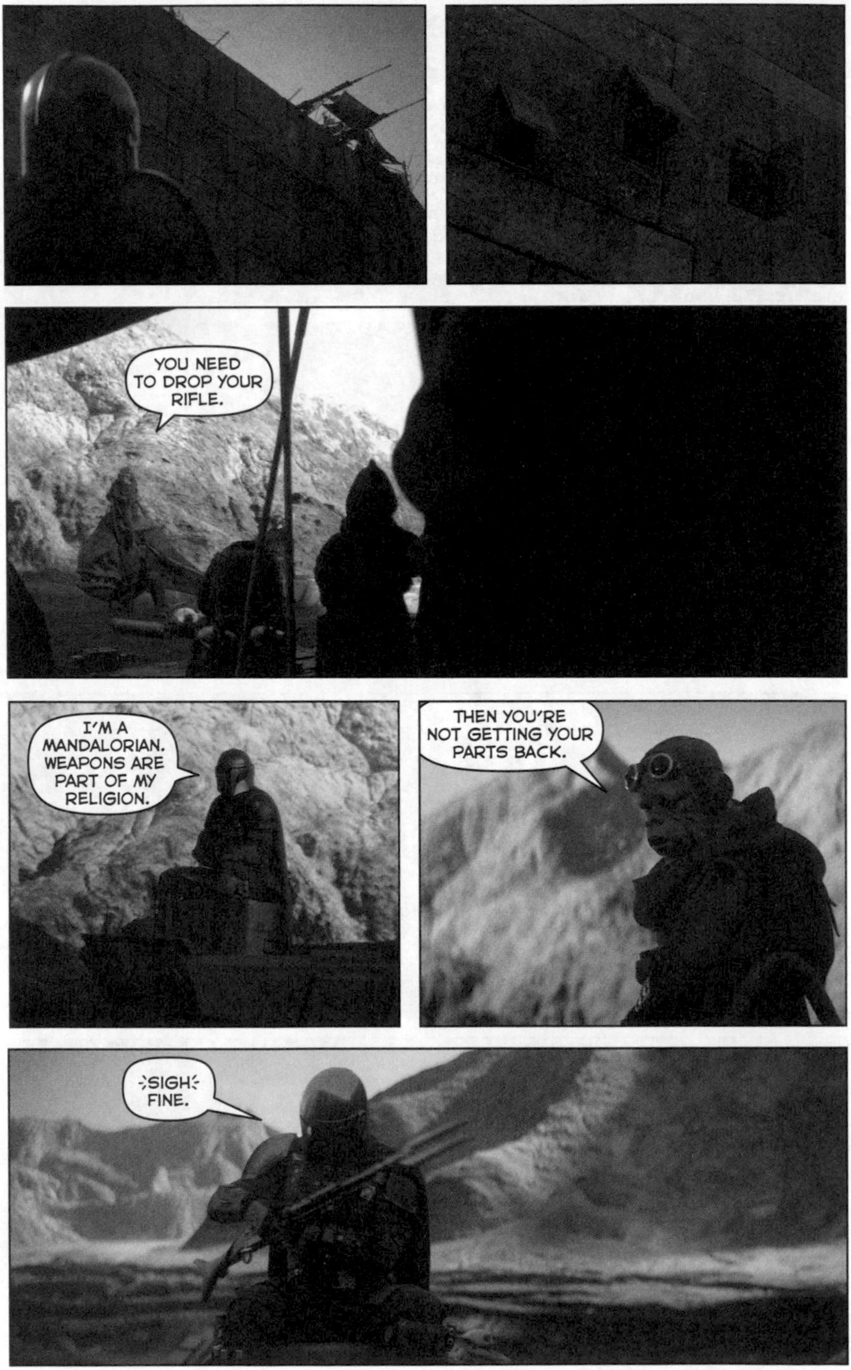
YOU NEED TO DROP YOUR RIFLE.
I'M A MANDALORIAN. WEAPONS ARE PART OF MY RELIGION.
THEN YOU'RE NOT GETTING YOUR PARTS BACK.
SIGH FINE.

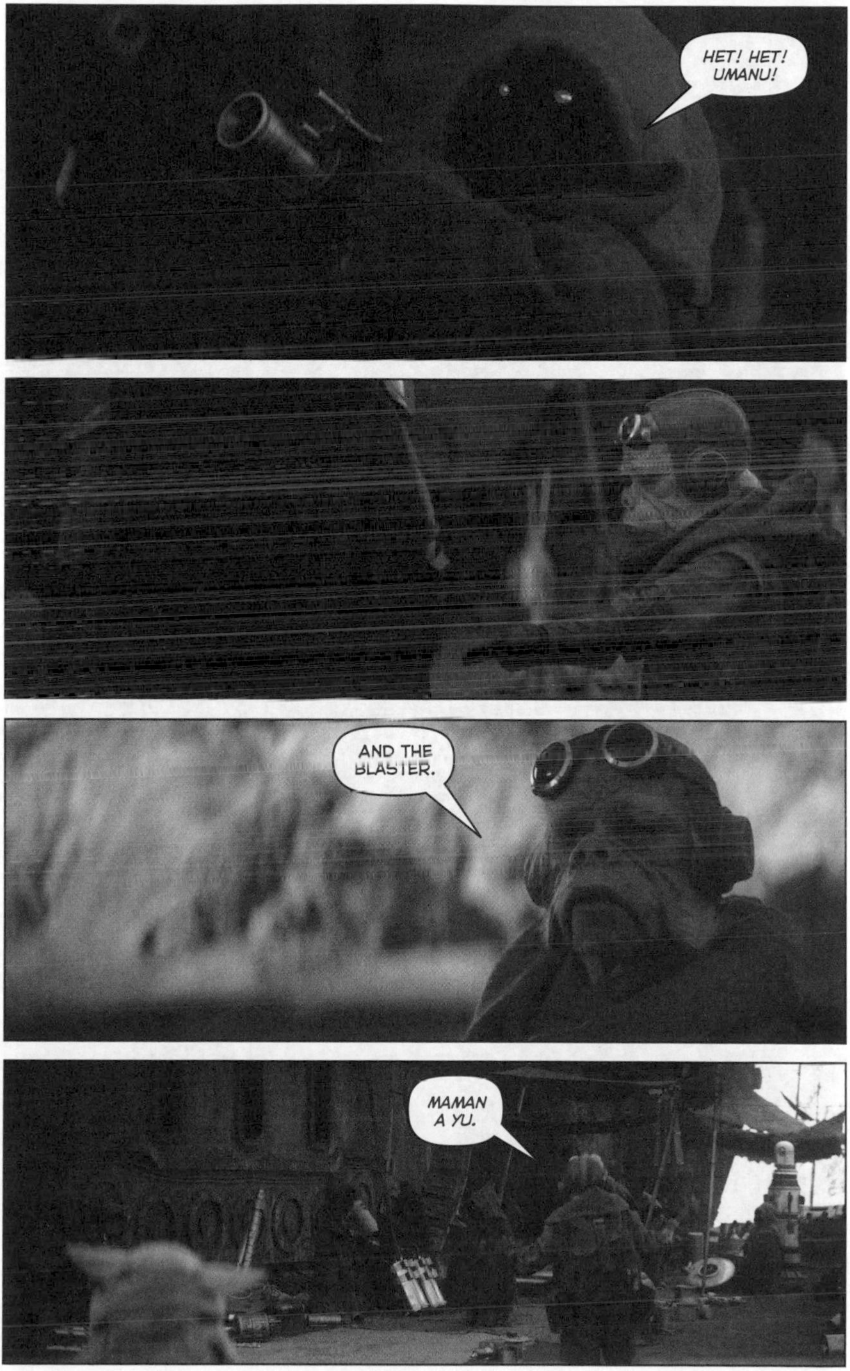
HET! HET! UMANU!
AND THE BLASTER.
MAMAN A YU.

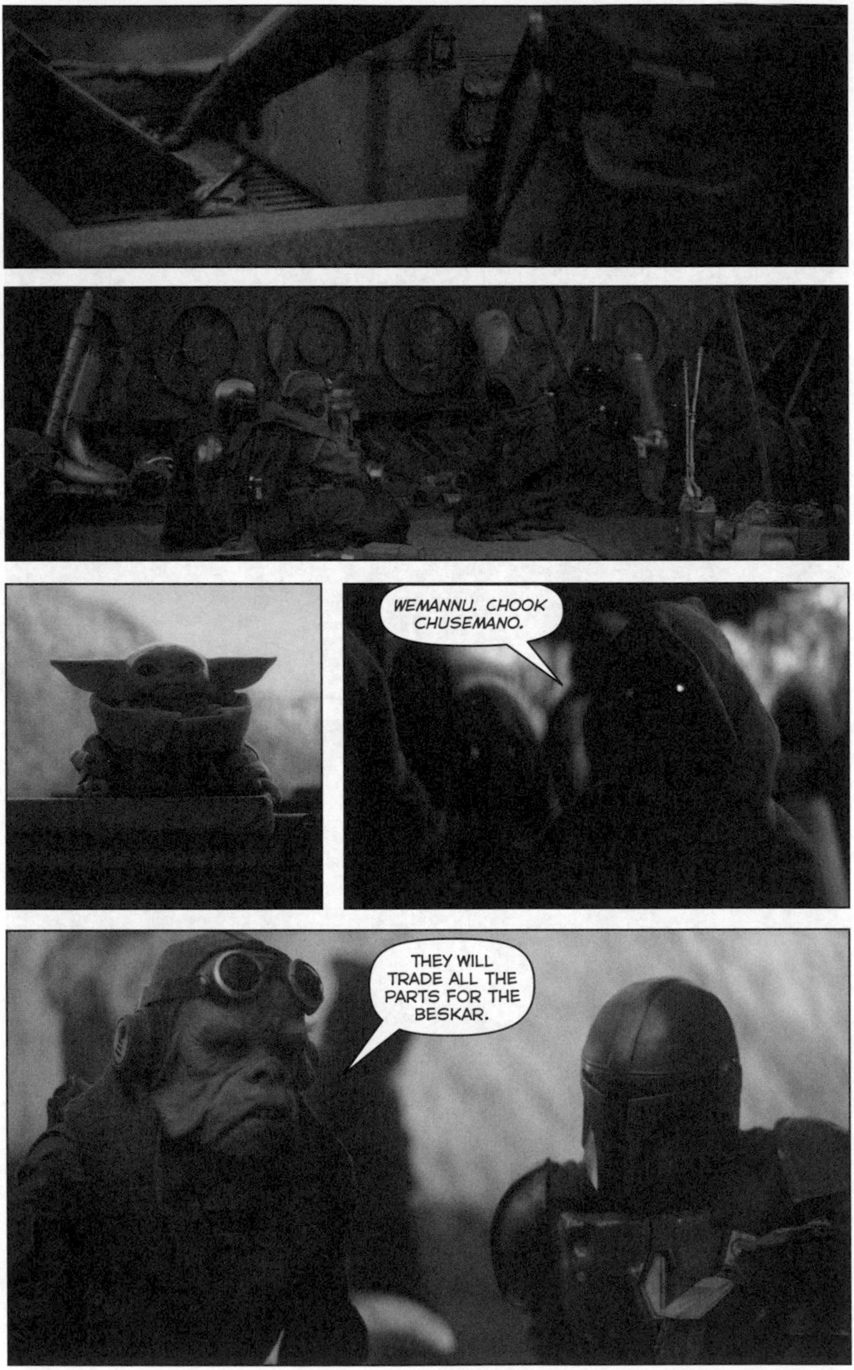
WEMANNU. CHOOK CHUSEMANO.
THEY WILL TRADE ALL THE PARTS FOR THE BESKAR.

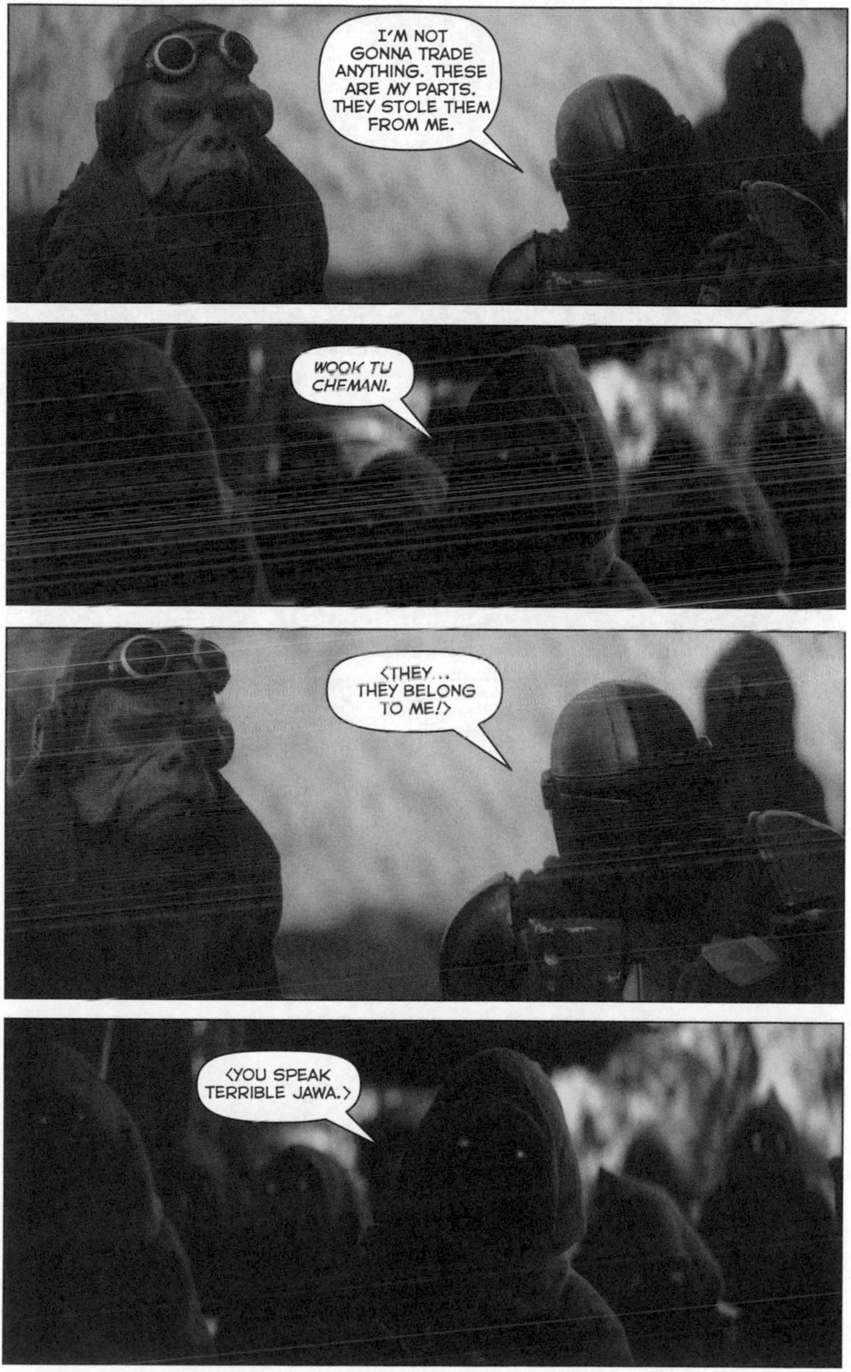
I'M NOT GONNA TRADE ANYTHING. THESE ARE MY PARTS. THEY STOLE THEM FROM ME.
WOOK TU CHEMANI.
<THEY... THEY BELONG TO ME!>
<YOU SPEAK TERRIBLE JAWA.>

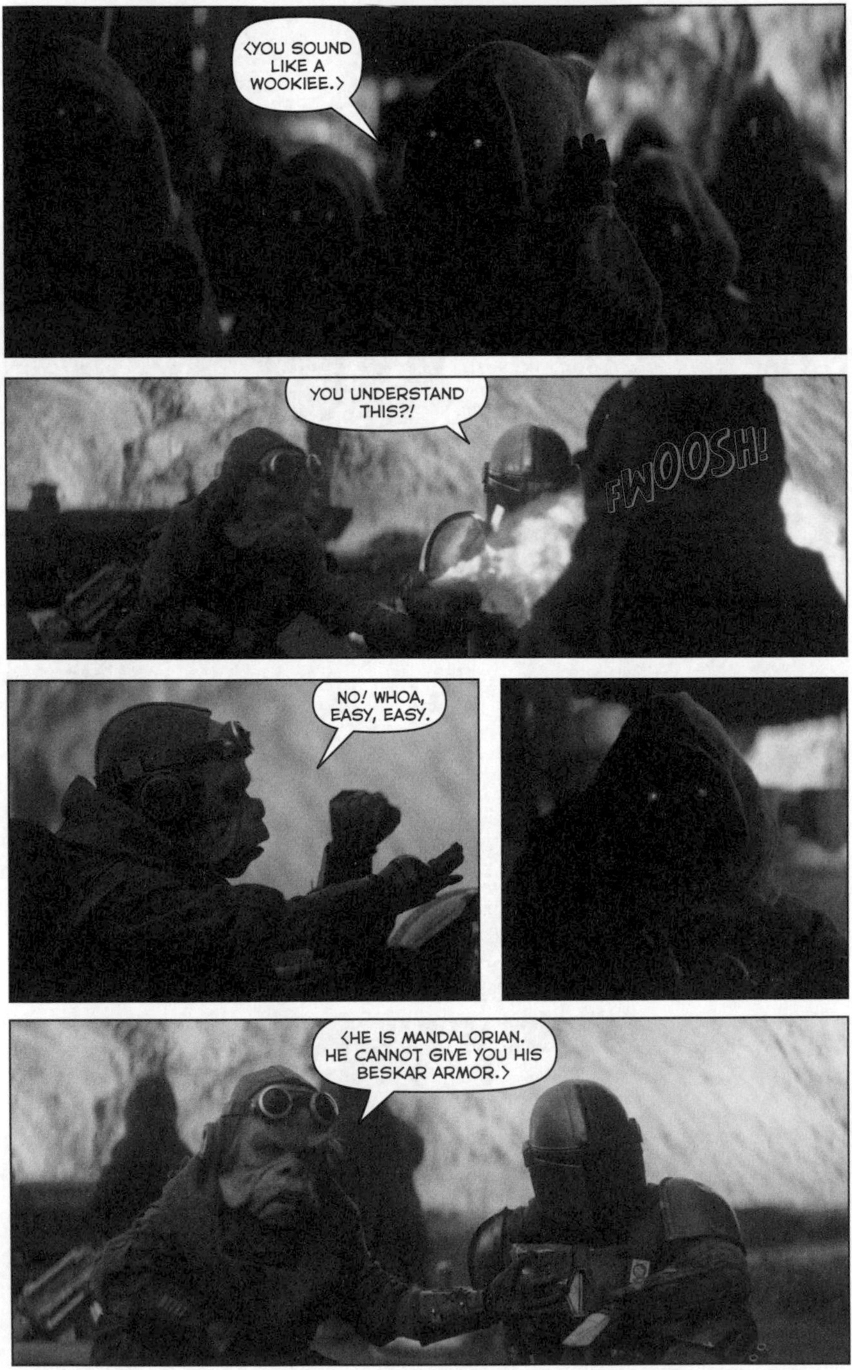
<YOU SOUND LIKE A WOOKIEE.>
YOU UNDERSTAND THIS?!
FWOOSH!
NO! WHOA, EASY, EASY.
<HE IS MANDALORIAN. HE CANNOT GIVE YOU HIS BESKAR ARMOR.>

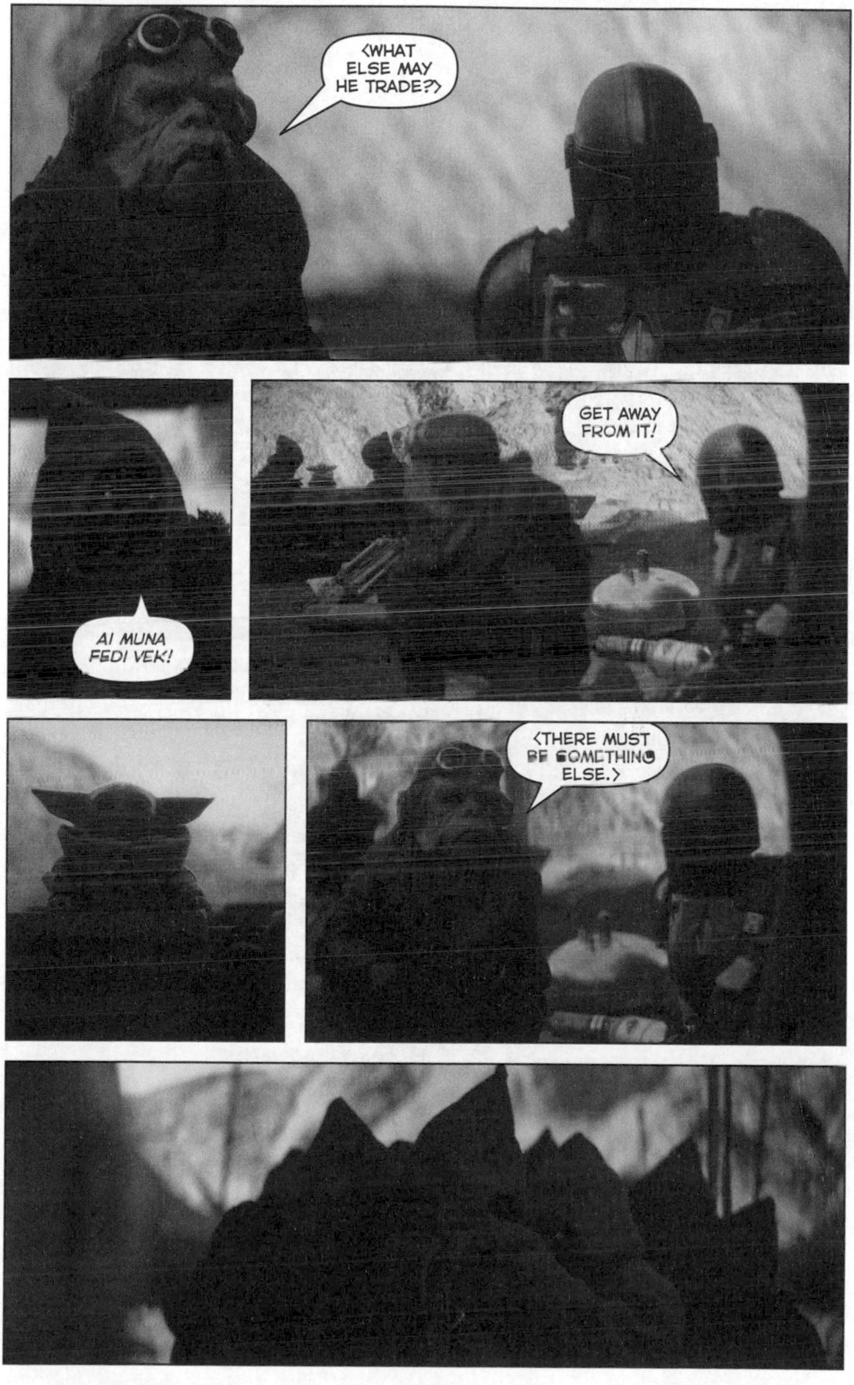
<WHAT ELSE MAY HE TRADE?>
AI MUNA FEDI VEK!
GET AWAY FROM IT!
<THERE MUST BE SOMETHING ELSE.>

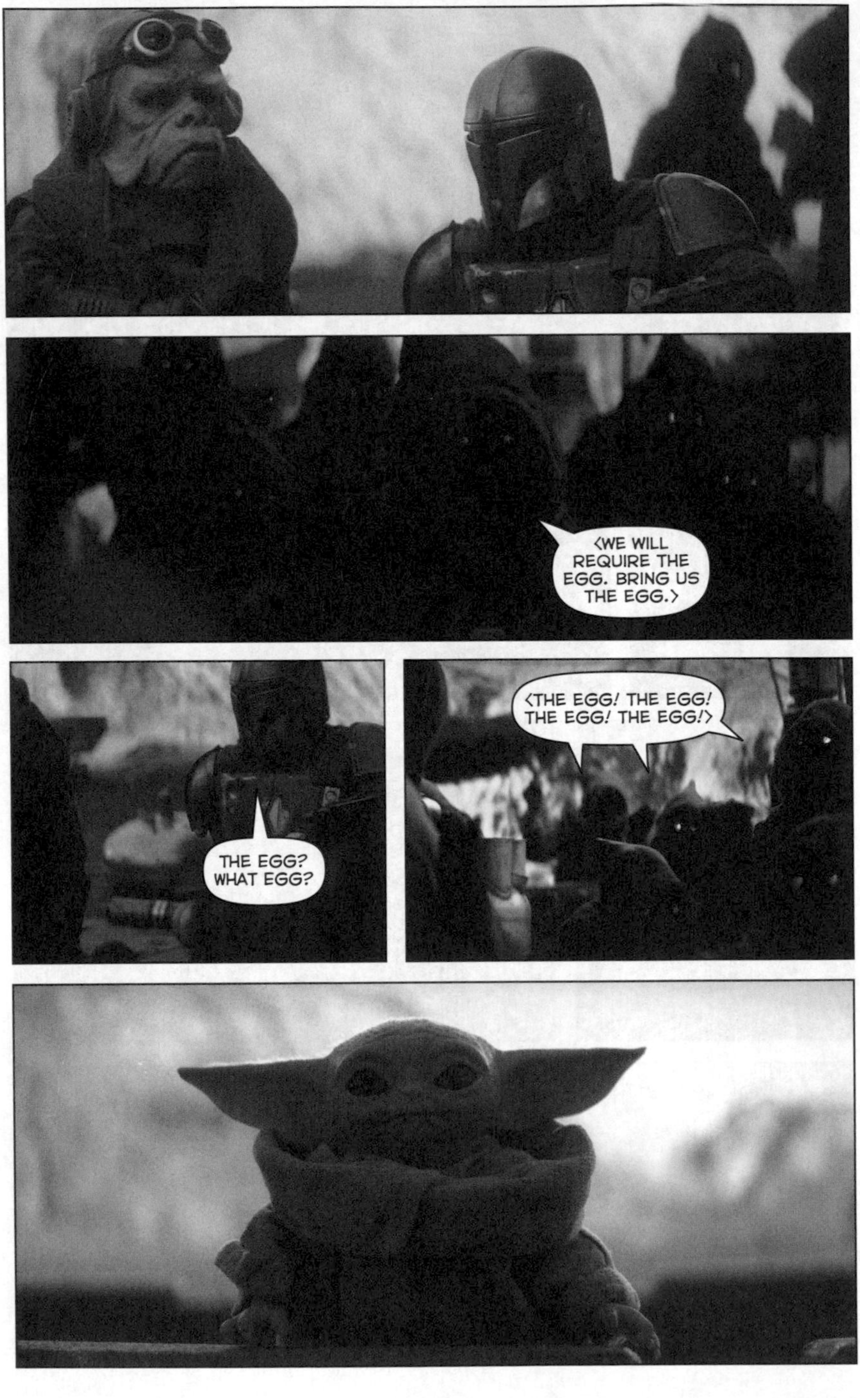

<WE WILL REQUIRE THE EGG. BRING US THE EGG.>
THE EGG? WHAT EGG?
<THE EGG! THE EGG! THE EGG! THE EGG!>

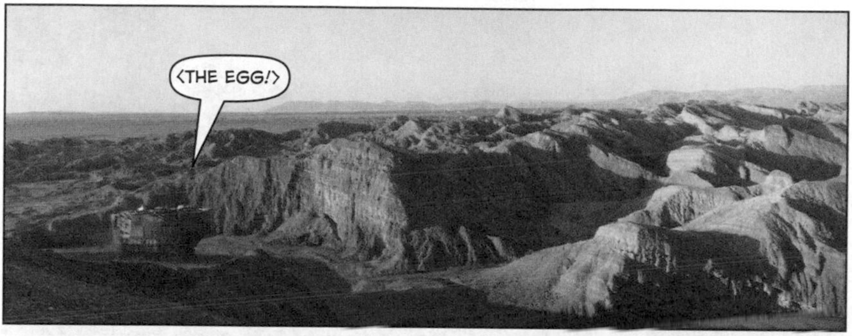
<THE EGG!>

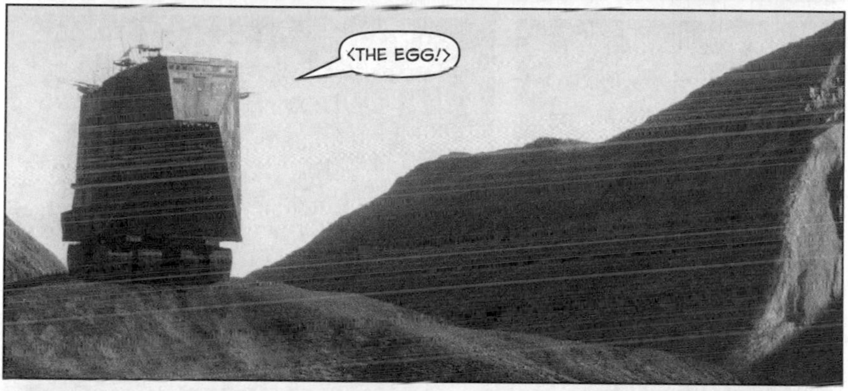
<THE EGG!>

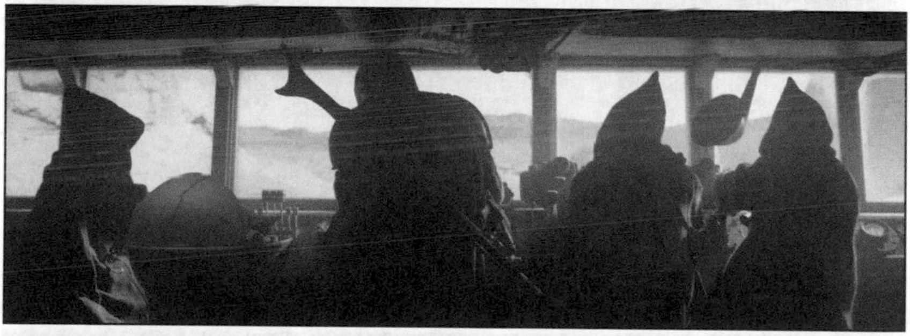

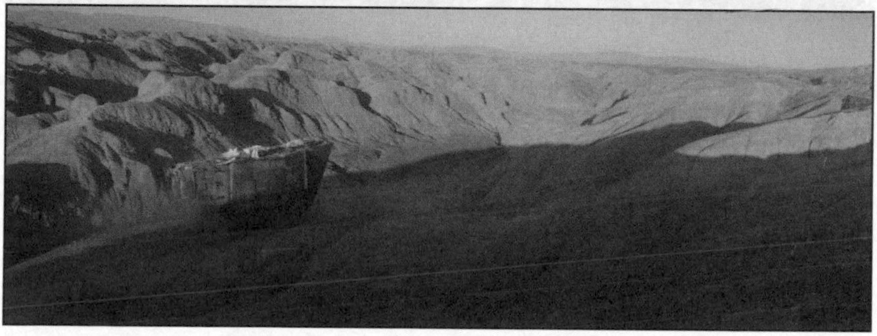

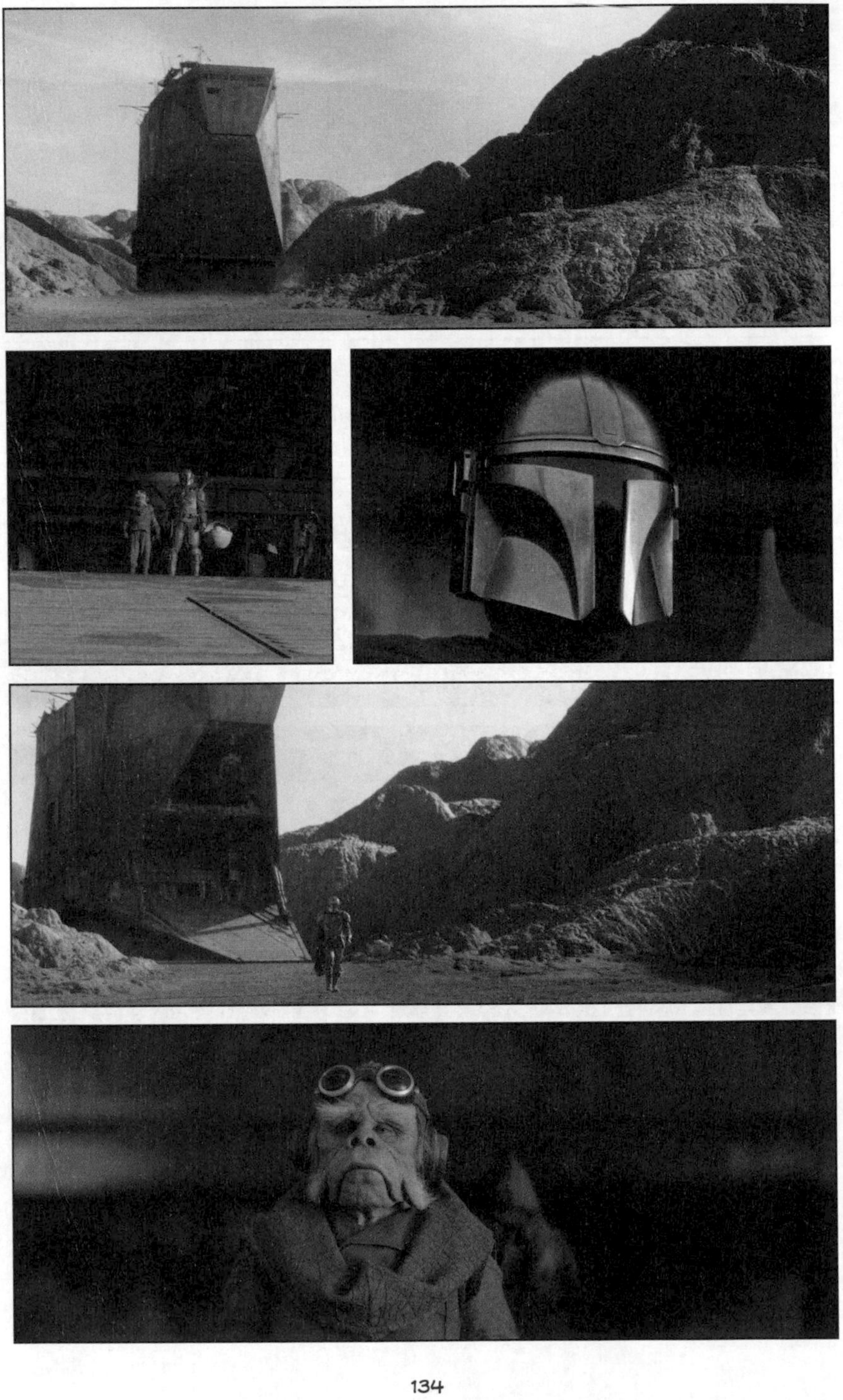

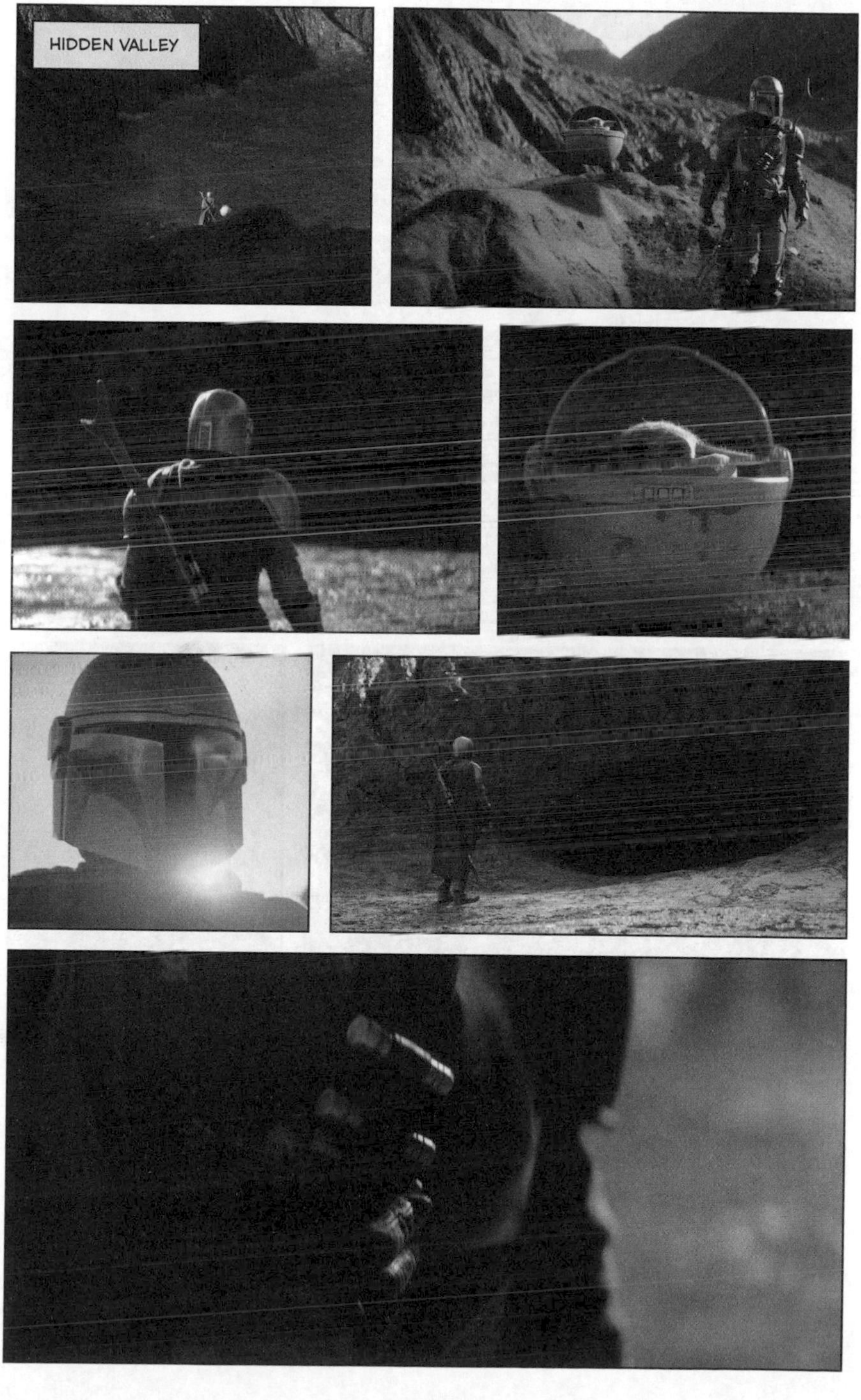
HIDDEN VALLEY

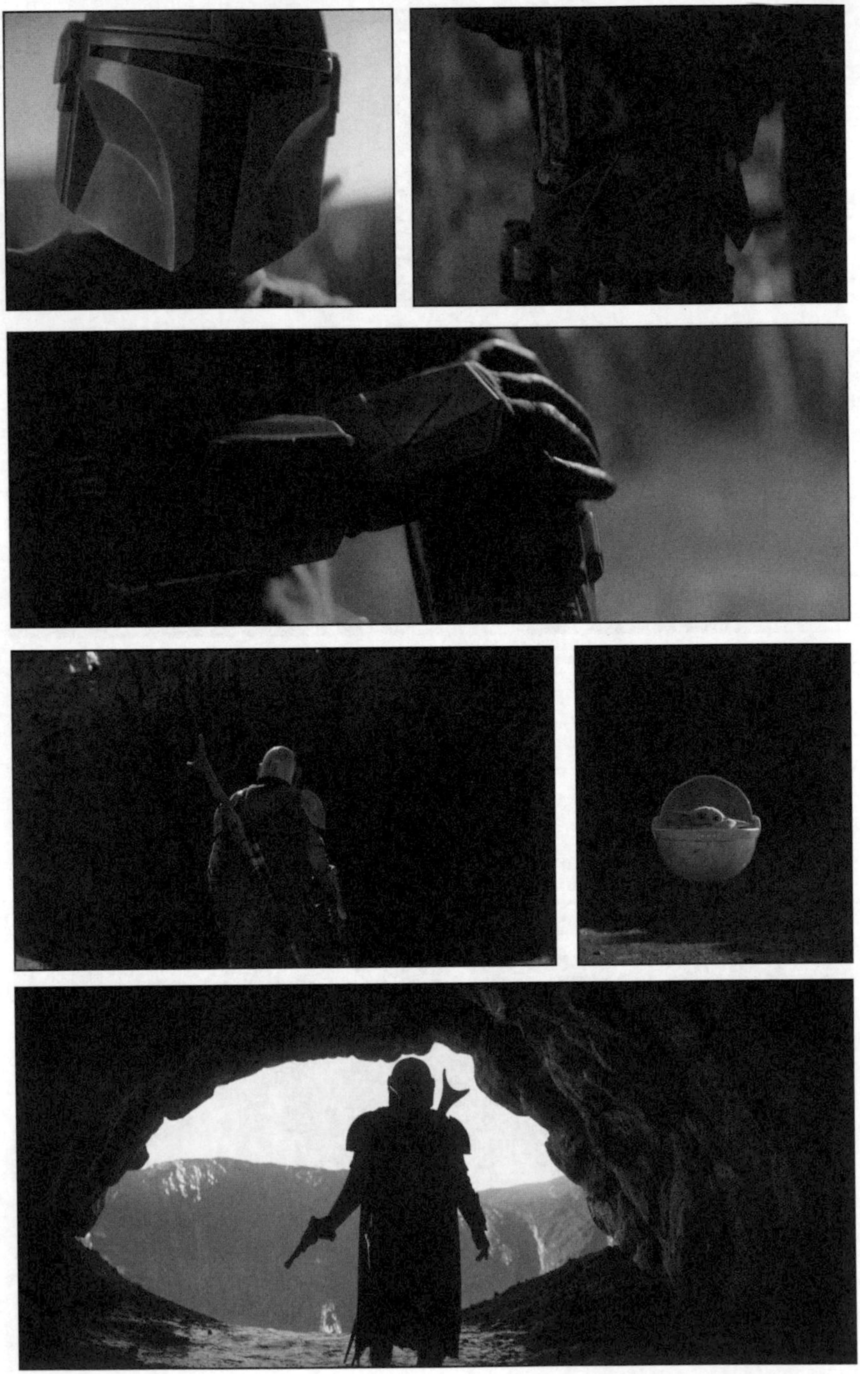

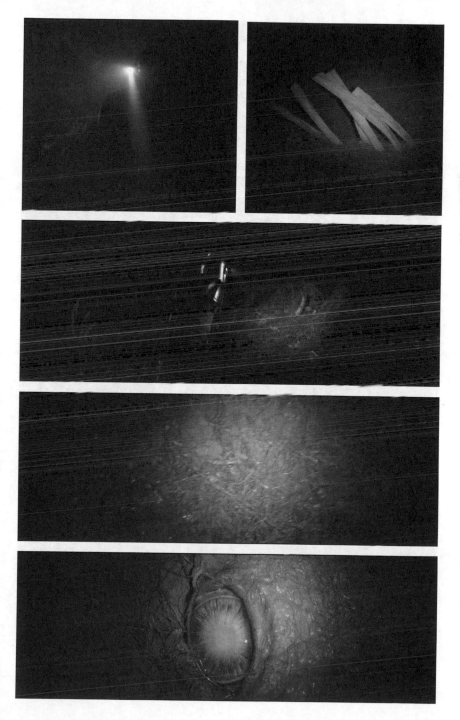

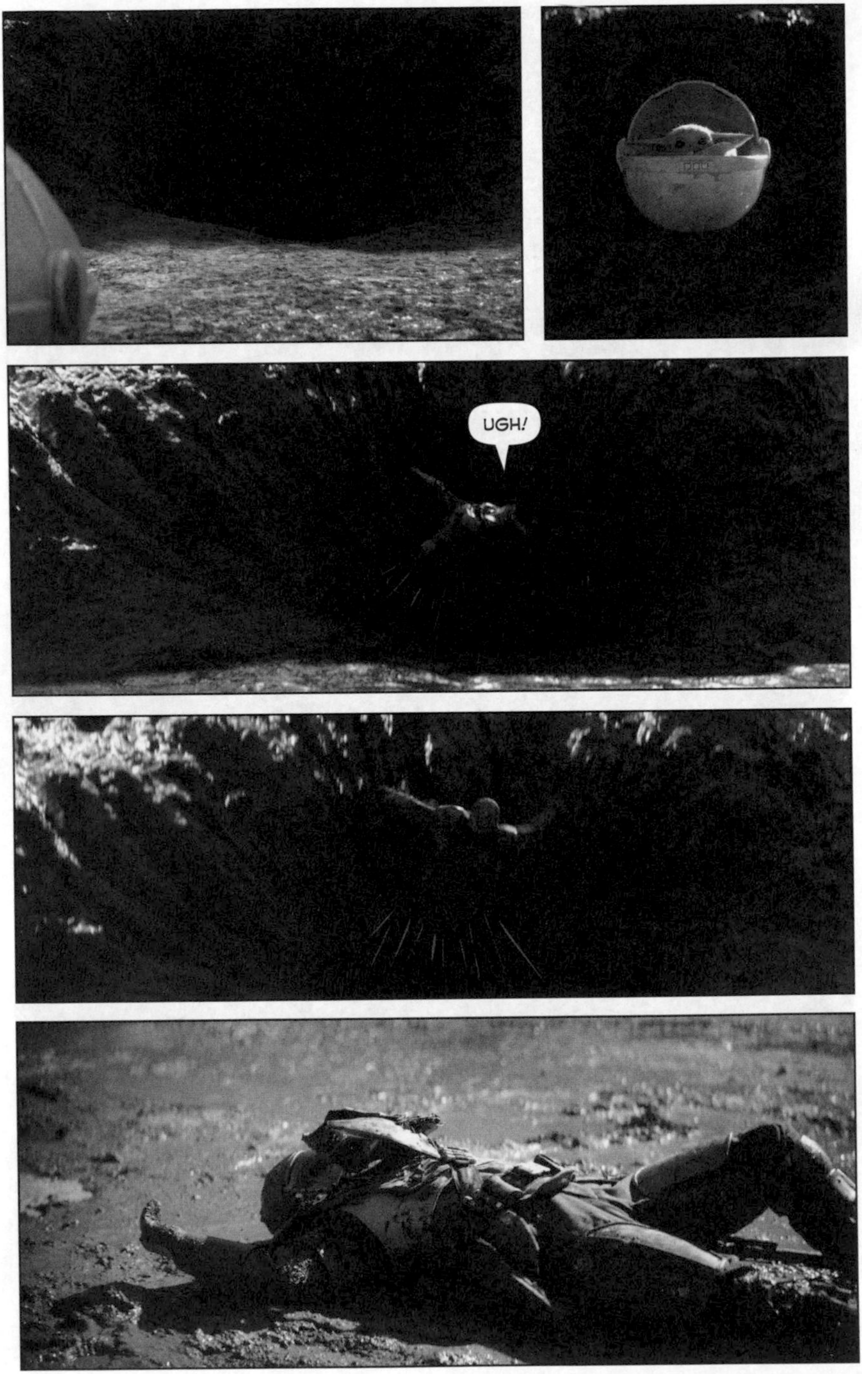
UGH!

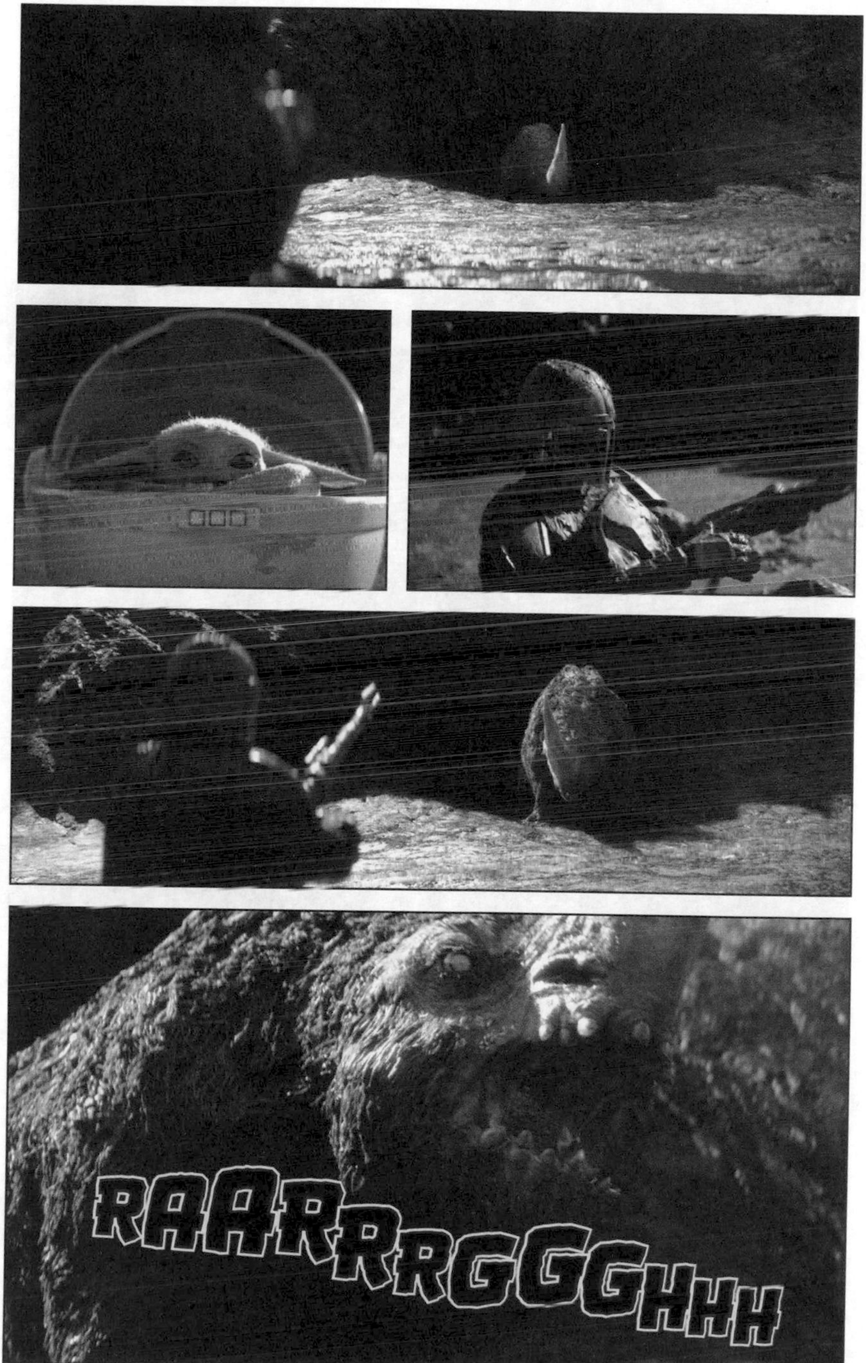
RAARRRGGGHHH

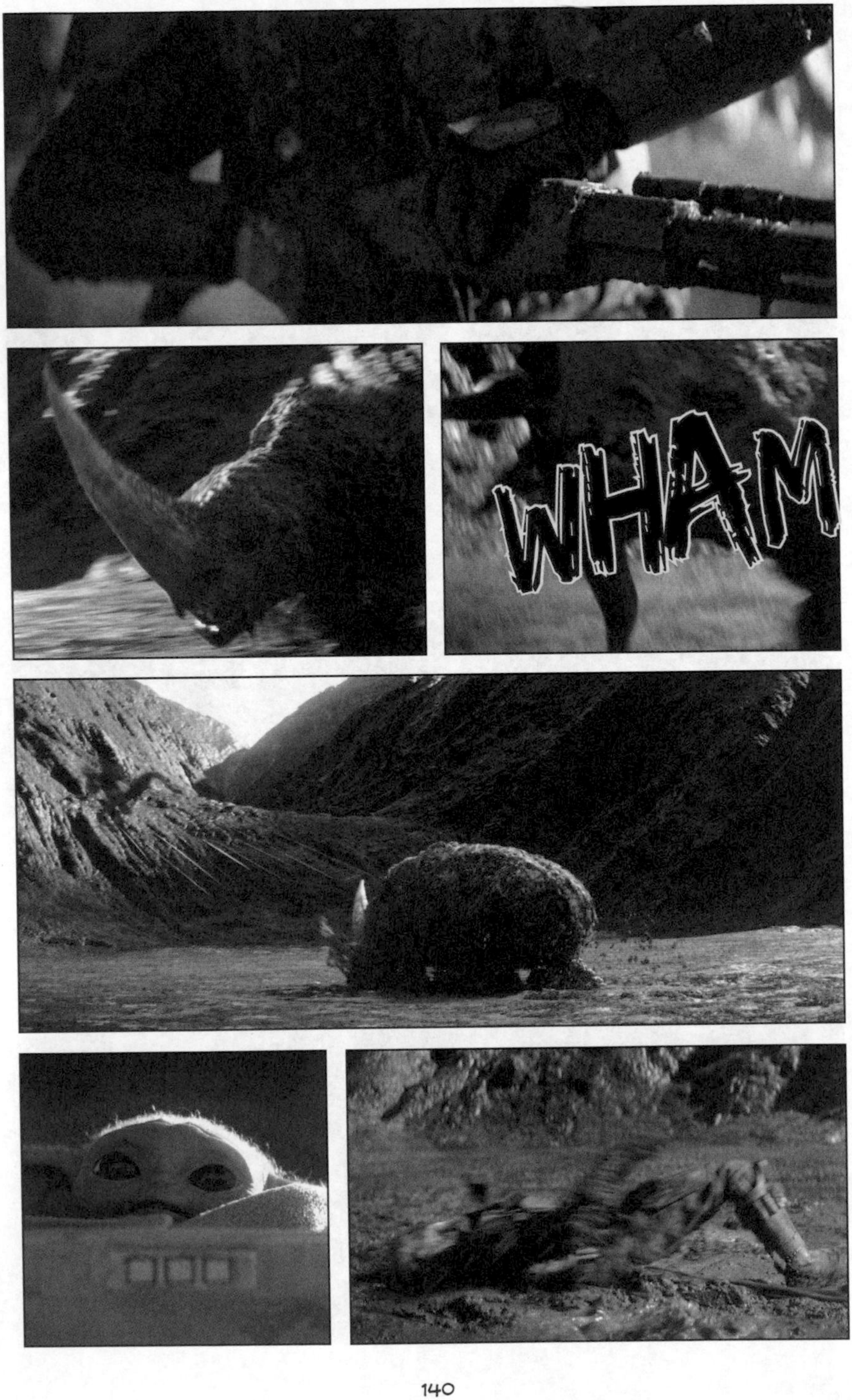
WHAM

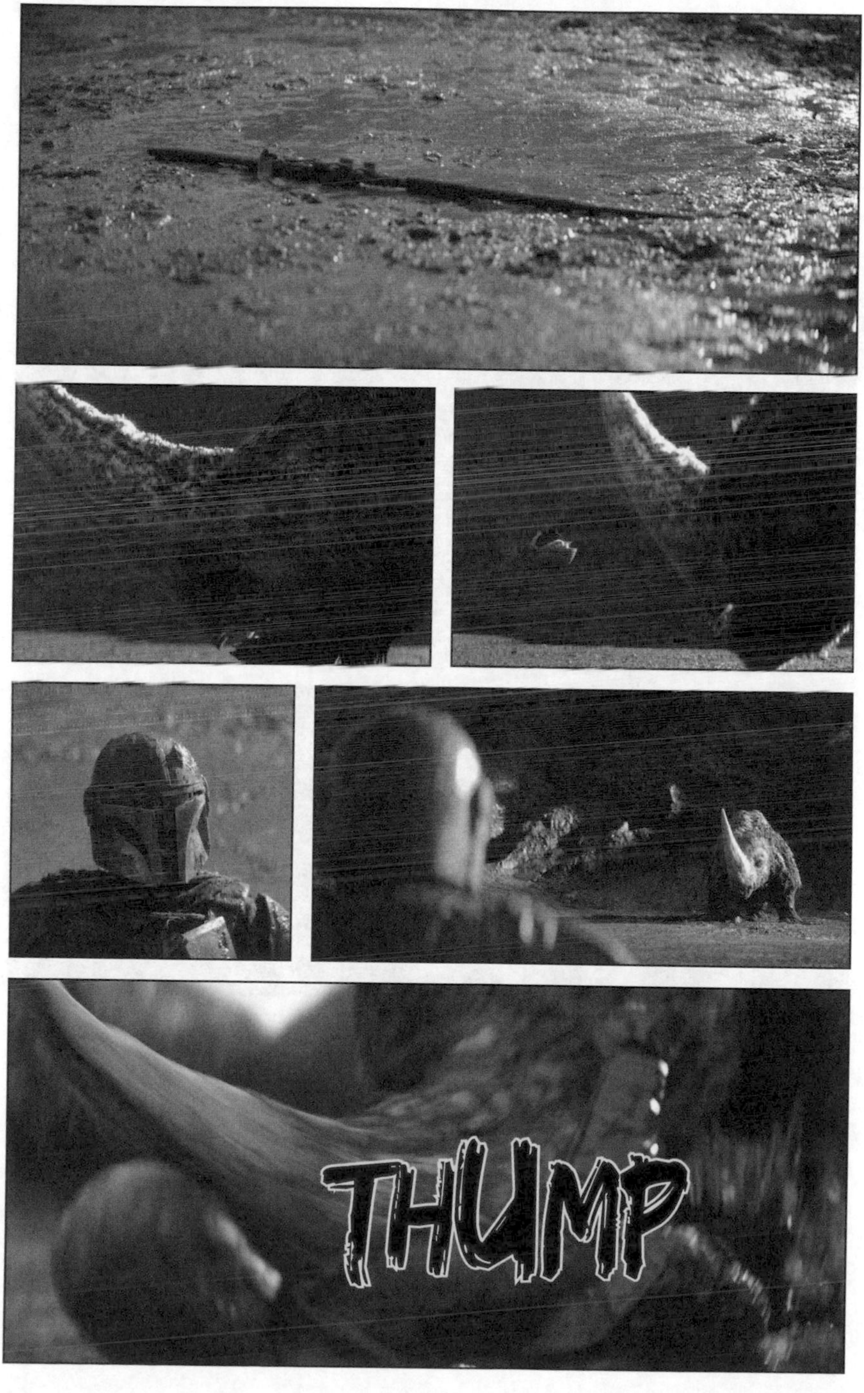
THUMP

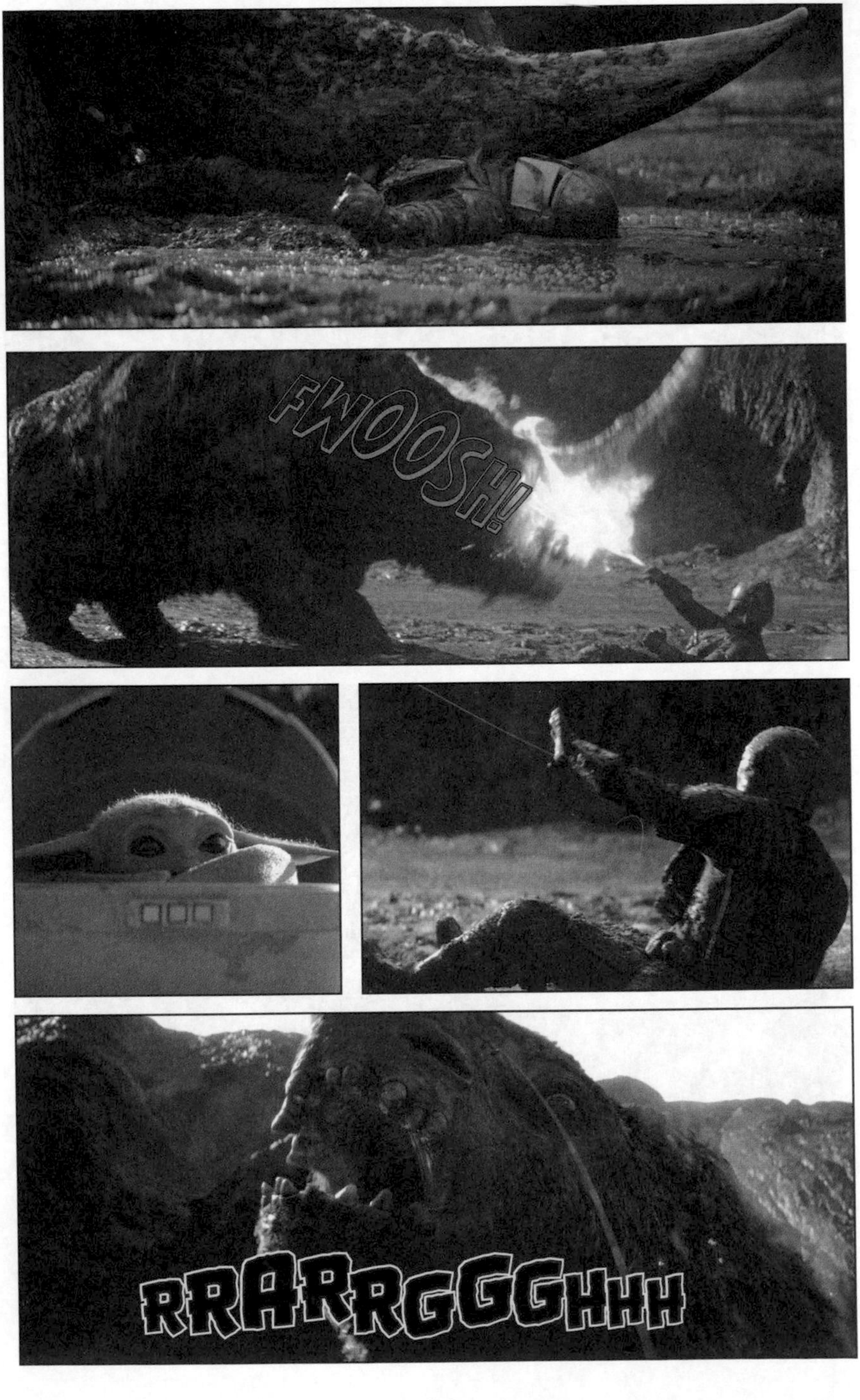
FWOOSH!
RRARRGGGHHH

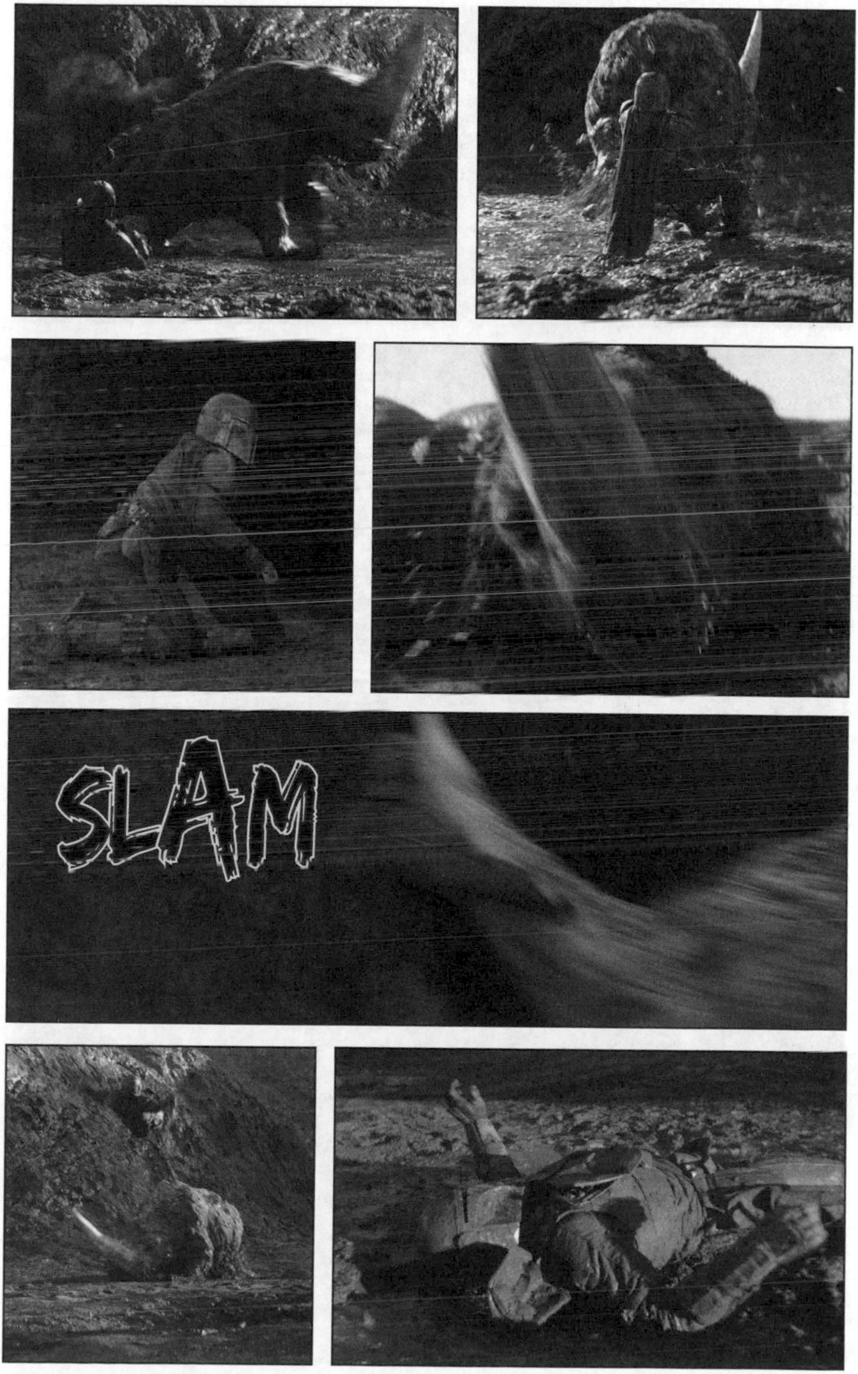
SLAM

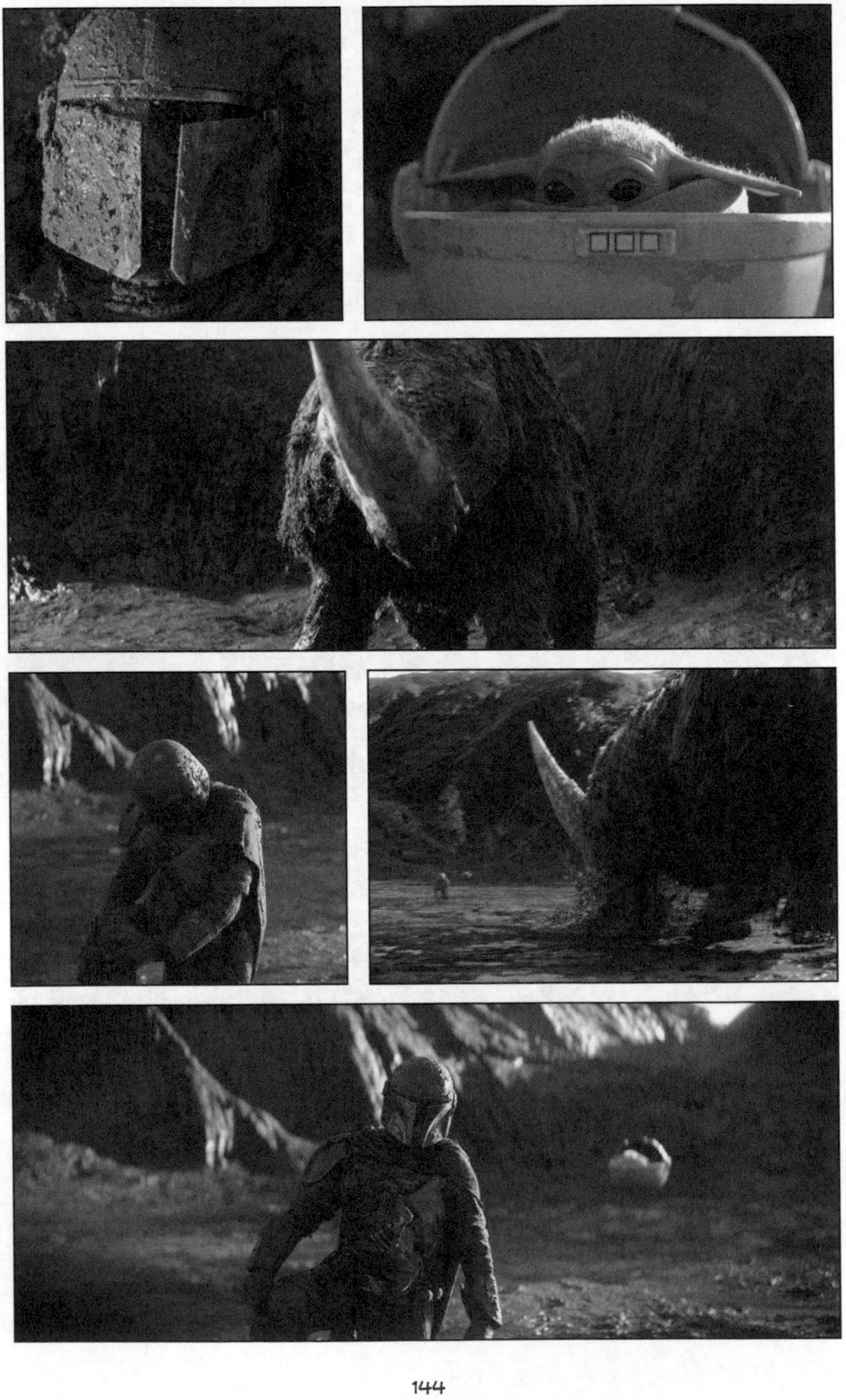

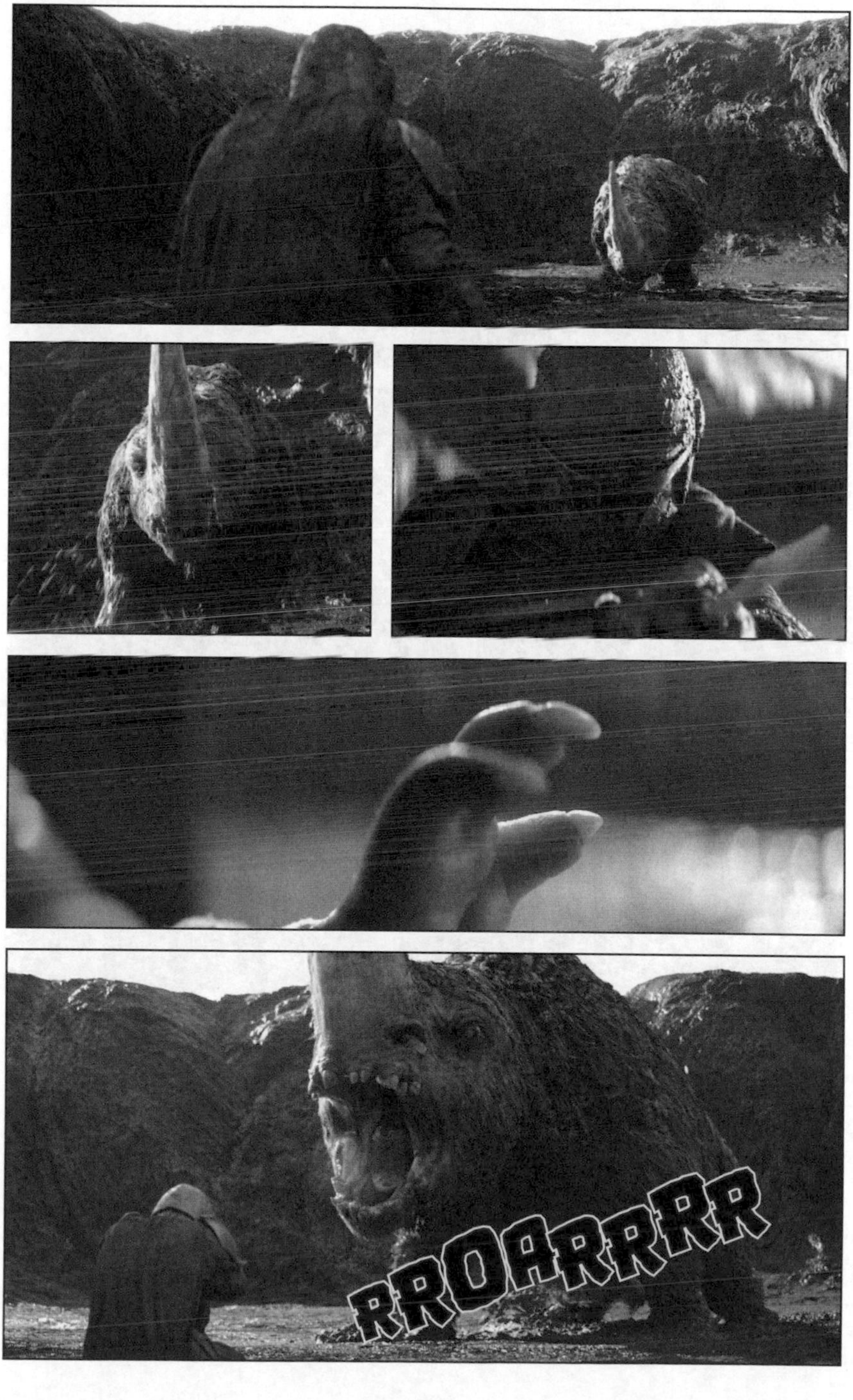
RROARRRRR

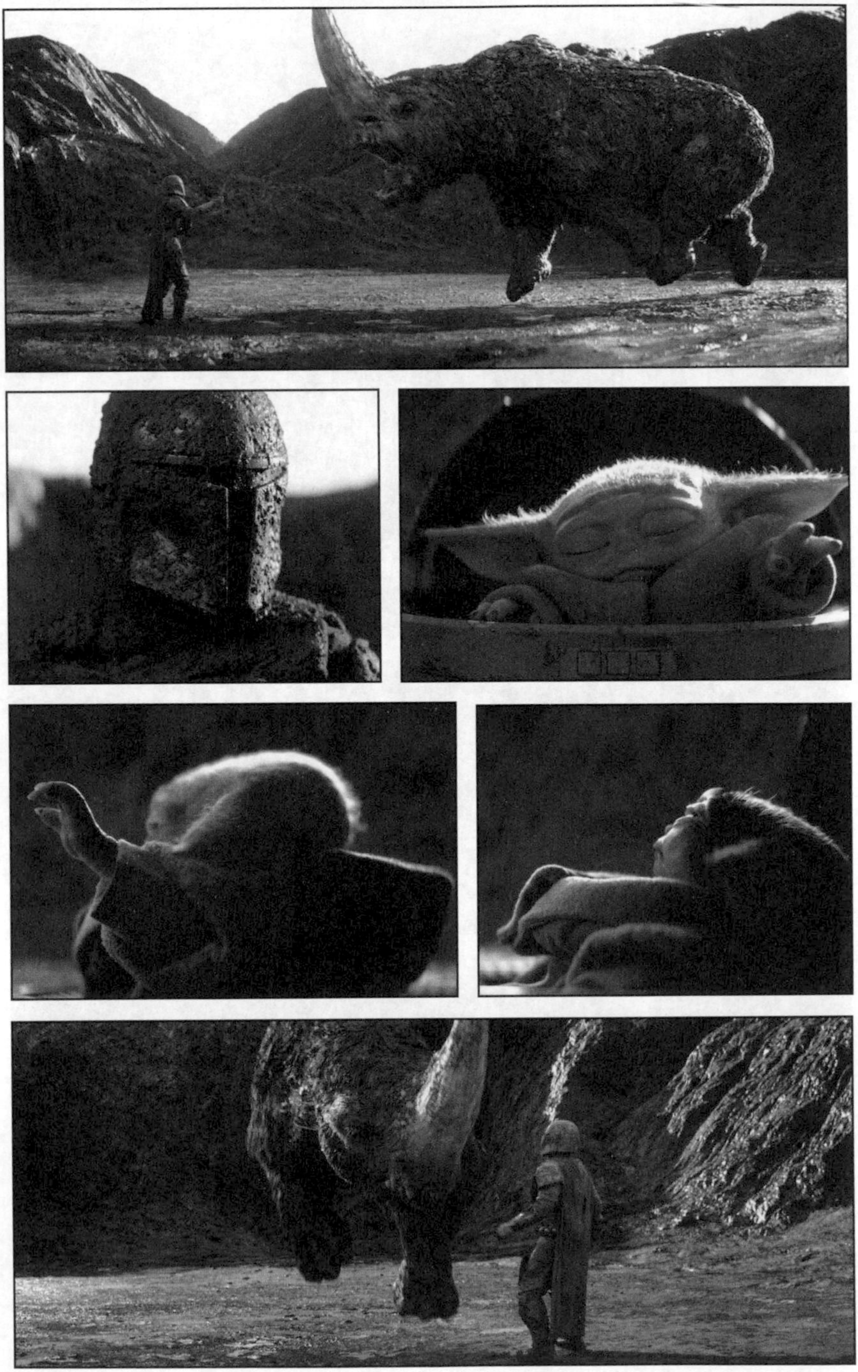

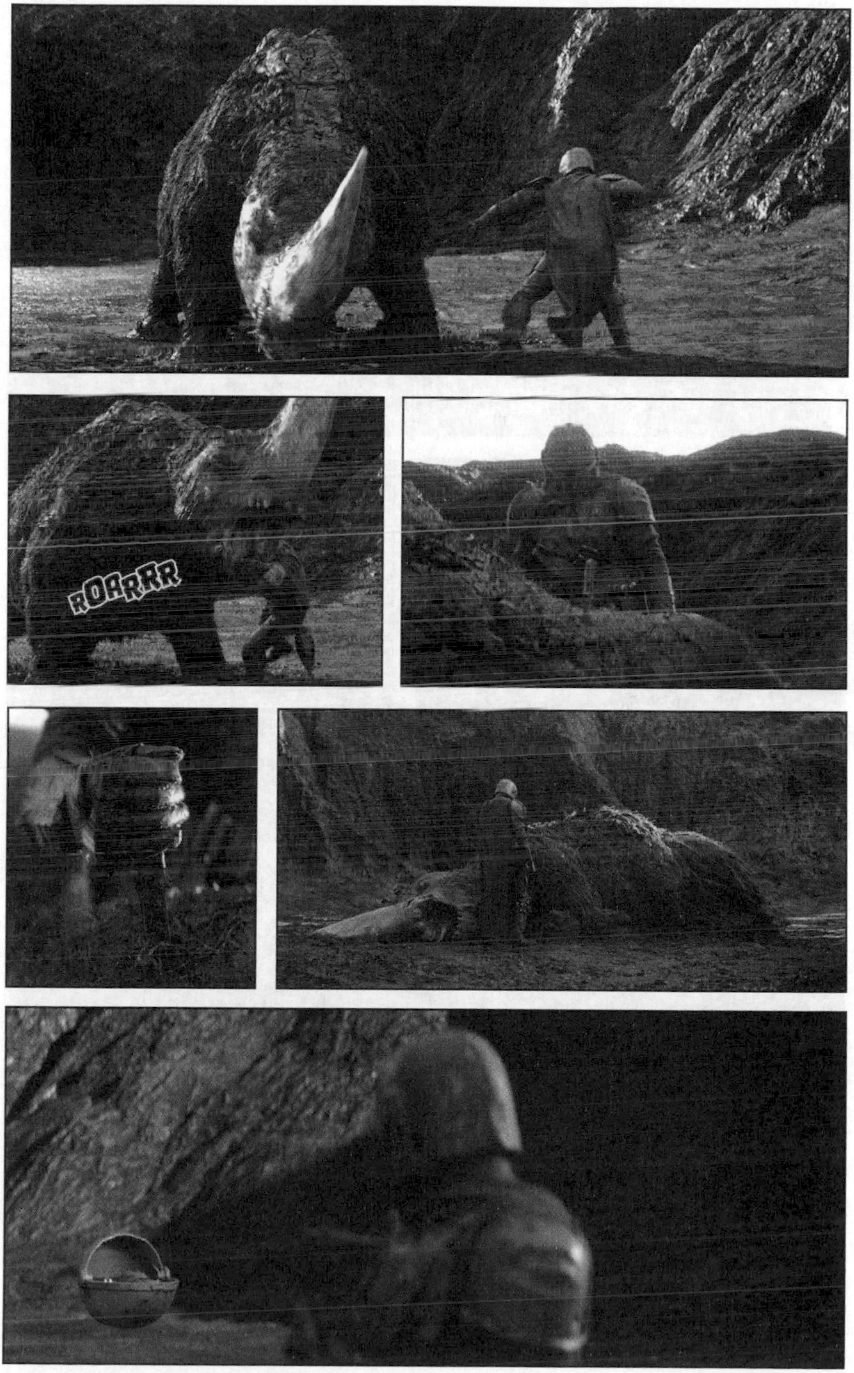
rOARRR

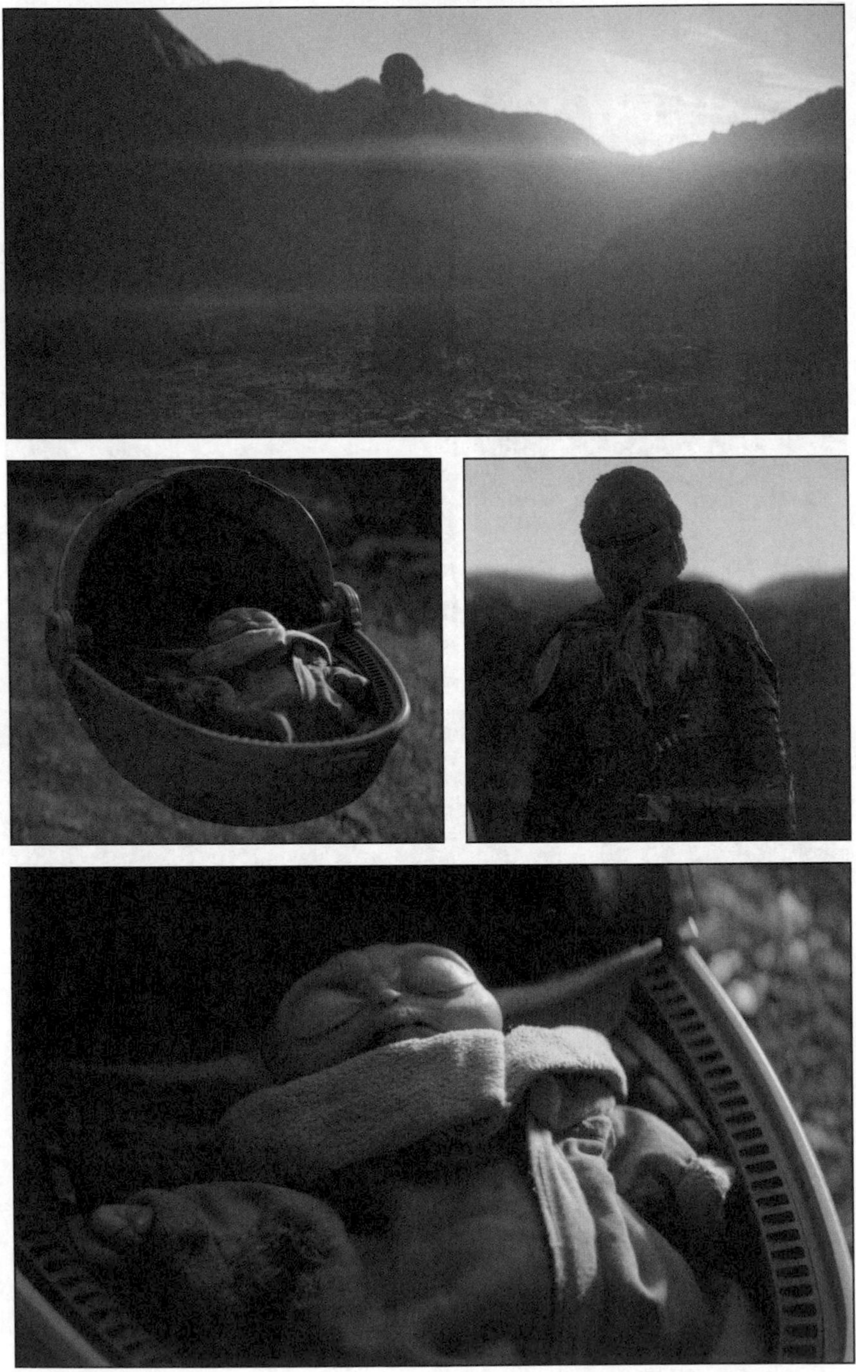

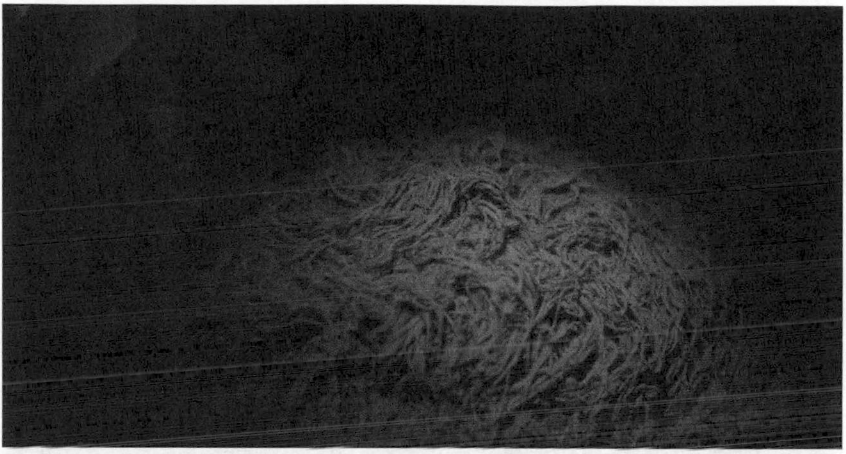

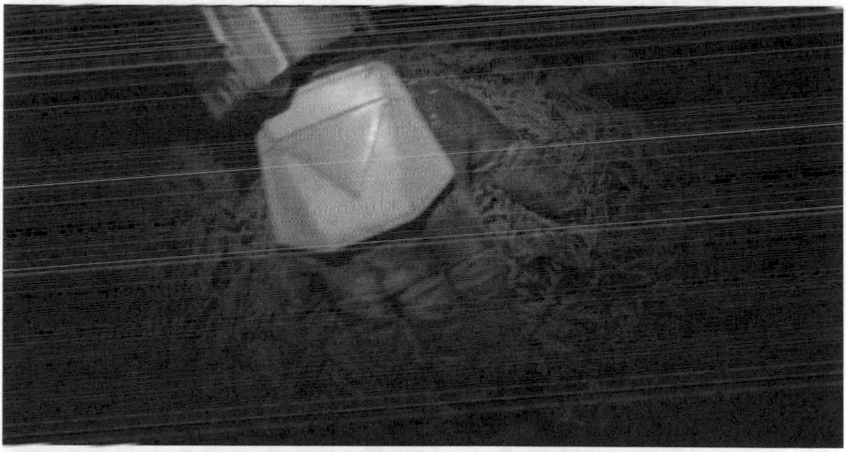

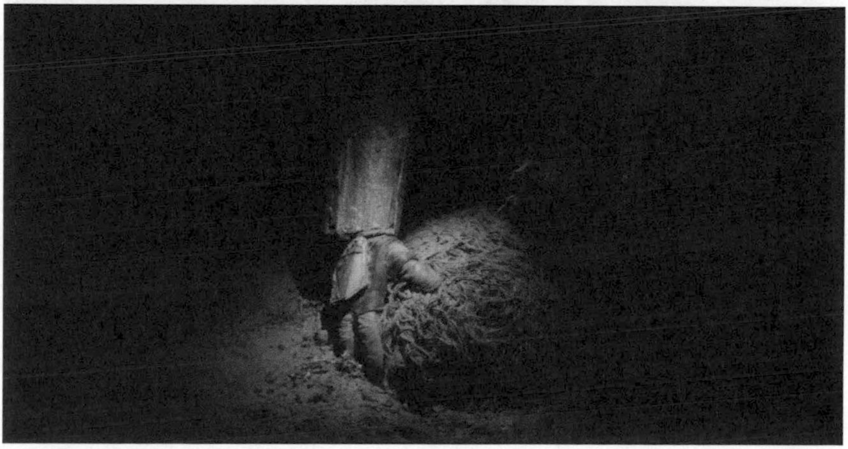

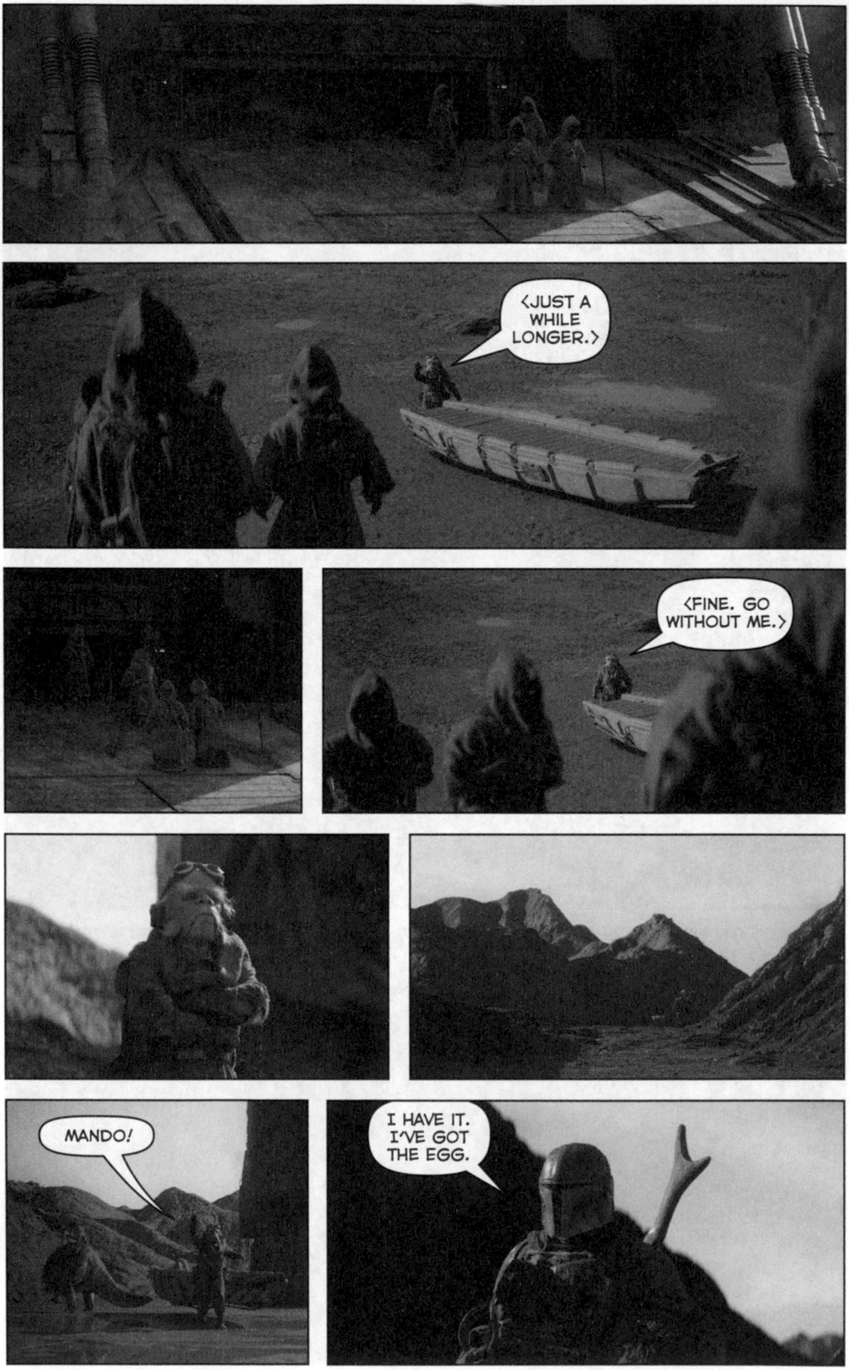
<JUST A WHILE LONGER.>
<FINE. GO WITHOUT ME.>
MANDO!
I HAVE IT. I'VE GOT THE EGG.

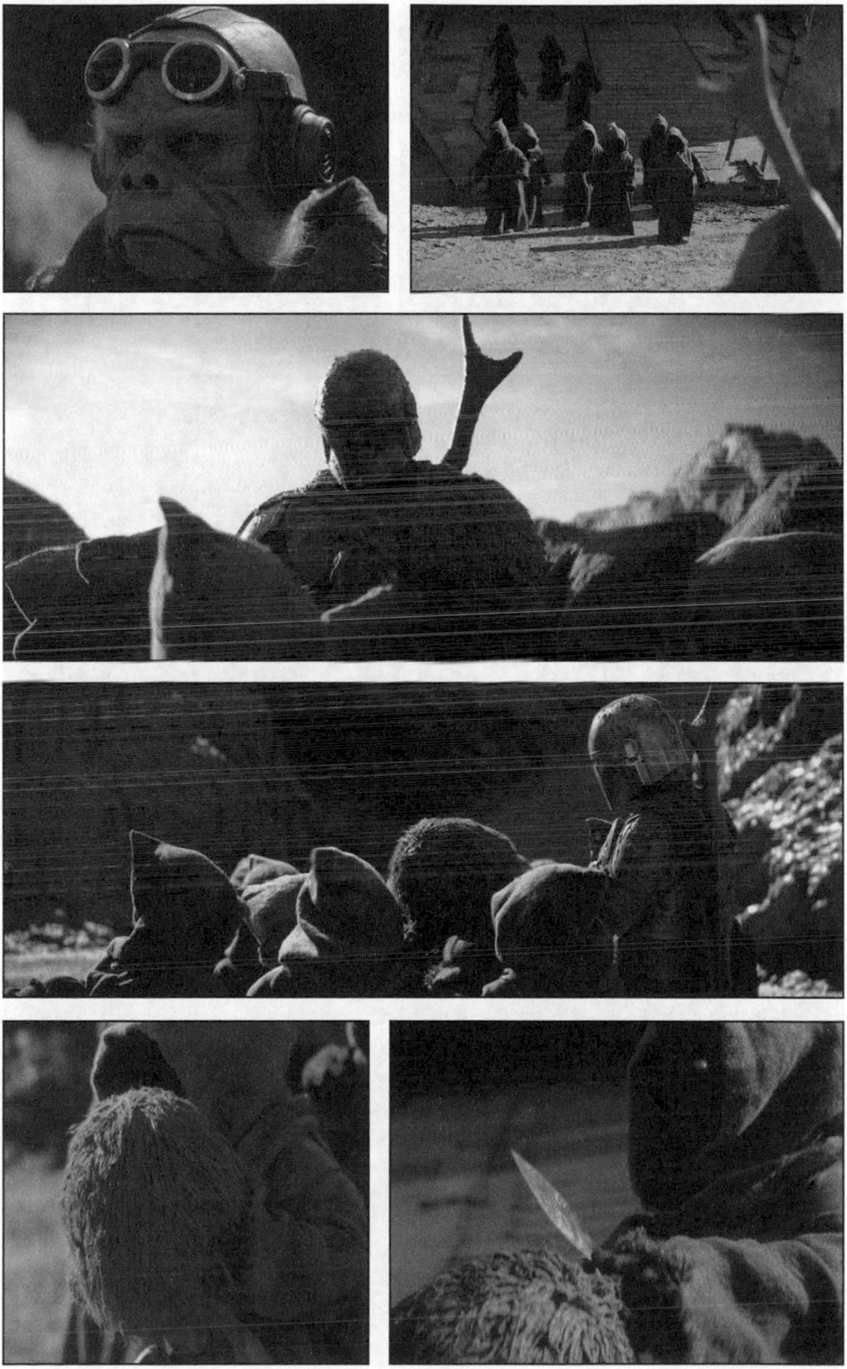

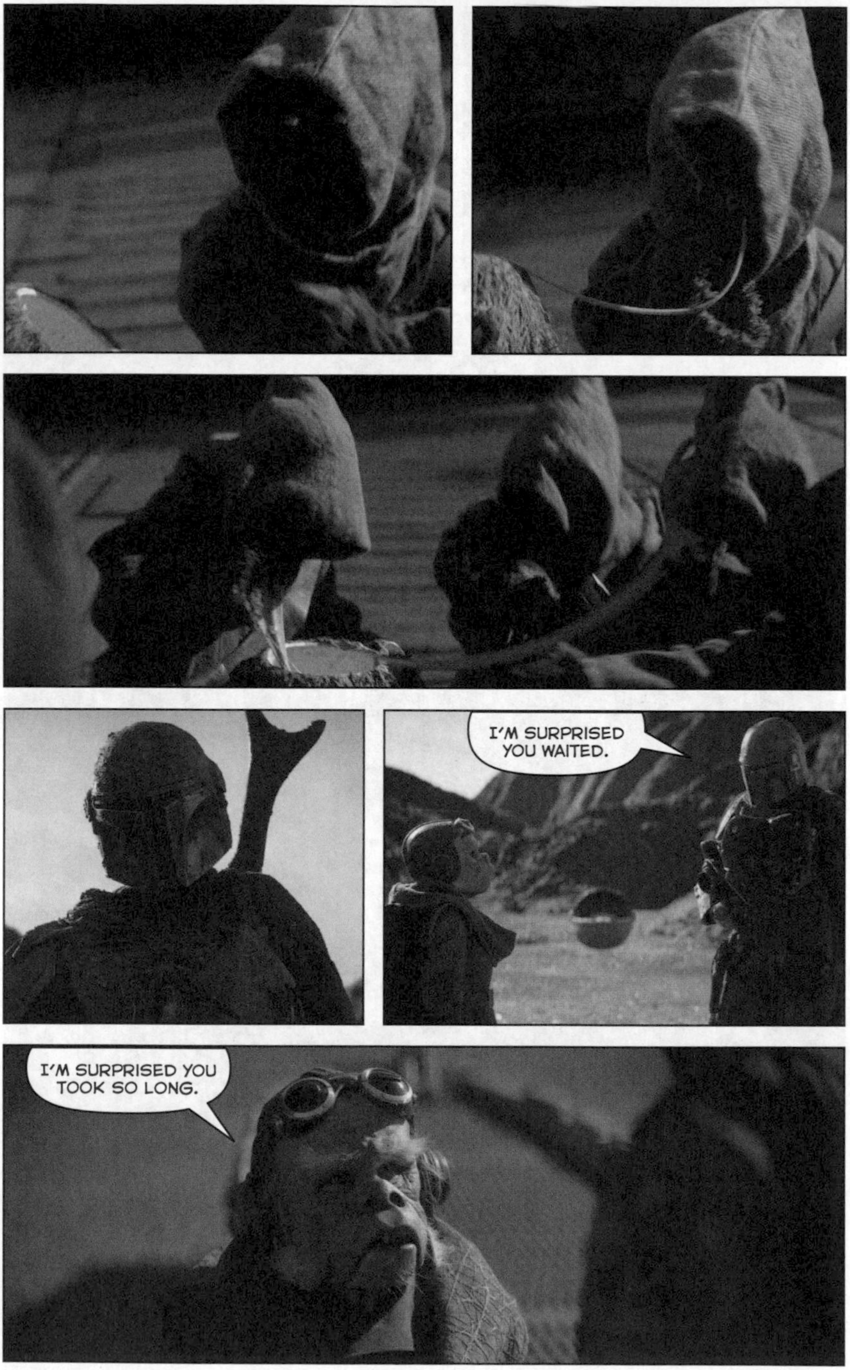
I'M SURPRISED YOU WAITED.
I'M SURPRISED YOU TOOK SO LONG.

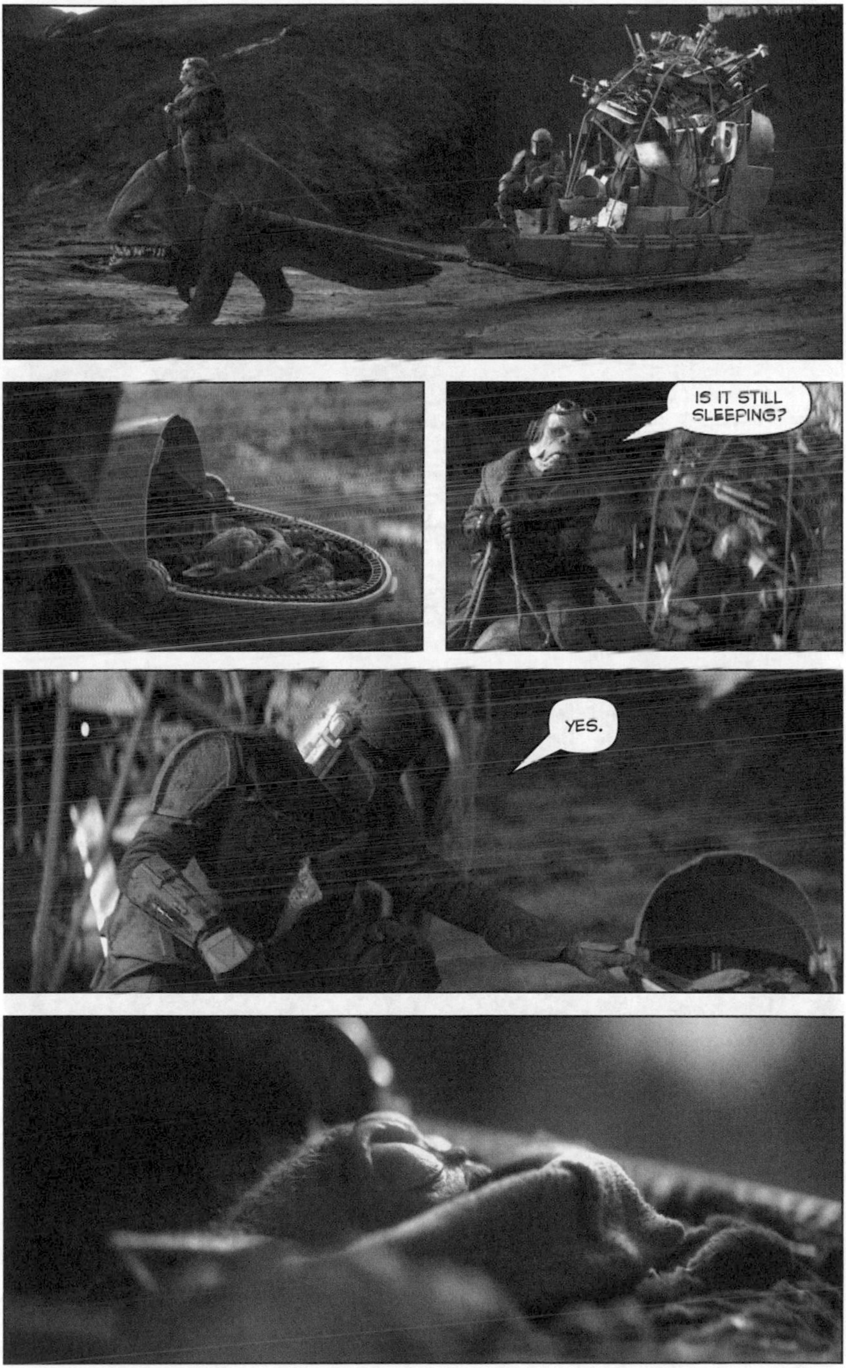
IS IT STILL SLEEPING?
YES.

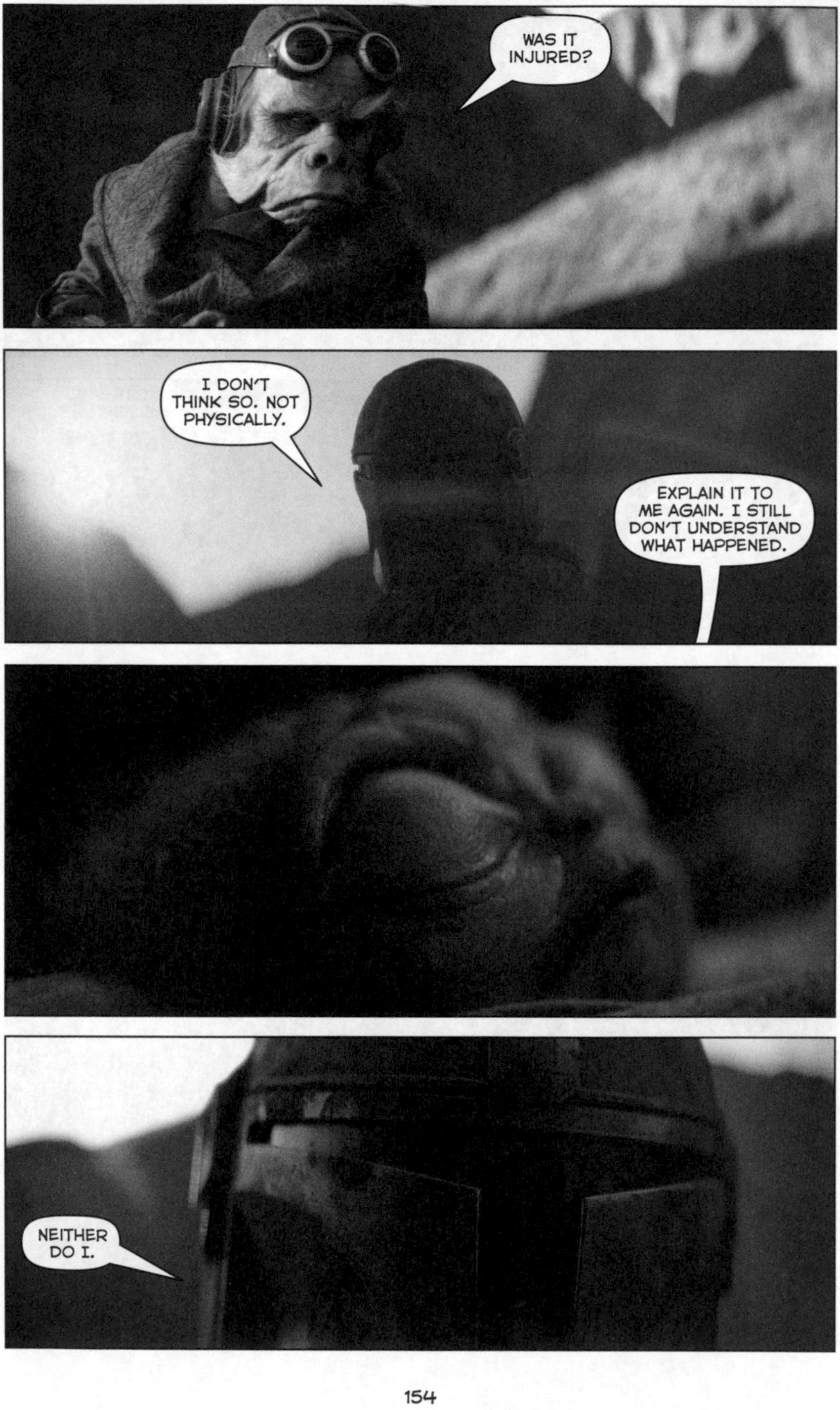
WAS IT INJURED?
I DON'T THINK SO. NOT PHYSICALLY.
EXPLAIN IT TO ME AGAIN. I STILL DON'T UNDERSTAND WHAT HAPPENED.
NEITHER DO I.

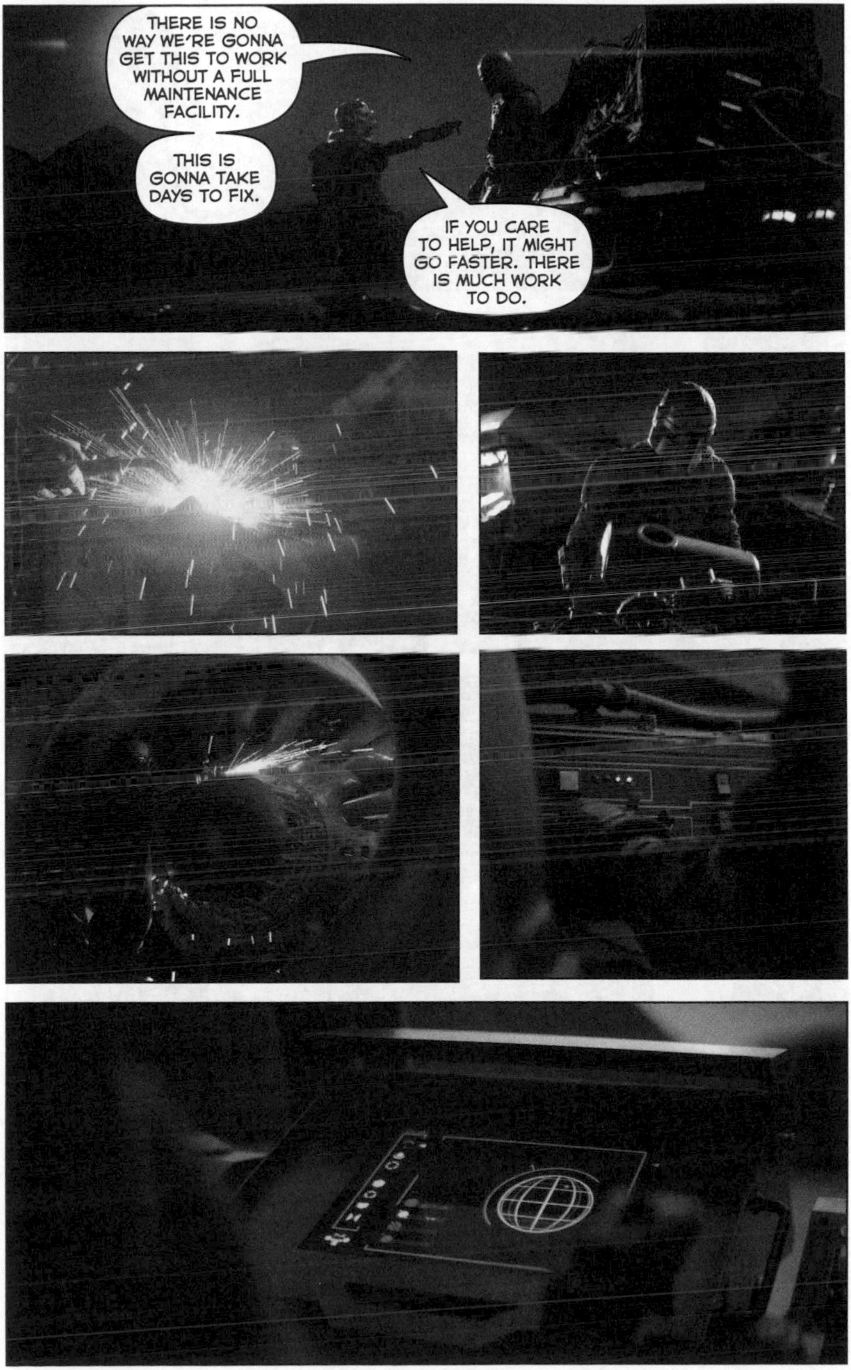
THERE IS NO WAY WE'RE GONNA GET THIS TO WORK WITHOUT A FULL MAINTENANCE FACILITY.
THIS IS GONNA TAKE DAYS TO FIX.
IF YOU CARE TO HELP, IT MIGHT GO FASTER. THERE IS MUCH WORK TO DO.

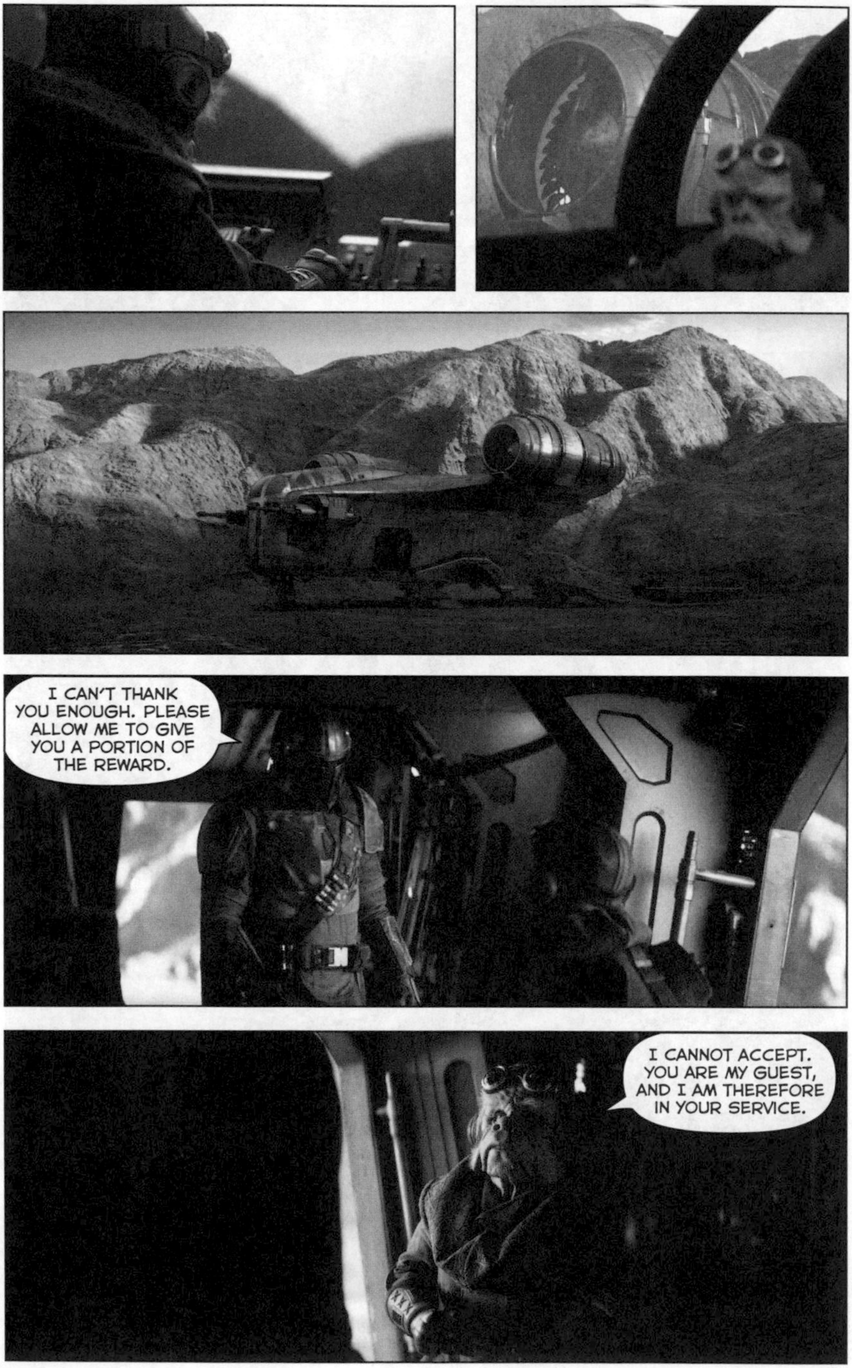
I CAN'T THANK YOU ENOUGH. PLEASE ALLOW ME TO GIVE YOU A PORTION OF THE REWARD.
I CANNOT ACCEPT. YOU ARE MY GUEST, AND I AM THEREFORE IN YOUR SERVICE.

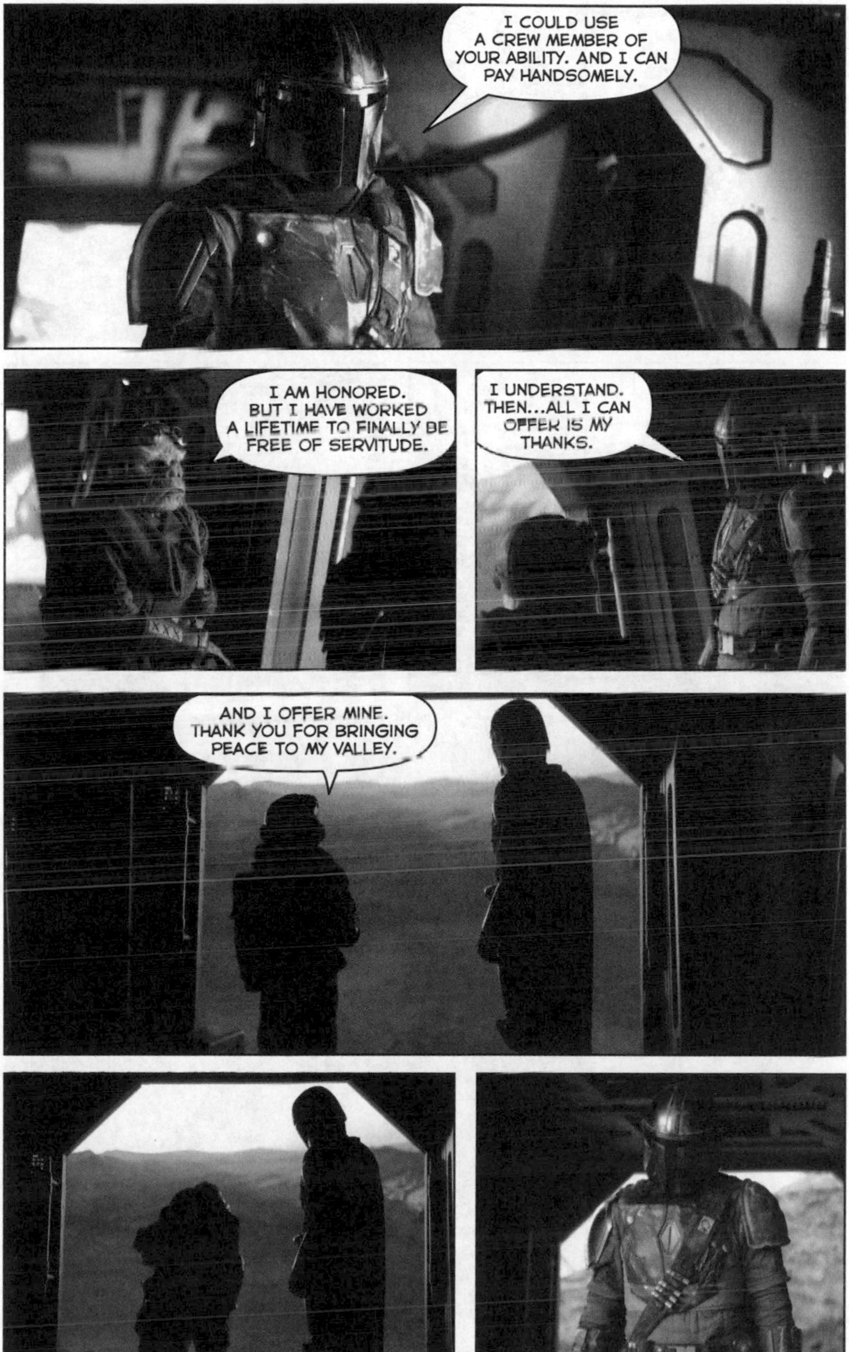
I COULD USE A CREW MEMBER OF YOUR ABILITY. AND I CAN PAY HANDSOMELY.
I AM HONORED. BUT I HAVE WORKED A LIFETIME TO FINALLY BE FREE OF SERVITUDE.
I UNDERSTAND. THEN...ALL I CAN OFFER IS MY THANKS.
AND I OFFER MINE. THANK YOU FOR BRINGING PEACE TO MY VALLEY.

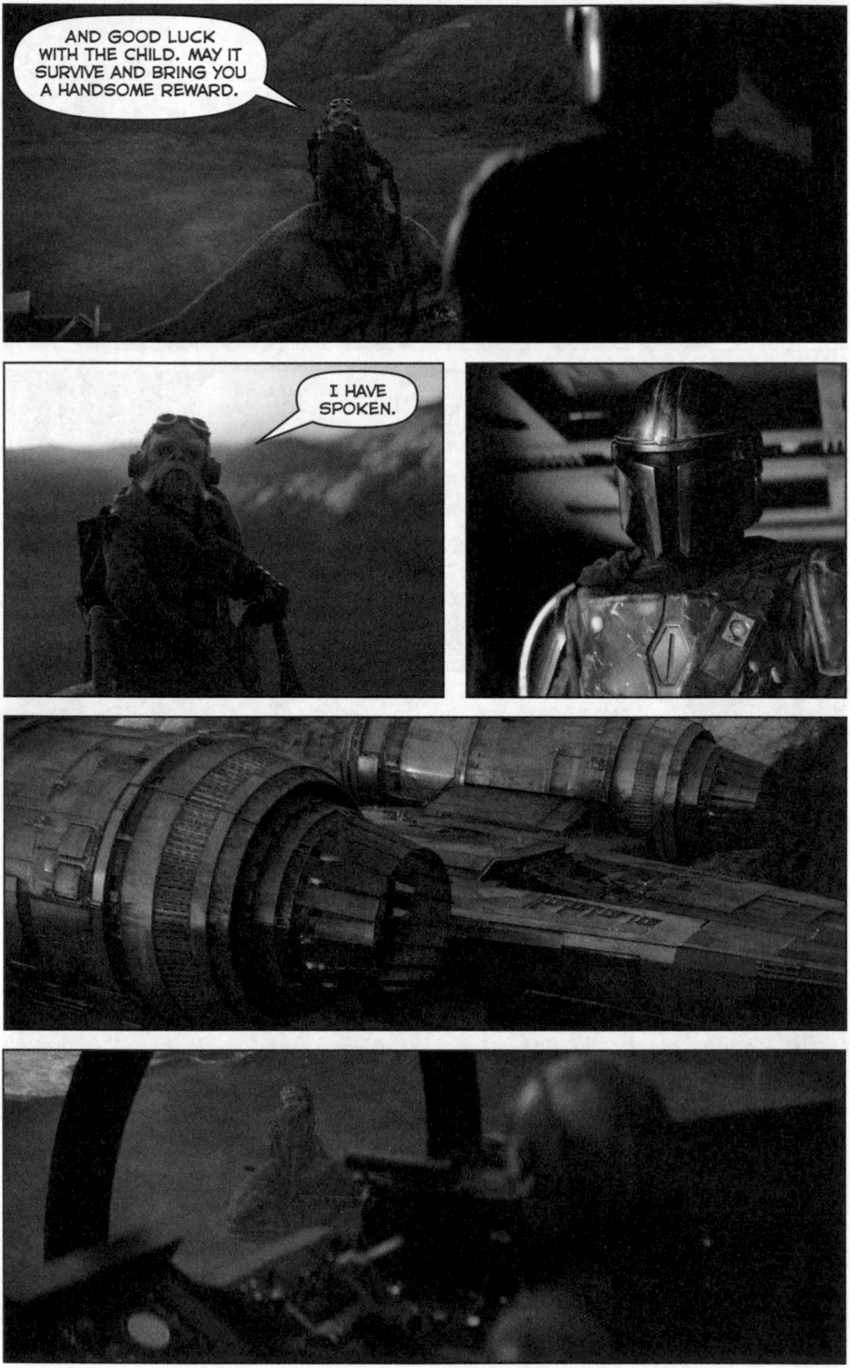
AND GOOD LUCK WITH THE CHILD. MAY IT SURVIVE AND BRING YOU A HANDSOME REWARD.
I HAVE SPOKEN.

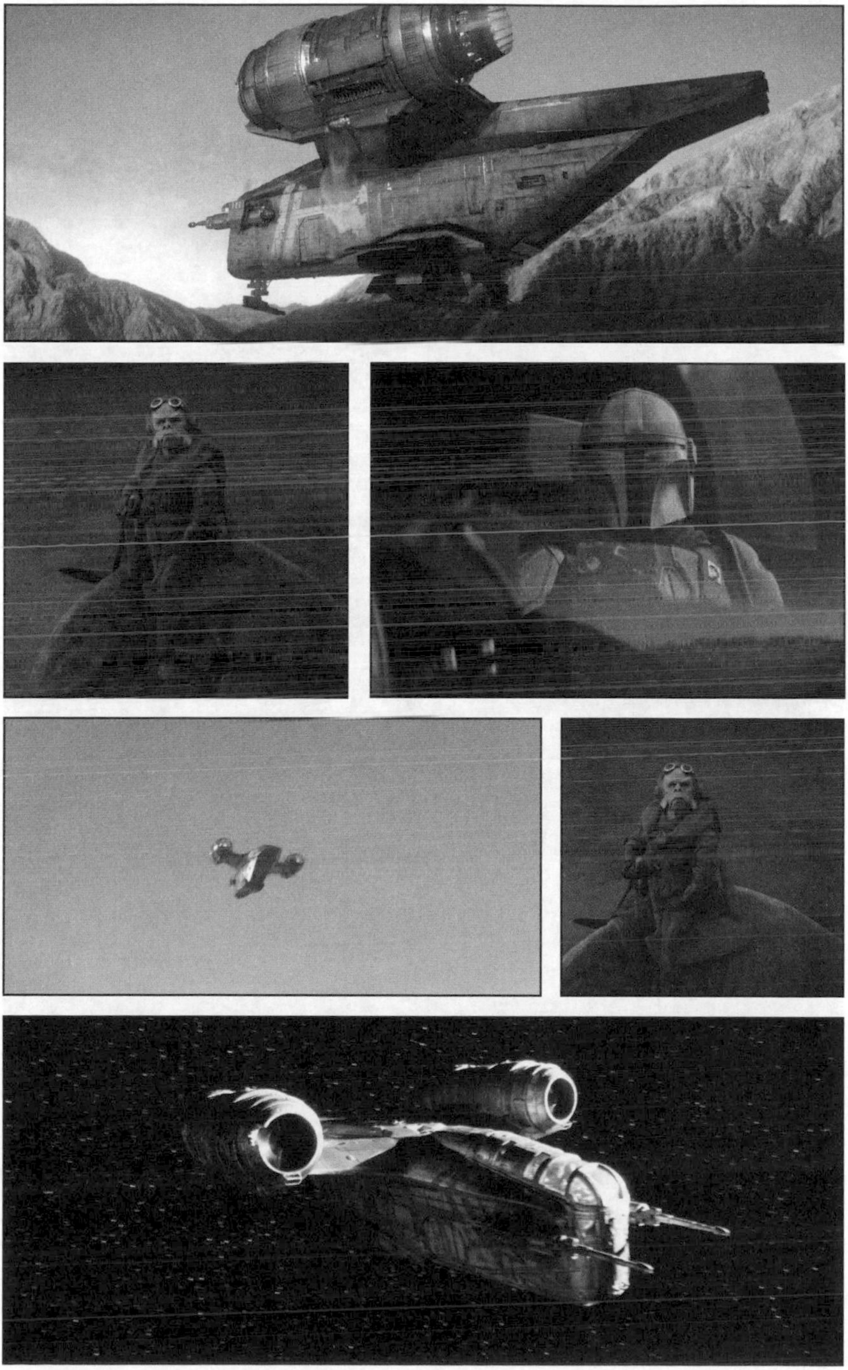

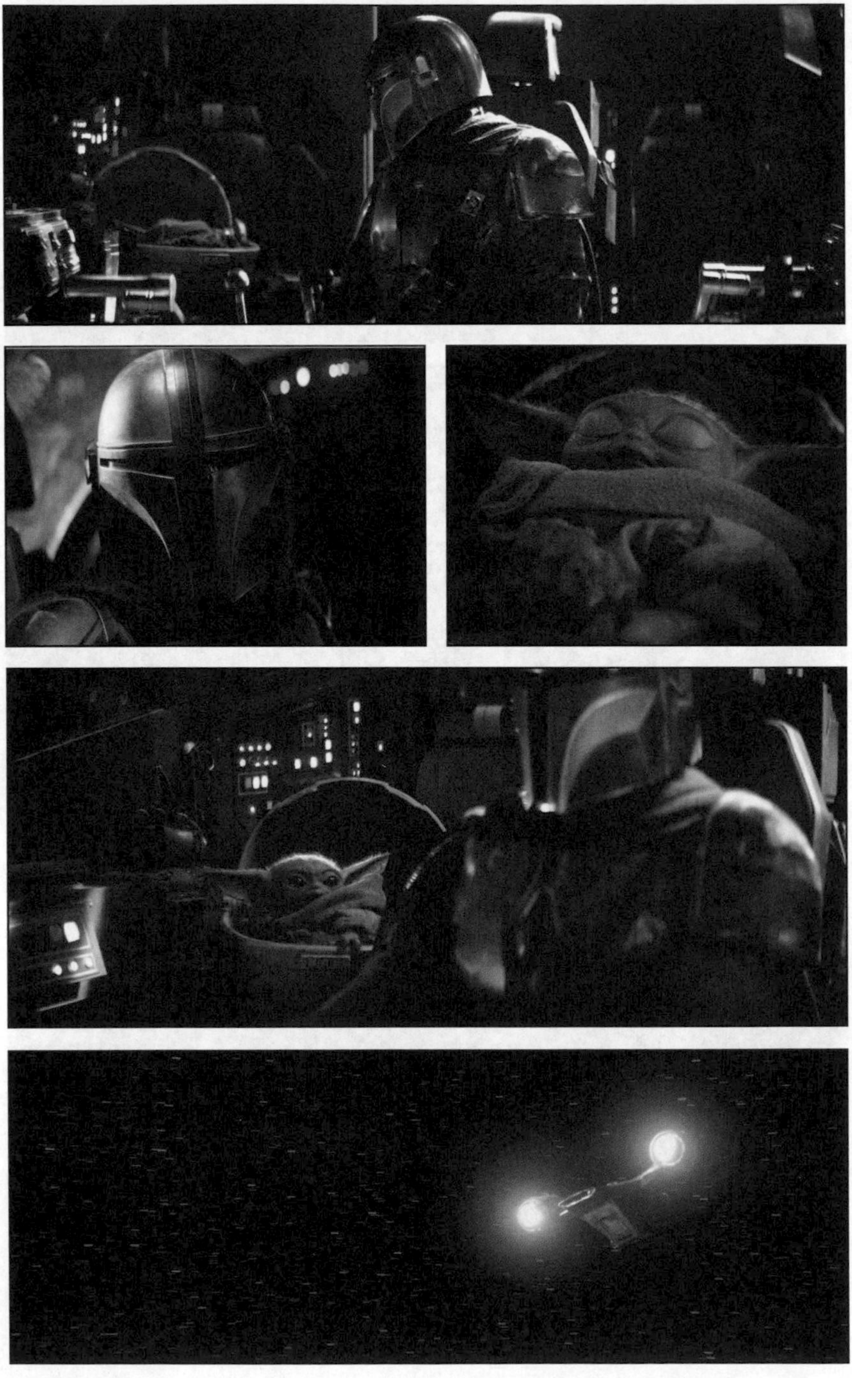

Chapter 3

THE SIN

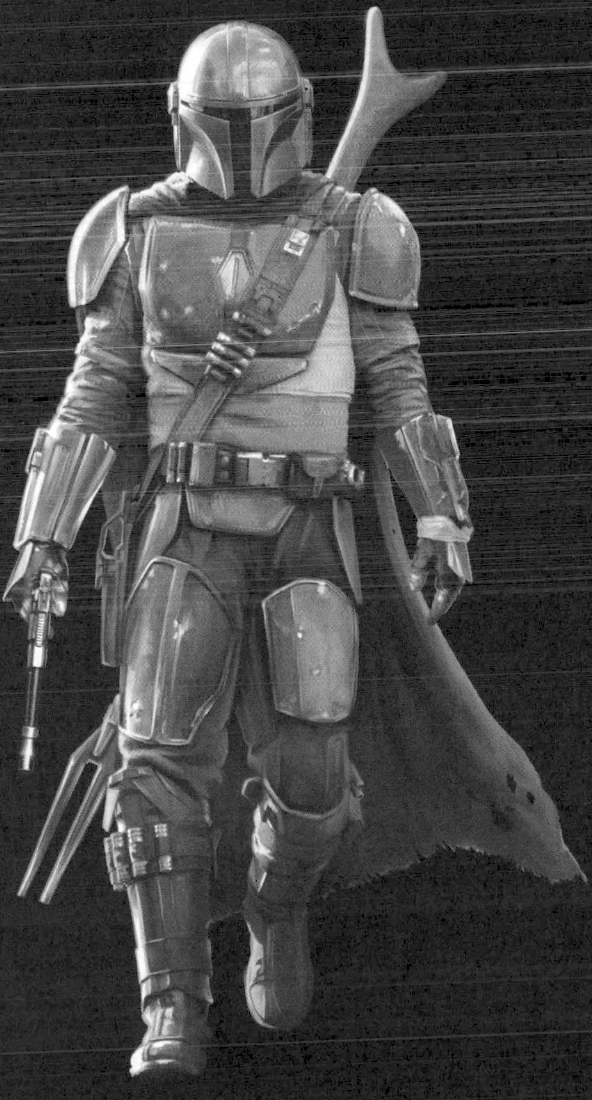

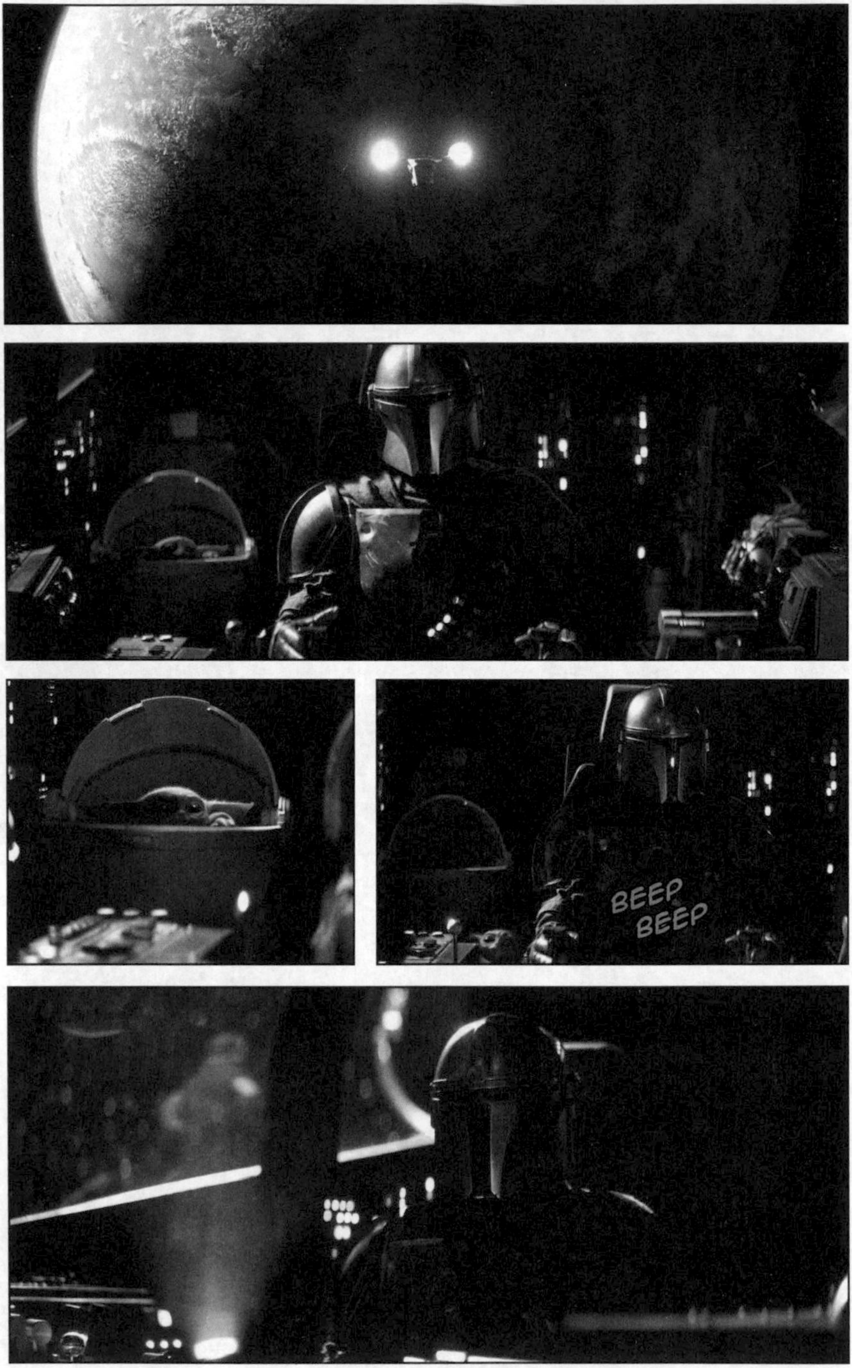
BEEP
BEEP

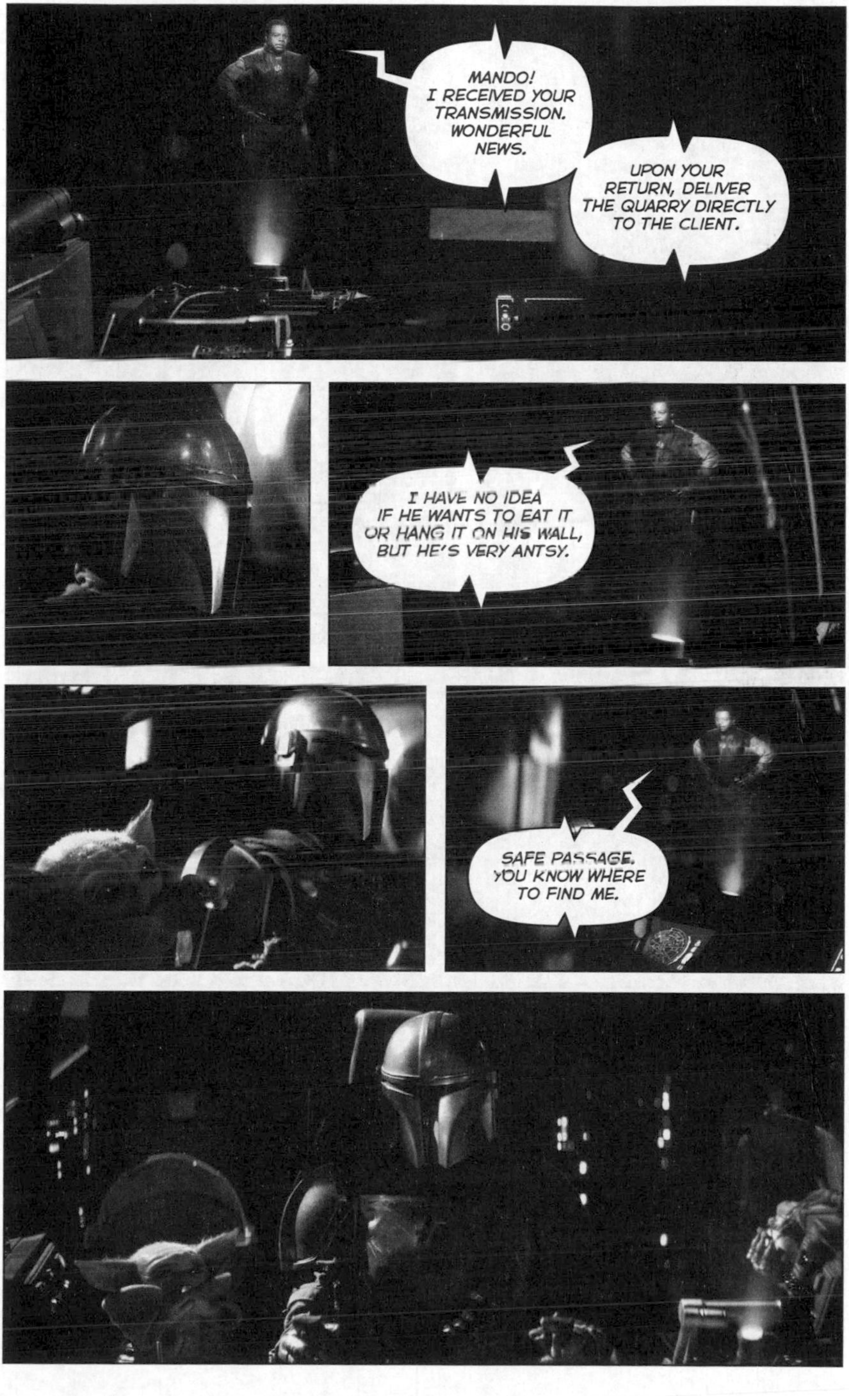
MANDO! I RECEIVED YOUR TRANSMISSION. WONDERFUL NEWS.
UPON YOUR RETURN, DELIVER THE QUARRY DIRECTLY TO THE CLIENT.
I HAVE NO IDEA IF HE WANTS TO EAT IT OR HANG IT ON HIS WALL, BUT HE'S VERY ANTSY.
SAFE PASSAGE. YOU KNOW WHERE TO FIND ME.

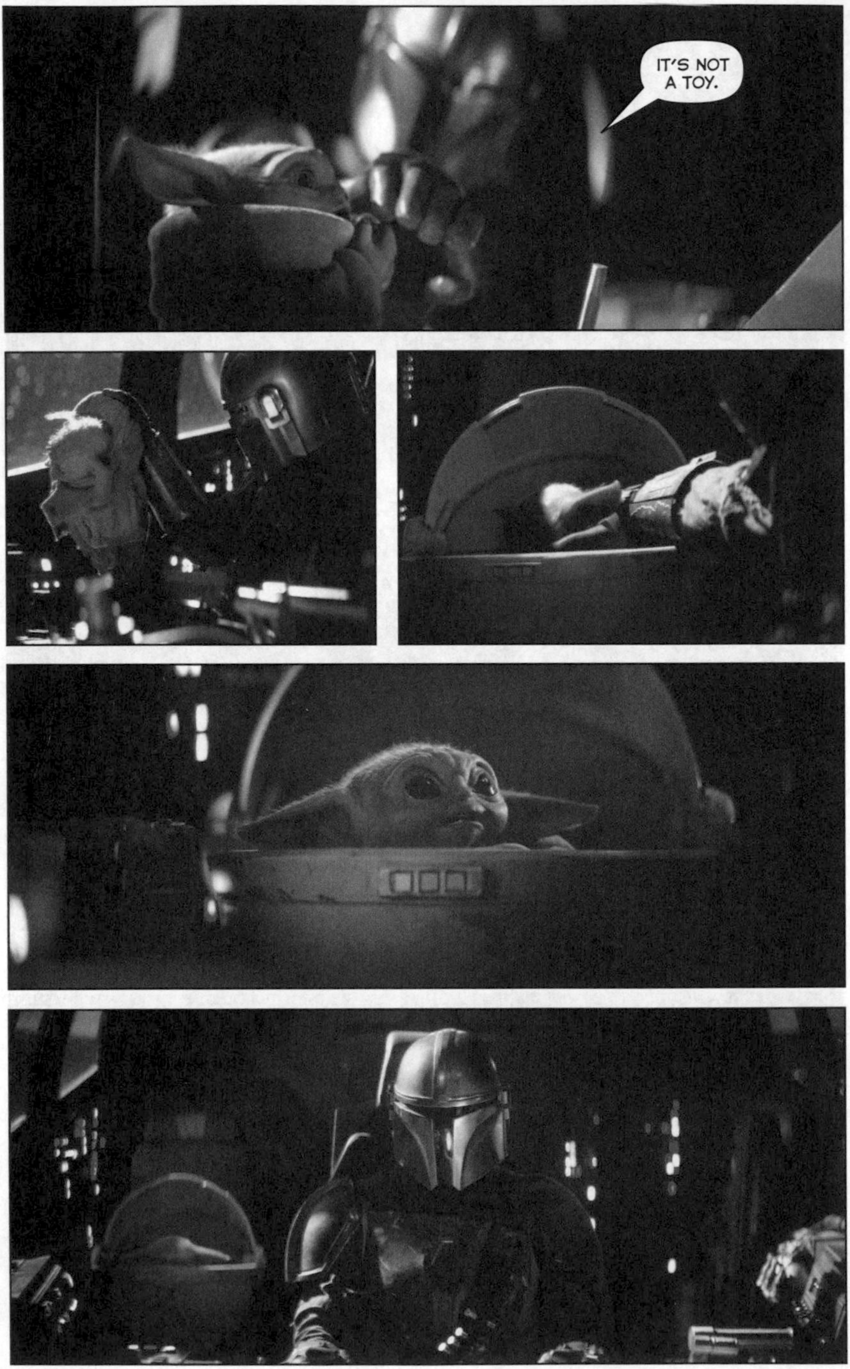
IT'S NOT
A TOY.

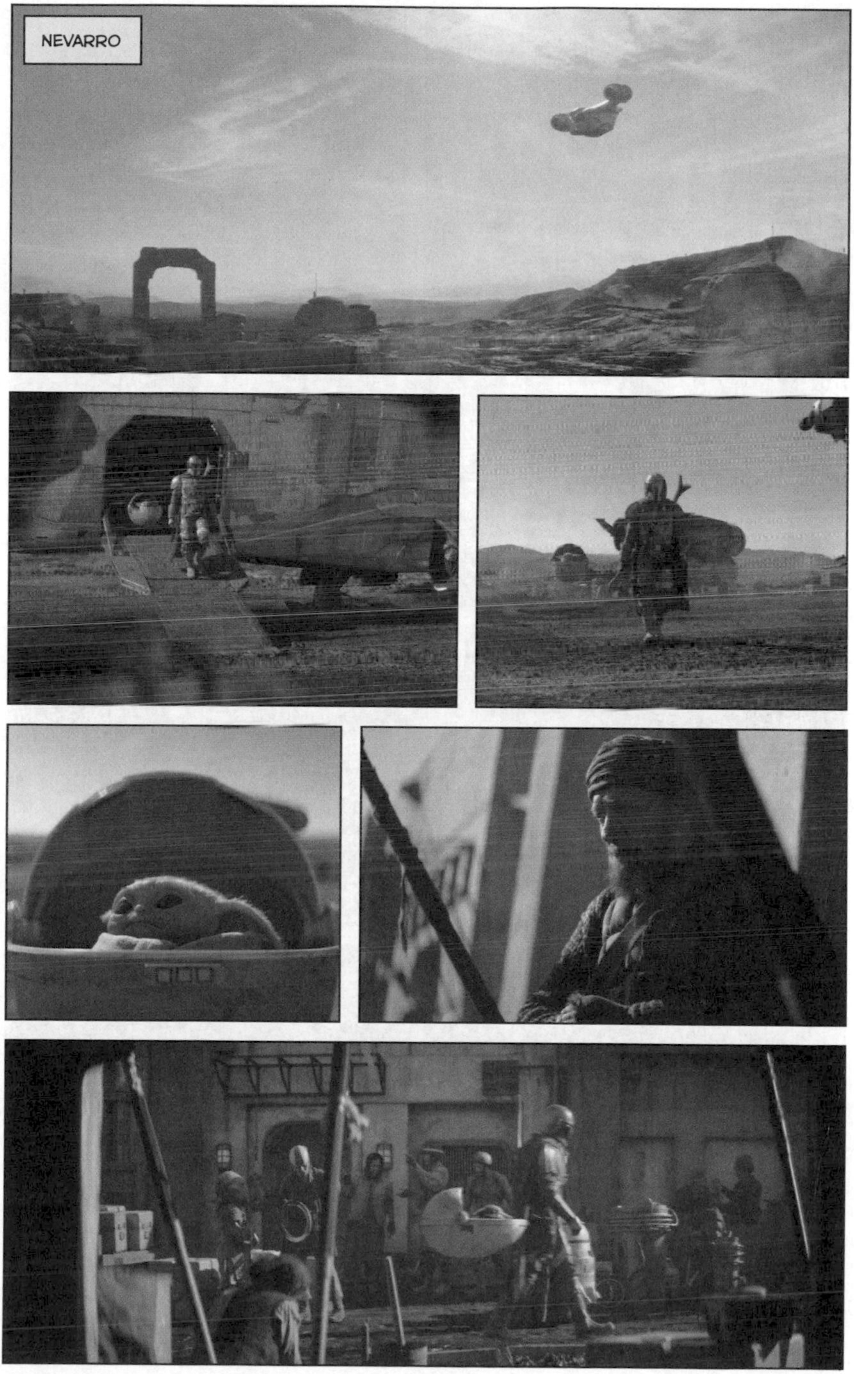
NEVARRO

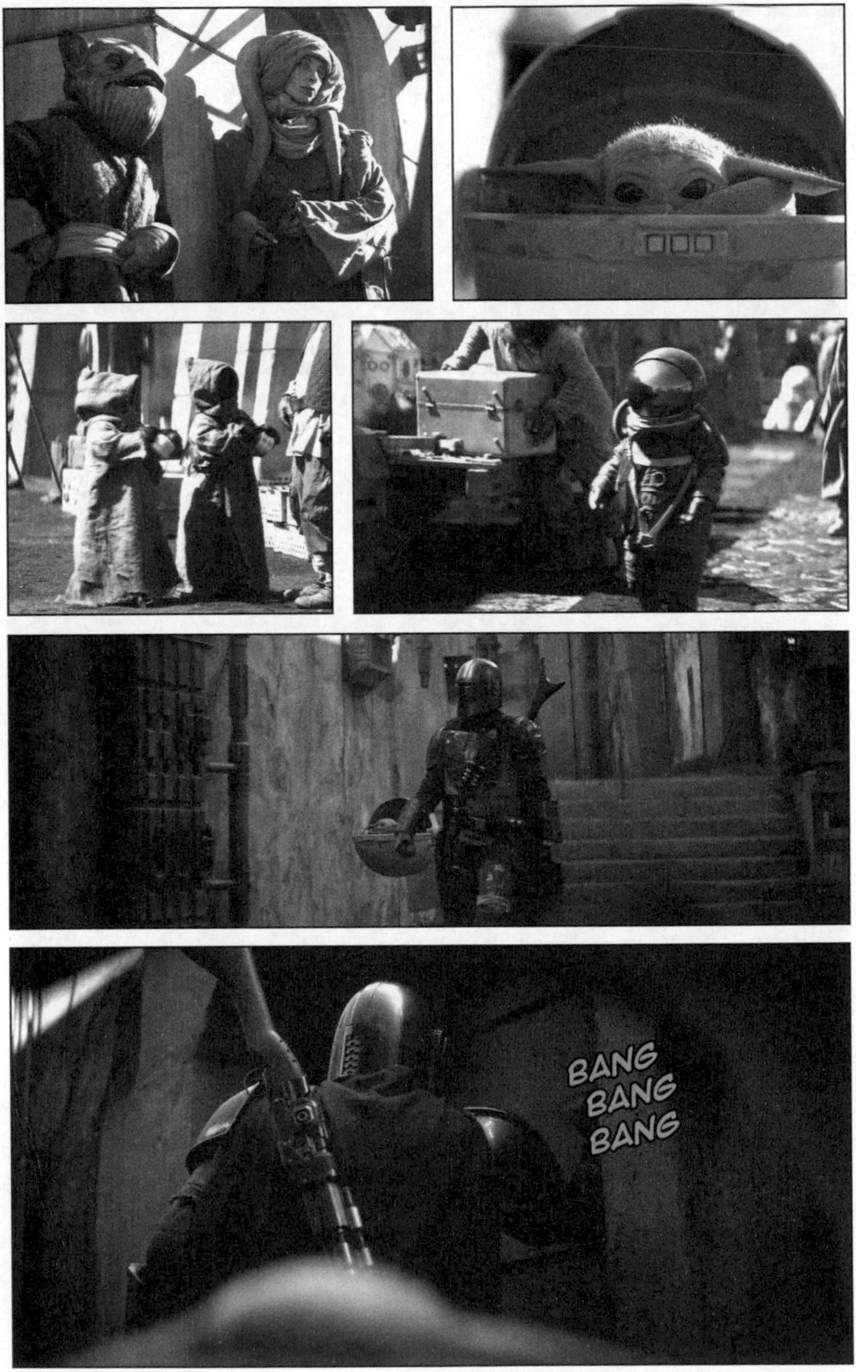
BANG
BANG
BANG

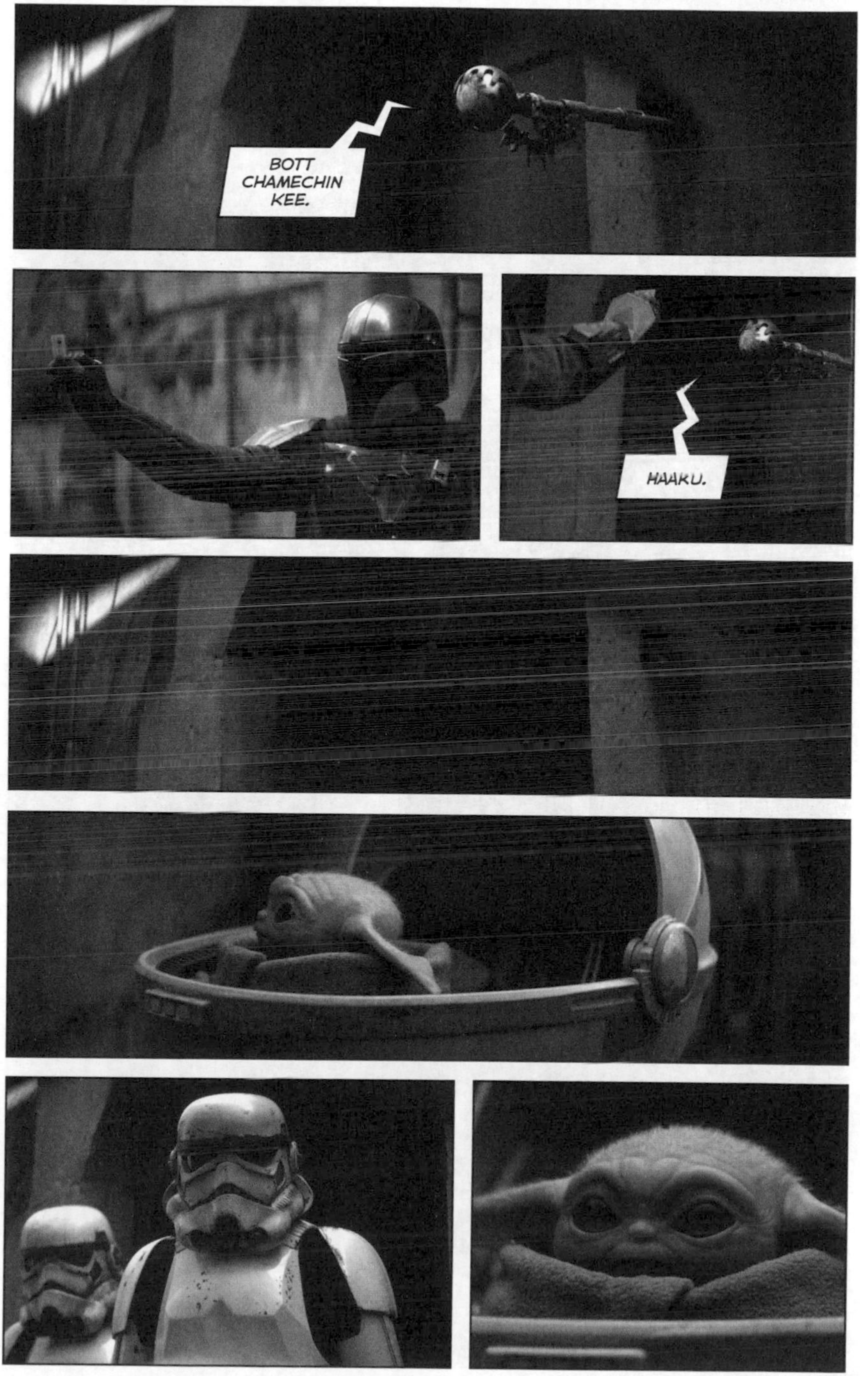
BOTT CHAMECHIN KEE.
HAARU.

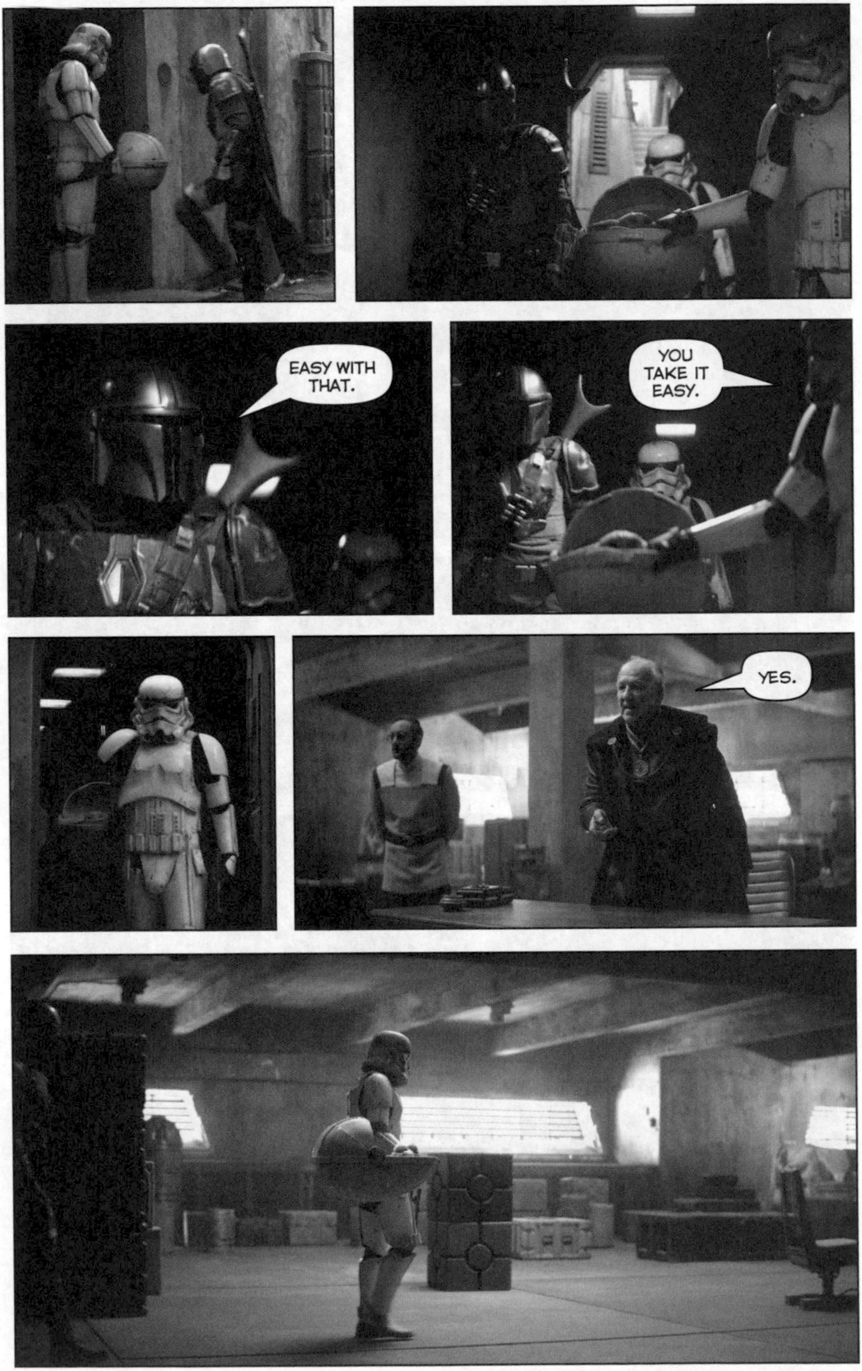
EASY WITH THAT.
YOU TAKE IT EASY.
YES.

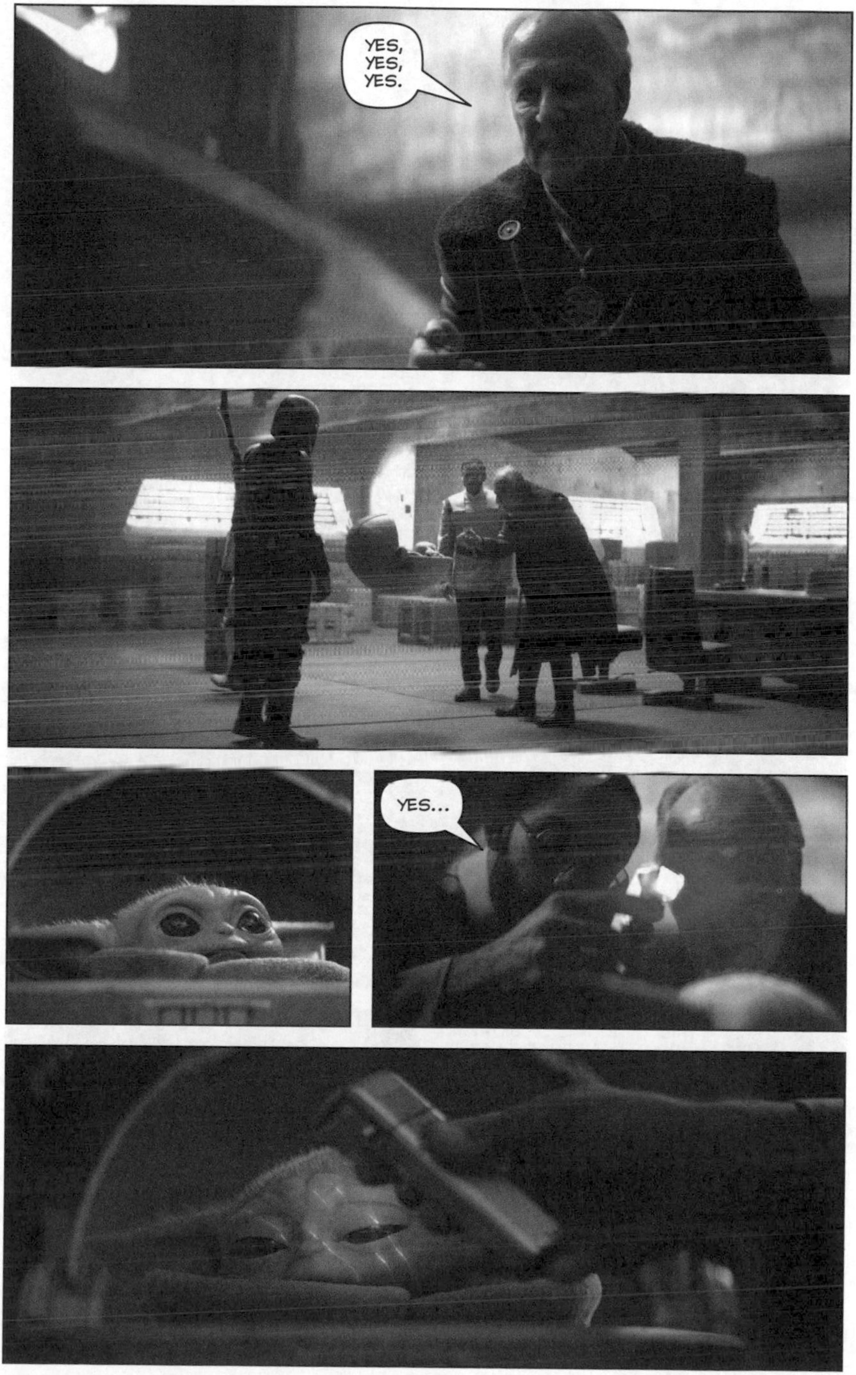
YES,
YES,
YES.
YES...

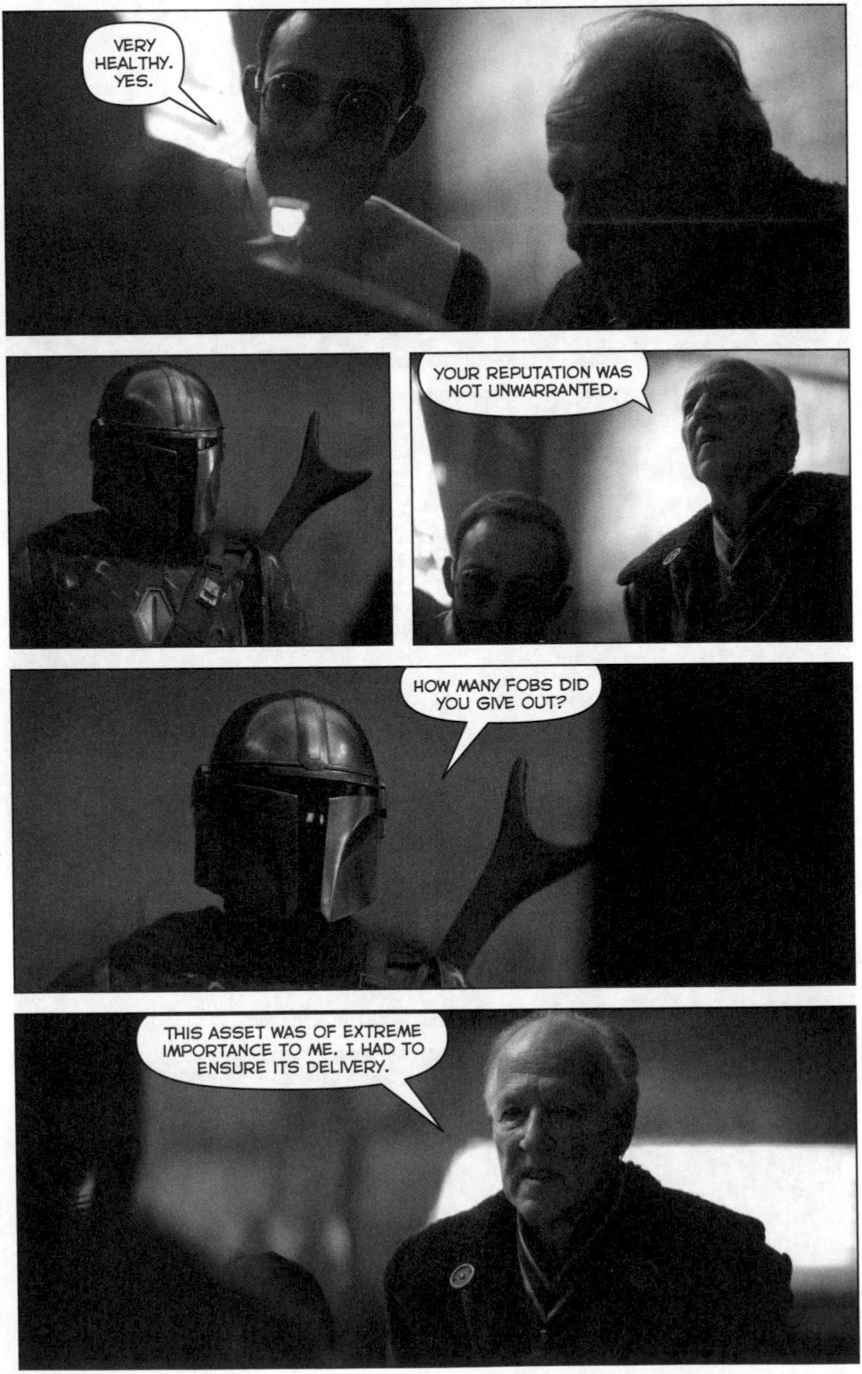
VERY HEALTHY. YES.
YOUR REPUTATION WAS NOT UNWARRANTED.
HOW MANY FOBS DID YOU GIVE OUT?
THIS ASSET WAS OF EXTREME IMPORTANCE TO ME. I HAD TO ENSURE ITS DELIVERY.

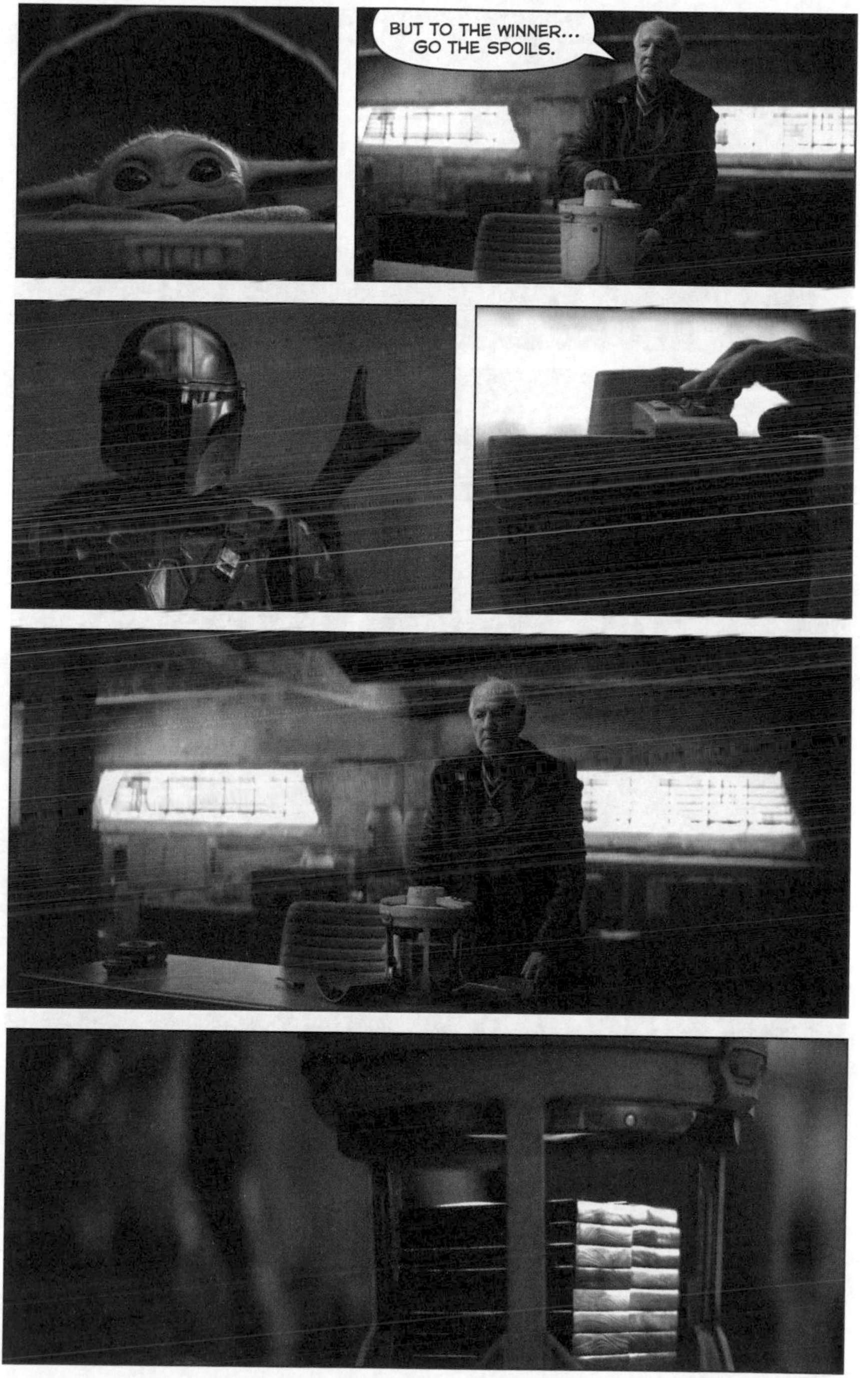
BUT TO THE WINNER...
GO THE SPOILS.

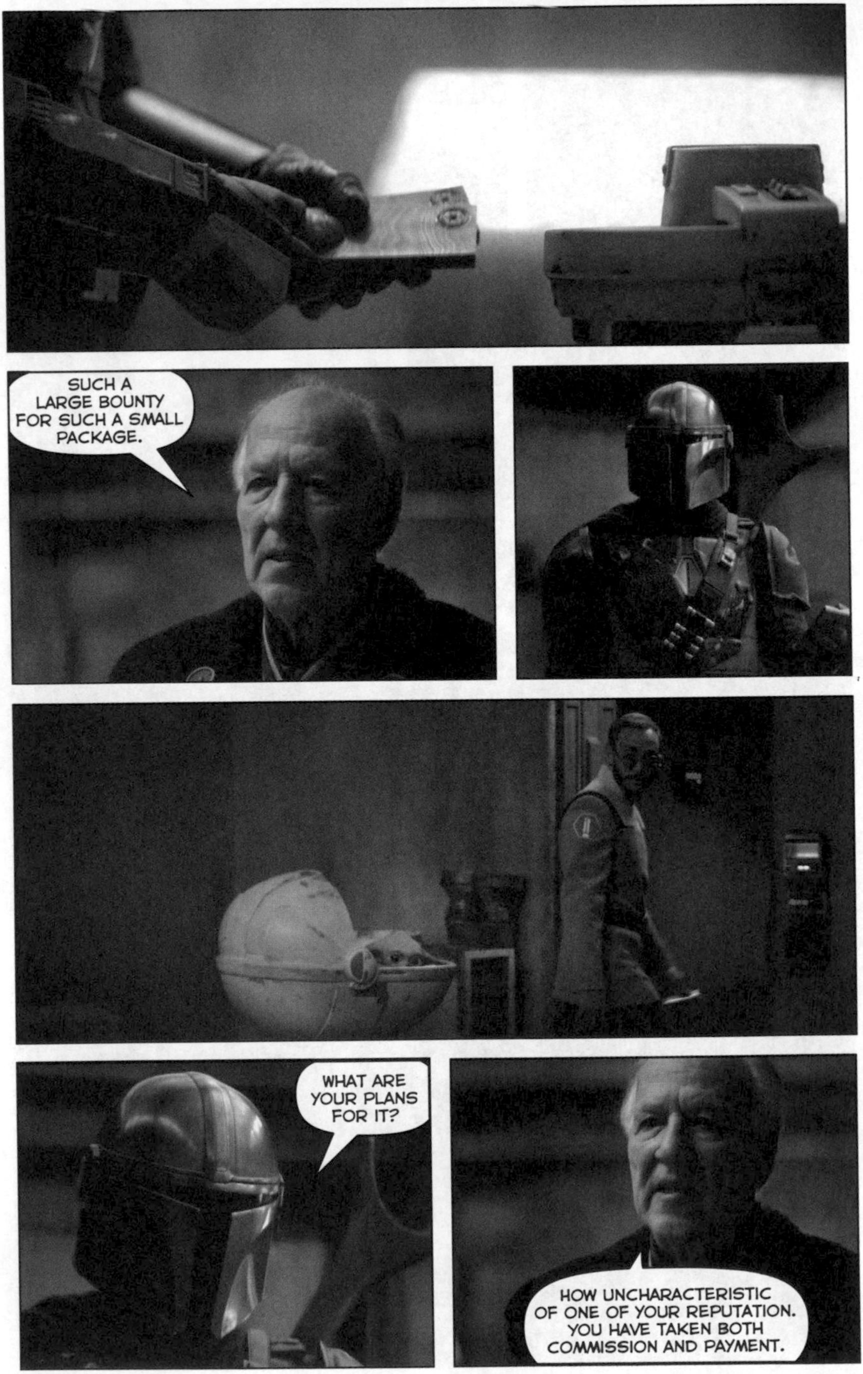
SUCH A LARGE BOUNTY FOR SUCH A SMALL PACKAGE.
WHAT ARE YOUR PLANS FOR IT?
HOW UNCHARACTERISTIC OF ONE OF YOUR REPUTATION. YOU HAVE TAKEN BOTH COMMISSION AND PAYMENT.

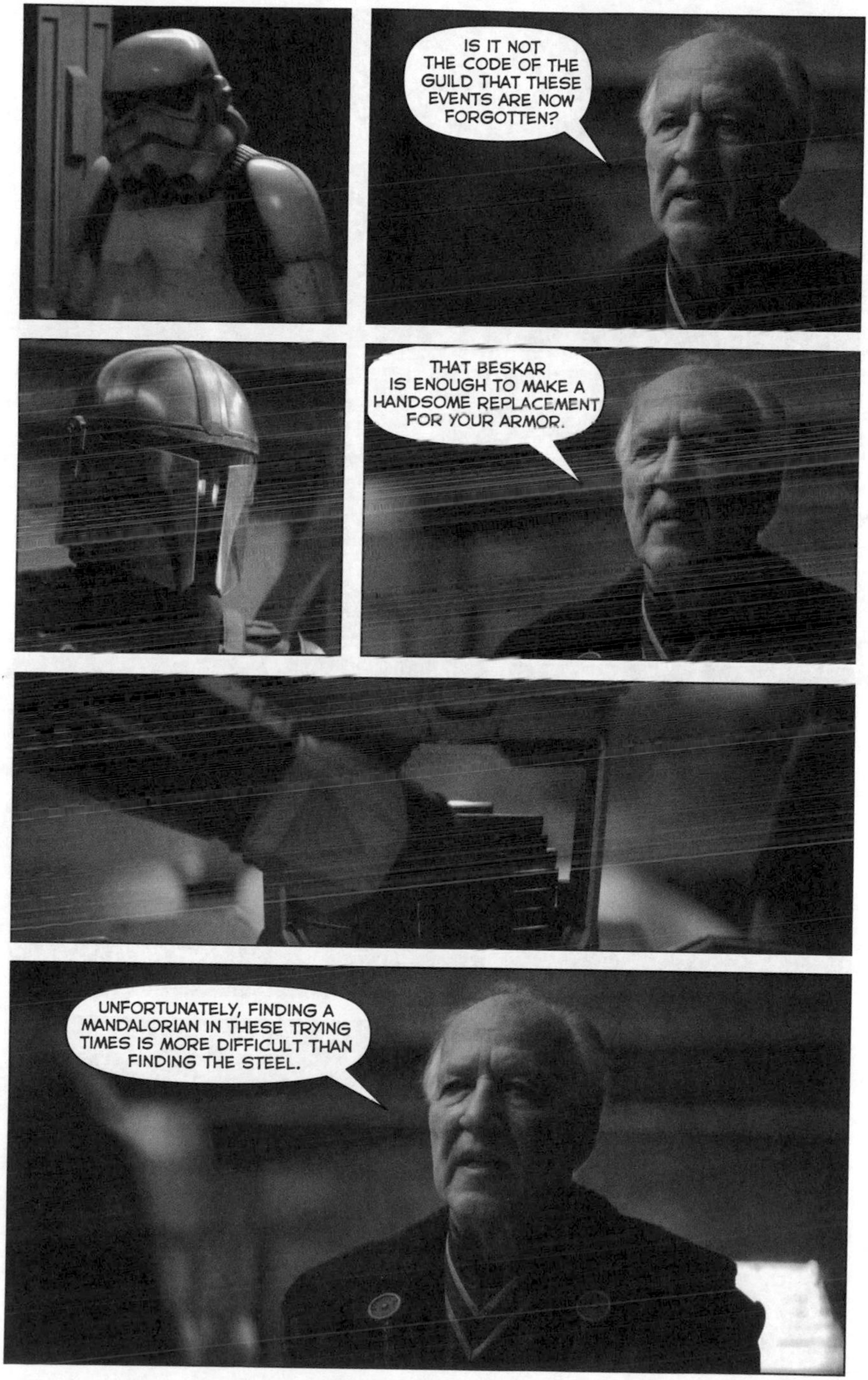
IS IT NOT THE CODE OF THE GUILD THAT THESE EVENTS ARE NOW FORGOTTEN?
THAT BESKAR IS ENOUGH TO MAKE A HANDSOME REPLACEMENT FOR YOUR ARMOR.
UNFORTUNATELY, FINDING A MANDALORIAN IN THESE TRYING TIMES IS MORE DIFFICULT THAN FINDING THE STEEL.

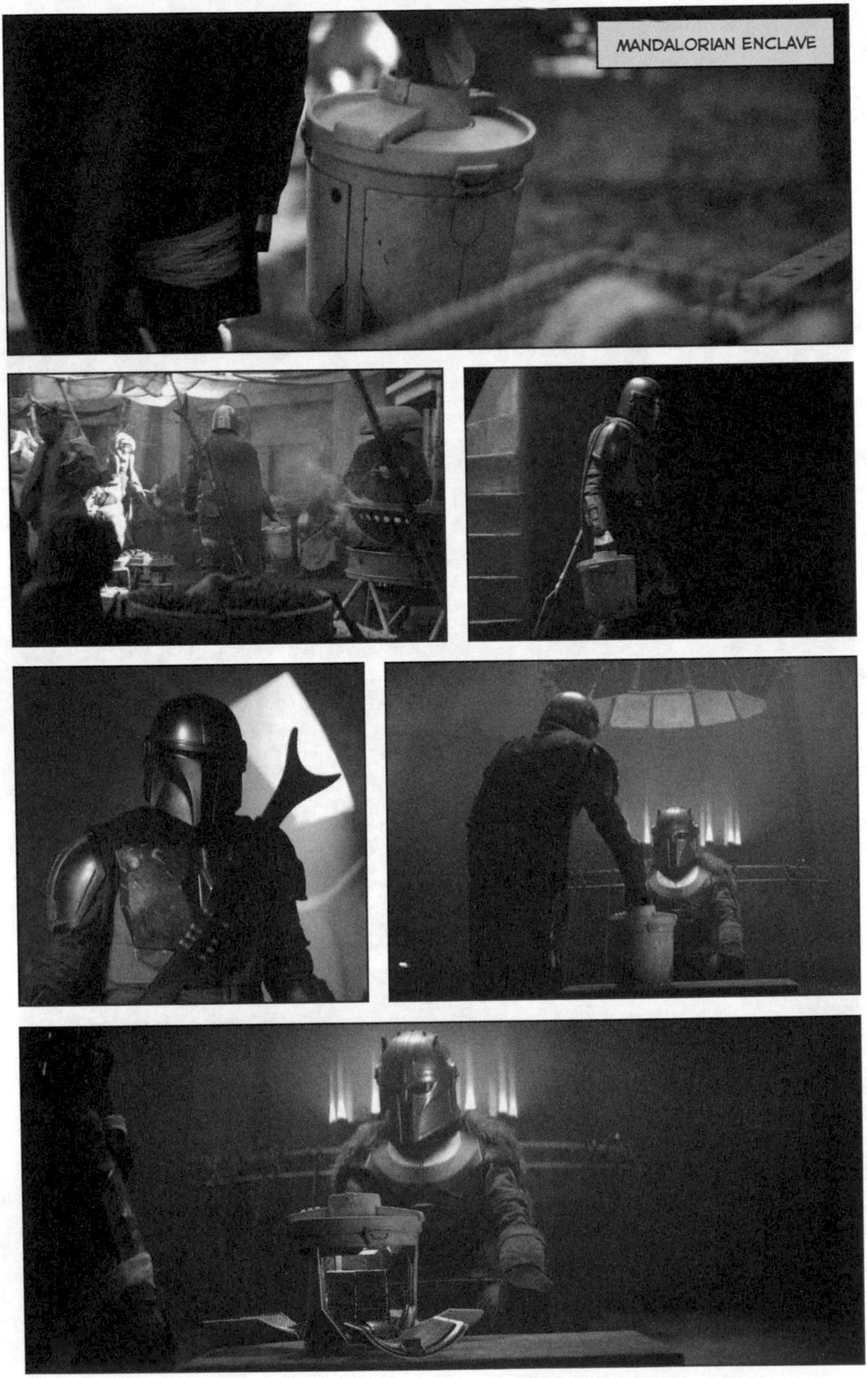
MANDALORIAN ENCLAVE

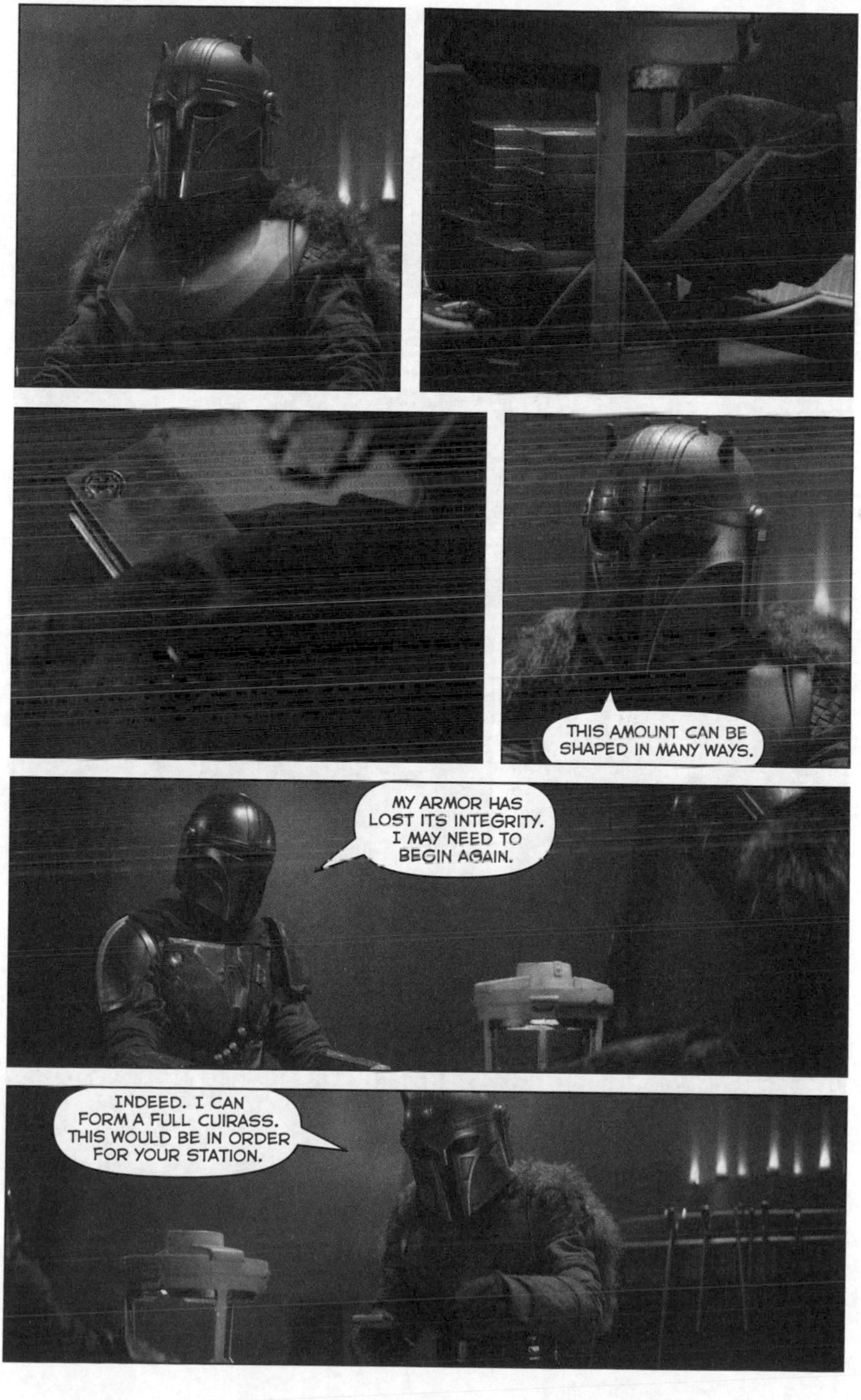
THIS AMOUNT CAN BE SHAPED IN MANY WAYS.
MY ARMOR HAS LOST ITS INTEGRITY. I MAY NEED TO BEGIN AGAIN.
INDEED. I CAN FORM A FULL CUIRASS. THIS WOULD BE IN ORDER FOR YOUR STATION.

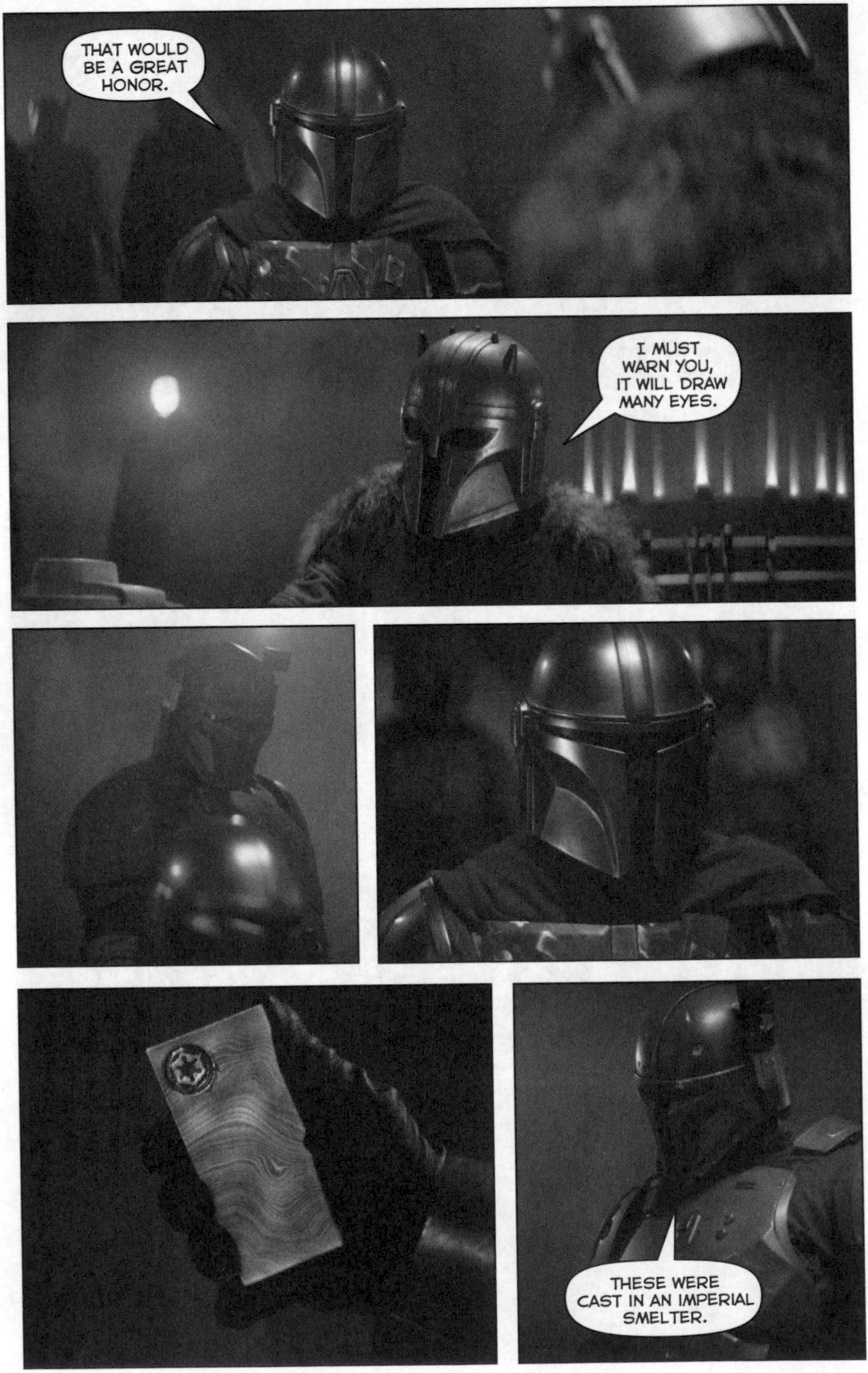
THAT WOULD BE A GREAT HONOR.
I MUST WARN YOU, IT WILL DRAW MANY EYES.
THESE WERE CAST IN AN IMPERIAL SMELTER.

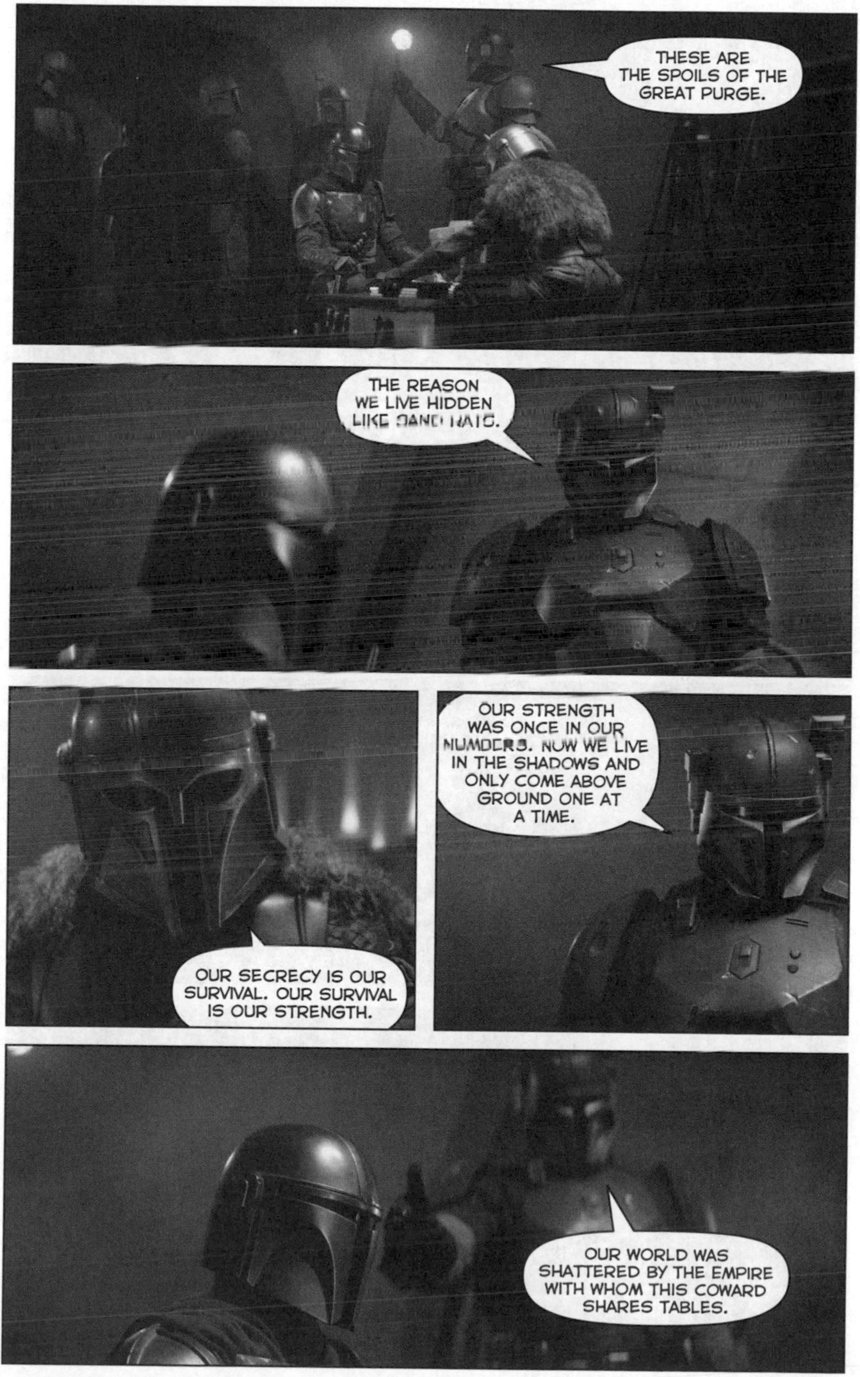
THESE ARE THE SPOILS OF THE GREAT PURGE.
THE REASON WE LIVE HIDDEN LIKE SAND RATS.
OUR SECRECY IS OUR SURVIVAL. OUR SURVIVAL IS OUR STRENGTH.
OUR STRENGTH WAS ONCE IN OUR NUMBERS. NOW WE LIVE IN THE SHADOWS AND ONLY COME ABOVE GROUND ONE AT A TIME.
OUR WORLD WAS SHATTERED BY THE EMPIRE WITH WHOM THIS COWARD SHARES TABLES.

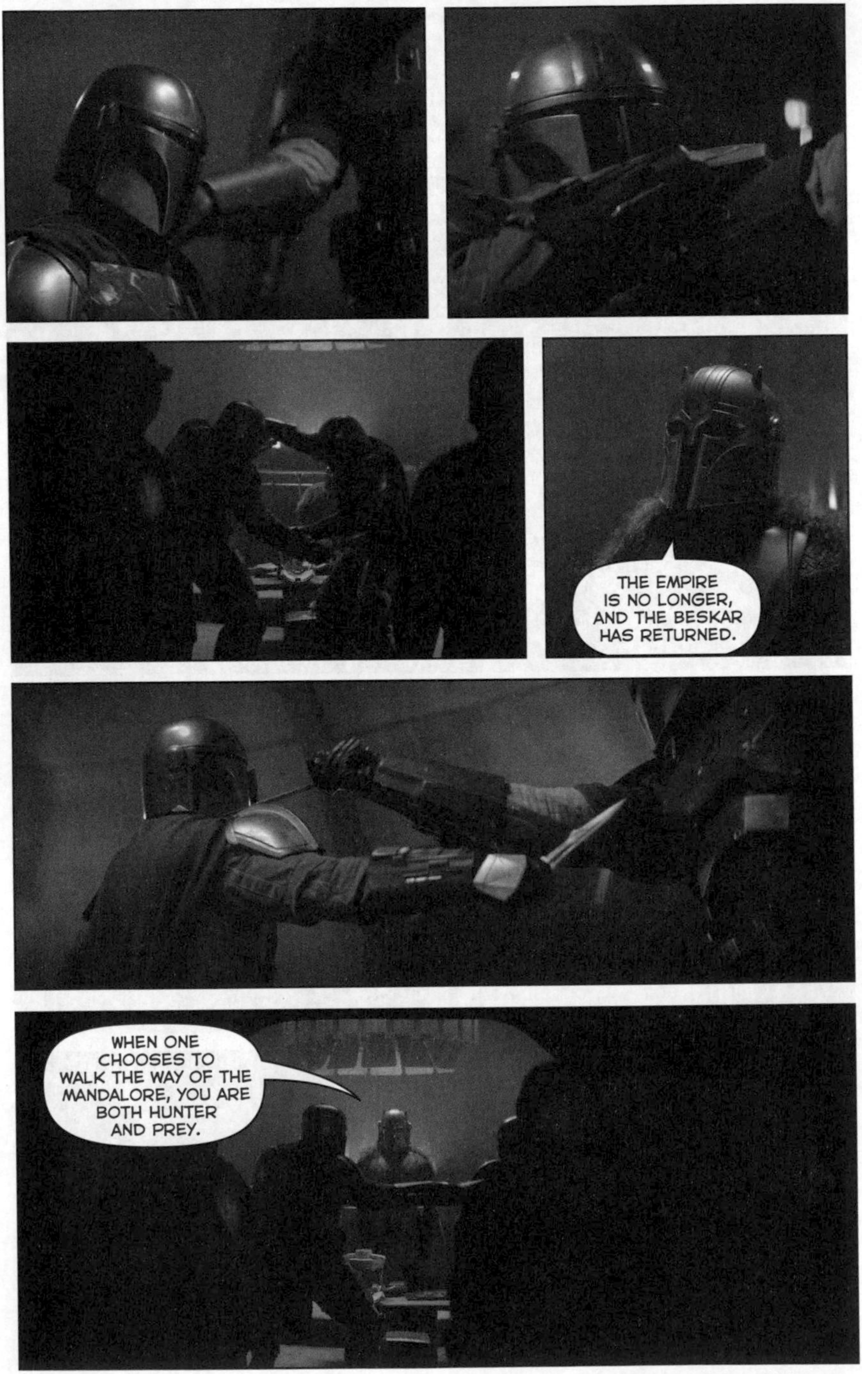
THE EMPIRE IS NO LONGER, AND THE BESKAR HAS RETURNED.
WHEN ONE CHOOSES TO WALK THE WAY OF THE MANDALORE, YOU ARE BOTH HUNTER AND PREY.

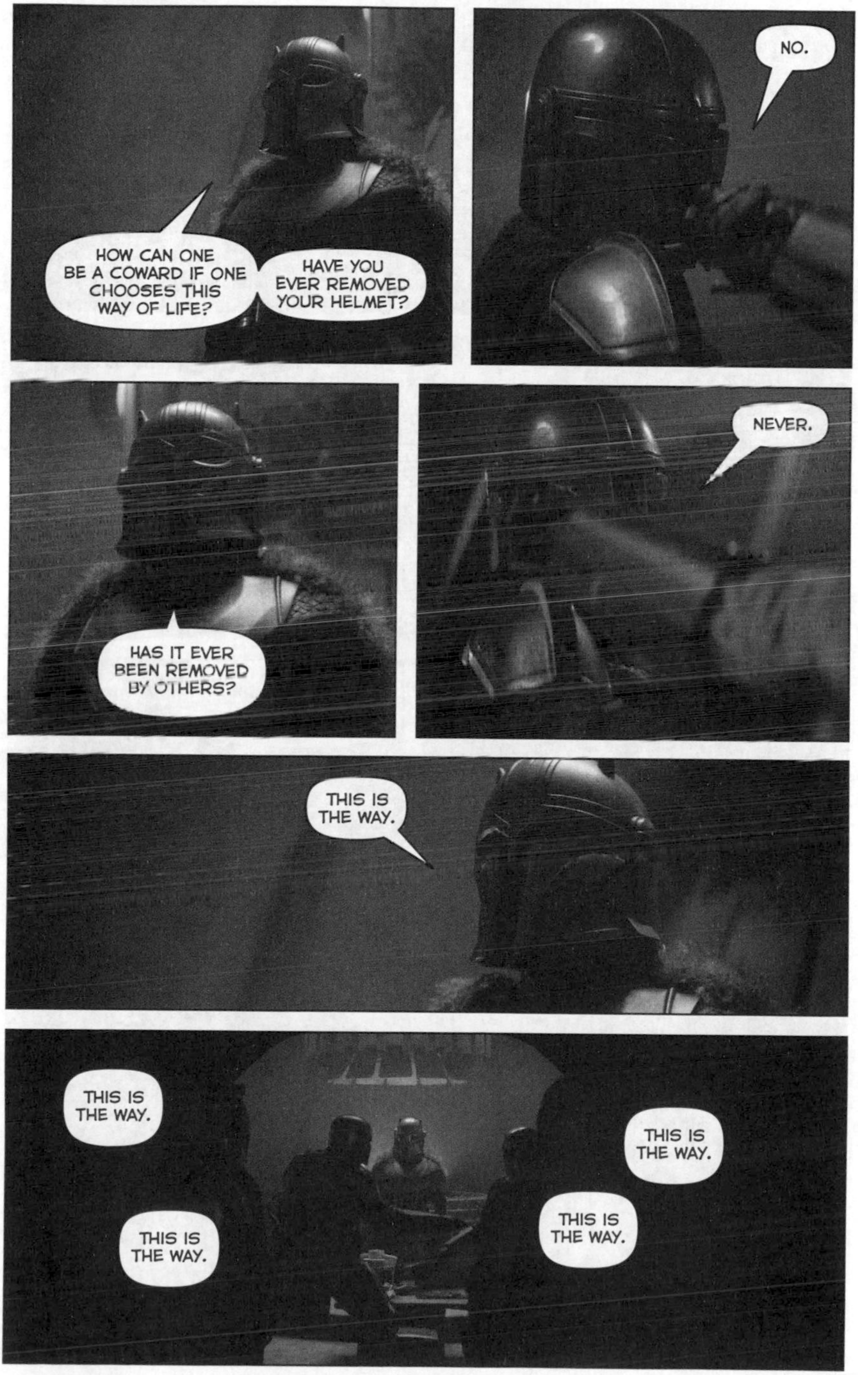
HOW CAN ONE BE A COWARD IF ONE CHOOSES THIS WAY OF LIFE?
HAVE YOU EVER REMOVED YOUR HELMET?
NO.
HAS IT EVER BEEN REMOVED BY OTHERS?
NEVER.
THIS IS THE WAY.
THIS IS THE WAY.
THIS IS THE WAY.
THIS IS THE WAY.
THIS IS THE WAY.

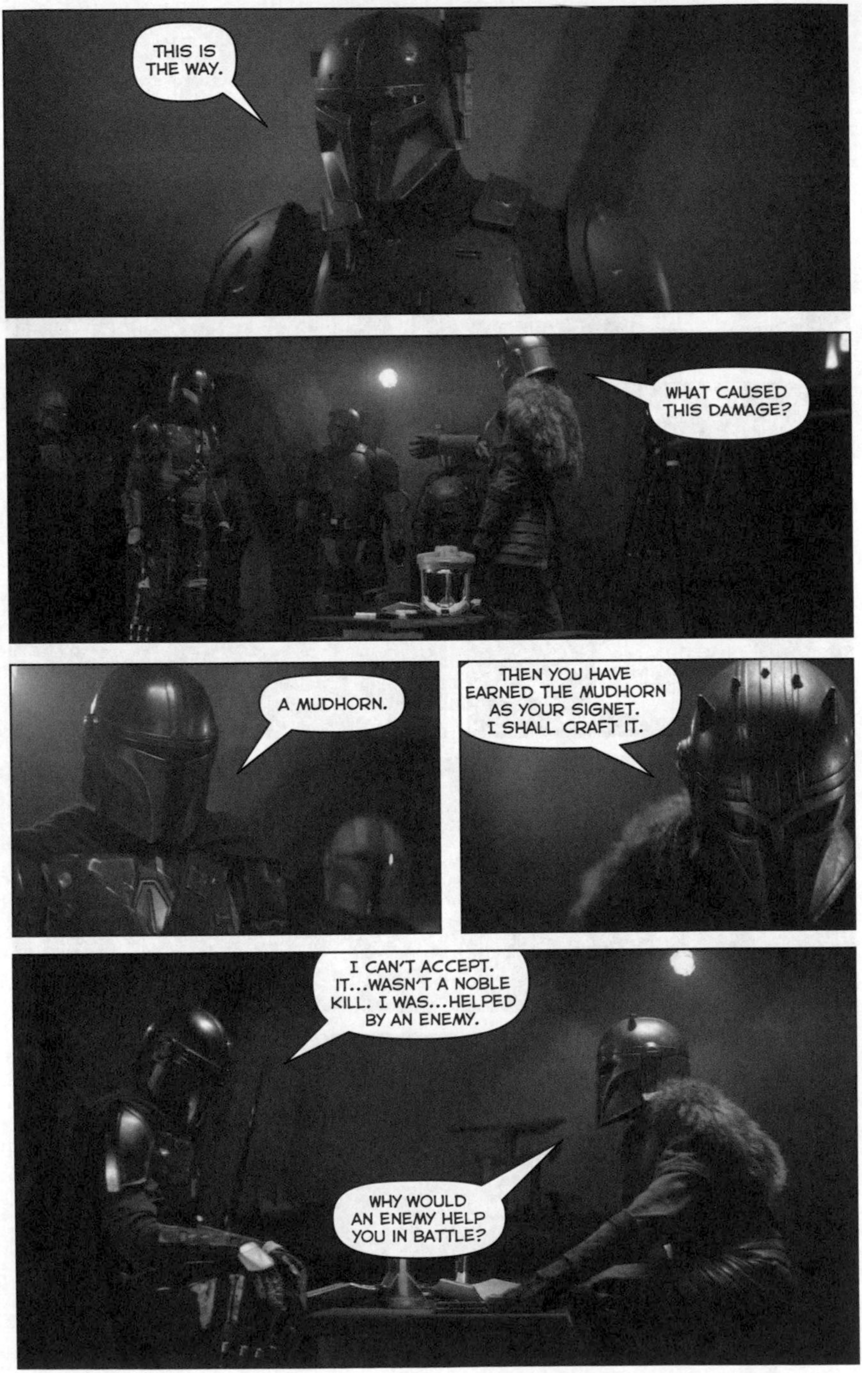
THIS IS THE WAY.
WHAT CAUSED THIS DAMAGE?
A MUDHORN.
THEN YOU HAVE EARNED THE MUDHORN AS YOUR SIGNET. I SHALL CRAFT IT.
I CAN'T ACCEPT. IT...WASN'T A NOBLE KILL. I WAS...HELPED BY AN ENEMY.
WHY WOULD AN ENEMY HELP YOU IN BATTLE?

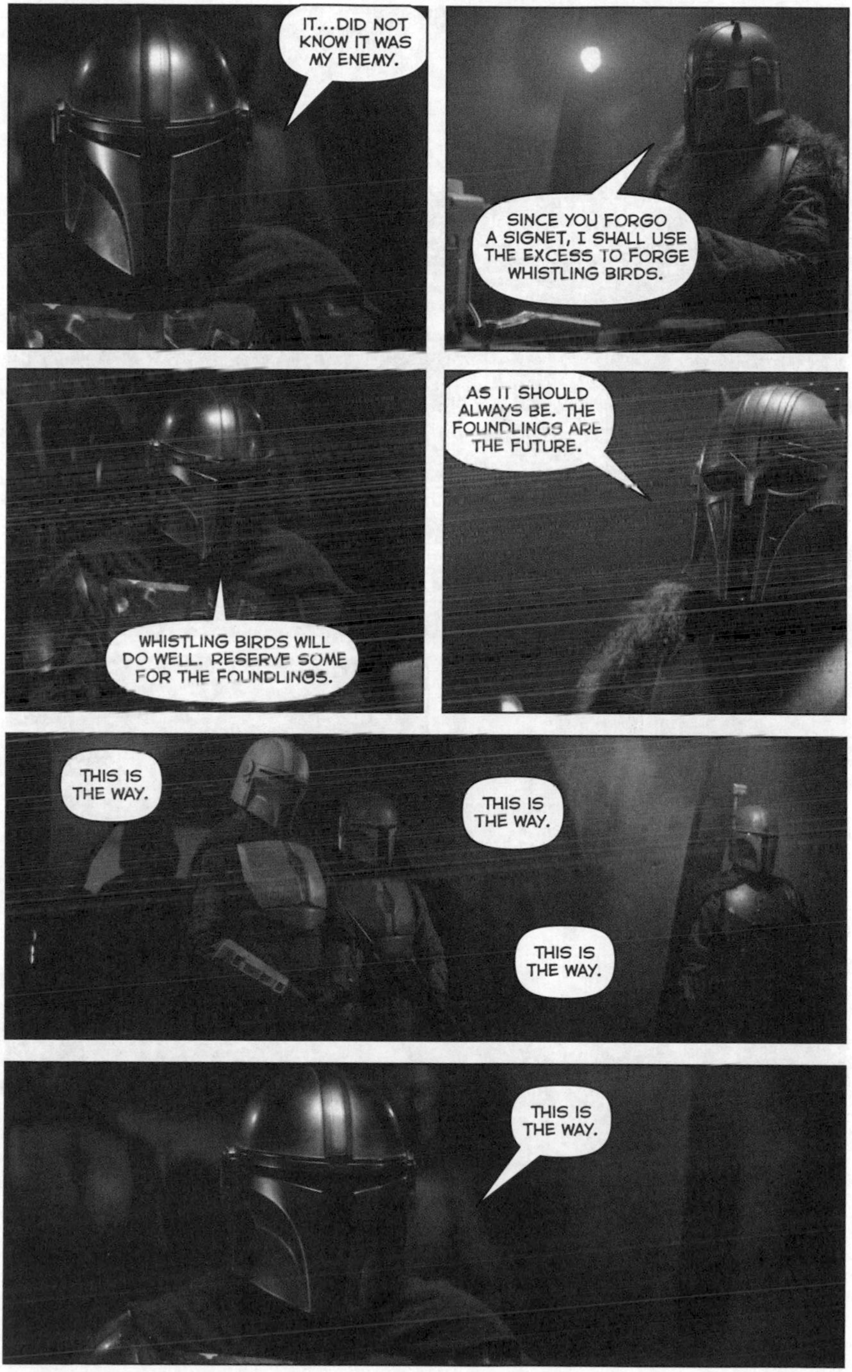
IT...DID NOT KNOW IT WAS MY ENEMY.
SINCE YOU FORGO A SIGNET, I SHALL USE THE EXCESS TO FORGE WHISTLING BIRDS.
WHISTLING BIRDS WILL DO WELL. RESERVE SOME FOR THE FOUNDLINGS.
AS IT SHOULD ALWAYS BE. THE FOUNDLINGS ARE THE FUTURE.
THIS IS THE WAY.
THIS IS THE WAY.
THIS IS THE WAY.
THIS IS THE WAY.

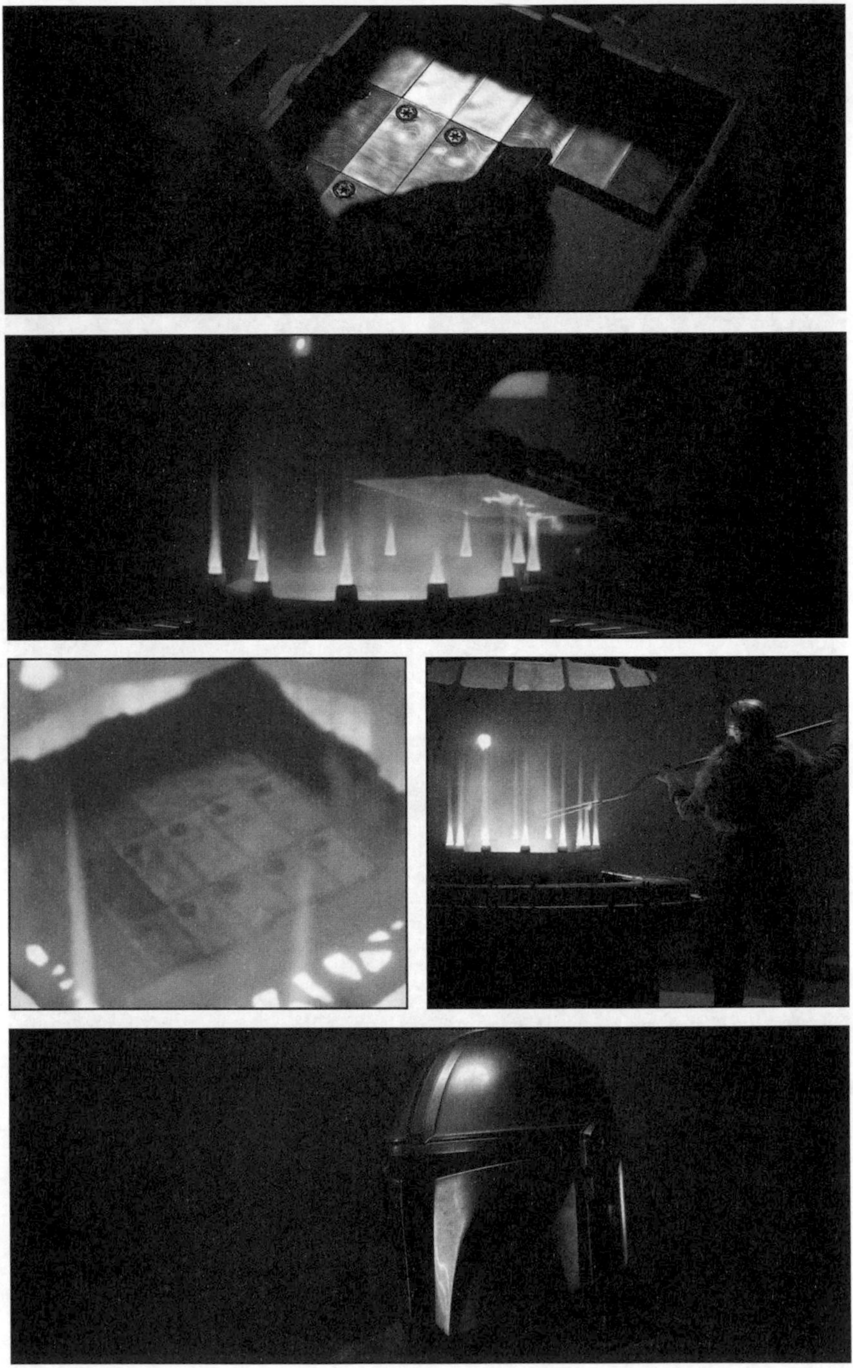

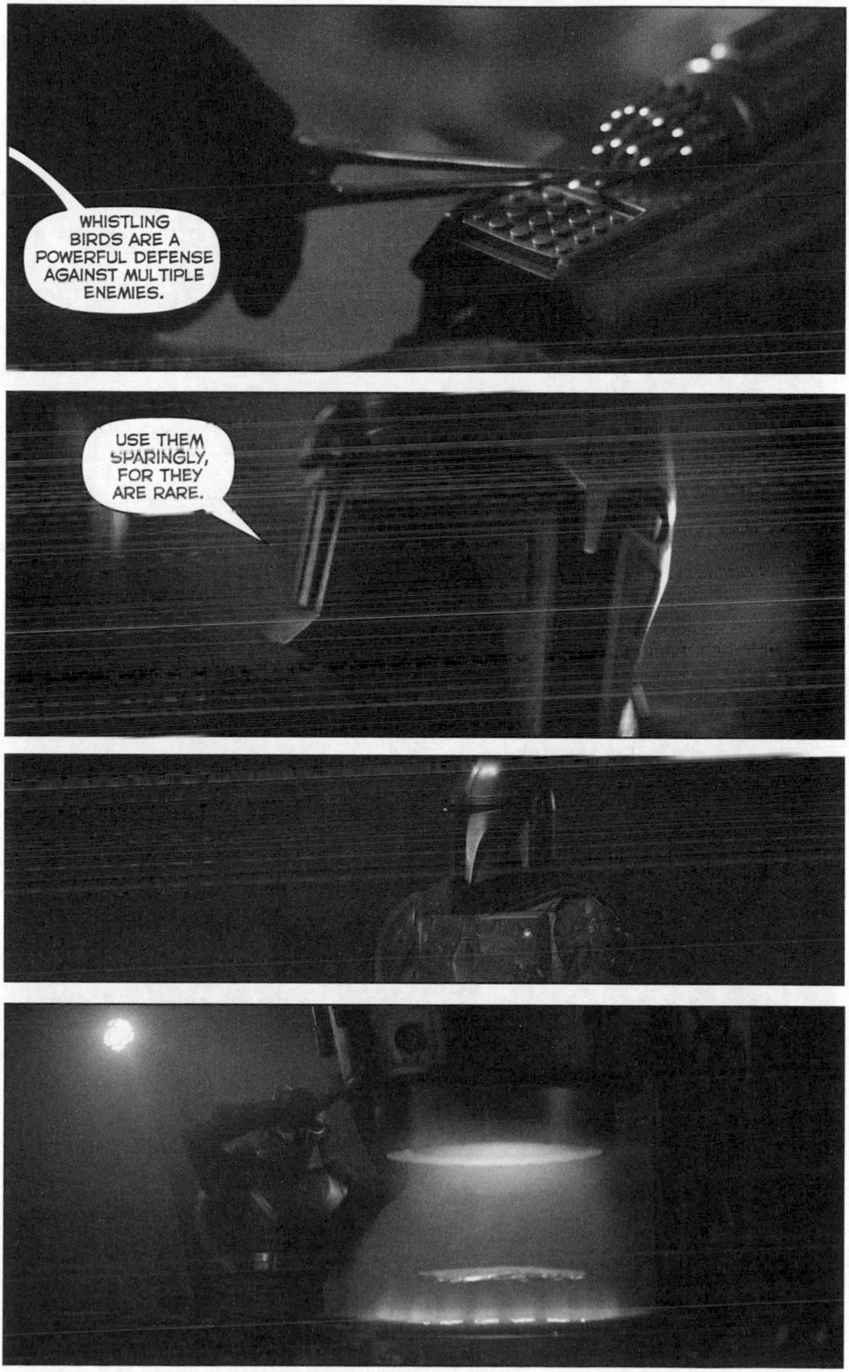
WHISTLING BIRDS ARE A POWERFUL DEFENSE AGAINST MULTIPLE ENEMIES.
USE THEM SPARINGLY, FOR THEY ARE RARE.

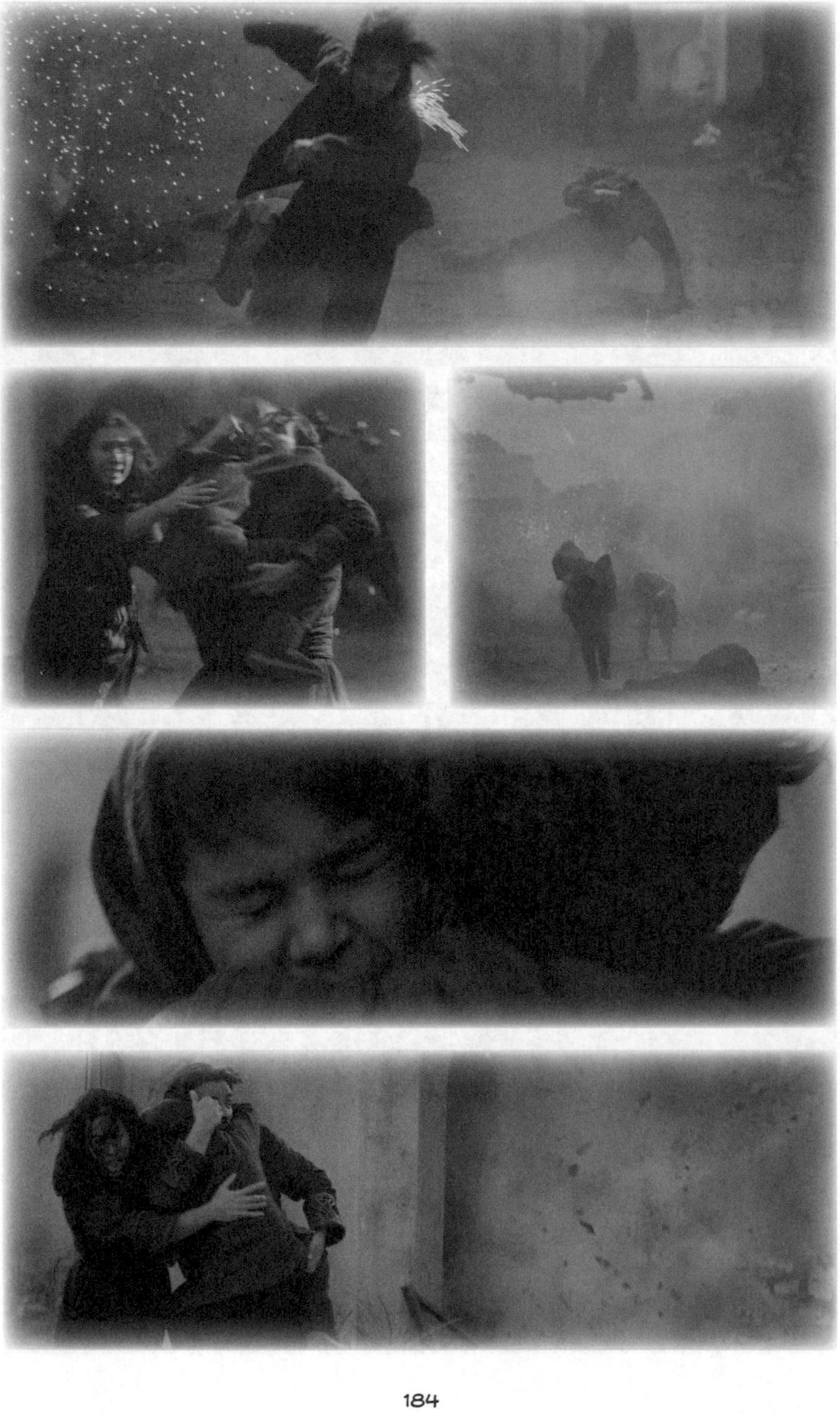

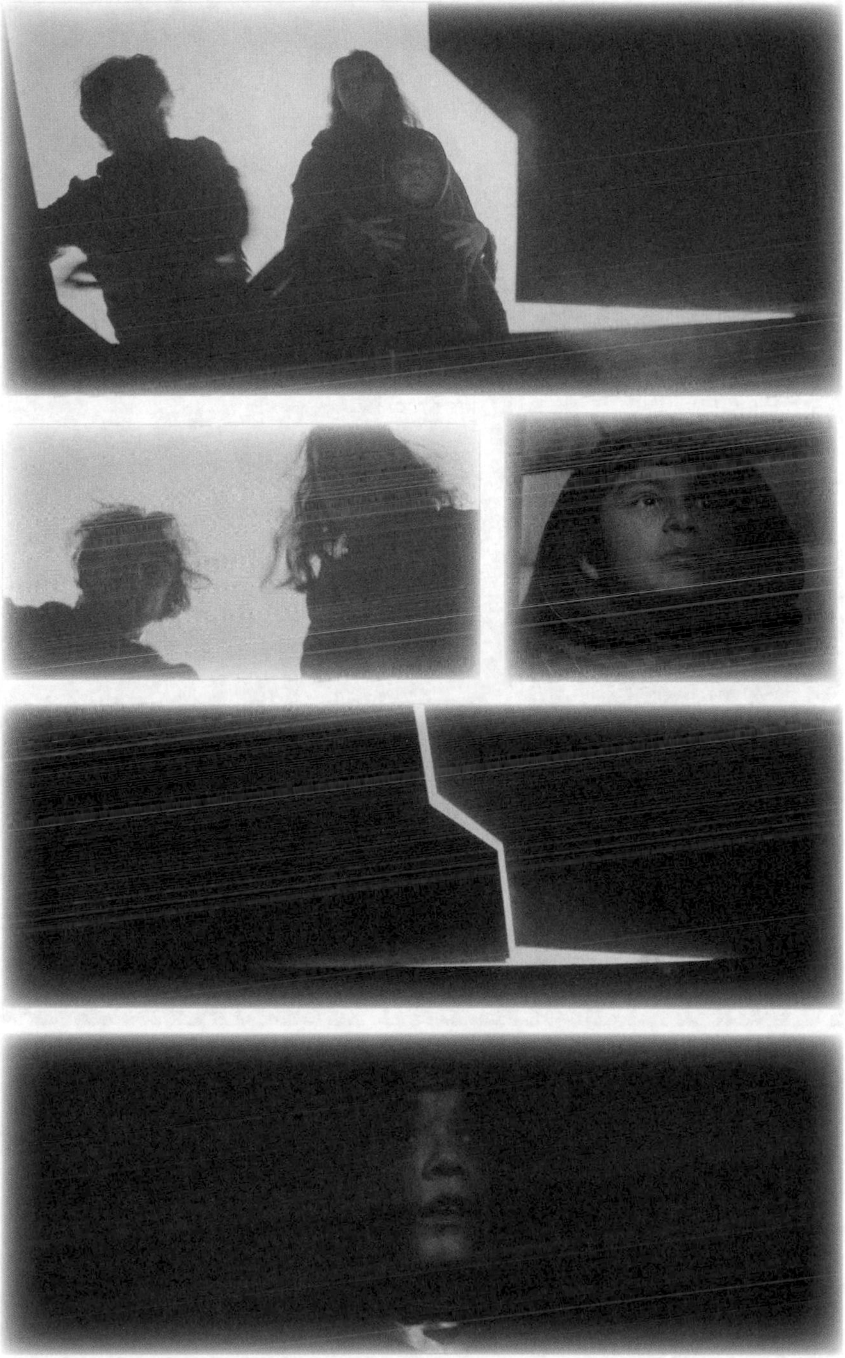

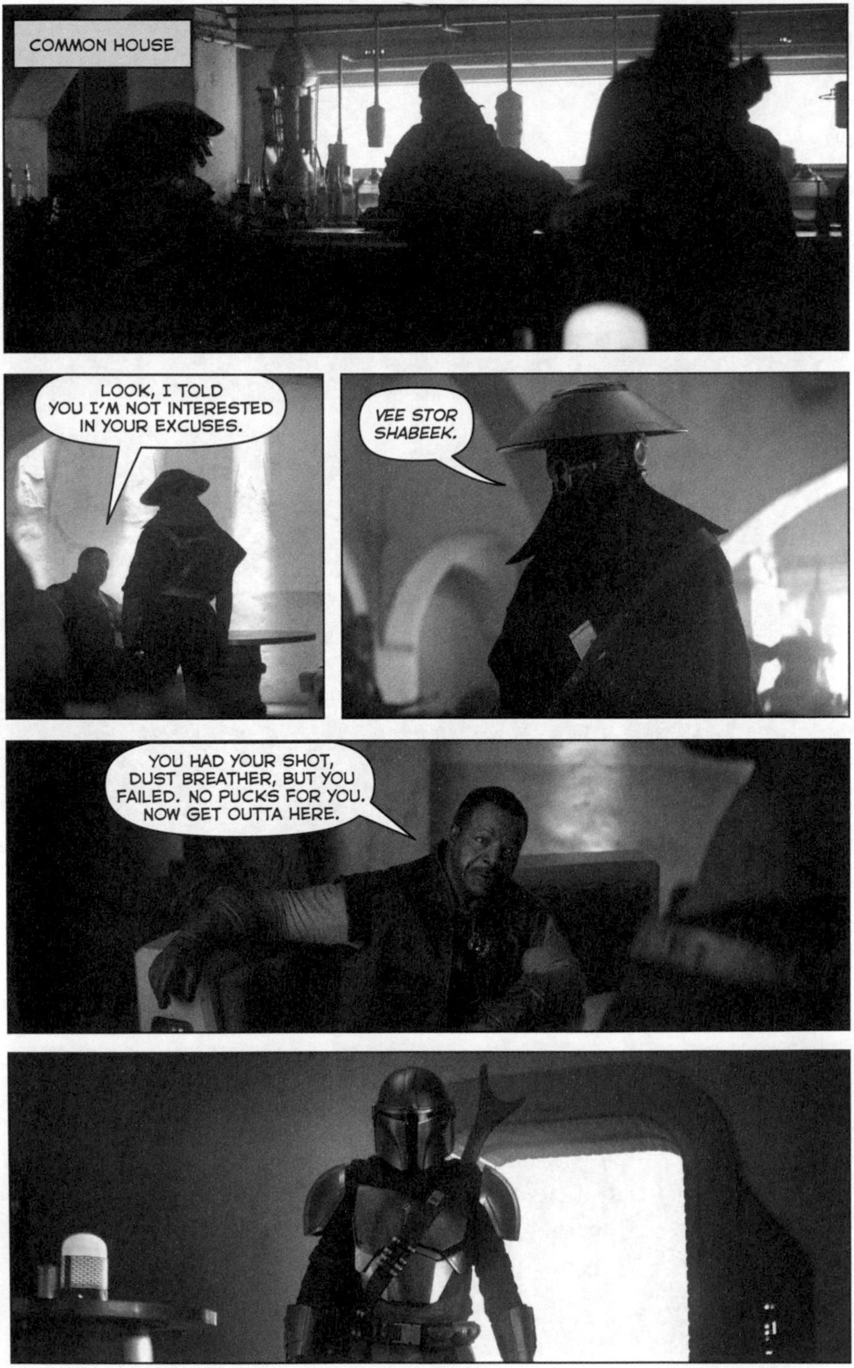
COMMON HOUSE
LOOK, I TOLD YOU I'M NOT INTERESTED IN YOUR EXCUSES.
VEE STOR SHABEEK.
YOU HAD YOUR SHOT, DUST BREATHER, BUT YOU FAILED. NO PUCKS FOR YOU. NOW GET OUTTA HERE.

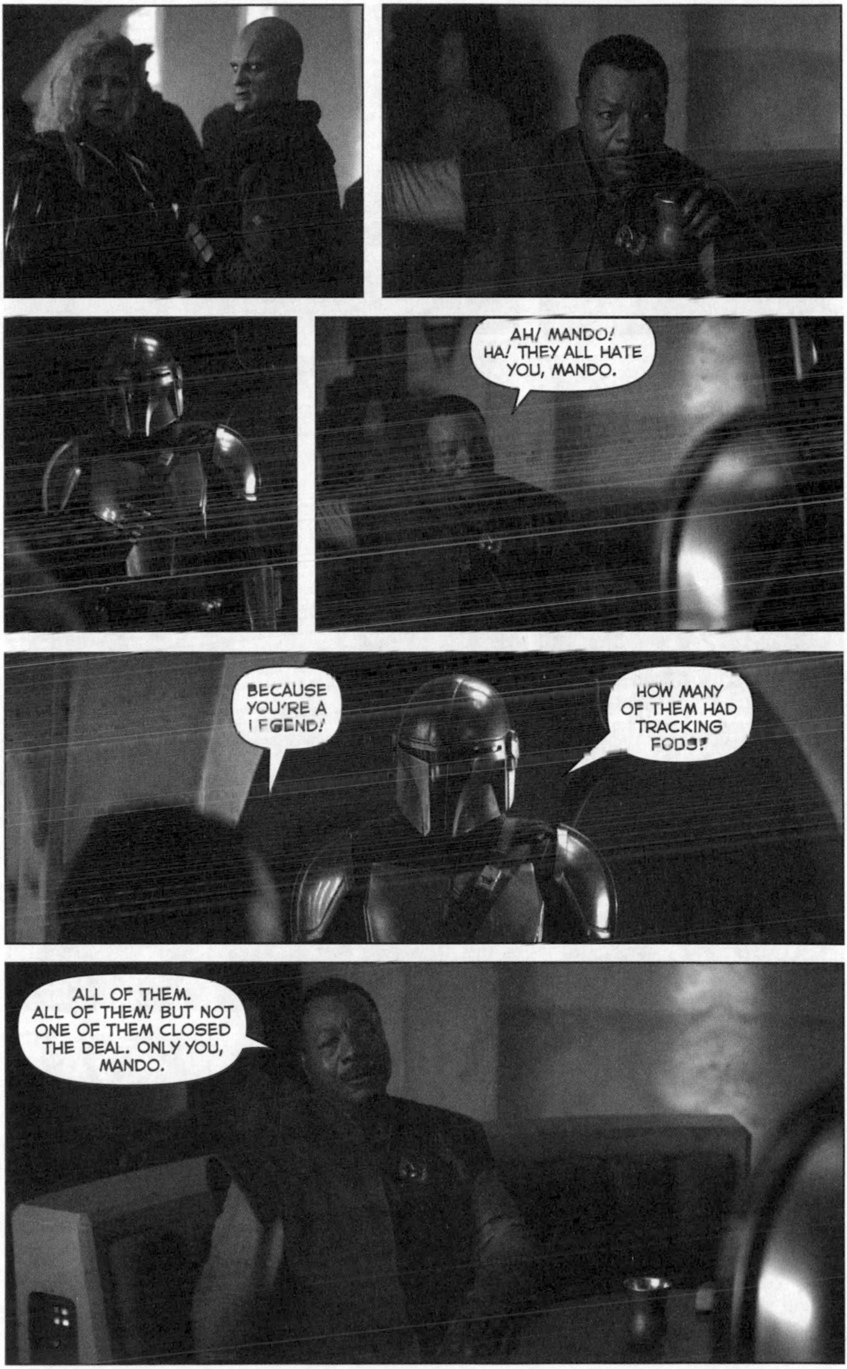
AH! MANDO! HA! THEY ALL HATE YOU, MANDO.
BECAUSE YOU'RE A LEGEND!
HOW MANY OF THEM HAD TRACKING FOBS?
ALL OF THEM. ALL OF THEM! BUT NOT ONE OF THEM CLOSED THE DEAL. ONLY YOU, MANDO.

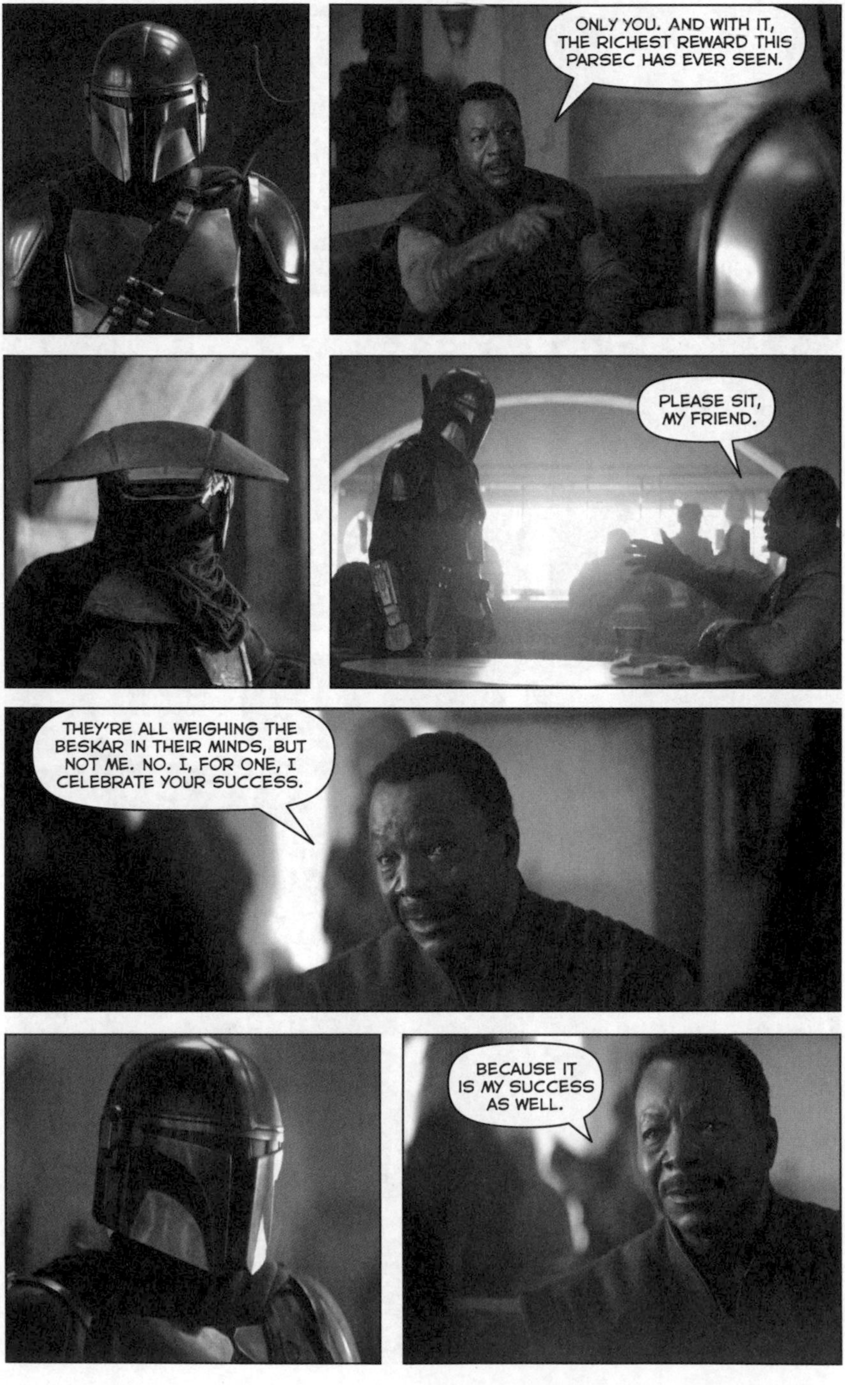
ONLY YOU. AND WITH IT, THE RICHEST REWARD THIS PARSEC HAS EVER SEEN.
PLEASE SIT, MY FRIEND.
THEY'RE ALL WEIGHING THE BESKAR IN THEIR MINDS, BUT NOT ME. NO. I, FOR ONE, I CELEBRATE YOUR SUCCESS.
BECAUSE IT IS MY SUCCESS AS WELL.

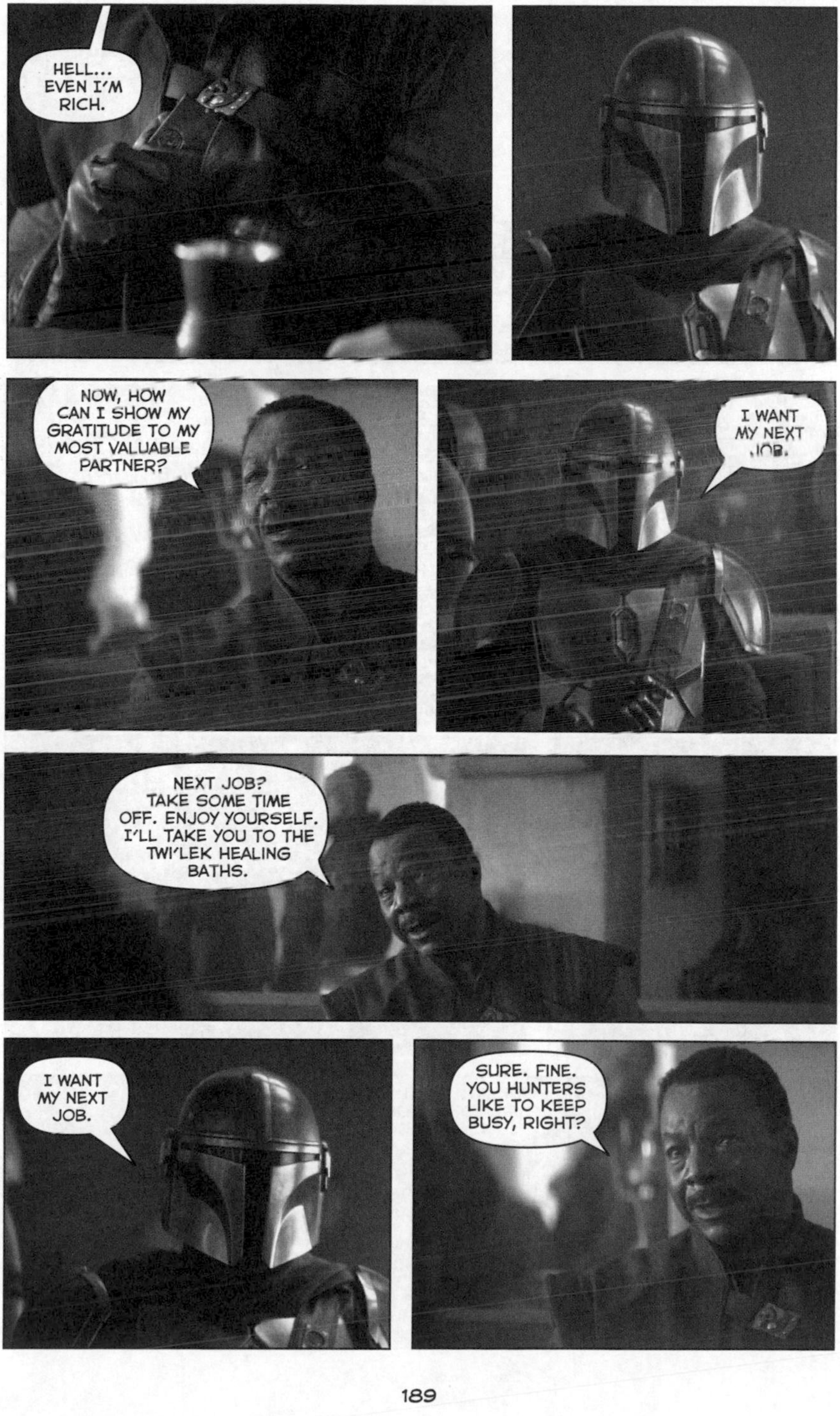
HELL... EVEN I'M RICH.
NOW, HOW CAN I SHOW MY GRATITUDE TO MY MOST VALUABLE PARTNER?
I WANT MY NEXT JOB.
NEXT JOB? TAKE SOME TIME OFF. ENJOY YOURSELF. I'LL TAKE YOU TO THE TWI'LEK HEALING BATHS.
I WANT MY NEXT JOB.
SURE. FINE. YOU HUNTERS LIKE TO KEEP BUSY, RIGHT?

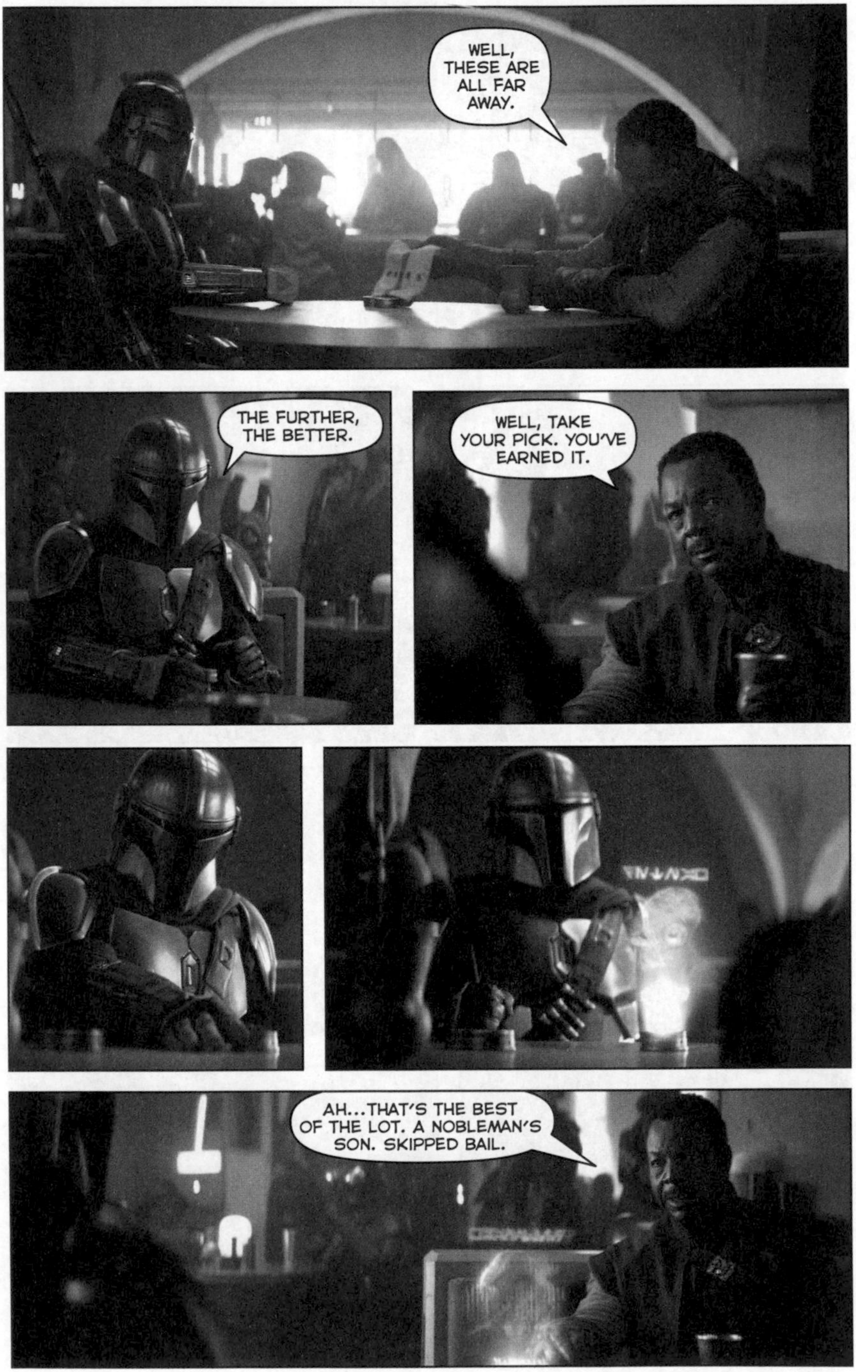

WELL, THESE ARE ALL FAR AWAY.
THE FURTHER, THE BETTER.
WELL, TAKE YOUR PICK. YOU'VE EARNED IT.
AH...THAT'S THE BEST OF THE LOT. A NOBLEMAN'S SON. SKIPPED BAIL.

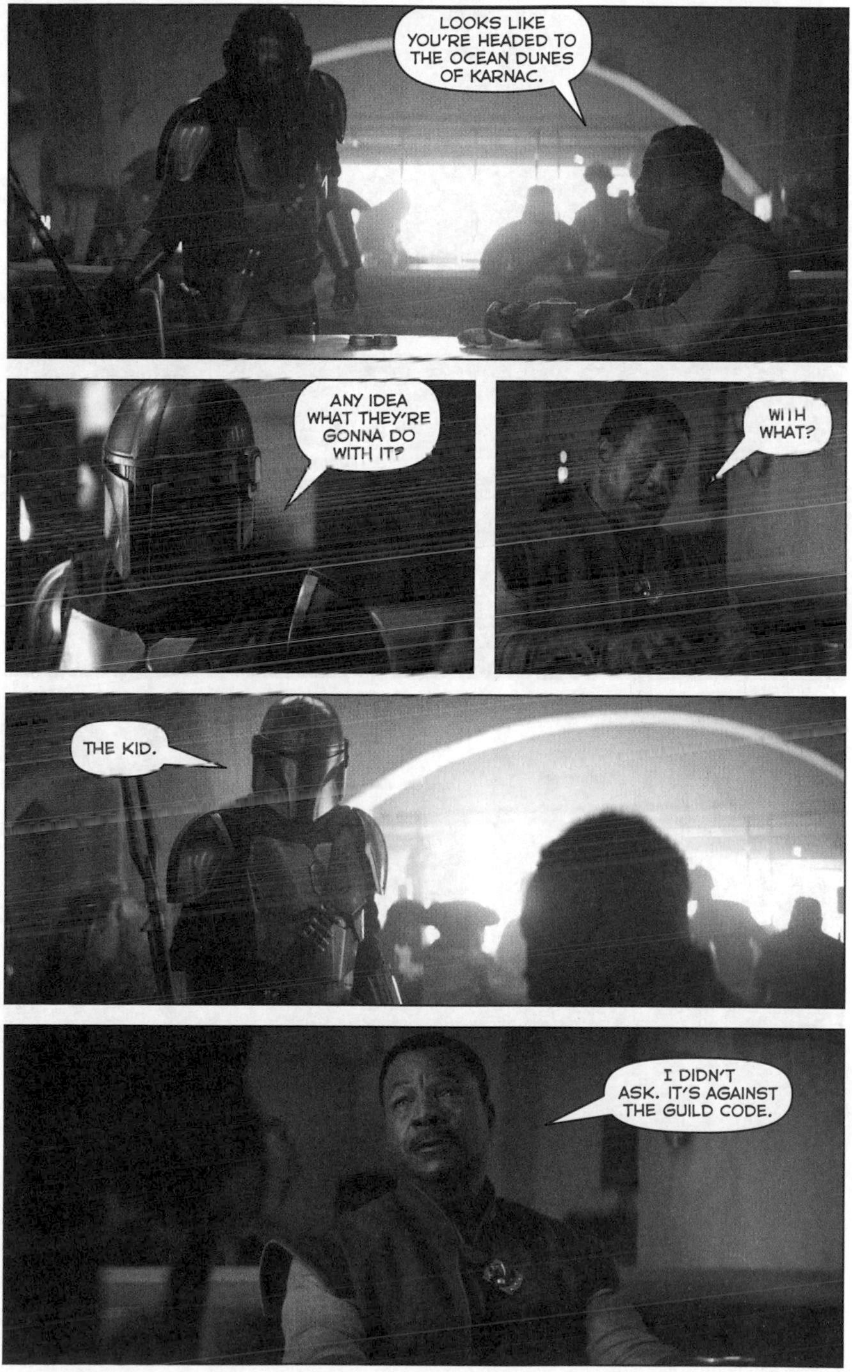
LOOKS LIKE YOU'RE HEADED TO THE OCEAN DUNES OF KARNAC.
ANY IDEA WHAT THEY'RE GONNA DO WITH IT?
WITH WHAT?
THE KID.
I DIDN'T ASK. IT'S AGAINST THE GUILD CODE.

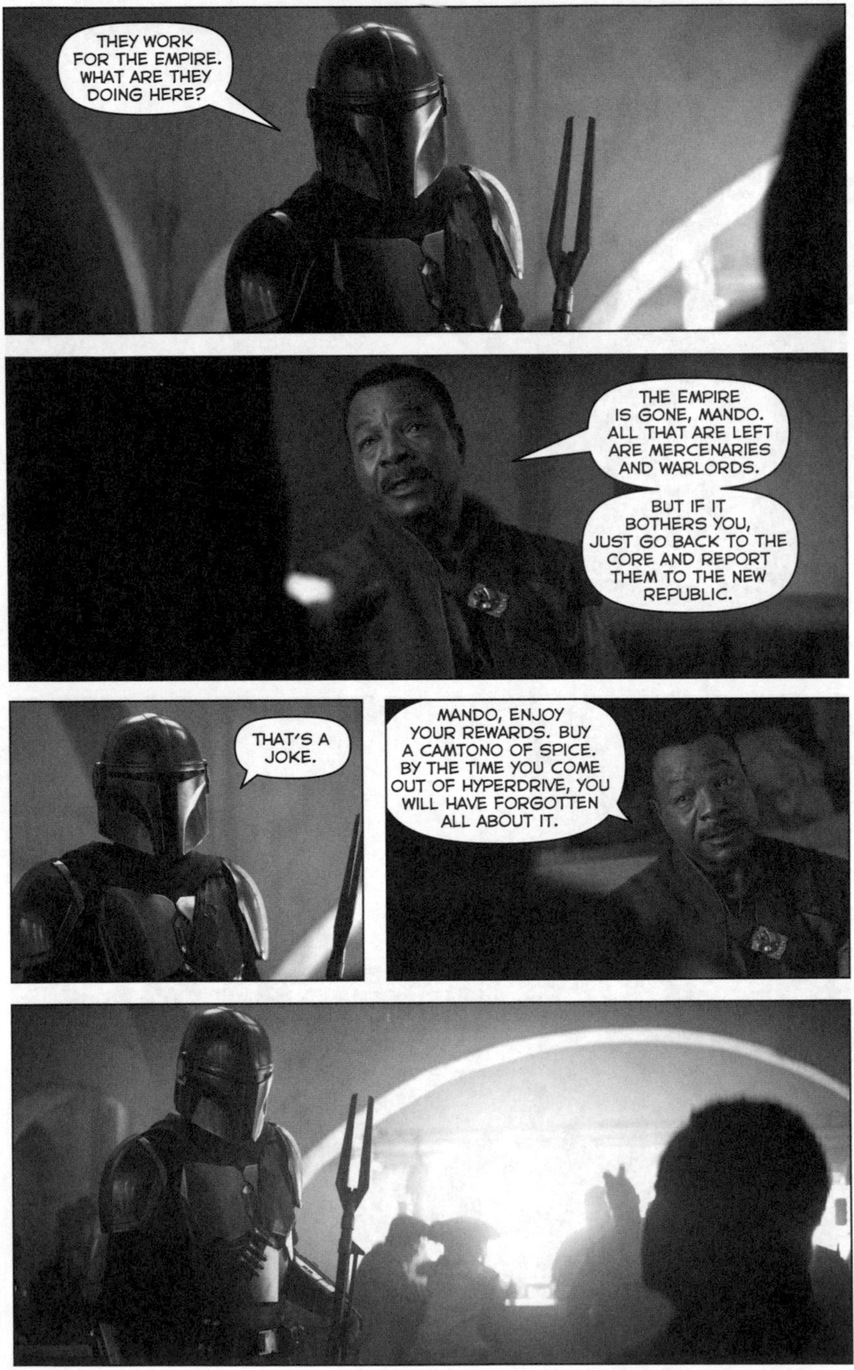
THEY WORK FOR THE EMPIRE. WHAT ARE THEY DOING HERE?
THE EMPIRE IS GONE, MANDO. ALL THAT ARE LEFT ARE MERCENARIES AND WARLORDS.
BUT IF IT BOTHERS YOU, JUST GO BACK TO THE CORE AND REPORT THEM TO THE NEW REPUBLIC.
THAT'S A JOKE.
MANDO, ENJOY YOUR REWARDS. BUY A CAMTONO OF SPICE. BY THE TIME YOU COME OUT OF HYPERDRIVE, YOU WILL HAVE FORGOTTEN ALL ABOUT IT.

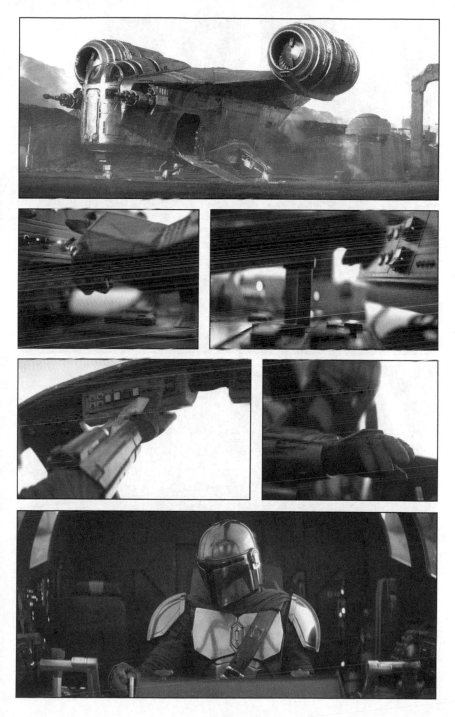

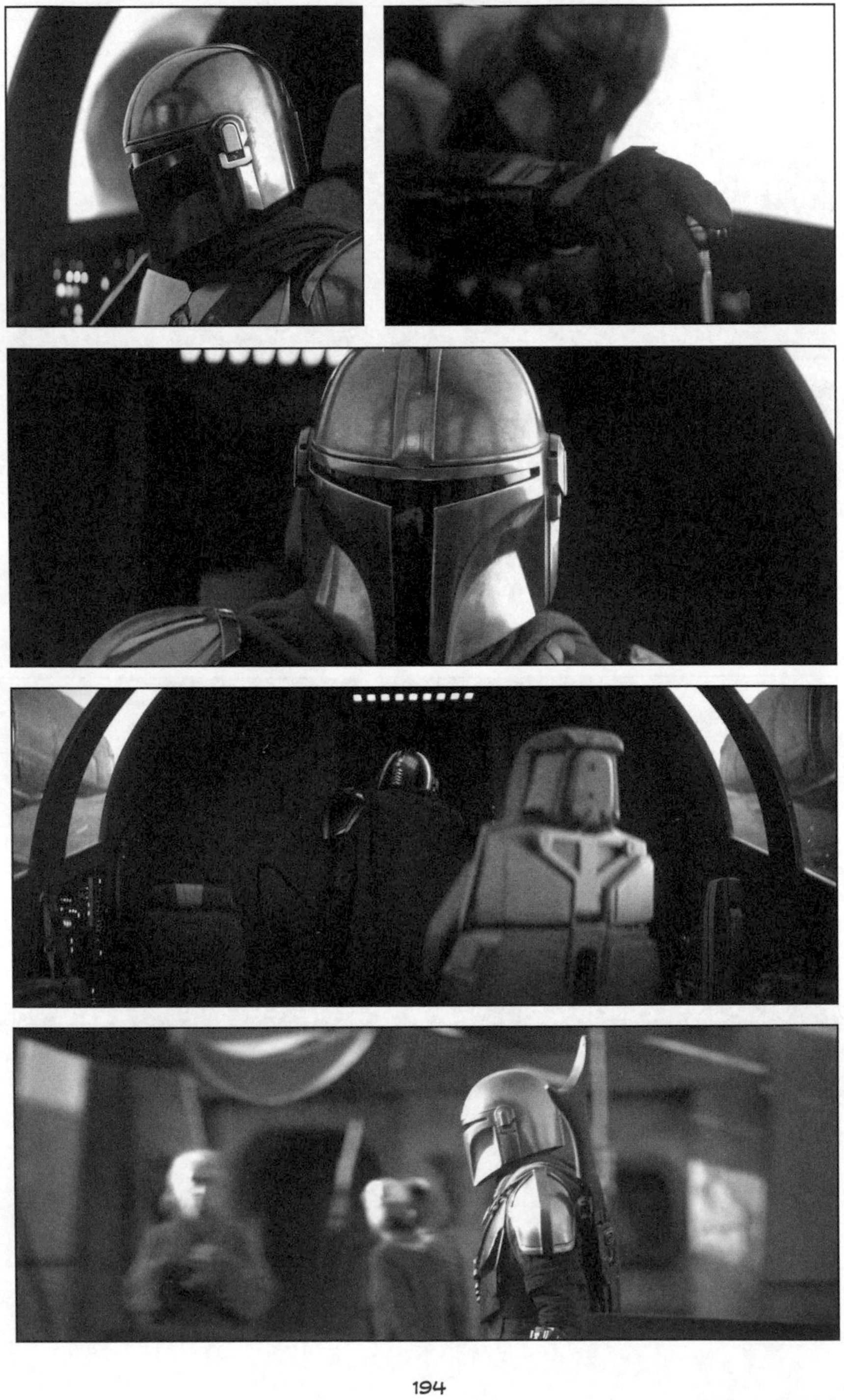

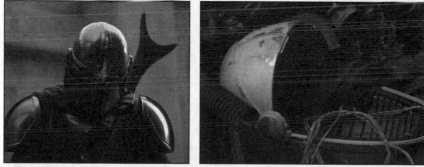

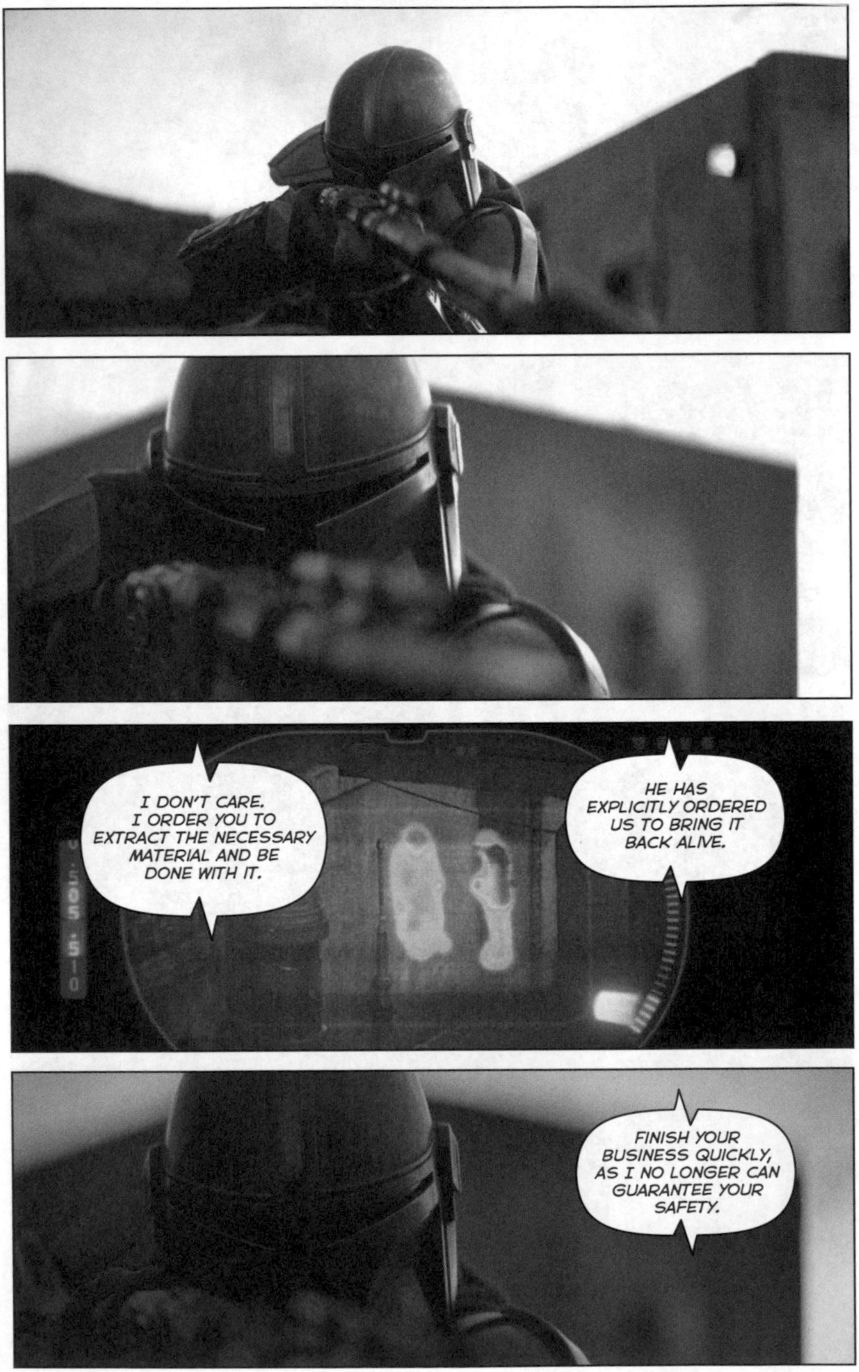
I DON'T CARE. I ORDER YOU TO EXTRACT THE NECESSARY MATERIAL AND BE DONE WITH IT.
HE HAS EXPLICITLY ORDERED US TO BRING IT BACK ALIVE.
FINISH YOUR BUSINESS QUICKLY, AS I NO LONGER CAN GUARANTEE YOUR SAFETY.

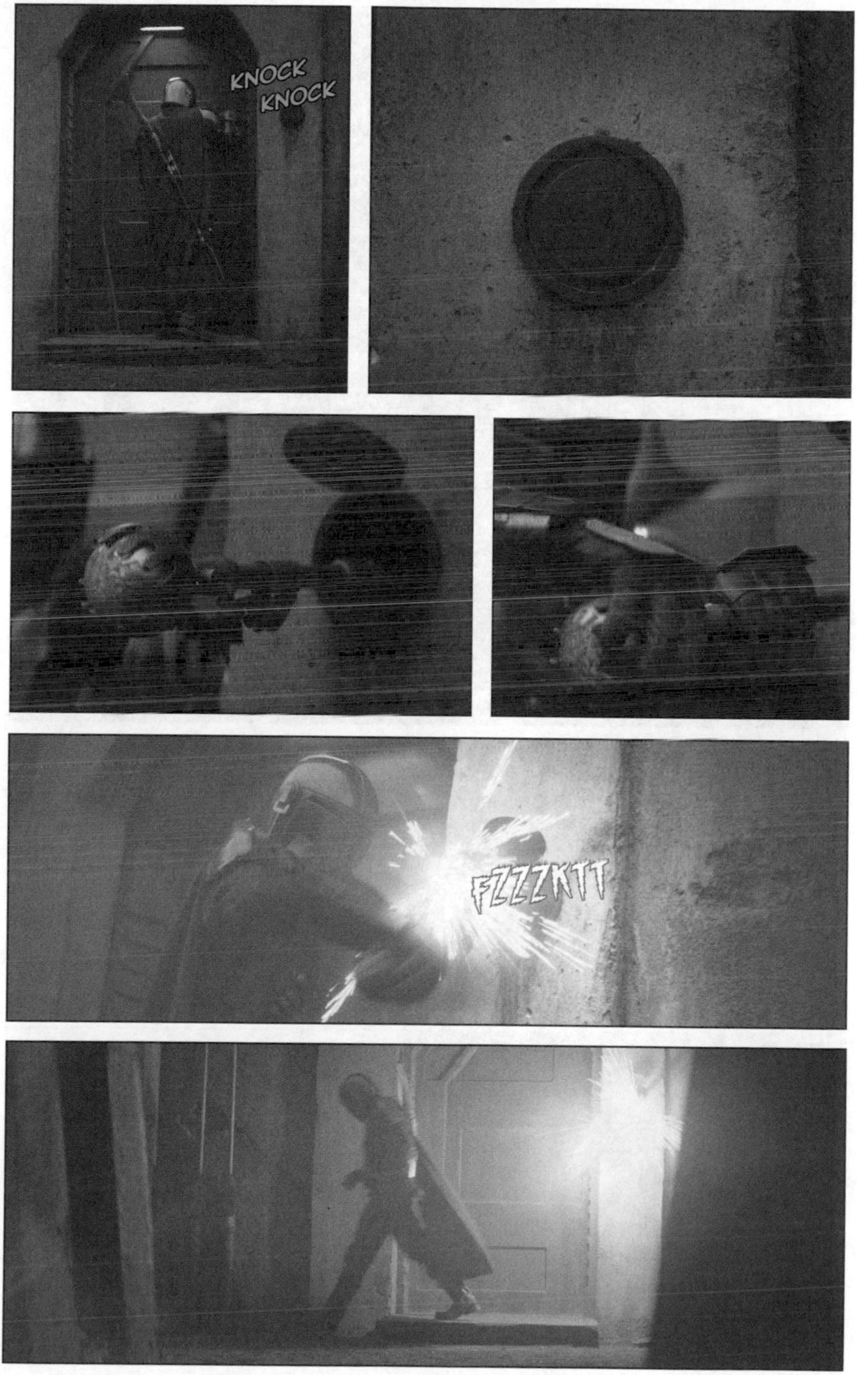
KNOCK
KNOCK
FZZZKTT

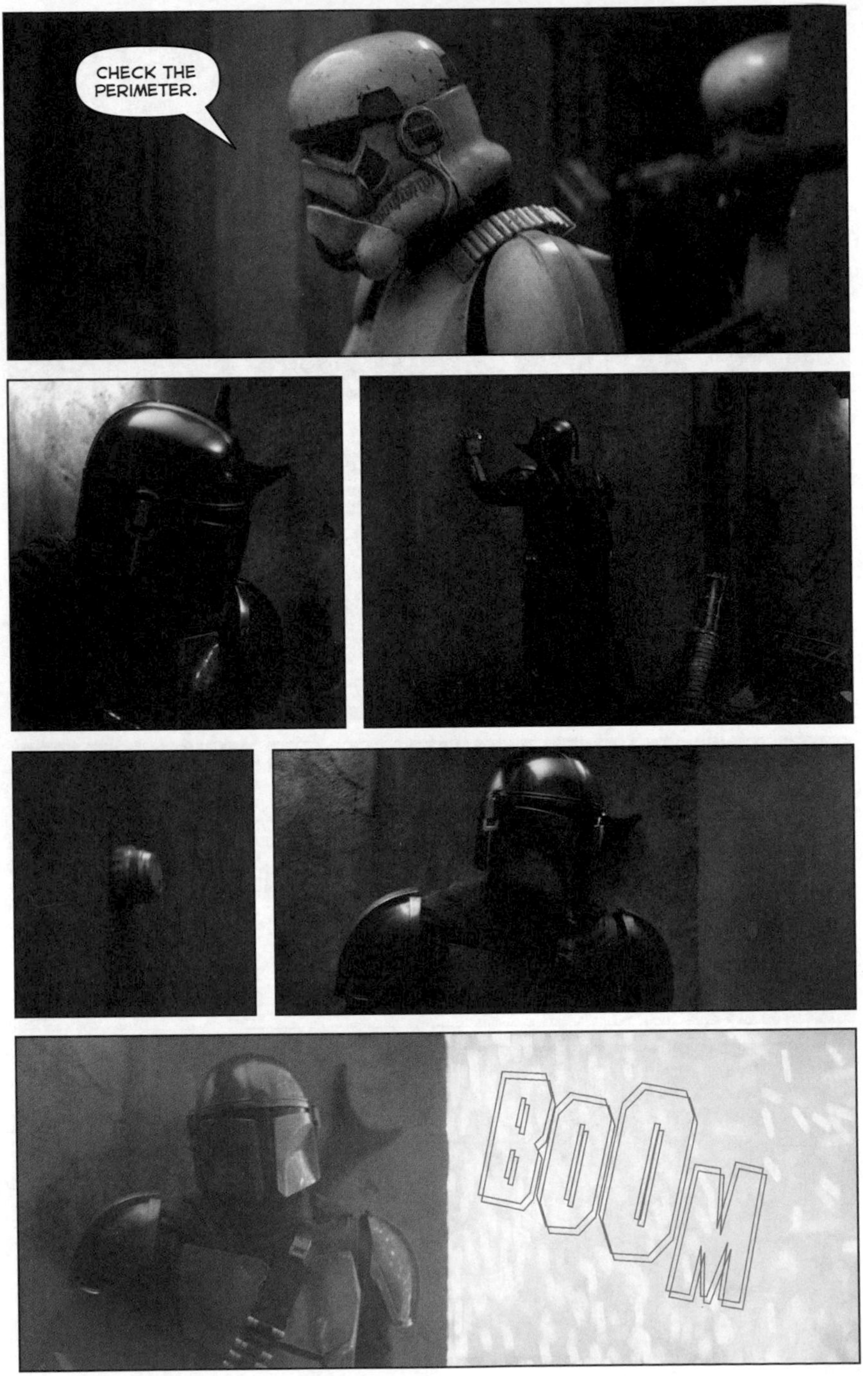
CHECK THE PERIMETER.
BOOM

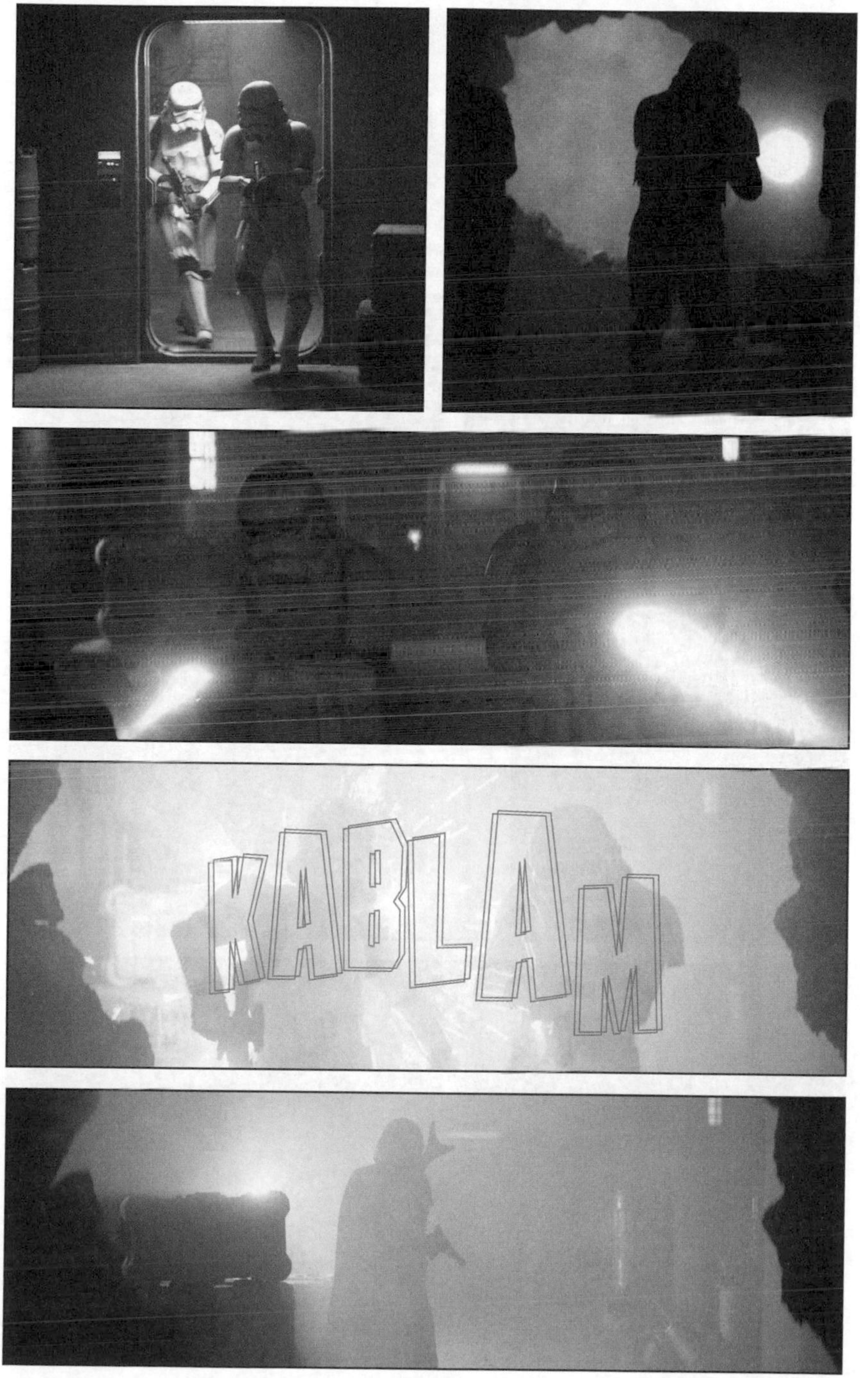
KABLAM

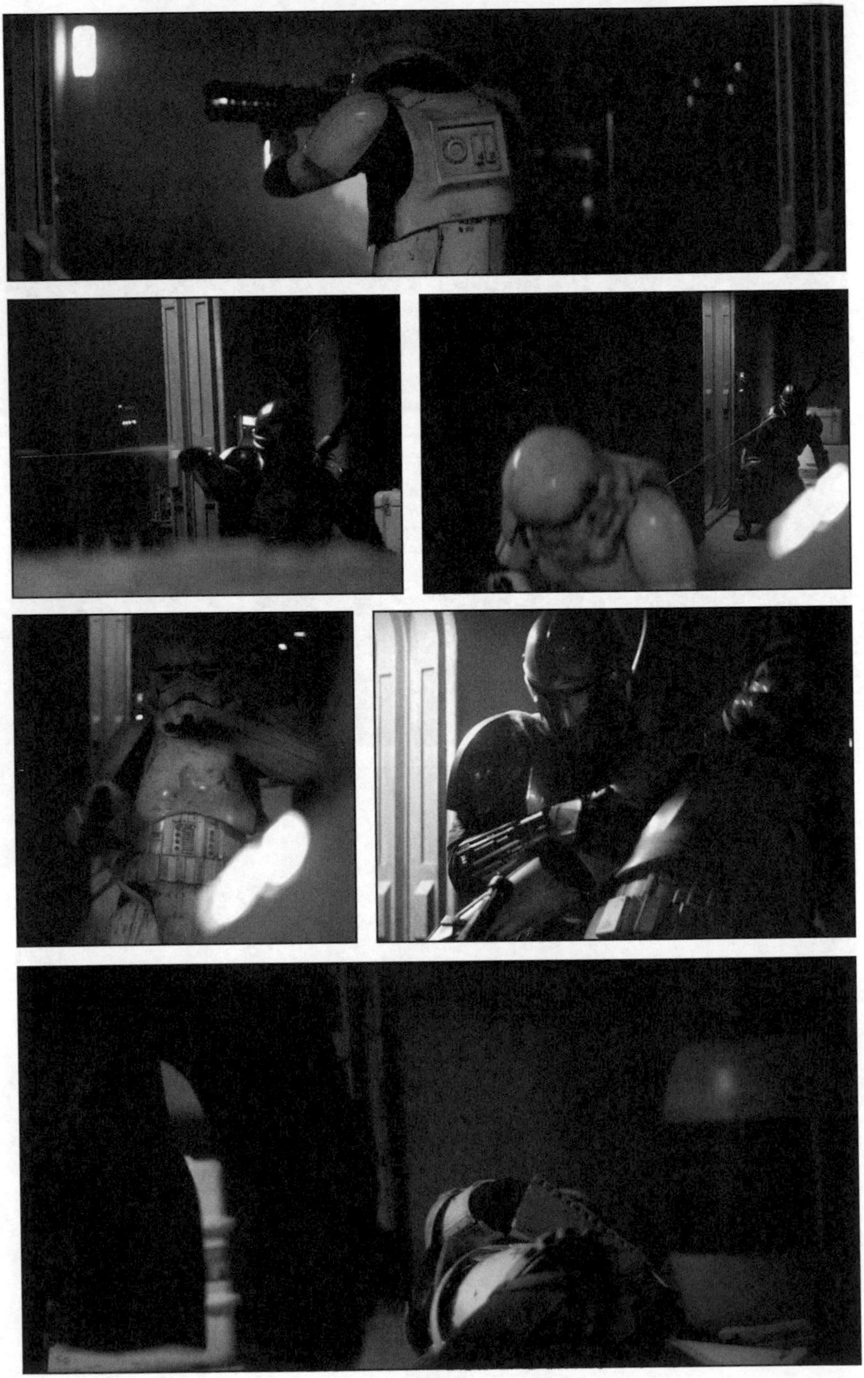

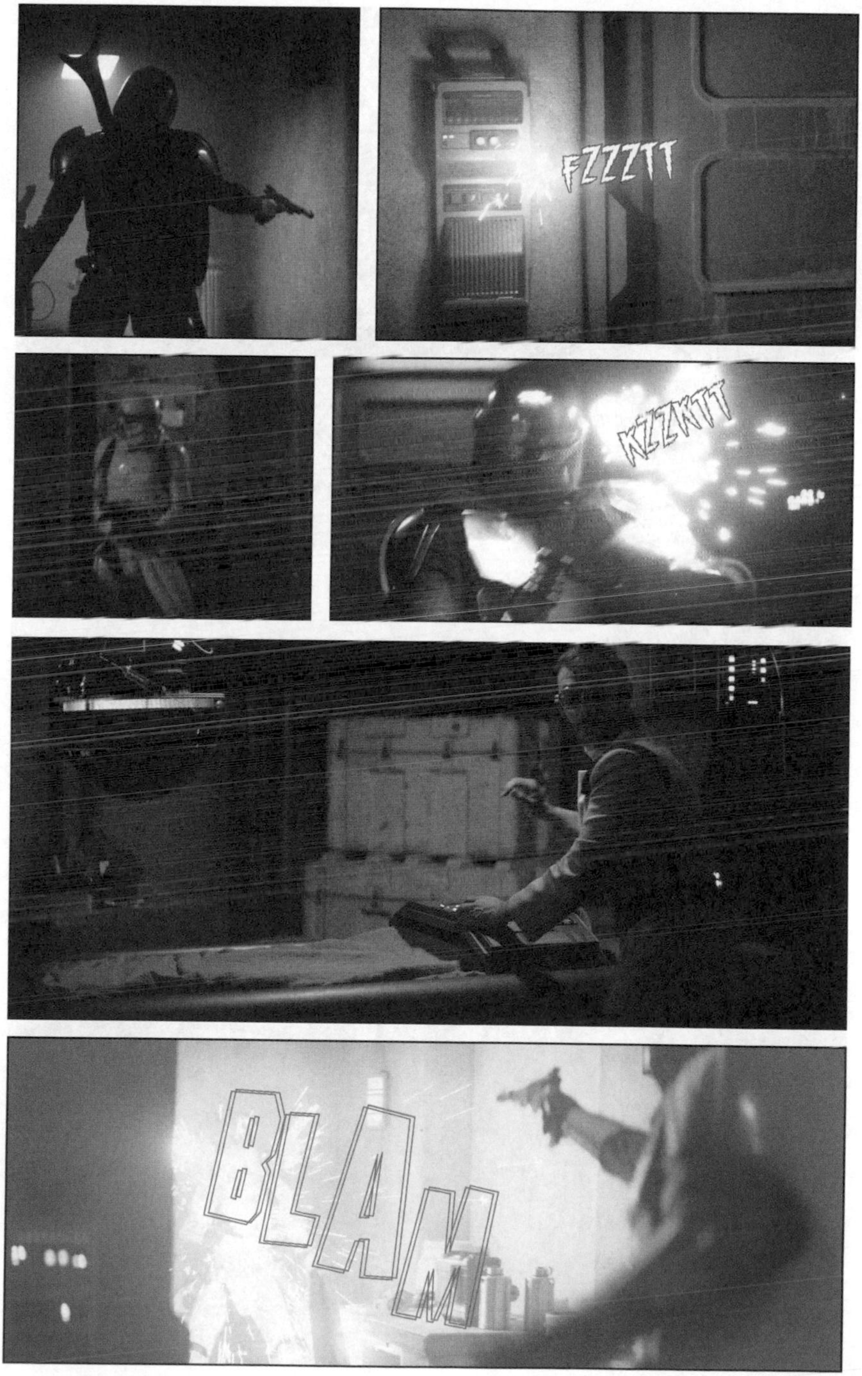
FZZZTT
KZZZKTT
BLAM

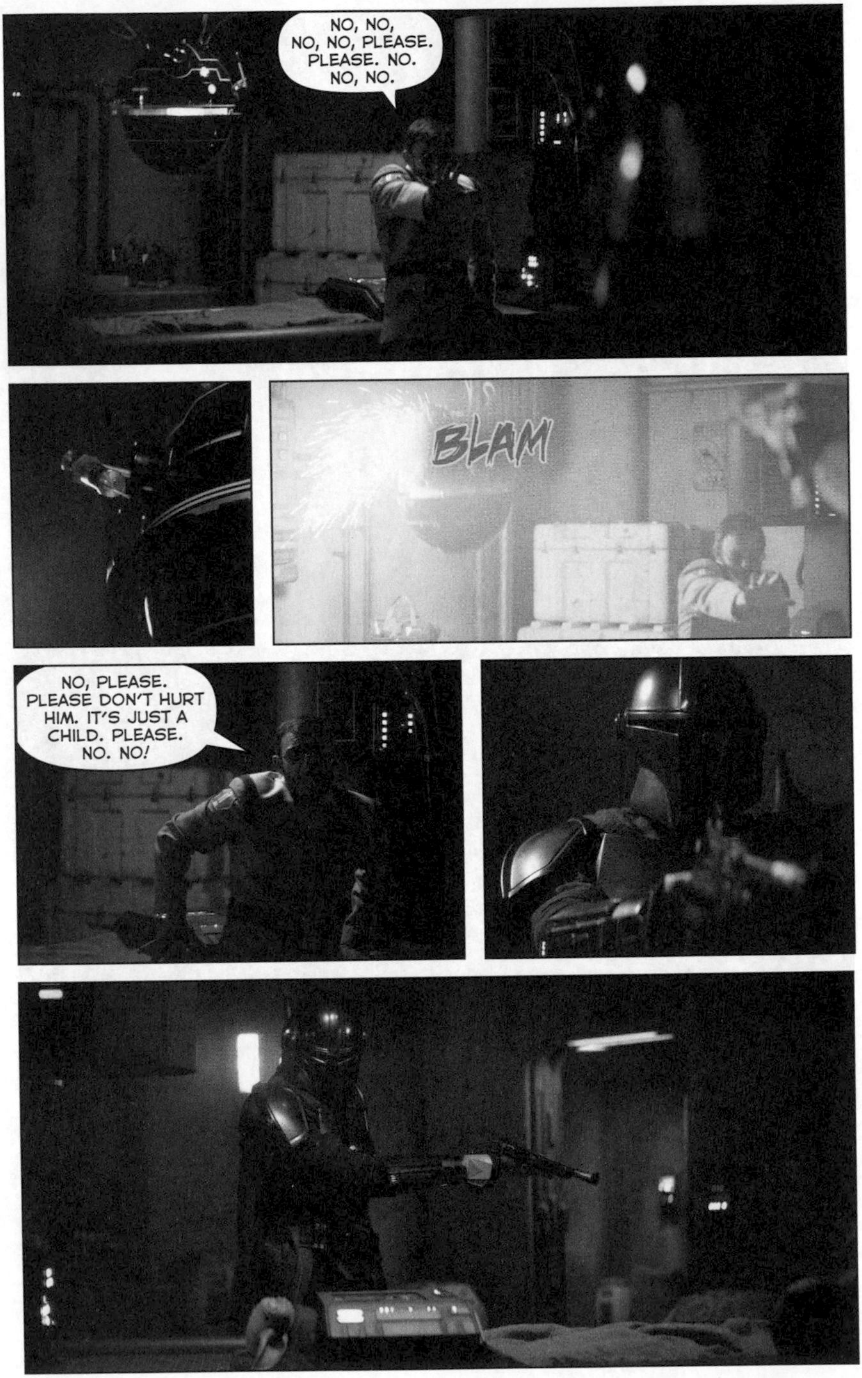
NO, NO,
NO, NO, PLEASE.
PLEASE. NO.
NO, NO.
BLAM
NO, PLEASE.
PLEASE DON'T HURT
HIM. IT'S JUST A
CHILD. PLEASE.
NO. NO!

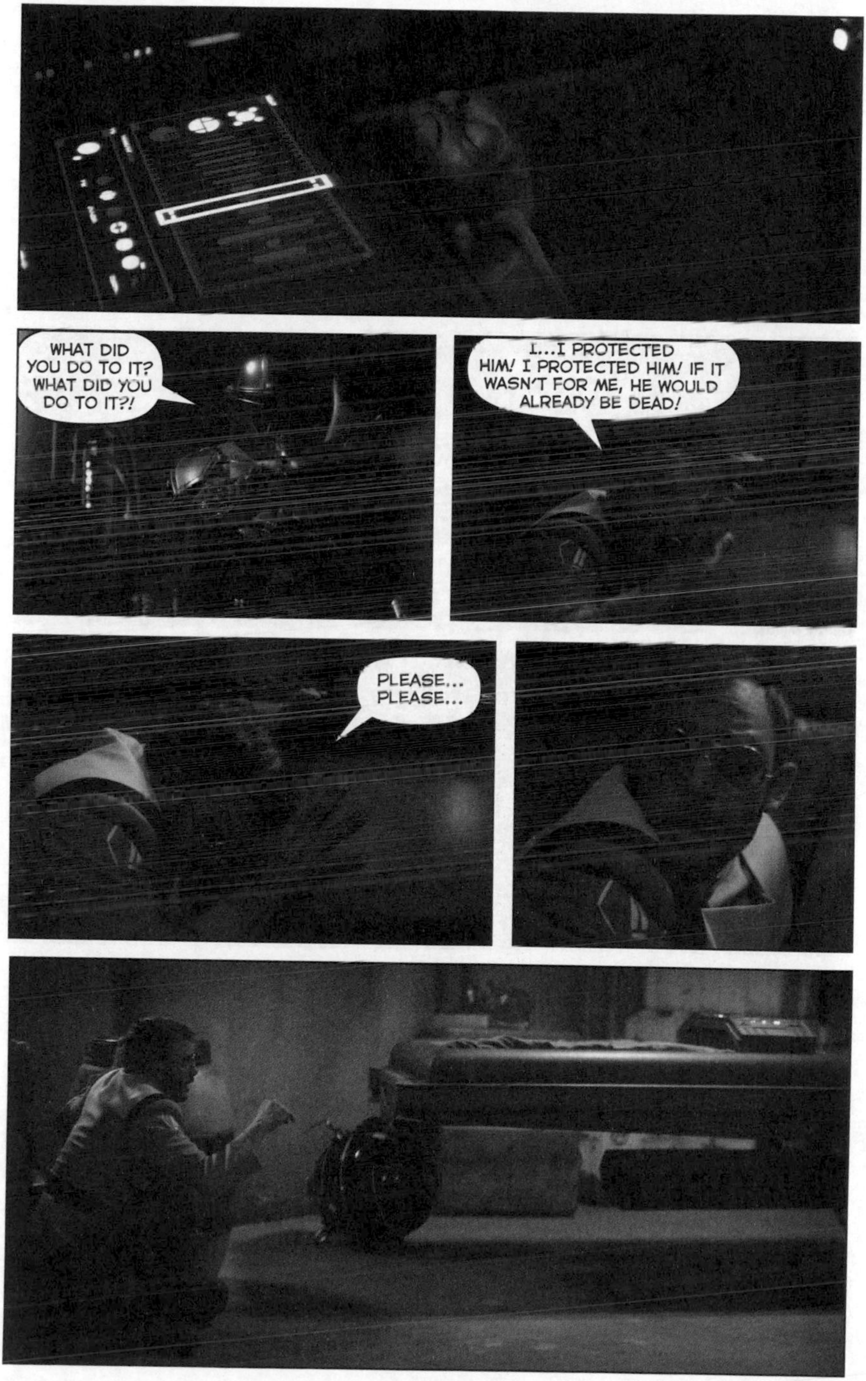
WHAT DID YOU DO TO IT? WHAT DID YOU DO TO IT?!
I...I PROTECTED HIM! I PROTECTED HIM! IF IT WASN'T FOR ME, HE WOULD ALREADY BE DEAD!
PLEASE... PLEASE...

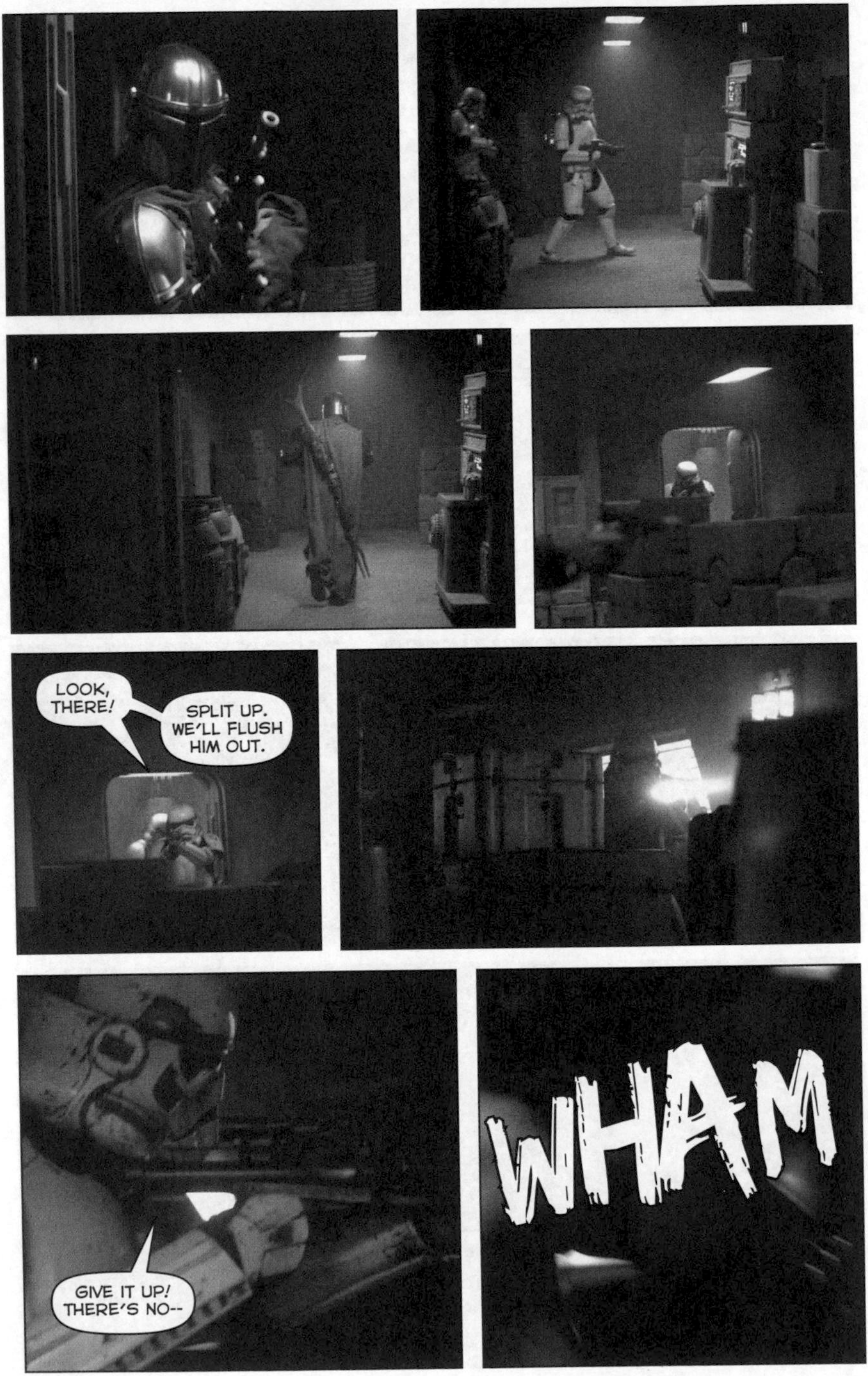
LOOK, THERE!
SPLIT UP. WE'LL FLUSH HIM OUT.
GIVE IT UP! THERE'S NO--
WHAM

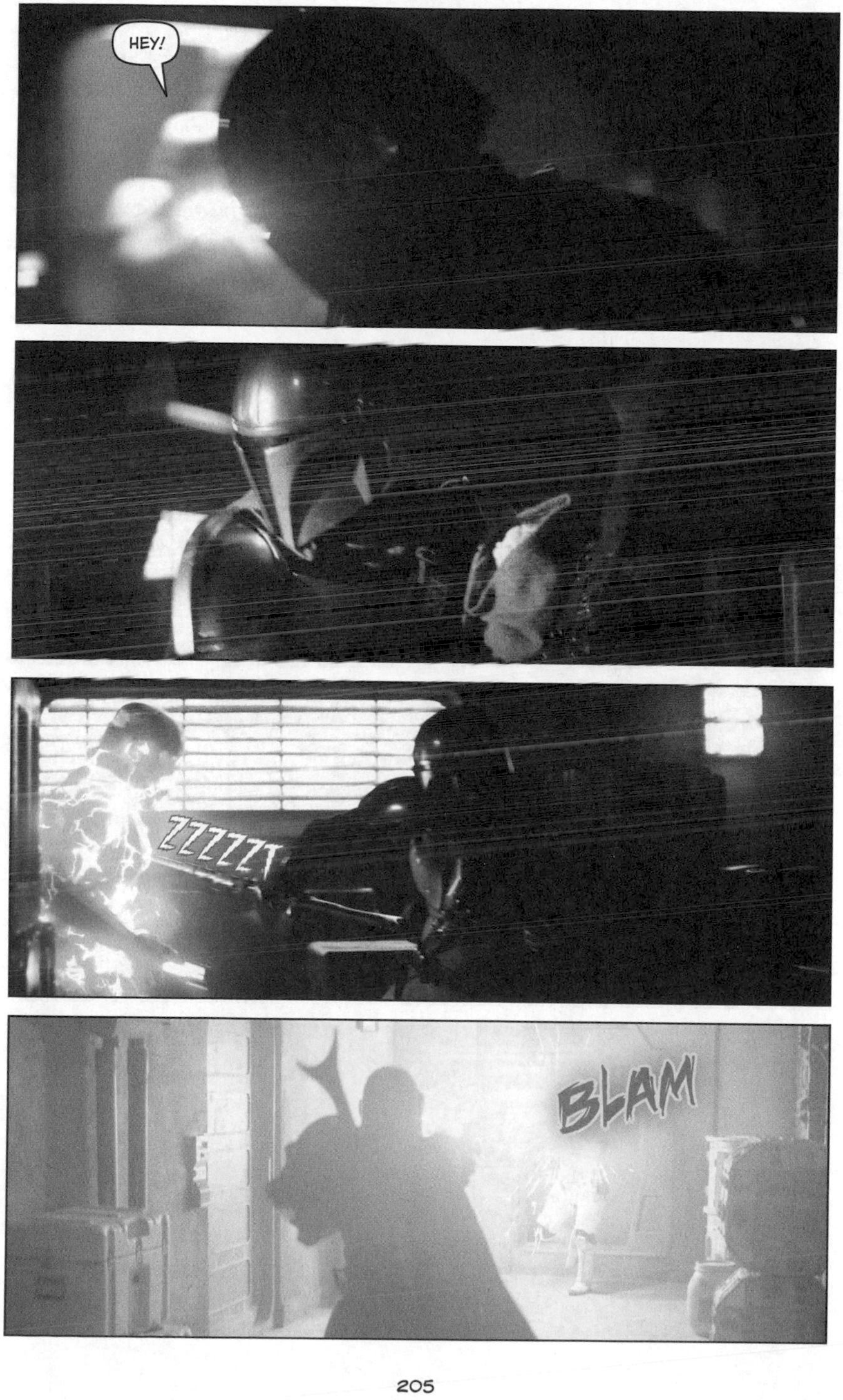
HEY!
ZZZZZT
BLAM

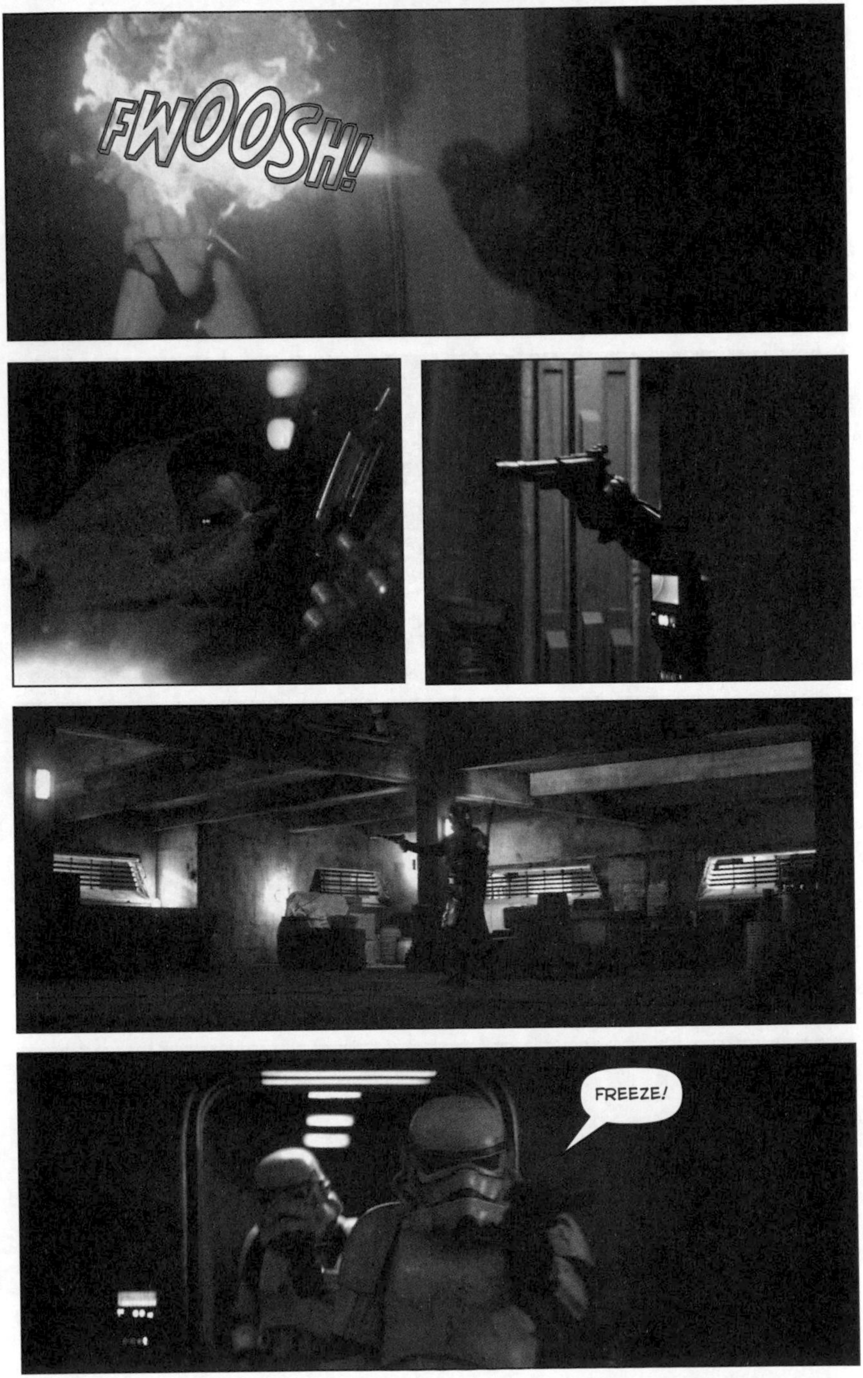
FWOOSH!
FREEZE!

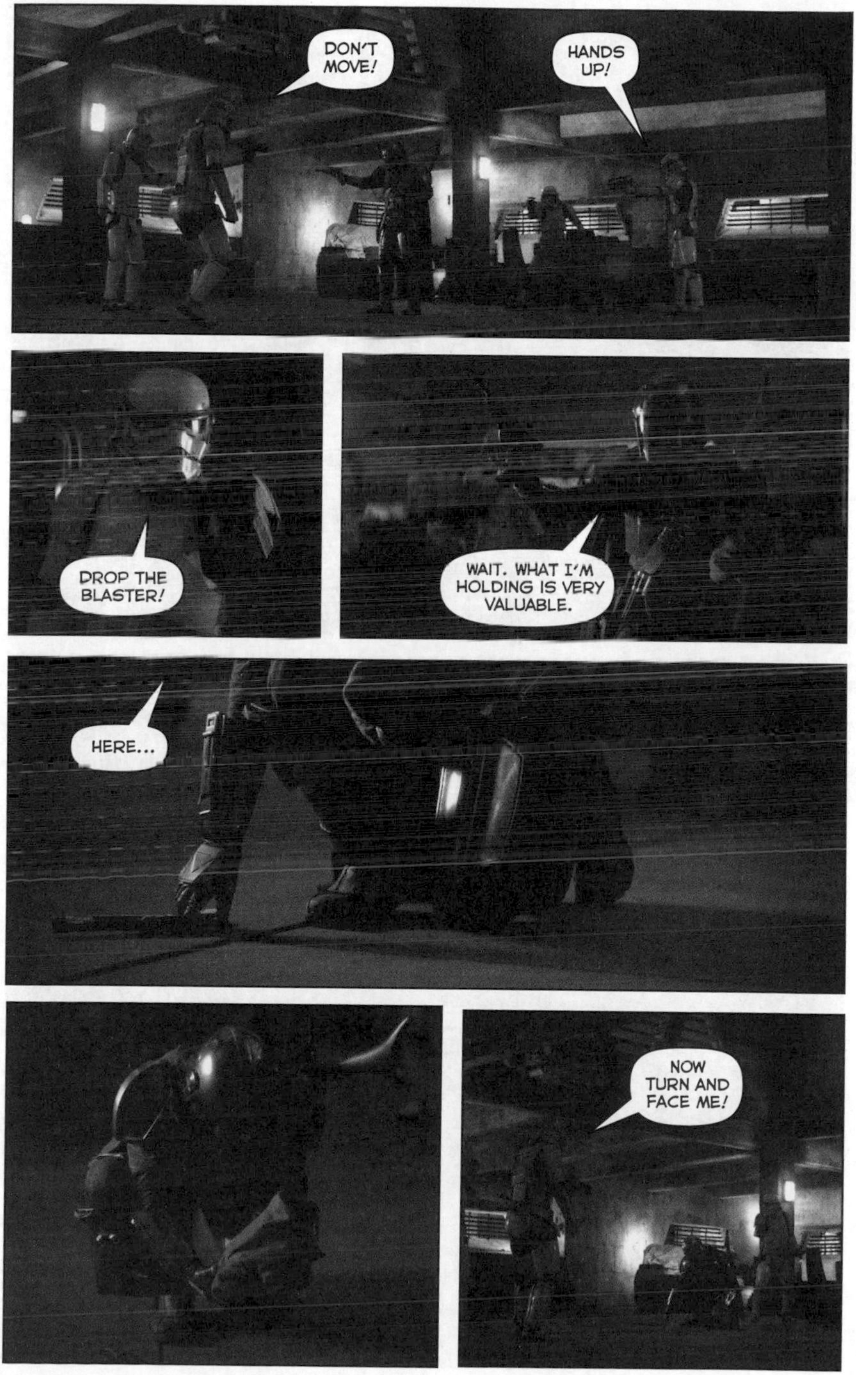
DON'T MOVE!
HANDS UP!
DROP THE BLASTER!
WAIT. WHAT I'M HOLDING IS VERY VALUABLE.
HERE...
NOW TURN AND FACE ME!

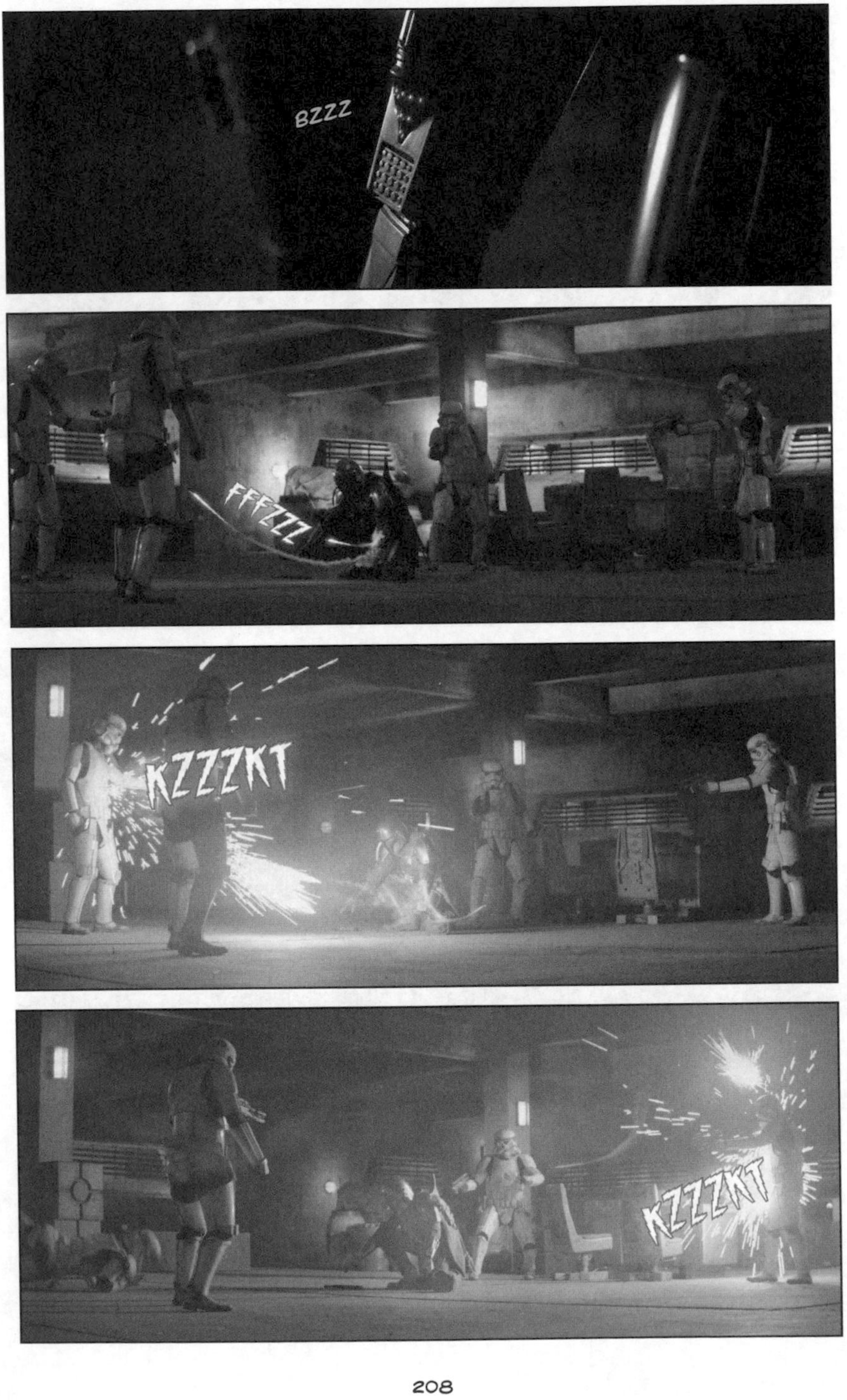
BZZZ
FFFZZZ
KZZZKT
KZZZKT

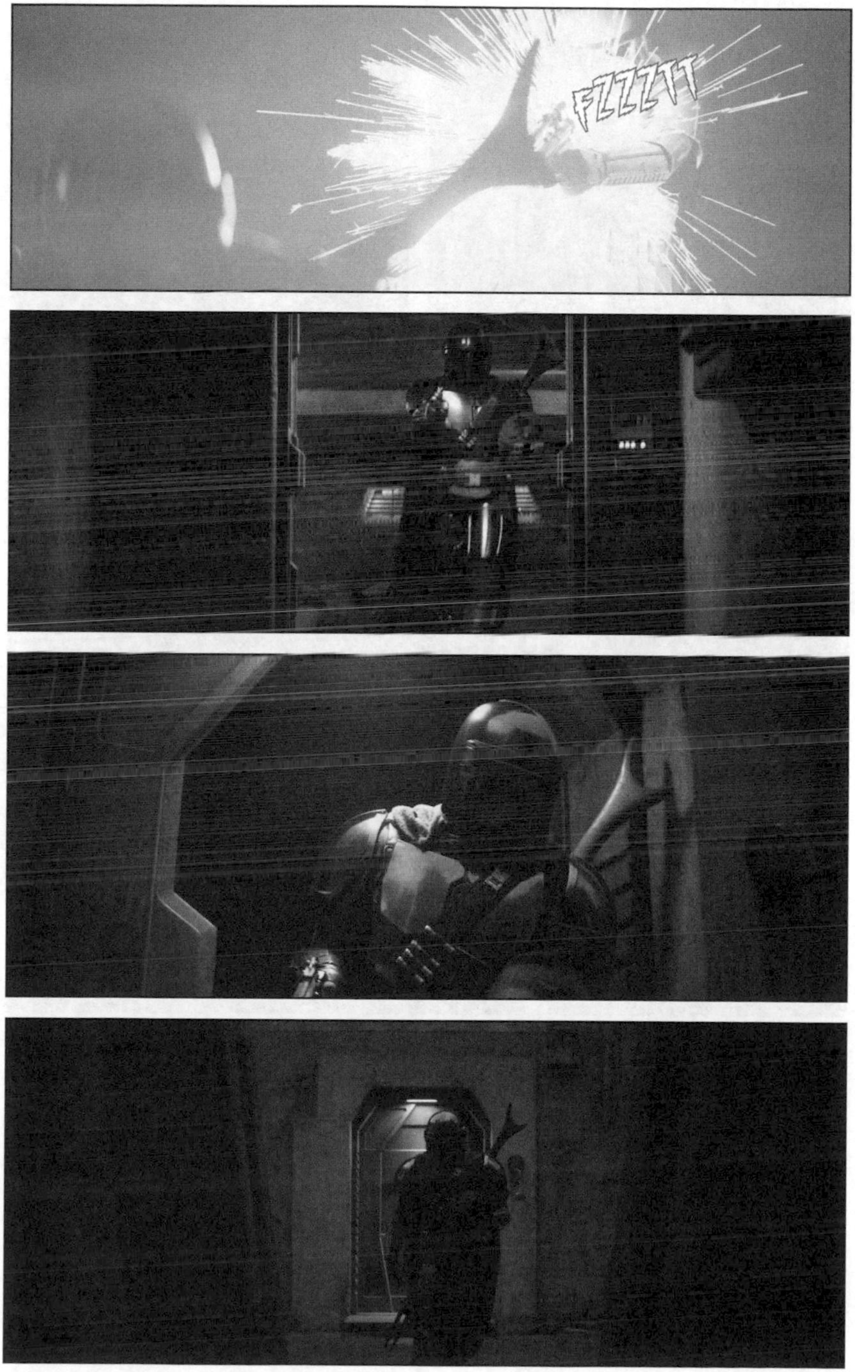
FZZZTT

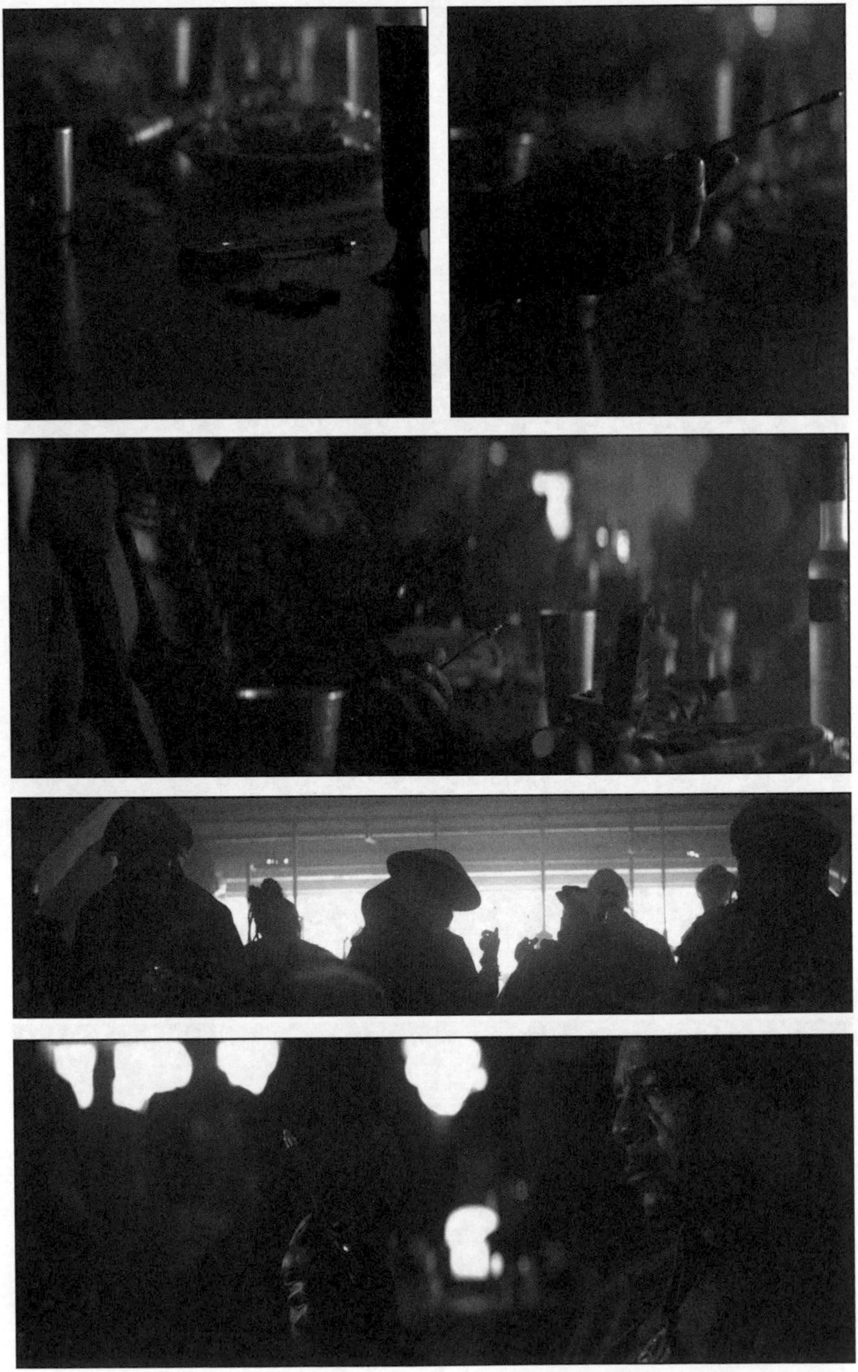

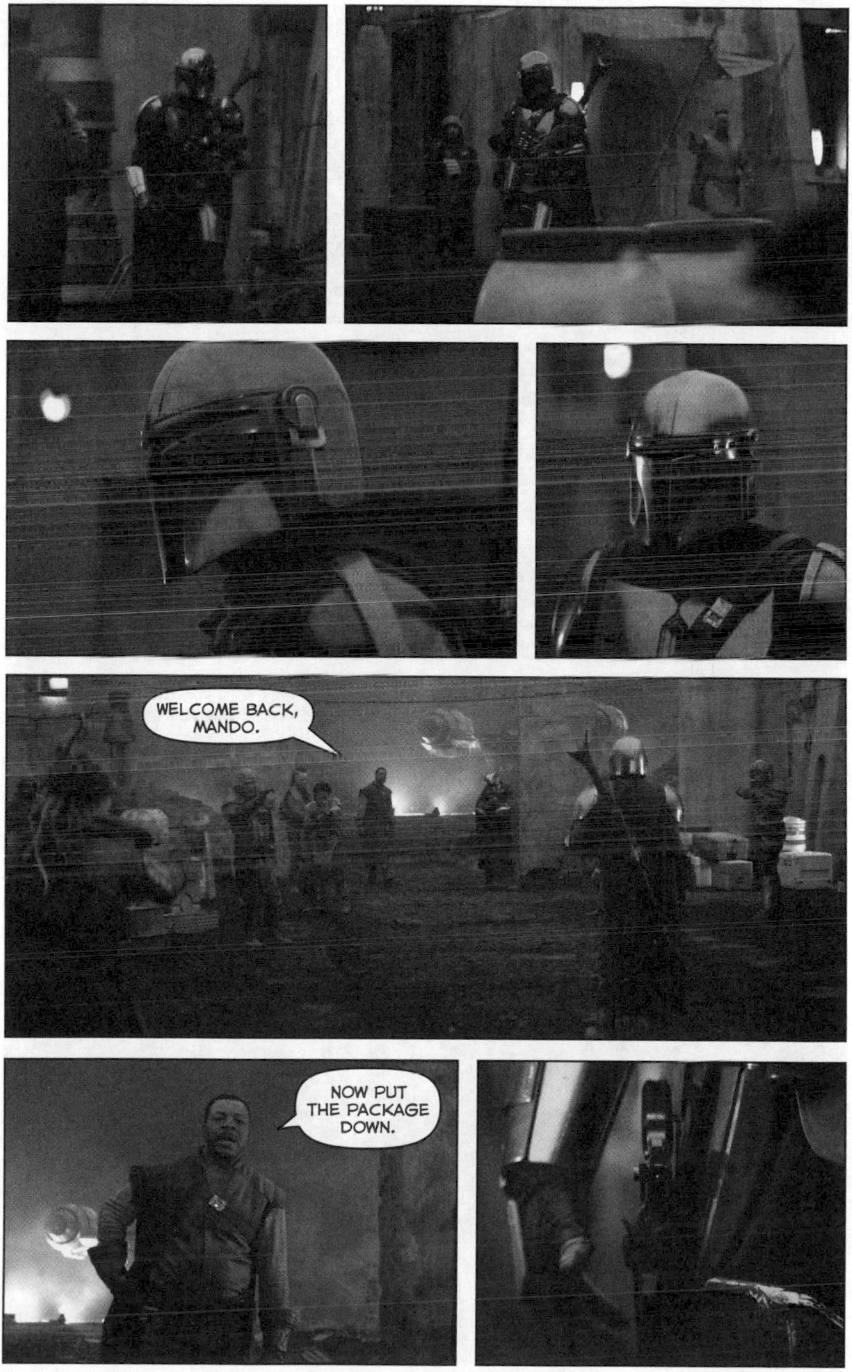
WELCOME BACK, MANDO.
NOW PUT THE PACKAGE DOWN.

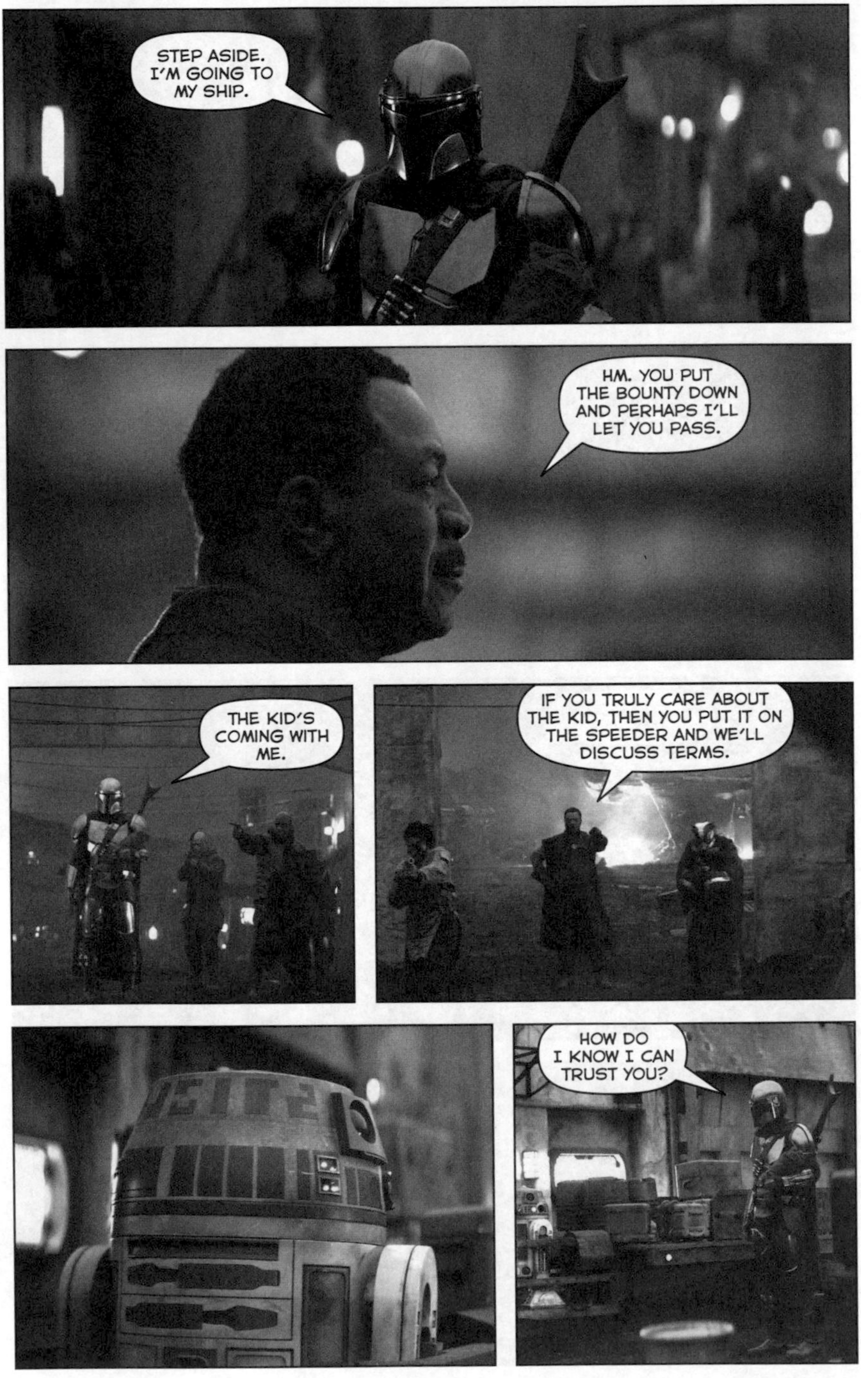
STEP ASIDE. I'M GOING TO MY SHIP.
HM. YOU PUT THE BOUNTY DOWN AND PERHAPS I'LL LET YOU PASS.
THE KID'S COMING WITH ME.
IF YOU TRULY CARE ABOUT THE KID, THEN YOU PUT IT ON THE SPEEDER AND WE'LL DISCUSS TERMS.
HOW DO I KNOW I CAN TRUST YOU?

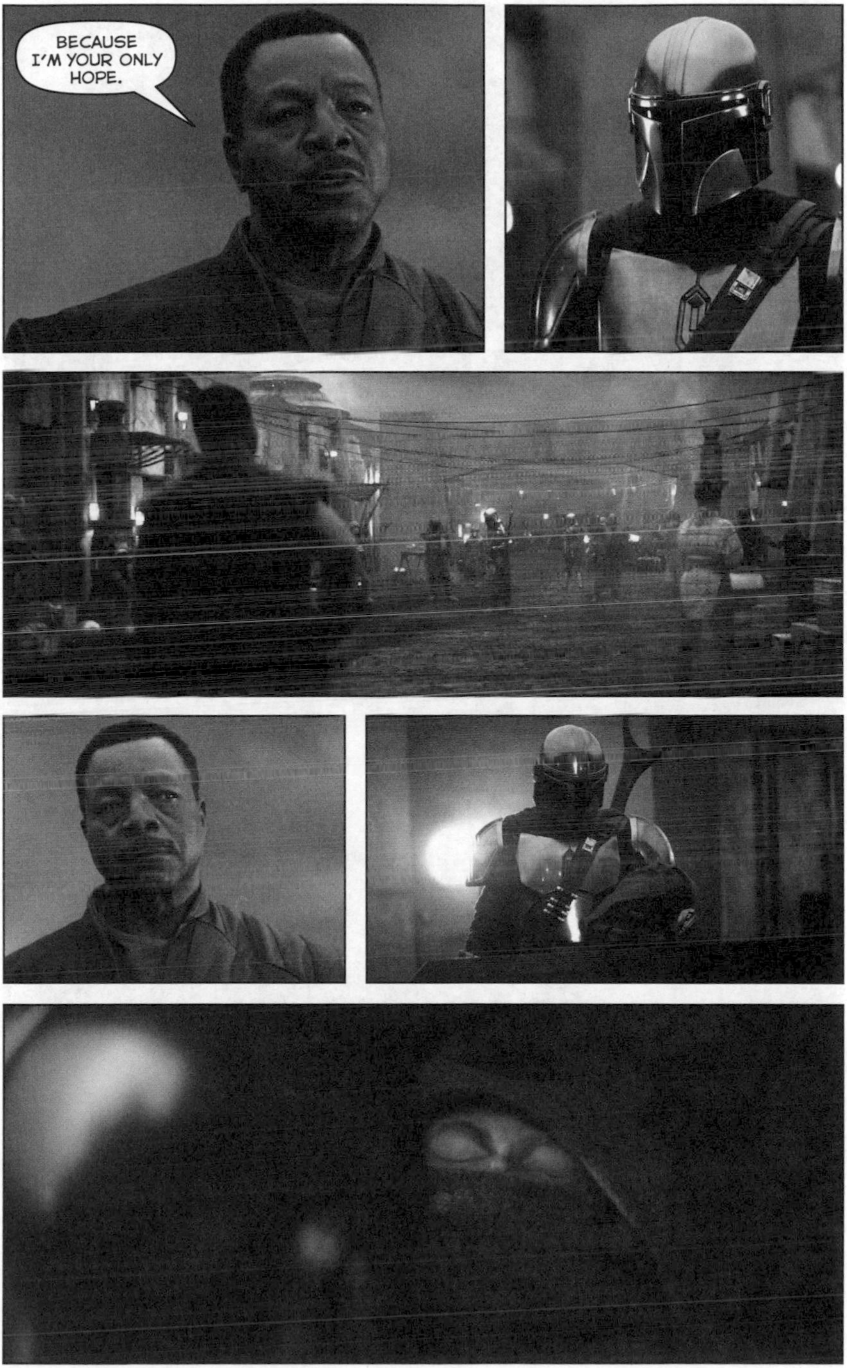
BECAUSE I'M YOUR ONLY HOPE.

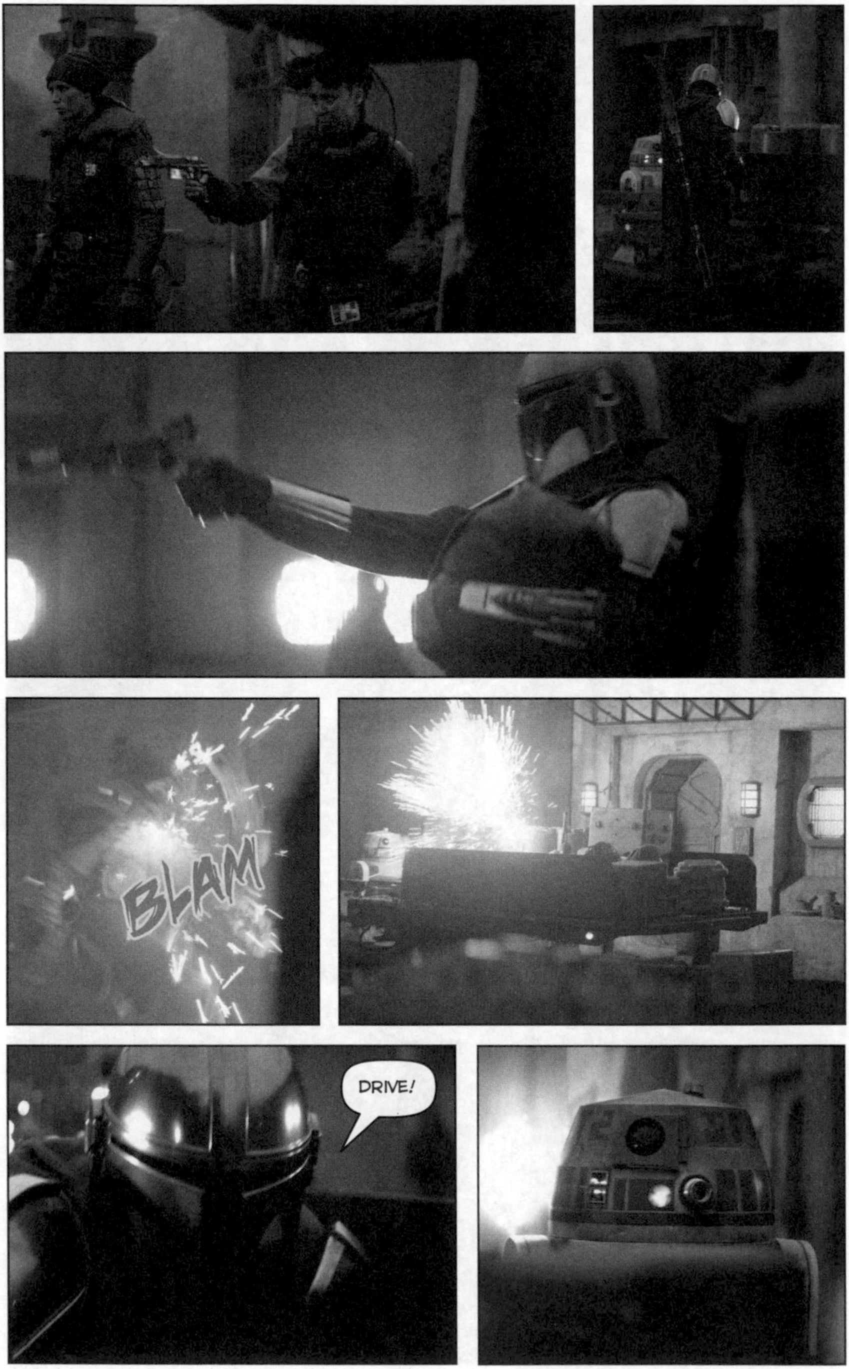
BLAM
DRIVE!

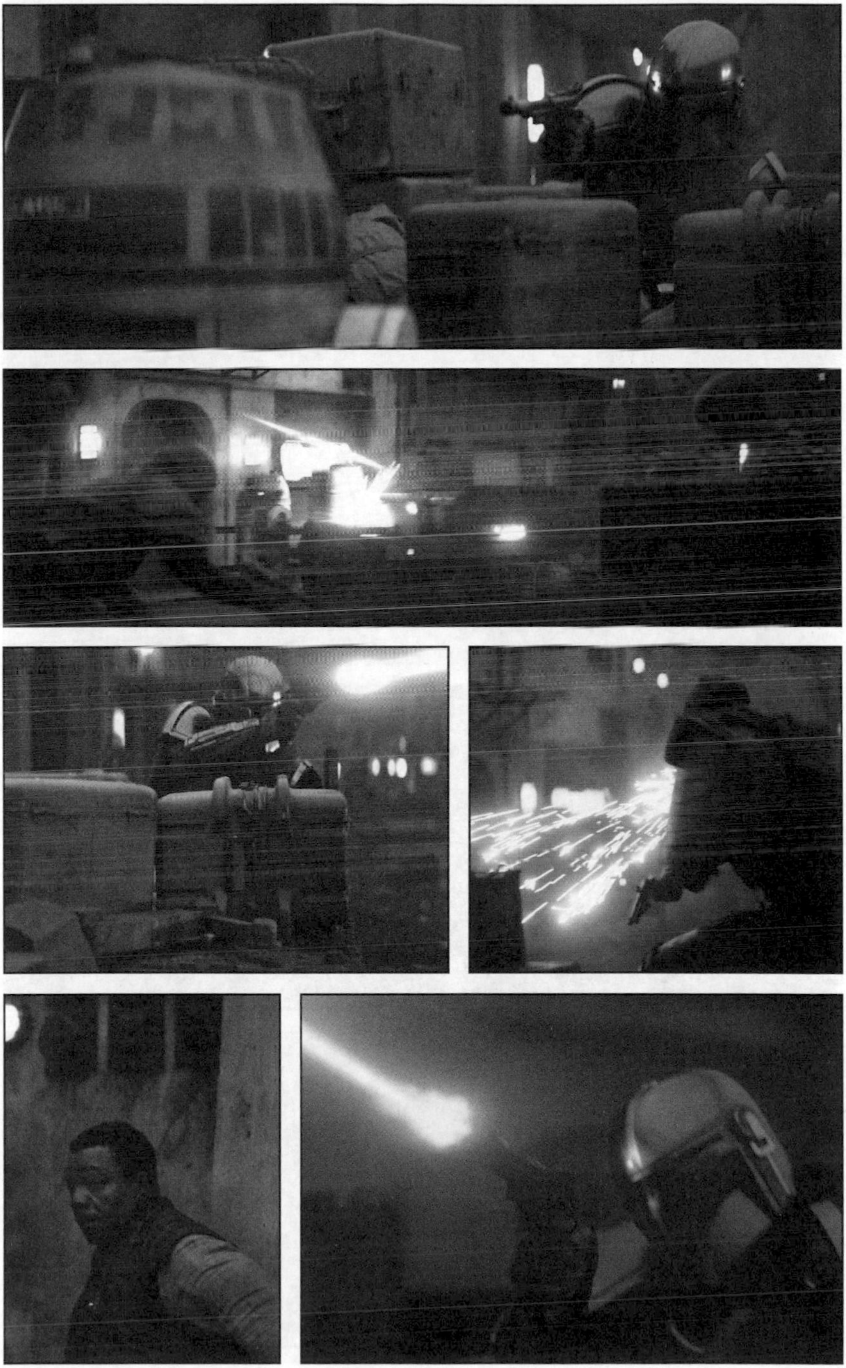

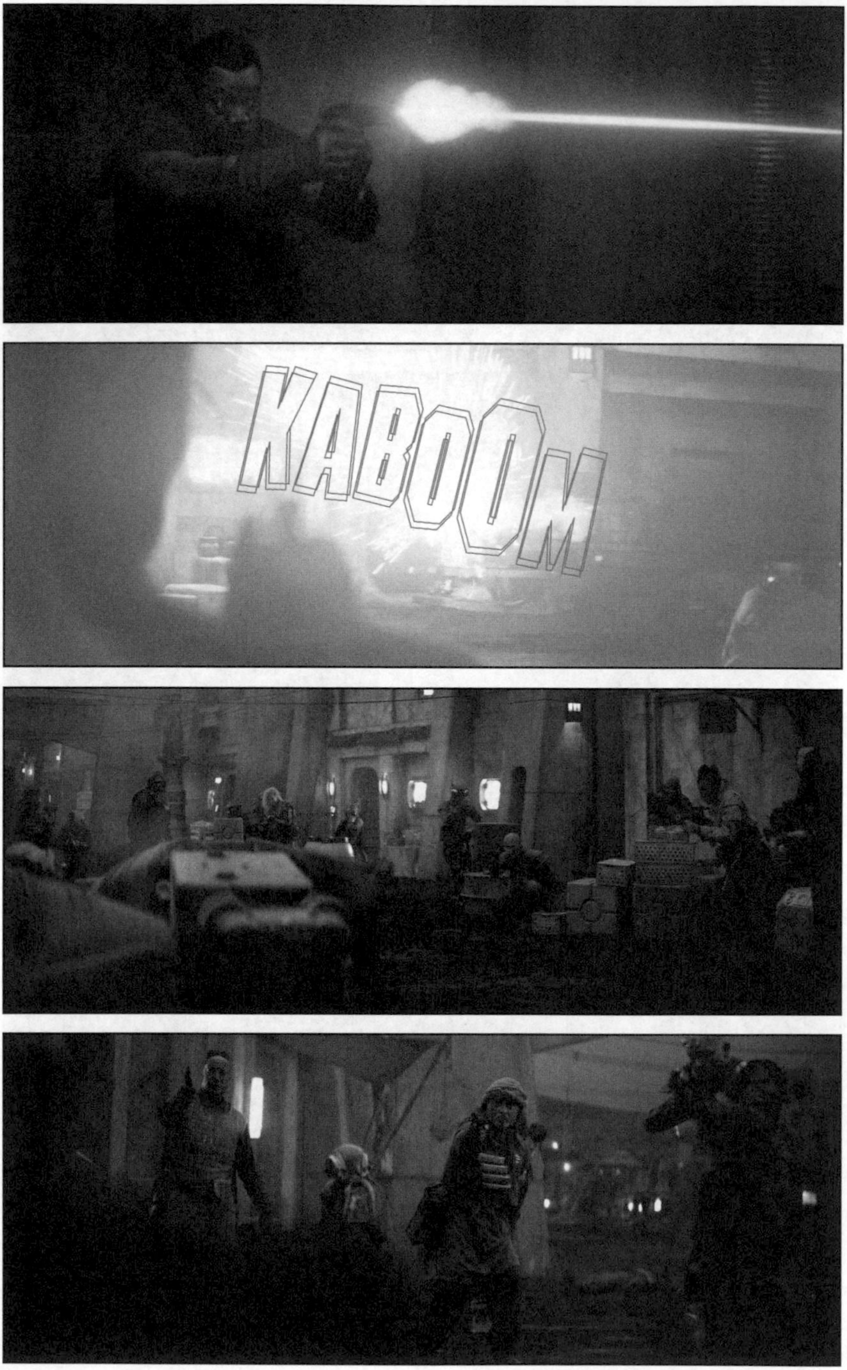
KABOOM

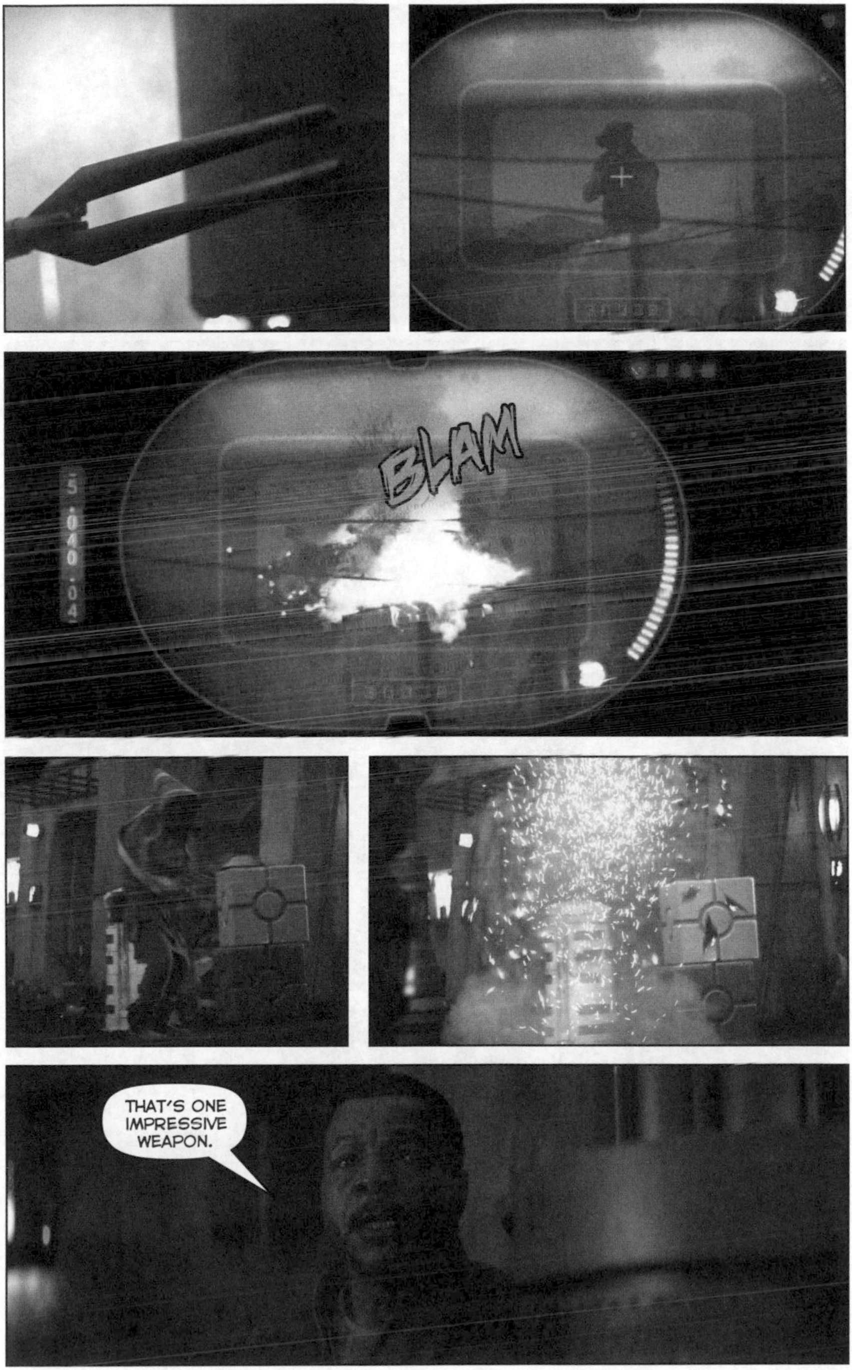
BLAM
THAT'S ONE IMPRESSIVE WEAPON.

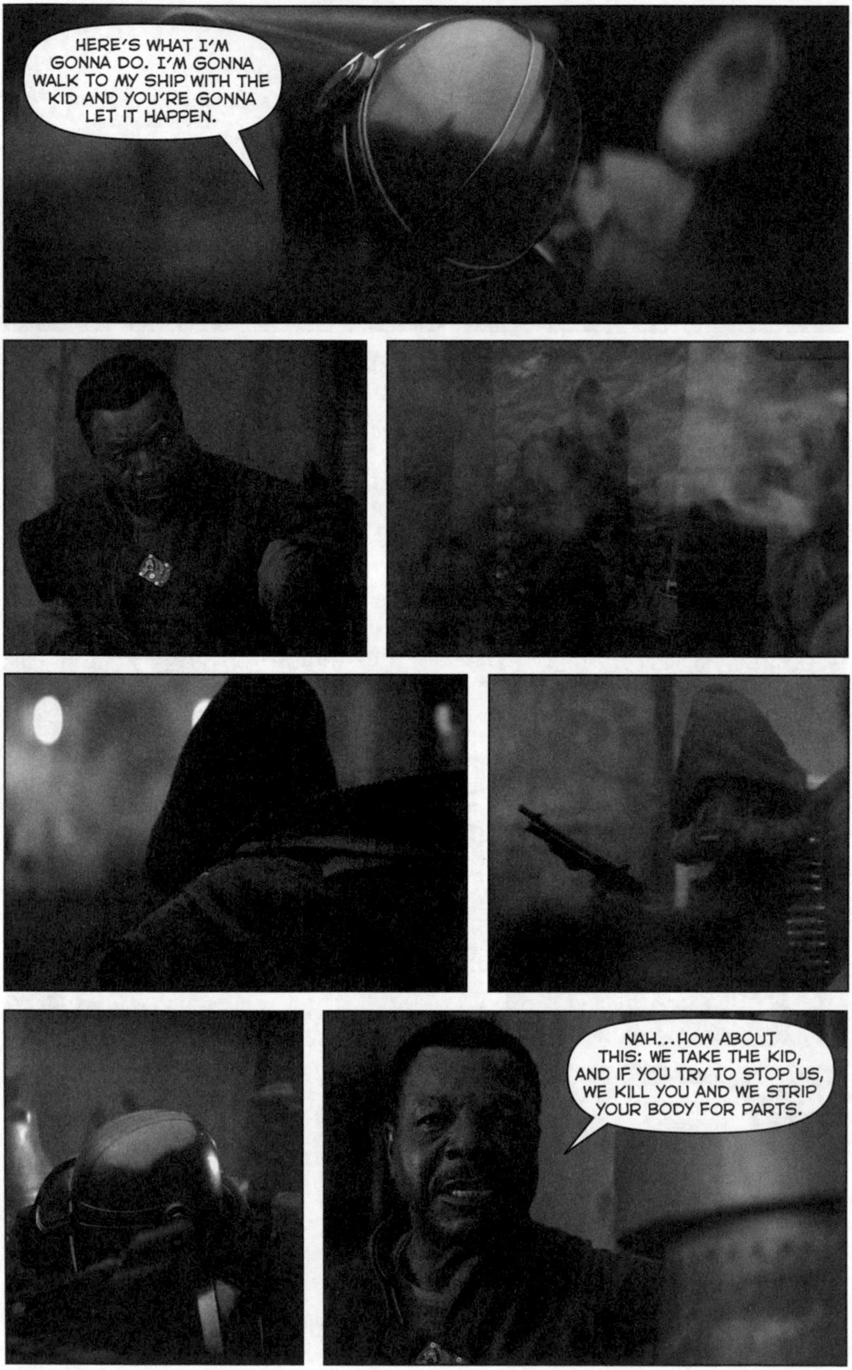
HERE'S WHAT I'M GONNA DO. I'M GONNA WALK TO MY SHIP WITH THE KID AND YOU'RE GONNA LET IT HAPPEN.
NAH...HOW ABOUT THIS: WE TAKE THE KID, AND IF YOU TRY TO STOP US, WE KILL YOU AND WE STRIP YOUR BODY FOR PARTS.

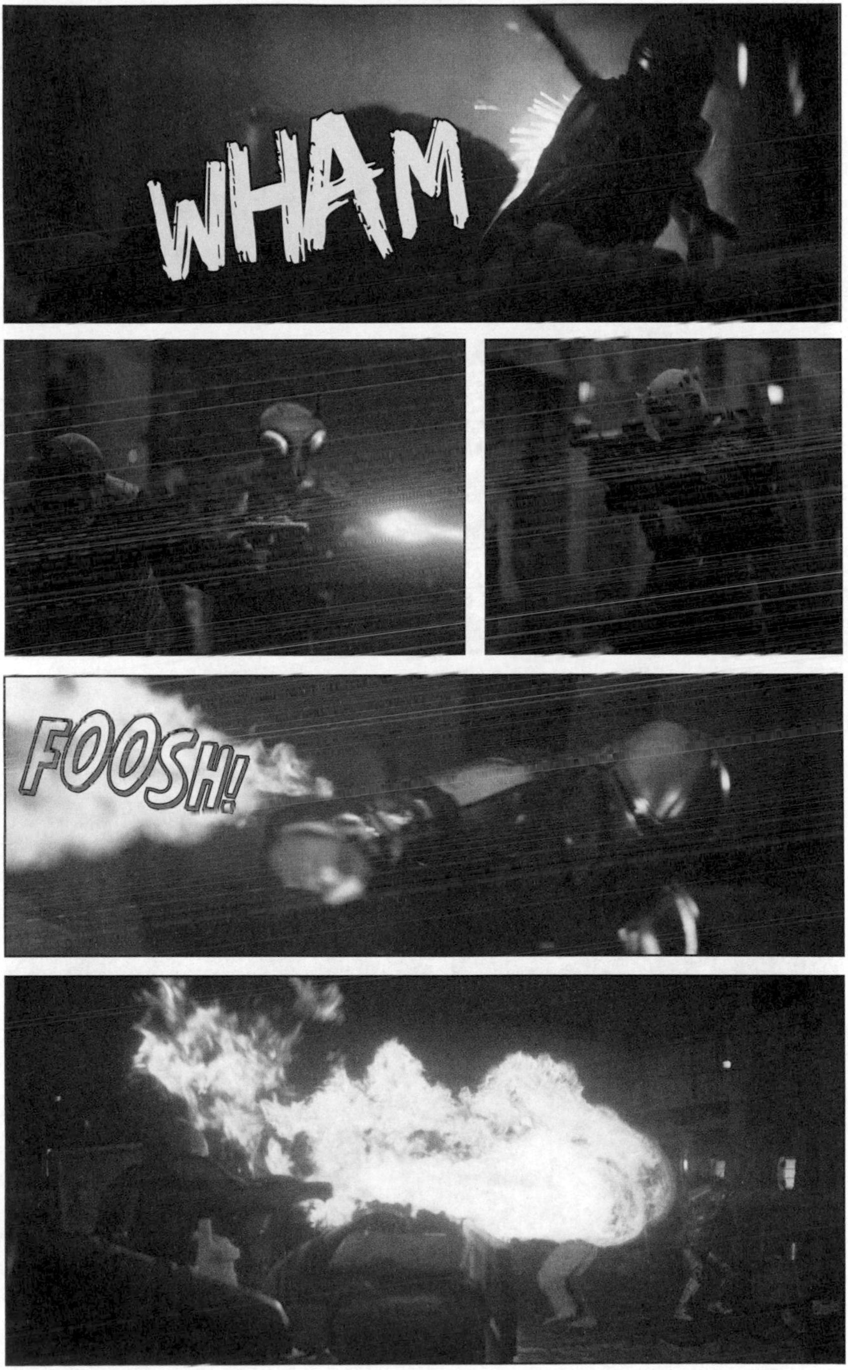
WHAM
FOOSH!

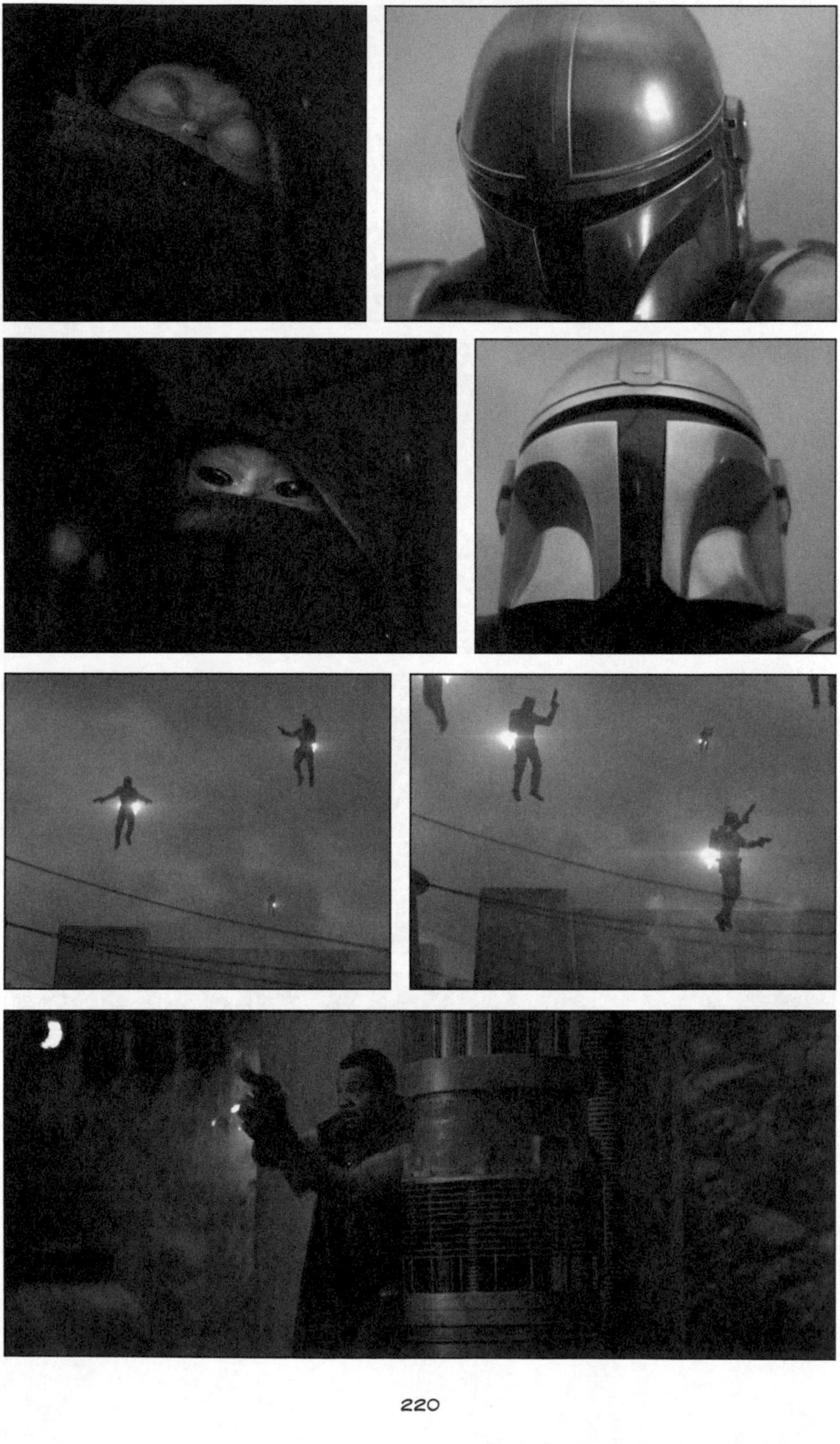

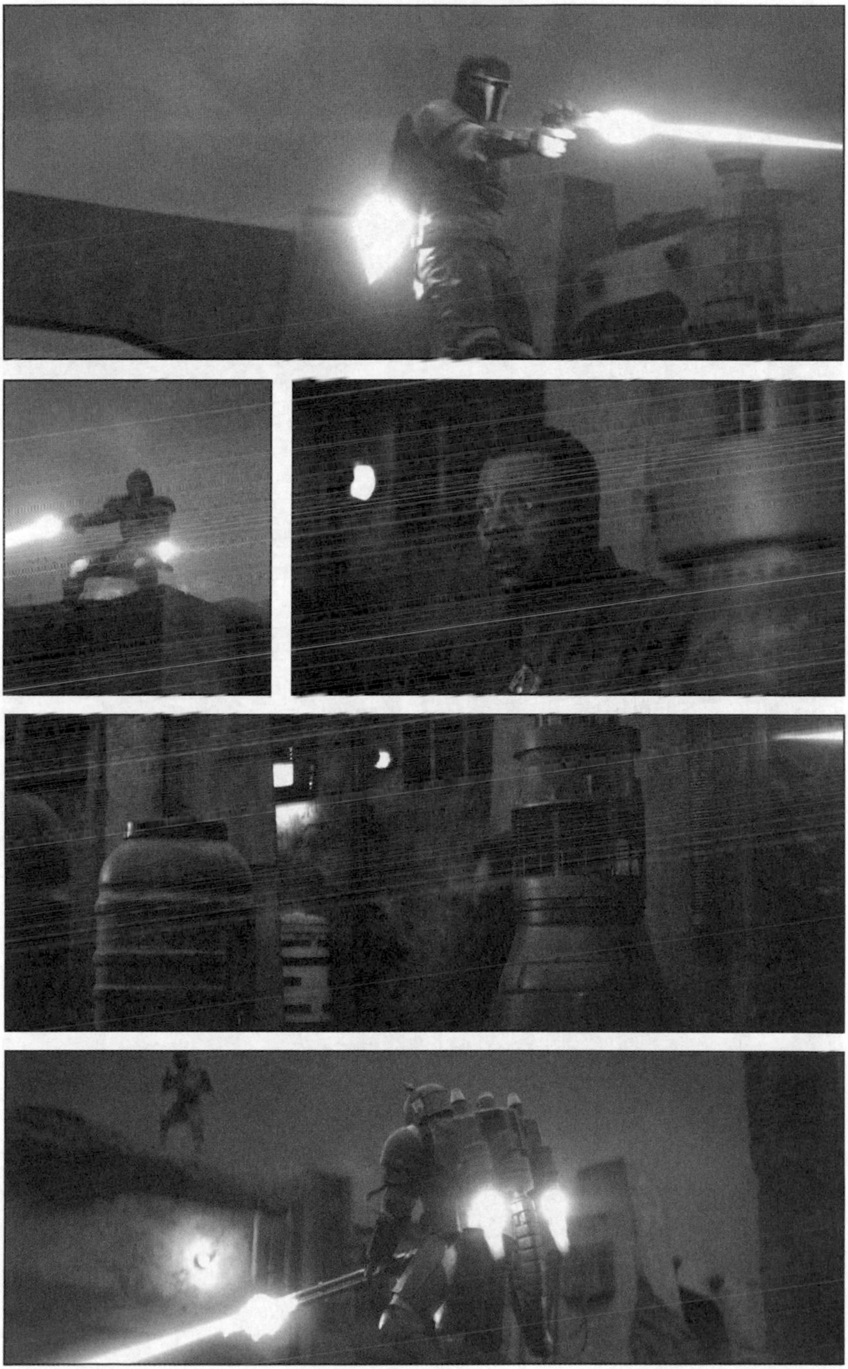

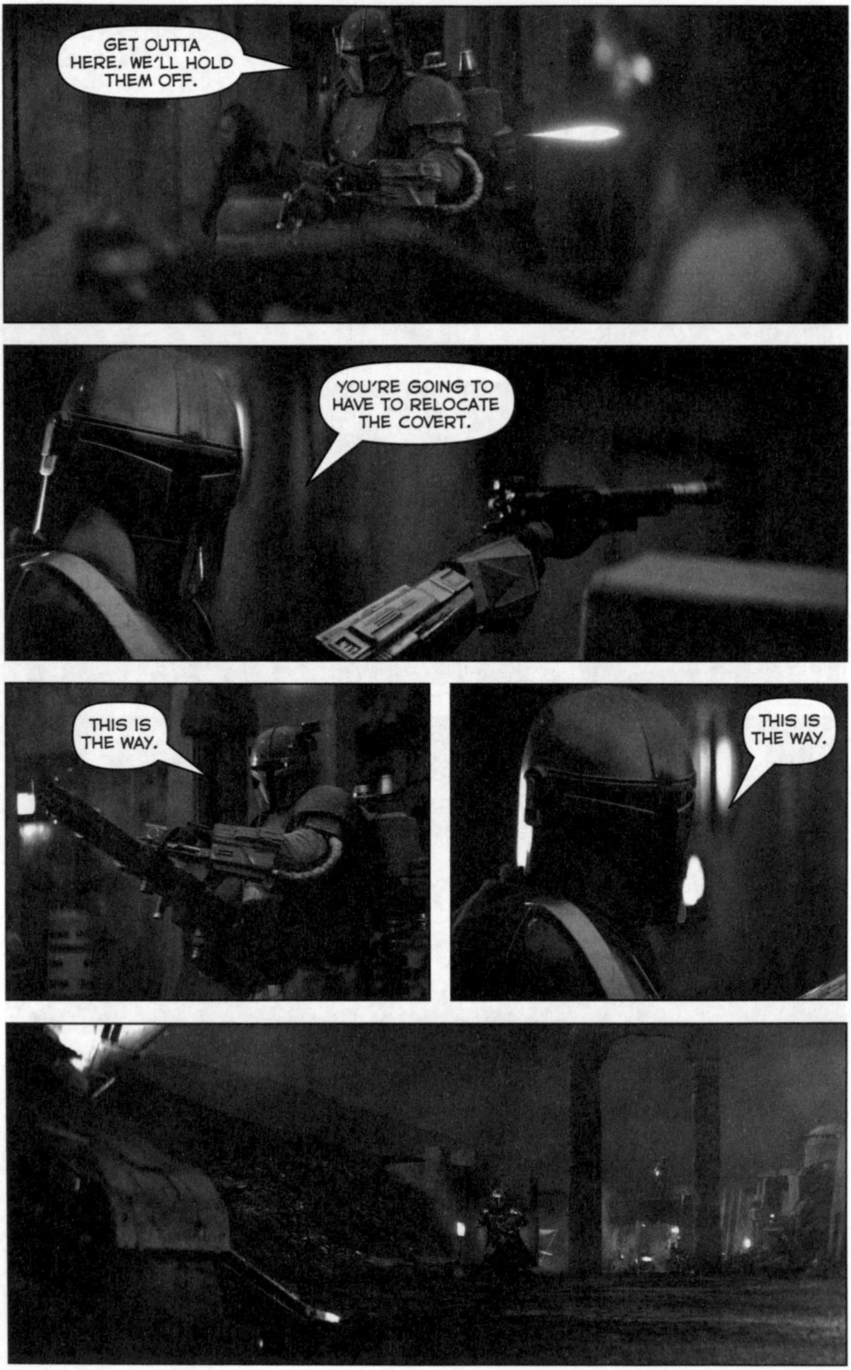
GET OUTTA HERE. WE'LL HOLD THEM OFF.
YOU'RE GOING TO HAVE TO RELOCATE THE COVERT.
THIS IS THE WAY.
THIS IS THE WAY.

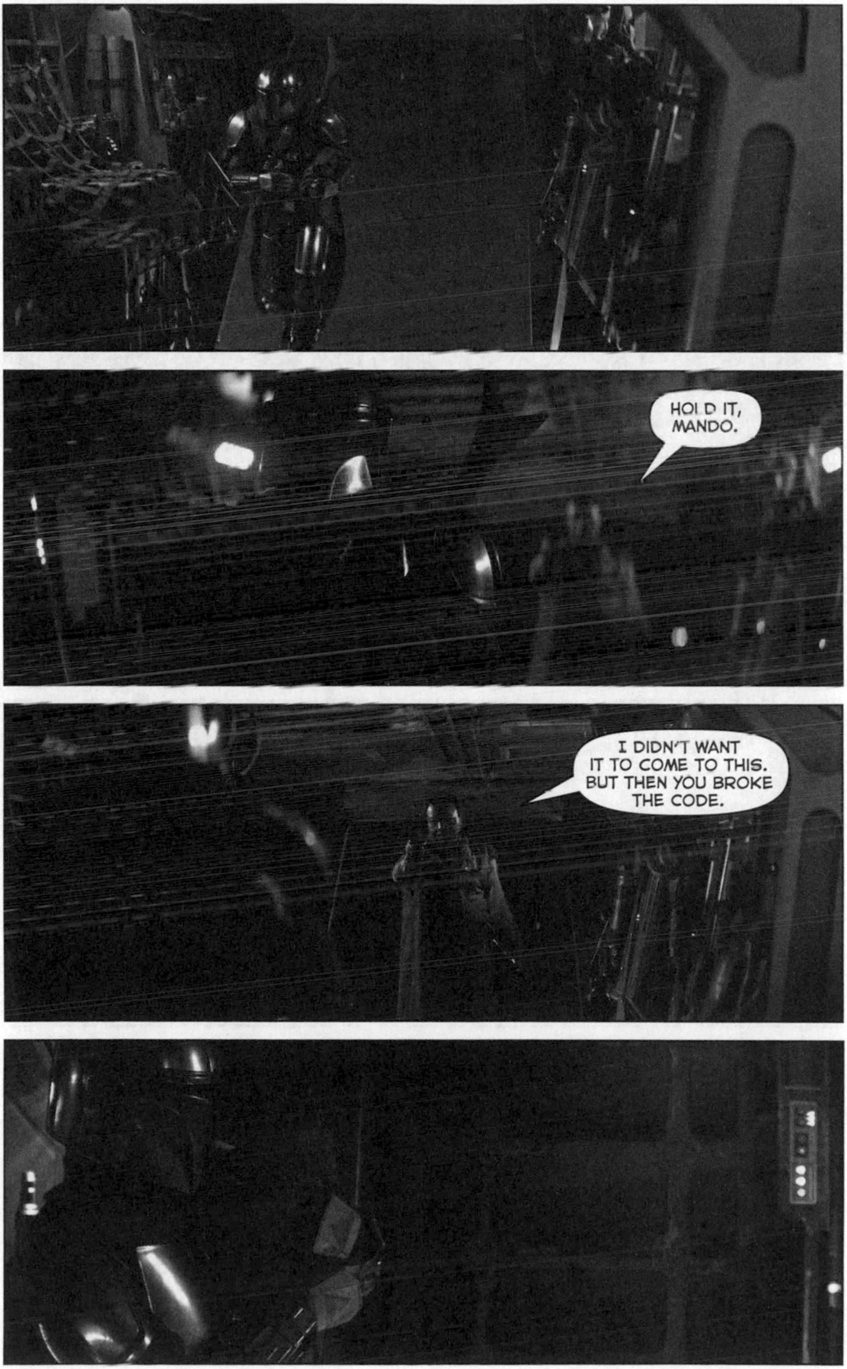
HOLD IT, MANDO.
I DIDN'T WANT IT TO COME TO THIS. BUT THEN YOU BROKE THE CODE.

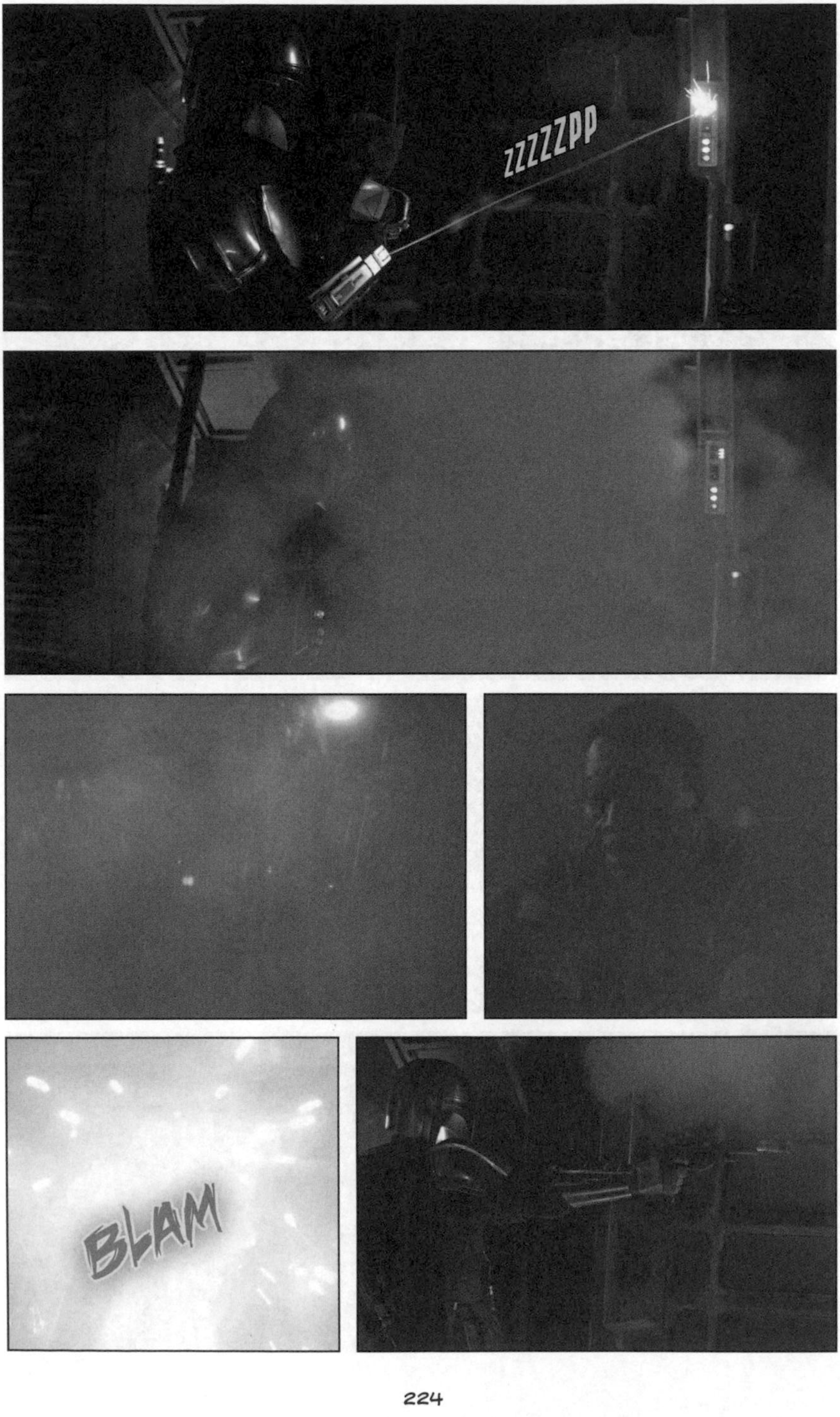
ZZZZZPP
BLAM

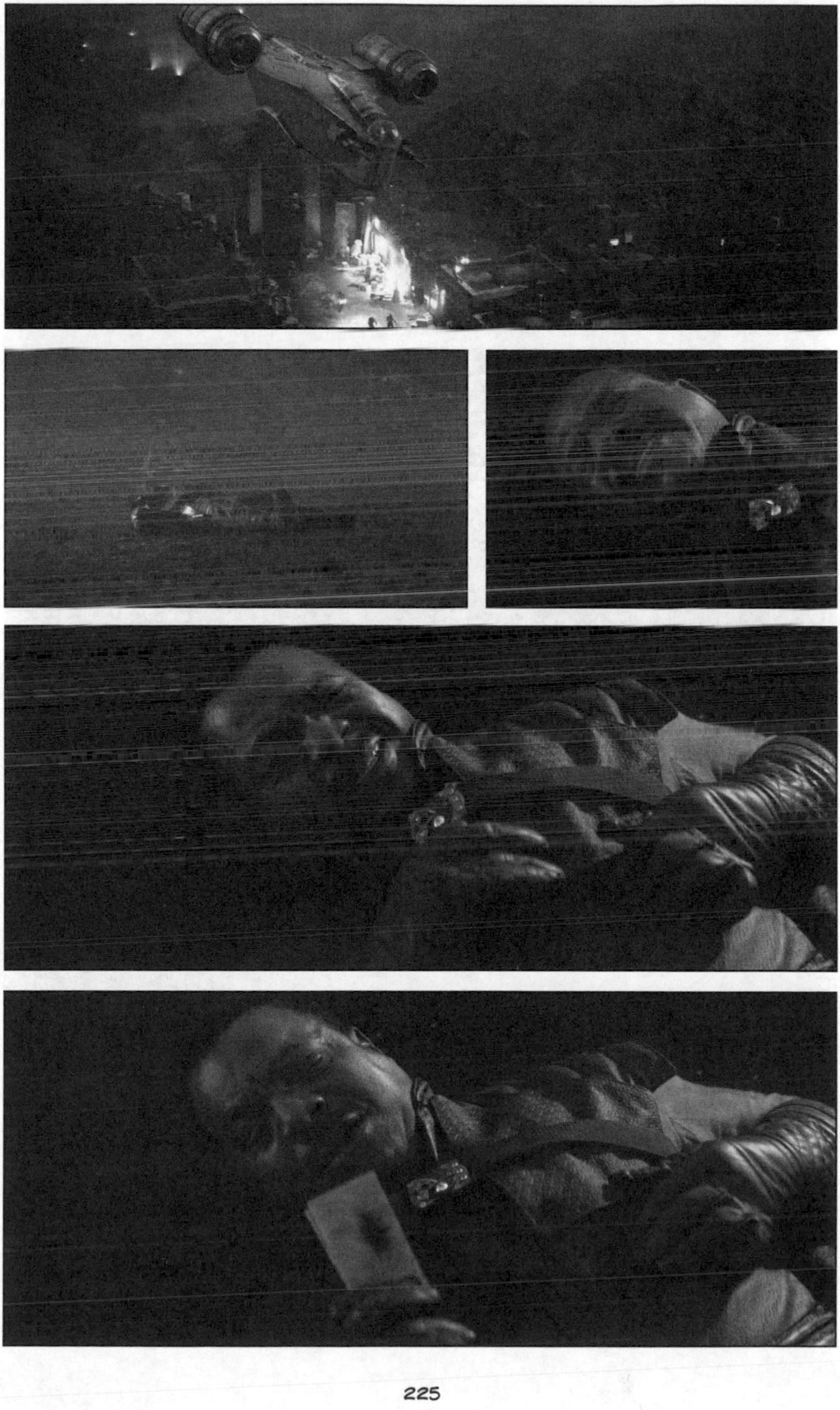

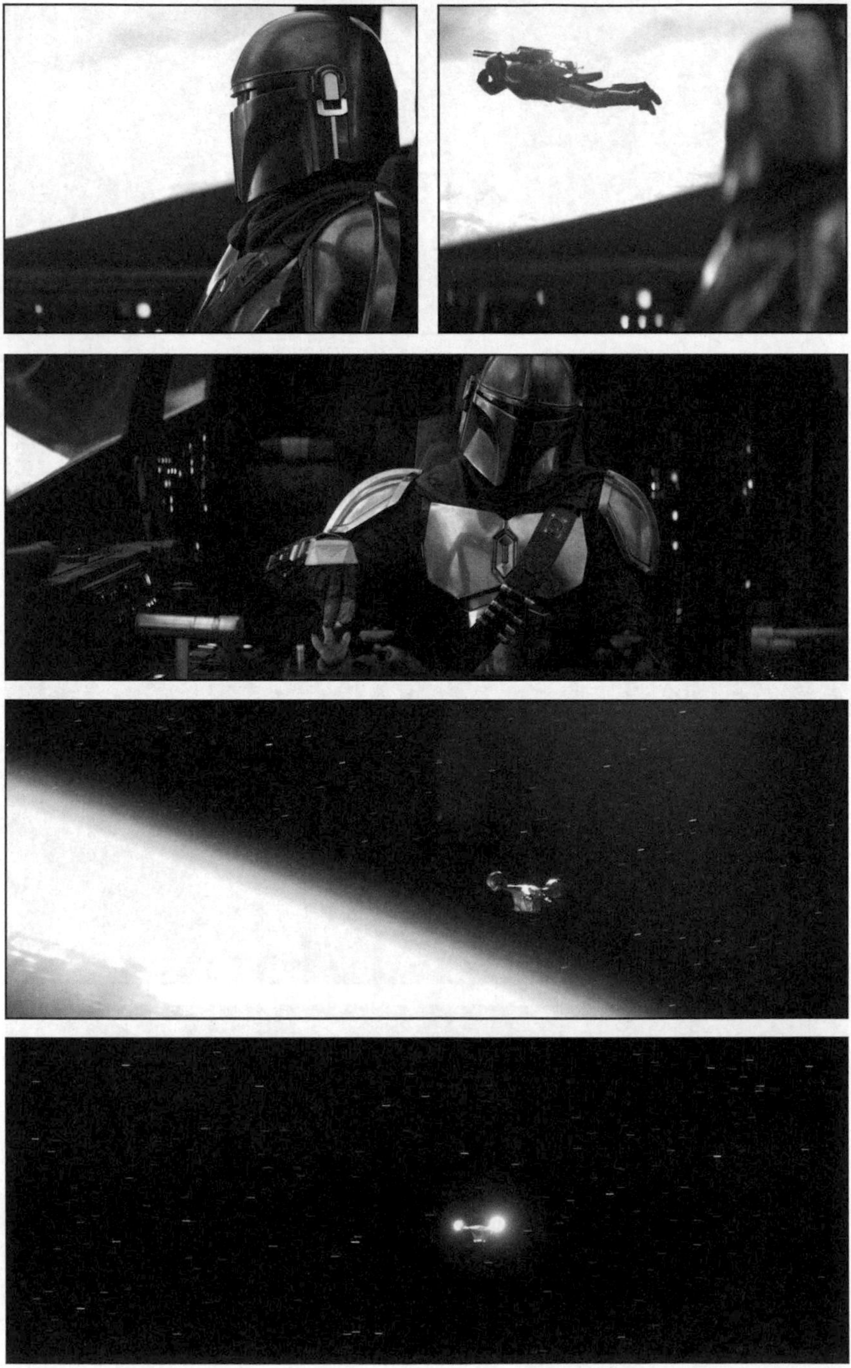

Chapter 4

SANCTUARY

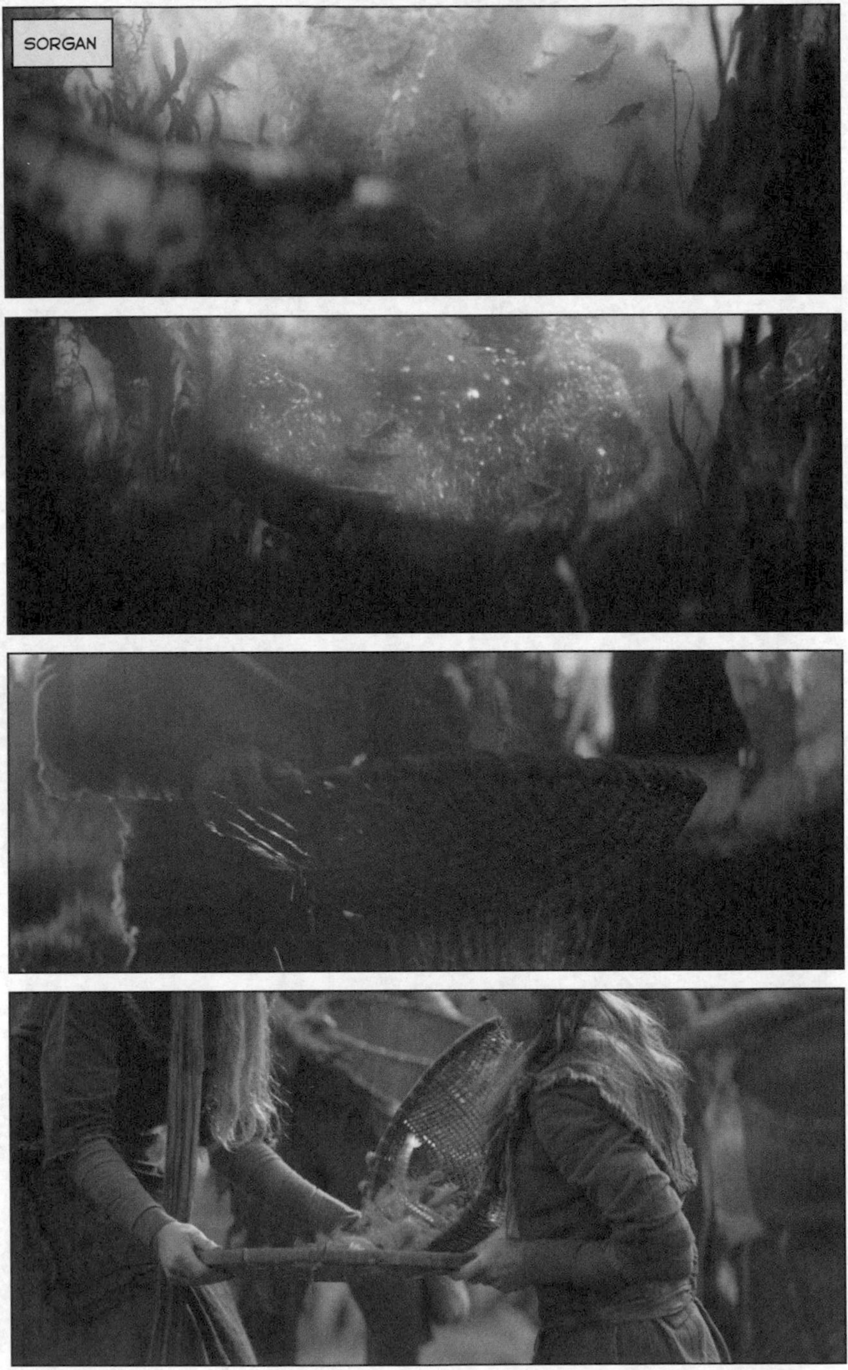
SORGAN

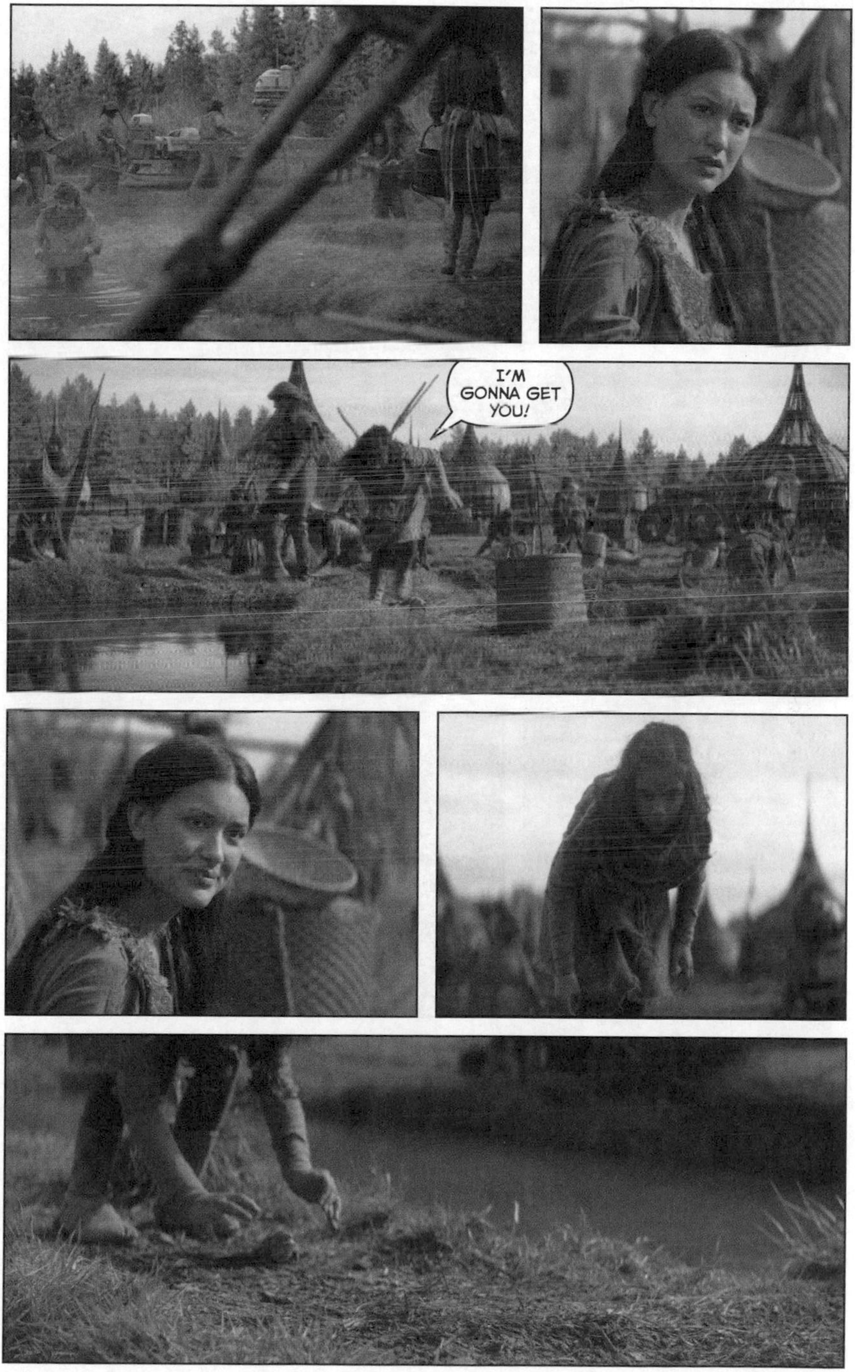
I'M GONNA GET YOU!

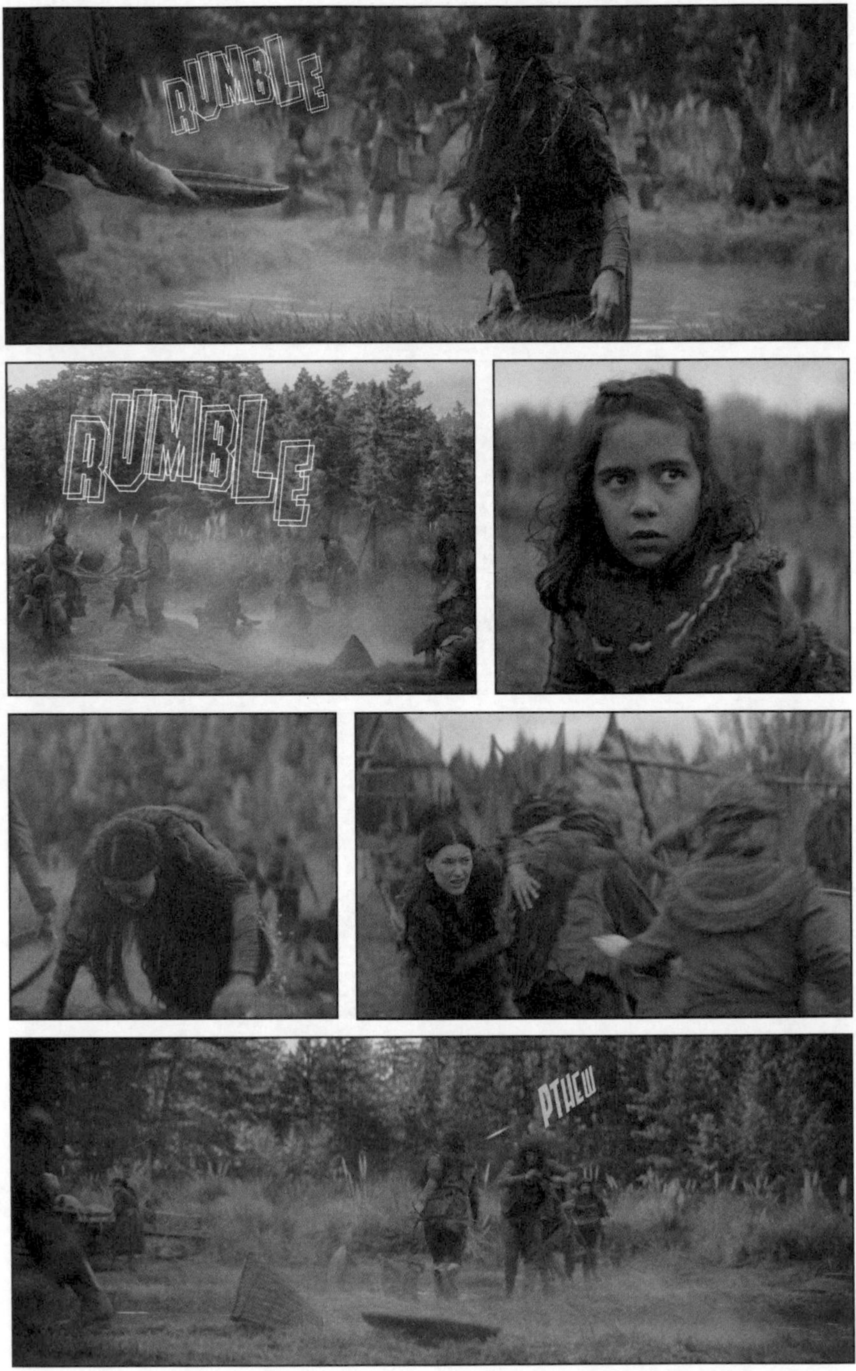
RUMBLE
RUMBLE
PTHEW

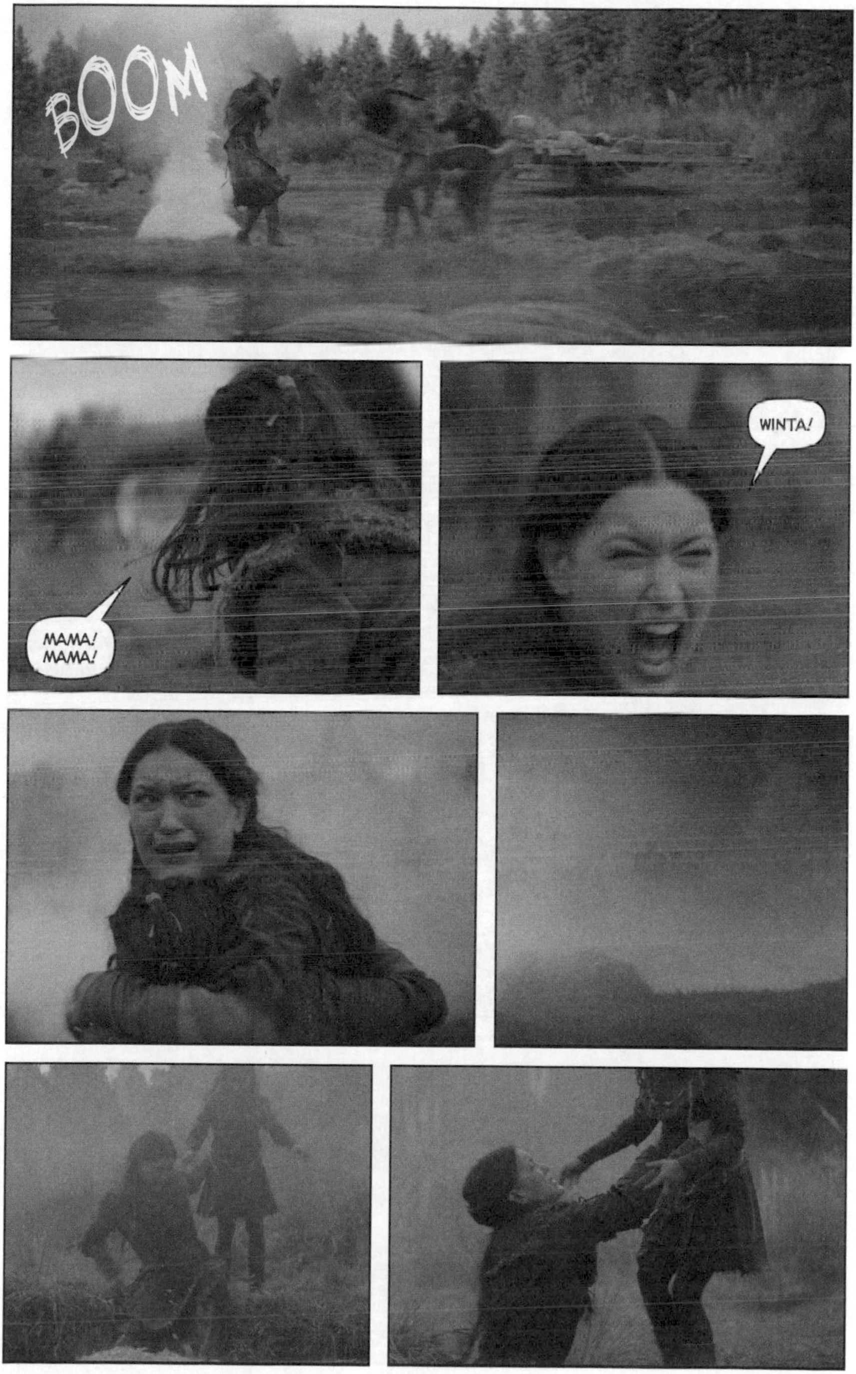
BOOM
MAMA! MAMA!
WINTA!

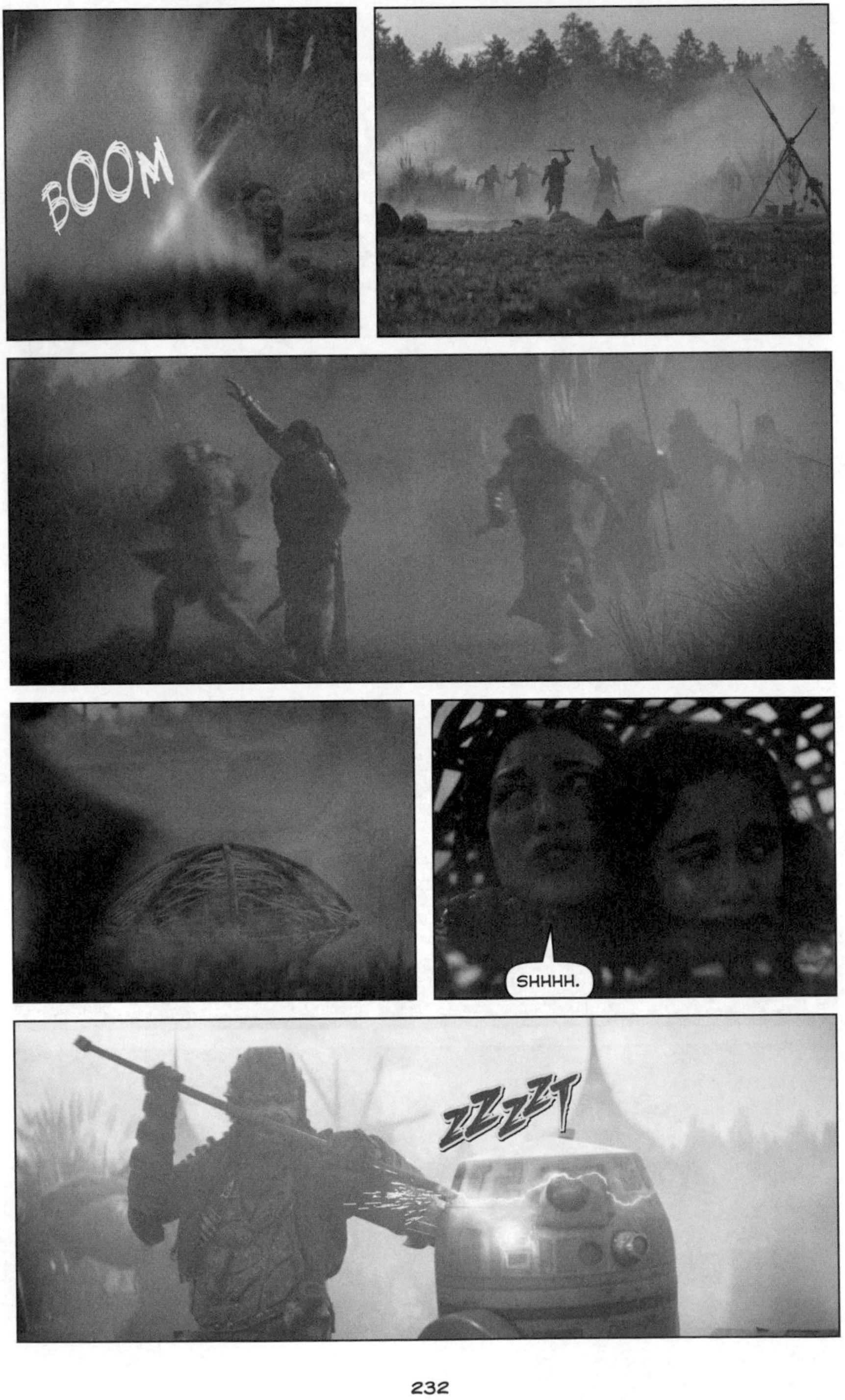
BOOM
SHHHH.
ZZZZT

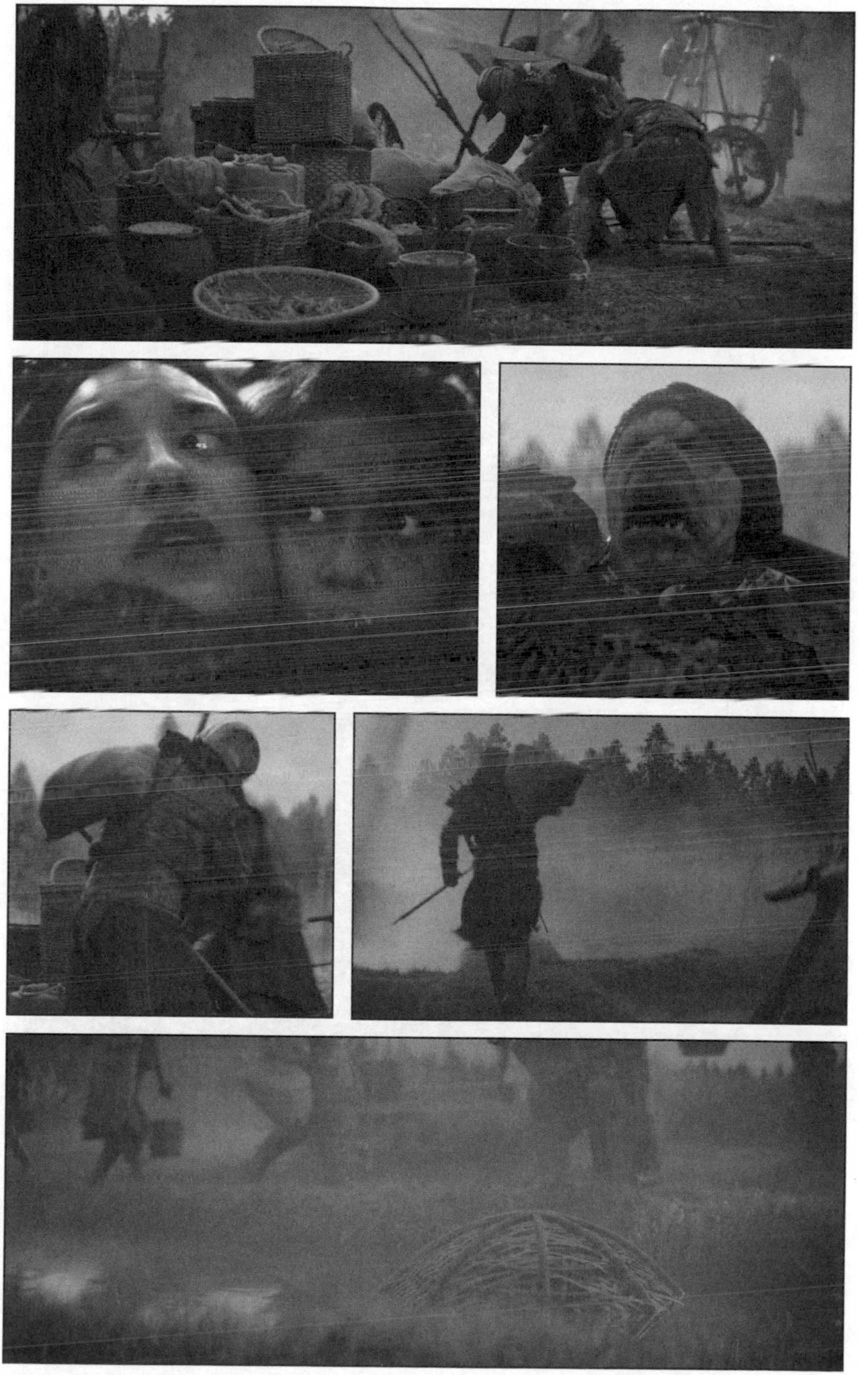

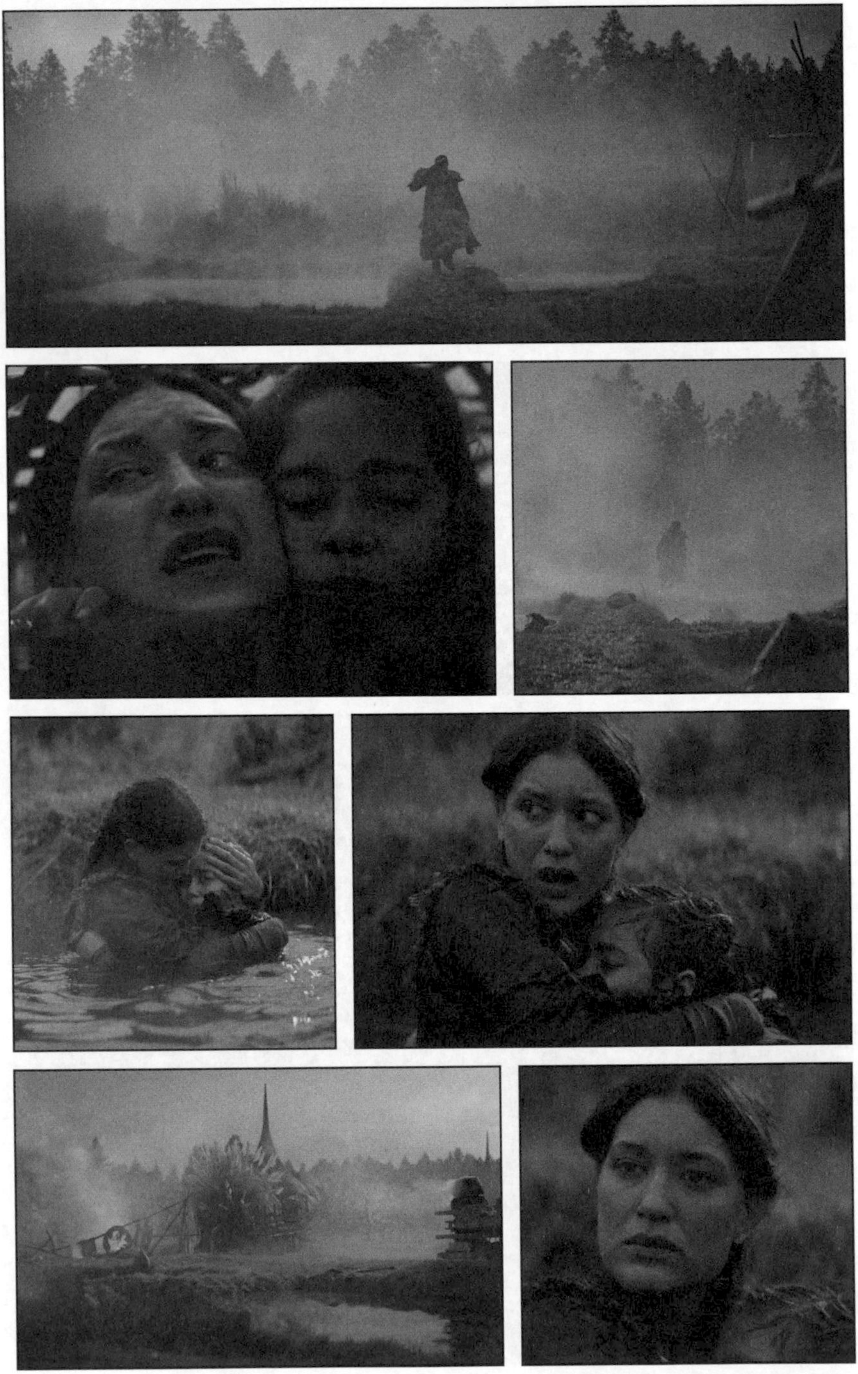

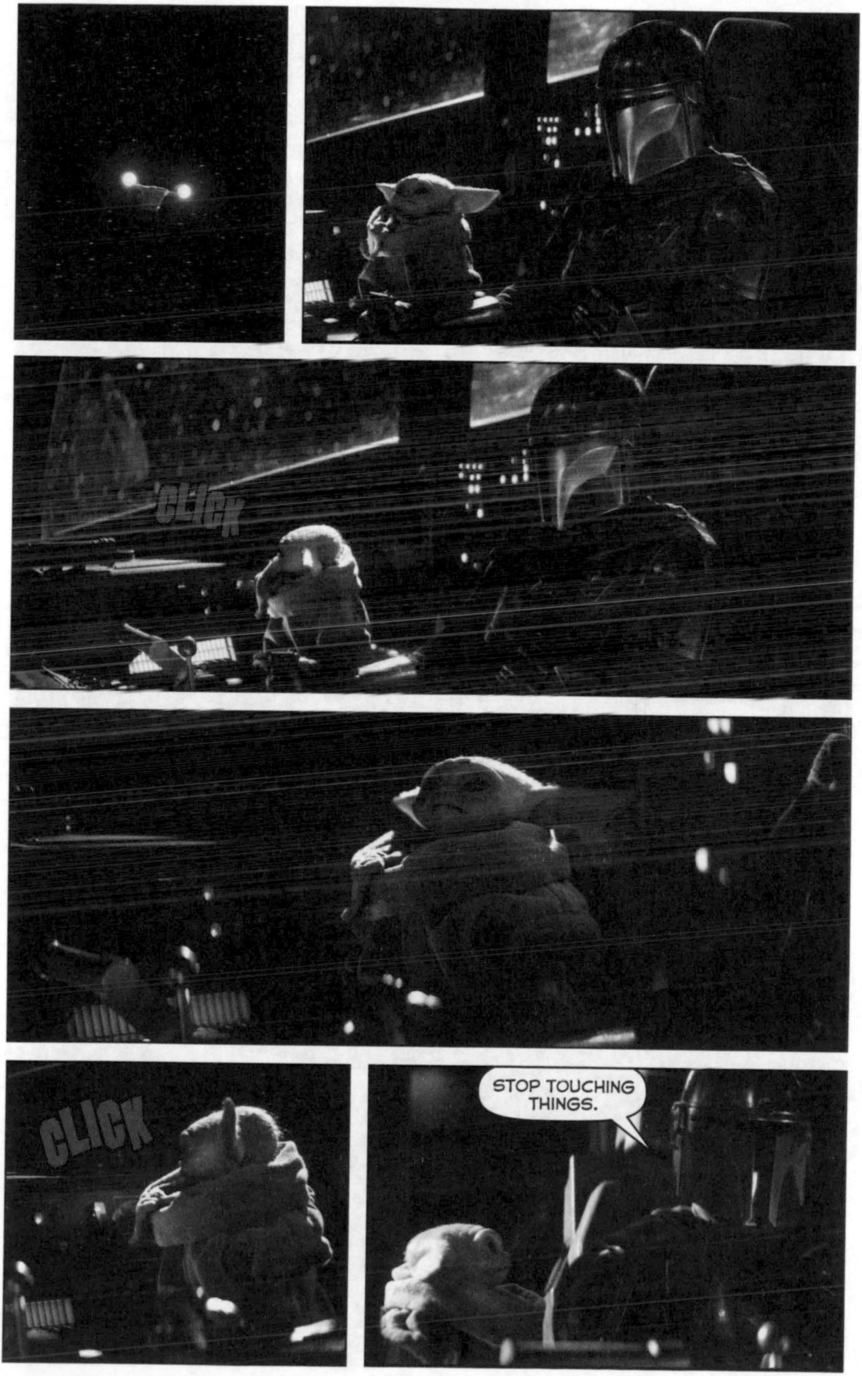
CLICK
CLICK
STOP TOUCHING THINGS.

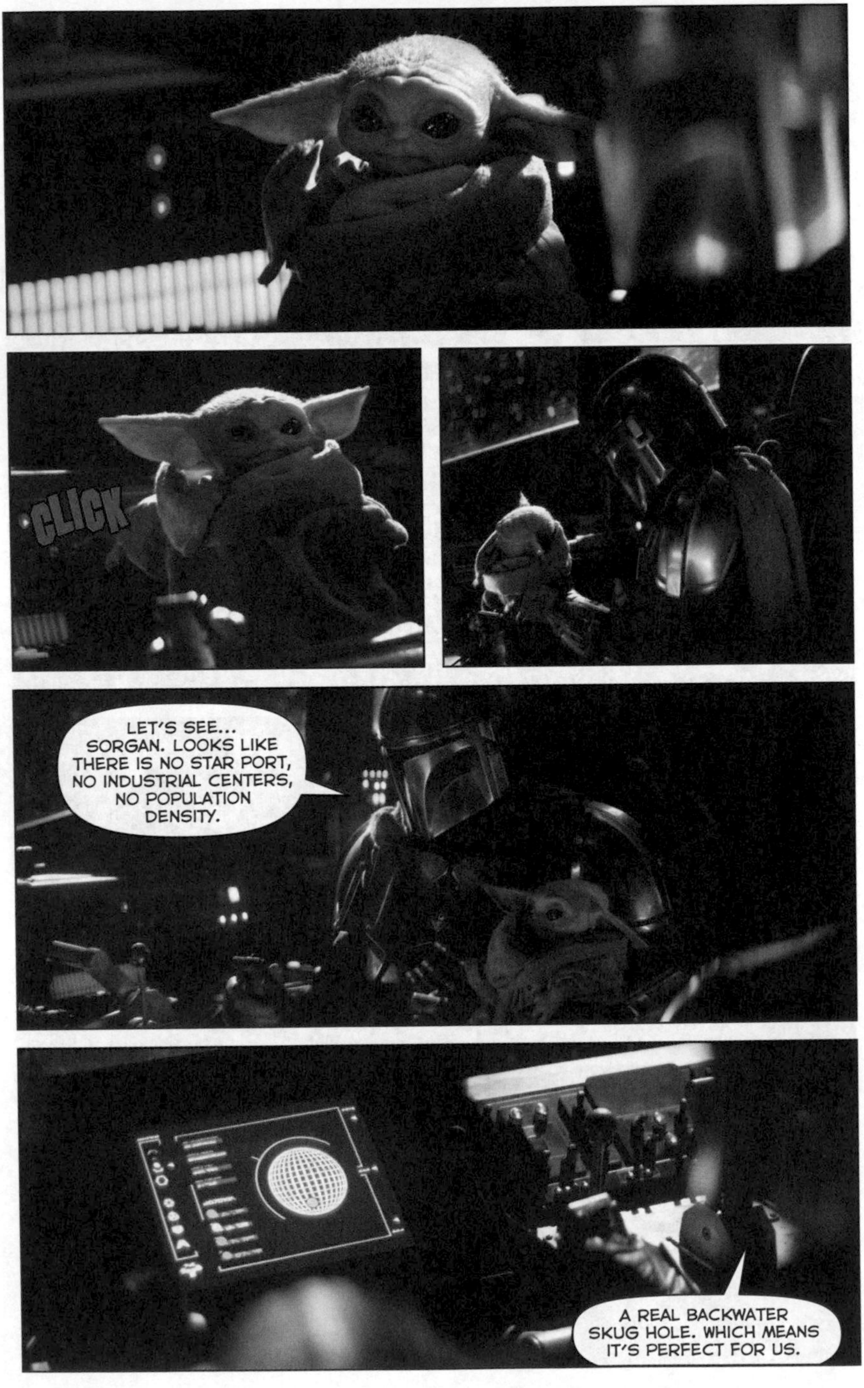
CLICK
LET'S SEE... SORGAN. LOOKS LIKE THERE IS NO STAR PORT, NO INDUSTRIAL CENTERS, NO POPULATION DENSITY.
A REAL BACKWATER SKUG HOLE. WHICH MEANS IT'S PERFECT FOR US.

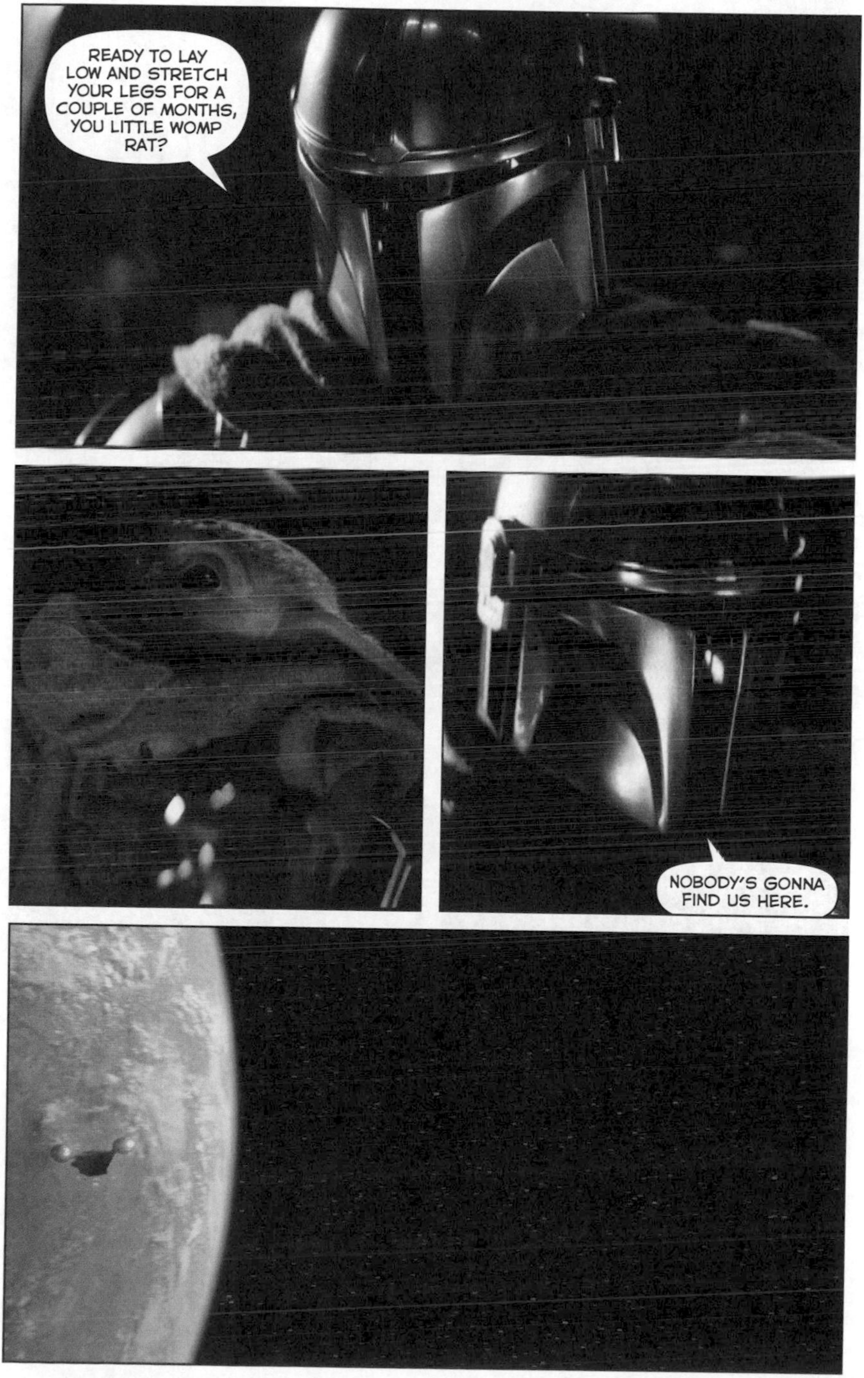
READY TO LAY LOW AND STRETCH YOUR LEGS FOR A COUPLE OF MONTHS, YOU LITTLE WOMP RAT?
NOBODY'S GONNA FIND US HERE.

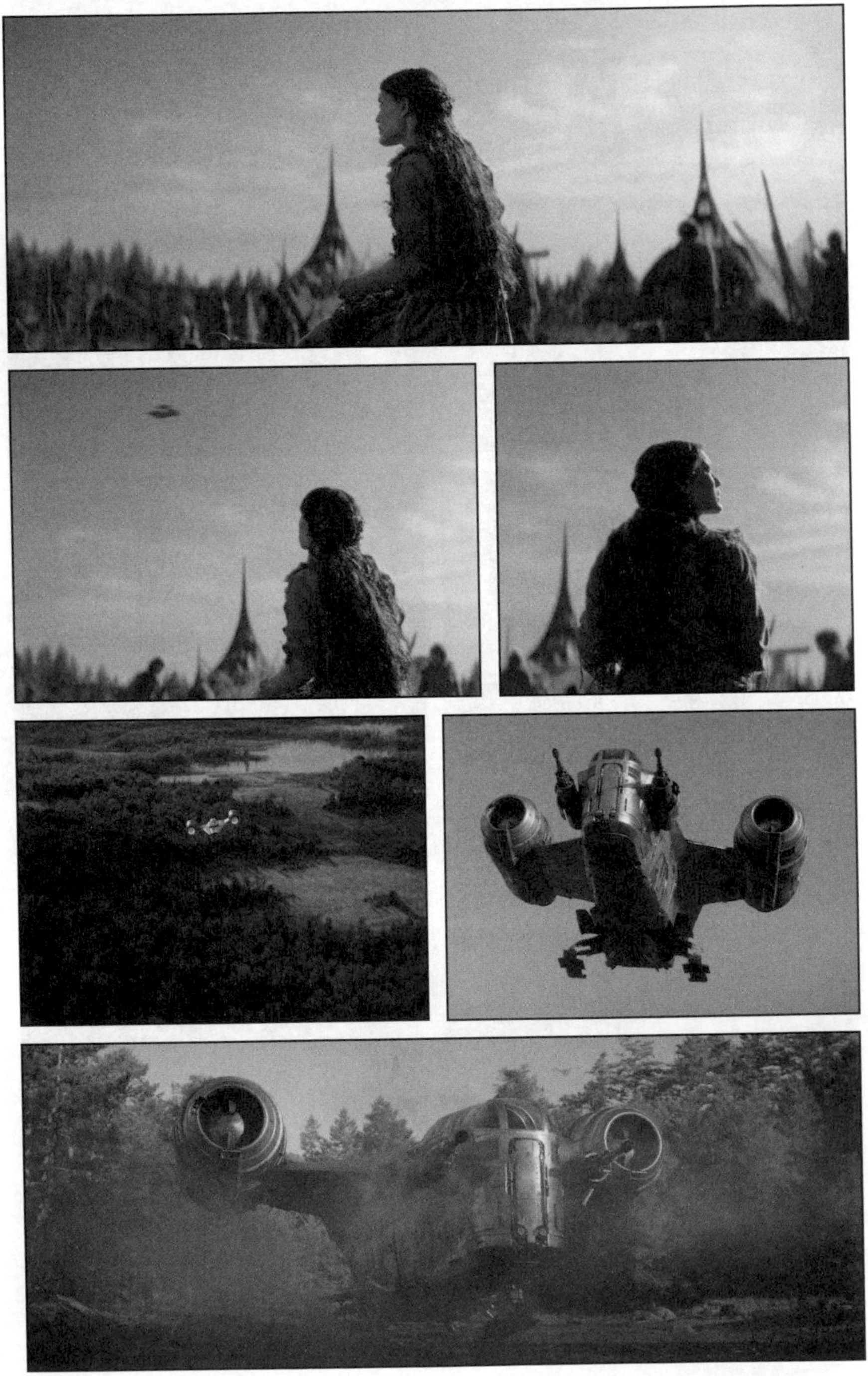

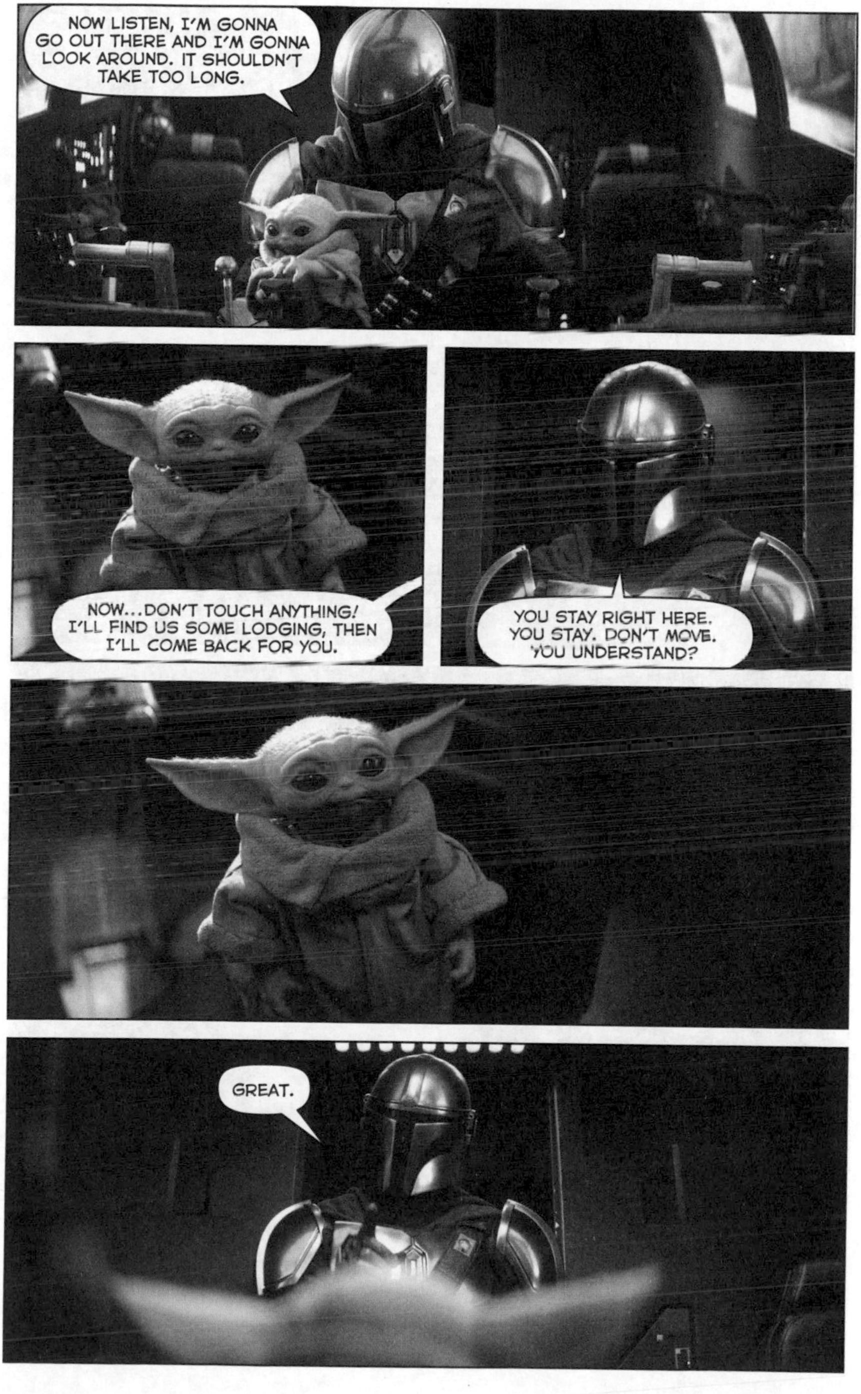
NOW LISTEN, I'M GONNA GO OUT THERE AND I'M GONNA LOOK AROUND. IT SHOULDN'T TAKE TOO LONG.
NOW...DON'T TOUCH ANYTHING! I'LL FIND US SOME LODGING, THEN I'LL COME BACK FOR YOU.
YOU STAY RIGHT HERE. YOU STAY. DON'T MOVE. YOU UNDERSTAND?
GREAT.

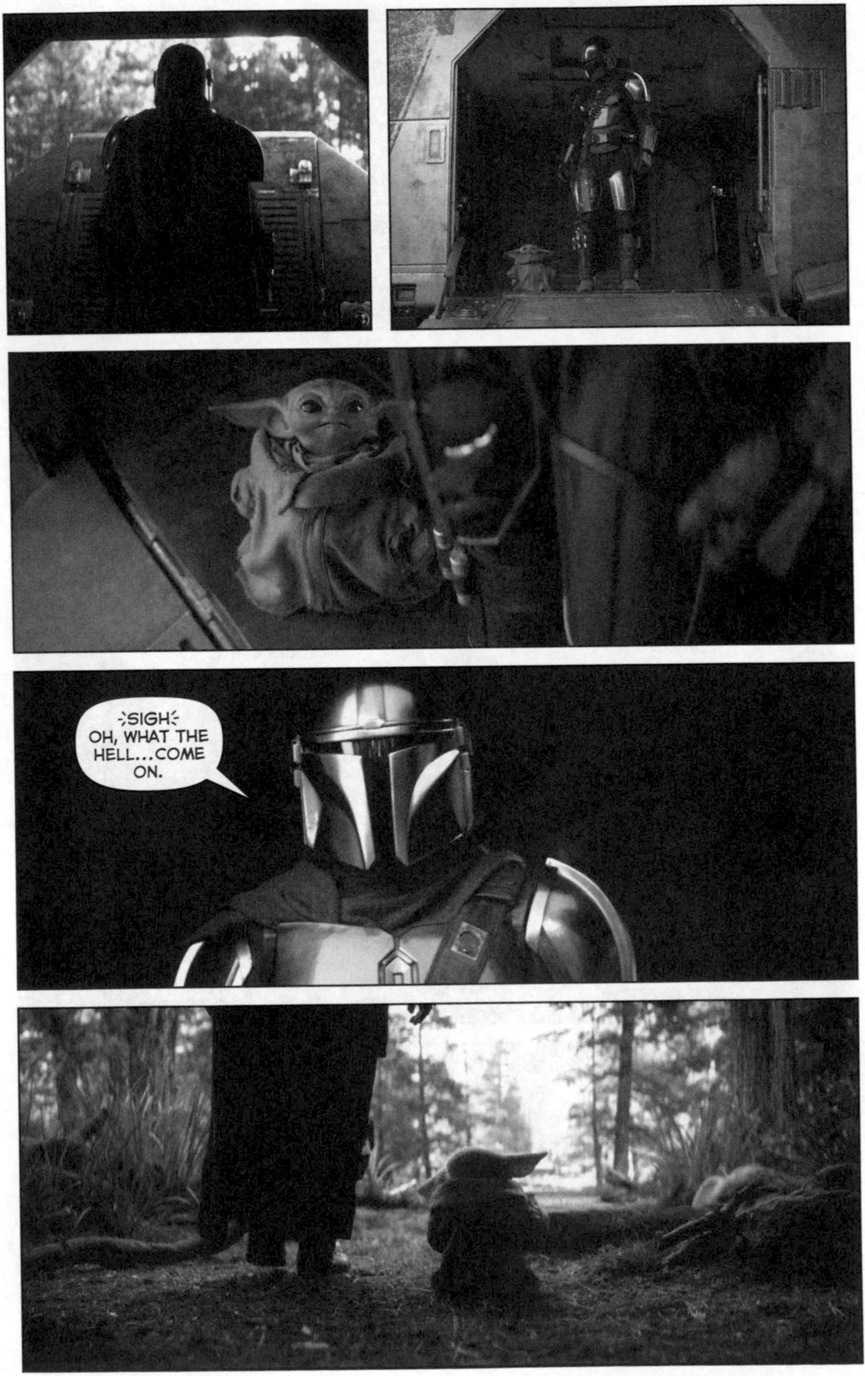

SIGH
OH, WHAT THE HELL...COME ON.

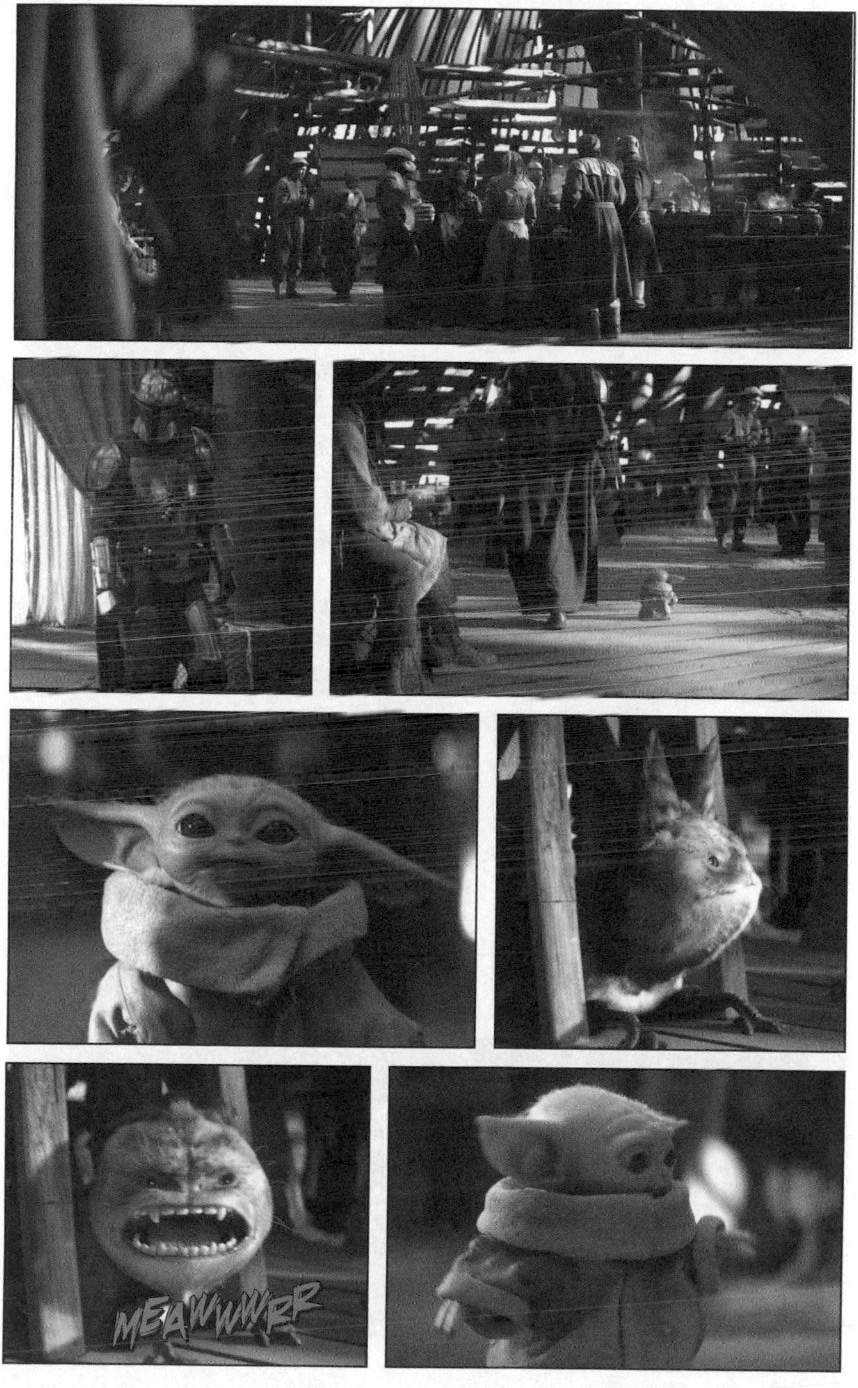
MEAWWWRR

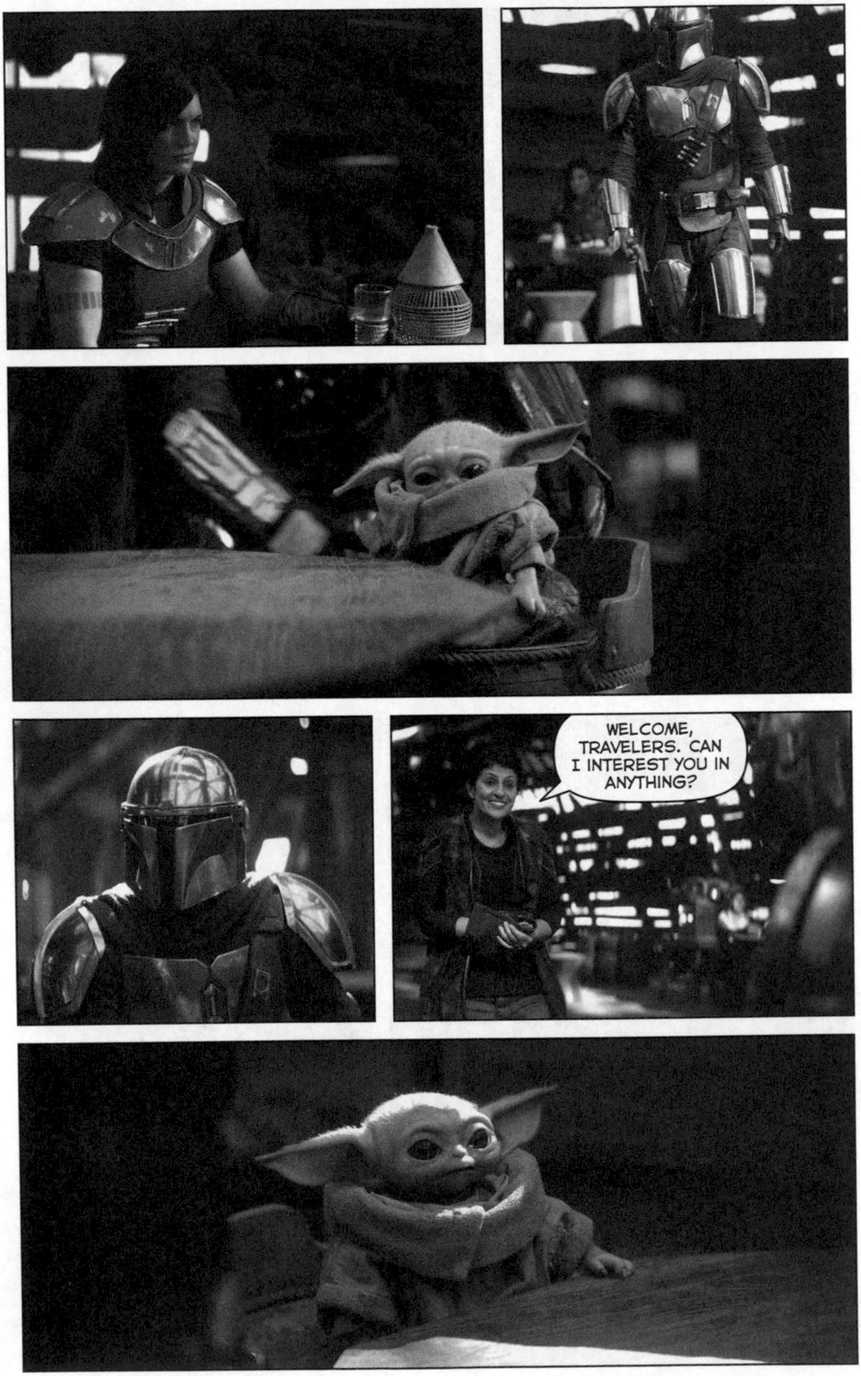
WELCOME, TRAVELERS. CAN I INTEREST YOU IN ANYTHING?

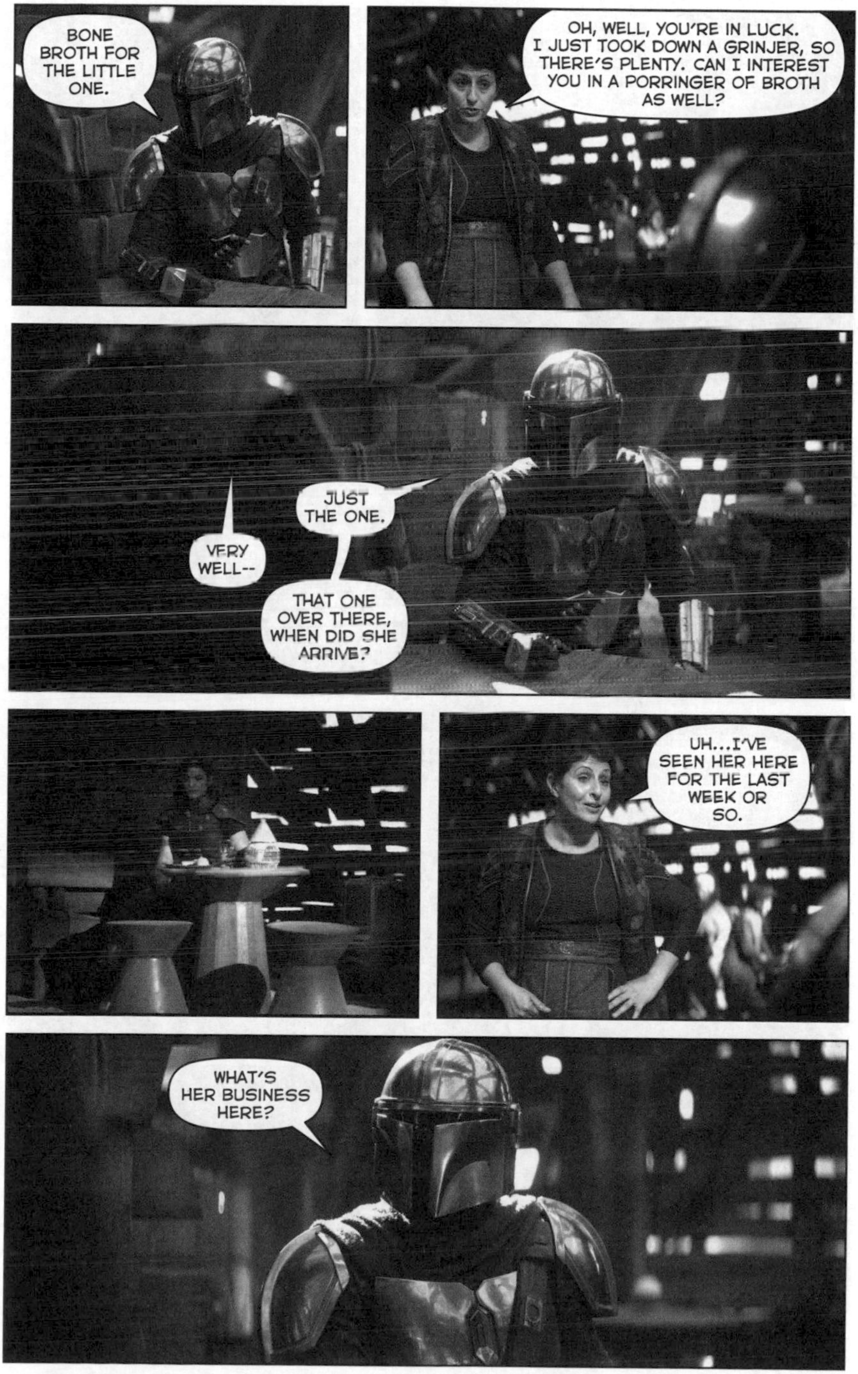
BONE BROTH FOR THE LITTLE ONE.
OH, WELL, YOU'RE IN LUCK. I JUST TOOK DOWN A GRINJER, SO THERE'S PLENTY. CAN I INTEREST YOU IN A PORRINGER OF BROTH AS WELL?
JUST THE ONE.
VERY WELL--
THAT ONE OVER THERE, WHEN DID SHE ARRIVE?
UH...I'VE SEEN HER HERE FOR THE LAST WEEK OR SO.
WHAT'S HER BUSINESS HERE?

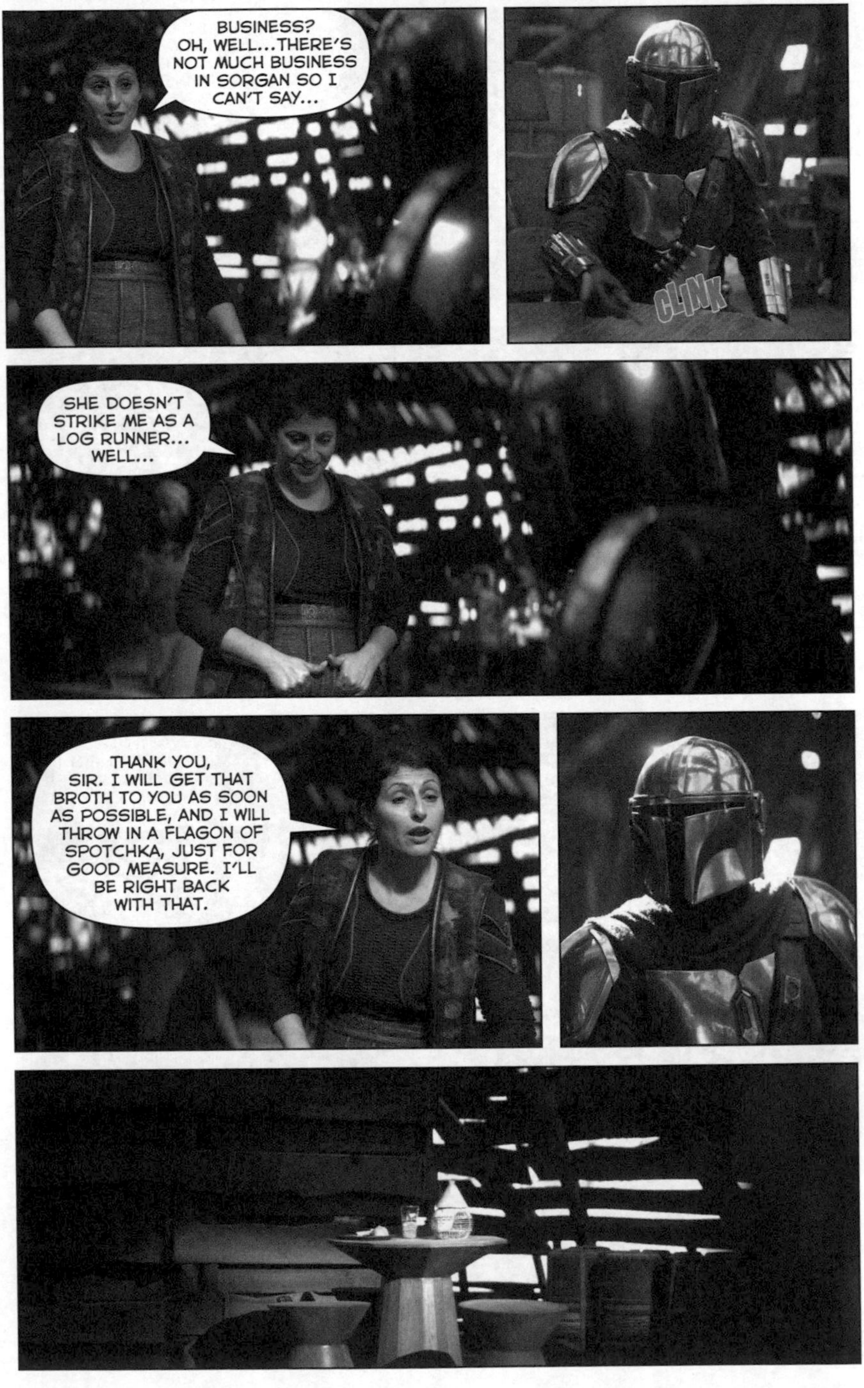
BUSINESS? OH, WELL...THERE'S NOT MUCH BUSINESS IN SORGAN SO I CAN'T SAY...
CLINK
SHE DOESN'T STRIKE ME AS A LOG RUNNER... WELL...
THANK YOU, SIR. I WILL GET THAT BROTH TO YOU AS SOON AS POSSIBLE, AND I WILL THROW IN A FLAGON OF SPOTCHKA, JUST FOR GOOD MEASURE. I'LL BE RIGHT BACK WITH THAT.

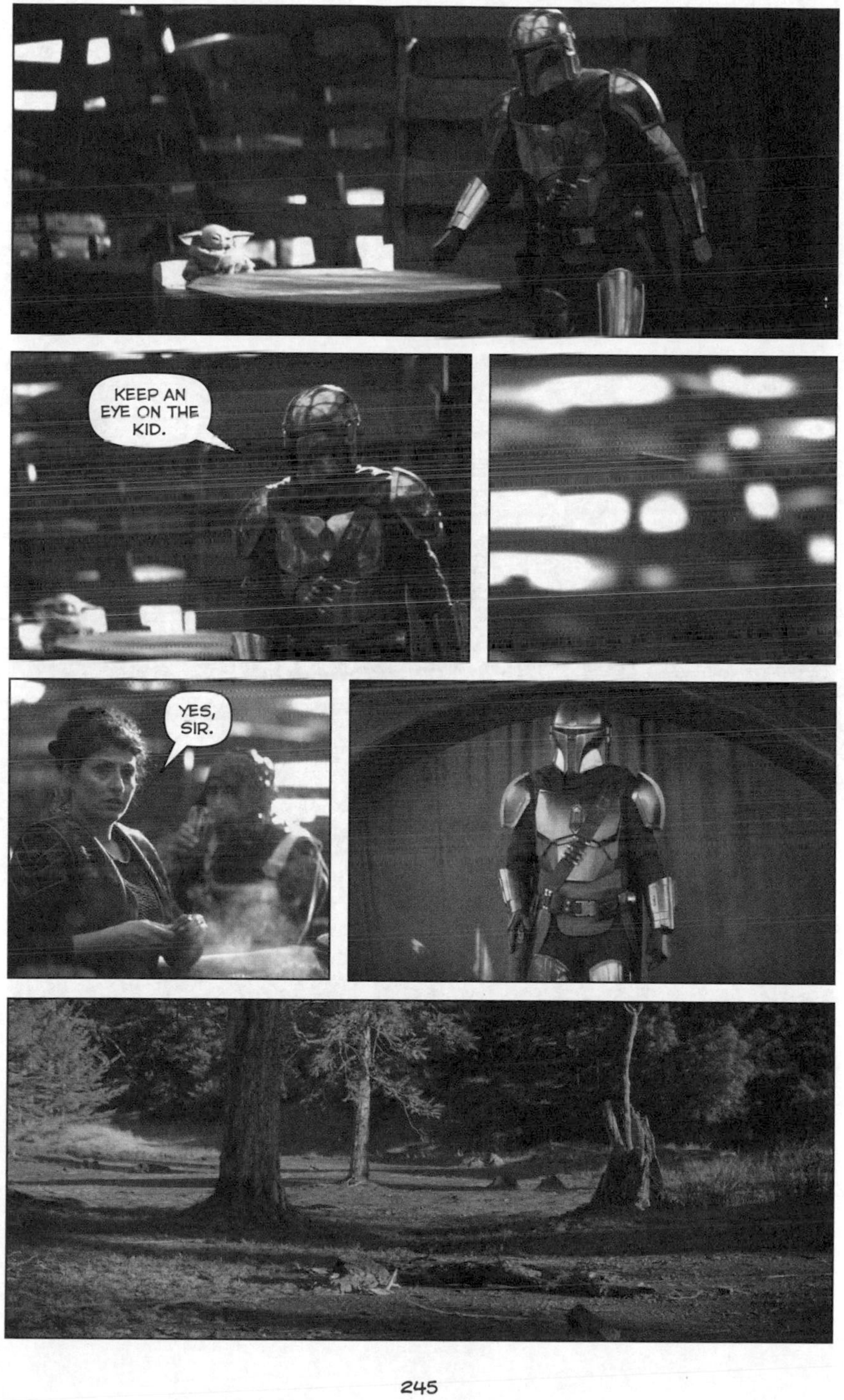
KEEP AN EYE ON THE KID.
YES, SIR.

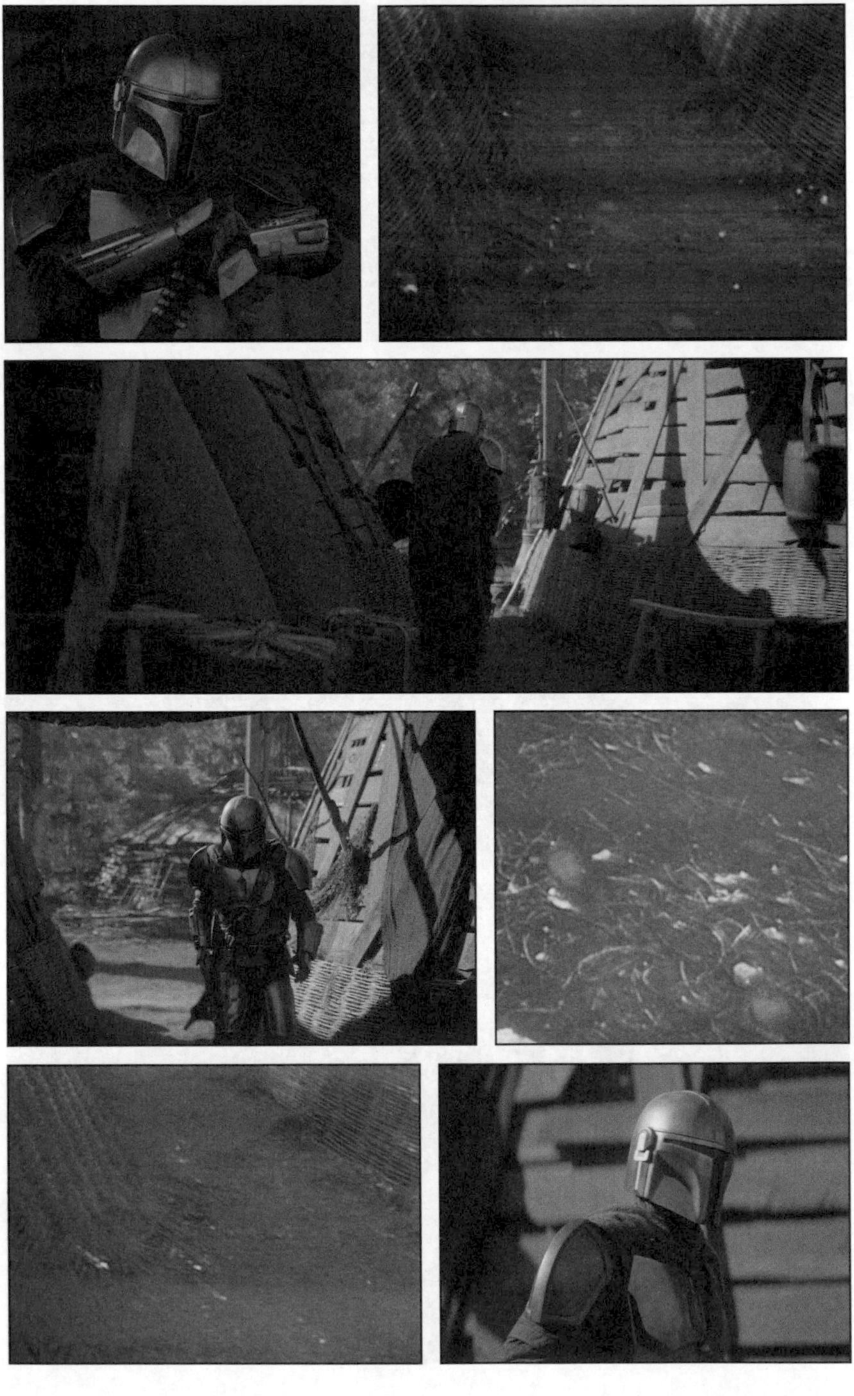

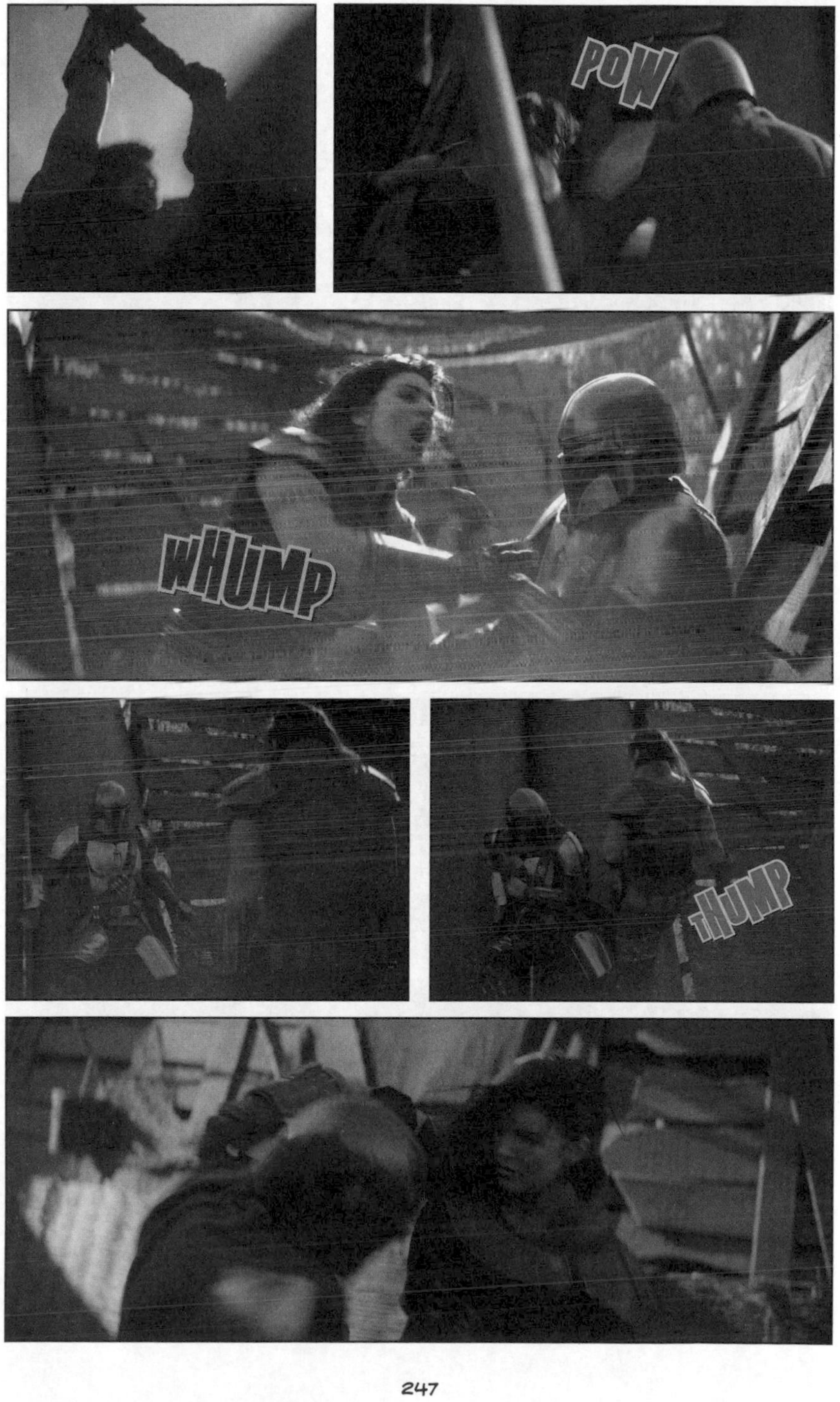
POW
WHUMP
THUMP

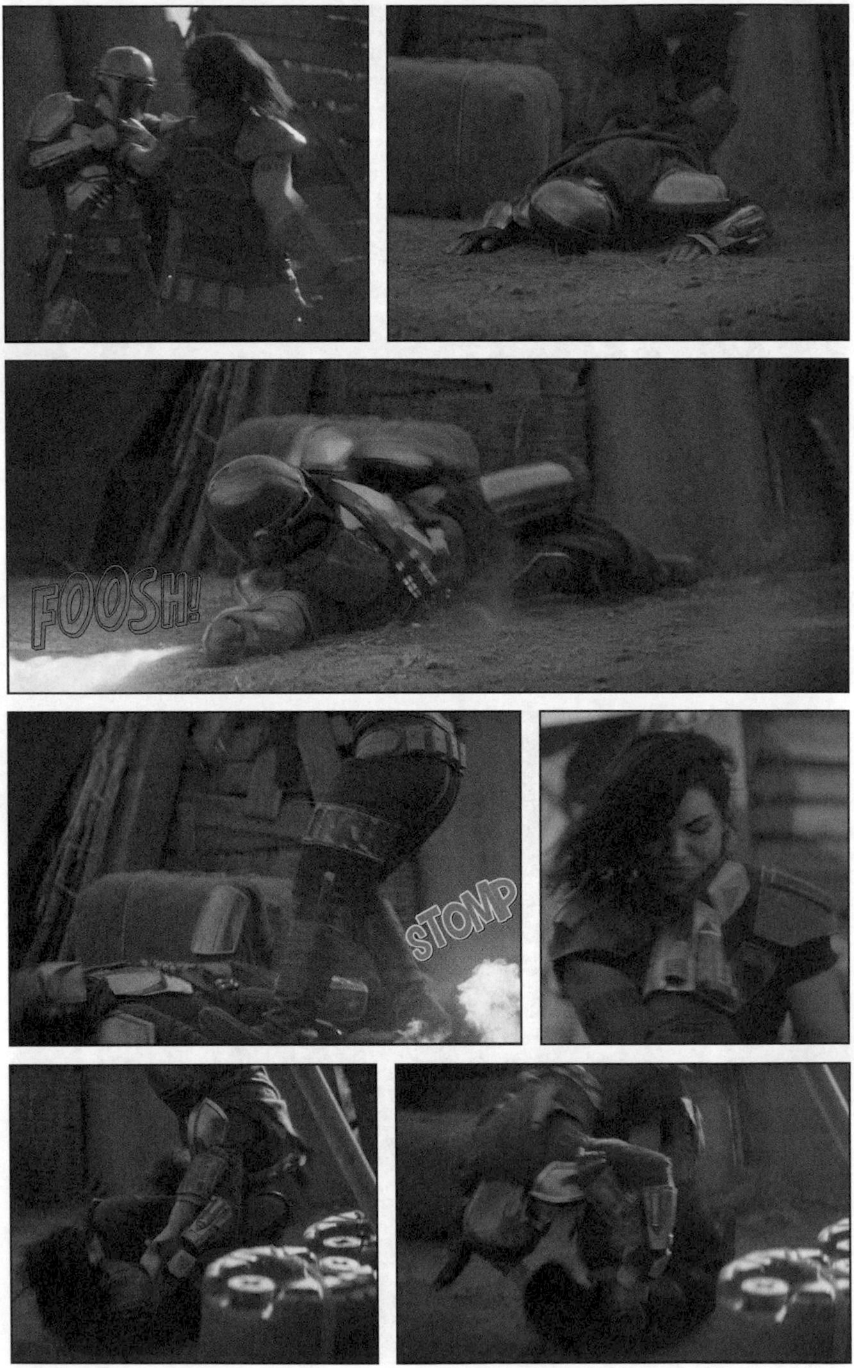
FOOSH!
STOMP

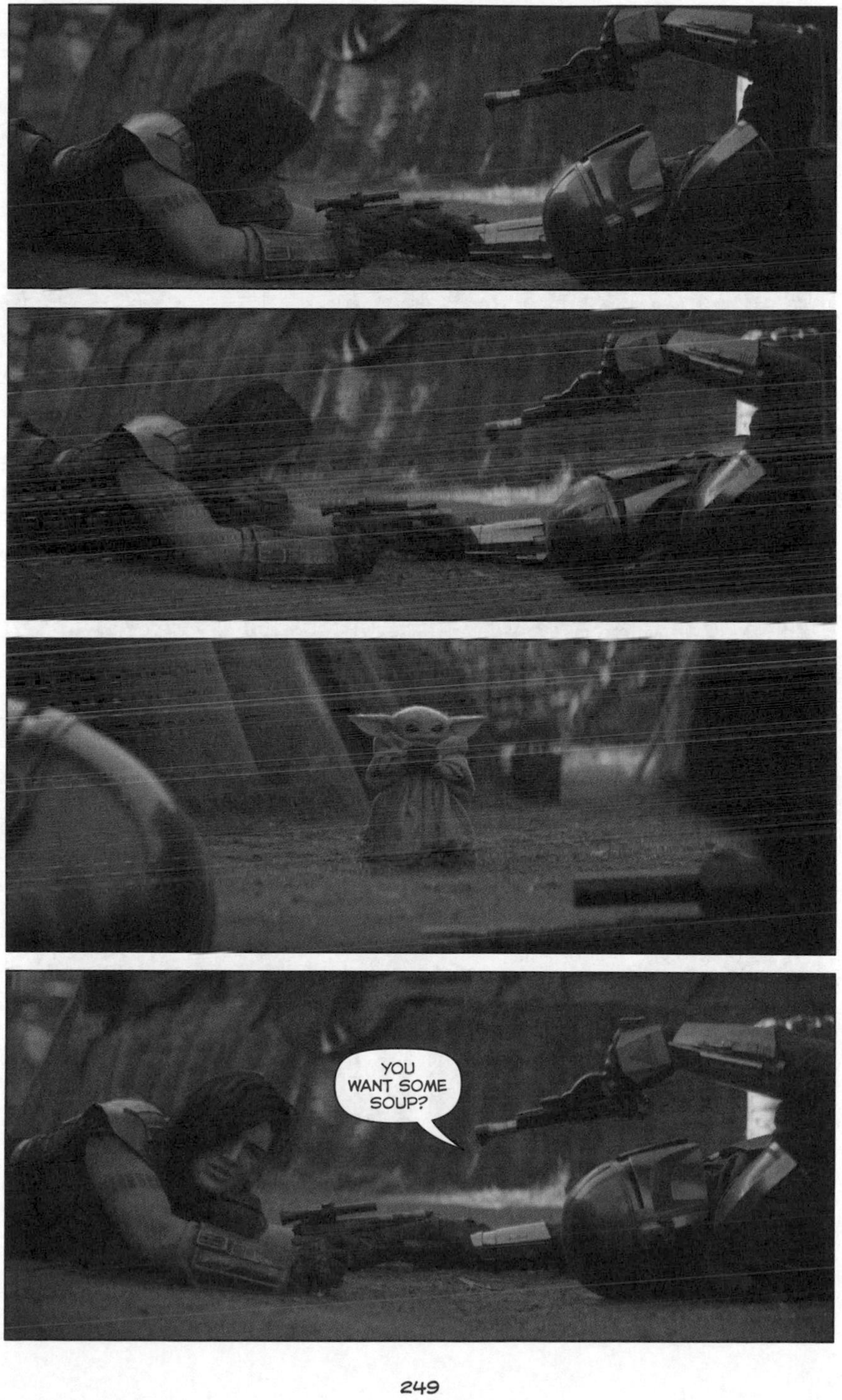
YOU WANT SOME SOUP?

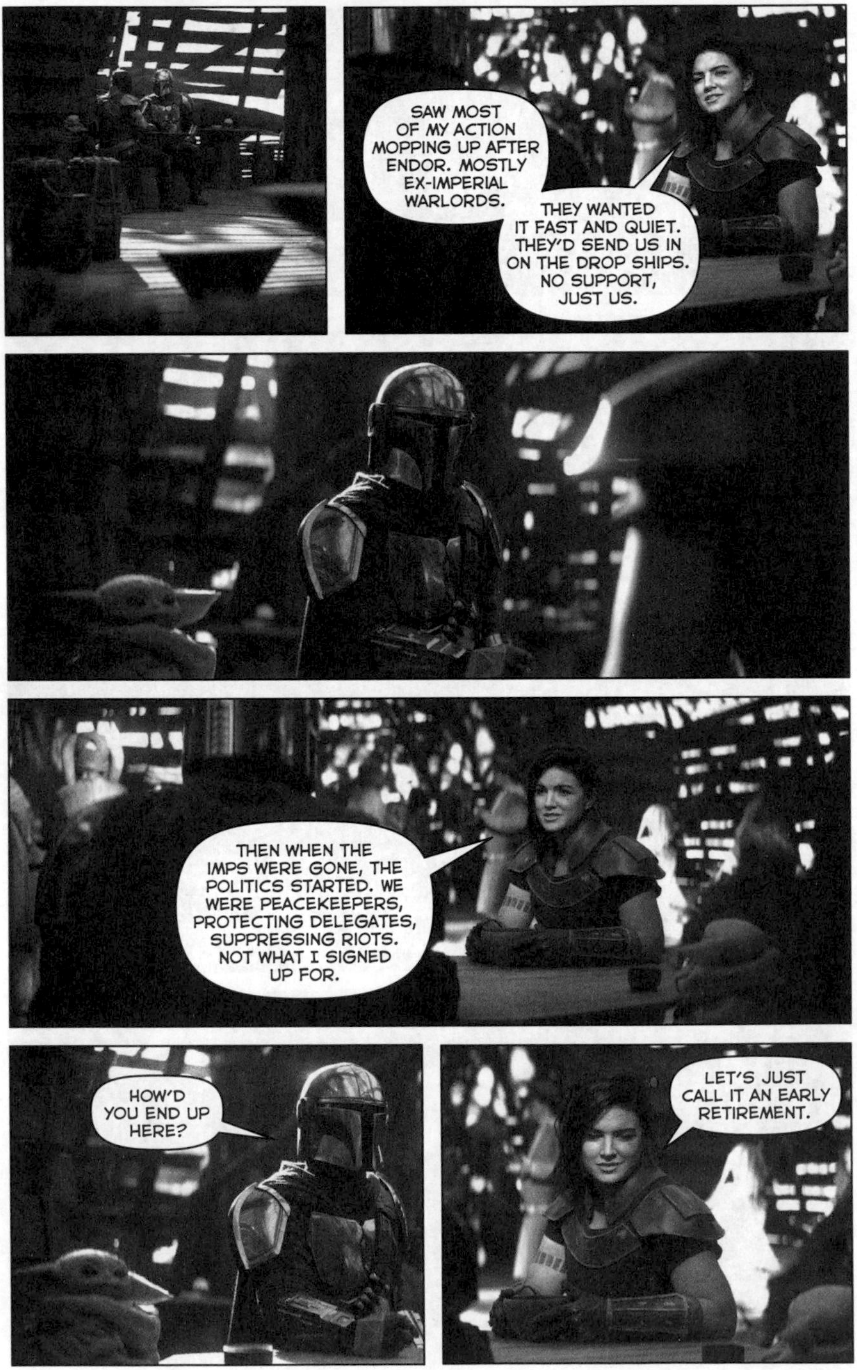
SAW MOST OF MY ACTION MOPPING UP AFTER ENDOR. MOSTLY EX-IMPERIAL WARLORDS.
THEY WANTED IT FAST AND QUIET. THEY'D SEND US IN ON THE DROP SHIPS. NO SUPPORT, JUST US.
THEN WHEN THE IMPS WERE GONE, THE POLITICS STARTED. WE WERE PEACEKEEPERS, PROTECTING DELEGATES, SUPPRESSING RIOTS. NOT WHAT I SIGNED UP FOR.
HOW'D YOU END UP HERE?
LET'S JUST CALL IT AN EARLY RETIREMENT.

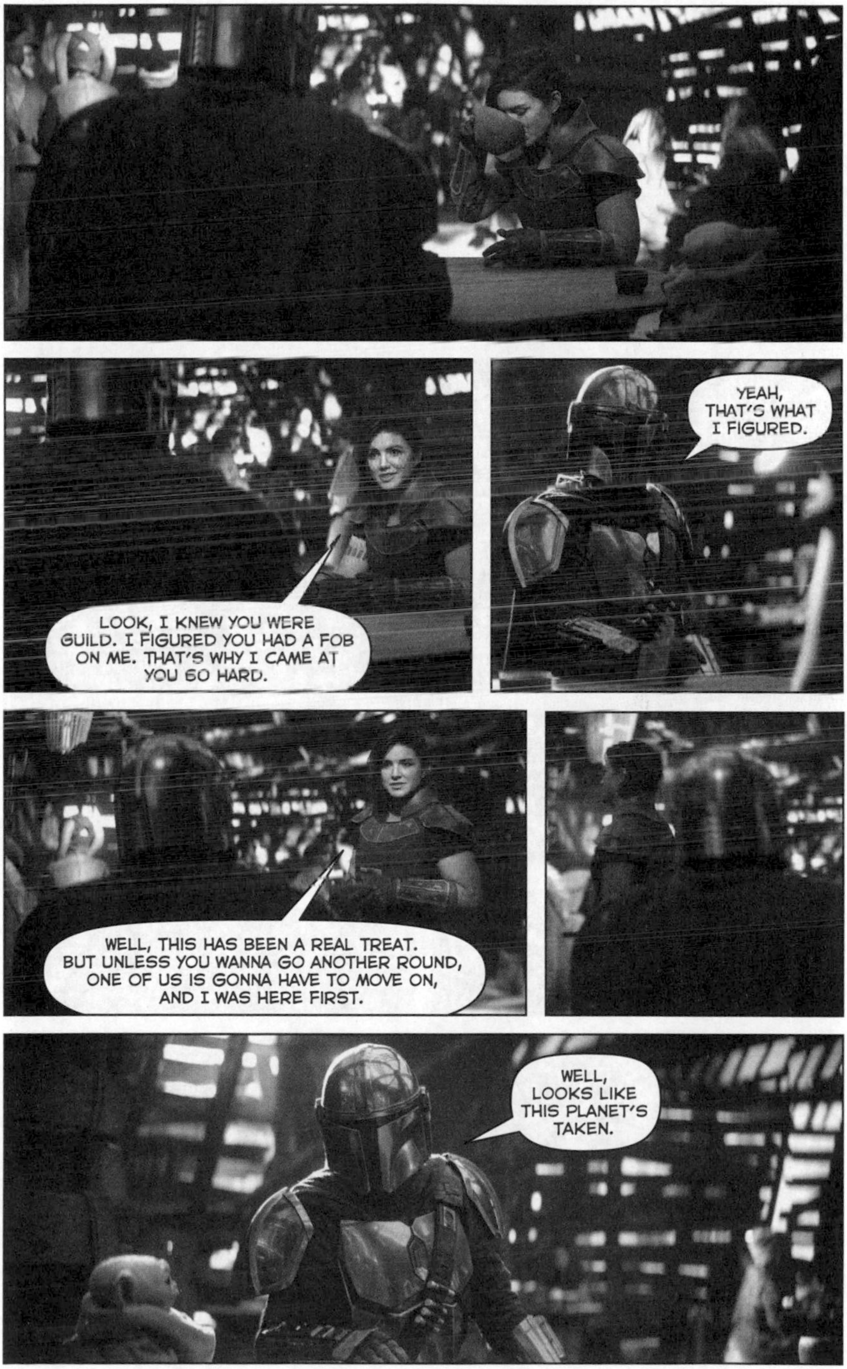
LOOK, I KNEW YOU WERE GUILD. I FIGURED YOU HAD A FOB ON ME. THAT'S WHY I CAME AT YOU SO HARD.
YEAH, THAT'S WHAT I FIGURED.
WELL, THIS HAS BEEN A REAL TREAT. BUT UNLESS YOU WANNA GO ANOTHER ROUND, ONE OF US IS GONNA HAVE TO MOVE ON, AND I WAS HERE FIRST.
WELL, LOOKS LIKE THIS PLANET'S TAKEN.

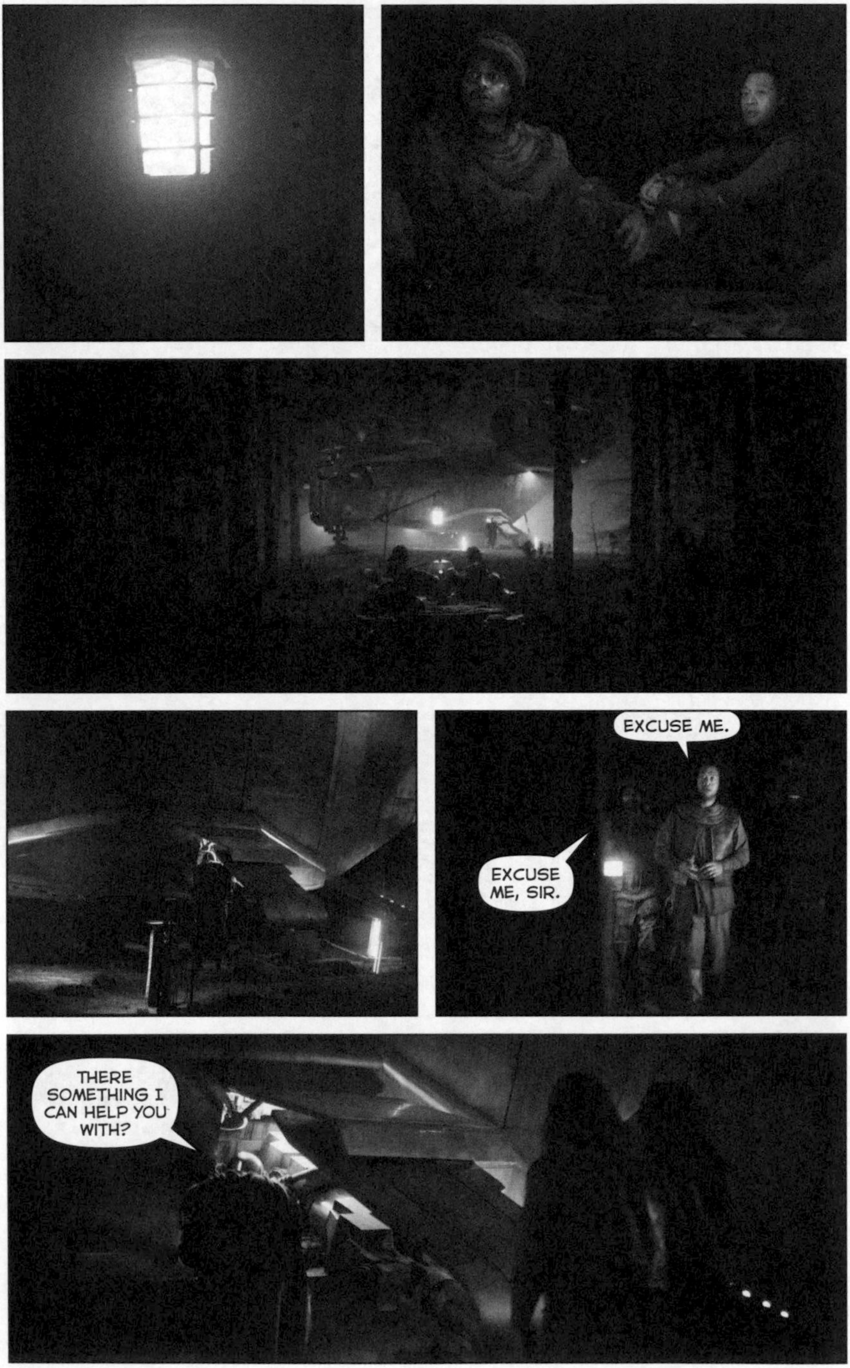
EXCUSE ME.
EXCUSE ME, SIR.
THERE SOMETHING I CAN HELP YOU WITH?

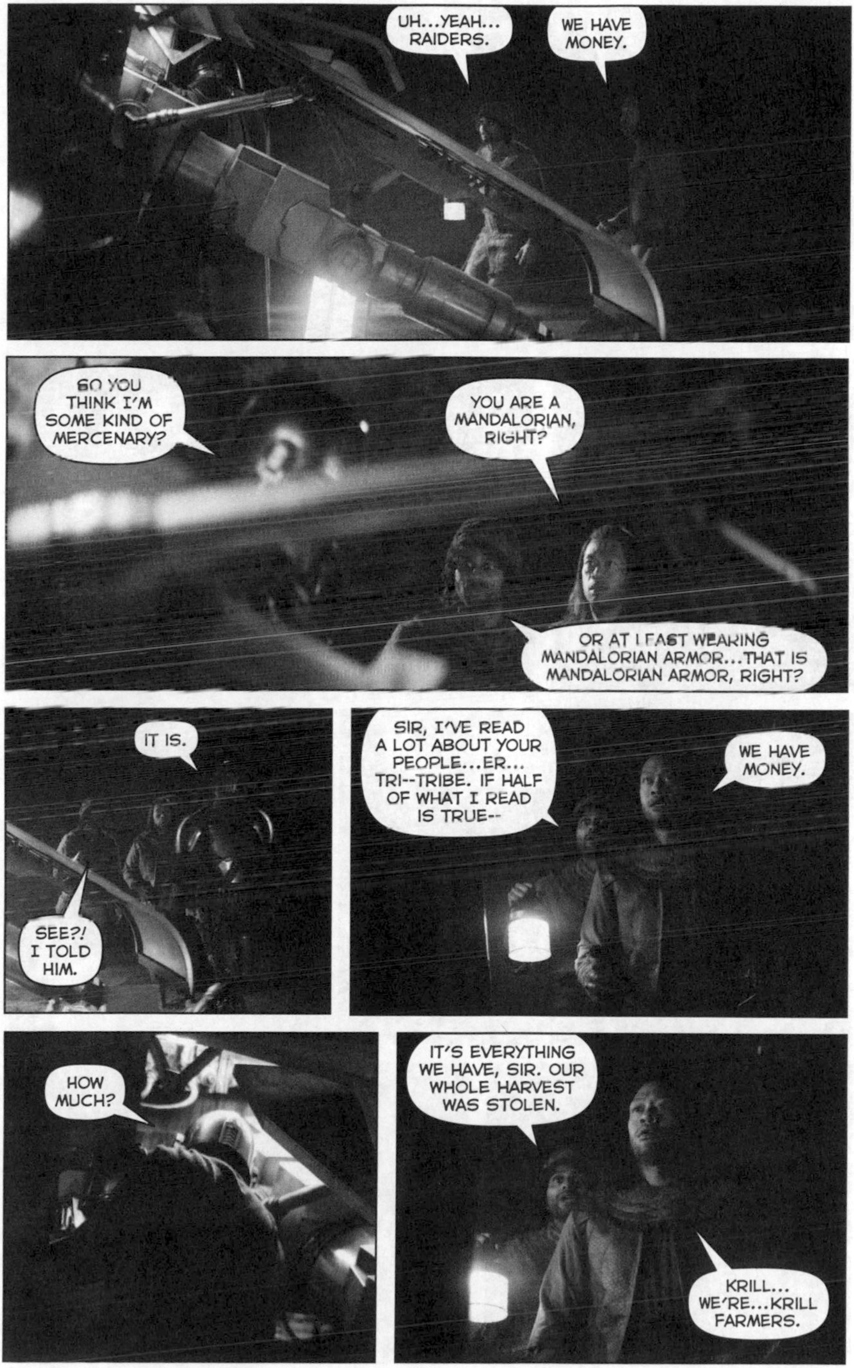
UH...YEAH... RAIDERS.
WE HAVE MONEY.
SO YOU THINK I'M SOME KIND OF MERCENARY?
YOU ARE A MANDALORIAN, RIGHT?
OR AT LEAST WEARING MANDALORIAN ARMOR...THAT IS MANDALORIAN ARMOR, RIGHT?
IT IS.
SEE?! I TOLD HIM.
SIR, I'VE READ A LOT ABOUT YOUR PEOPLE...ER... TRI--TRIBE. IF HALF OF WHAT I READ IS TRUE--
WE HAVE MONEY.
HOW MUCH?
IT'S EVERYTHING WE HAVE, SIR. OUR WHOLE HARVEST WAS STOLEN.
KRILL... WE'RE...KRILL FARMERS.

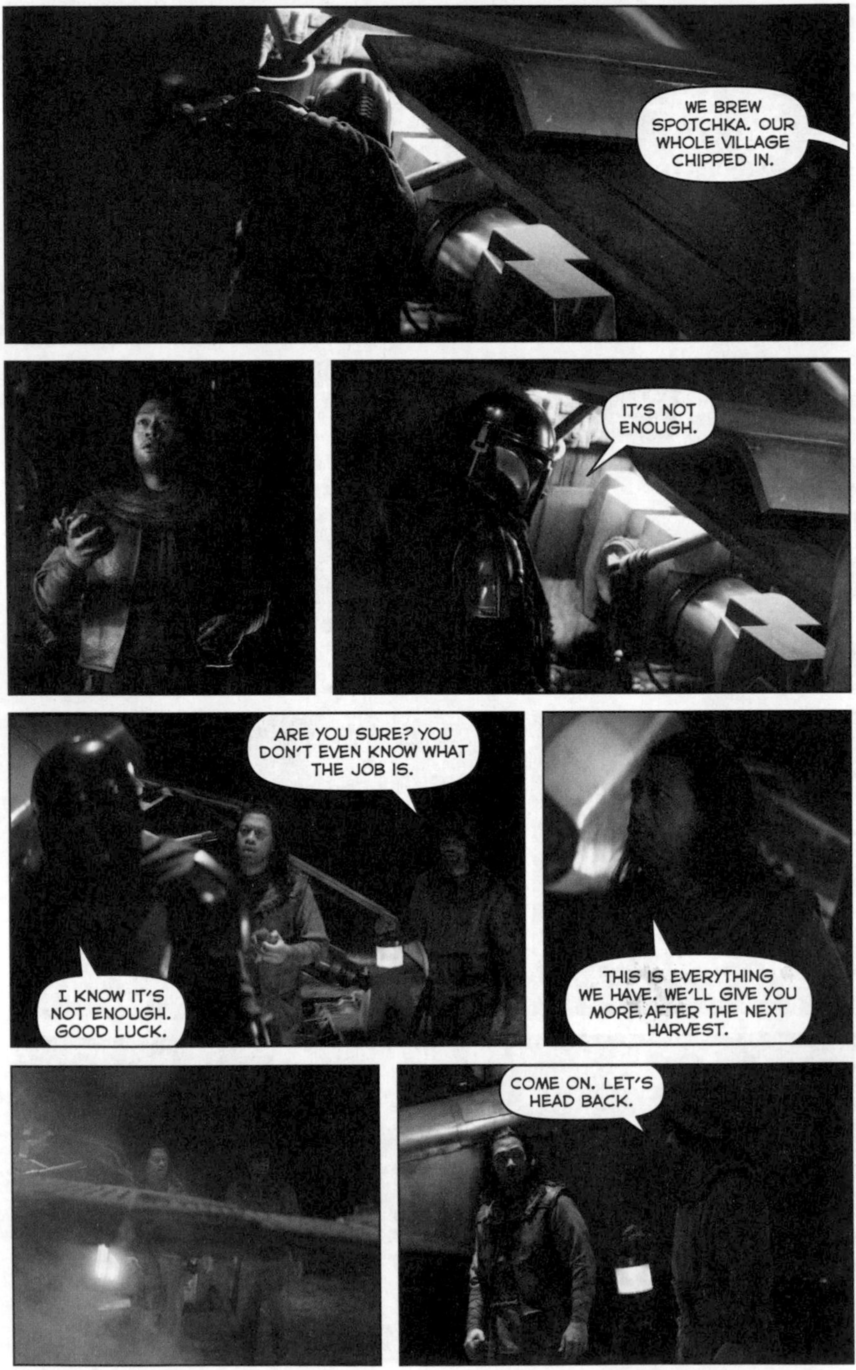
WE BREW SPOTCHKA. OUR WHOLE VILLAGE CHIPPED IN.
IT'S NOT ENOUGH.
ARE YOU SURE? YOU DON'T EVEN KNOW WHAT THE JOB IS.
I KNOW IT'S NOT ENOUGH. GOOD LUCK.
THIS IS EVERYTHING WE HAVE. WE'LL GIVE YOU MORE AFTER THE NEXT HARVEST.
COME ON. LET'S HEAD BACK.

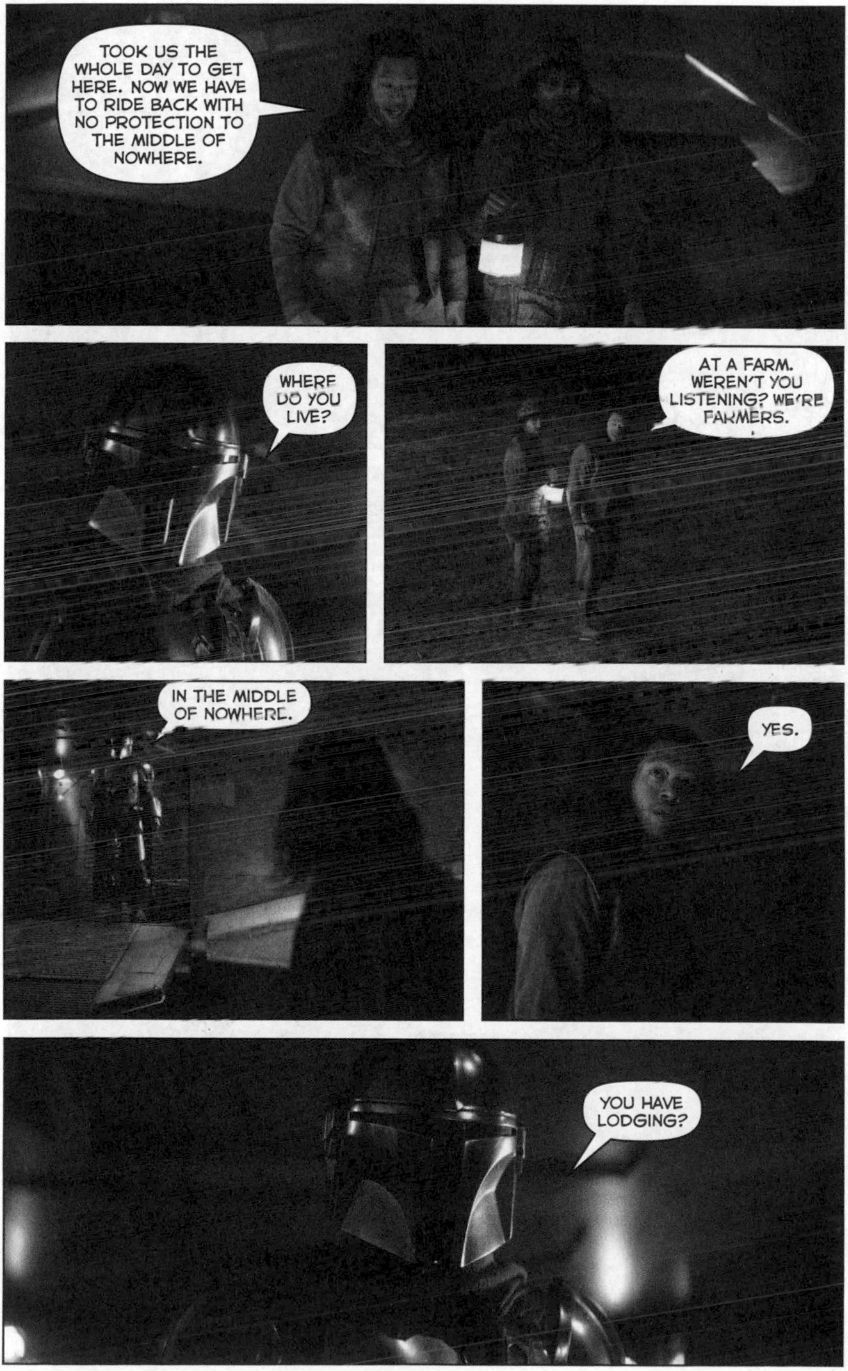
TOOK US THE WHOLE DAY TO GET HERE. NOW WE HAVE TO RIDE BACK WITH NO PROTECTION TO THE MIDDLE OF NOWHERE.
WHERE DO YOU LIVE?
AT A FARM. WEREN'T YOU LISTENING? WE'RE FARMERS.
IN THE MIDDLE OF NOWHERE.
YES.
YOU HAVE LODGING?

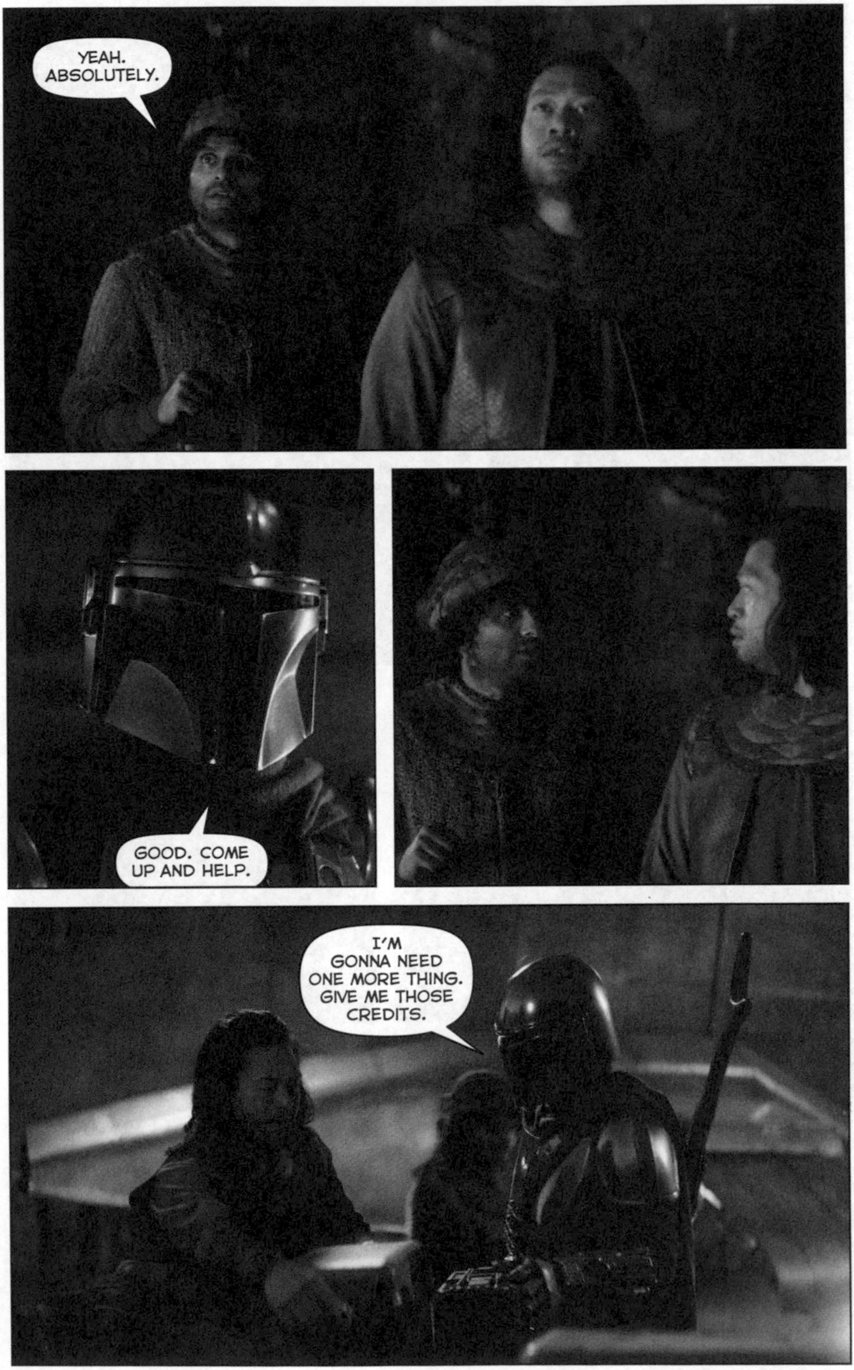
YEAH. ABSOLUTELY.
GOOD. COME UP AND HELP.
I'M GONNA NEED ONE MORE THING. GIVE ME THOSE CREDITS.

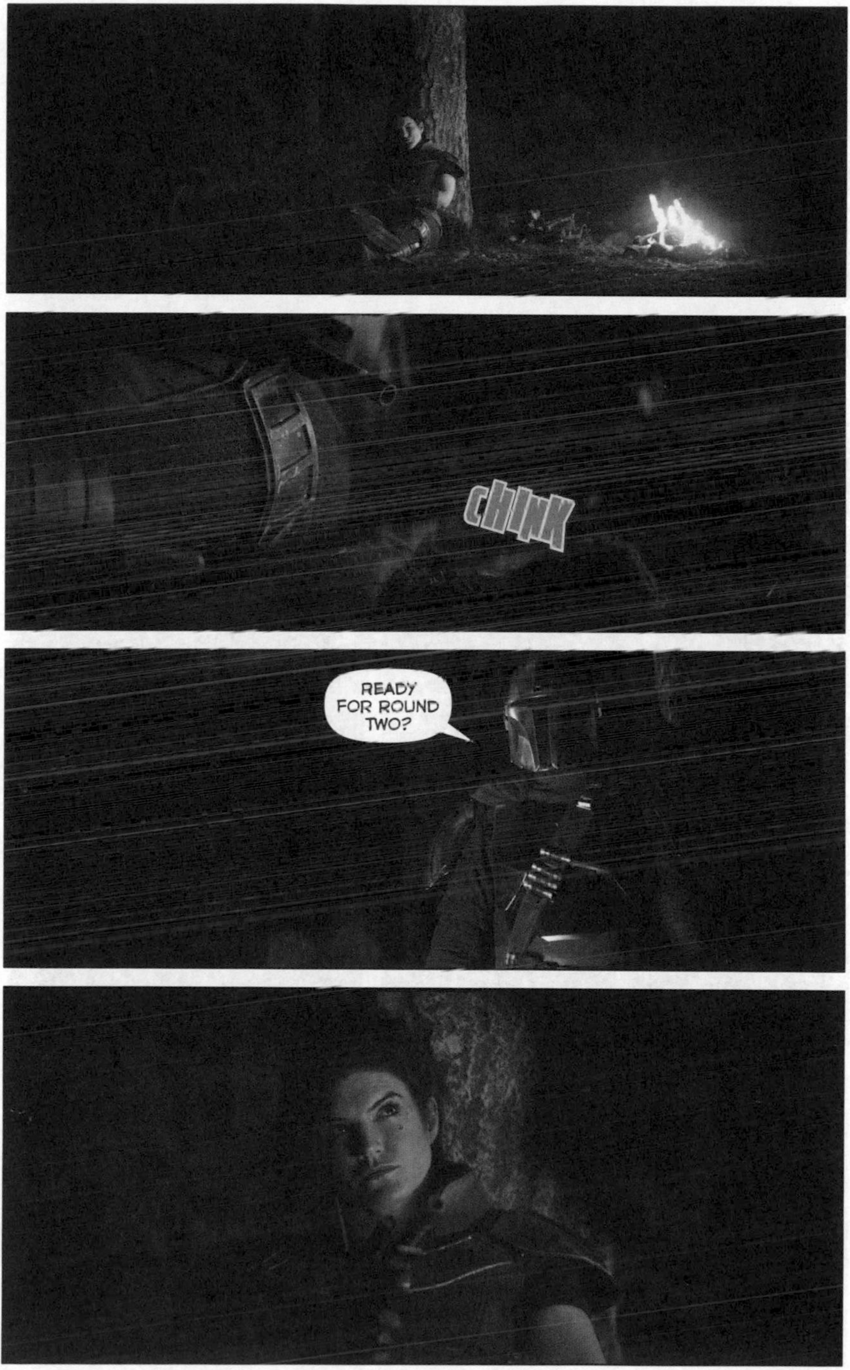
CHINK
READY FOR ROUND TWO?

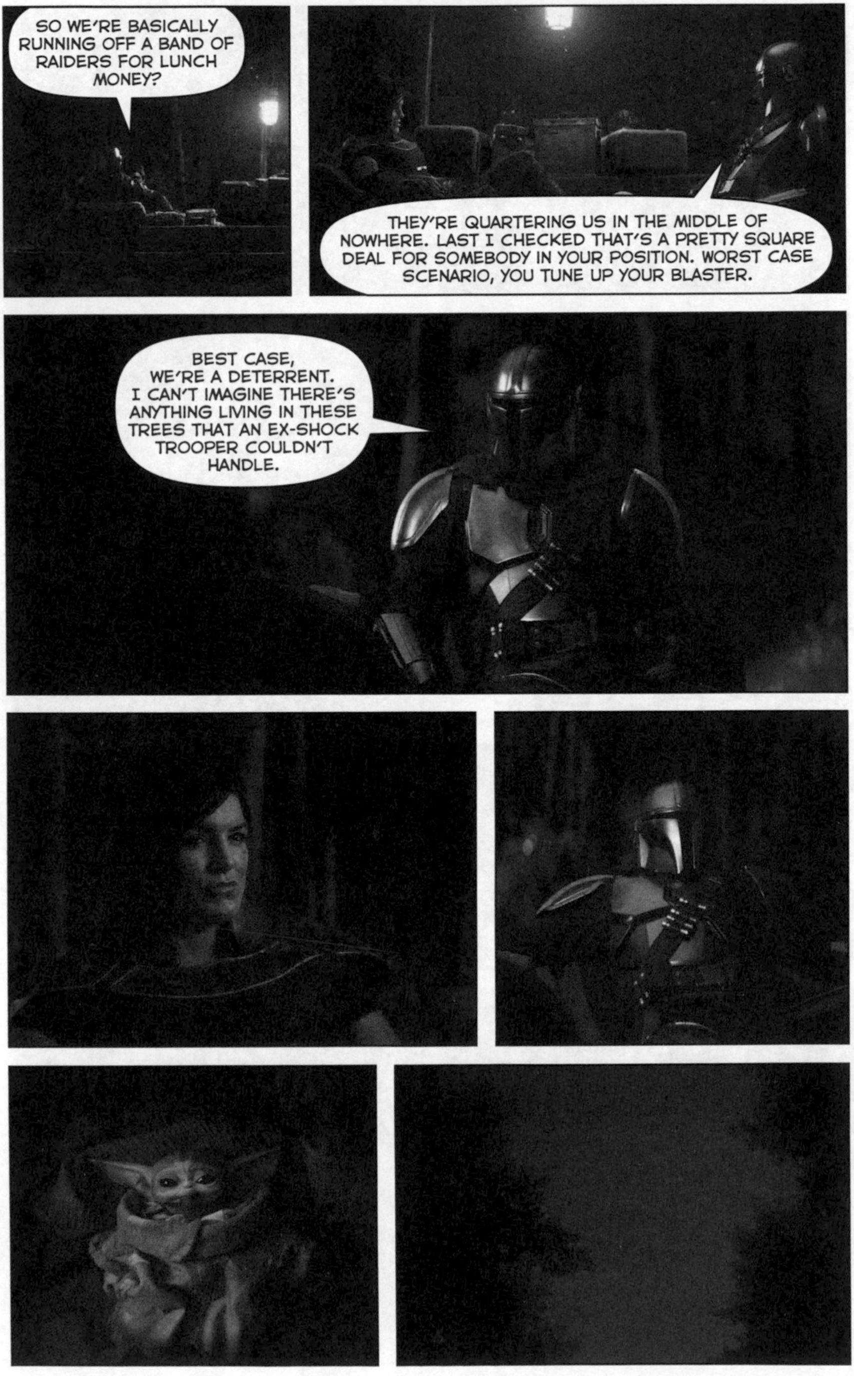
SO WE'RE BASICALLY RUNNING OFF A BAND OF RAIDERS FOR LUNCH MONEY?
THEY'RE QUARTERING US IN THE MIDDLE OF NOWHERE. LAST I CHECKED THAT'S A PRETTY SQUARE DEAL FOR SOMEBODY IN YOUR POSITION. WORST CASE SCENARIO, YOU TUNE UP YOUR BLASTER.
BEST CASE, WE'RE A DETERRENT. I CAN'T IMAGINE THERE'S ANYTHING LIVING IN THESE TREES THAT AN EX-SHOCK TROOPER COULDN'T HANDLE.

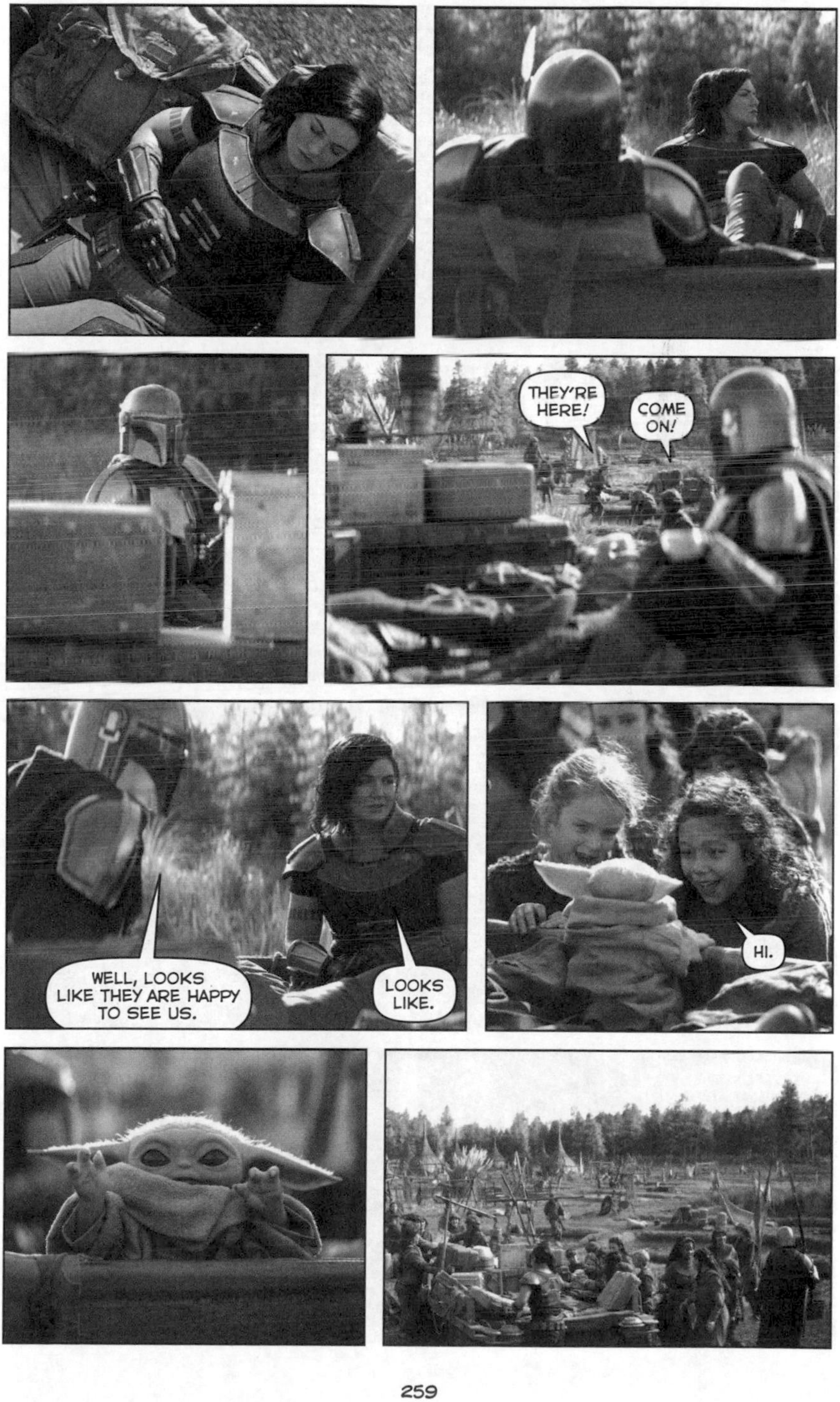
THEY'RE HERE!
COME ON!
WELL, LOOKS LIKE THEY ARE HAPPY TO SEE US.
LOOKS LIKE.
HI.

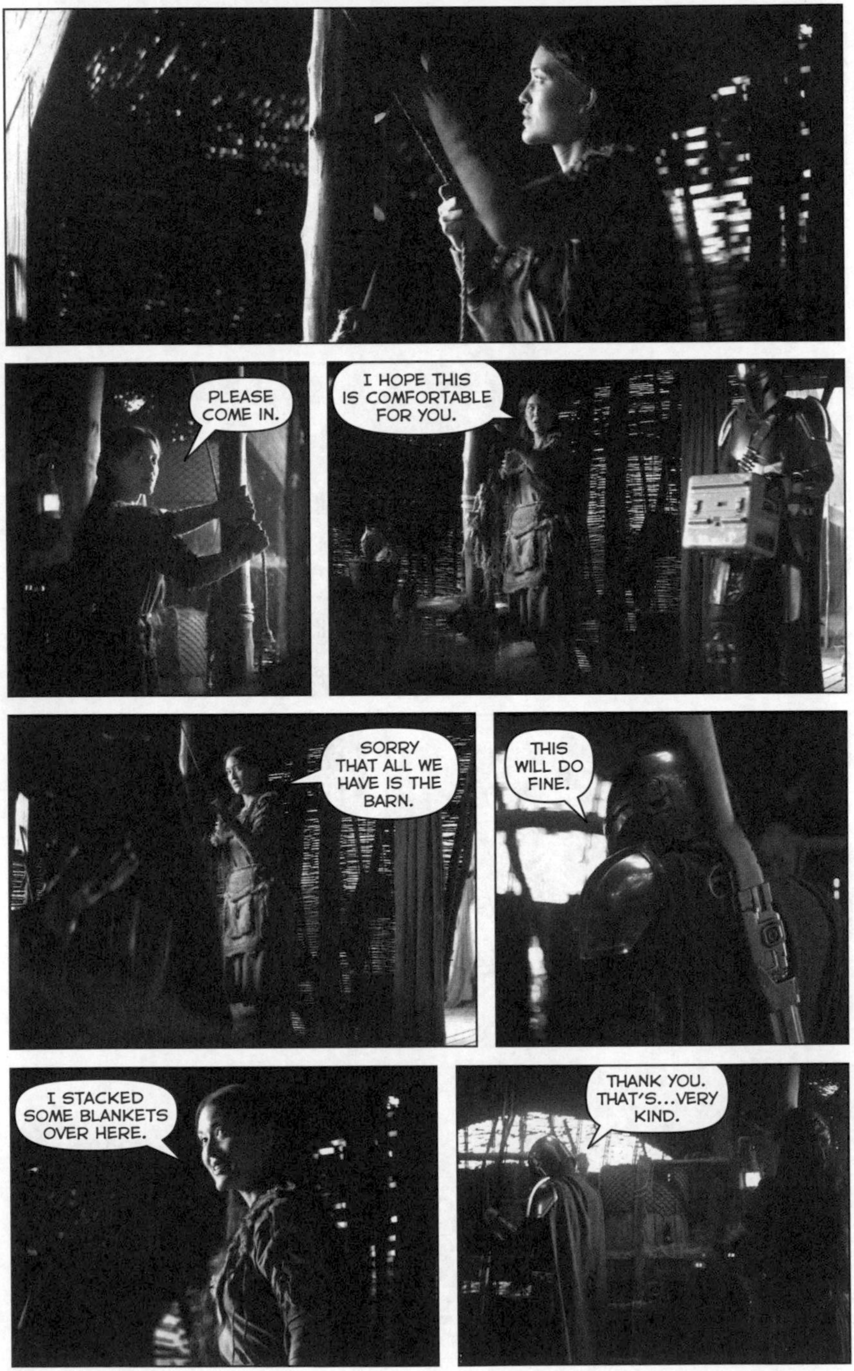
PLEASE COME IN.
I HOPE THIS IS COMFORTABLE FOR YOU.
SORRY THAT ALL WE HAVE IS THE BARN.
THIS WILL DO FINE.
I STACKED SOME BLANKETS OVER HERE.
THANK YOU. THAT'S...VERY KIND.

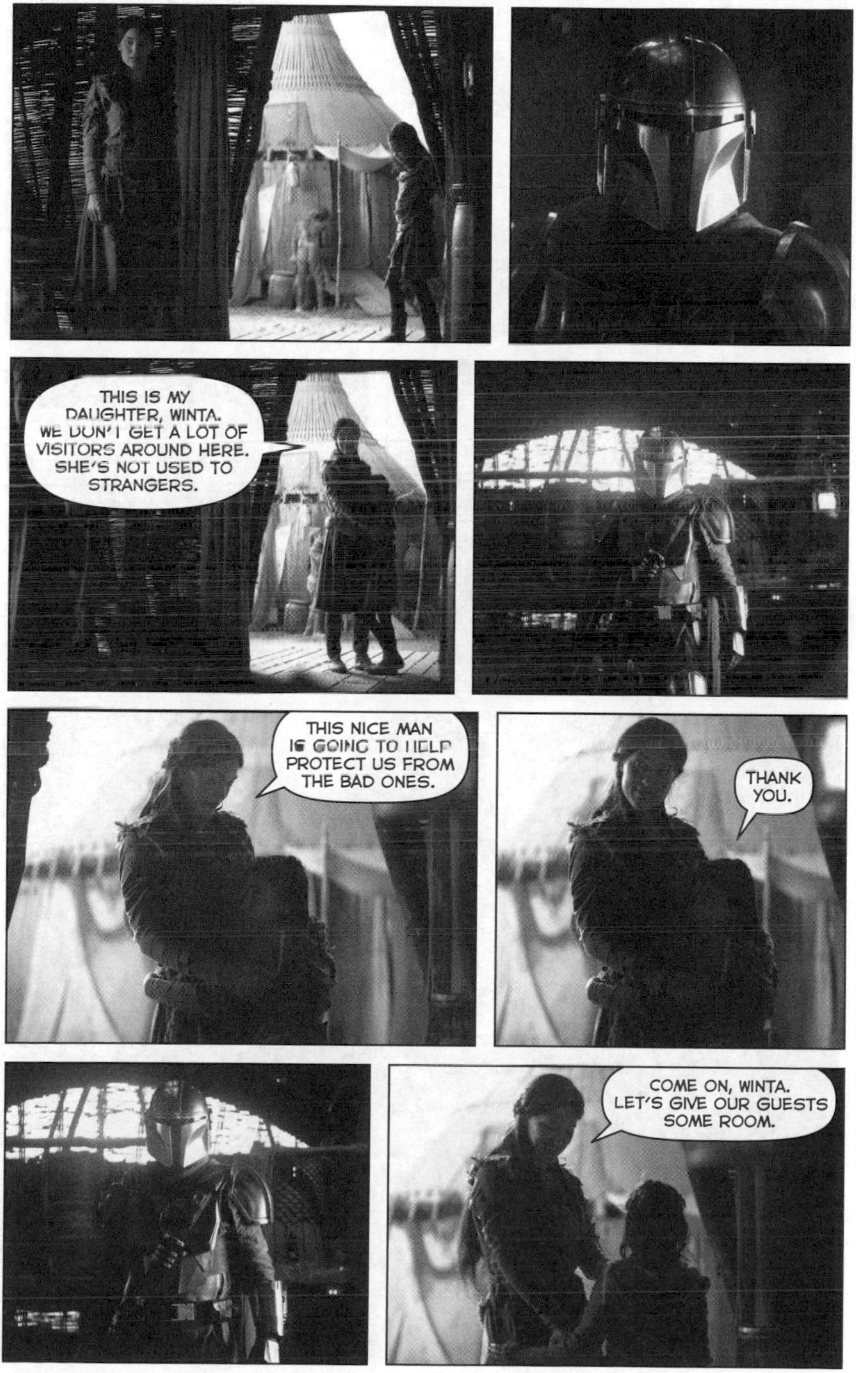
THIS IS MY DAUGHTER, WINTA. WE DON'T GET A LOT OF VISITORS AROUND HERE. SHE'S NOT USED TO STRANGERS.
THIS NICE MAN IS GOING TO HELP PROTECT US FROM THE BAD ONES.
THANK YOU.
COME ON, WINTA. LET'S GIVE OUR GUESTS SOME ROOM.

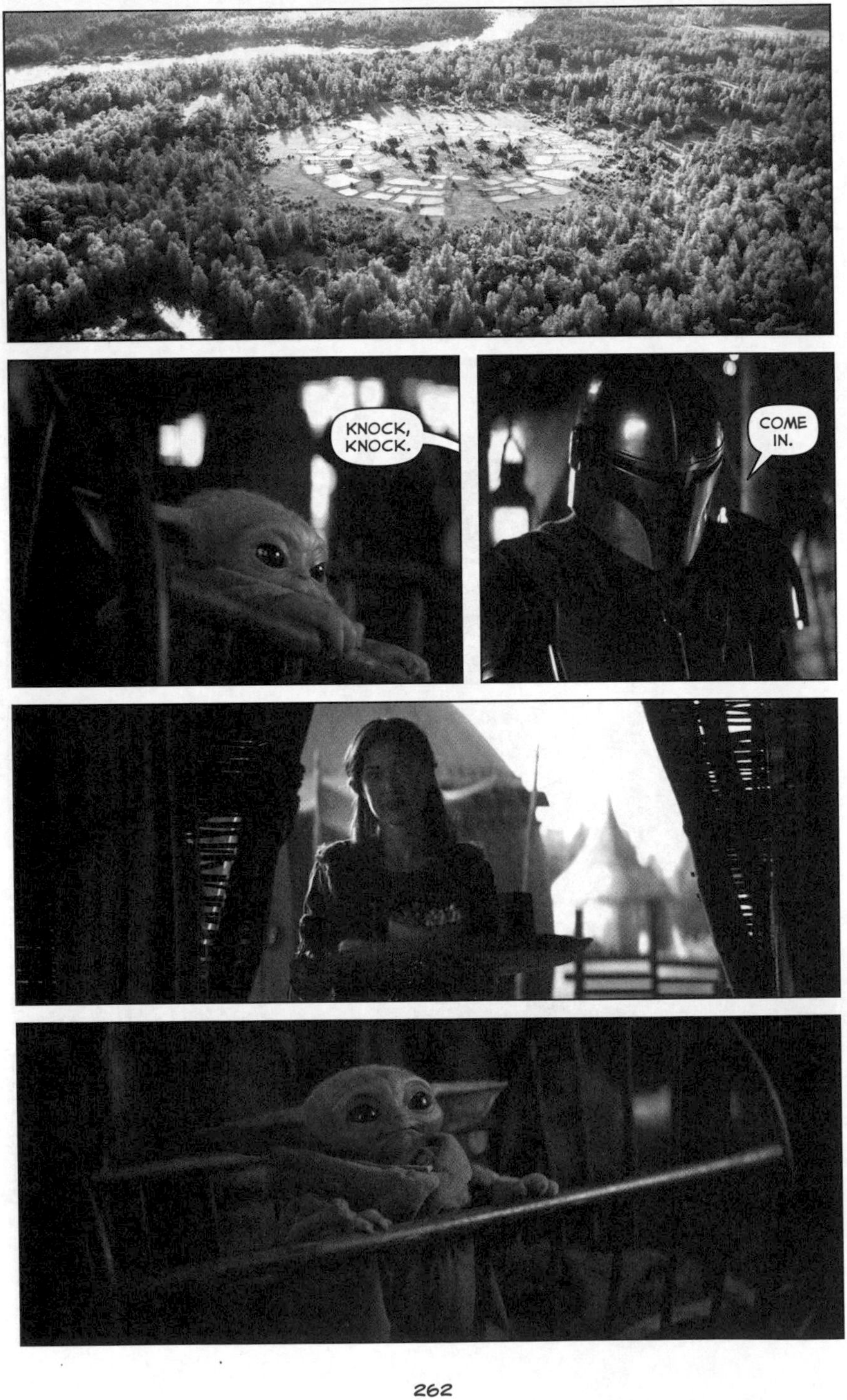
KNOCK, KNOCK.
COME IN.

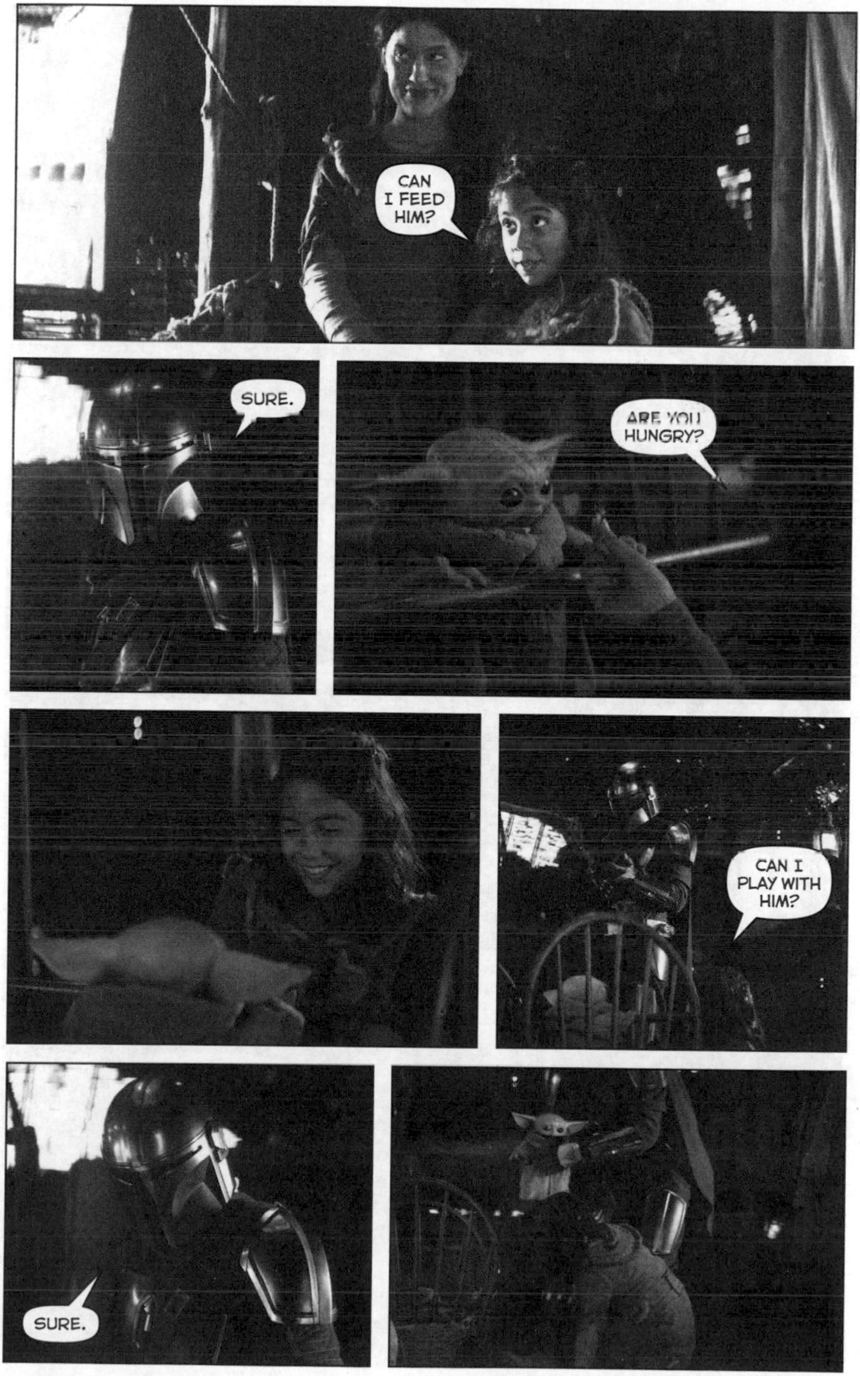
CAN I FEED HIM?
SURE.
ARE YOU HUNGRY?
CAN I PLAY WITH HIM?
SURE.

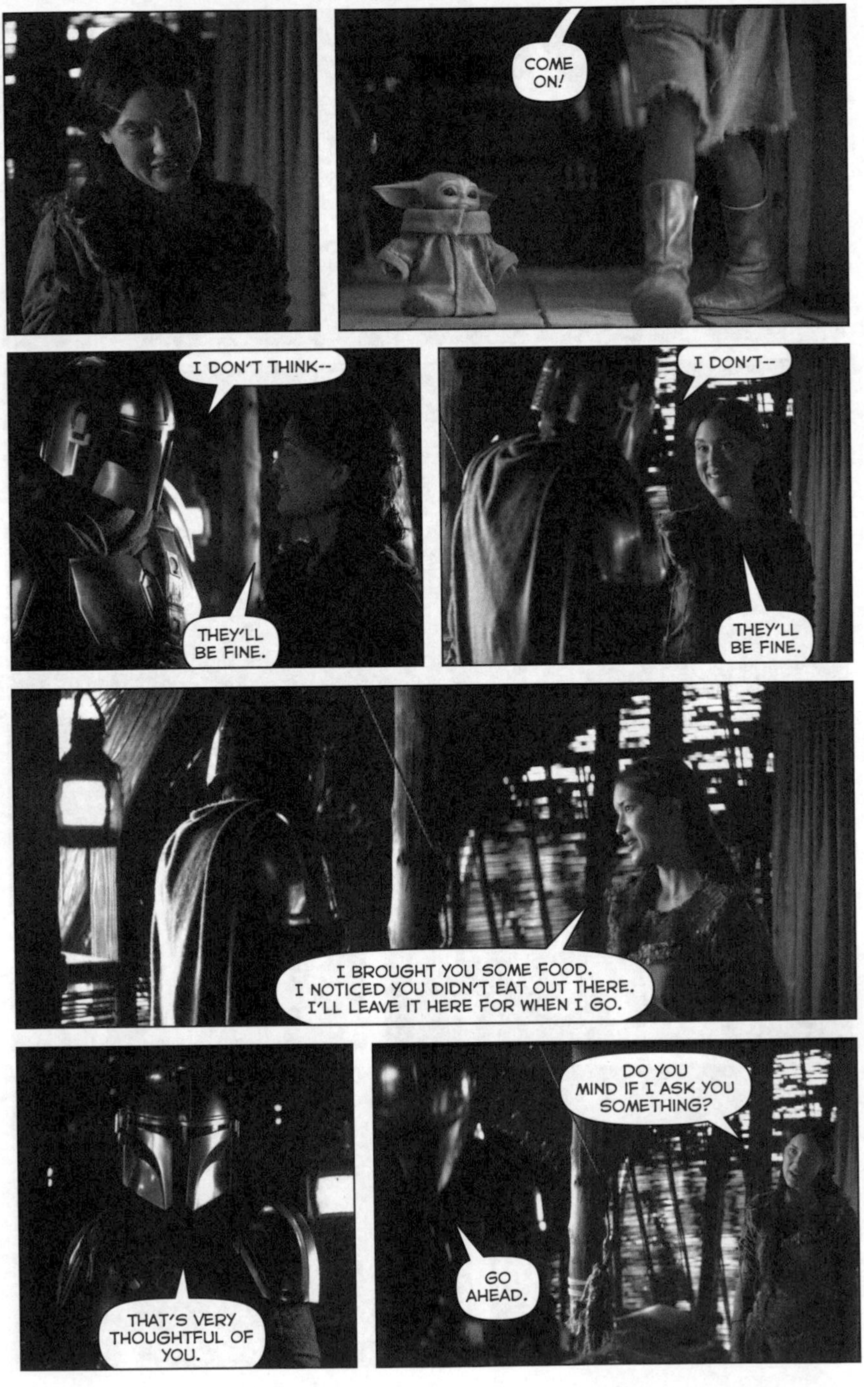
COME ON!
I DON'T THINK--
THEY'LL BE FINE.
I DON'T--
THEY'LL BE FINE.
I BROUGHT YOU SOME FOOD. I NOTICED YOU DIDN'T EAT OUT THERE. I'LL LEAVE IT HERE FOR WHEN I GO.
THAT'S VERY THOUGHTFUL OF YOU.
DO YOU MIND IF I ASK YOU SOMETHING?
GO AHEAD.

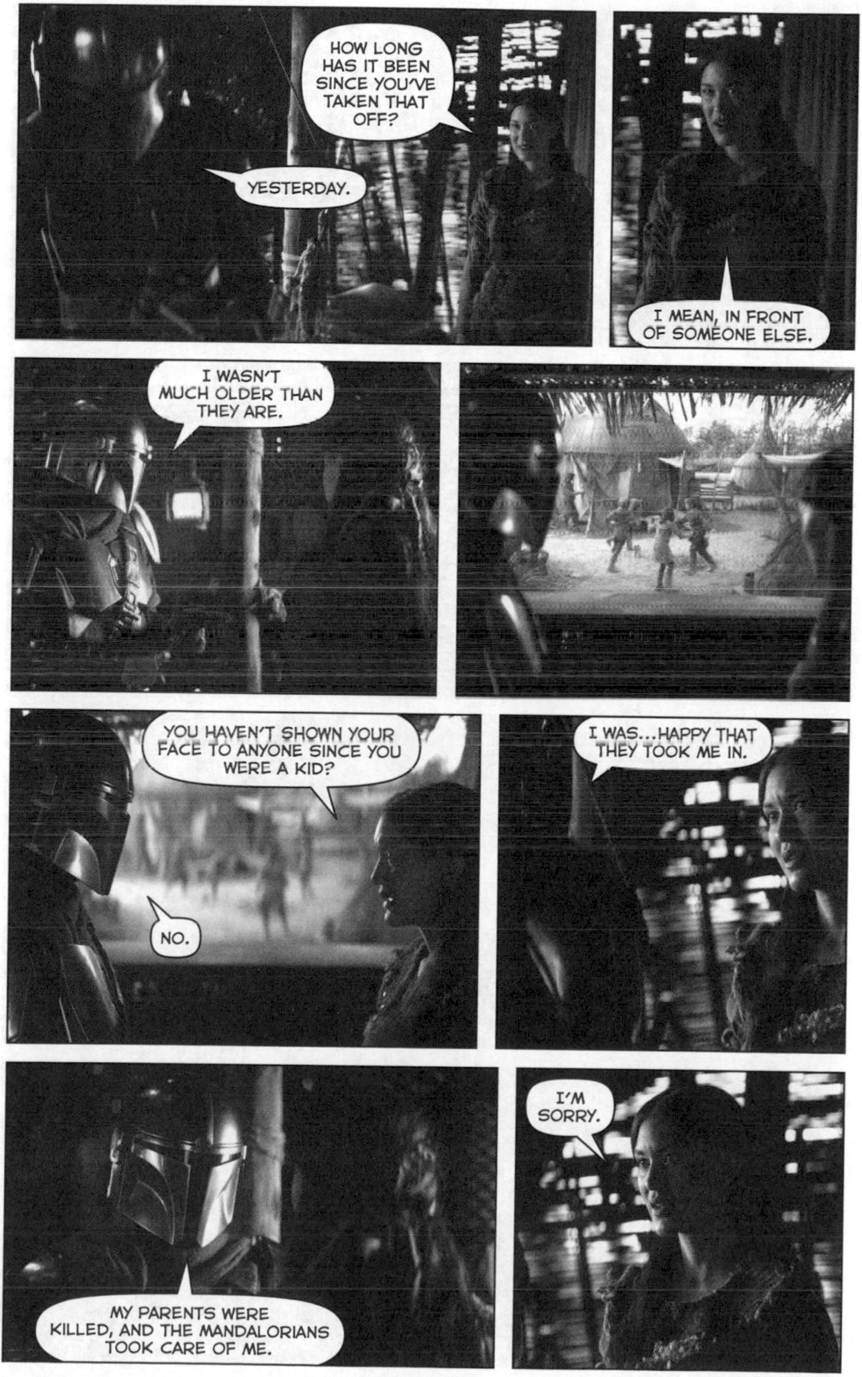
HOW LONG HAS IT BEEN SINCE YOU'VE TAKEN THAT OFF?
YESTERDAY.
I MEAN, IN FRONT OF SOMEONE ELSE.
I WASN'T MUCH OLDER THAN THEY ARE.
YOU HAVEN'T SHOWN YOUR FACE TO ANYONE SINCE YOU WERE A KID?
NO.
I WAS...HAPPY THAT THEY TOOK ME IN.
MY PARENTS WERE KILLED, AND THE MANDALORIANS TOOK CARE OF ME.
I'M SORRY.

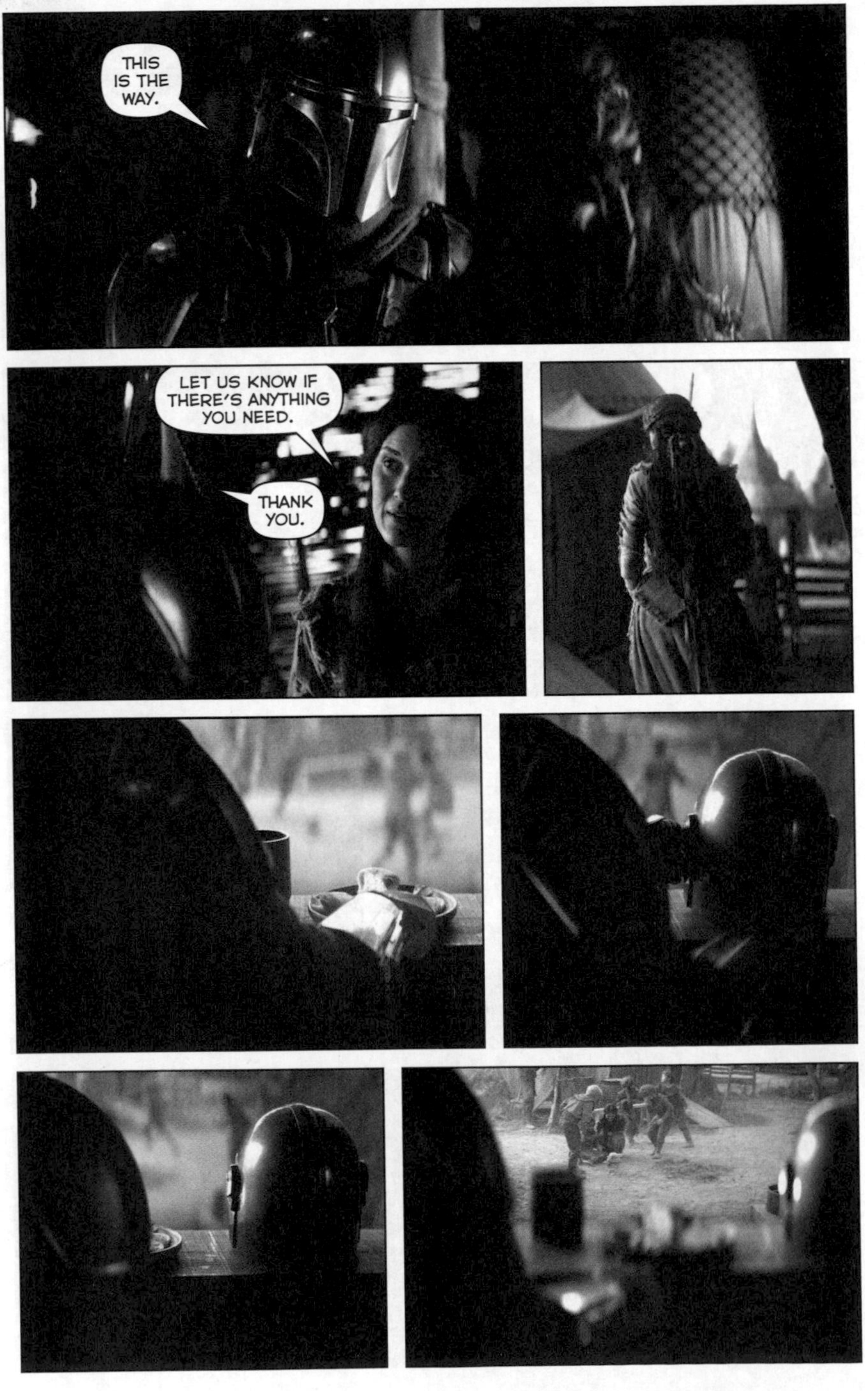
THIS IS THE WAY.
LET US KNOW IF THERE'S ANYTHING YOU NEED.
THANK YOU.

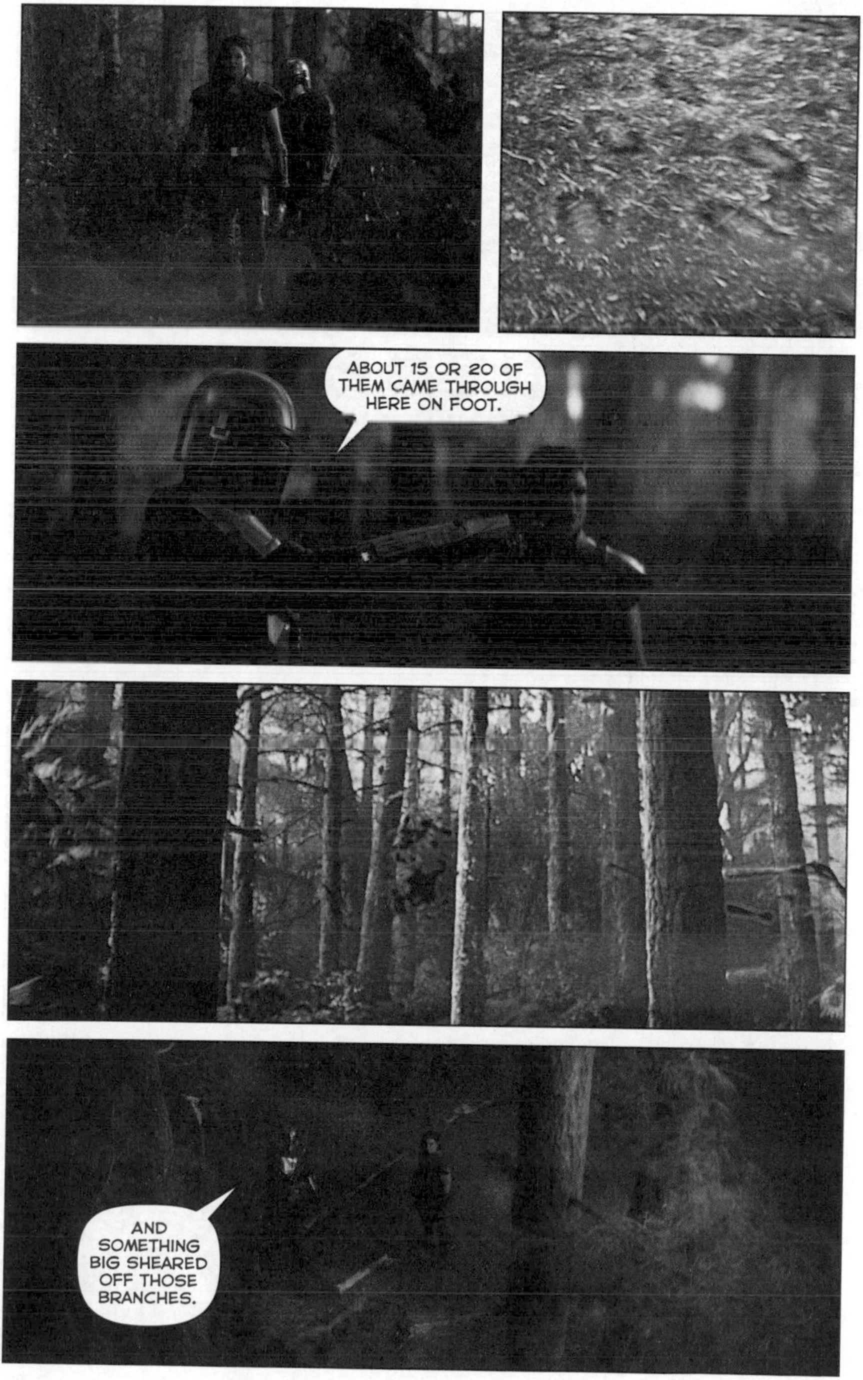
ABOUT 15 OR 20 OF THEM CAME THROUGH HERE ON FOOT.
AND SOMETHING BIG SHEARED OFF THOSE BRANCHES.

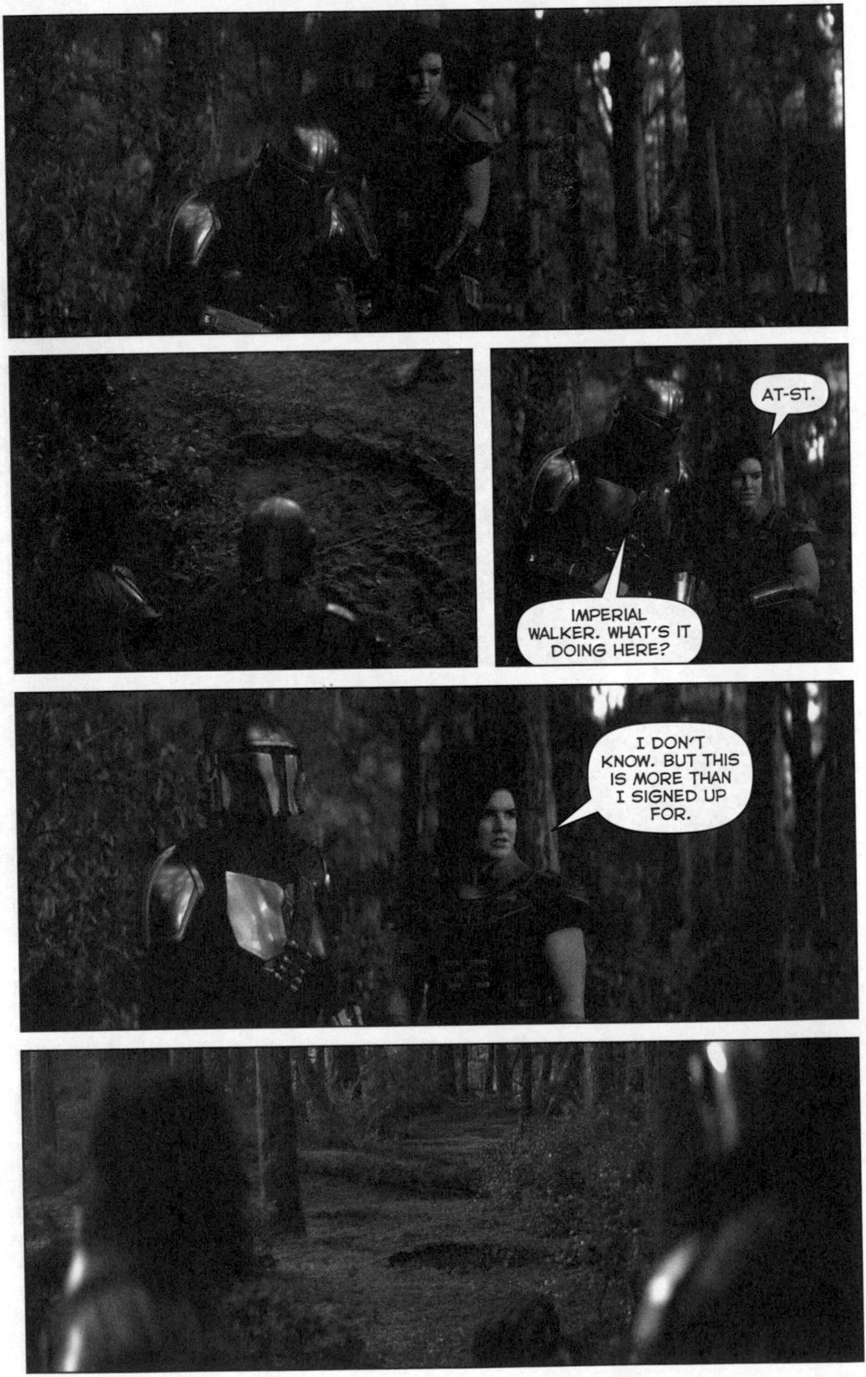
AT-ST.
IMPERIAL WALKER. WHAT'S IT DOING HERE?
I DON'T KNOW. BUT THIS IS MORE THAN I SIGNED UP FOR.

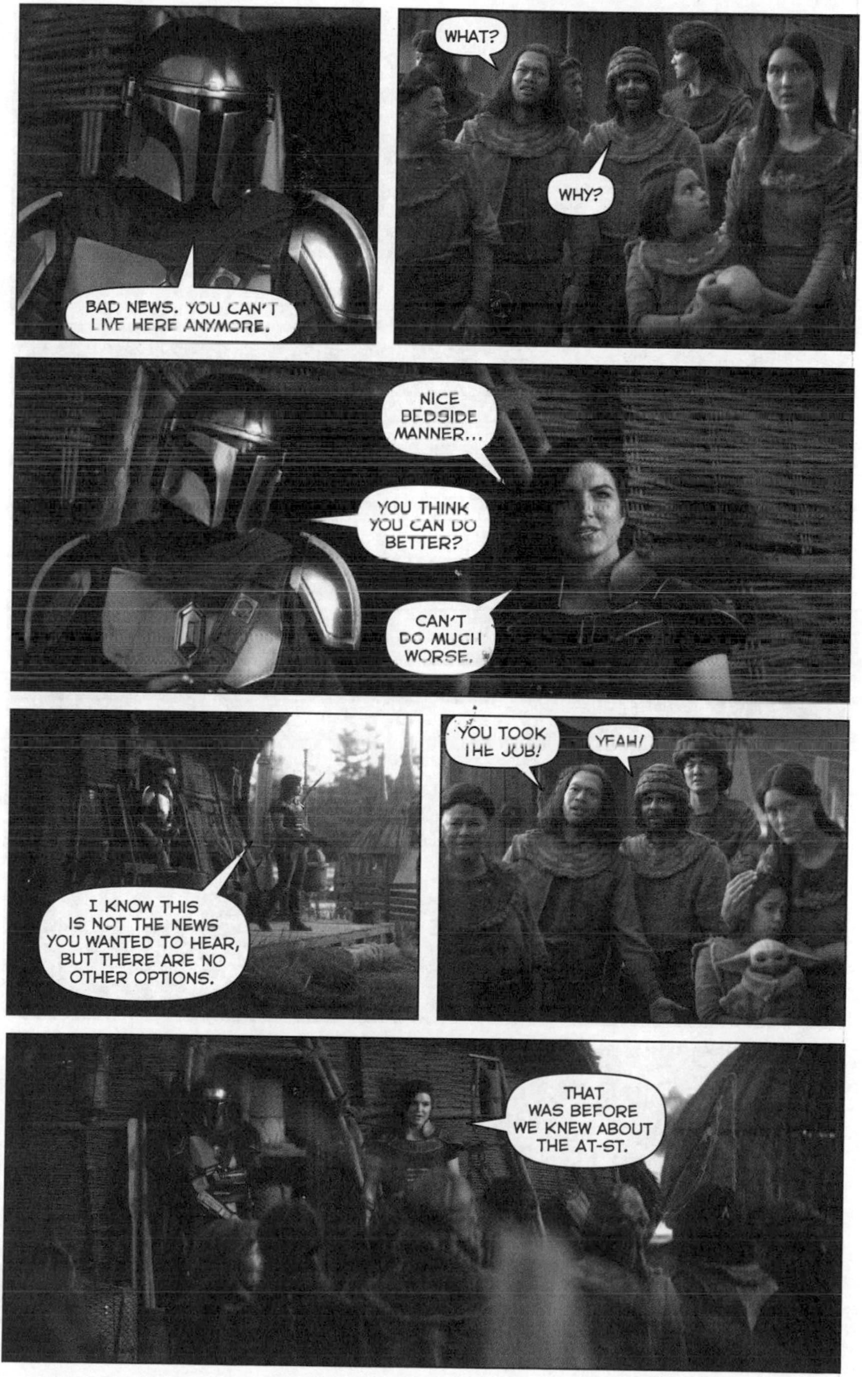
BAD NEWS. YOU CAN'T LIVE HERE ANYMORE.
WHAT?
WHY?
NICE BEDSIDE MANNER...
YOU THINK YOU CAN DO BETTER?
CAN'T DO MUCH WORSE.
I KNOW THIS IS NOT THE NEWS YOU WANTED TO HEAR, BUT THERE ARE NO OTHER OPTIONS.
YOU TOOK THE JOB!
YEAH!
THAT WAS BEFORE WE KNEW ABOUT THE AT-ST.

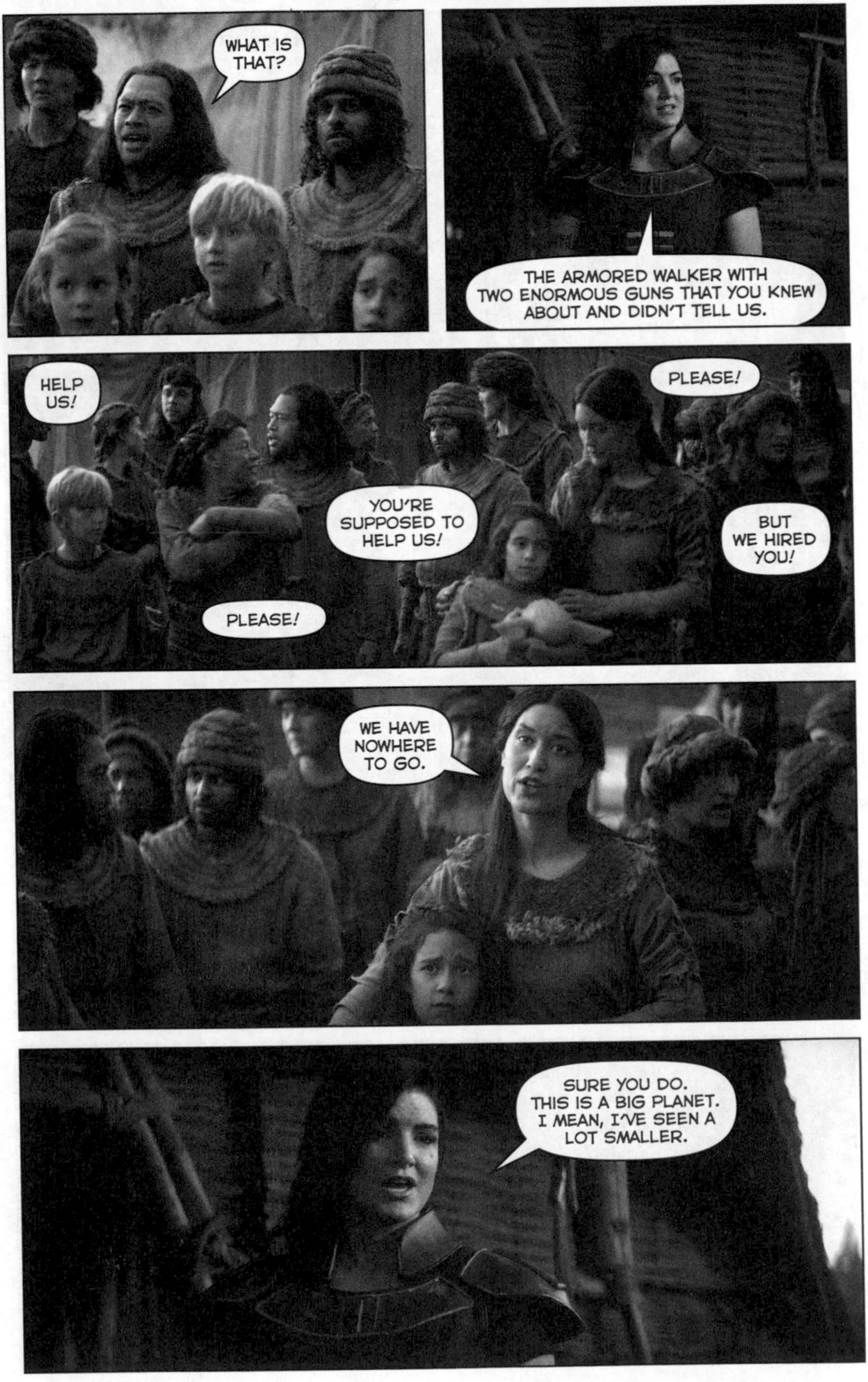
WHAT IS THAT?
THE ARMORED WALKER WITH TWO ENORMOUS GUNS THAT YOU KNEW ABOUT AND DIDN'T TELL US.
HELP US!
PLEASE!
YOU'RE SUPPOSED TO HELP US!
BUT WE HIRED YOU!
PLEASE!
WE HAVE NOWHERE TO GO.
SURE YOU DO. THIS IS A BIG PLANET. I MEAN, I'VE SEEN A LOT SMALLER.

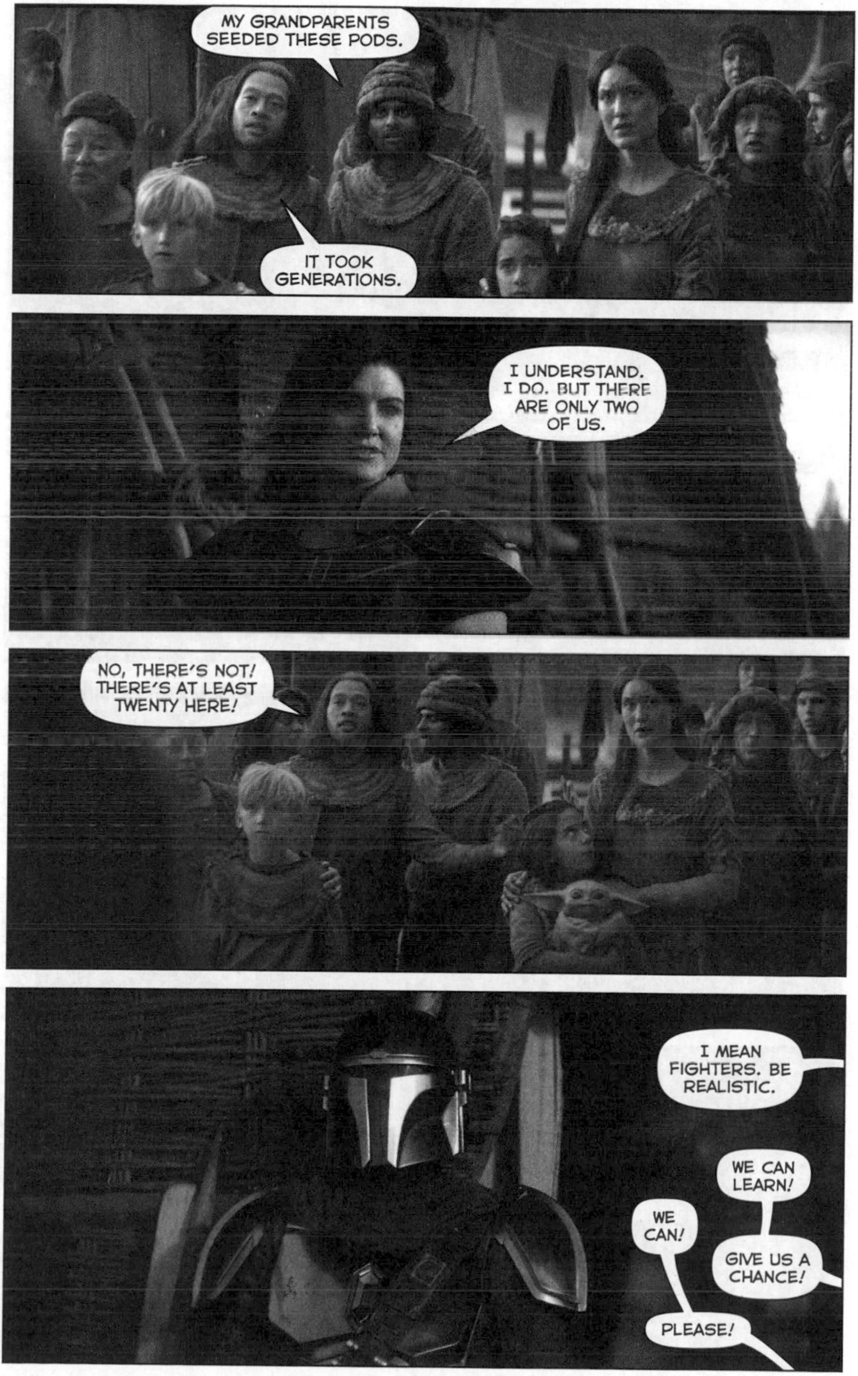
MY GRANDPARENTS SEEDED THESE PODS.
IT TOOK GENERATIONS.
I UNDERSTAND. I DO. BUT THERE ARE ONLY TWO OF US.
NO, THERE'S NOT! THERE'S AT LEAST TWENTY HERE!
I MEAN FIGHTERS. BE REALISTIC.
WE CAN LEARN!
WE CAN!
GIVE US A CHANCE!
PLEASE!

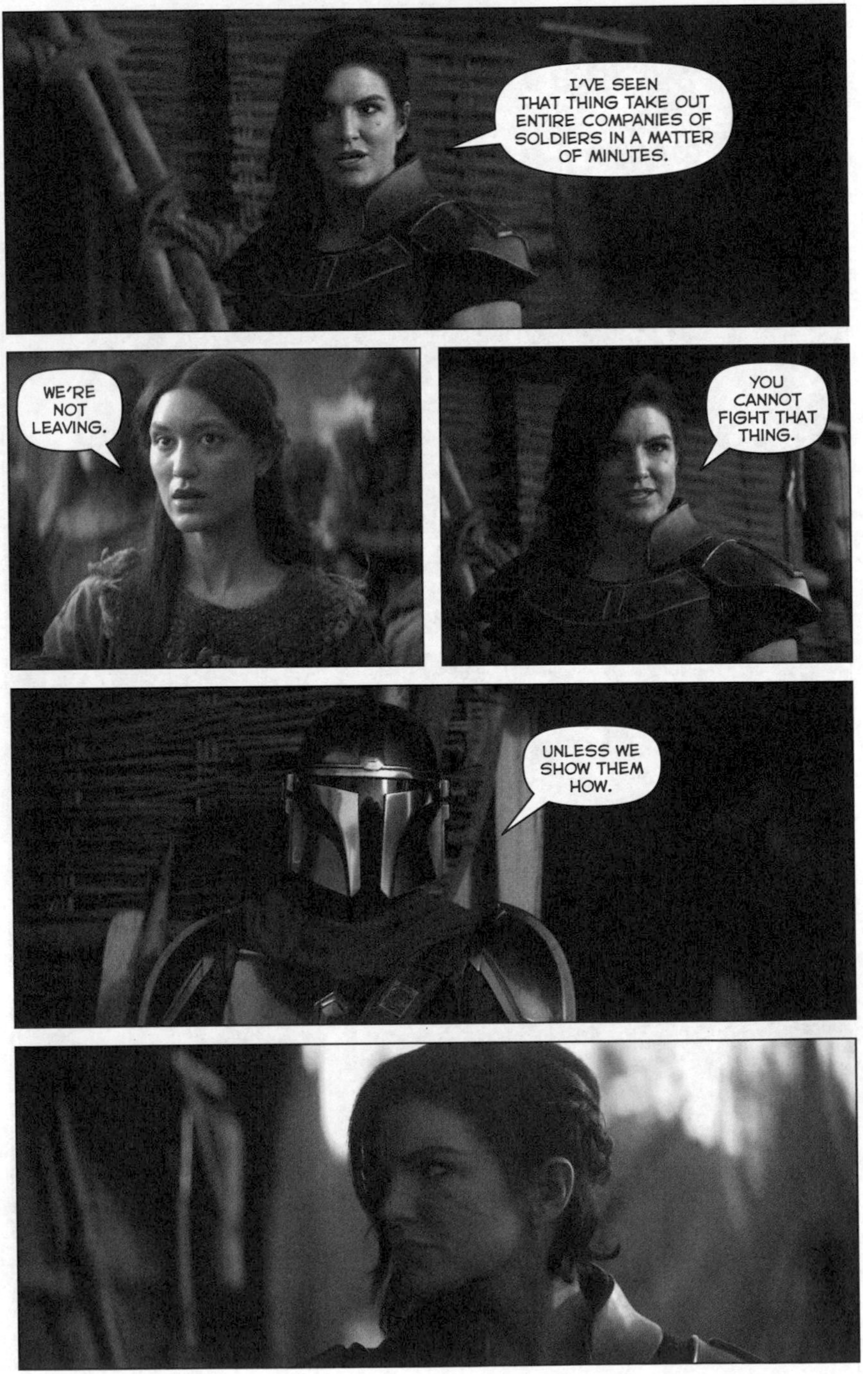
I'VE SEEN THAT THING TAKE OUT ENTIRE COMPANIES OF SOLDIERS IN A MATTER OF MINUTES.
WE'RE NOT LEAVING.
YOU CANNOT FIGHT THAT THING.
UNLESS WE SHOW THEM HOW.

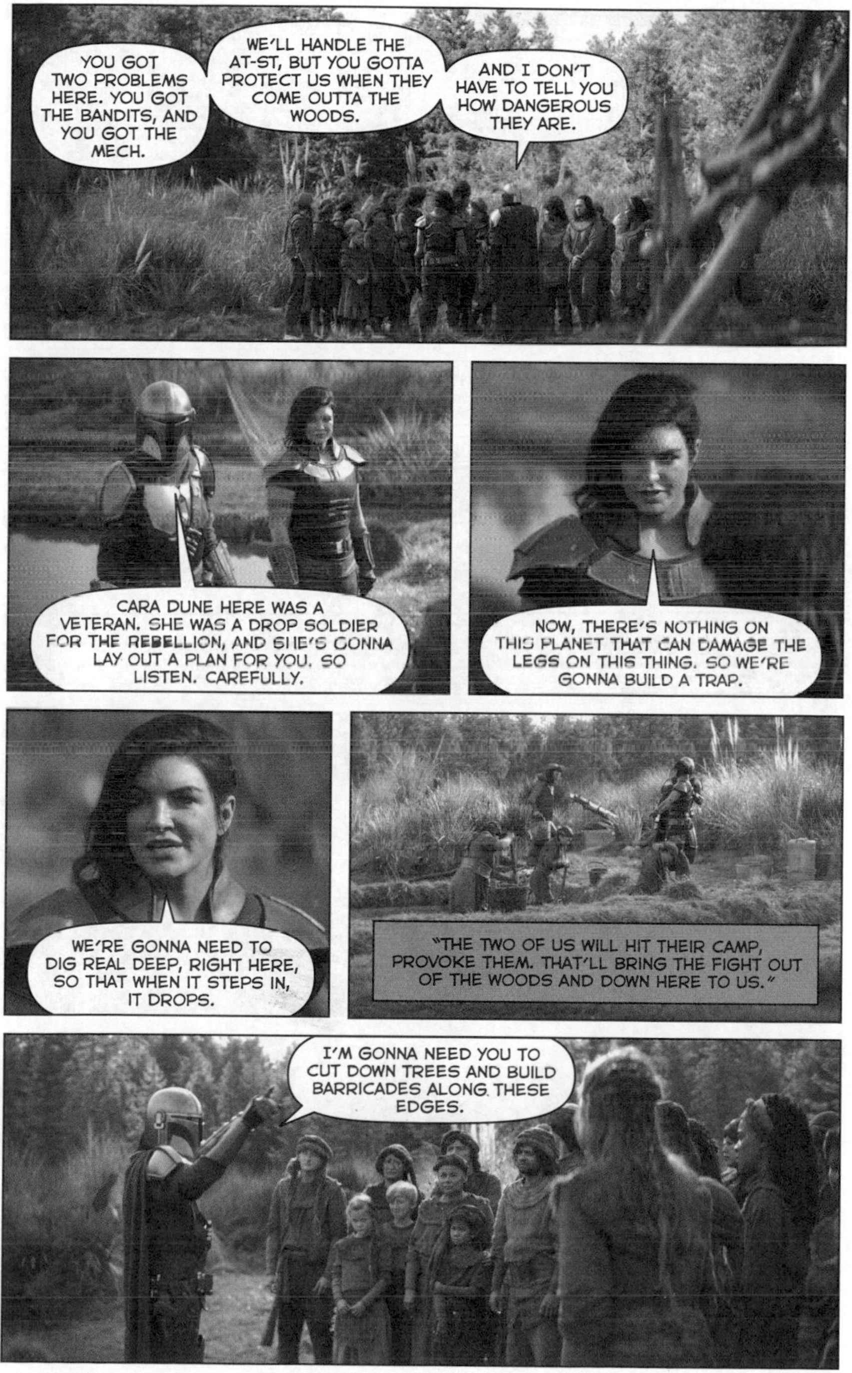
YOU GOT TWO PROBLEMS HERE. YOU GOT THE BANDITS, AND YOU GOT THE MECH.
WE'LL HANDLE THE AT-ST, BUT YOU GOTTA PROTECT US WHEN THEY COME OUTTA THE WOODS.
AND I DON'T HAVE TO TELL YOU HOW DANGEROUS THEY ARE.
CARA DUNE HERE WAS A VETERAN. SHE WAS A DROP SOLDIER FOR THE REBELLION, AND SHE'S GONNA LAY OUT A PLAN FOR YOU. SO LISTEN. CAREFULLY.
NOW, THERE'S NOTHING ON THIS PLANET THAT CAN DAMAGE THE LEGS ON THIS THING. SO WE'RE GONNA BUILD A TRAP.
WE'RE GONNA NEED TO DIG REAL DEEP, RIGHT HERE, SO THAT WHEN IT STEPS IN, IT DROPS.
"THE TWO OF US WILL HIT THEIR CAMP, PROVOKE THEM. THAT'LL BRING THE FIGHT OUT OF THE WOODS AND DOWN HERE TO US."
I'M GONNA NEED YOU TO CUT DOWN TREES AND BUILD BARRICADES ALONG THESE EDGES.

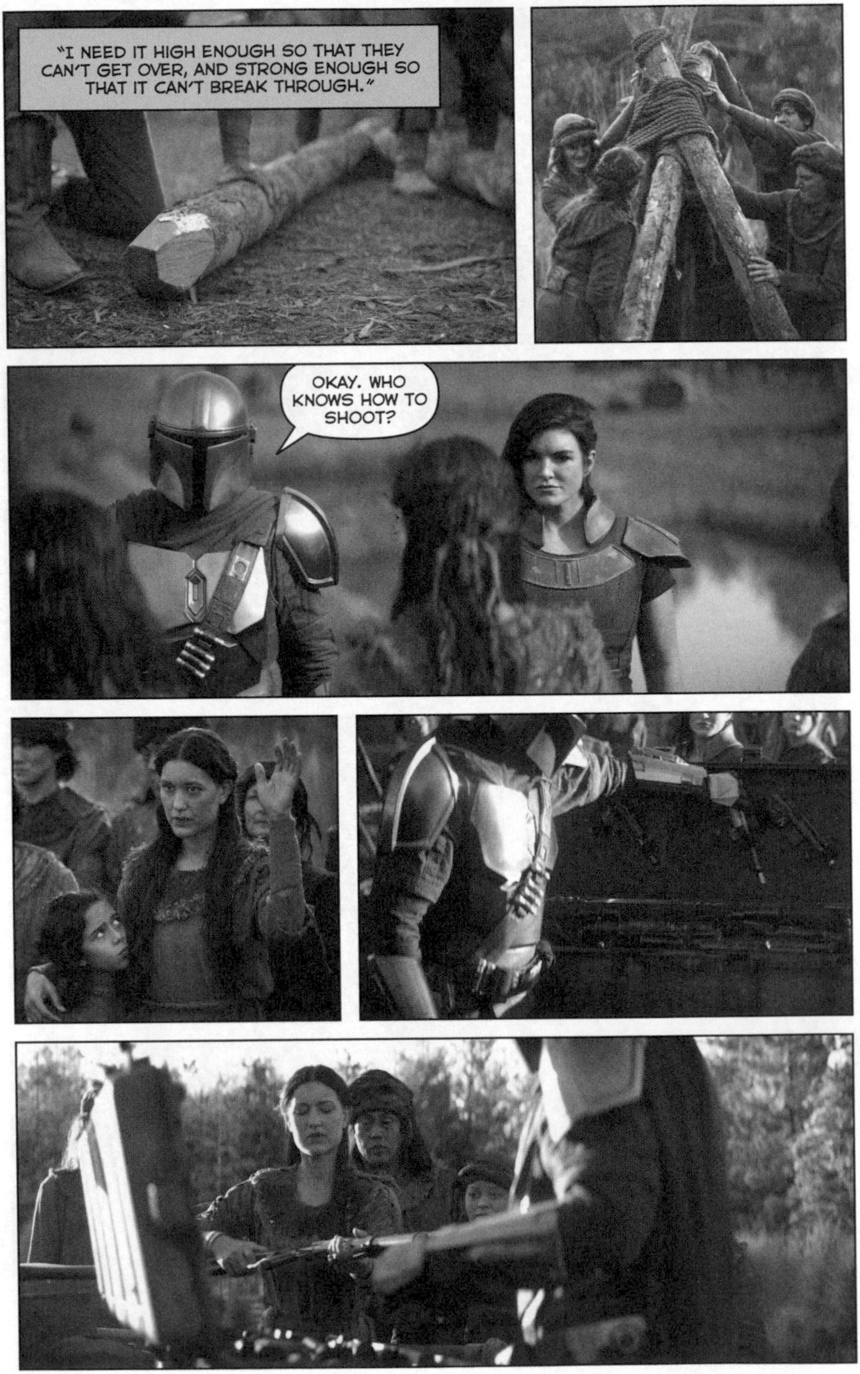
"I NEED IT HIGH ENOUGH SO THAT THEY CAN'T GET OVER, AND STRONG ENOUGH SO THAT IT CAN'T BREAK THROUGH."
OKAY. WHO KNOWS HOW TO SHOOT?

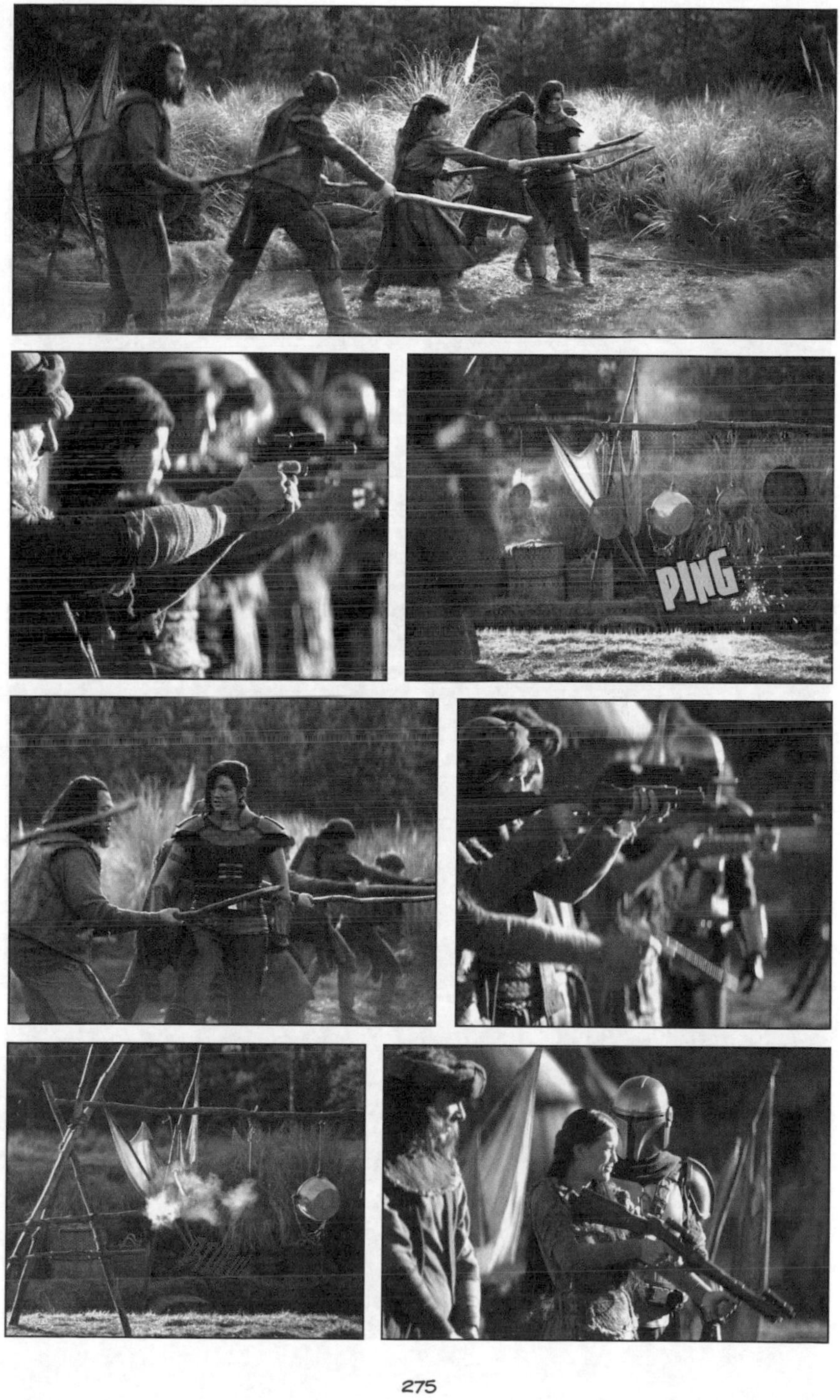
PING

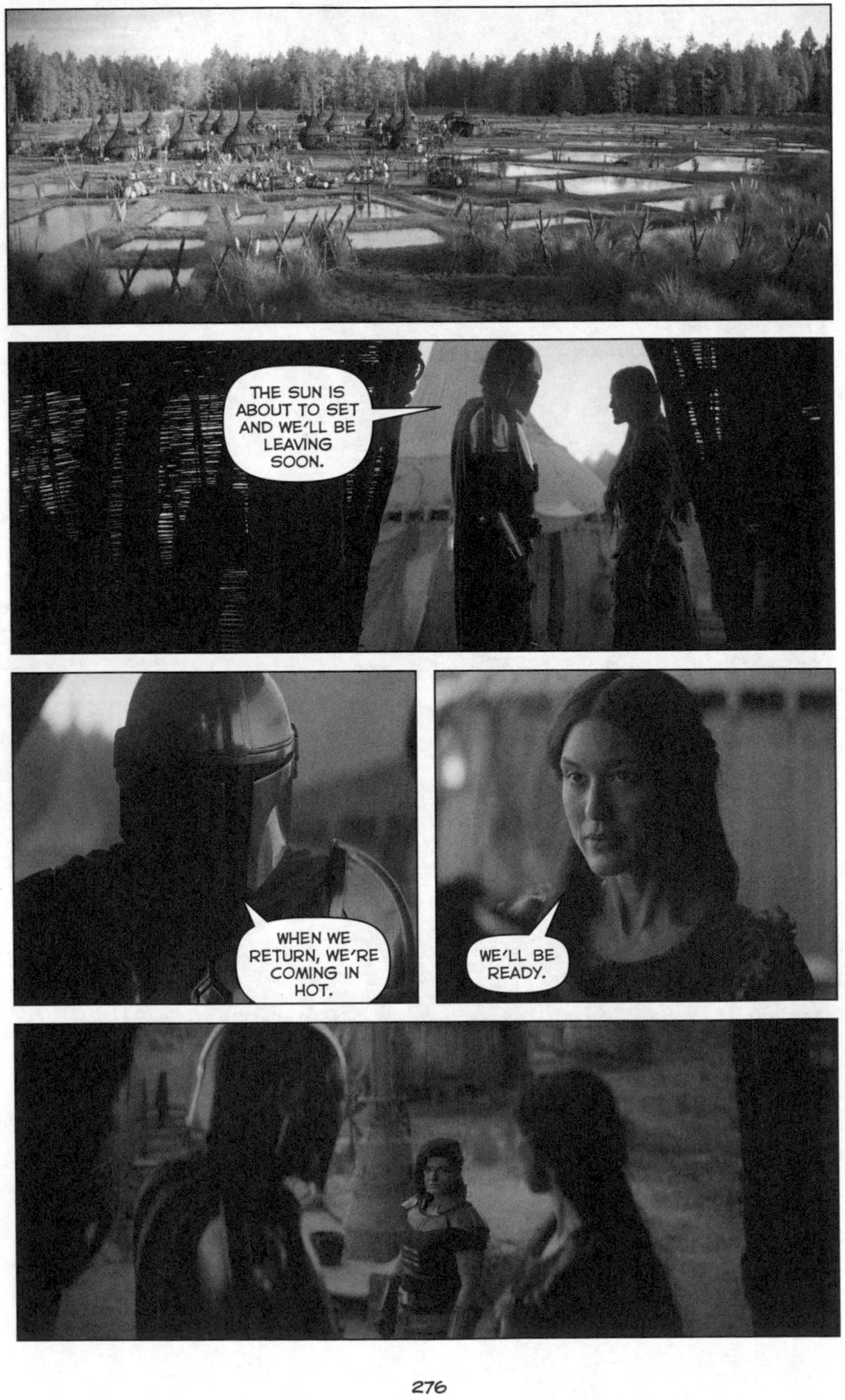
THE SUN IS ABOUT TO SET AND WE'LL BE LEAVING SOON.
WHEN WE RETURN, WE'RE COMING IN HOT.
WE'LL BE READY.

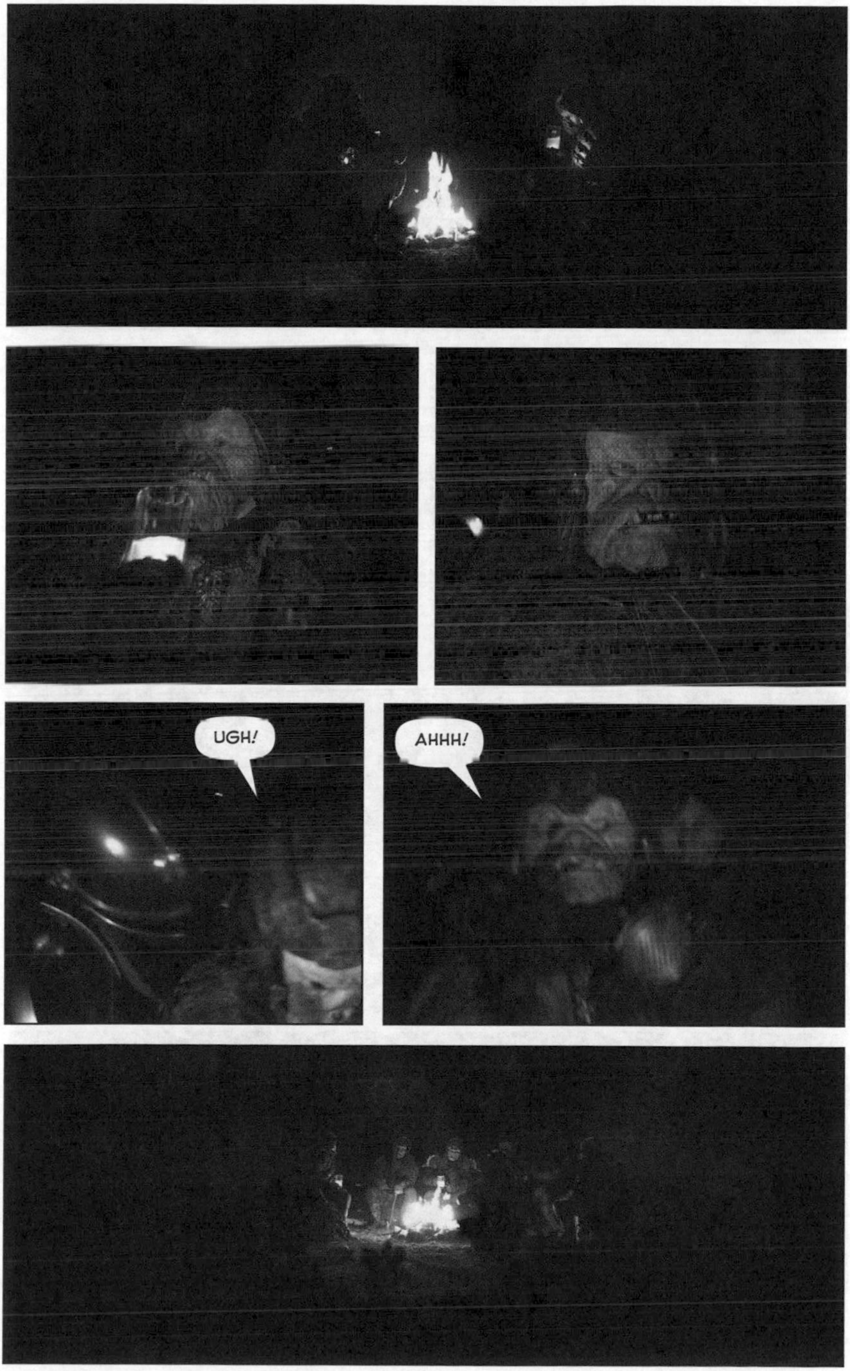
UGH!
AHHH!

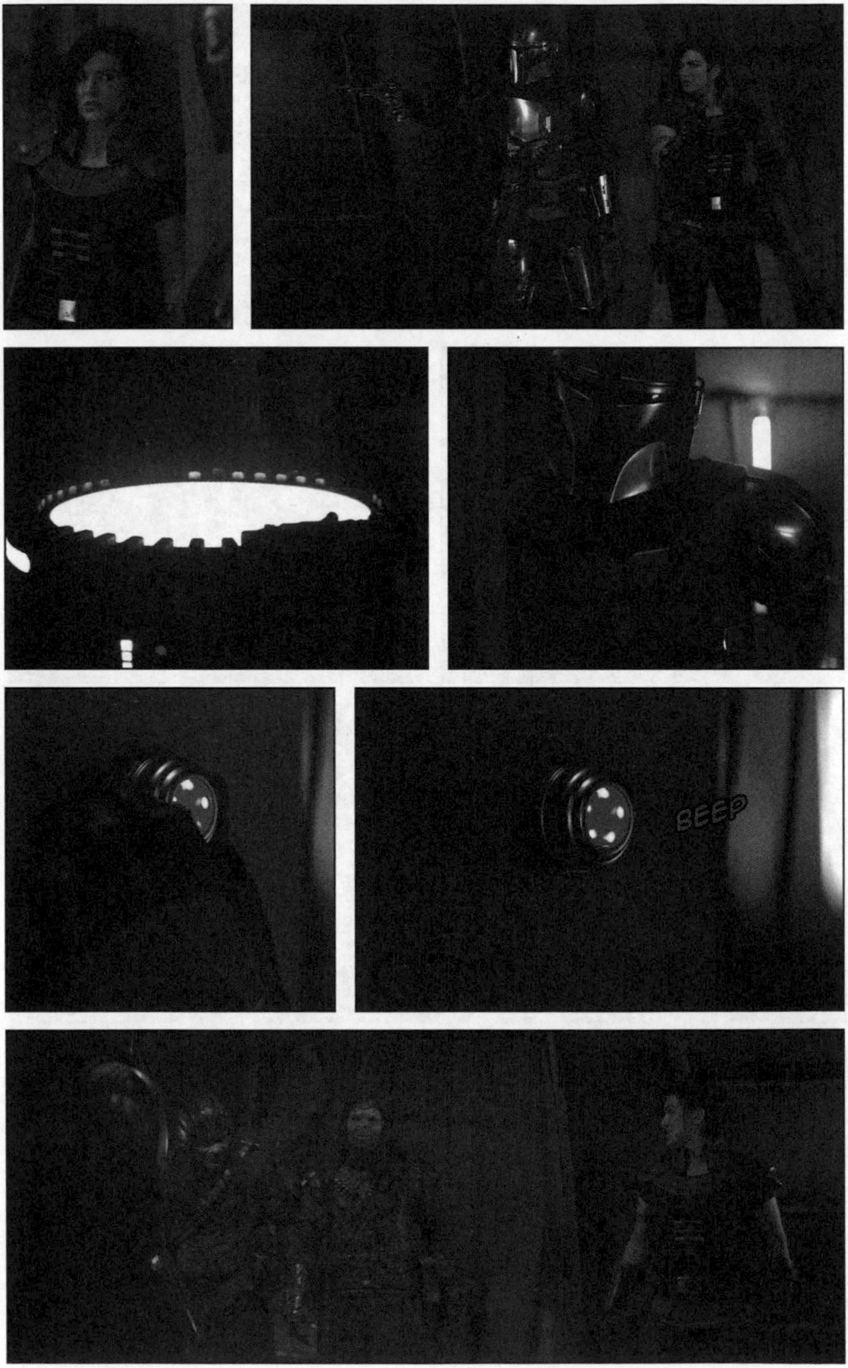
BEEP

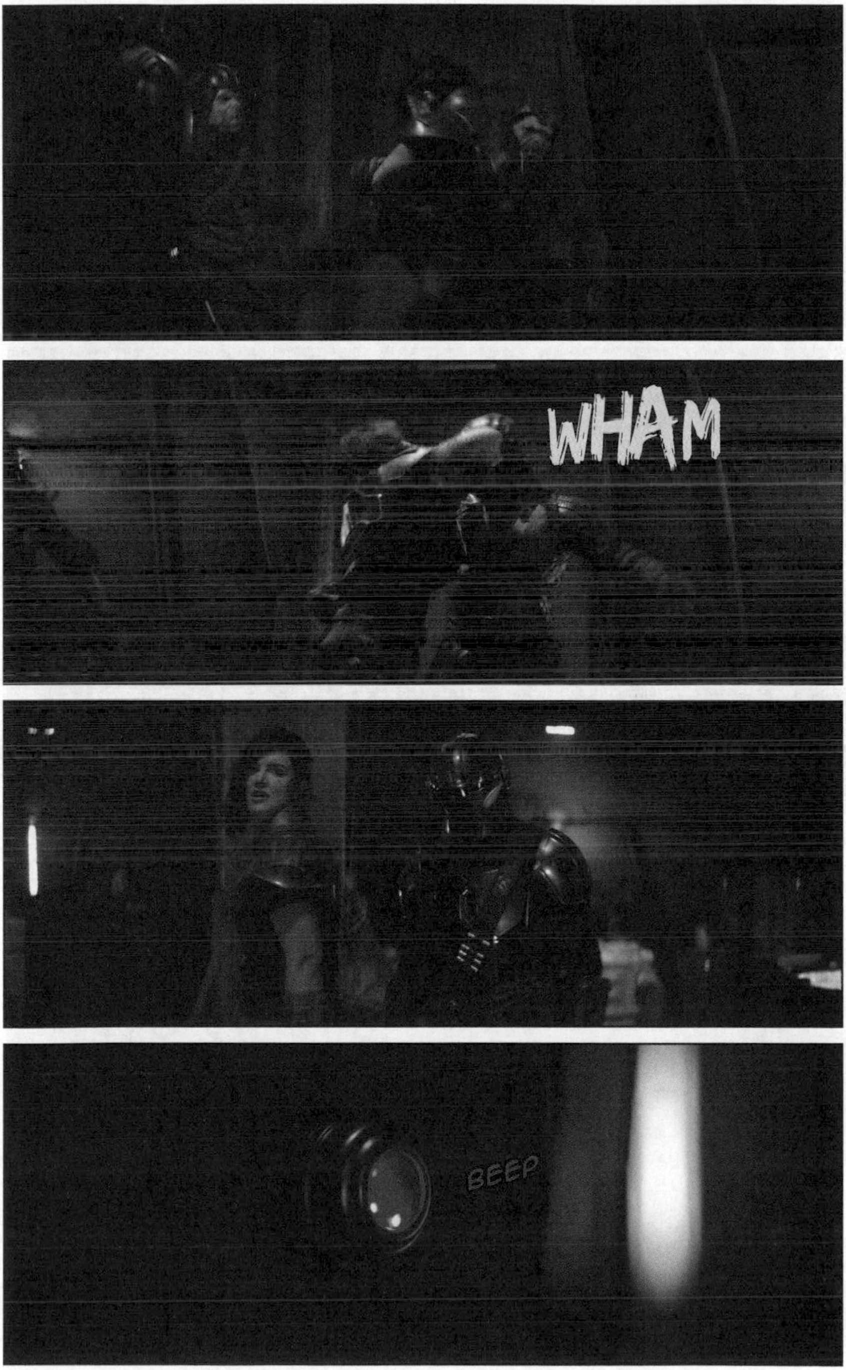
WHAM
BEEP

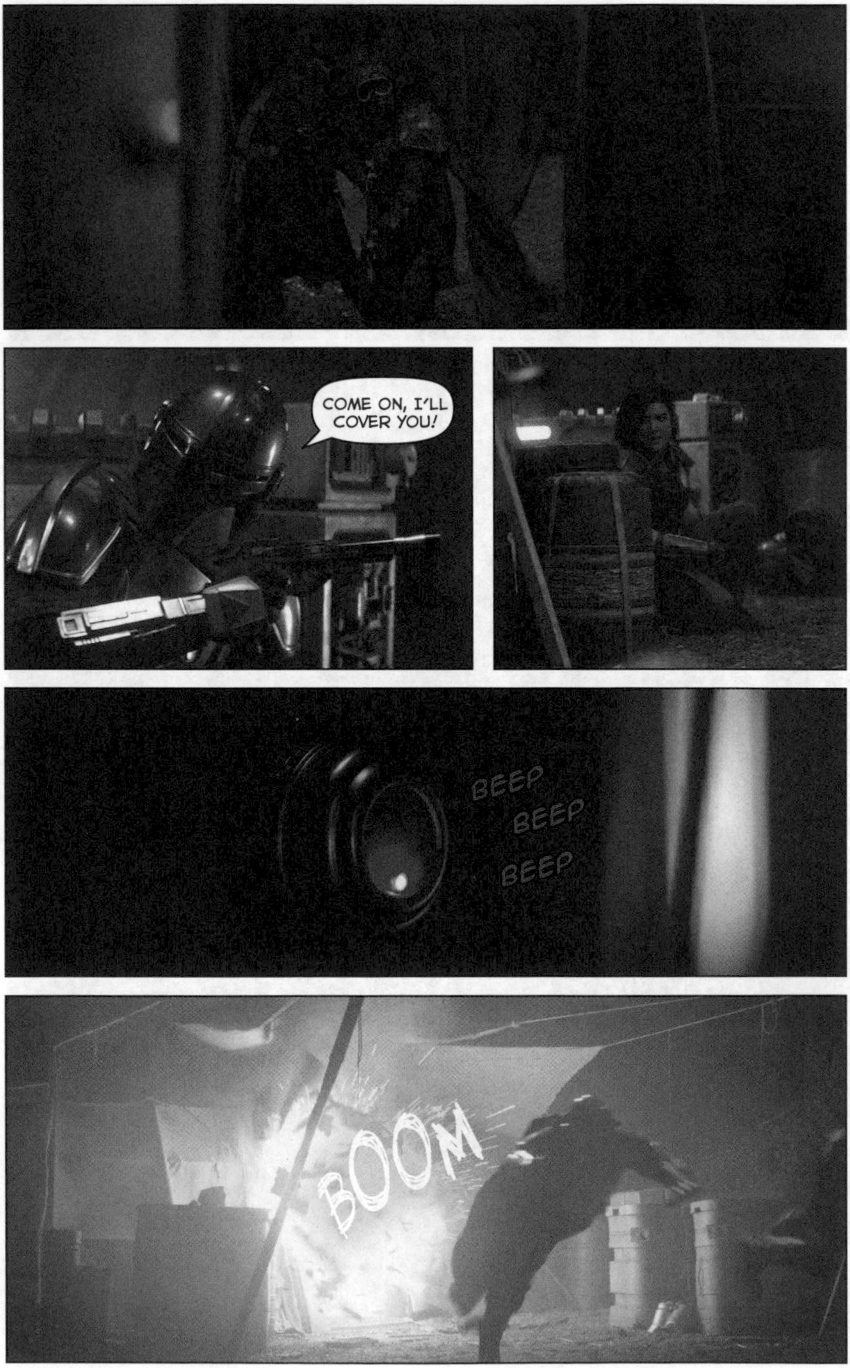
COME ON, I'LL COVER YOU!
BEEP
BEEP
BEEP
BOOM

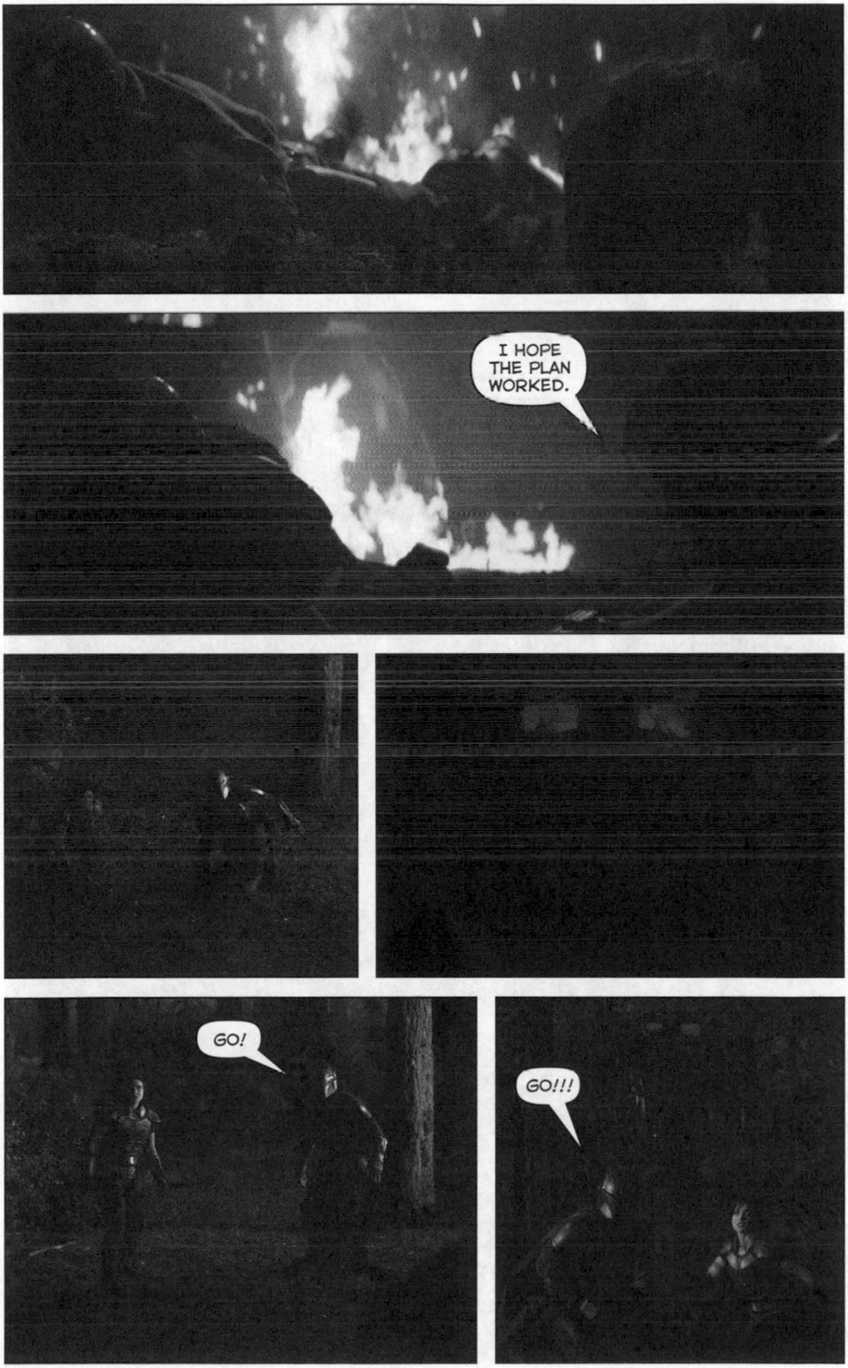
I HOPE THE PLAN WORKED.
GO!
GO!!!

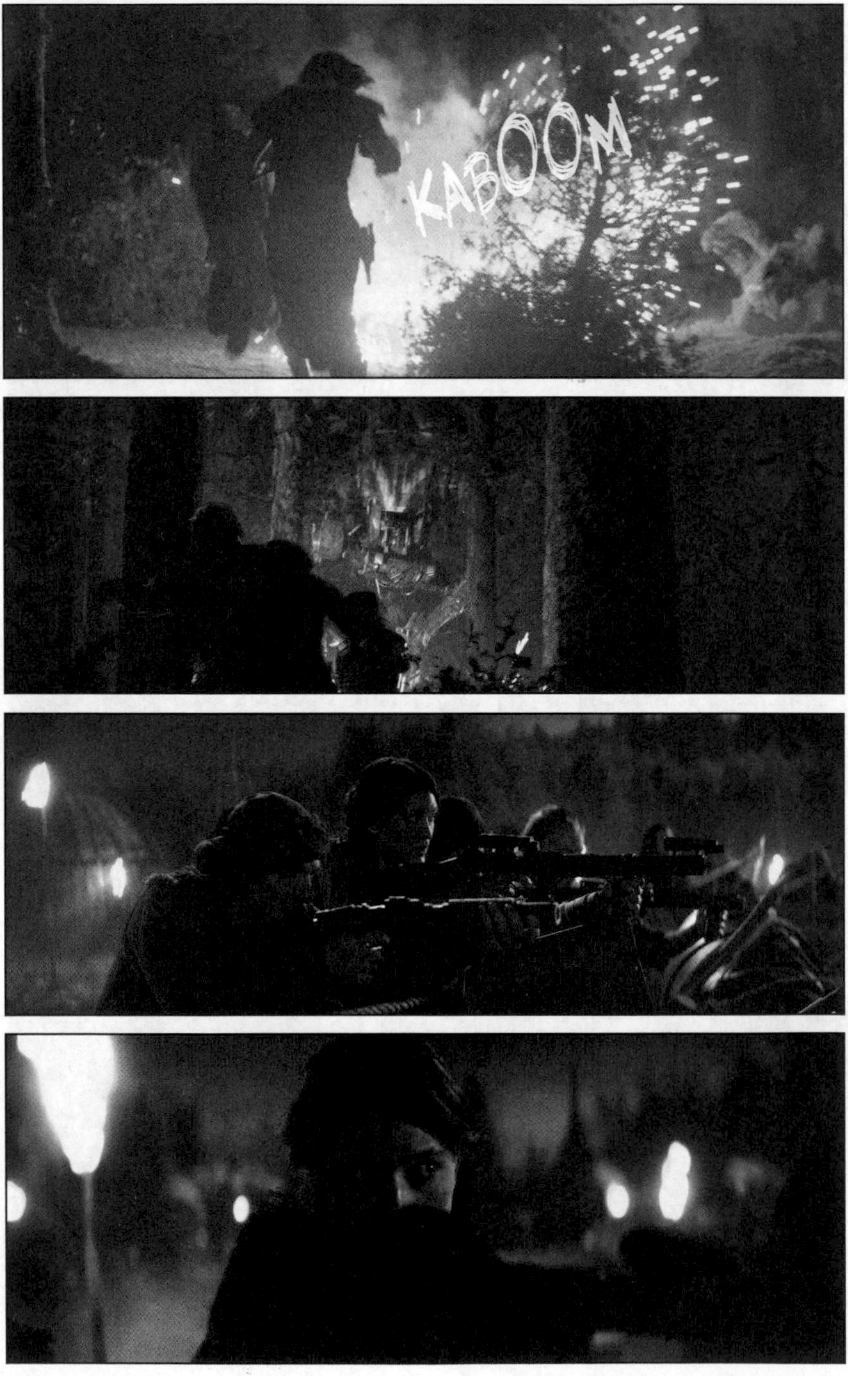
KABOOM

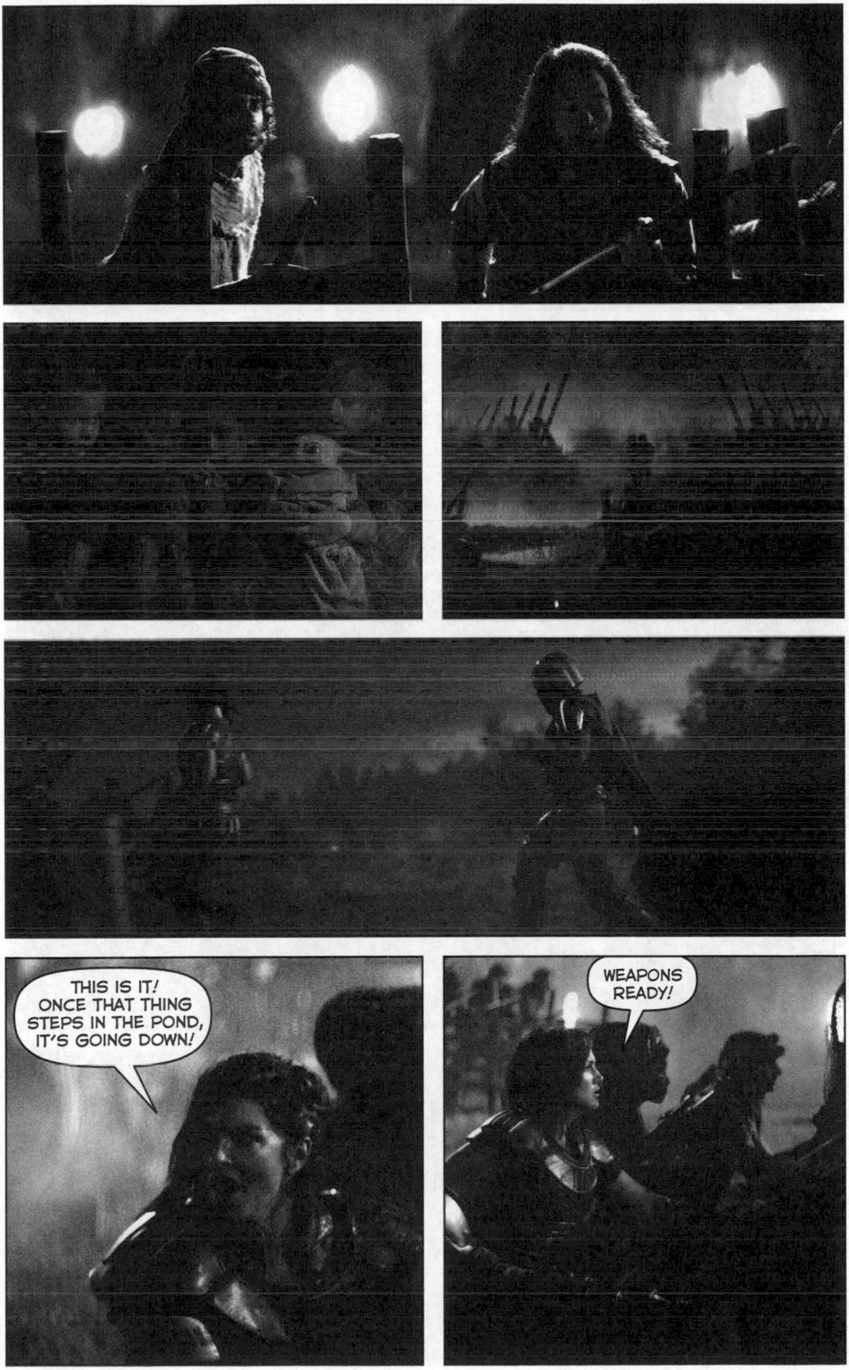
THIS IS IT! ONCE THAT THING STEPS IN THE POND, IT'S GOING DOWN!
WEAPONS READY!

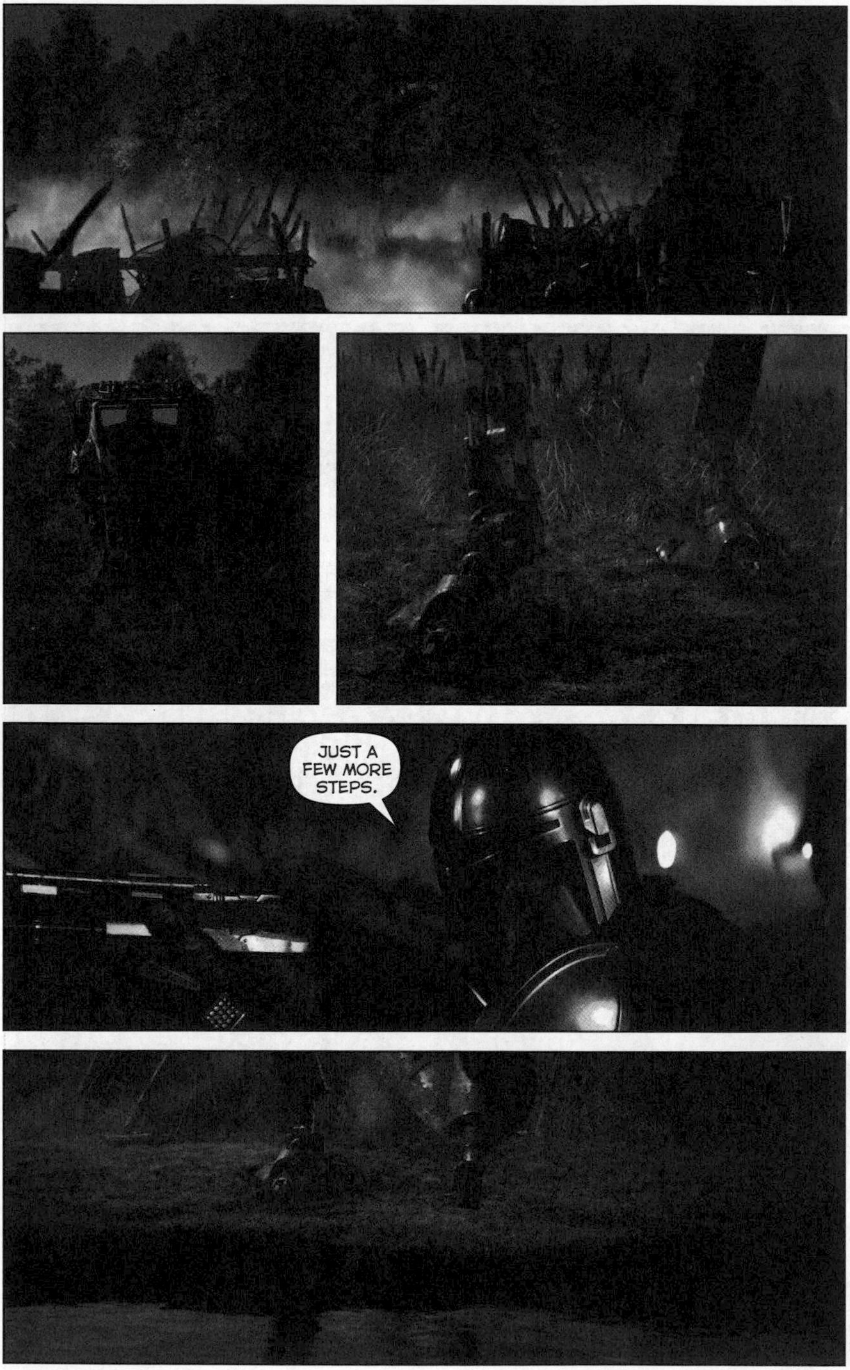
JUST A FEW MORE STEPS.

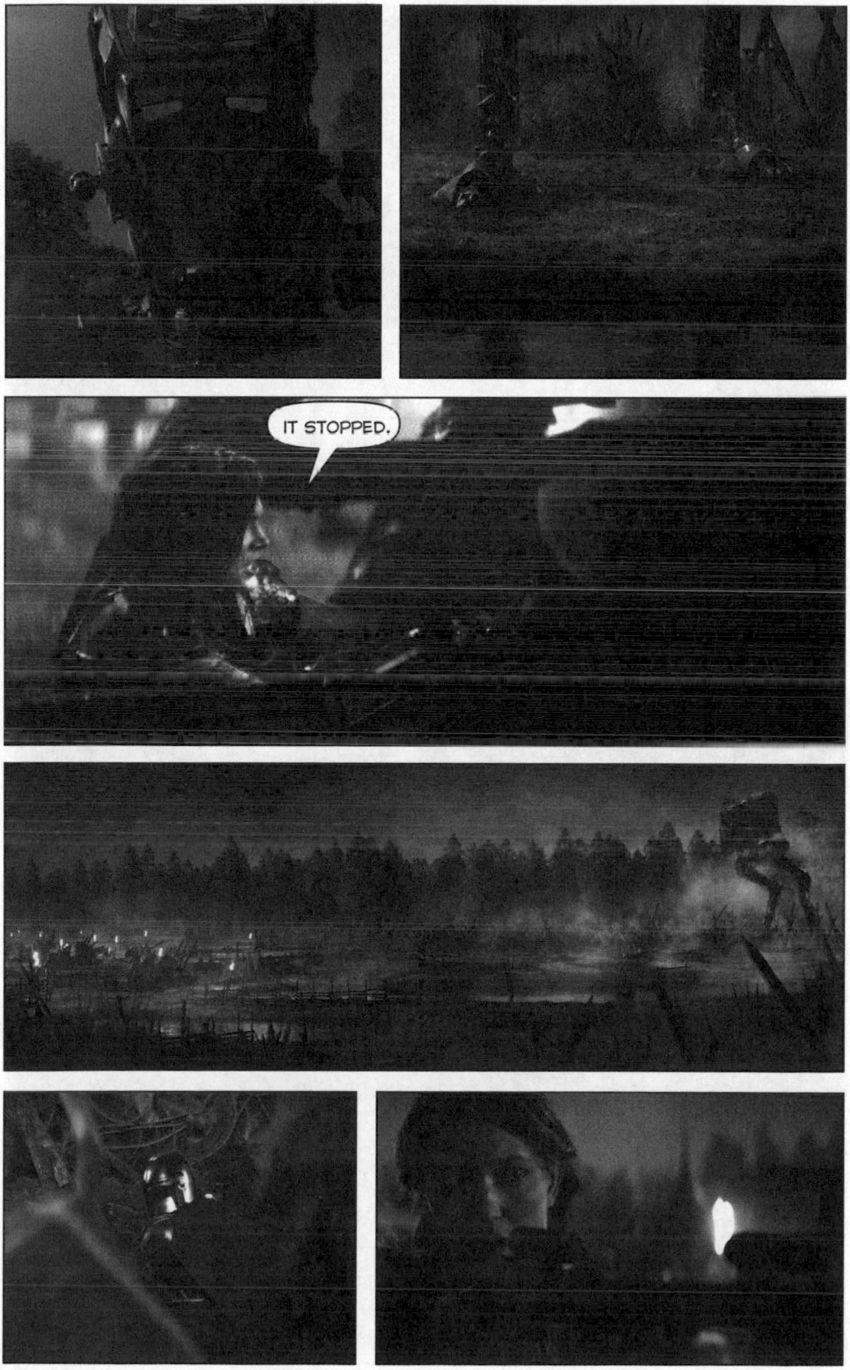
IT STOPPED.

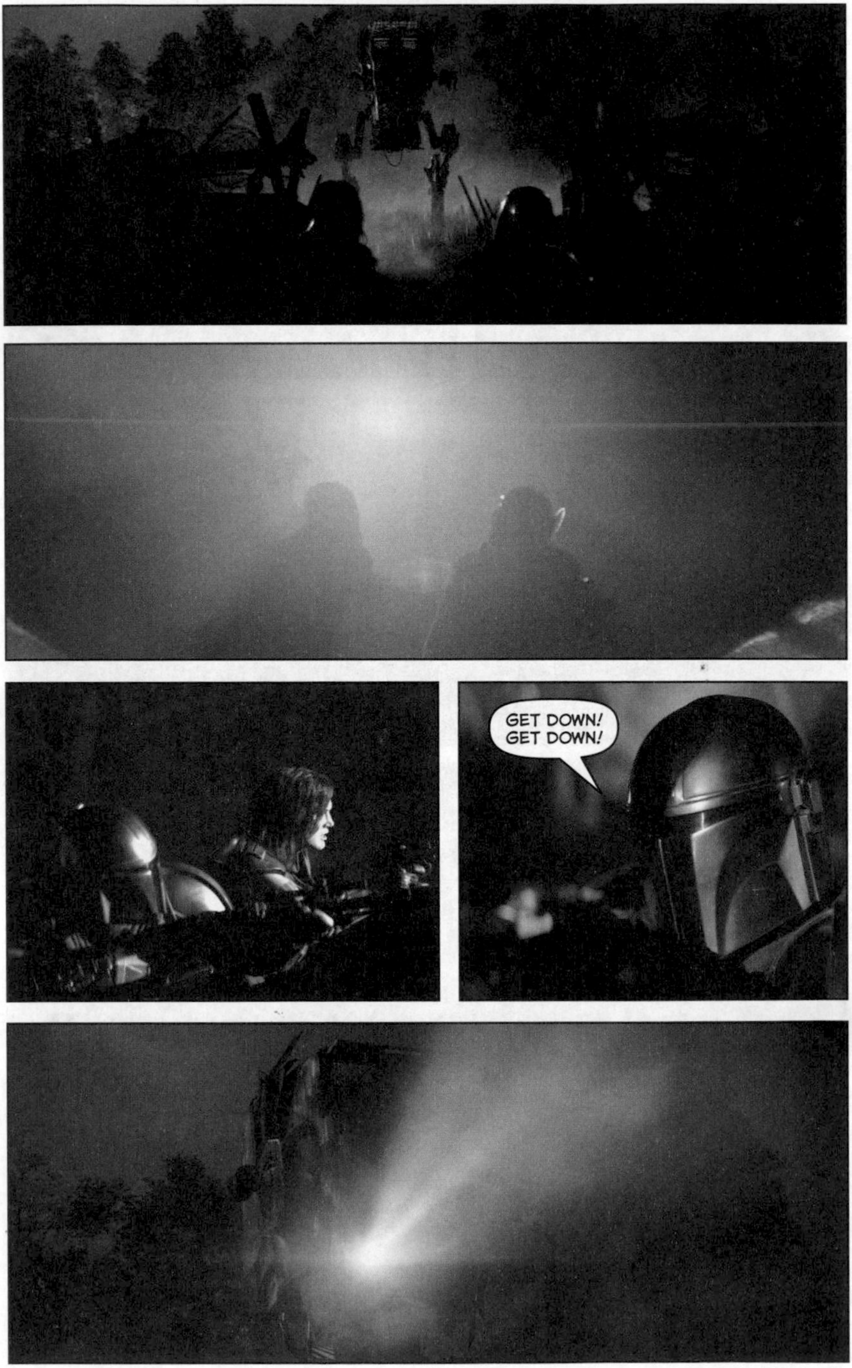
GET DOWN!
GET DOWN!

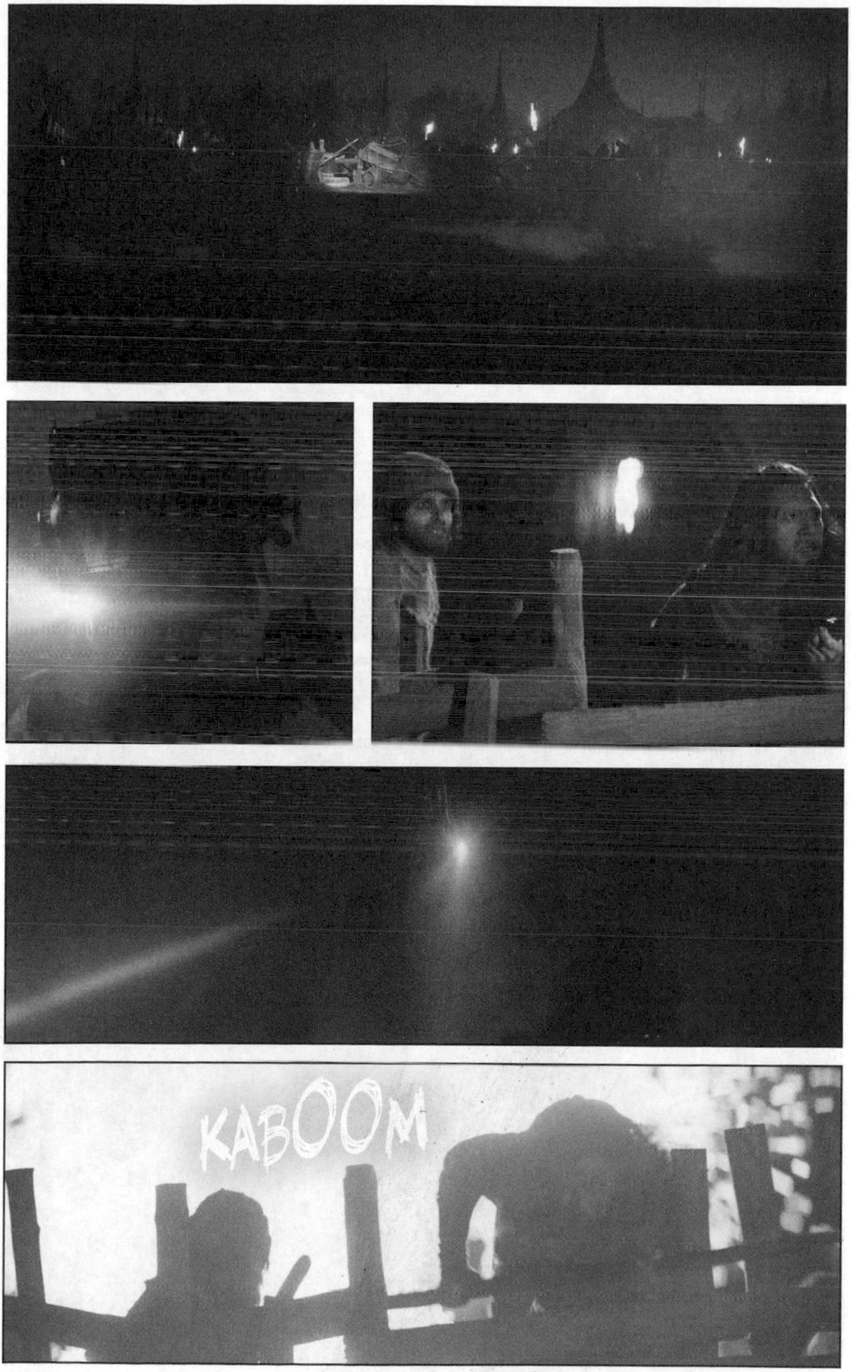
KABOOM

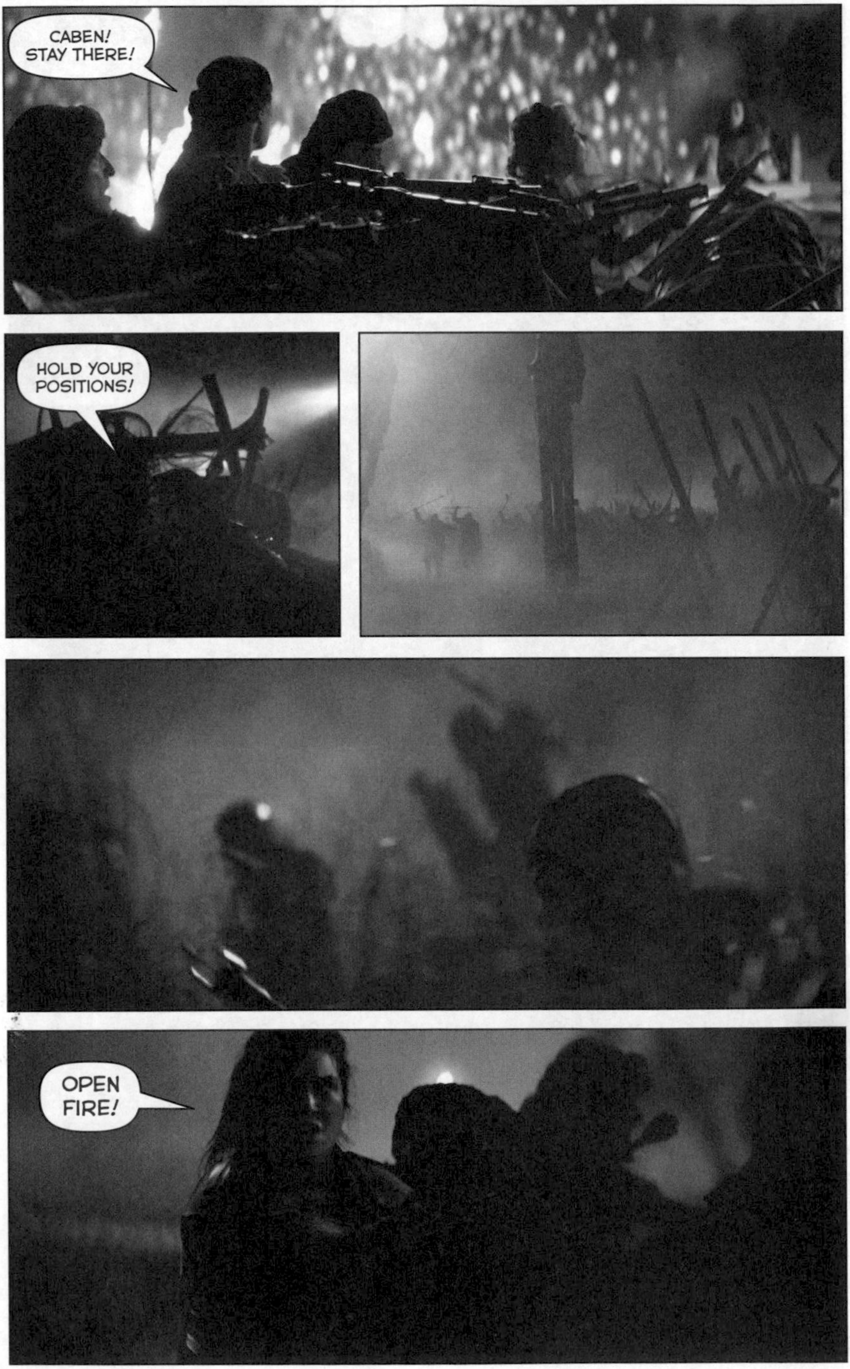
CABEN! STAY THERE!
HOLD YOUR POSITIONS!
OPEN FIRE!

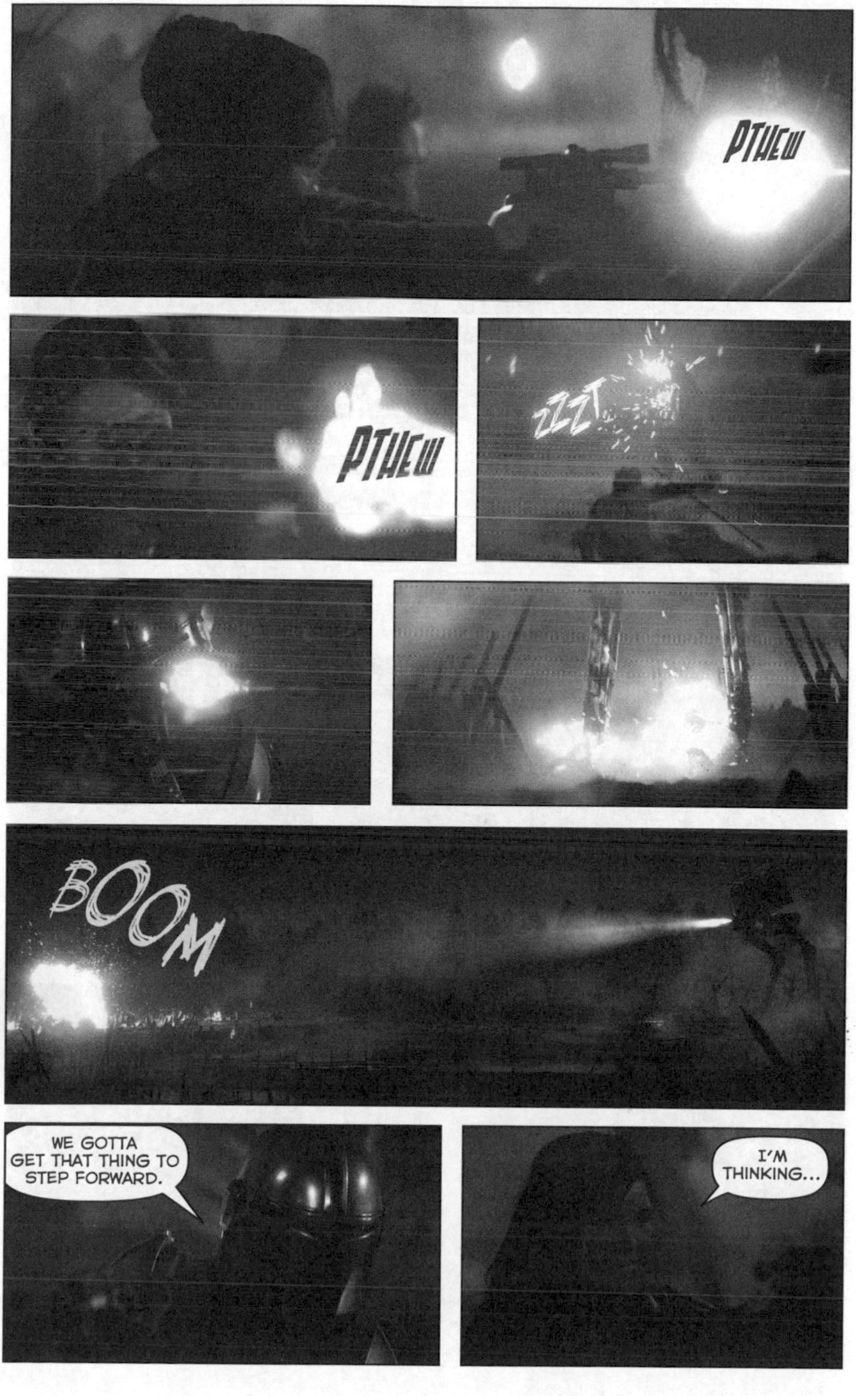
PTHEW
PTHEW
ZZZT
BOOM
WE GOTTA GET THAT THING TO STEP FORWARD.
I'M THINKING...

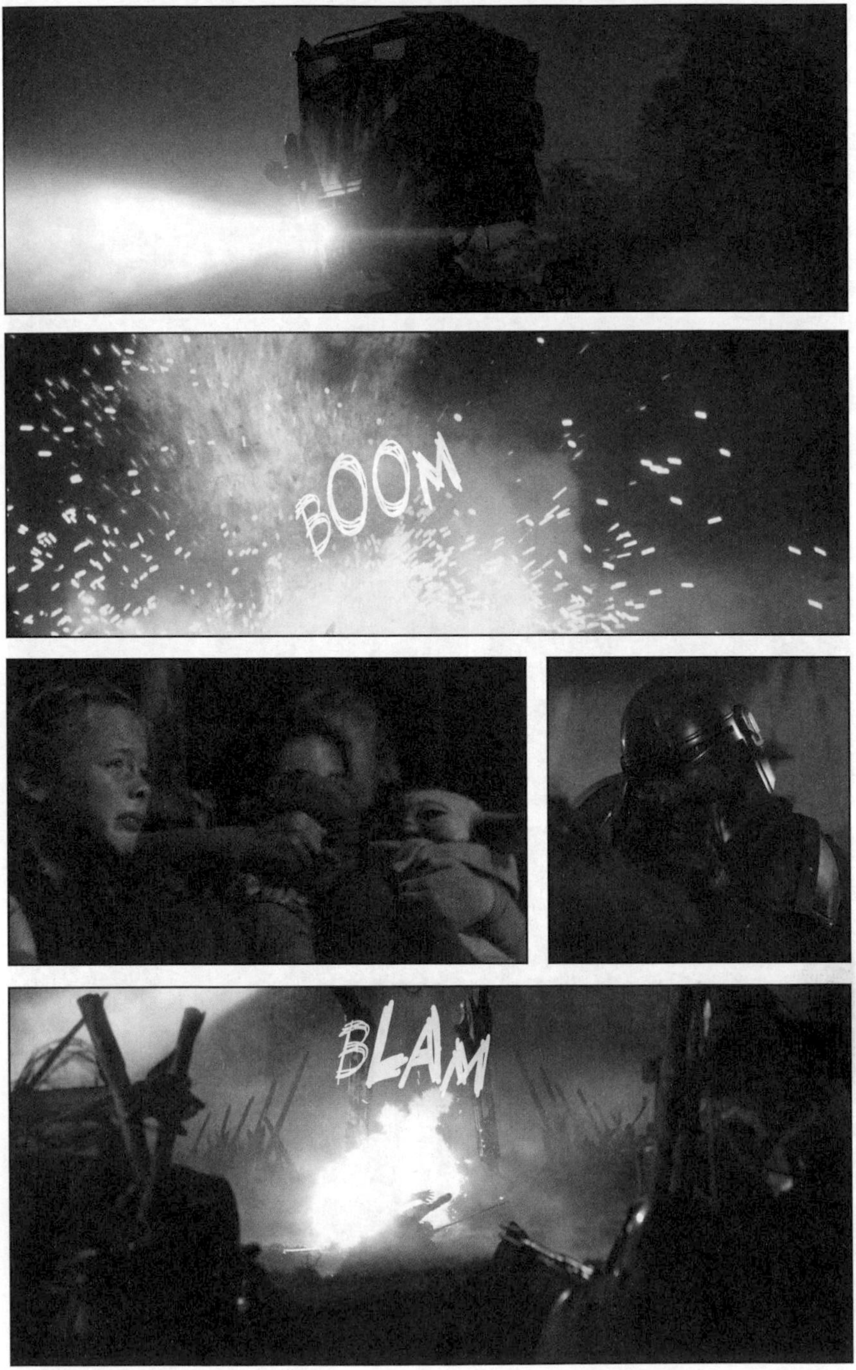
BOOM
BLAM

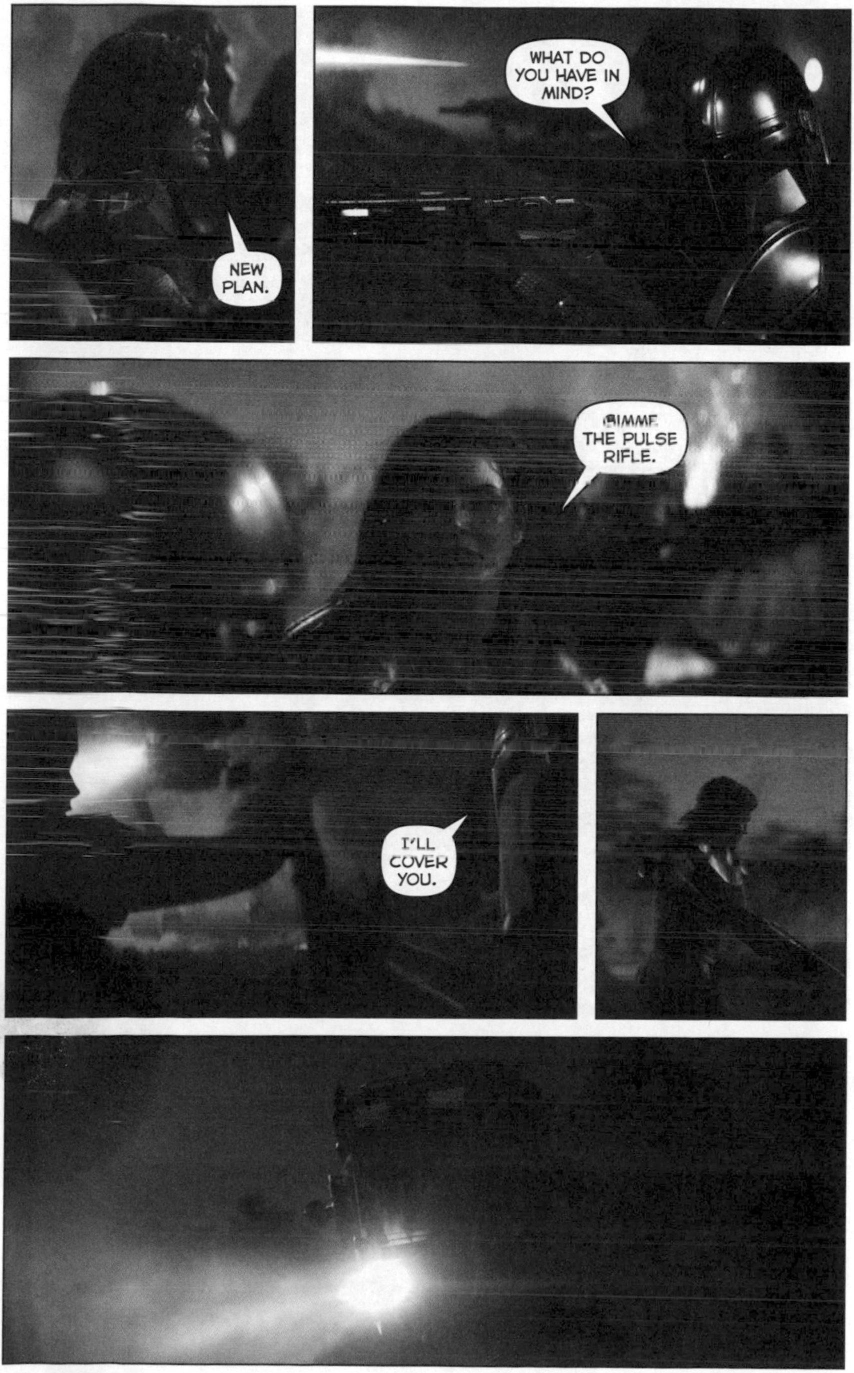
NEW PLAN.
WHAT DO YOU HAVE IN MIND?
GIMME THE PULSE RIFLE.
I'LL COVER YOU.

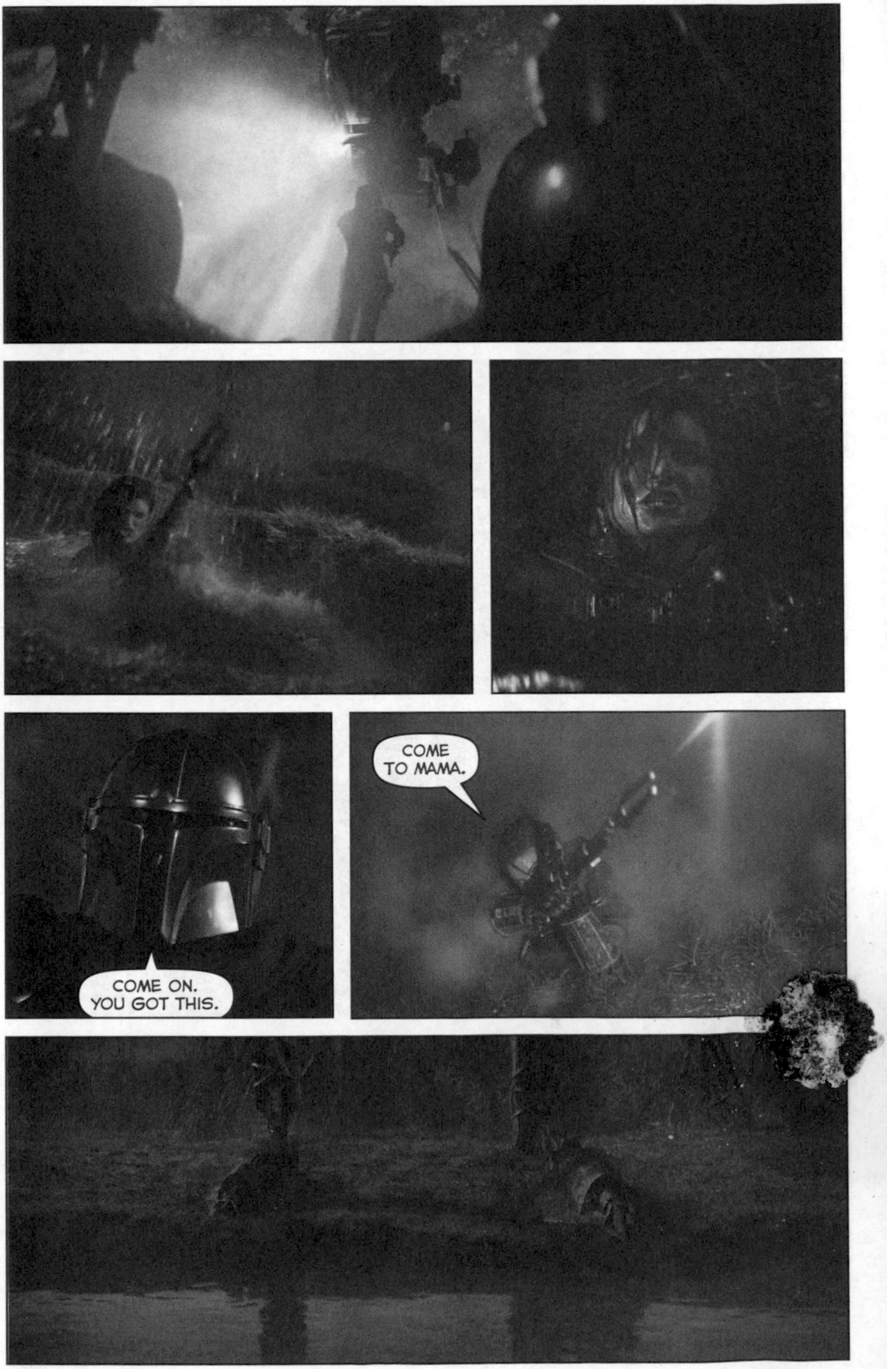
COME ON. YOU GOT THIS.
COME TO MAMA.

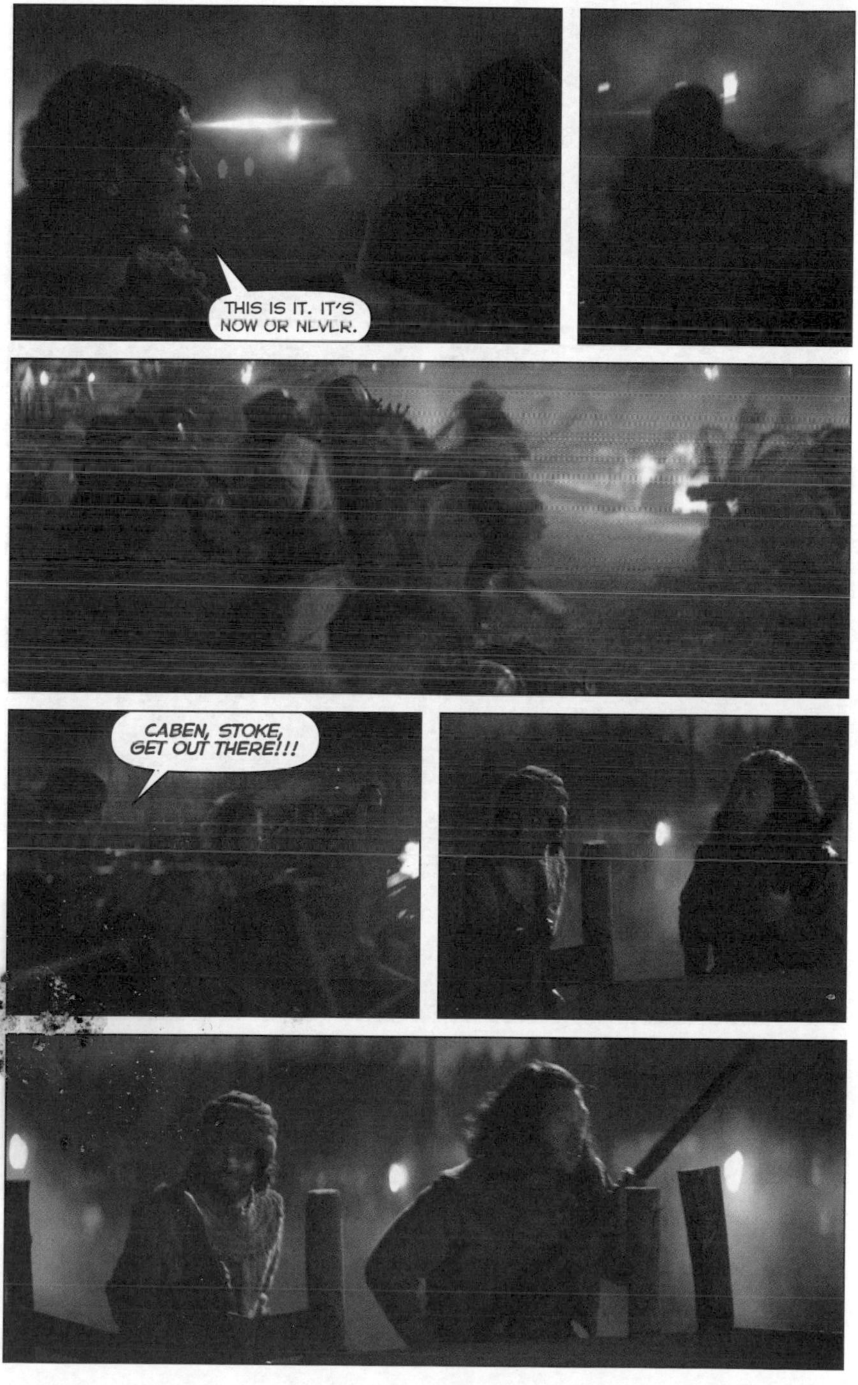
THIS IS IT. IT'S NOW OR NEVER.
CABEN, STOKE, GET OUT THERE!!!

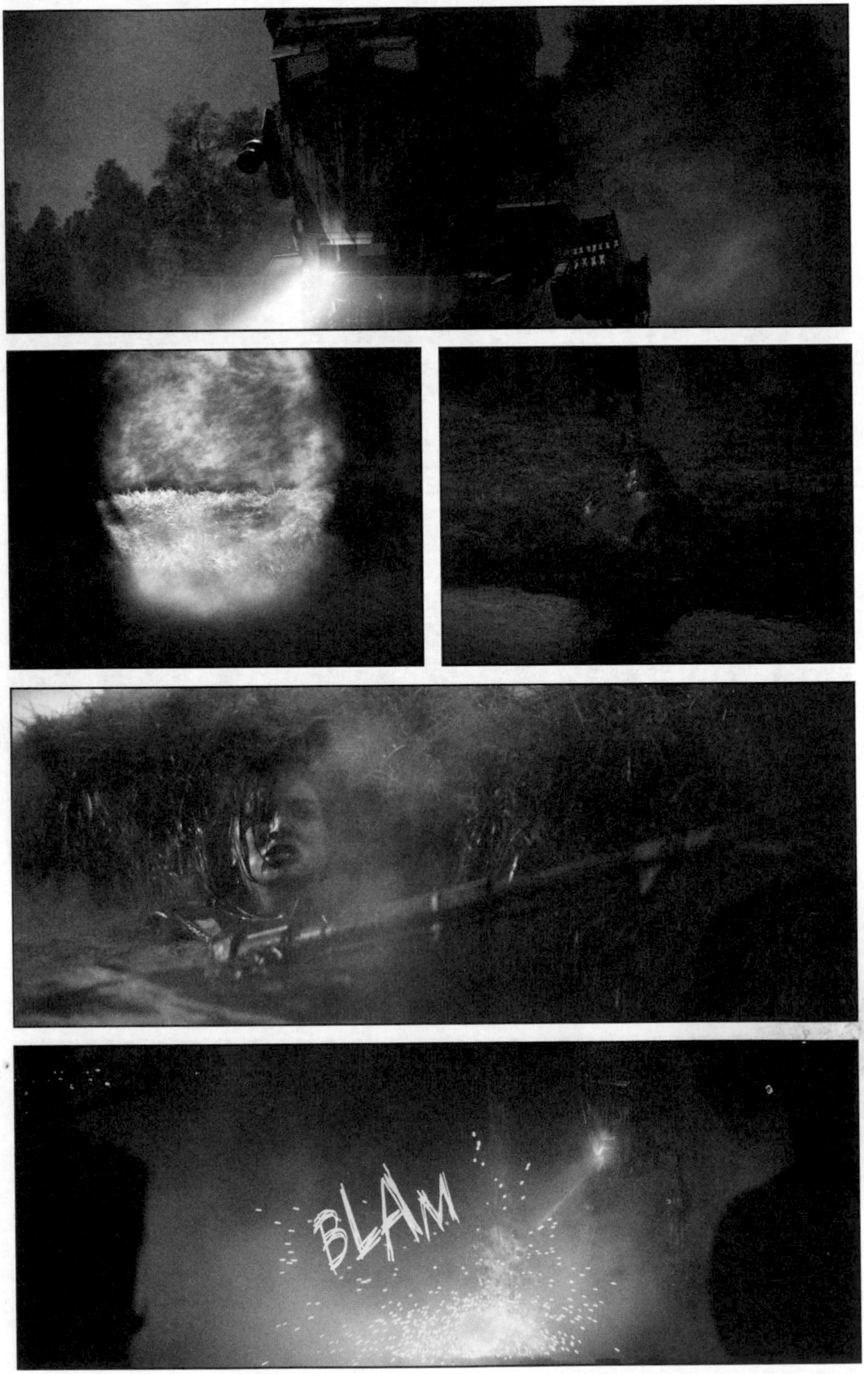
BLAM

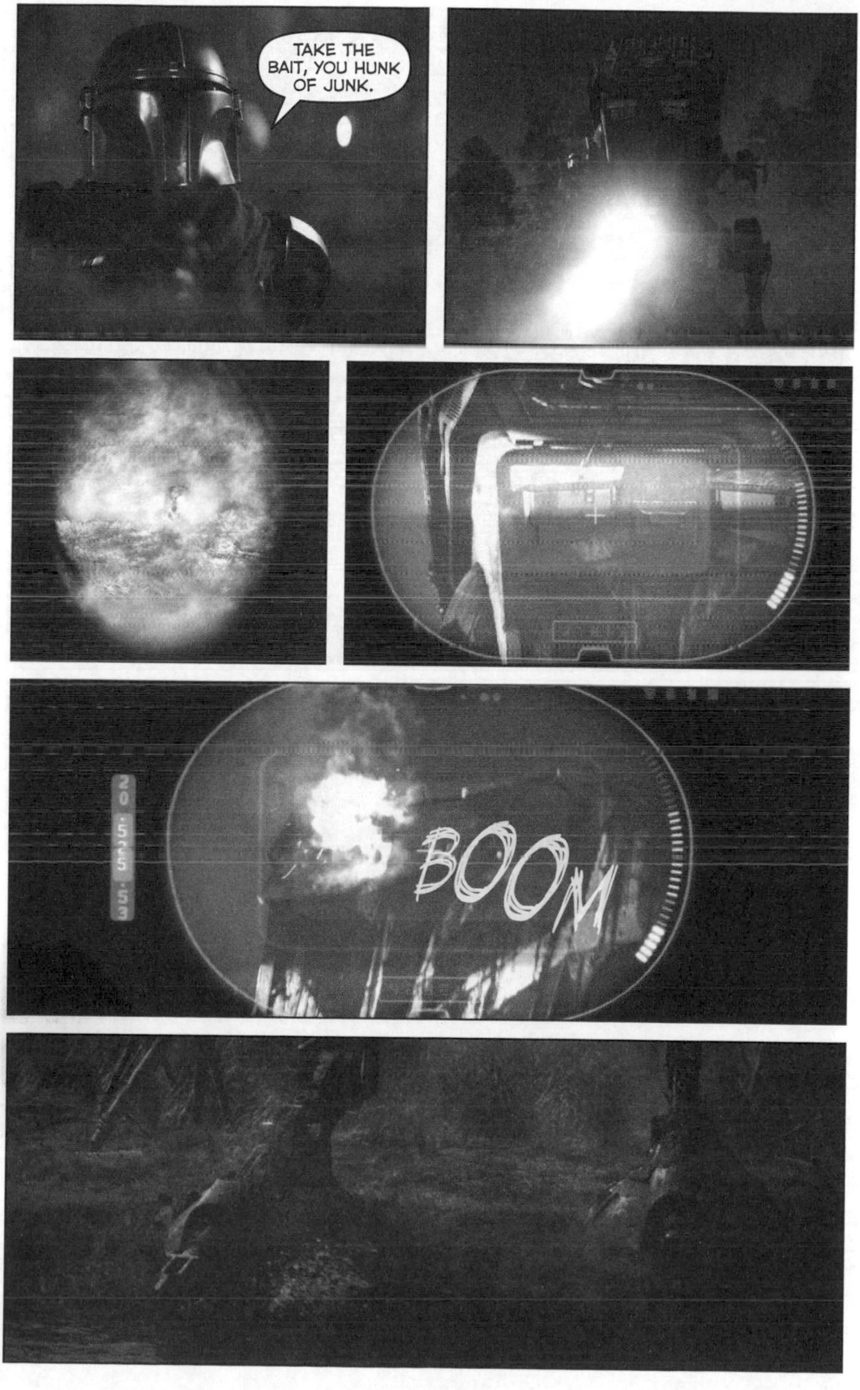
TAKE THE BAIT, YOU HUNK OF JUNK.
BOOM

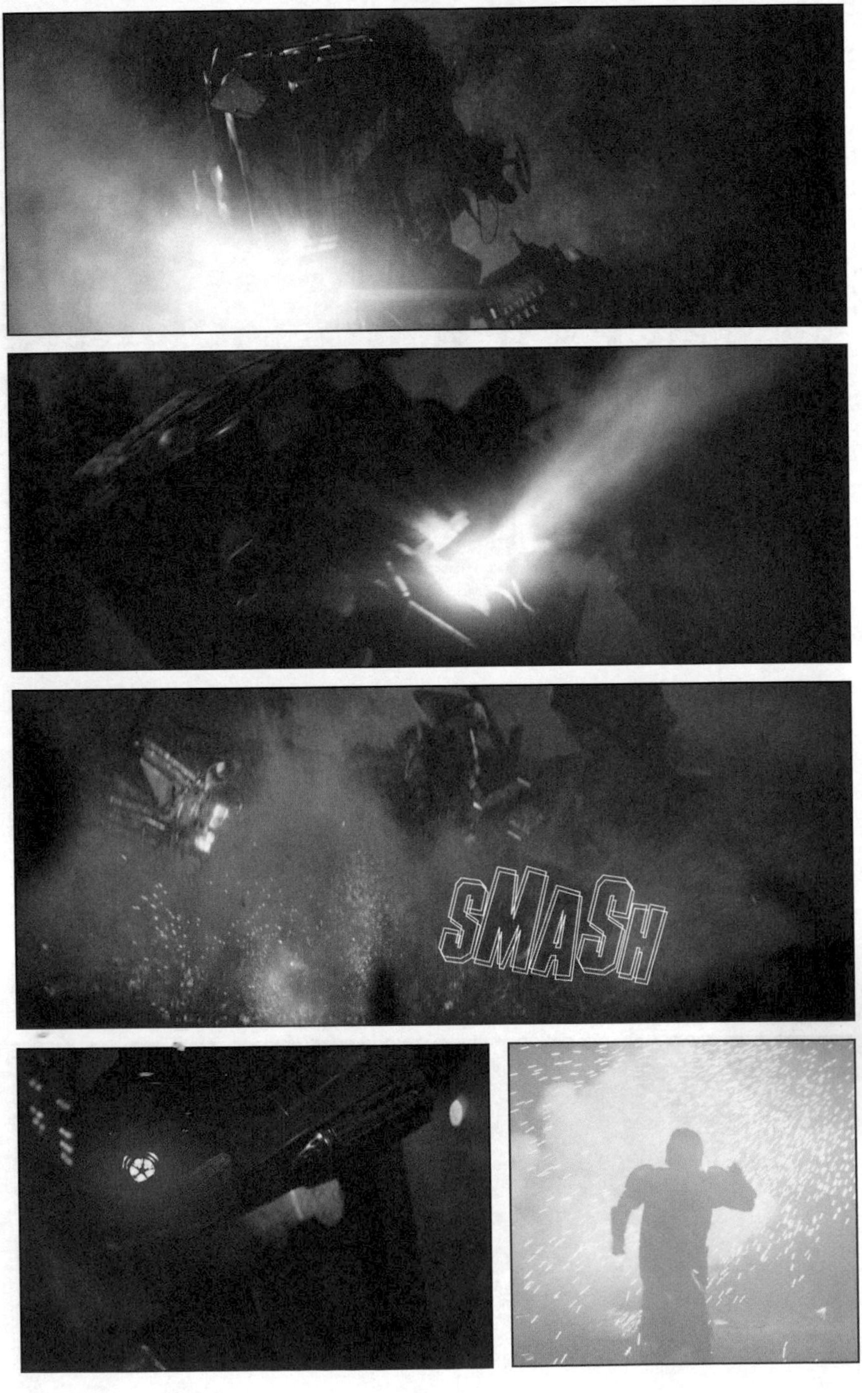
SMASH

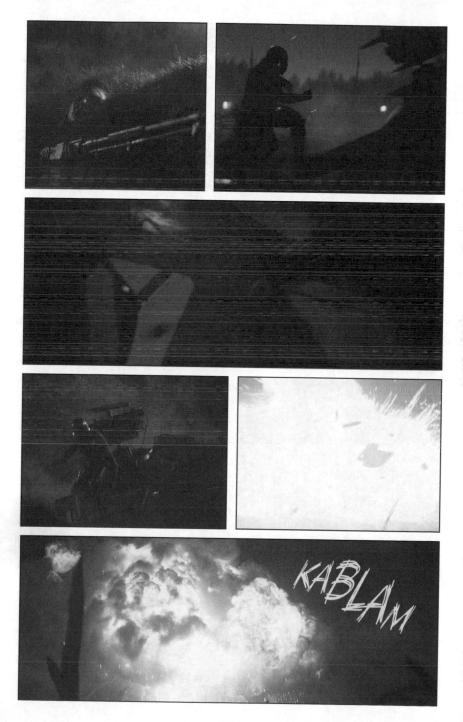

KABLAM

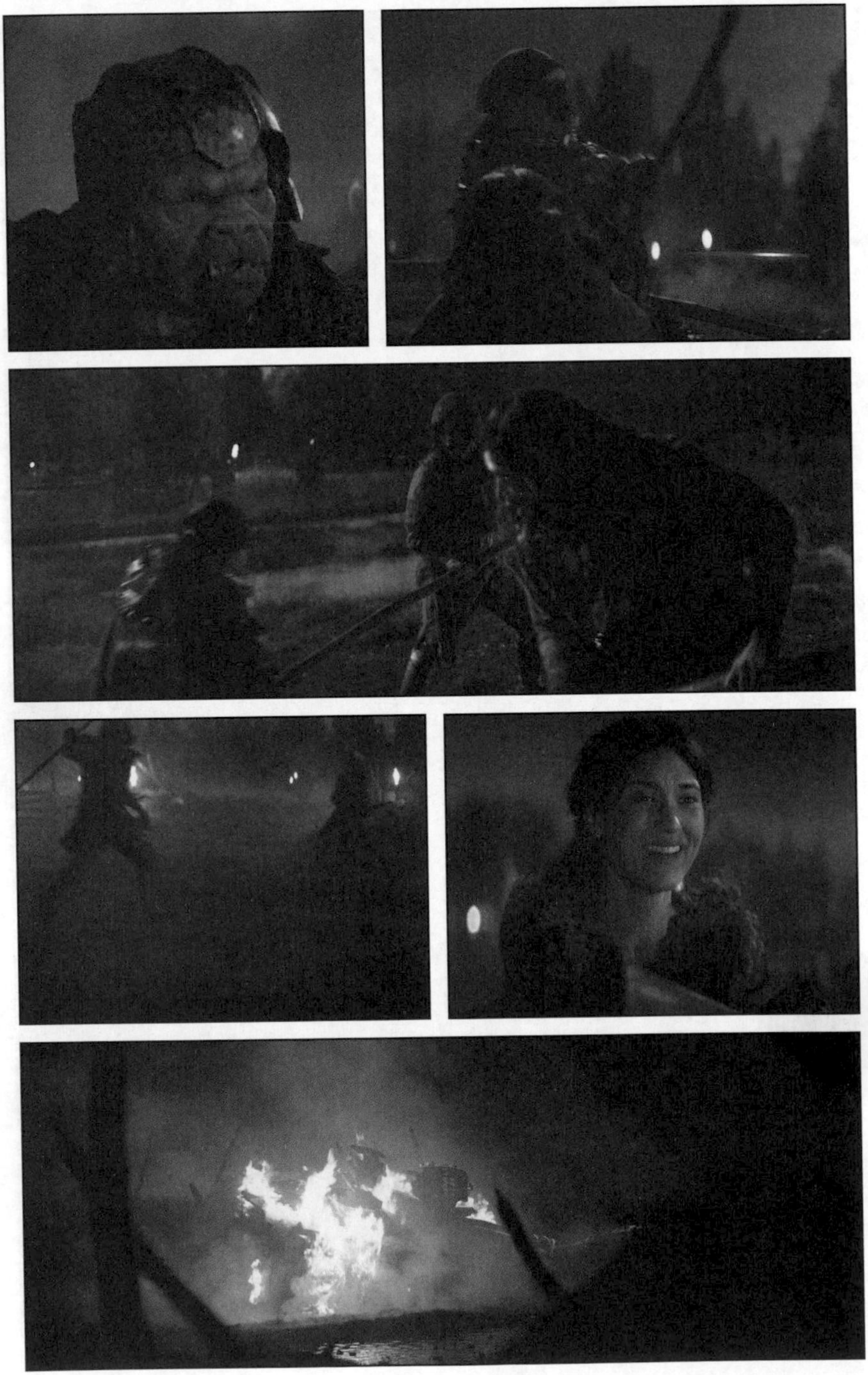

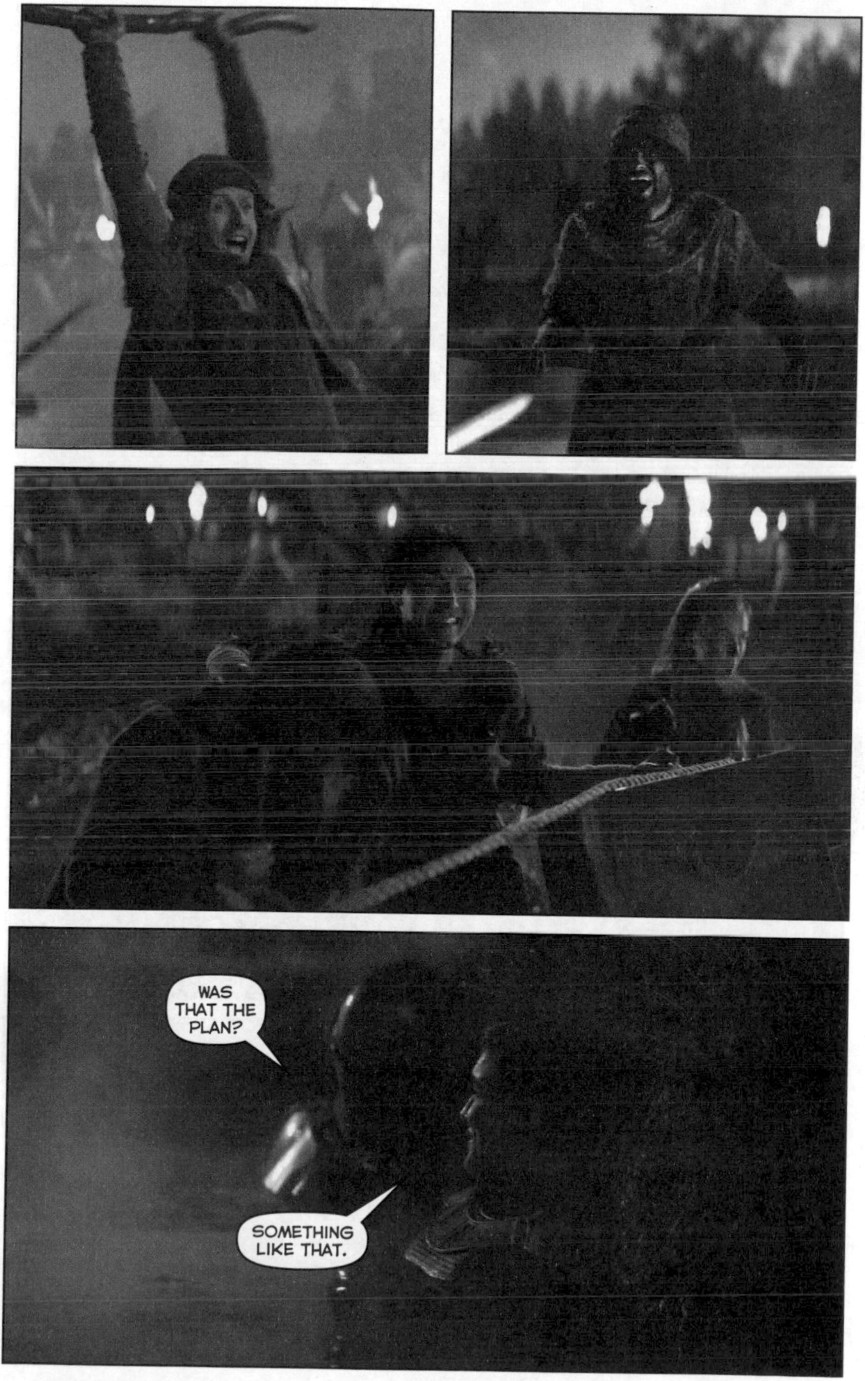
WAS THAT THE PLAN?
SOMETHING LIKE THAT.

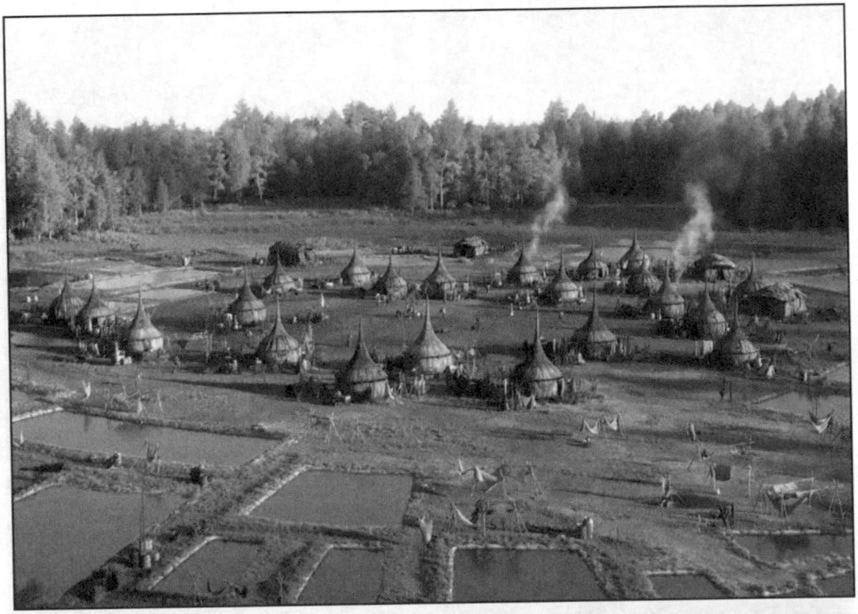

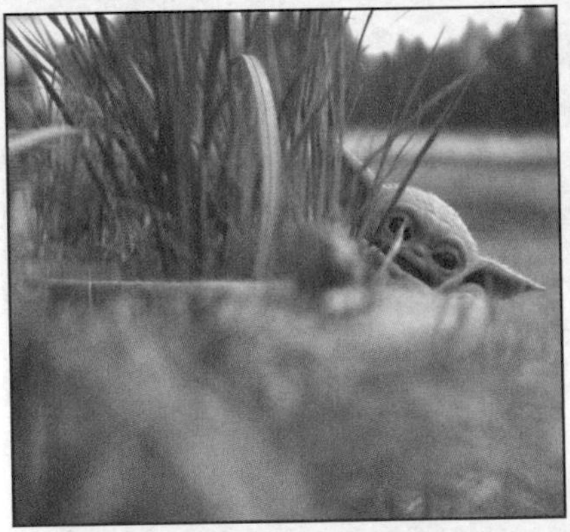

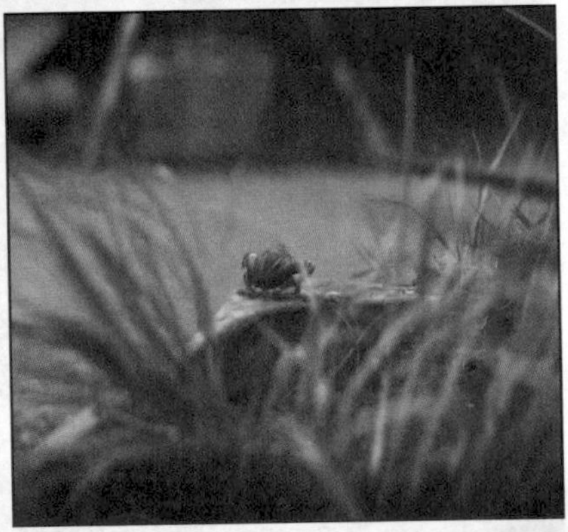

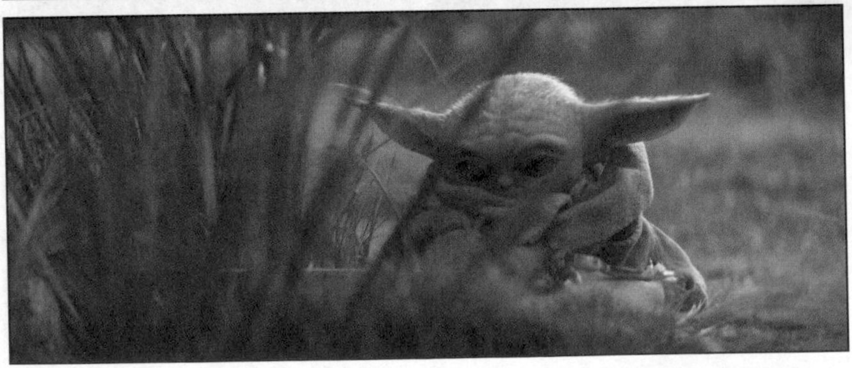

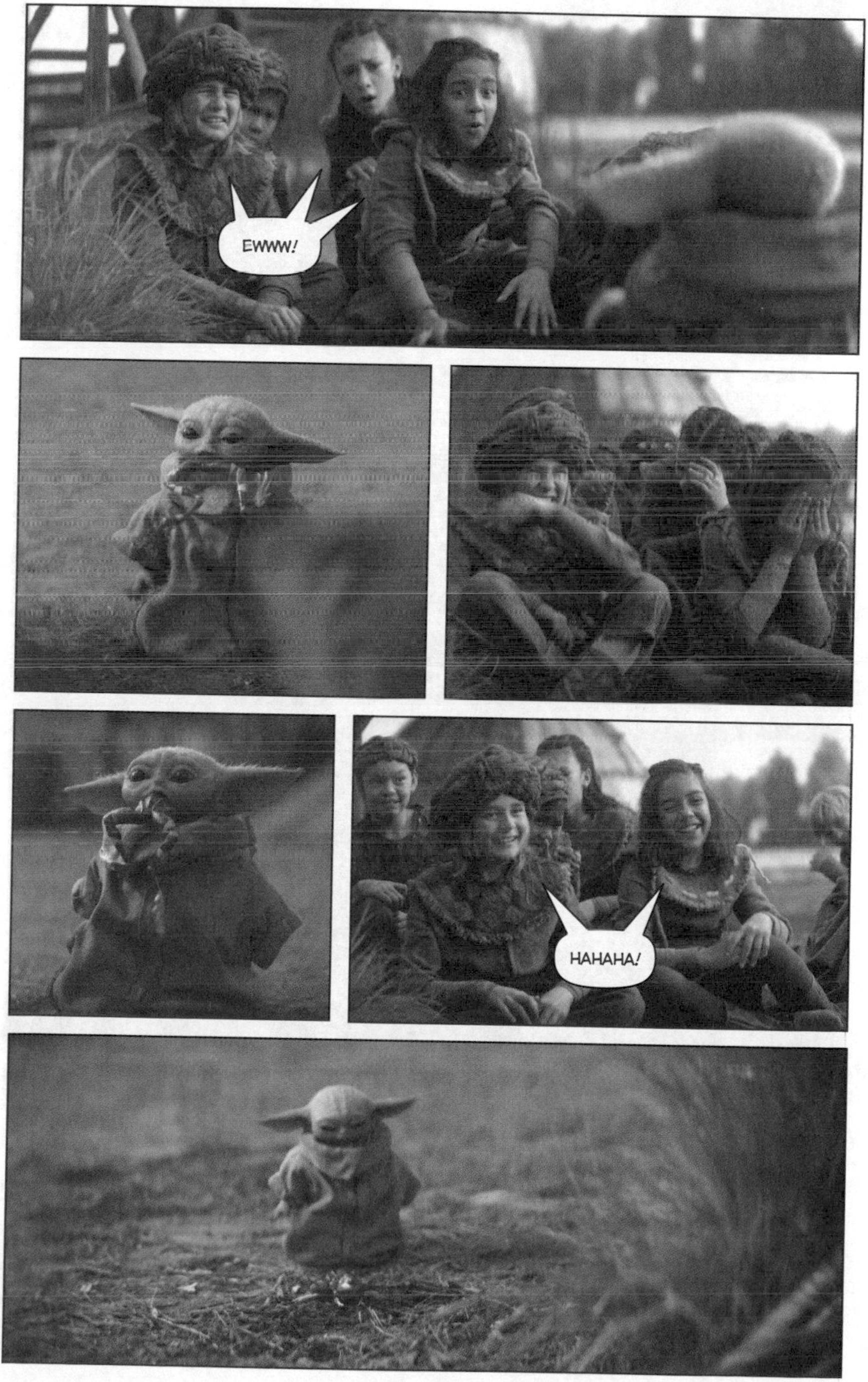
EWWW!
HAHAHA!

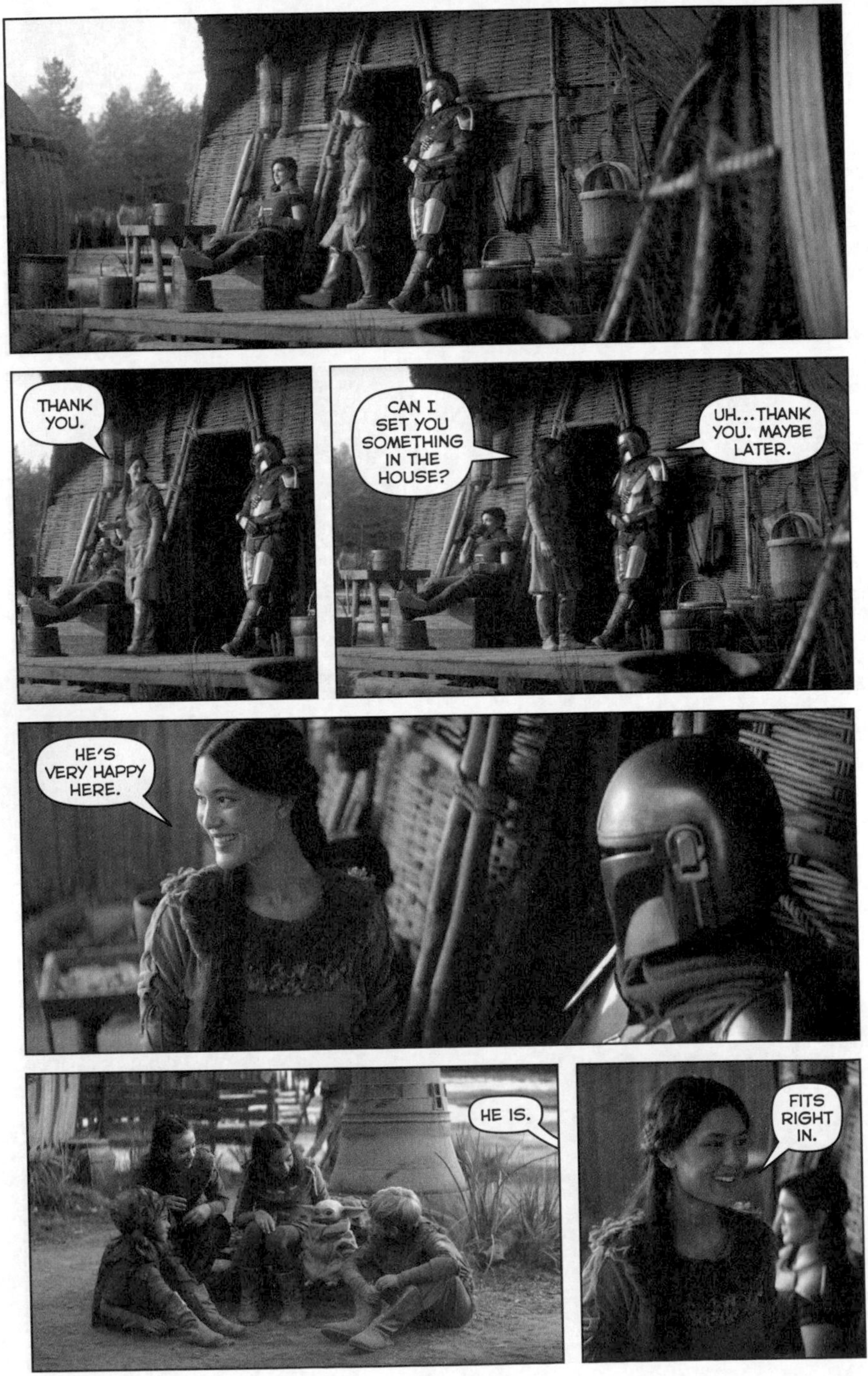
THANK YOU.
CAN I SET YOU SOMETHING IN THE HOUSE?
UH...THANK YOU. MAYBE LATER.
HE'S VERY HAPPY HERE.
HE IS.
FITS RIGHT IN.

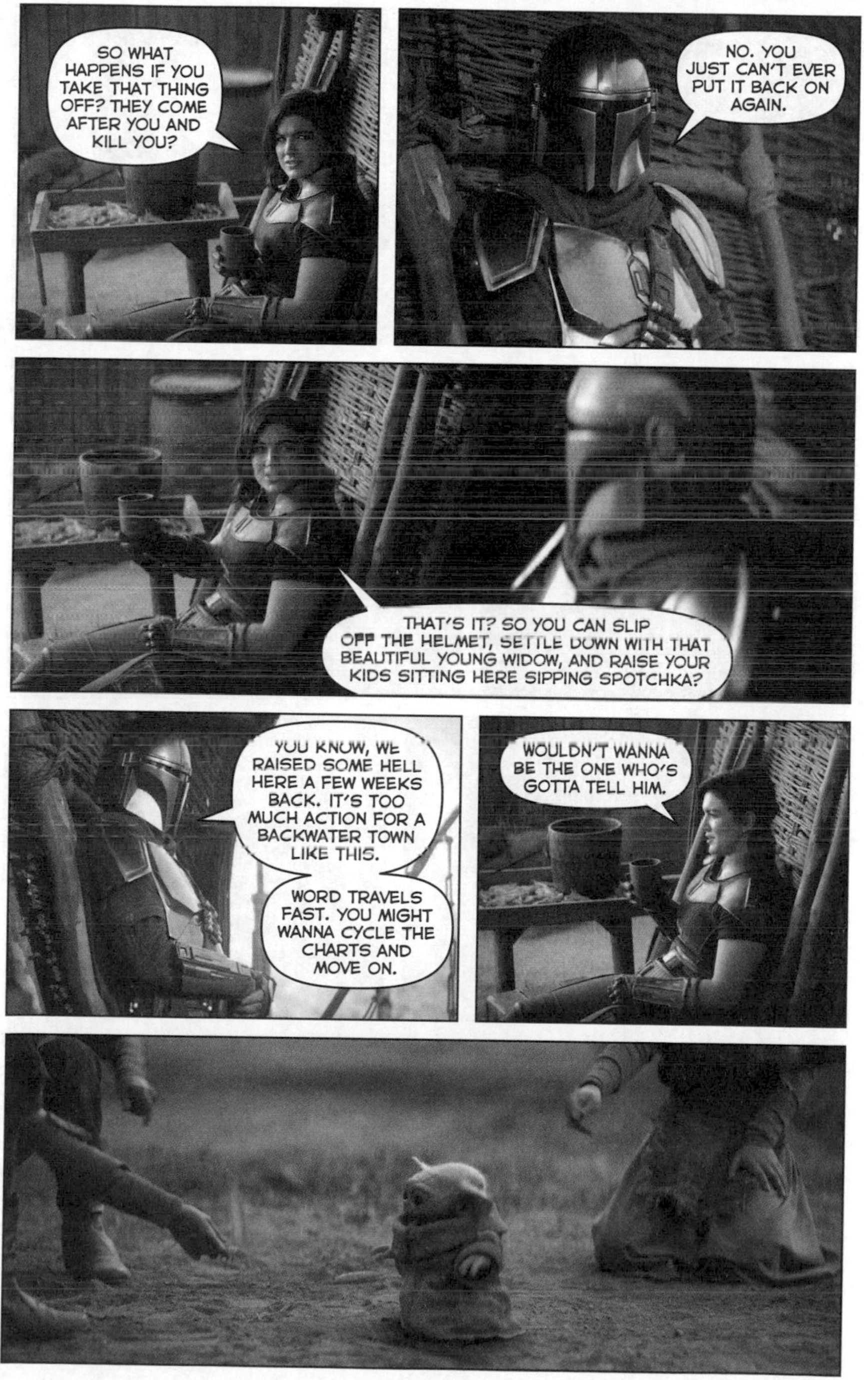
SO WHAT HAPPENS IF YOU TAKE THAT THING OFF? THEY COME AFTER YOU AND KILL YOU?
NO. YOU JUST CAN'T EVER PUT IT BACK ON AGAIN.
THAT'S IT? SO YOU CAN SLIP OFF THE HELMET, SETTLE DOWN WITH THAT BEAUTIFUL YOUNG WIDOW, AND RAISE YOUR KIDS SITTING HERE SIPPING SPOTCHKA?
YOU KNOW, WE RAISED SOME HELL HERE A FEW WEEKS BACK. IT'S TOO MUCH ACTION FOR A BACKWATER TOWN LIKE THIS.
WORD TRAVELS FAST. YOU MIGHT WANNA CYCLE THE CHARTS AND MOVE ON.
WOULDN'T WANNA BE THE ONE WHO'S GOTTA TELL HIM.

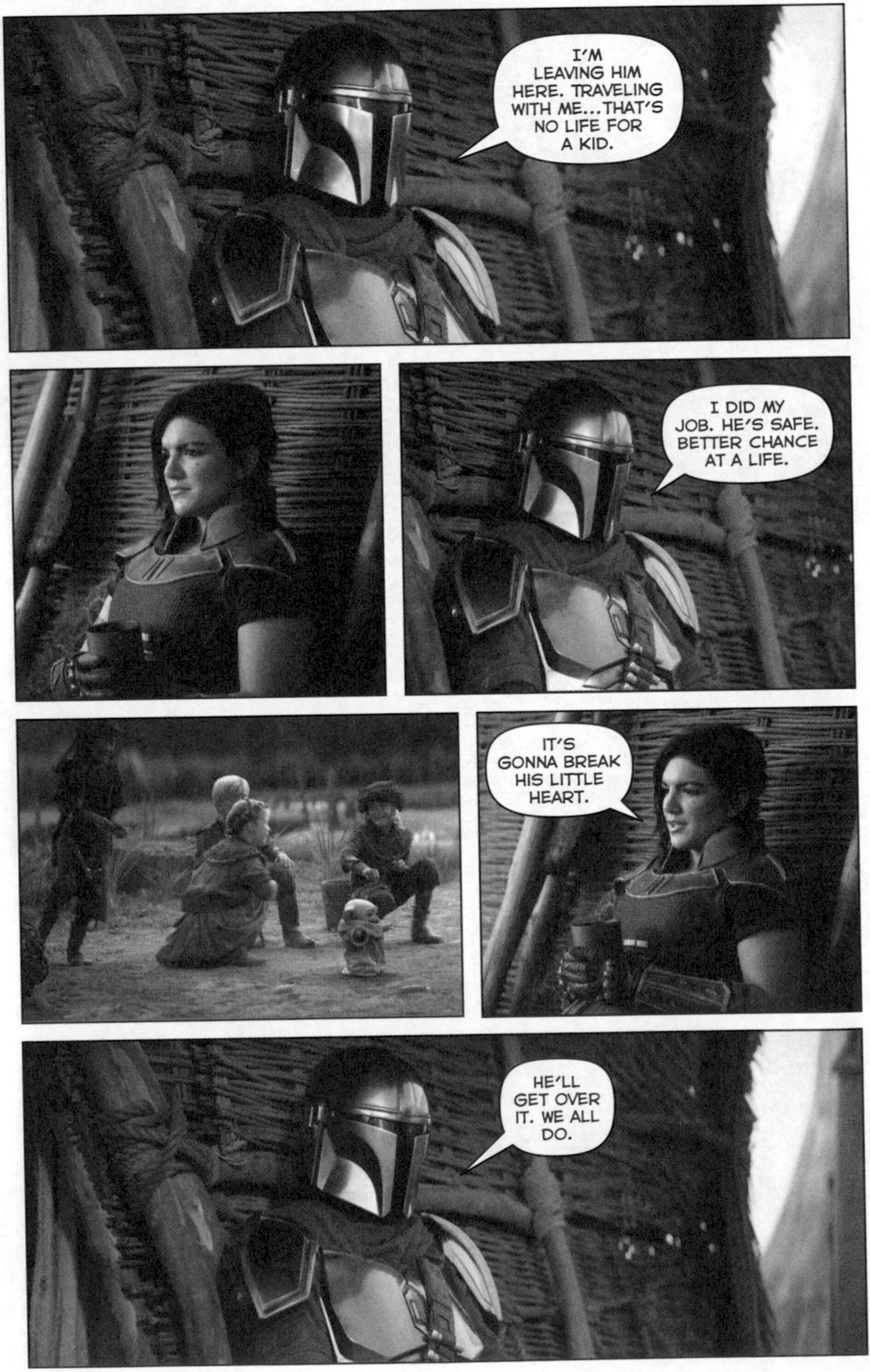
I'M LEAVING HIM HERE. TRAVELING WITH ME...THAT'S NO LIFE FOR A KID.
I DID MY JOB. HE'S SAFE. BETTER CHANCE AT A LIFE.
IT'S GONNA BREAK HIS LITTLE HEART.
HE'LL GET OVER IT. WE ALL DO.

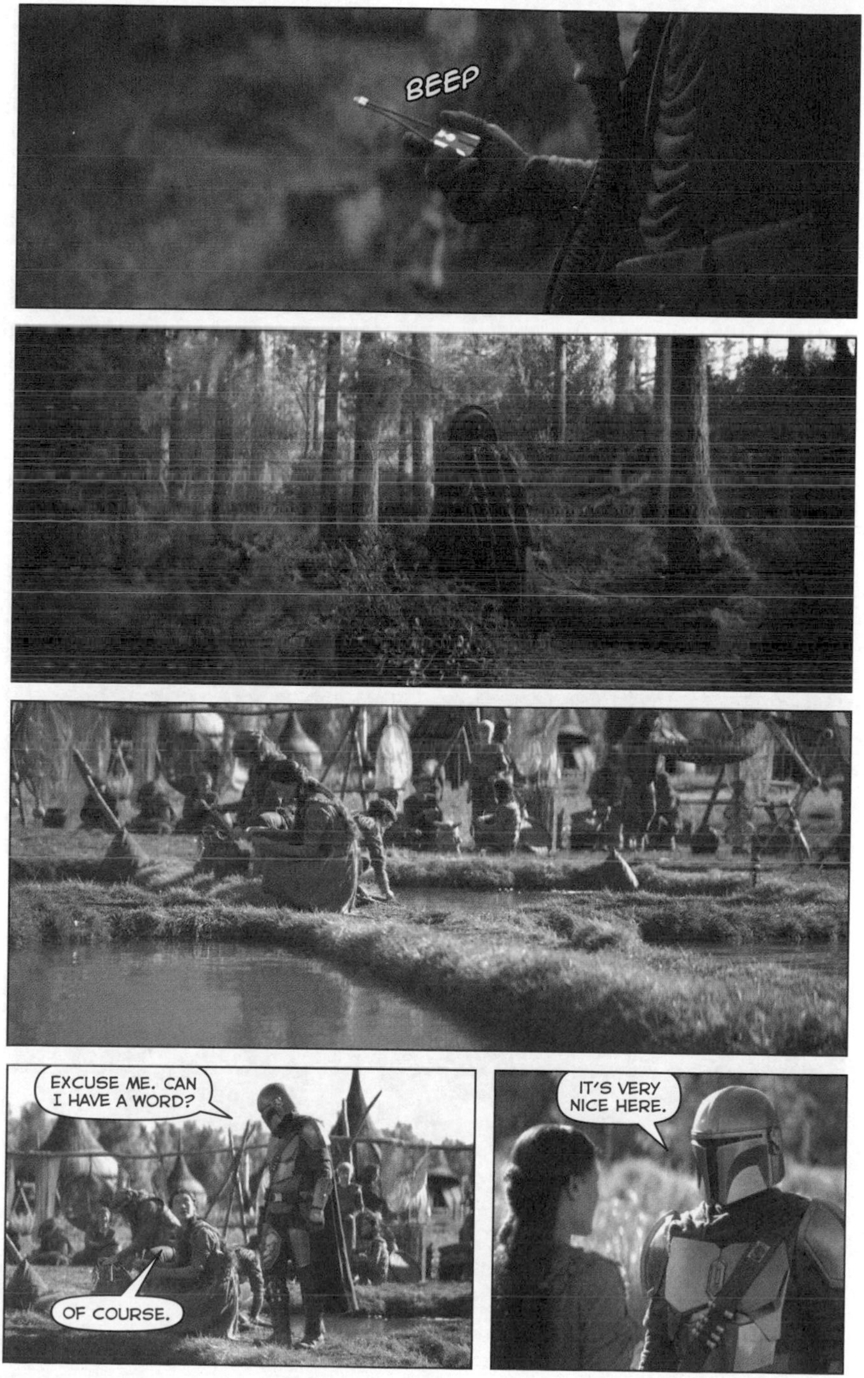
BEEP
EXCUSE ME. CAN I HAVE A WORD?
OF COURSE.
IT'S VERY NICE HERE.

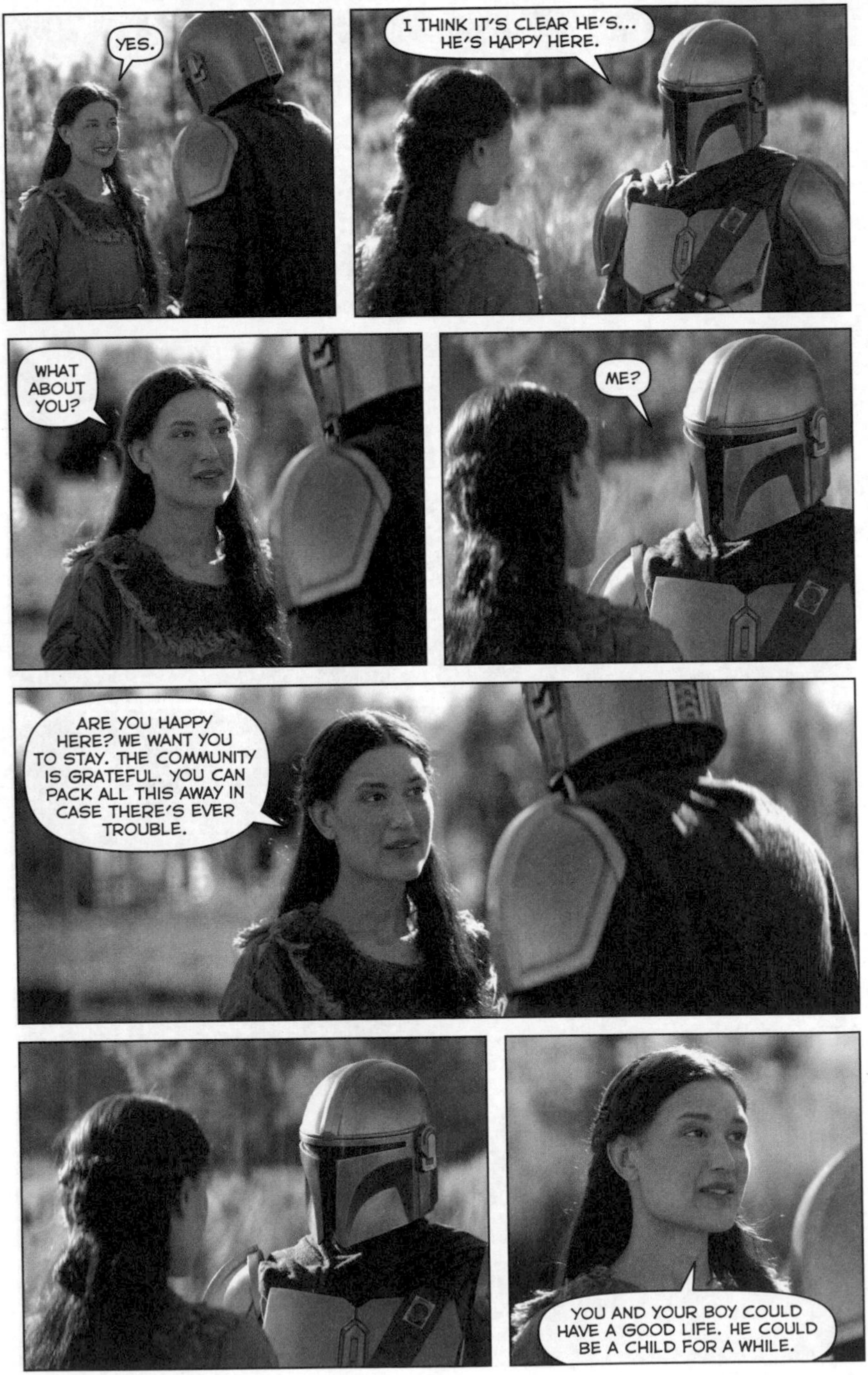
YES.
I THINK IT'S CLEAR HE'S... HE'S HAPPY HERE.
WHAT ABOUT YOU?
ME?
ARE YOU HAPPY HERE? WE WANT YOU TO STAY. THE COMMUNITY IS GRATEFUL. YOU CAN PACK ALL THIS AWAY IN CASE THERE'S EVER TROUBLE.
YOU AND YOUR BOY COULD HAVE A GOOD LIFE. HE COULD BE A CHILD FOR A WHILE.

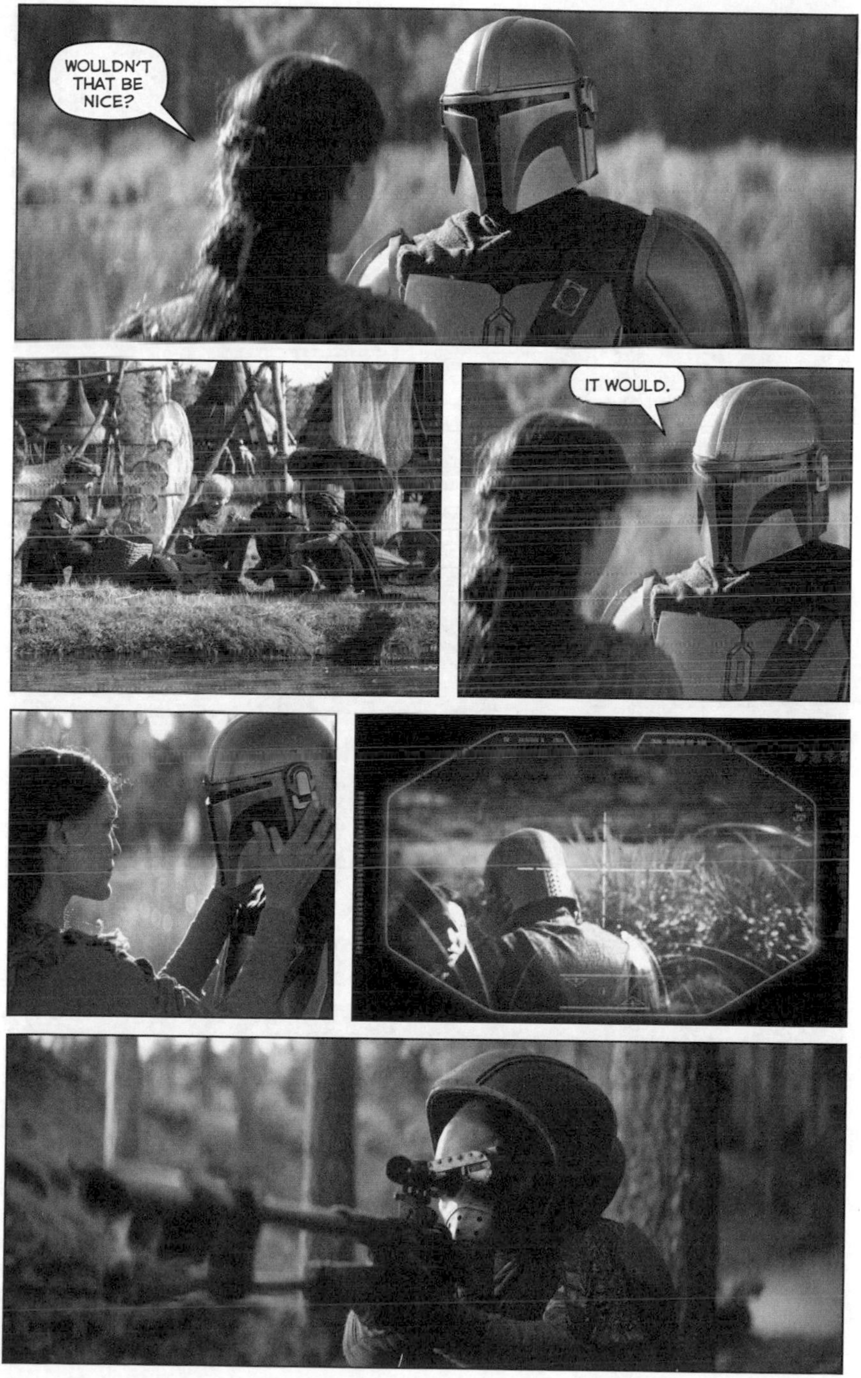
WOULDN'T THAT BE NICE?
IT WOULD.

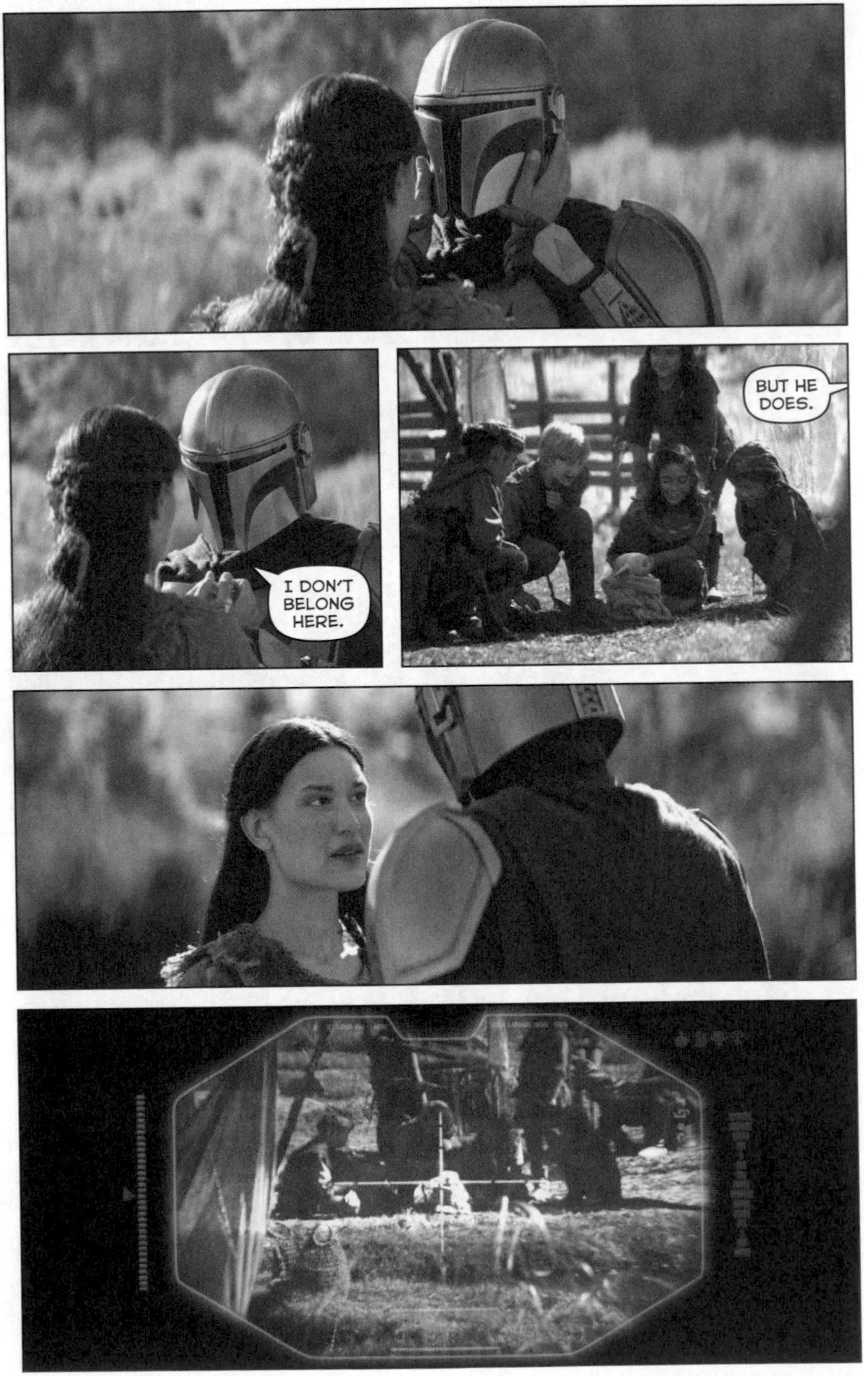
I DON'T BELONG HERE.
BUT HE DOES.

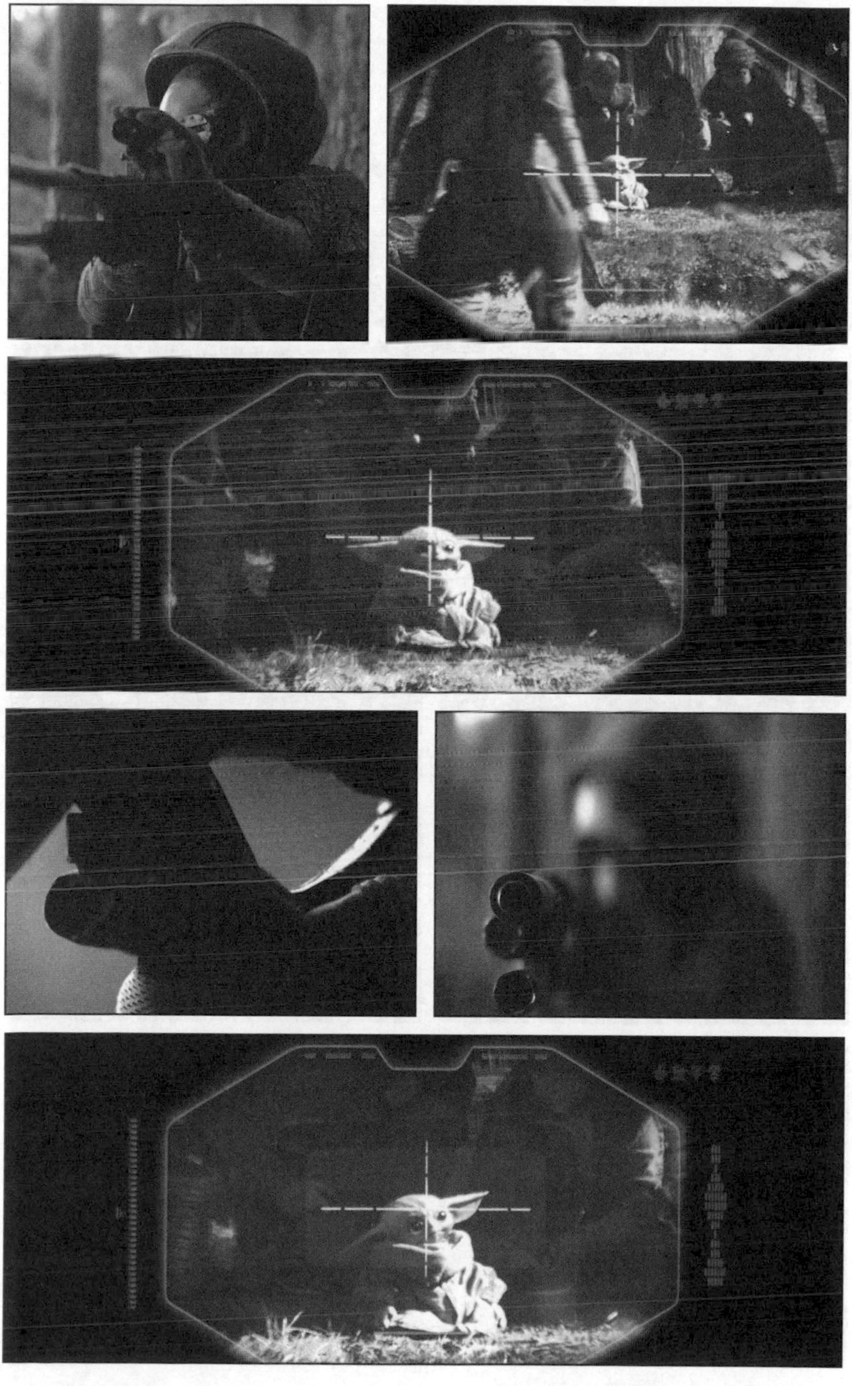

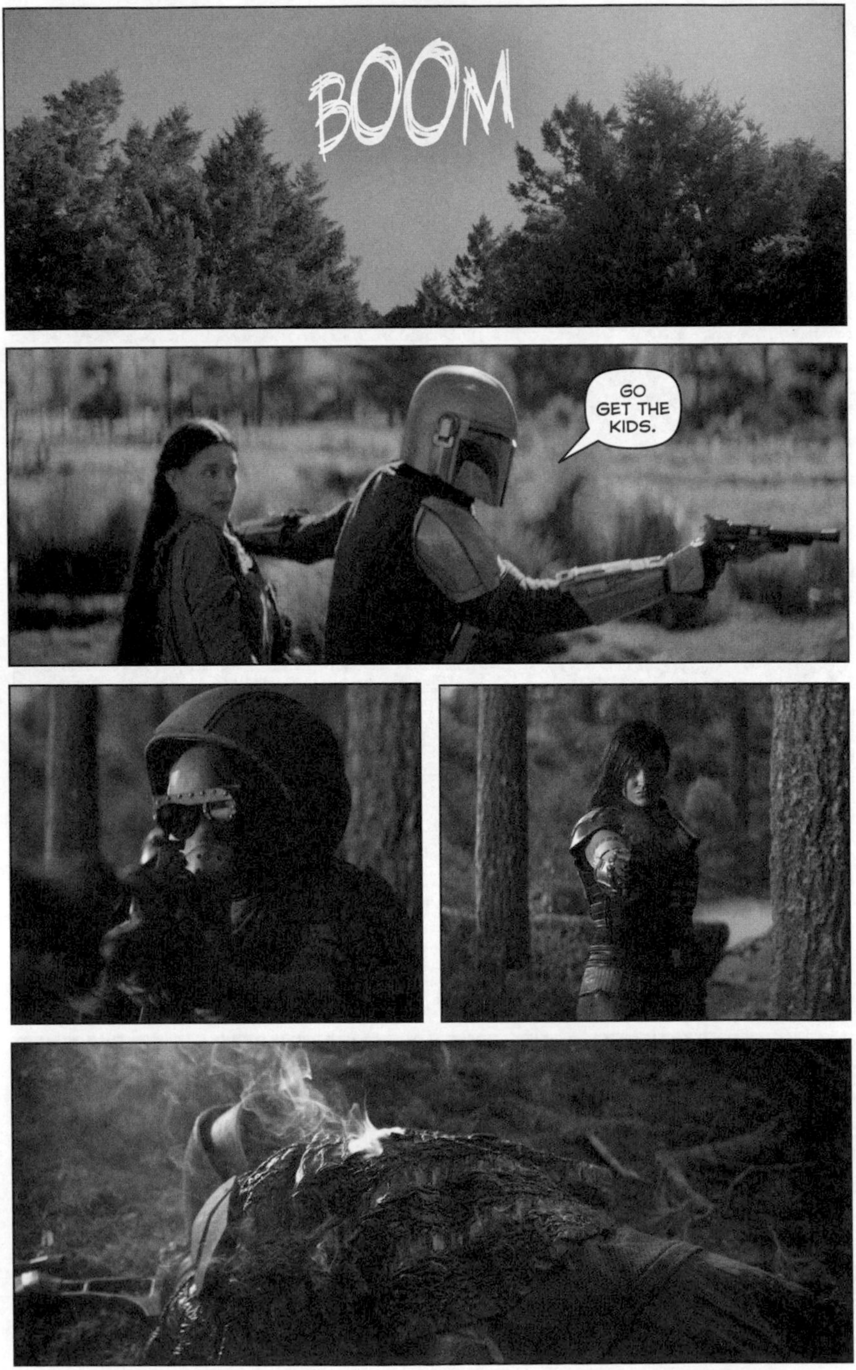
BOOM
GO GET THE KIDS.

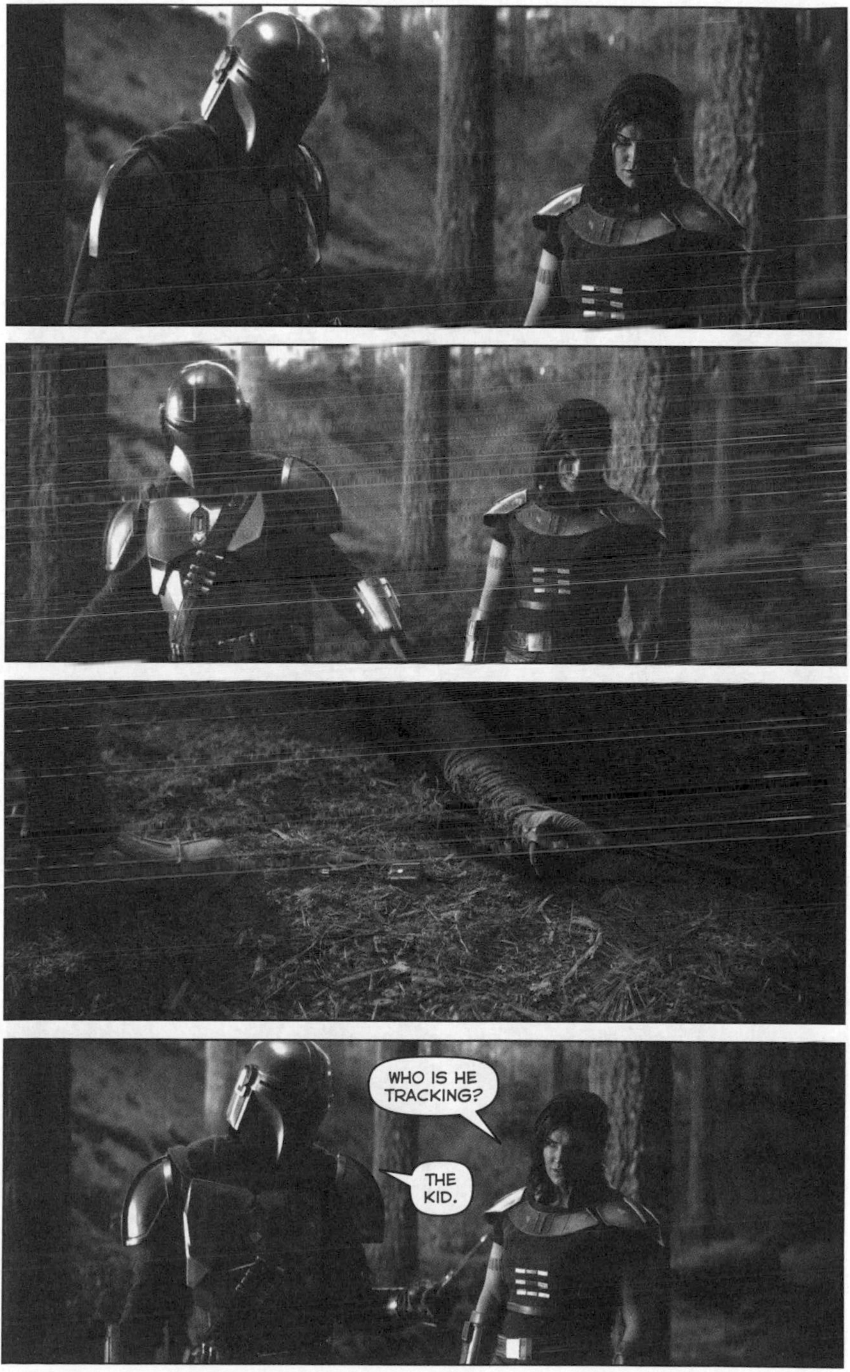
WHO IS HE TRACKING?
THE KID.

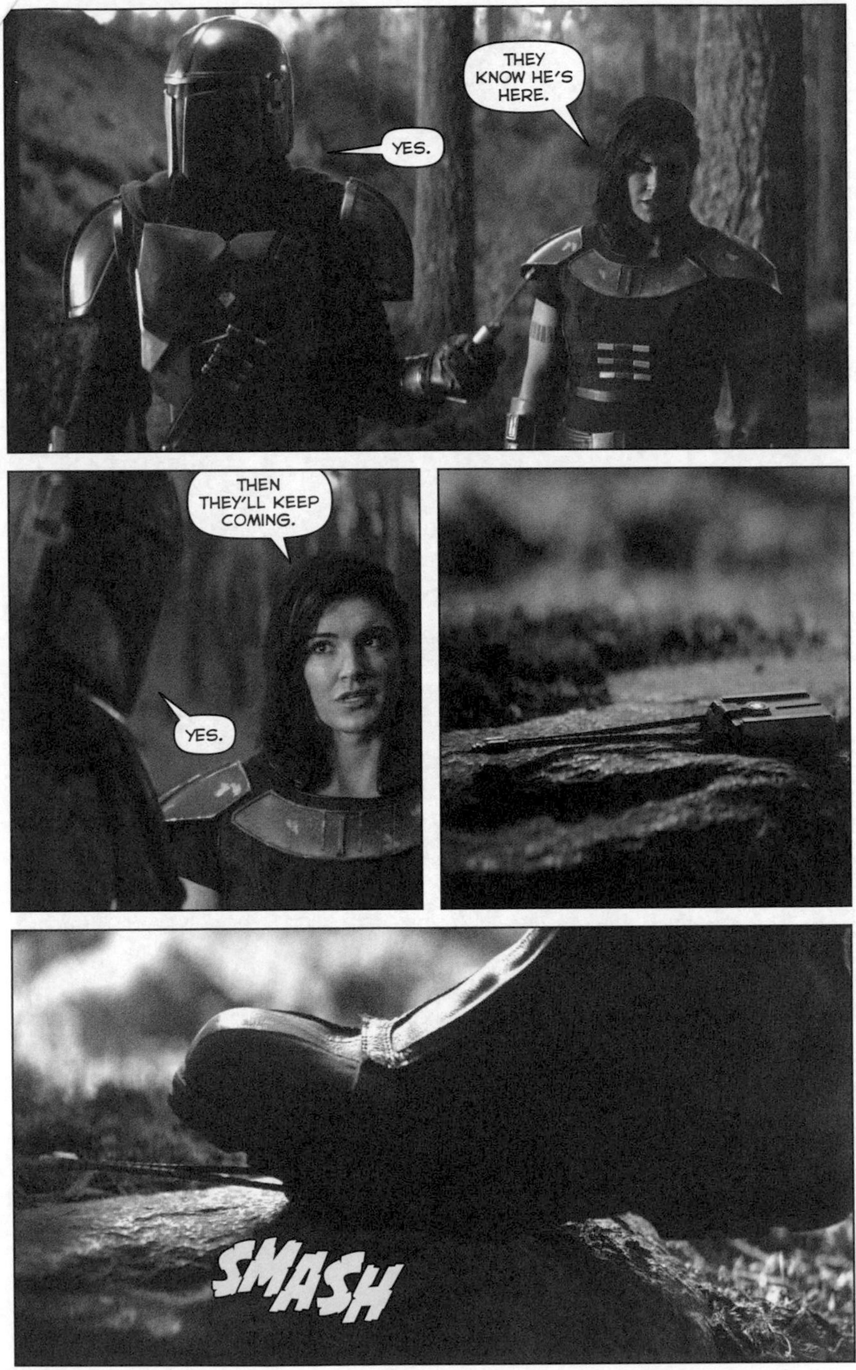
THEY KNOW HE'S HERE.
YES.
THEN THEY'LL KEEP COMING.
YES.
SMASH

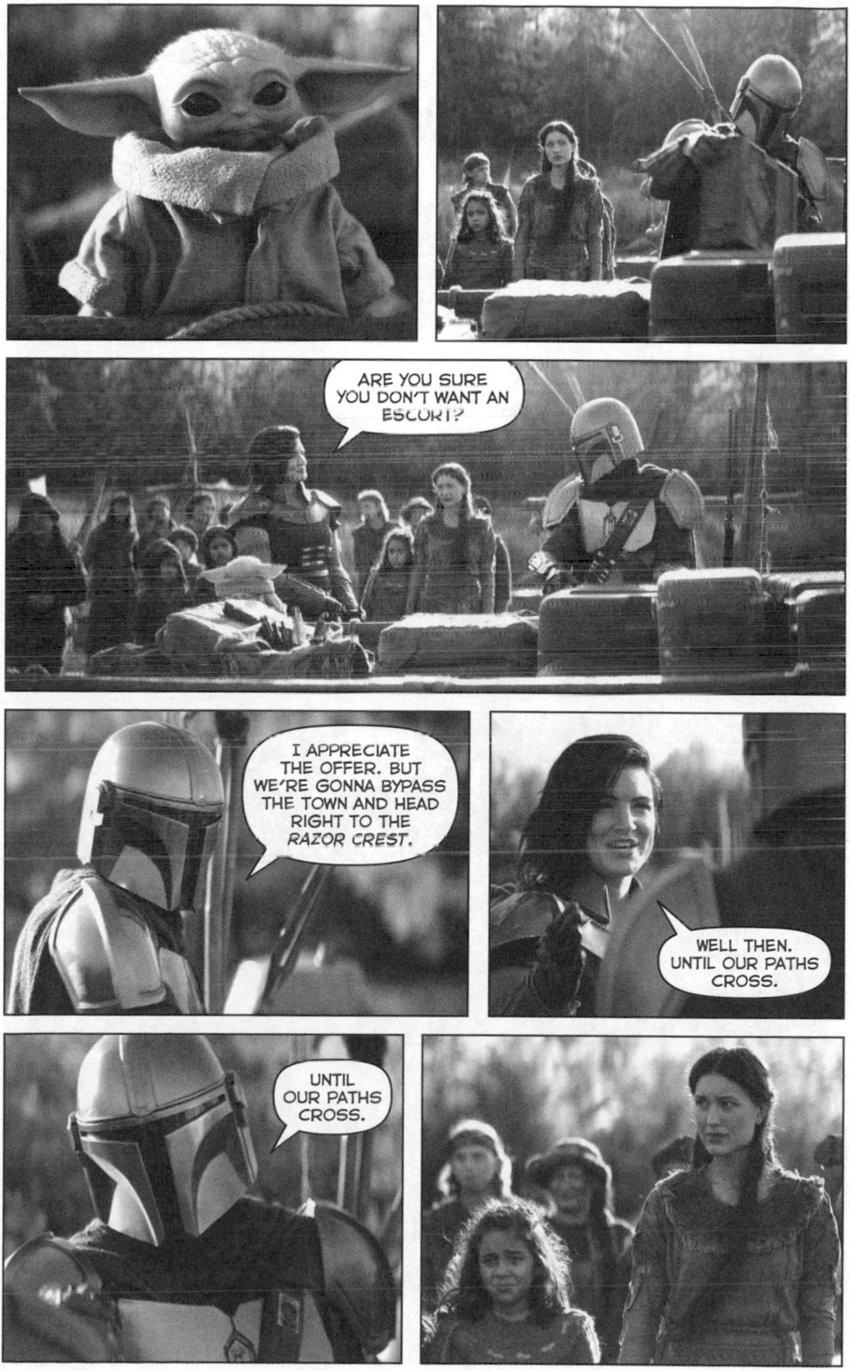
ARE YOU SURE YOU DON'T WANT AN ESCORT?
I APPRECIATE THE OFFER. BUT WE'RE GONNA BYPASS THE TOWN AND HEAD RIGHT TO THE *RAZOR CREST*.
WELL THEN. UNTIL OUR PATHS CROSS.
UNTIL OUR PATHS CROSS.

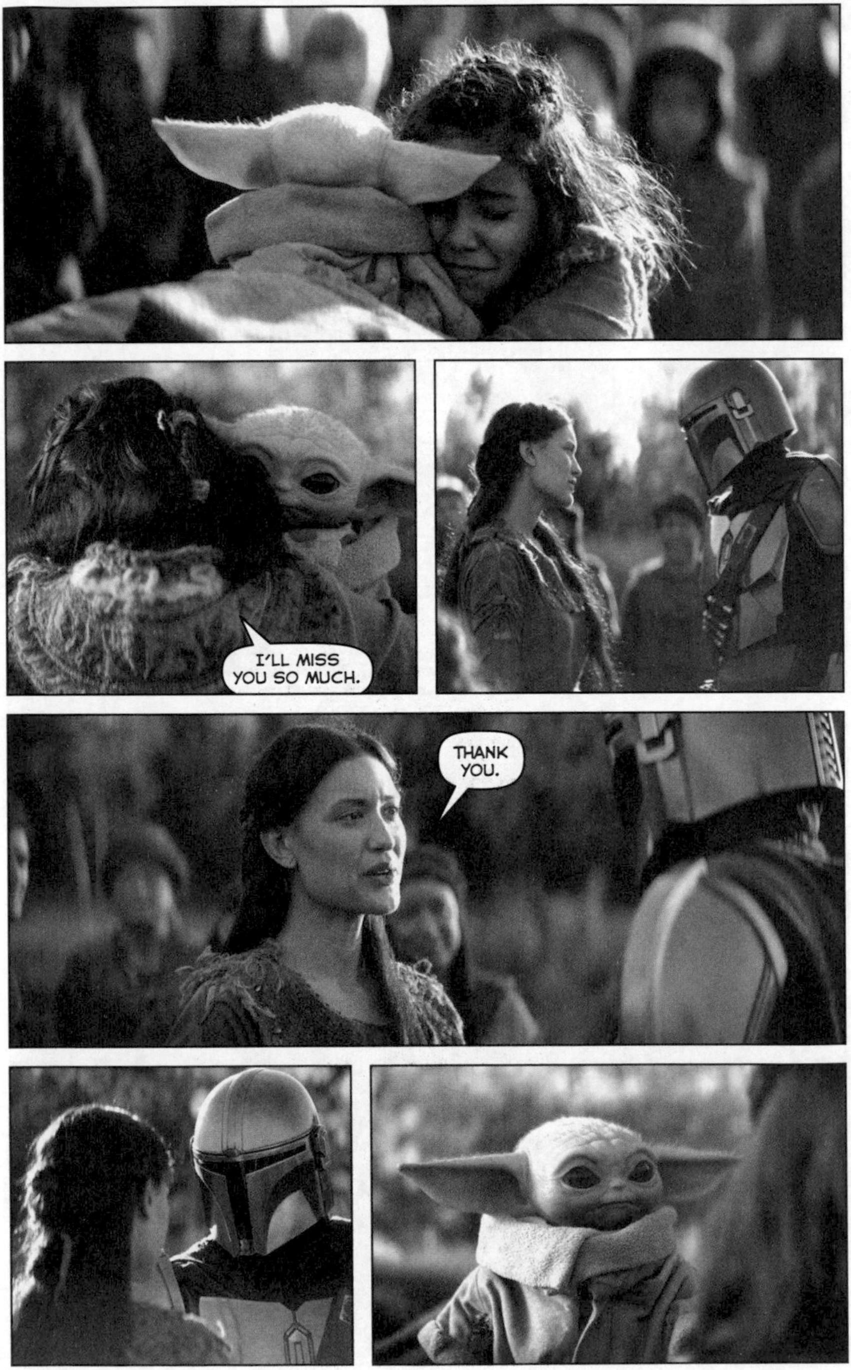
I'LL MISS YOU SO MUCH.
THANK YOU.

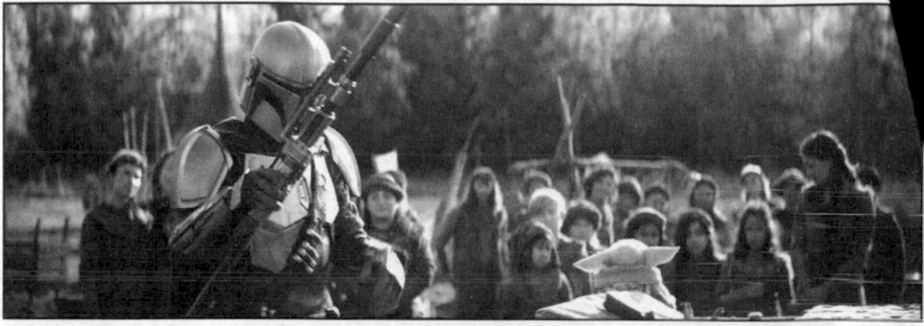
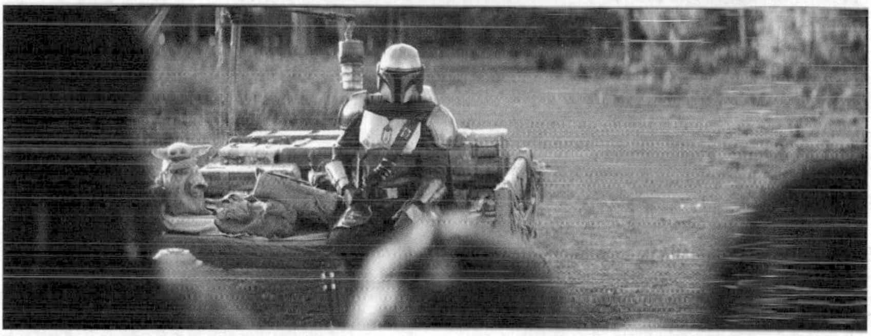
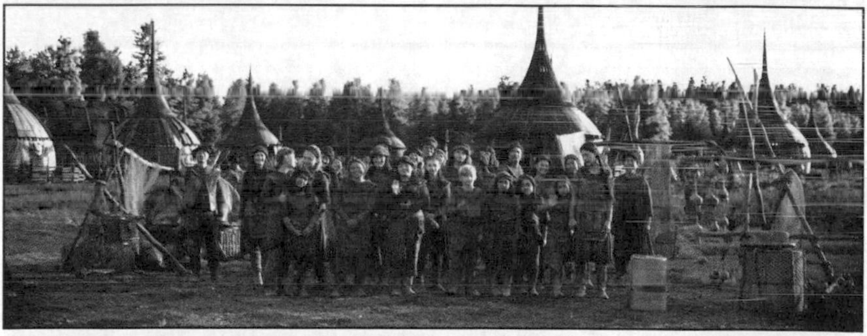
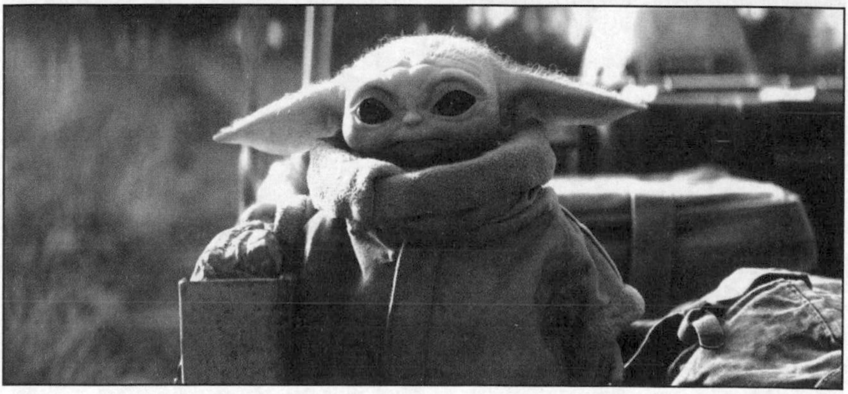

CREDITS

THE MANDALORIAN

Executive Producers
Jon Favreau
Dave Filoni
Kathleen Kennedy
Colin Wilson

Directed by
Dave Filoni

Written by
Jon Favreau

THE CHILD

Executive Producers
Jon Favreau
Dave Filoni
Kathleen Kennedy
Colin Wilson

Directed by
Rick Famuyiwa

Written by
Jon Favreau

THE SIN

Executive Producers
Jon Favreau
Dave Filoni
Kathleen Kennedy
Colin Wilson

Directed by
Deborah Chow

Written by
Jon Favreau

SANCTUARY

Executive Producers
Jon Favreau
Dave Filoni
Kathleen Kennedy
Colin Wilson

Directed by
Bryce Dallas Howard

Written by
Jon Favreau